'What a very, very
LUCKY
person you are.

Spread out before you are the
FINEST and **FUNNIEST**
words from the finest and funniest writer
the past century ever knew. '

Stephen Fry

D0177217

Pelham Grenville Wodehouse (always known as 'Plum') wrote more than ninety novels and some three hundred short stories over 73 years. He is widely recognised as the greatest 20th-century writer of humour in the English language.

Wodehouse mixed the high culture of his classical education with the popular slang of the suburbs in both England and America, becoming a 'cartoonist of words'. Drawing on the antics of a near-contemporary world, he placed his Drones, Earls, Ladies (including draconian aunts and eligible girls) and Valets, in a recently vanished society, whose reality is transformed by his remarkable imagination into something timeless and enduring.

Perhaps best known for the escapades of Bertie Wooster and Jeeves, Wodehouse also created the world of Blandings Castle, home to Lord Emsworth and his cherished pig, the Empress of Blandings. His stories include gems concerning the irrepressible and disreputable Ukridge; Psmith, the elegant socialist; the ever-so-slightly-unscrupulous Fifth Earl of Ickenham, better known as Uncle Fred; and those related by Mr Mulliner, the charming raconteur of The Angler's Rest, and the Oldest Member at the Golf Club.

Wodehouse collaborated with a variety of partners on straight plays and worked principally alongside Guy Bolton on providing the lyrics and script for musical comedies with such composers as George Gershwin, Irving Berlin and Cole Porter. He liked to say that the royalties for 'Just My Bill', which Jerome Kern incorporated into *Showboat*, were enough to keep him in tobacco and whisky for the rest of his life.

In 1936 he was awarded the Mark Twain Prize for 'having made an outstanding and lasting contribution to the happiness of the world'. He was made a Doctor of Letters by Oxford University in 1939 and in 1975, aged 93, he was knighted by Queen Elizabeth II. He died shortly afterwards, on St Valentine's Day.

To have created so many characters that require no introduction places him in a very select group of writers, led by Shakespeare and Dickens.

'You don't analyse such sunlit
PERFECTION
you just bask in its warmth and splendour'

Stephen Fry

'Wodehouse is the
GREATEST
comic writer'

Douglas Adams

'**SUBLIME**
comic genius . . . light as a feather, but fabulous'

Ben Elton

'The
FUNNIEST
writer ever to put words on paper'

Hugh Laurie

'P. G. Wodehouse wrote
THE BEST
English comic novels of the century'

Sebastian Faulks

'**WITTY**
and effortlessly fluid. His books are laugh-out-loud funny'

Arabella Weir

'**THE HEAD**
of my profession'

Hilaire Belloc

'Wodehouse was quite simply
THE BEE'S KNEES.
And then some'

Joseph Connolly

'Mr Wodehouse's
IDYLLIC WORLD CAN NEVER STALE.
He will continue to release future generations from captivity
that may be more irksome than our own. He has made a
world for us to live in and delight in'

Evelyn Waugh

'**THE ULTIMATE IN COMFORT READING**
because nothing bad ever happens in P. G. Wodehouse land. Or
even if it does, it's always sorted out by the end of the book. For as
long as I'm immersed in a P. G. Wodehouse book, it's possible to
keep the real world at bay and live in a far, far nicer, funnier
one where happy endings are the order of the day'

Marian Keyes

'You should read Wodehouse when you're well
and when you're poorly; when you're travelling,
and when you're not; when you're feeling clever, and when
you're feeling utterly dim. Wodehouse
ALWAYS LIFTS YOUR SPIRITS,
no matter how high they happen to be already'

Lynne Truss

'P. G. Wodehouse remains the greatest chronicler of
A CERTAIN KIND OF ENGLISHNESS,
that no one else has ever captured quite so sharply, or with
quite as much wit and affection'

Julian Fellowes

'Not only the funniest English novelist who
ever wrote but one of our finest stylists.
His world is **PERFECT**, his stories are
PERFECT, his writing is **PERFECT**.
What more is there to be said?'

Susan Hill

'One of my (few) proud boasts is that I once spent a day interviewing P. G. Wodehouse at his home in America. He was exactly as I'd expected: a lovely, modest man. He could have walked out of one of his own novels. It's dangerous to use the word

GENIUS

to describe a writer, but I'll risk it with him'

John Humphrys

'The

INCOMPARABLE AND TIMELESS

genius – perfect for readers of all ages, shapes and sizes!'

Kate Mosse

'COMPULSORY READING

for anyone who has a pig, an aunt – or a sense of humour!'

Lindsey Davis

'A genius ...

ELUSIVE, DELICATE BUT LASTING.

He created such a credible world that, sadly, I suppose, never really existed but what a delight it always is to enter it and the temptation to linger there is sometimes almost overwhelming'

Alan Ayckbourn

'I've recorded all the Jeeves books, and I can tell you this: it's like singing Mozart. The perfection of the phrasing is

A PHYSICAL PLEASURE.

I doubt if any singer in the English language has more perfect music'

Simon Callow

'I constantly find myself drooling with admiration at the

SUBLIME

way Wodehouse plays with the English language'

Simon Brett

'To pick up a Wodehouse novel is to find oneself in the presence of genius – no writer has ever given me so much **PURE ENJOYMENT**'

John Julius Norwich

'P. G. Wodehouse is **THE GOLD STANDARD OF ENGLISH WIT**'

Christopher Hitchens

'Wodehouse is so **UTTERLY, PROPERLY, SIMPLY FUNNY**'

Adele Parks

'To dive into a Wodehouse novel is to swim in some of the most **ELEGANTLY TURNED PHRASES** in the English language'

Ben Schott

'P. G. Wodehouse should be prescribed to treat depression. Cheaper, more effective than valium and far, far more **ADDICTIVE**'

Olivia Williams

'My only problem with Wodehouse is deciding which of his **ENCHANTING** books to take to my desert island'

Ruth Dudley Edwards

'Quite simply, **THE MASTER OF COMIC WRITING** at work'

Jane Moore

P. G. WODEHOUSE

The World of Jeeves

arrow books

17 19 20 18 16

Arrow Books
20 Vauxhall Bridge Road
London SW1V 2SA

Arrow Books is part of the Penguin Random House group of companies
whose addresses can be found at global.penguinrandomhouse.com

Penguin
Random House
UK

Copyright © The Trustees of the Wodehouse Estate

The Trustees of the Wodehouse Estate have asserted P.G. Wodehouse's
right to be identified as the author of this Work in accordance with the
Copyright, Designs and Patents Act 1988.

First published in Great Britain by Herbert Jenkins Ltd in 1967
First published by Arrow Books in 2008

www.penguin.co.uk

A CIP catalogue record for this book is available from the British Library.

ISBN 9780099514237

Typeset by SX Composing DTP, Rayleigh, Essex
Printed and bound in Great Britain by Clays Ltd, Elcograf S.p.A

Penguin Random House is committed to a sustainable future for our business,
our readers and our planet. This book is made from Forest Stewardship
Council® certified paper.

MIX
Paper from
responsible sources
FSC
www.fsc.org   FSC® C018179

CONTENTS

This trackless desert of print which we see before us, winding on and on into the purple distance, represents my first Omnibus Book: and I must confess that, as I contemplate it, I cannot overcome a slight feeling of chestiness, just the faint beginning of that offensive conceit against which we authors have to guard so carefully. I mean, it isn't everyone . . . I mean to say, an Omnibus Book . . . Well, dash it, you can't say it doesn't mark an epoch in a fellow's career and put him just a bit above the common herd. P. G. Wodehouse, O.B. Not such a very distant step from P. G. Wodehouse, O.M.

Mingled with this pride there is a certain diffidence. Hitherto, I have administered Jeeves and Bertie to the public in reasonably small doses, spread over a lapse of time. (Fifteen years, to be exact.) How will my readers react to the policy of the Solid Slab?

There is, of course, this to be said for the Omnibus Book in general and this one in particular. When you buy it, you have got something. The bulk of this volume makes it almost the ideal paper-weight. The number of its pages assures its possessor of plenty of shaving paper on his vacation. Placed upon the waist-line and jerked up and down each morning, it will reduce embonpoint and strengthen the abdominal muscles. And those still at their public school will find that between – say Caesar's Commentaries in limp cloth and this Jeeves book there is no comparison as a missile in an inter-study brawl.

The great trouble with a book like this is that the purchaser is tempted to read too much of it at one time. He sees this hideous mass confronting him and he wants to get at it and have done with it. This is a mistake. I would not recommend anyone to attempt to finish this volume at a sitting. It can be done – I did it myself when correcting the proofs – but it leaves one weak and is really not worth doing just for the sake of saying you have done it.

Take it easy. Spread it out. Assimilate it little by little. Here, for instance, is a specimen day's menu, as advocated by a well-known West End physician.

Breakfast

Toast.
Marmalade.
Coffee.
Soft-boiled egg.
JEEVES AND THE HARD-BOILED EGG.

Luncheon

Hors d'oeuvres.
Cauliflower au gratin.
Lamb cutlet.
JEEVES AND THE KID CLEMENTINA.

Dinner

Clear soup.
Halibut.
Chicken en casserole.
Savoury.
JEEVES AND THE OLD SCHOOL CHUM.

Before Retiring

Liver pill.
JEEVES AND THE IMPENDING DOOM.

Should insomnia supervene, add ten minutes of one of the other stories.

I find it curious, now that I have written so much about him, to recall how softly and undramatically Jeeves first entered my little world. Characteristically, he did not thrust himself forward. On that occasion, he spoke just two lines.

The first was:

'Mrs. Gregson to see you, sir.'

The second:

'Very good, sir, which suit will you wear?'

That was in a story in a volume entitled THE MAN WITH TWO LEFT FEET. It was only some time later, when I was going into the strange affair which is related under the title of 'The Artistic Career of Corky', that the man's qualities dawned upon me. I still blush to think of the off-hand way I treated him at our first encounter.

One great advantage in being a historian to a man like Jeeves is that his mere personality prevents one selling one's artistic soul for gold. In recent years I have had lucrative offers for his services from theatrical managers, motion-picture magnates, the proprietors of one or two widely advertised commodities, and even the editor of the comic supplement of an American newspaper, who wanted him for a 'comic strip'. But, tempting though the terms were, it only needed Jeeves deprecating cough and his murmured 'I would scarcely advocate it, sir,' to put the jack under my better nature. Jeeves knows his place, and it is between the covers of a book.

A sudden thought comes to me at this point and causes me a little anxiety. Never having been mixed up in this Omnibus Book business before, I am ignorant of the rules of the game. And what is worrying me is this – Does the publication of an Omnibus Book impose a moral obligation on the author, a sort of gentleman's agreement that he will not write any more about the characters included in it? I hope not, for as regards Jeeves and Bertie all has not yet been told. The world at present knows nothing of Young Thos and his liver-pad, of the curious affair of old Boko and the Captain Kidd costume, or of the cook

Anatole and the unwelcome birthday present. Nor has the infamy wrought by Tuppy Glossop upon Bertie been avenged.

Before we go any further, I must have it distinctly understood that the end is not yet.

The end certainly was not yet. Indeed, it would be difficult to think of an end that was less yetter. Since those words were written – thirty-five years ago come Lammas Eve – the Messrs. Herbert Jenkins Ltd. have published nine full-length Jeeves novels and at any moment I may be starting on another. It just shows how easily one can become an addict. You tell yourself that you can take Jeeves stories or leave them alone, that one more can't possibly hurt you, because you know you can pull up whenever you feel like it, but it is merely wishful thinking. The craving has gripped you and there is no resisting it. You have passed the point of no return.

Taking typewriter in hand to tack on these few words to the Introduction of the 1931 edition, I must confess that a blush mantles my cheek as I read that bit about selling one's soul for gold. It is true that Jeeves has not appeared in a comic strip, but when the B.B.C. wanted to do him on Television, I did not draw myself to my full height and issue a cold *nolle prosequi;* I just asked them how much gold they had in mind. And now Guy Bolton and I have celebrated the fiftieth year of our collaboration by writing a Jeeves musical, making the twenty-first of these merry melanges of mirth and music which we have done together. One's views change with the years. One loses one's . . . what is it, Jeeves? Austerity, I fancy, is the word for which you are groping, sir. That's right, thank you, Jeeves. Not at all, sir. Yes, one tends to lose one's austerity, and today I should not object very strongly if someone wanted to do JEEVES ON ICE. But I still feel, as I felt when I wrote the original Introduction, that his place is between the covers of a book.

P. G. WODEHOUSE

1 · JEEVES TAKES CHARGE

Now, touching this business of old Jeeves – my man, you know – how do we stand? Lots of people think I'm much too dependent on him. My Aunt Agatha, in fact, has even gone so far as to call him my keeper. Well, what I say is: Why not? The man's a genius. From the collar upward he stands alone. I gave up trying to run my own affairs within a week of his coming to me. That was about half a dozen years ago, directly after the rather rummy business of Florence Craye, my Uncle Willoughby's book, and Edwin, the Boy Scout.

The thing really began when I got back to Easeby, my uncle's place in Shropshire. I was spending a week or so there, as I generally did in the summer; and I had had to break my visit to come back to London to get a new valet. I had found Meadowes, the fellow I had taken to Easeby with me, sneaking my silk socks, a thing no bloke of spirit could stick at any price. It transpiring, moreover, that he had looted a lot of other things here and there about the place, I was reluctantly compelled to hand the misguided blighter the mitten and go to London to ask the registry office to dig up another specimen for my approval. They sent me Jeeves.

I shall always remember the morning he came. It so happened that the night before I had been present at a rather cheery little supper, and I was feeling pretty rocky. On top of this I was trying to read a book Florence Craye had given me. She had been one of the house-party at Easeby, and two or three days before I left we had got engaged. I was due back at the end of the week, and I knew she would expect me to have finished the book by then. You see, she was particularly keen on boosting me up a bit nearer her own plane of intellect. She was a girl with a wonderful profile, but steeped to the gills in serious purpose. I can't give you a better idea of the way things stood than by telling you that the book she'd given me to read was called *Types of Ethical Theory*, and that when I opened it at random I struck a page beginning:

> *The postulate or common understanding involved in speech is certainly coextensive, in the obligation it carries, with the social organism of which language is the instrument, and the ends of which it is an effort to subserve.*

All perfectly true, no doubt; but not the sort of thing to spring on a lad with a morning head.

I was doing my best to skim through this bright little volume when the bell rang. I crawled off the sofa and opened the door. A kind of darkish sort of respectful Johnnie stood without.

'I was sent by the agency, sir,' he said. 'I was given to understand that you required a valet.'

I'd have preferred an undertaker; but I told him to stagger in, and he floated noiselessly through the doorway like a healing zephyr. That impressed me from the start. Meadowes had had flat feet and used to clump. This fellow didn't seem to have any feet at all. He just streamed in. He had a grave, sympathetic face, as if he, too, knew what it was to sup with the lads.

'Excuse me, sir,' he said gently.

Then he seemed to flicker, and wasn't there any longer. I heard him moving about in the kitchen, and presently he came back with a glass on a tray.

'If you would drink this, sir,' he said, with a kind of bedside manner, rather like the royal doctor shooting the bracer into the sick prince. 'It is a little preparation of my own invention. It is the Worcester Sauce that gives it its colour. The raw egg makes it nutritious. The red pepper gives it its bite. Gentlemen have told me they have found it extremely invigorating after a late evening.'

I would have clutched at anything that looked like a life-line that morning. I swallowed the stuff. For a moment I felt as if somebody had touched off a bomb inside the old bean and was strolling down my throat with a lighted torch, and then everything seemed suddenly to get all right. The sun shone in through the window; birds twittered in the tree-tops; and, generally speaking, hope dawned once more.

'You're engaged!' I said, as soon as I could say anything.

I perceived clearly that this cove was one of the world's workers, the sort no home should be without.

'Thank you, sir. My name is Jeeves.'

'You can start in at once?'

'Immediately, sir.'

'Because I'm due down at Easeby, in Shropshire, the day after tomorrow.'

'Very good, sir.' He looked past me at the mantelpiece. 'That is an excellent likeness of Lady Florence Craye, sir. It is two years since I saw her ladyship. I was at one time in Lord Worplesdon's employment. I tendered my resignation because I could not see eye to eye with his lordship in his desire to dine in dress trousers, a flannel shirt, and a shooting coat.'

He couldn't tell me anything I didn't know about the old boy's eccentricity. This Lord Worplesdon was Florence's father. He was the old buster who, a few years later, came down to breakfast one morning, lifted the first cover he saw, said 'Eggs! Eggs! Eggs! Damn all eggs!' in an overwrought sort of voice, and instantly legged it for France, never to return to the bosom of his family. This, mind you, being a bit of luck for the bosom of the f., for old Worplesdon had the worst temper in the county.

I had known the family ever since I was a kid, and from

boyhood up this old boy had put the fear of death into me. Time, the great healer, could never remove from my memory the occasion when he found me – then a stripling of fifteen – smoking one of his special cigars in the stables. He got after me with a hunting-crop just at the moment when I was beginning to realise that what I wanted most on earth was solitude and repose, and chased me more than a mile across difficult country. If there was a flaw, so to speak, in the pure joy of being engaged to Florence, it was the fact that she rather took after her father, and one was never certain when she might not erupt. She had a wonderful profile, though.

'Lady Florence and I are engaged, Jeeves,' I said.

'Indeed, sir?'

You know, there was a kind of rummy something about his manner. Perfectly all right and all that, but not what you'd call chirpy. It somehow gave me the impression that he wasn't keen on Florence. Well, of course, it wasn't my business. I supposed that while he had been valeting old Worplesdon she must have trodden on his toes in some way. Florence was a dear girl, and, seen sideways, most awfully good-looking; but if she had a fault it was a tendency to be a bit imperious with the domestic staff.

At this point in the proceedings there was another ring at the front door. Jeeves shimmered out and came back with a telegram. I opened it. It ran:

Return immediately. Extremely urgent. Catch first train. Florence.

'Rum!' I said.

'Sir?'

'Oh, nothing!'

It shows how little I knew Jeeves in those days that I didn't go a bit deeper into the matter with him. Nowadays I would never dream of reading a rummy communication without asking him what he thought of it. And this one was devilish odd. What I mean is, Florence knew I was going back to Easeby the day after tomorrow, anyway; so why the hurry call? Something must have happened, of course; but I couldn't see what on earth it could be.

'Jeeves,' I said, 'we shall be going down to Easeby this afternoon. Can you manage it?

'Certainly, sir.'

'You can get your packing done and all that?'

'Without any difficulty, sir. Which suit will you wear for the journey?

'This one.'

I had on a rather sprightly young check that morning, to which I was a good deal attached; I fancied it, in fact, more than a little. It was perhaps rather sudden till you got used to it, but nevertheless an extremely sound effort, which many lads at the club and elsewhere had admired unrestrainedly.

'Very good, sir.'

Again there was that kind of rummy something in his manner. It was the way he said it, don't you know. He didn't like the suit. I pulled myself together to assert myself. Something seemed to tell me that, unless I was jolly careful and nipped this lad in the bud, he would be starting to boss me. He had the aspect of a distinctly resolute blighter.

Well, I wasn't going to have any of that sort of thing, by Jove! I'd seen so many cases of fellows who had become perfect slaves to their valets. I remember poor old Aubrey Fothergill tell me – with absolute tears in his eyes, poor chap! – one night at the club, that he had been compelled to give up a favourite pair of brown shoes simply because Meekyn, his man, disapproved of them. You have to keep these fellows in their place, don't you know. You have to work the good old iron-hand-in-the-velvet-glove wheeze. If you give them a what's-its-name, they take a thingummy.

'Don't you like this suit, Jeeves?' I said coldly.

'Oh, yes, sir.'

'Well, what don't you like about it?'

'It is a very nice suit, sir.'

'Well, what's wrong with it? Out with it, dash it!'

'If I might make the suggestion, sir, a simple brown or blue, with a hint of some quiet twill—'

'What absolute rot!'

'Very good, sir.'

'Perfectly blithering, my dear man!'

'As you say, sir.'

I felt as if I had stepped on the place where the last stair ought to have been but wasn't. I felt defiant, if you know what I mean, and there didn't seem anything to defy.

'All right, then,' I said.

'Yes, sir.'

And then he went away to collect his kit, while I started in again on *Types of Ethical Theory* and took a stab at a chapter headed 'Idiopsychological Ethics'.

Most of the way down in the train that afternoon, I was wondering what could be up at the other end. I simply couldn't see what could have happened, Easeby wasn't one of those country houses you read about in the society novels, where young girls are lured on to play baccarat and then skinned to the bone of their jewellery, and so on. The house-party I had left had consisted entirely of law-abiding birds like myself.

Besides, my uncle wouldn't have let anything of that kind go on in his house. He was a rather stiff, precise sort of old boy, who liked a quiet life. He was just finishing a history of the family or something, which he had been working on for the last year, and didn't stir much from the library. He was rather a good instance of what they say about its being a good scheme for a fellow to sow his wild oats. I'd been told that in his youth Uncle Willoughby had been a bit of a bounder. You would never have thought it to look at him now.

When I got to the house, Oakshott, the butler, told me that Florence was in her room, watching her maid pack. Apparently there was a dance on at a house about twenty miles away that night, and she was motoring over with some of the Easeby lot and would be away some nights. Oakshott said she had told him to tell her the moment I arrived; so I trickled into the smoking-room and waited, and presently in she came. A glance showed me that she was perturbed, and even peeved. Her eyes had a goggly look, and altogether she appeared considerably pipped.

'Darling!' I said, and attempted the good old embrace; but she side-stepped like a bantam weight.

'Don't!'

'What's the matter?'

'Everything's the matter! Bertie, you remember asking me, when you left, to make myself pleasant to your uncle?'

'Yes.'

The idea being, of course, that as at that time I was more or less dependent on Uncle Willoughby I couldn't very well marry without his approval. And though I knew he wouldn't have any objection to Florence, having known her father since they were at Oxford together, I hadn't wanted to take any chances; so I had told her to make an effort to fascinate the old boy.

'You told me it would please him particularly if I asked him to read me some of his history of the family.'

'Wasn't he pleased?'

'He was delighted. He finished writing the thing yesterday afternoon, and read me nearly all of it last night. I have never had such a shock in my life. The book is an outrage. It is impossible. It is horrible!'

'But, dash it, the family weren't so bad as all that.'

'It is not a history of the family at all. Your uncle has written his reminiscences! He calls them *Recollections of a Long Life*!'

I began to understand. As I say, Uncle Willoughby had been somewhat on the tabasco side as a young man, and it began to look as if he might have turned out something pretty fruity if he had started recollecting his long life.

'If half of what he has written is true,' said Florence, 'your uncle's youth must have been perfectly appalling. The moment we began to read he plunged straight into a most scandalous story of how he and my father were thrown out of a music-hall in 1887!'

'Why?'

'I decline to tell you why.'

It must have been something pretty bad. It took a lot to make them chuck people out of music-halls in 1887.

'Your uncle specifically states that father had drunk a quart and a half of champagne before beginning the evening,' she went on. 'The book is full of stories like that. There is a dreadful one about Lord Emsworth.'

'Lord Emsworth? Not the one we know? Not the one at Blandings?'

A most respectable old Johnnie, don't you know. Doesn't do a thing nowadays but dig in the garden with a spud.

'The very same. That is what makes the book so unspeakable. It is full of stories about people one knows who are the essence of propriety today, but who seem to have behaved, when they were in London in the 'eighties, in a manner that would not have been tolerated in the fo'c'sle of a whaler. Your uncle seems to remember everything disgraceful that happened to anybody when he was in his early twenties. There is a story about Sir Stanley Gervase-Gervase at the White City which is ghastly in its perfection of detail. It seems that Sir Stanley – but I can't tell you!'

'Have a dash!'

'No!'

'Oh, well, I shouldn't worry. No publisher will print the book if it's as bad as all that.'

'On the contrary, your uncle told me that all negotiations are settled with Riggs and Ballinger, and he's sending off the manuscript tomorrow for immediate publication. They make a special thing of that sort of book. They published Lady Carnaby's *Memories of Eighty Interesting Years*.'

'I read 'em!'

'Well, then, when I tell you that Lady Carnaby's Memories are simply not to be compared with your uncle's Recollections, you will understand my state of mind. And father appears in nearly every story in the book! I am horrified at the things he did when he was a young man!'

'What's to be done?'

'The manuscript must be intercepted before it reaches Riggs and Ballinger, and destroyed!'

I sat up.

This sounded rather sporting.

'How are you going to do it?' I inquired.

'How can I do it? Didn't I tell you the parcel goes off tomorrow? I am going to the Murgatroyds' dance tonight and shall not be back till Monday. You must do it. That is why I telegraphed to you.'

'What!'

She gave me a look.

'Do you mean to say you refuse to help me, Bertie?'

'No; but – I say!'

'It's quite simple.'

'But even if I— What I mean is— Of course, anything I can do – but – if you know what I mean—'

'You say you want to marry me, Bertie?'

'Yes, of course; but still—'

For a moment she looked exactly like her old father.

'I will never marry you if those Recollections are published.'

'But, Florence, old thing!'

'I mean it. You may look on it as a test, Bertie. If you have the resource and courage to carry this thing through, I will take it as evidence that you are not the vapid and shiftless person most people think you. If you fail, I shall know that your Aunt Agatha was right when she called you a spineless invertebrate. It will be perfectly simple for you to intercept the manuscript, Bertie. It only requires a little resolution.'

'But suppose Uncle Willoughby catches me at it? He'd cut me off with a bob.'

'If you care more for your uncle's money than for me—'

'No, no! Rather not!'

'Very well, then. The parcel containing the manuscript will, of course, be placed on the hall table tomorrow for Oakshott to take to the village with the letters. All you have to do is to take it away and destroy it. Then your uncle will think it has been lost in the post.'

It sounded thin to me.

'Hasn't he got a copy of it?'

'No; it has not been typed. He is sending the manuscript just as he wrote it.'

'But he could write it over again.'

'As if he would have the energy!'

'But—'

'If you are going to do nothing but make absurd objections, Bertie—'

'I was only pointing things out.'

'Well, don't! Once and for all, will you do me this quite simple act of kindness?'

The way she put it gave me an idea.

'Why not get Edwin to do it? Keep it in the family, kind of, don't you know. Besides, it would be a boon to the kid.'

A jolly bright idea it seemed to me. Edwin was her young brother, who was spending his holidays at Easeby. He was a ferret-faced kid, whom I had disliked since birth. As a matter of fact, talking of Recollections and Memories, it was young blighted Edwin who, nine years before, had led his father to where I was smoking his cigar and caused all the unpleasantness. He was fourteen now and had just joined the Boy Scouts. He was one of those thorough kids, and took his responsibilities pretty seriously. He was always in a sort of fever because he was dropping behind schedule with his daily acts of kindness. However hard he tried, he'd fall behind; and then you would find him prowling about the house, setting such a clip to try and catch up with himself that Easeby was rapidly becoming a perfect hell for man and beast.

The idea didn't seem to strike Florence.

'I shall do nothing of the kind, Bertie. I wonder you can't appreciate the compliment I am paying you – trusting you like this.'

'Oh, I see that all right, but what I mean is, Edwin would do it so much better than I would. These Boy Scouts are up to all sorts of dodges. They spoor, don't you know, and take cover and creep about, and what not.'

'Bertie, will you or will you not do this perfectly trivial thing for me? If not, say so now, and let us end this farce of pretending that you care a snap of the fingers for me.'

'Dear old soul, I love you devotedly!'

'Then will you or will you not—'

'Oh, all right,' I said. 'All right! All right! All right!'

And then I tottered forth to think it over. I met Jeeves in the passage just outside.

'I beg your pardon, sir. I was endeavouring to find you.'

'What's the matter?'

'I felt that I should tell you, sir, that somebody has been putting black polish on your brown walking shoes.'

'What! Who? Why?'

'I could not say, sir.'

'Can anything be done with them?'

'Nothing, sir.'

'Damn!'

'Very good, sir.'

I've often wondered since then how these murderer fellows manage to keep in shape while they're contemplating their next effort. I had a much simpler sort of job on hand, and the thought of it rattled me to such an extent in the night watches that I was a perfect wreck next day. Dark circles under the eyes – I give you my word! I had to call on Jeeves to rally round with one of those life-savers of his.

From breakfast on I felt like a bag-snatcher at a railway station. I had to hang about waiting for the parcel to be put on the hall table, and it wasn't put. Uncle Willoughby was a fixture in the library, adding the finishing touches to the great work, I supposed, and the more I thought the thing over the less I liked it. The chances against my pulling it off seemed about three to two, and the thought of what would happen if I didn't gave me cold shivers down the spine. Uncle Willoughby was a pretty mild sort of old boy, as a rule, but I've known him to cut up rough, and, by Jove, he was scheduled to extend himself if he caught me trying to get away with his life work.

It wasn't till nearly four that he toddled out of the library with the parcel under his arm, put it on the table, and toddled off again. I was hiding a bit to the south-east at the moment, behind a suit of armour. I bounded out and legged it for the table. Then I nipped upstairs to hide the swag. I charged in like a mustang and nearly stubbed my toe on young blighted Edwin, the Boy Scout. He was standing at the chest of drawers, confound him, messing about with my ties.

'Hallo!' he said.

'What are you doing here?'

'I'm tidying your room. It's my last Saturday's act of kindness.'

'Last Saturday's?'

'I'm five days behind. I was six till last night, but I polished your shoes.'

'Was it you—'

'Yes. Did you see them? I just happened to think of it. I was in here, looking round. Mr. Berkeley had this room while you were away. He left this morning. I thought perhaps he might have left something in it that I could have sent on. I've often done acts of kindness that way.'

'You must be a comfort to one and all!'

It became more and more apparent to me that this infernal kid must somehow be turned out eftsoons or right speedily. I had hidden the parcel behind my back; and I didn't think he had seen it; but I wanted to get at that chest of drawers quick, before anyone else came along.

'I shouldn't bother about tidying the room,' I said.

'I like tidying it. It's not a bit of trouble – really.'

'But it's quite tidy now.'

'Not so tidy as I shall make it.'

This was getting perfectly rotten. I didn't want to murder the kid, and yet there didn't seem any other way of shifting him. I pressed down the mental accelerator. The old lemon throbbed fiercely. I got an idea.

'There's something much kinder than that which you could do,' I said. 'You see that box of cigars? Take it down to the smoking-room and snip off the ends for me. That would save me no end of trouble. Stagger along, laddie.'

He seemed a bit doubtful; but he staggered. I shoved the parcel into a drawer, locked it, trousered the key, and felt better. I might be a chump, but, dash it, I could out-general a mere kid with a face like a ferret. I went downstairs again. Just as I was passing the smoking-room door out curveted Edwin. It seemed to me that if he wanted to do a real act of kindness he would commit suicide.

'I'm snipping them,' he said.

'Snip on! Snip on!'

'Do you like them snipped much, or only a bit?'

'Medium.'

'All right. I'll be getting on, then.'

'I should.'

And we parted.

Fellows who know all about that sort of thing – detectives, and so on – will tell you that the most difficult thing in the world is to get rid of the body. I remembered, as a kid, having to learn by heart a poem about a bird by the name of Eugene Aram, who had the deuce of a job in this respect. All I can recall of the actual poetry is the bit that goes:

'Tum-tum, tum-tum, tum-tumty-tum, I slew him, tum-tum tum!'

But I recollect that the poor blighter spent much of his valuable time dumping the corpse into ponds and burying it, and what not, only to have it pop out at him again. It was about an hour after I had shoved the parcel into the drawer when I realised that I had let myself in for just the same sort of thing.

Florence had talked in an airy sort of way about destroying the manuscript; but when one came down to it, how the deuce can a chap destroy a great chunky mass of paper in somebody else's house in the middle of summer? I couldn't ask to have a fire in my bedroom, with the thermometer in the eighties. And if I didn't burn the thing, how else could I get rid of it? Fellows on the battlefield eat dispatches to keep them from falling into the hands of the enemy, but it would have taken me a year to eat Uncle Willoughby's Recollections.

I'm bound to say the problem absolutely baffled me. The only thing seemed to be to leave the parcel in the drawer and hope for the best.

I don't know whether you have ever experienced it, but it's a dashed unpleasant thing having a crime on one's conscience. Towards the end of the day the mere sight of the drawer began to depress me. I found myself getting all on edge; and once when Uncle Willoughby trickled silently into the smoking-room when I was alone there and spoke to me before I knew he was there, I broke the record for the sitting high jump.

I was wondering all the time when Uncle Willoughby would sit up and take notice. I didn't think he would have time to suspect that anything had gone wrong till Saturday morning, when he would be expecting, of course, to get the acknowledgment of the manuscript from the publishers. But early on Friday evening he came out of the library as I was passing and asked me to step in. He was looking considerably rattled.

'Bertie,' he said – he always spoke in a precise sort of pompous kind of way – 'an exceedingly disturbing thing has happened. As you know, I dispatched the manuscript of my book to Messrs. Riggs and Ballinger, the publishers, yesterday afternoon. It should have reached them by the first post this morning. Why I should have been uneasy I cannot say, but my mind was not altogether at rest respecting the safety of the parcel. I therefore telephoned to Messrs. Riggs and Ballinger a few moments back to make inquiries. To my consternation they informed me that they were not yet in receipt of my manuscript.'

'Very rum!'

'I recollect distinctly placing it myself on the hall table in good time to be taken to the village. But here is a sinister thing. I have spoken to Oakshott, who took the rest of the letters to the post office, and he cannot recall seeing it there. He is, indeed, unswerving in his assertions that when he went to the hall to collect the letters there was no parcel among them.'

'Sounds funny!'

'Bertie, shall I tell you what I suspect?'

'What's that?'

'The suspicion will no doubt sound to you incredible, but it alone seems to fit the facts as we know them. I incline to the belief that the parcel has been stolen.'

'Oh, I say! Surely not!'

'Wait! Hear me out. Though I have said nothing to you before, or to anyone else, concerning the matter, the fact remains that during the past few weeks a number of objects – some valuable, others not – have disappeared in this house. The conclusion to which one is irresistibly impelled is that we have a kleptomaniac in our midst. It is a peculiarity of kleptomania, as you are no doubt aware, that the subject is unable to differentiate between the intrinsic values of objects.

He will purloin an old coat as readily as a diamond ring, or a tobacco pipe costing but a few shillings with the same eagerness as a purse of gold. The fact that this manuscript of mine could be of no possible value to any outside person convinces me that—'

'But, Uncle, one moment; I know all about those things that were stolen. It was Meadowes, my man, who pinched them. I caught him snaffling my silk socks. Right in the act, by Jove!'

He was tremendously impressed.

'You amaze me, Bertie! Send for the man at once and question him.'

'But he isn't here. You see, directly I found that he was a sock-sneaker I gave him the boot. That's why I went to London – to get a new man.'

'Then, if the man Meadowes is no longer in the house it could not be he who purloined my manuscript. The whole thing is inexplicable.'

After which we brooded for a bit. Uncle Willoughby pottered about the room, registering baffledness, while I sat sucking at a cigarette, feeling rather like a chappie I'd once read about in a book, who murdered another cove and hid the body under the dining-room table, and then had to be the life and soul of a dinner party, with it there all the time. My guilty secret oppressed me to such an extent that after a while I couldn't stick it any longer. I lit another cigarette and started for a stroll in the grounds, by way of cooling off.

It was one of those still evenings you get in the summer, when you can hear a snail clear its throat a mile away. The sun was sinking over the hills and the gnats were fooling about all over the place, and everything smelled rather topping – what with the falling dew and so on – and I was just beginning to feel a little soothed by the peace of it all when suddenly I heard my name spoken.

'It's about Bertie.'

It was the loathsome voice of young blighted Edwin! For a

moment I couldn't locate it. Then I realised that it came from the library. My stroll had taken me within a few yards of the open window.

I had often wondered how those Johnnies in books did it – I mean the fellows with whom it was the work of a moment to do about a dozen things that ought to have taken them about ten minutes. But, as a matter of fact, it was the work of a moment with me to chuck away my cigarette, swear a bit, leap about ten yards, dive into a bush that stood near the library window, and stand there with my ears flapping. I was as certain as I've ever been of anything that all sorts of rotten things were in the offing.

'About Bertie?' I heard Uncle Willoughby say.

'About Bertie and your parcel. I heard you talking to him just now. I believe he's got it.'

When I tell you that just as I heard these frightful words a fairly substantial beetle of sorts dropped from the bush down the back of my neck, and I couldn't even stir to squash the same, you will understand that I felt pretty rotten. Everything seemed against me.

'What do you mean, boy? I was discussing the disappearance of my manuscript with Bertie only a moment back, and he professed himself as perplexed by the mystery as myself!'

'Well, I was in his room yesterday afternoon, doing him an act of kindness, and he came in with a parcel. I could see it, though he tried to keep it behind his back. And then he asked me to go to the smoking-room and snip some cigars for him; and about two minutes afterwards he came down – and he wasn't carrying anything. So it must be in his room.'

I understand they deliberately teach these dashed Boy Scouts to cultivate their powers of observation and deduction and what not. Devilish thoughtless and inconsiderate of them, I call it. Look at the trouble it causes.

'It sounds incredible,' said Uncle Willoughby, thereby bucking me up a trifle.

'Shall I go and look in his room?' asked young blighted Edwin. 'I'm sure the parcel's there.'

'But what could be his motive for perpetrating this extraordinary theft?'

'Perhaps he's a – what you said just now.'

'A kleptomaniac? Impossible!'

'It might have been Bertie who took all those things from the very start,' suggested the little brute hopefully. 'He may be like Raffles.'

'Raffles?'

'He's a chap in a book who went about pinching things.'

'I cannot believe that Bertie would – ah – go about pinching things.'

'Well, I'm sure he's got the parcel. I'll tell you what you might do. You might say that Mr. Berkeley wired that he had left something here. He had Bertie's room, you know. You might say you wanted to look for it.'

'That would be possible. I—'

I didn't wait to hear any more. Things were getting too hot. I sneaked softly out of my bush and raced for the front door. I sprinted up to my room and made for the drawer where I had put the parcel. And then I found I hadn't the key. It wasn't for the deuce of a time that I recollected I had shifted it to my evening trousers the night before and must have forgotten to take it out again.

Where the dickens were my evening things? I had looked all over the place before I remembered that Jeeves must have taken them away to brush. To leap at the bell and ring it was, with me, the work of a moment. I had just rung it when there was a footstep outside, and in came Uncle Willoughby.

'Oh, Bertie,' he said, without a blush, 'I have – ah – received a telegram from Berkeley, who occupied this room in your absence, asking me to forward him his – er – his cigarette-case, which, it would appear, he inadvertently omitted to take with him when he left the house. I cannot find it downstairs; and it has, therefore, occurred to me that he may have left it in this room. I will – er – just take a look round.'

It was one of the most disgusting spectacles I've ever seen – this white-haired old man, who should have been thinking of the hereafter, standing there lying like an actor.

'I haven't seen it anywhere,' I said.

'Nevertheless, I will search. I must – ah – spare no effort.'

'I should have seen it if it had been here – what?'

'It may have escaped your notice. It is – er – possibly in one of the drawers.'

He began to nose about. He pulled out drawer after drawer, pottering round like an old bloodhound, and babbling from time to time about Berkeley and his cigarette-case in a way that struck me as perfectly ghastly. I just stood there, losing weight every moment.

Then he came to the drawer where the parcel was.

'This appears to be locked,' he said, rattling the handle.

'Yes; I shouldn't bother about that one. It – it's – er – locked, and all that sort of thing.'

'You have not the key?'

A soft, respectful voice spoke behind me.

'I fancy, sir, that this must be the key you require. It was in the pocket of your evening trousers.'

It was Jeeves. He had shimmered in, carrying my evening things, and was standing there holding out the key. I could have massacred the man.

'Thank you,' said my uncle.

'Not at all, sir.'

The next moment Uncle Willoughby had opened the drawer. I shut my eyes.

'No,' said Uncle Willoughby, 'there is nothing here. The drawer is empty. Thank you, Bertie. I hope I have not disturbed you. I fancy – er – Berkeley must have taken his case with him after all.'

When he had gone I shut the door carefully. Then I turned to Jeeves. The man was putting my evening things out on a chair.

'Er – Jeeves!'

'Sir?'

'Oh, nothing.'

It was deuced difficult to know how to begin.

'Er – Jeeves!'

'Sir?'

'Did you— Was there— Have you by chance—'

'I removed the parcel this morning sir.'

'Oh – ah – why?'

'I considered it more prudent, sir.'

I mused for a while.

'Of course, I suppose all this seems tolerably rummy to you, Jeeves?'

'Not at all, sir. I chanced to overhear you and Lady Florence speaking of the matter the other evening, sir.'

'Did you, by Jove?'

'Yes, sir.'

'Well – er – Jeeves, I think that, on the whole, if you were to – as it were – freeze on to that parcel until we get back to London—'

'Exactly, sir.'

'And then we might – er – so to speak – chuck it away somewhere – what?'

'Precisely, sir.'

'I'll leave it in your hands.'

'Entirely, sir.'

'You know, Jeeves, you're by way of being rather a topper.'

'I endeavour to give satisfaction, sir.'

'One in a million, by Jove!'

'It is very kind of you to say so, sir.'

'Well, that's about all, then, I think.'

'Very good, sir.'

Florence came back on Monday. I didn't see her till we were all having tea in the hall. It wasn't till the crowd had cleared away a bit that we got a chance of having a word together.

'Well, Bertie?' she said.

'It's all right.'

'You have destroyed the manuscript?'

'Not exactly; but—'

'What do you mean?'

'I mean I haven't absolutely—'

'Bertie, your manner is furtive!'

'It's all right. It's this way—'

And I was just going to explain how things stood when out of the library came leaping Uncle Willoughby, looking as braced as a two-year-old. The old boy was a changed man.

'A most remarkable thing, Bertie! I have just been speaking with Mr. Riggs on the telephone, and he tells me he received my manuscript by the first post this morning. I cannot imagine what can have caused the delay. Our postal facilities are extremely inadequate in the rural districts. I shall write to head-quarters about it. It is insufferable if valuable parcels are to be delayed in this fashion.'

I happened to be looking at Florence's profile at the moment, and at this juncture she swung round and gave me a look that went right through me like a knife. Uncle Willoughby meandered back to the library, and there was a silence that you could have dug bits out of with a spoon.

'I can't understand it,' I said at last. 'I can't understand it, by Jove!'

'I can. I can understand it perfectly, Bertie. Your heart failed you. Rather than risk offending your uncle you—'

'No, no! Absolutely!'

'You preferred to lose me rather than risk losing the money. Perhaps you did not think I meant what I said. I meant every word. Our engagement is ended.'

'But – I say!'

'Not another word!'

'But, Florence, old thing!'

'I do not wish to hear any more. I see now that your Aunt

Agatha was perfectly right. I consider that I have had a very lucky escape. There was a time when I thought that, with patience, you might be moulded into something worth while. I see now that you are impossible!'

And she popped off, leaving me to pick up the pieces. When I had collected the *débris* to some extent I went to my room and rang for Jeeves. He came in looking as if nothing had happened or was ever going to happen. He was the calmest thing in captivity.

'Jeeves!' I yelled. 'Jeeves, that parcel has arrived in London!'

'Yes, sir?'

'Did you send it?'

'Yes, sir. I acted for the best, sir. I think that both you and Lady Florence overestimated the danger of people being offended at being mentioned in Sir Willoughby's Recollections. It has been my experience, sir, that the normal person enjoys seeing his or her name in print, irrespective of what is said about them. I have an aunt, sir, who a few years ago was a martyr to swollen limbs. She tried Walkinshaw's Supreme Ointment and obtained considerable relief – so much so that she sent them an unsolicited testimonial. Her pride at seeing her photograph in the daily papers in connexion with descriptions of her lower limbs before taking, which were nothing less than revolting, was so intense that it led me to believe that publicity, of whatever sort, is what nearly everybody desires. Moreover, if you have ever studied psychology, sir, you will know that respectable old gentlemen are by no means averse to having it advertised that they were extremely wild in their youth. I have an uncle—'

I cursed his aunts and his uncles and him and all the rest of the family.

'Do you know that Lady Florence has broken off her engagement with me?

'Indeed, sir?'

Not a bit of sympathy! I might have been telling him it was a fine day.

'You're sacked!'

'Very good, sir.'

He coughed gently.

'As I am no longer in your employment, sir, I can speak freely without appearing to take a liberty. In my opinion you and Lady Florence were quite unsuitably matched. Her ladyship is of a highly determined and arbitrary temperament, quite opposed to your own. I was in Lord Worplesdon's service for nearly a year, during which time I had ample opportunities of studying her ladyship. The opinion of the servants' hall was far from favourable to her. Her ladyship's temper caused a good deal of adverse comment among us. It was at times quite impossible. You would not have been happy, sir!'

'Get out!'

'I think you would also have found her educational methods a little trying, sir. I have glanced at the book her ladyship gave you – it has been lying on your table since our arrival – and it is, in my opinion, quite unsuitable. You would not have enjoyed it. And I have it from her ladyship's own maid, who happened to overhear a conversation between her ladyship and one of the gentlemen staying here – Mr. Maxwell, who is employed in an editorial capacity by one of the reviews – that it was her intention to start you almost immediately upon Nietzsche. You would not enjoy Nietzsche, sir. He is fundamentally unsound.'

'Get out!'

'Very good, sir.'

It's rummy how sleeping on a thing often makes you feel quite different about it. It's happened to me over and over again. Somehow or other, when I woke next morning the old heart didn't feel half so broken as it had done. It was a perfectly topping day, and there was something about the way the sun came in at the window and the row the birds were kicking up in the ivy that made me half wonder whether Jeeves wasn't right. After all, though she had a wonderful profile, was it such a catch being engaged to Florence Craye as the casual observer might imagine? Wasn't there something in what Jeeves had said about her character? I began to realise that my ideal wife was something quite different, something a lot more clinging and drooping and prattling, and what not.

I had got as far as this in thinking the thing out when that *Types of Ethical Theory* caught my eye. I opened it, and I give you my honest word this was what hit me:

> *Of the two antithetic terms in the Greek philosophy one only was real and self-subsisting; and that one was Ideal Thought as opposed to that which it has to penetrate and mould. The other corresponding to our Nature, was in itself phenomenal, unreal, without any permanent footing, having no predicates that held true for two moments together; in short, redeemed from negation only by including indwelling realities appearing through.*

Well – I mean to say – what? And Nietzsche, from all accounts, a lot worse than that!

'Jeeves,' I said, when he came in with my morning tea, 'I've been thinking it over. You're engaged again.'

'Thank you, sir.'

I sucked down a cheerful mouthful. A great respect for this bloke's judgment began to soak through me.

'Oh, Jeeves,' I said; 'about that check suit.'

'Yes, sir?'

'Is it really a frost?'

'A trifle too bizarre, sir, in my opinion.'

'But lots of fellows have asked me who my tailor is.'

'Doubtless in order to avoid him, sir.'

'He's supposed to be one of the best men in London.'

'I am saying nothing against his moral character, sir.'

I hesitated a bit. I had a feeling that I was passing into this chappie's clutches, and that if I gave in now I should become just like poor old Aubrey Fothergill, unable to call my soul my own. On the other hand, this was obviously a cove of rare intelligence, and it would be a comfort in a lot of ways to have him doing the thinking for me. I made up my mind.

'All right, Jeeves,' I said. 'You know! Give the bally thing away to somebody!'

He looked down at me like a father gazing tenderly at the wayward child.

'Thank you, sir. I gave it to the under-gardener last night. A little more tea, sir?'

'Jeeves,' I said, coming away from the window.

'Sir?' said Jeeves. He had been clearing the breakfast things, but at the sound of the young master's voice he cheesed it courteously.

'It's a topping morning, Jeeves.'

'Decidedly, sir.'

'Spring and all that.'

'Yes, sir.'

'In the spring, Jeeves, a livelier iris gleams upon the burnished dove.'

'So I have been informed, sir.'

'Right-o! Then bring me my whangee, my yellowest shoes, and the old green Homburg. I'm going into the park to do pastoral dances.'

'Very good, sir.'

I don't know if you know that sort of feeling you get on these days round about the end of April and the beginning of May, when the sky's a light blue with cotton-wool clouds and there's a bit of a breeze blowing from the west? Kind of uplifted feeling. Romantic, if you know what I mean. I'm not much of a ladies' man, but on this particular morning it seemed to me that what I really wanted was some charming girl to buzz up and ask me to save her from assassins or something. So that it was a bit of an anti-climax when I merely ran into young Bingo Little, looking perfectly foul in a crimson satin tie decorated with horseshoes.

'Hallo, Bertie,' said Bingo.

'My God, man!' I gargled. 'The cravat! The gent's neckwear! Why? For what reason?'

'Oh, the tie?' He blushed. 'I – er – I was given it.'

He seemed embarrassed, so I dropped the subject. Always the gentleman. We toddled along a bit, and sat down on a couple of chairs by the Serpentine. Conversation languished. Bingo was staring straight ahead of him in a glassy sort of manner.

'I say, Bertie,' he said, after a pause of about an hour and a quarter.

'Hallo!'

'Do you like the name Mabel?'

'No.'

'No?'

'No.'

'You don't think there's a kind of music in the word, like the wind rustling gently through the treetops?'

'No.'

He seemed disappointed for a moment; then cheered up.

'Of course, you wouldn't. You always were a fat-headed worm without any soul, weren't you?'

'Just as you say. Who is she? Tell me all.'

For I realised now that poor old Bingo was going through it once again. Ever since I have known him – and we were at school together – he has been perpetually falling in love with someone, generally in the spring, which seems to act on him like magic. At school he had the finest collection of actresses' photographs of anyone of his time; and at Oxford his romantic nature was a byword.

'You'd better come along and meet her at lunch,' he said, looking at his watch.

'A ripe suggestion,' I said. 'Where are you meeting her? At the Ritz?'

'Near the Ritz.'

He was geographically accurate. About fifty yards east of the Ritz there is one of those blighted tea-and-bun shops you see dotted about all over London, and into this, if you'll believe me, young Bingo dived like a homing rabbit; and before I had time to say a word we were wedged in at a table, on the brink of a silent pool of coffee left there by an early luncher.

I'm bound to say I couldn't quite follow the development of the scenario. Bingo, while not absolutely rolling in the stuff, has always had a fairish amount of the ready. Apart from what he got from his uncle old Mortimer Little; you've probably heard of Little's Liniment (It Limbers Up The Legs): he ran that till he turned it into a company and retired with a pile – I say, apart from what he got from the above, who gave him a pretty decent allowance, Bingo being his only relative and presumably his heir, I knew that Bingo had finished up the jumping season well on the right side of the ledger, having collected a parcel over the Lincolnshire. Why, then, was he lunching the girl at this Godforsaken eatery? It couldn't be because he was hard up.

Just then the waitress arrived. Rather a pretty girl.

'Aren't we going to wait—?' I started to say to Bingo, thinking it somewhat thick that, in addition to asking a girl to lunch with him in a place like this, he should fling himself on the foodstuffs before she turned up, when I caught sight of his face, and stopped.

The man was goggling. His entire map was suffused with a rich blush. He looked like the Soul's Awakening done in pink.

'Hallo, Mabel!' he said, with a sort of gulp.

'Hallo!' said the girl.

'Mabel,' said Bingo, 'this is Bertie Wooster, a pal of mine.'

'Please to meet you,' she said. 'Nice morning.'

'Fine,' I said.

'You see I'm wearing the tie,' said Bingo.

'It suits you beautiful,' said the girl.

Personally, if anyone had told me that a tie like that suited me, I should have risen and struck them on the mazzard, regardless of their age and sex; but poor old Bingo simply got all flustered with gratification, and smirked in the most gruesome manner.

'Well, what's it going to be today?' asked the girl, introducing the business touch into the conversation.

Bingo studied the menu devoutly.

'I'll have a cup of cocoa, cold veal and ham pie, slice of fruit cake, and a macaroon. Same for you, Bertie?'

I gazed at the man, revolted. That he could have been a pal of mine all these years and think me capable of insulting the old turn with this sort of stuff cut me to the quick.

'Or how about a bit of hot steak-pudding, with a sparkling limado to wash it down?' said Bingo.

You know the way love can change a fellow is really frightful to contemplate. This bird before me, who spoke in this absolutely careless way of macaroons and limado, was the man I had seen in happier days telling the head-waiter at Claridge's exactly how he wanted the *chef to* prepare the *sole frit au gourmet aux champignons,* and saying he would jolly well sling it back if it wasn't just right. Ghastly! Ghastly!

A roll and butter and a small coffee seemed the only things on the list that hadn't been specially prepared by the nastier-minded members of the Borgia family for people they had a particular grudge against, so I chose them, and Mabel hopped it.

'Well?' said Bingo, rapturously.

I took it that he wanted my opinion of the female poisoner who had just left us.

'Very nice,' I said.

He seemed dissatisfied.

'You don't think she's the most wonderful girl you ever saw?' he said, wistfully.

'Oh, absolutely!' I said, to appease the blighter. 'Where did you meet her?'

'At a Subscription dance at Camberwell.'

'What on earth were you doing at a Subscription dance at Camberwell?'

'Your man Jeeves asked me if I would buy a couple of tickets. It was in aid of some charity or other.'

'Jeeves? I didn't know he went in for that sort of thing.'

'Well, I suppose he has to relax a bit every now and then. Anyway, he was there, swinging a dashed efficient shoe. I hadn't meant to go at first, but I turned up for a lark. Oh, Bertie, think what I might have missed!'

'What might you have missed?' I asked, the old lemon being slightly clouded.

'Mabel, you chump. If I hadn't gone I shouldn't have met Mabel.'

'Oh, ah!'

At this point Bingo fell into a species of trance, and only came out of it to wrap himself round the pie and macaroon.

'Bertie,' he said, 'I want your advice.'

'Carry on.'

'At least, not your advice, because that wouldn't be much good to anybody. I mean, you're a pretty consummate old ass, aren't you? Not that I want to hurt your feelings, of course.'

'No, no, I see that.'

'What I wish you would do is to put the whole thing to that fellow Jeeves of yours, and see what he suggests. You've often told me that he has helped other pals of yours out of messes. From what you tell me, he's by way of being the brains of the family.'

'He's never let me down yet.'

'Then put my case to him.'

'What case?'

'My problem.'

'What problem?'

'Why, you poor fish, my uncle, of course. What do you think my uncle's going to say to all this? If I sprang it on him cold, he'd tie himself in knots on the hearth-rug.'

'One of these emotional johnnies, eh?'

'Somehow or other his mind has got to be prepared to receive the news. But how?'

'Ah!'

'That's a lot of help, that "ah"! You see, I'm pretty well dependent on the old boy. If he cut off my allowance, I should be very much in the soup. So you put the whole binge up to Jeeves and see if he can't scare up a happy ending somehow. Tell him my future is in his hands, and that, if the wedding bells ring out, he can rely on me, even unto half my kingdom. Well, call it ten quid. Jeeves would exert himself with ten quid on the horizon, what?'

'Undoubtedly,' I said.

I wasn't in the least surprised at Bingo wanting to lug Jeeves into his private affairs like this. It was the first thing I would have thought of doing myself if I had been in any hole of any description. Most fellows, no doubt, are all for having their valets confine their activities to creasing trousers and what not without trying to run the home; but it's different with Jeeves. Right from the first day he came to me, I have looked on him as a sort of guide, philosopher, and friend. He is a bird of the ripest intellect, full of bright ideas. If anybody could fix things for poor old Bingo, he could.

I stated the case to him that night after dinner.

'Jeeves.'

'Sir?'

'Are you busy just now?'

'No, sir.'

'I mean, not doing anything in particular?'

'No, sir. It is my practice at this hour to read some improving book: but, if you desire my services, this can easily be postponed, or indeed, abandoned altogether.'

'Well, I want your advice. It's about Mr. Little.'

'Young Mr. Little, sir, or the elder Mr. Little, his uncle, who lives in Pounceby Gardens?'

Jeeves seemed to know everything. Most amazing thing. I'd been pally with Bingo practically all my life, and yet I didn't remember ever having heard that his uncle lived anywhere in particular.

'How did you know he lived in Pounceby Gardens?' I said.

'I am on terms of some intimacy with the elder Mr. Little's cook, sir. In fact, there is an understanding.'

I'm bound to say that this gave me a bit of a start. Somehow I'd never thought of Jeeves going in for that sort of thing.

'Do you mean you're engaged?'

'It may be said to amount to that, sir.'

'Well, well!'

'She is a remarkably excellent cook, sir,' said Jeeves, as though he felt called on to give some explanation. 'What was it you wished to ask me about Mr. Little?'

I sprang the details on him.

'And that's how the matter stands, Jeeves,' I said. 'I think we ought to rally round a trifle and help poor old Bingo put the thing through. Tell me about old Mr. Little. What sort of a chap is he?'

'A somewhat curious character, sir. Since retiring from business he has become a great recluse, and now devotes himself almost entirely to the pleasures of the table.'

'Greedy hog, you mean?'

'I would not, perhaps, take the liberty of describing him in precisely those terms, sir. He is what is usually called a gourmet. Very particular about what he eats, and for that reason sets a high value on Miss Watson's services.'

'The cook?'

'Yes, sir.'

'Well, it looks to me as though our best plan would be to shoot young Bingo on to him after dinner one night. Melting mood, I mean to say, and all that.'

'The difficulty is, sir, that at the moment Mr. Little is on a diet, owing to an attack of gout.'

'Things begin to look wobbly.'

'No, sir, I fancy that the elder Mr. Little's misfortune may be turned to the younger Mr. Little's advantage. I was speaking only the other day to Mr. Little's valet, and he was telling me that it has become his principal duty to read to Mr. Little in the evenings. If I were in your place, sir, I should send young Mr. Little to read to his uncle.'

'Nephew's devotion, you mean? Old man touched by kindly action, what?'

'Partly that, sir. But I would rely more on young Mr. Little's choice of literature.'

'That's no good. Jolly old Bingo has a kind face, but when it comes to literature he stops at the *Sporting Times*.'

'That difficulty may be overcome. I would be happy to select books for Mr. Little to read. Perhaps I might explain my idea further?'

'I can't say I quite grasp it yet.'

'The method which I advocate is what, I believe, the advertisers call Direct Suggestion, sir, consisting as it does of driving an idea home by constant repetition. You may have had experience of the system?'

'You mean they keep on telling you that some soap or other is the best, and after a bit you come under the influence and charge round the corner and buy a cake?'

'Exactly, sir. The same method was the basis of all the most valuable propaganda during the world war. I see no reason why it should not be adopted to bring about the desired result with regard to the subject's views on class distinctions. If young Mr. Little were to read day after day to his uncle a series of narratives in which marriage with young persons of an inferior social status was held up as both feasible and admirable, I fancy it would prepare the elder Mr. Little's mind for the reception of the information that his nephew wishes to marry a waitress in a tea-shop.'

'*Are* there any books of that sort nowadays? The only ones I ever see mentioned in the papers are about married couples who find life grey, and can't stick each other at any price.'

'Yes, sir, there are a great many, neglected by the reviewers but widely read. You have never encountered *All for Love*, by Rosie M. Banks?'

'No.'

'Nor *A Red, Red Summer Rose*, by the same author?'

'No.'

'I have an aunt, sir, who owns an almost complete set of Rosie M. Banks. I could easily borrow as many volumes as young Mr. Little might require. They make very light, attractive reading.'

'Well, it's worth trying.'

'I should certainly recommend the scheme, sir.'

'All right, then. Toddle round to your aunt's tomorrow and grab a couple of the fruitiest. We can but have a dash at it.'

'Precisely, sir.'

Bingo reported three days later that Rosie M. Banks was the goods and beyond a question the stuff to give the troops. Old Little had jibbed somewhat at first at the proposed change of literary diet, he not being much of a lad for fiction and having stuck hitherto exclusively to the heavier monthly reviews; but Bingo had got chapter one of *All for Love* past his guard before he knew what was happening, and after that there was nothing to it. Since then they had finished *A Red, Red Summer Rose*, *Madcap Myrtle*, and *Only a Factory Girl* and were halfway through *The Courtship of Lord Strathmorlick*.

Bingo told me all this in a husky voice over an egg beaten up in sherry. The only blot on the thing from his point of view was that it wasn't doing a bit of good to the old vocal chords, which were beginning to show signs of cracking under the strain. He had been looking his symptoms up in a medical dictionary, and he thought he had got 'clergyman's throat'. But against this you had to set the fact that he was making an undoubted hit in the right quarter, and also that after the evening's reading he always stayed on to dinner; and, from what he told me, the dinners turned out by old Little's cook had to be tasted to be believed. There were tears in the old blighter's eyes as he got on the subject of the clear soup. I suppose to a fellow who for weeks had been tackling macaroons and limado it must have been like Heaven.

Old Little wasn't able to give any practical assistance at these banquets, but Bingo said that he came to the table and had his whack of arrowroot, and sniffed the dishes, and told stories of *entrés* he had had in the past, and sketched out scenarios of what he was going to do to the bill of fare in the future, when the doctor put him in shape; so I suppose he enjoyed himself, too, in a way. Anyhow, things seemed to be buzzing along quite satisfactorily, and Bingo said he had got an idea which, he thought, was going to clinch the thing. He wouldn't tell me what it was, but he said it was a pippin.

'We make progress, Jeeves,' I said.

'That is very satisfactory, sir.'

'Mr. Little tells me that when he came to the big scene in *Only a Factory Girl*, his uncle gulped like a stricken bull-pup.'

'Indeed, sir?'

'Where Lord Claude takes the girl in his arms, you know, and says—'

'I am familiar with the passage, sir. It is distinctly moving. It was a great favourite of my aunt's.'

'I think we're on the right track.'

'It would seem so, sir.'

'In fact, this looks like being another of your successes. I've always said, and I always shall say, that for sheer brain, Jeeves, you stand alone. All the other great thinkers of the age are simply in the crowd, watching you go by.'

'Thank you very much, sir. I endeavour to give satisfaction.'

About a week after this, Bingo blew in with the news that his uncle's gout had ceased to trouble him, and that on the morrow he would be back at the old stand working away with knife and fork as before.

'And, by the way,' said Bingo, 'he wants you to lunch with him tomorrow.'

'Me? Why me? He doesn't know I exist.'

'Oh, yes, he does. I've told him about you.'

'What have you told him?'

'Oh, various things. Anyhow, he wants to meet you. And take my tip, laddie – you go! I should think tomorrow would be something special.'

I don't know why it was, but even then it struck me that there was something dashed odd – almost sinister, if you know what I mean – about young Bingo's manner. The old egg had the air of one who has something up his sleeve.

'There is more in this than meets the eye,' I said. 'Why should your uncle ask a fellow to lunch whom he's never seen?'

'My dear old fathead, haven't I just said that I've been telling him all about you – that you're my best pal – at school together, and all that sort of thing?'

'But even then – and another thing. Why are you so dashed keen on my going?'

Bingo hesitated for a moment.

'Well, I told you I'd got an idea. This is it. I want you to spring the news on him. I haven't the nerve myself.'

'What! I'm hanged if I do!'

'And you call yourself a pal of mine!'

'Yes, I know; but there are limits.'

'Bertie,' said Bingo, reproachfully, 'I saved your life once.'

'When?'

'Didn't I? It must have been some other fellow, then. Well, anyway, we were boys together and all that. You can't let me down.'

'Oh, all right,' I said. 'But, when you say you haven't nerve enough for any dashed thing in the world, you misjudge yourself. A fellow who—'

'Bung-oh!' said young Bingo. 'One-thirty tomorrow. Don't be late.'

I'm bound to say that the more I contemplated the binge, the less I liked it. It was all very well for Bingo to say that I was slated for a magnificent lunch; but what good is the best possible lunch to a fellow if he is slung out into the street on his ear during the soup course? However, the word of a Wooster is his bond and all that sort of rot, so at one-thirty next day I tottered up the steps of No. 16, Pounceby Gardens, and punched the bell. And half a minute later I was up in the drawing-room, shaking hands with the fattest man I have ever seen in my life.

The motto of the Little family was evidently 'variety'. Young Bingo is long and thin and hasn't had a superfluous ounce on him since we first met; but the uncle restored the average and a bit over. The hand which grasped mine wrapped it round and enfolded it till I began to wonder if I'd ever get it out without excavating machinery.

'Mr. Wooster, I am gratified – I am proud – I am honoured.'

It seemed to me that young Bingo must have boosted me to some purpose.

'Oh, ah!' I said.

He stepped back a bit, still hanging on to the good right hand.

'You are very young to have accomplished so much!'

I couldn't follow the train of thought. The family, especially my Aunt Agatha, who has savaged me incessantly from childhood up, have always rather made a point of the fact that mine is a wasted life, and that, since I won a prize at my first school for the best collection of wild flowers made during the summer holidays, I haven't done a dam' thing to land me on the nation's scroll of fame. I was wondering if he couldn't have got me mixed up with someone else, when the telephone-bell rang outside in the hall, and the maid came in to say that I was wanted. I buzzed down, and found it was young Bingo.

'Hallo!' said young Bingo. 'So you've got there? Good man! I knew I could rely on you. I say, did my uncle seem pleased to see you?'

'Absolutely all over me. I can't make it out.'

'Oh, that's all right. I just rang up to explain. The fact is, old man, I know you won't mind, but I told him that you were the author of those books I've been reading to him.'

'What!'

'Yes, I said, that "Rosie M. Banks" was your pen-name, and you didn't want it generally known, because you were a modest, retiring sort of chap. He'll listen to you now. Absolutely hang on your words. A brightish idea, what? I doubt if Jeeves in person could have thought up a better one than that. Well, pitch it strong, old lad, and keep steadily before you the fact that I must have my allowance raised. I can't possibly marry on what I've got now. If this film is to end with the slow fade-out on the embrace, at least double is indicated. Well, that's that. Cheerio!'

And he rang off. At that moment the gong sounded, and the genial host came tumbling downstairs like the delivery of a ton of coals.

I always look back to that lunch with a sort of aching regret. It was the lunch of a lifetime, and I wasn't in a fit state to appreciate it. Subconsciously, if you know what I mean, I could see it was pretty special, but I had got the wind up to such a frightful extent over the ghastly situation in which young Bingo had landed me that its deeper meaning never really penetrated. Most of the time I might have been eating sawdust for all the good it did me.

Old Little struck the literary note right from the start.

'My nephew has probably told you that I have been making a close study of your books of late?' he began.

'Yes. He did mention it. How – er – how did you like the bally things?'

He gazed reverently at me.

'Mr. Wooster, I am not ashamed to say that the tears came into my eyes as I listened to them. It amazes me that a man as young as you can have been able to plumb human nature so surely to its depths; to play with so unerring a hand on the quivering heartstrings of your reader; to write novels so true, so human, so moving, so vital!'

'Oh, it's just a knack,' I said.

The good old persp. was bedewing my forehead by this time in a pretty lavish manner. I don't know when I've been so rattled.

'Do you find the room a trifle warm?'

'Oh no, no, rather not. Just right.'

'Then it's the pepper. If my cook has a fault – which I am not prepared to admit – it is that she is inclined to stress the pepper a trifle in her made dishes. By the way, do you like her cooking?'

I was so relieved that we had got off the subject of my literary output that I shouted approval in a ringing baritone.

'I am delighted to hear it, Mr. Wooster. I may be prejudiced, but to my mind that woman is a genius.'

'Absolutely!' I said.

'She has been with me many years, and in all that time I have not known her guilty of a single lapse from the highest standard. Except once, in the winter of 1917, when a purist might have condemned a certain mayonnaise of hers as lacking in creaminess. But one must make allowances. There had been several air-raids about that time, and no doubt the poor woman was shaken. But nothing is perfect in this world, Mr. Wooster, and I have had my cross to bear. All these years I have lived in constant apprehension lest some evilly-disposed person might lure her from my employment. To my certain knowledge she has received offers, lucrative offers, to accept service elsewhere. You may judge of my dismay, Mr. Wooster, when only this morning the bolt fell. She gave notice!'

'Good Lord!'

'Your consternation does credit, if I may say so, to the heart of the author of *A Red, Red Summer Rose*. But I am thankful to

53

say the worst has not happened. The matter has been adjusted. Jane is not leaving me.'

'Good egg!'

'Good egg, indeed – though the expression is not familiar to me. I do not remember having come across it in your books. And, speaking of your books, may I say that what has impressed me about them even more than the moving poignancy of the actual narrative is your philosophy of life. If there were more like you, Mr. Wooster, London would be a better place.'

This was dead opposite to my Aunt Agatha's philosophy of life, she having always rather given me to understand that it is the presence in it of fellows like me that makes London more or less of a plague-spot; but I let it go.

'Let me tell you, Mr. Wooster, that I appreciate your splendid defiance of the outworn fetishes of a purblind social system. I appreciate it! *You* are big enough to see that rank is but the guinea stamp and that, in the magnificent words of Lord Bletchmore in *Only a Factory Girl,* "Be her origin ne'er so humble, a good woman is the equal of the finest lady on earth!"'

I sat up.

'I say! Do you think that?'

'I do, Mr. Wooster. I am ashamed to say that there was a time when I was, like other men, a slave to the idiotic convention which we call Class Distinction. But, since I read your books—'

I might have known it. Jeeves had done it again.

'You think it's all right for a bloke in what you might call a certain social position to marry a girl of what you might describe as the lower classes?'

'Most assuredly I do, Mr. Wooster.'

I took a deep breath, and slipped him the good news.

'Young Bingo – your nephew, you know – wants to marry a waitress,' I said.

'I honour him for it.'

'You don't object?'

54

'On the contrary.'

I took another deep breath, and shifted to the sordid side of the business.

'I hope you won't think I'm butting in, don't you know,' I said, 'but – er – well, how about it?'

'I fear I do not quite follow you.'

'Well, I mean to say, his allowance and all that. The money you're good enough to give him. He was rather hoping that you might see your way to jerking up the total a bit.'

Old Little shook his head regretfully.

'I fear that can hardly be managed. You see, a man in my position is compelled to save every penny. I will gladly continue my nephew's existing allowance, but beyond that I cannot go. It would not be fair to my wife.'

'What! But you're not married?'

'Not yet. But I propose to enter upon that holy state almost immediately. The lady who for years has cooked so well for me honoured me by accepting my hand this very morning.' A cold gleam of triumph came into his eye. 'Now let 'em try to get her away from me!' he muttered, defiantly.

'Young Mr. Little has been trying frequently during the afternoon to reach you on the telephone, sir,' said Jeeves that night, when I got home.

'I'll bet he has,' I said. I had sent poor old Bingo an outline of the situation by messenger-boy shortly after lunch.

'He seemed a trifle agitated.'

'I don't wonder. Jeeves,' I said, 'brace up and bite the bullet. I'm afraid I've bad news for you.'

'Sir?'

'That scheme of yours – reading those books to old Mr. Little and all that – has blown out a fuse.'

'They did not soften him?'

'They did. That's the whole bally trouble. Jeeves, I'm sorry to say that *fiancée* of yours – Miss Watson, you know – the cook, you know – well, the long and the short of it is that she's chosen riches instead of honest worth, if you know what I mean.'

'Sir?'

'She's handed you the mitten and gone and got engaged to old Mr. Little!'

'Indeed, sir?'

'You don't seem much upset?'

'The fact is, sir, I had anticipated some such outcome.'

I stared at him. 'Then what on earth did you suggest the scheme for?'

'To tell you the truth, sir, I was not wholly averse from a severance of my relations with Miss Watson. In fact, I greatly desired it. I respect Miss Watson exceedingly, but I have seen for a long time that we were not suited. Now the other young person with whom I have an understanding—'

'Great Scot, Jeeves! There isn't another?'

'Yes, sir.'

'How long has this been going on?'

'For some weeks, sir. I was greatly attracted by her when I first met her at a Subscription dance at Camberwell.'

'My sainted aunt! Not—'

Jeeves inclined his head gravely.

'Yes, sir. By an odd coincidence it is the same young person that young Mr. Little – I have placed the cigarettes on the small table. Good night, sir.'

It gave me a nasty jar, I can tell you. You see, what happened was this. Once a year Jeeves takes a couple of weeks' vacation and biffs off to the sea or somewhere to restore his tissues. Pretty rotten for me, of course, while he's away. But it has to be stuck, so I stick it; and I must admit that he usually manages to get hold of a fairly decent fellow to look after me in his absence.

Well, the time had come round again, and Jeeves was in the kitchen giving the understudy a few tips about his duties. I happened to want a stamp or something, or a bit of string or something, and I toddled down the passage to ask him for it. The silly ass had left the kitchen door open, and I hadn't gone two steps when his voice caught me squarely in the ear-drum.

'You will find Mr. Wooster,' he was saying to the substitute chappie, 'an exceedingly pleasant and amiable young gentleman, but not intelligent. By no means intelligent. Mentally he is negligible – quite negligible.'

Well, I mean to say, what!

I suppose, strictly speaking, I ought to have charged in and ticked the blighter off properly in no uncertain voice. But I doubt whether it's humanly possible to tick Jeeves off. Personally, I didn't even have a dash at it. I merely called for my hat and stick in a marked manner and legged it. But the memory rankled, if you know what I mean. We Woosters do not lightly forget. At least, we do – somethings – appointments, and people's birthdays, and letters to post, and all that – but not an absolute bally insult like the above. I brooded like the dickens.

I was still brooding when I dropped in at the oyster-bar at Buck's for a quick bracer. I needed a bracer rather particularly at the moment, because I was on my way to lunch with my Aunt Agatha. A pretty frightful ordeal, believe me or believe me not. Practically the nearest thing to being disembowelled. I had just had one quick and another rather slower, and was feeling about as cheerio as was possible under the circs, when a muffled voice hailed me from the north-east, and turning round, I saw young Bingo Little propped up in a corner, wrapping himself round a sizable chunk of bread and cheese.

'Hallo-allo-allo!' I said. 'Haven't seen you for ages. You've not been in here lately, have you?'

'No. I've been living out in the country.'

'Eh?' I said, for Bingo's loathing for the country was well known. 'Whereabouts?'

'Down in Hampshire, at a place called Ditteredge.'

'No really? I know some people who've got a house there. The Glossops. Have you met them?'

'Why, that's where I'm staying!' said young Bingo. 'I'm tutoring the Glossop kid.'

'What for?' I said. I couldn't seem to see young Bingo as a tutor. Though, of course, he did get a degree of sorts at Oxford, and I suppose you can always fool some of the people some of the time.

'What for? For money, of course! An absolute sitter came unstitched in the second race at Haydock Park,' said young Bingo, with some bitterness, 'and I dropped my entire month's allowance. I hadn't the nerve to touch my uncle for any more, so it was a case of buzzing round to the agents and getting a job. I've been down there three weeks.'

'I haven't met the Glossop kid.'

'Don't!' advised Bingo, briefly.

'The only one of the family I really know is the girl.'

I had hardly spoken these words when the most extraordinary change came over young Bingo's face. His eyes bulged, his cheeks flushed, and his Adam's apple hopped about like one of those indiarubber balls on the top of the fountain in a shooting-gallery.

'Oh, Bertie!' he said, in a strangled sort of voice.

I looked at the poor fish anxiously. I knew that he was always falling in love with someone, but it didn't seem possible that even he could have fallen in love with Honoria Glossop. To me the girl was simply nothing more nor less than a pot of poison. One of those dashed large, brainy, strenuous, dynamic girls you see so many of these days. She had been at Girton, where, in addition to enlarging her brain to the most frightful extent, she had gone in for every kind of sport and developed the physique of a middle-weight catch-as-catch-can wrestler. I'm not sure she didn't box for the 'Varsity while she was up. The effect she had on me whenever she appeared was to make me want to slide into a cellar and lie low till they blew the All-Clear.

Yet here was young Bingo obviously all for her. There was no mistaking it. The love-light was in the blighter's eyes.

'I worship her, Bertie! I worship the very ground she treads on!' continued the patient, in a loud penetrating voice. One or two fellows had come in, and McGarry, the chap behind the bar, was listening with his ears flapping. But there's no reticence about Bingo. He always reminds me of the hero of a musical comedy who takes the centre of the stage, gathers the boys round him in a circle, and tells them all about his love at the top of his voice.

'Have you told her?'

'No. I haven't had the nerve. But we walk together in the garden most evenings, and it sometimes seems to me that there is a look in her eyes.'

'I know that look. Like a sergeant-major.'

'Nothing of the kind! Like a tender goddess.'

'Half a second, old thing,' I said. 'Are you sure we're talking about the same girl? The one I mean is Honoria. Perhaps there's a younger sister or something I've not heard of?'

'Her name is Honoria,' bawled Bingo, reverently.

'And she strikes you as a tender goddess?'

'She does.'

'God bless you!' I said.

'She walks in beauty like the night of cloudless climes and starry skies; and all that's best of dark and bright meet in her aspect and her eyes. Another bit of bread and cheese,' he said to the lad behind the bar.

'You're keeping your strength up,' I said.

'This is my lunch. I've got to meet Oswald at Waterloo at one-fifteen, to catch the train back. I brought him up to town to see the dentist.'

'Oswald? Is that the kid?'

'Yes. Pestilential to a degree.'

'Pestilential! That reminds me, I'm lunching with my Aunt Agatha. I'll have to pop off now, or I'll be late.'

In Society circles, I believe, my Aunt Agatha has a fairly fruity reputation as a hostess. But then, I take it she doesn't ballyrag her other guests the way she does me. I don't think I can remember a single meal with her since I was a kid of tender years at which she didn't turn the conversation sooner or later to the subject of my frightfulness. Today, she started in on me with the fish.

'Bertie,' she said – in part and chattily – 'it is young men like you who make the person with the future of the race at heart despair!'

'What-ho!' I said.

'Cursed with too much money, you fritter away in selfish idleness a life which might have been made useful, helpful, and profitable. You do nothing but waste your time on frivolous pleasures. You are simply an anti-social animal, a drone—' She fixed me with a glittering eye. 'Bertie, you must marry!'

'No, dash it all!'

'Yes! You should be breeding children to—'

'No, really, I say, please!' I said, blushing richly. Aunt Agatha belongs to two or three of these women's clubs, and she keeps forgetting she isn't in the smoking-room.

'You want somebody strong, self-reliant, and sensible, to counterbalance the deficiencies and weaknesses of your own character. And by great good luck I have found the very girl. She is of excellent family – plenty of money, though that does not matter in your case. She has met you; and, while there is naturally much in you of which she disapproves, she does not dislike you. I know this, for I have sounded her – guardedly, of course – and I am sure that you have only to make the first advances—'

'Who is it?' I would have said it long before, but the shock had made me swallow a bit of roll the wrong way, and I had only just finished turning purple and trying to get a bit of air back into the old windpipe. 'Who is it?'

'Sir Roderick Glossop's daughter, Honoria.'

'No, no!' I cried, paling beneath the tan.

'Don't be silly, Bertie. She is just the wife for you.'

'Yes, but look here—'

'She will mould you.'

'But I don't want to be moulded.'

Aunt Agatha gave me the kind of look she used to give me when I was a kid and had been found in the jam cupboard.

'Bertie! I hope you are not going to be troublesome.'

'Well, but I mean—'

'Lady Glossop has very kindly invited you to Ditteredge Hall for a few days. I told her you would be delighted to come down tomorrow.'

'I'm sorry, but I've got a dashed important engagement tomorrow.'

'What engagement?'

'Well – er—'

'You have no engagement. And, even if you had, you must put it off. I shall be very seriously annoyed, Bertie, if you do not go to Ditteredge Hall tomorrow.'

'Oh, right-o!' I said.

A man may be down, but he is never out. It wasn't two minutes after I had parted from Aunt Agatha before the old fighting spirit of the Woosters reasserted itself. Ghastly as the peril was which loomed before me, I was conscious of a rummy sort of exhilaration. It was a tight corner, but the tighter the corner, I felt, the more juicily should I score off Jeeves when I got myself out of it without a bit of help from him. Ordinarily, of course, I should have consulted him and trusted to him to solve the difficulty; but after what I had heard him saying in the kitchen, I was dashed if I was going to demean myself. When I got home I addressed the man with light abandon.

'Jeeves,' I said, 'I'm in a bit of difficulty.'

'I'm sorry to hear that, sir.'

'Yes, quite a bad hole. In fact, you might say on the brink of a precipice, and faced by an awful doom.'

'If I could be of any assistance, sir—'

'Oh, no. No, no. Thanks very much, but no, no. I won't trouble you. I've no doubt I shall be able to get out of it all right by myself.'

'Very good, sir.'

So that was that. I'm bound to say I'd have welcomed a bit more curiosity from the fellow, but that is Jeeves all over. Cloaks his emotions, if you know what I mean. Wears the mask and what not.

Honoria was away when I got to Ditteredge on the following afternoon. Her mother told me that she was staying with some people named Braythwayt in the neighbourhood, and would be back next day, bringing the daughter of the house with her for a visit. She said I would find Oswald out in the grounds, and such is a mother's love that she spoke as if that were a bit of a boost for the grounds and an inducement to go there.

Rather decent, the grounds at Ditteredge. A couple of terraces, a bit of lawn with a cedar on it, a bit of shrubbery, and finally a small but goodish lake with a stone bridge running across it. Directly I'd worked my way round the shrubbery I spotted young Bingo leaning against the bridge smoking a cigarette. Sitting on the stone work, fishing, was a species of kid whom I took to be Oswald the Plague-Spot.

Bingo was both surprised and delighted to see me, and introduced me to the kid. If the latter was surprised and delighted, too, he concealed it like a diplomat. He just looked at me, raised his eyebrows slightly, and went on fishing. He was one of those supercilious striplings, who give you the impression that you went to the wrong school and that your clothes don't fit.

'This is Oswald,' said Bingo.

'What,' I replied, cordially, 'could be sweeter? How are you?'

'Oh, all right,' said the kid.

'Nice place, this.'

'Oh, all right,' said the kid.

'Having a good time fishing?'

'Oh, all right,' said the kid.

Young Bingo led me off to commune apart.

'Doesn't Oswald's incessant flow of prattle make your head ache sometimes?' I asked.

Bingo sighed.

'It's a hard job.'

'What's a hard job?'

'Loving him.'

'Do you love him?' I asked, surprised. I shouldn't have thought it could be done.

'I try to,' said young Bingo, 'for Her sake. She's coming back tomorrow, Bertie.'

'So I heard.'

'She is coming, my love, my own—'

'Absolutely,' I said. 'But touching on young Oswald once more. Do you have to be with him all day? How do you manage to stick it?'

'Oh, he doesn't give much trouble. When we aren't working he sits on the bridge all the time, trying to catch tiddlers.'

'Why don't you shove him in?'

'Shove him in?'

'It seems to me distinctly the thing to do,' I said, regarding the stripling's back with a good deal of dislike. 'It would wake him up a bit, and make him take an interest in things.'

Bingo shook his head a bit wistfully.

'Your proposition attracts me,' he said, 'but I'm afraid it can't be done. You see, She would never forgive me. She is devoted to the little brute.'

'Great Scot!' I cried. 'I've got it!'

I don't know if you know that feeling when you get an inspiration, and tingle all down your spine from the soft collar as now worn to the very soles of the old Waukeesis? Jeeves, I suppose, feels that way more or less all the time, but it isn't often it comes to me. But now all Nature seemed to be shouting at me, 'You've clicked!' and I grabbed young Bingo by the arm in a way that must have made him feel as if a horse had bitten him. His finely-chiselled features were twisted with agony, and he asked me what the dickens I thought I was playing at.

'Bingo,' I said, 'what would Jeeves have done?'

'How do you mean, what would Jeeves have done?'

'I mean what would he have advised in a case like yours? I mean you wanting to make a hit with Honoria Glossop and all that. Why, take it from me laddie, he would have shoved you behind that clump of bushes over there; he would have got me to lure Honoria on to the bridge somehow; then, at the proper time, he would have told me to give the kid a pretty hefty jab in the small of the back, so as to shoot him into the water; and then you would have dived in and hauled him out. How about it?'

'You didn't think that out by yourself, Bertie?' said young Bingo, in a hushed sort of voice.

'Yes, I did. Jeeves isn't the only fellow with ideas.'

'But it's absolutely wonderful.'

'Just a suggestion.'

'The only objection I can see is that it would be so dashed awkward for you. I mean to say, suppose the kid turned round and said you had shoved him in, that would make you frightfully unpopular with Her.'

'I don't mind risking that.'

The man was deeply moved.

'Bertie, this is noble.'

'No, no.'

He clasped my hand silently, then chuckled like the last bit of water going down the waste-pipe in a bath.

'Now what?' I said.

'I was only thinking,' said young Bingo, 'how fearfully wet Oswald will get. Oh, happy day!'

I don't know if you've noticed it, but it's rummy how nothing in this world ever seems to be absolutely perfect. The drawback to this otherwise singularly bright binge was, of course, the fact that Jeeves wouldn't be on the spot to watch me in action. Still, apart from that there wasn't a flaw. The beauty of the thing was, you see, that nothing could possibly go wrong. You know how it is, as a rule, when you want to get Chappie A on Spot B at exactly the same moment when Chappie C is on Spot D. There's always a chance of a hitch. Take the case of a general, I mean to say, who's planning out a big movement. He tells one regiment to capture the hill with the windmill on it at the exact moment when another regiment is taking the bridgehead or something down in the valley; and everything gets all messed up. And then, when they're chatting the thing over in camp that night, the colonel of the first regiment says, 'Oh, sorry! Did you say the hill with the windmill? I thought you said the one with the flock of sheep.' And there you are! But, in this case, nothing like that could happen, because Oswald and Bingo would be on the spot right along, so that all I had to worry about was getting Honoria there in due season. And I managed that all right, first shot, by asking her if she would come for a stroll in the grounds with me, as I had something particular to say to her. She had arrived shortly after lunch in the car with the Braythwayt girl. I was introduced to the latter, a tallish girl with blue eyes and fair hair. I rather took to her – she was so unlike Honoria – and, if I had been able to spare the time, I shouldn't have minded talking to her for a bit. But business was business – I had fixed it up with Bingo to be behind the bushes at three sharp, so I got hold of Honoria and steered her out through the grounds in the direction of the lake.

'You're very quiet, Mr. Wooster,' she said.

Made me jump a bit. I was concentrating pretty tensely at the moment. We had just come in sight of the lake, and I was casting a keen eye over the ground to see that everything was in order. Everything appeared to be as arranged. The kid Oswald was hunched up on the bridge; and, as Bingo wasn't visible, I took it that he had got into position. My watch made it two minutes after the hour.

'Eh?' I said. 'Oh, ah, yes. I was just thinking.'

'You said you had something important to say to me.'

'Absolutely!' I had decided to open the proceedings by sort of paving the way for young Bingo. I mean to say, without actually mentioning his name, I wanted to prepare the girl's mind for the fact that, surprising as it might seem, there was someone who had long loved her from afar and all that sort of rot. 'It's like this,' I said. 'It may sound rummy and all that, but there's somebody who's frightfully in love with you and so forth – a friend of mind, you know.'

'A friend of yours?'

'Yes.'

She gave a kind of a laugh.

'Well, why doesn't he tell me so?'

'Well, you see, that's the sort of chap he is. Kind of shrinking, diffident kind of fellow. Hasn't got the nerve. Thinks you so much above him, don't you know. Looks on you as a sort of goddess. Worships the ground you tread on, but can't whack up the ginger to tell you so.'

'This is very interesting.'

'Yes. He's not a bad chap, you know, in his way. Rather an ass, perhaps, but well-meaning. Well, that's the posish. You might just bear it in mind, what?'

'How funny you are!'

She chucked back her head and laughed with considerable vim. She had a penetrating sort of laugh. Rather like a train going into a tunnel. It didn't sound over-musical to me, and on the kid Oswald it appeared to jar not a little. He gazed at us with a good deal of dislike.

'I wish the dickens you wouldn't make that row,' he said. 'Scaring all the fish away.'

It broke the spell a bit. Honoria changed the subject.

'I do wish Oswald wouldn't sit on the bridge like that,' she said. 'I'm sure it isn't safe. He might easily fall in.'

'I'll go and tell him,' I said.

I suppose the distance between the kid and me at this juncture was about five yards, but I got the impression that it was nearer a hundred. And, as I started to toddle across the intervening space, I had a rummy feeling that I'd done this very thing before. Then I remembered. Years ago, at a country-house party, I had been roped in to play the part of a butler in some amateur theatricals in aid of some ghastly charity or other; and I had had to open the proceedings by walking across the empty stage from left upper entrance and shoving a tray on a table down right. They had impressed it on me at rehearsals that I mustn't take the course at a quick heel-and-toe, like a chappie finishing strongly in a walking-race; and the result was that I kept the brakes on to such an extent that it seemed to me as if I was never going to get to the bally table at all. The stage seemed to stretch out in front of me like a trackless desert, and there was a kind of breathless hush as if all Nature had paused to concentrate its attention on me personally. Well, I felt just like that now. I had a kind of dry gulping in my throat, and the more I walked the farther away the kid seemed to get, till suddenly I found myself standing just behind him without quite knowing how I'd got there.

'Hallo!' I said, with a sickly sort of grin – wasted on the kid, because he didn't bother to turn round and look at me. He merely wiggled his left ear in a rather peevish manner. I don't know when I've met anybody in whose life I appeared to mean so little.

'Hallo!' I said. 'Fishing?'

I laid my hand in a sort of elder-brotherly way on his shoulder.

'Here, look out!' said the kid, wobbling on his foundations.

It was one of those things that want doing quickly or not at all. I shut my eyes and pushed. Something seemed to give. There was a scrambling sound, a kind of yelp, a scream in the offing, and a splash. And so the long day wore on, so to speak.

I opened my eyes. The kid was just coming to the surface.

'Help!' I shouted, cocking an eye on the bush from which young Bingo was scheduled to emerge.

Nothing happened. Young Bingo didn't emerge to the slightest extent whatever.

'I say! Help!' I shouted again.

I don't want to bore you with reminiscences of my theatrical career, but I must just touch once more on that appearance of mine as the butler. The scheme on that occasion had been that when I put the tray on the table the heroine would come on and say a few words to get me off. Well, on the night the misguided female forgot to stand by, and it was a full minute before the search-party located her and shot her on to the stage. And all that time I had to stand there, waiting. A rotten sensation, believe me, and this was just the same, only worse. I understood what these writers mean when they talk about time standing still.

Meanwhile, the kid Oswald was presumably being cut off in his prime, and it began to seem to me that some sort of steps ought to be taken about it. What I had seen of the lad hadn't particularly endeared him to me, but it was undoubtedly a bit thick to let him pass away. I don't know when I have seen anything more grubby and unpleasant than the lake as viewed from the bridge; but the thing apparently had to be done. I chucked off my coat and vaulted over.

It seems rummy that water should be so much wetter when you go into it with your clothes on than when you're just bathing, but take it from me that it does. I was only under about three seconds, I suppose, but I came up feeling like the bodies you read of in the paper which 'had evidently been in the water several days'. I felt clammy and bloated.

At this point the scenario struck another snag. I had assumed that directly I came to the surface I should get hold of the kid and steer him courageously to shore. But he hadn't waited to be steered. When I had finished getting the water out of my eyes and had time to take a look round, I saw him about ten yards away, going strongly and using, I think, the Australian crawl. The spectacle took all the heart out of me, I mean to say, the whole essence of a rescue, if you know what I mean, is that the party of the second part shall keep fairly still and in one spot. If he starts swimming off on his own account and can obviously give you at least forty yards in the hundred, where are you? The whole thing falls through. It didn't seem to me that there was much to be done except get ashore, so I got ashore. By the time I had landed, the kid was half-way to the house. Look at it from whatever angle you like, the thing was a wash-out.

I was interrupted in my meditations by a noise like the Scotch express going under a bridge. It was Honoria Glossop laughing. She was standing at my elbow, looking at me in a rummy manner.

'Oh, Bertie, you are funny!' she said. And even in that moment there seemed to me something sinister in the words. She had never called me anything except 'Mr. Wooster' before. 'How wet you are!'

'Yes, I am wet.'

'You had better hurry into the house and change.'

'Yes.'

I wrung a gallon or two of water out of my clothes.

'You *are* funny!' she said again. 'First proposing in that extraordinary roundabout way, and then pushing poor little Oswald into the lake so as to impress me by saving him.'

I managed to get the water out of my throat sufficiently to try to correct this fearful impression.

'No, no!'

'He said you pushed him in, and I saw you do it. Oh, I'm not angry, Bertie. I think it was too sweet of you. But I'm quite sure it's time that I took you in hand. You certainly want someone to look after you. You've been seeing too many moving-pictures. I suppose the next thing you would have done would have been to set the house on fire so as to rescue me.' She looked at me in a proprietary sort of way. 'I think,' she said, 'I shall be able to make something of you, Bertie. It is true yours has been a wasted life up to the present, but you are still young, and there is a lot of good in you.'

'No, really there isn't.'

'Oh, yes, there is. It simply wants bringing out. Now you run straight up to the house and change your wet clothes or you will catch cold.'

And, if you know what I mean, there was a sort of motherly note in her voice which seemed to tell me, even more than her actual words, that I was for it.

As I was coming downstairs after changing, I ran into young Bingo, looking festive to a degree.

'Bertie!' he said. 'Just the man I wanted to see. Bertie, a wonderful thing has happened.'

'You blighter!' I cried. 'What became of you? Do you know—?'

'Oh, you mean about being in those bushes? I hadn't time to tell you about that. It's all off.'

'All off?'

'Bertie, I was actually starting to hide in those bushes when the most extraordinary thing happened. Walking across the lawn I saw the most radiant, the most beautiful girl in the world. There is none like her, none. Bertie, do you believe in love at first sight? You do believe in love at first sight, don't you, Bertie, old man? Directly I saw her, she seemed to draw me like a magnet. I seemed to forget everything. We two were alone in a world of music and sunshine. I joined her. I got into conversation. She was a Miss Braythwayt, Bertie – Daphne Braythwayt. Directly our eyes met I realised that what I had imagined to be my love for Honoria Glossop had been a mere passing whim. Bertie, you do believe in love at first sight, don't you? She is so wonderful, so sympathetic. Like a tender goddess—'

At this point I left the blighter.

Two days later I got a letter from Jeeves.

'. . . The weather,' it ended, 'continues fine. I have had one exceedingly enjoyable bathe.'

I gave one of those hollow, mirthless laughs, and went downstairs to join Honoria. I had an appointment with her in the drawing-room. She was going to read Ruskin to me.

The blow fell at precisely one forty-five (summer-time). Benson, my Aunt Agatha's butler, was offering me the fried potatoes at the moment, and such was my emotion that I lofted six of them on the sideboard with the spoon. Shaken to the core, if you know what I mean.

I've told you how I got engaged to Honoria Glossop in my efforts to do young Bingo Little a good turn. Well, on this particular morning she had lugged me round to Aunt Agatha's for lunch, and I was just saying 'Death, where is thy sting?' when I realised that the worst was yet to come.

'Bertie,' she said, suddenly, as if she had just remembered it, 'what is the name of that man of yours – your valet?'

'Eh? Oh, Jeeves.'

'I think he's a bad influence for you,' said Honoria. 'When we are married you must get rid of Jeeves.'

It was at this point that I jerked the spoon and sent six of the best and crispest sailing on to the sideboard, with Benson gambolling after them like a dignified old retriever.

'Get rid of Jeeves!' I gasped.

'Yes. I don't like him.'

'I don't like him,' said Aunt Agatha.

'But I can't. I mean – why, I couldn't carry on for a day without Jeeves.'

'You will have to,' said Honoria. 'I don't like him at all'

'I don't like him at all,' said Aunt Agatha. 'I never did.'

Ghastly, what? I'd always had an idea that marriage was a bit of a wash-out, but I'd never dreamed that it demanded such frightful sacrifices from a fellow. I passed the rest of the meal in a sort of stupor.

The scheme had been, if I remember, that after lunch I should go off and caddy for Honoria on a shopping tour down Regent Street; but when she got up and started collecting me and the rest of her things, Aunt Agatha stopped her.

'You run along, dear,' she said. 'I want to say a few words to Bertie.'

So Honoria legged it, and Aunt Agatha drew up her chair and started in.

'Bertie,' she said, 'dear Honoria does not know it, but a little difficulty has arisen about your marriage.'

'By Jove! not really?' I said, hope starting to dawn.

'Oh, it's nothing at all, of course. It is only a little exasperating. The fact is, Sir Roderick is being rather troublesome.'

'Thinks I'm not a good bet? Wants to scratch the fixture? Well, perhaps he's right.'

'Pray do not be so absurd, Bertie. It is nothing so serious as that. But the nature of Sir Roderick's profession unfortunately makes him – over-cautious.'

I didn't get it.

'Over-cautious?'

'Yes. I suppose it is inevitable. A nerve specialist with his extensive practice can hardly help taking a rather warped view of humanity.'

I got what she was driving at now. Sir Roderick Glossop, Honoria's father, is always called a nerve specialist, because it sounds better, but everybody knows that he's really a sort of janitor to the looneybin. I mean to say, when your uncle the Duke begins to feel the strain a bit and you find him in the blue drawing-room sticking straws in his hair, old Glossop is the first person you send for. He toddles round, gives the patient the once-over, talks about over-excited nervous systems, and recommends complete rest and seclusion and all that sort of thing. Practically every posh family in the country has called him in at one time or another, and I suppose that, being in that position – I mean constantly having to sit on people's heads while their nearest and dearest 'phone to the asylum to send round the wagon – does tend to make a chappie take what you might call a warped view of humanity.

'You mean he thinks I may be a looney, and he doesn't want a looney son-in-law?' I said.

Aunt Agatha seemed rather peeved than otherwise at my ready intelligence.

'Of course, he does not think anything so ridiculous. I told you he was simply exceedingly cautious. He wants to satisfy himself that you are perfectly normal.' Here she paused, for Benson had come in with the coffee. When he had gone, she went on: 'He appears to have got hold of some extraordinary story about your having pushed his son Oswald into the lake at Ditteredge Hall. Incredible of course. Even you would hardly do a thing like that.'

'Well, I did sort of lean against him, you know, and he shot off the bridge.'

'Oswald definitely accuses you of having pushed him into the water. That has disturbed Sir Roderick, and unfortunately it has caused him to make inquiries, and he has heard about your poor Uncle Henry.'

She eyed me with a good deal of solemnity, and I took a grave sip of coffee. We were peeping into the family cupboard and having a look at the good old skeleton. My late Uncle Henry, you see, was by way of being the blot on the Wooster escutcheon. An extremely decent chappie personally, and one who had always endeared himself to me by tipping me with considerable lavishness when I was at school; but there's no doubt he did at times do rather rummy things, notably keeping eleven pet rabbits in his bedroom; and I suppose a purist might have considered him more or less off his onion. In fact, to be perfectly frank, he wound up his career, happy to the last and completely surrounded by rabbits, in some sort of a home.

'It is very absurd, of course,' continued Aunt Agatha. 'If any of the family had inherited poor Henry's eccentricity – and it was nothing more – it would have been Claude and Eustace, and there could not be two brighter boys.'

Claude and Eustace were twins, and had been kids at school with me in my last summer term. Casting my mind back, it seemed to me that 'bright' just about described them. The whole of that term, as I remembered it, had been spent in getting them out of a series of frightful rows.

'Look how well they are doing at Oxford. Your Aunt Emily had a letter from Claude only the other day saying that they hoped to be elected shortly to a very important college club, called "The Seekers".'

'Seekers?' I couldn't recall any club of the name in my time at Oxford. 'What do they seek?'

'Claude did not say. Truth or Knowledge, I should imagine. It is evidently a very desirable club to belong to, for Claude added that Lord Rainsby, the Earl of Datchet's son, was one of his fellow-candidates. However, we are wandering from the point, which is that Sir Roderick wants to have a quiet talk with you quite alone. Now I rely on you, Bertie, to be – I won't say intelligent, but at least sensible. Don't giggle nervously: try to keep that horrible glassy expression out of your eyes: don't yawn or fidget: and remember that Sir Roderick is the president of the West London branch of the anti-gambling league, so please do not talk about horse-racing. He will lunch with you at your flat tomorrow at one-thirty. Please remember that he drinks no wine, strongly disapproves of smoking, and can only eat the simplest food, owing to an impaired digestion. Do not offer him coffee, for he considers it the root of half the nerve-trouble in the world.'

'I should think a dog-biscuit and a glass of water would about meet the case, what?'

'Bertie!'

'Oh, all right. Merely persiflage.'

'Now it is precisely that sort of idiotic remark that would be calculated to arouse Sir Roderick's worst suspicions. Do please try to refrain from any misguided flippancy when you are with him. He is a very serious-minded man. . . . Are you going? Well, please remember all I have said. I rely on you, and, if anything goes wrong I shall never forgive you.'

'Right ho!' I said.

And so home, with a jolly day to look forward to.

I breakfasted pretty late next morning and went for a stroll afterwards. It seemed to me that anything I could do to clear the old lemon ought to be done, and a bit of fresh air generally relieves that rather foggy feeling that comes over a fellow early in the day. I had taken a stroll in the Park, and got back as far as Hyde Park Corner, when some blighter sloshed me between the shoulder-blades. It was young Eustace, my cousin. He was arm-in-arm with two other fellows, the one on the outside being my cousin Claude and the one in the middle a pink-faced chappie with light hair and an apologetic sort of look.

'Bertie, old egg!' said young Eustace, affably.

'Hallo!' I said, not frightfully chirpily.

'Fancy running into you, the one man in London who can support us in the style we are accustomed to! By the way, you've never met old Dog-Face, have you? Dog-Face, this is my cousin Bertie. Lord Rainsby – Mr. Wooster. We've just been round to your flat, Bertie. Bitterly disappointed that you were out, but were hospitably entertained by old Jeeves. That man's a corker, Bertie. Stick to him.'

'What are you doing in London?' I asked.

'Oh, buzzing round. We're just up for the day. Flying visit, strictly unofficial. We oil back on the three-ten. And now touching that lunch you very decently volunteered to stand us, which shall it be? Ritz? Savoy? Carlton? Or, if you're a member of Ciro's or the Embassy, that would do just as well.'

'I can't give you lunch. I've got an engagement myself. And by Jove,' I said, taking a look at my watch, 'I'm late.' I hailed a taxi. 'Sorry.'

'As man to man, then,' said Eustace, 'lend us a fiver.'

I hadn't time to stop and argue. I unbelted the fiver and hopped into the cab. It was twenty to two when I got to the flat. I bounded into the sitting-room, but it was empty.

Jeeves shimmied in.

'Sir Roderick has not yet arrived, sir.'

'Good egg!' I said. 'I thought I should find him smashing up the furniture.' My experience is that the less you want a fellow, the more punctual he's bound to be, and I had had a vision of the old lad pacing the rug in my sitting-room, saying 'He cometh not!' and generally hotting up. 'Is everything in order?'

'I fancy you will find the arrangements quite satisfactory, sir.'

'What are you giving us?'

'Cold consomme, a cutlet, and a savoury, sir. With lemon-squash, iced.'

'Well, I don't see how that can hurt him. Don't go getting carried away by the excitement of the thing and start bringing in coffee.'

'No, sir.'

'And don't let your eyes get glassy, because, if you do, you're apt to find yourself in a padded cell before you know where you are.'

'Very good, sir.'

There was a ring at the bell.

'Stand by, Jeeves,' I said. 'We're off!'

I had met Sir Roderick Glossop before, of course, but only when I was with Honoria; and there is something about Honoria which makes almost anybody you meet in the same room seem sort of under-sized and trivial by comparison. I had never realised till this moment what an extraordinarily formidable old bird he was. He had a pair of shaggy eyebrows which gave his eyes a piercing look which was not at all the sort of thing a fellow wanted to encounter on an empty stomach. He was fairly tall and fairly broad, and he had the most enormous head, with practically no hair on it, which made it seem bigger and much more like the dome of St. Paul's. I suppose he must have taken about a nine or something in hats. Shows what a rotten thing it is to let your brain develop too much.

'What ho! What ho! What ho!' I said, trying to strike the genial note, and then had a sudden feeling that that was just the sort of thing I had been warned not to say. Dashed difficult it is to start things going properly on an occasion like this. A fellow living in a London flat is so handicapped. I mean to say, if I had been the young squire greeting the visitor in the country, I could have said 'Welcome to Meadowsweet Hall!' or something zippy like that. It sounds silly to say: 'Welcome to Number 6a, Crichton Mansions, Berkeley Street, W.1.'

'I am afraid I am a little late,' he said, as we sat down. 'I was detained at my club by Lord Alastair Hungerford, the Duke of Ramfurline's son. His Grace, he informed me, had exhibited a renewal of the symptoms which have been causing the family so much concern. I could not leave him immediately. Hence my unpunctuality, which I trust has not discommoded you.'

'Oh, not at all. So the Duke is off his rocker, what?'

'The expression which you use is not precisely the one I should have employed myself with reference to the head of perhaps the noblest family in England, but there is no doubt that cerebral excitement does, as you suggest, exist in no small degree.' He sighed as well as he could with his mouth full of cutlet. 'A profession like mine is a great strain, a great strain.'

'Must be.'

'Sometimes I am appalled at what I see around me.' He stopped suddenly and sort of stiffened. 'Do you keep a cat, Mr. Wooster?'

'Eh? What? Cat? No, no cat.'

'I was conscious of a distinct impression that I had heard a cat mewing either in the room or very near to where we are sitting.'

'Probably a taxi or something in the street.'

'I fear I do not follow you.'

'I mean to say, taxis squawk, you know. Rather like cats in a sort of way.'

'I had not observed the resemblance,' he said, rather coldly.

'Have some lemon-squash,' I said. The conversation seemed to be getting rather difficult.

'Thank you. Half a glassful, if I may.' The hell-brew appeared to buck him up, for he resumed in a slightly more pally manner: 'I have a particular dislike for cats. But I was saying – Oh, yes. Sometimes I am positively appalled at what I see around me. It is not only the cases which come under my professional notice, painful as many of those are. It is what I see as I go about London. Sometimes it seems to me that the whole world is mentally unbalanced. This very morning, for example, a most singular and distressing occurrence took place as I was driving from my house to the club. The day being clement, I had instructed my chauffeur to open my landaulette, and I was leaning back, deriving no little pleasure from the sunshine, when our progress was arrested in the middle of the thoroughfare by one of those blocks in the traffic which are inevitable in so congested a system as that of London.'

I supposed I had been letting my mind wander a bit, for when he stopped and took a sip of lemon-squash I had a feeling that I was listening to a lecture and was expected to say something.

'Hear, hear!' I said.

'I beg your pardon?'

'Nothing, nothing. You were saying—'

'The vehicles proceeding in the opposite direction had also been temporarily arrested; but after a moment they were permitted to proceed. I had fallen into a meditation, when suddenly the most extraordinary thing took place. My hat was snatched abruptly from my head! And as I looked back I perceived it being waved in a kind of feverish triumph from the interior of a taxi-cab, which, even as I looked, disappeared through a gap in the traffic and was lost to sight.'

I didn't laugh, but I distinctly heard a couple of my floating ribs part from their moorings under the strain.

'Must have been meant for a practical joke,' I said. 'What?'

This suggestion didn't seem to please the old boy.

'I trust,' he said, 'I am not deficient in an appreciation of the humorous, but I confess that I am at a loss to detect anything akin to pleasantry in the outrage. The action was beyond all question that of a mentally unbalanced subject. These mental lesions may express themselves in almost any form. The Duke of Ramfurline, to whom I had occasion to allude just now, is under the impression – this is in the strictest confidence – that he is a canary; and his seizure today, which so perturbed Lord Alastair, was due to the fact that a careless footman had neglected to bring him his morning lump of sugar. Cases are common, again, of . . . Mr. Wooster, there *is* a cat close at hand! It is *not* in the street! The mewing appears to come from the adjoining room.'

This time I had to admit there was no doubt about it. There was a distinct sound of mewing coming from the next room. I punched the bell for Jeeves, who drifted in and stood waiting with an air of respectful devotion.

'Sir?'

'Oh, Jeeves,' I said. 'Cats! What about it? Are there any cats in the flat?'

'Only the three in your bedroom, sir.'

'What!'

'Cats in his bedroom!' I heard Sir Roderick whisper in a kind of stricken way, and his eyes hit me amidships like a couple of bullets.

'What do you mean,' I said, 'only the three in my bedroom?'

'The black one, the tabby, and the small lemon-coloured animal, sir.'

'What on earth—?'

I charged round the table in the direction of the door. Unfortunately, Sir Roderick had just decided to edge in that direction himself, with the result that we collided in the doorway with a good deal of force, and staggered out into the hall together. He came smartly out of the clinch and grabbed an umbrella from the rack.

'Stand back!' he shouted, waving it over his head. 'Stand back, sir! I am armed!'

It seemed to me that the moment had come to be soothing.

'Awfully sorry I barged into you,' I said. 'Wouldn't have had it happen for worlds. I was just dashing out to have a look into things.'

He appeared a trifle reassured, and lowered the umbrella. But just then the most frightful shindy started in the bedroom. It sounded as though all the cats in London, assisted by delegates from outlying suburbs, had got together to settle their differences once for all. A sort of augmented orchestra of cats.

'This noise is unendurable,' yelled Sir Roderick. 'I cannot hear myself speak.'

'I fancy, sir,' said Jeeves, respectfully, 'that the animals may have become somewhat exhilarated as the result of having discovered the fish under Mr. Wooster's bed.'

The old boy tottered.

'Fish! Did I hear you rightly?'

'Sir?'

'Did you say that there was a fish under Mr. Wooster's bed?'

'Yes, sir.'

Sir Roderick gave a low moan, and reached for his hat and stick.

'You aren't going?' I said.

'Mr. Wooster, I *am* going! I prefer to spend my leisure time in less eccentric society.'

'But I say. Here, I must come with you. I'm sure the whole business can be explained. Jeeves, my hat.'

Jeeves rallied round I took the hat from him and shoved it on my head.

'Good heavens!'

Beastly shock it was! The bally thing had absolutely engulfed me, if you know what I mean. Even as I was putting it on I got a sort of impression that it was a trifle roomy; and no sooner had I let go of it than it settled down over my ears like a kind of extinguisher.

'I say! This isn't my hat!'

'It is *my* hat!' said Sir Roderick in about the coldest, nastiest voice I'd ever heard. 'The hat which was stolen from me this morning as I drove in my car.'

'But—'

I suppose Napoleon or somebody like that would have been equal to the situation, but I'm bound to say it was too much for me. I just stood there goggling in a sort of coma, while the old boy lifted the hat off me and turned to Jeeves.

'I should be glad, my man,' he said, 'if you would accompany me a few yards down the street. I wish to ask you some questions.'

'Very good, sir.'

'Here, but, I say—!' I began, but he left me standing. He stalked out, followed by Jeeves. And at that moment the row in the bedroom started again, louder than ever.

I was about fed up with the whole thing. I mean, cats in your bedroom – a bit thick, what? I didn't know how the dickens they had got in, but I was jolly well resolved that they weren't going to stay picnicking there any longer. I flung open the door. I got a momentary flash of about a hundred and fifteen cats of all sizes and colours scrapping in the middle of the room, and then they all shot past me with a rush and out of the front door; and all that was left of the mobscene was the head of a whacking big fish, lying on the carpet and staring up at me in a rather austere sort of way, as if it wanted a written explanation and apology.

There was something about the thing's expression that

absolutely chilled me, and I withdrew on tip-toe and shut the door. And, as I did so, I bumped into someone.

'Oh, sorry!' he said.

I spun round. It was the pink-faced chappie, Lord Something or other, the fellow I had met with Claude and Eustace.

'I say,' he said, apologetically, 'awfully sorry to bother you, but those weren't my cats I met just now legging it downstairs, were they? They looked like my cats.'

'They came out of my bedroom.'

'Then they *were* my cats!' he said, sadly. 'Oh dash it!'

'Did you put cats in my bedroom?'

'Your man, what's his name, did. He rather decently said I could keep them there till my train went. I'd just come to fetch them. And now they've gone! Oh, well, it can't be helped, I suppose. I'll take the hat and the fish, anyway.'

I was beginning to dislike this bird.

'Did you put that bally fish there, too?'

'No, that was Eustace's. The hat was Claude's.' I sank limply into a chair.

'I say, you couldn't explain this, could you?' I said.

The chappie gazed at me in mild surprise.

'Why, don't you know all about it? I say!' He blushed profusely. 'Why, if you don't know about it, I shouldn't wonder if the whole thing didn't seem rather rummy to you.'

'Rummy is the word.'

'It was for The Seekers, you know.'

'The Seekers?'

'Rather a blood club, you know, up at Oxford, which your cousins and I are rather keen on getting into. You have to pinch something you know, to get elected. Some sort of a souvenir, you know. A policeman's helmet, you know, or a door-knocker or something, you know. The room's decorated with the things at the annual dinner, and everybody makes speeches and all that sort of thing. Rather jolly. Well, we wanted rather to make a sort of special effort and do the thing in style, if you understand, so we came up to London to see if we couldn't pick up something here that would be a bit out of the ordinary. And we had the most amazing luck right from the start. Your cousin Claude managed to collect a quite decent top-hat out of a passing car, and your cousin Eustace got away with a really goodish salmon or something from Harrods, and I snaffled three excellent cats all in the first hour. We were fearfully braced, I can tell you. And then the difficulty was to know where to park the things till our train went. You look so beastly conspicuous, you know, tooling about London with a fish and a lot of cats. And then Eustace remembered you, and we all came on here in a cab. You were out, but your man said it would be all right. When we met you, you were in such a hurry that we hadn't time to explain. Well, I think I'll be taking the hat if you don't mind.'

'It's gone.'

'Gone?'

'The fellow you pinched it from happened to be the man who was lunching here. He took it away with him.'

'Oh, I say! Poor old Claude will be upset. Well, how about the goodish salmon or something?'

'Would you care to view the remains?'

He seemed all broken up when he saw the wreckage.

'I doubt if the committee would accept that,' he said, sadly. 'There isn't a frightful lot of it left, what?'

'The cats ate the rest.'

He sighed deeply.

'No cats, no fish, no hat. We've had all our trouble for nothing. I do call that hard! And on top of that – I say, I hate to ask you, but you couldn't lend me a tenner, could you?'

'A tenner? What for?'

'Well, the fact is, I've got to pop round and bail Claude and Eustace out. They've been arrested.'

'Arrested!'

'Yes. You see, what with the excitement of collaring the hat and the salmon or something, added to the fact that we had rather a festive lunch, they got a bit above themselves, poor chaps, to pinch a motor lorry. Silly of course, because I don't see how they could have got the thing to Oxford and shown it to the committee. Still, there wasn't any reasoning with them, and, when the driver started making a fuss, there was a bit of a mix-up, and Claude and Eustace are more or less languishing in Vine Street police station till I pop round and bail them out. So if you could manage a tenner – Oh, thanks, that's fearfully good of you. It would have been too bad to leave them there, what? I mean, they're both such frightfully good chaps, you know. Everybody likes them up at the 'Varsity. They're fearfully popular.'

'I bet they are!' I said.

When Jeeves came back, I was waiting for him on the mat. I wanted speech with the blighter.

'Well?' I said.

'Sir Roderick asked me a number of questions, sir, respecting your habits and mode of life, to which I replied guardedly.'

'I don't care about that. What I want to know is why you didn't explain the whole thing to him right at the start? A word from you would have put everything clear.'

'Yes, sir.'

'Now he's gone off thinking me a looney.'

'I should not be surprised, from his conversation with me, sir, if some such idea had not entered his head.'

I was just starting in to speak, when the telephone-bell rang. Jeeves answered it.

'No, madam, Mr. Wooster is not in. No, madam, I do not know when he will return. No, madam, he left no message. Yes, madam, I will inform him.' He put back the receiver.

'Mrs. Gregson, sir.'

Aunt Agatha! I had been expecting it. Ever since the luncheon-party had blown out a fuse, her shadow had been hanging over me, so to speak.

'Does she know? Already?'

'I gather that Sir Roderick has been speaking to her on the telephone, sir, and—'

'No wedding bells for me, what?'

Jeeves coughed.

'Mrs. Gregson did not actually confide in me, sir, but I fancy that some such thing may have occurred. She seemed decidedly agitated, sir.'

It's a rummy thing, but I'd been so snootered by the old boy and the cats and the fish and the hat and the pink-faced chappie and all the rest of it that the bright side simply hadn't occurred to me till now. By Jove, it was like a bally weight rolling off my chest! I gave a yelp of pure relief.

'Jeeves,' I said, 'I believe you worked the whole thing!'

'Sir?'

'I believe you had the jolly old situation in hand right from the start.'

'Well, sir, Benson, Mrs. Gregson's butler, who inadvertently chanced to overhear something of your conversation when you were lunching at the house, did mention certain of the details to me; and I confess that, though it may be a liberty to say so, I entertained hopes that something might occur to prevent the match. I doubt if the young lady was entirely suitable to you, sir.'

'And she would have shot you out on your ear five minutes after the ceremony.'

'Yes, sir. Benson informed me that she had expressed some such intention. Mrs. Gregson wishes you to call upon her immediately, sir.'

'She does, eh? What do you advise, Jeeves?'

'I think a trip to the south of France might prove enjoyable, sir.'

'Jeeves,' I said, 'you are right, as always. Pack the old suitcase, and meet me at Victoria in time for the boat-train. I think that's the manly, independent course, what?'

'Absolutely, sir!' said Jeeves.

'Jeeves,' I said, 'we've backed a winner.'

'Sir?'

'Coming to this place, I mean. Here we are in a topping hotel, with fine weather, good cooking, golf, bathing, gambling of every variety, and my Aunt Agatha miles away on the other side of the English Channel. I ask you, what could be sweeter?'

I had had to leg it, if you remember, with considerable speed from London because my Aunt Agatha was on my track with a hatchet as the result of the breaking-off of my engagement to Honoria Glossop. The thing hadn't been my fault, but I couldn't have convinced Aunt Agatha of that if I'd argued for a week: so it had seemed to me that the judicious course to pursue was to buzz briskly off while the buzzing was good. I was standing now at the window of the extremely decent suite which I'd taken at the Hotel Splendide at Roville on the French coast, and, as I looked down at the people popping to and fro in the sunshine, and reflected that in about a quarter of an hour I was due to lunch with a girl who was the exact opposite of Honoria Glossop in every way, I felt dashed uplifted. Gay, genial, happy-go-lucky, and devil-may-care, if you know what I mean.

I had met this girl – Aline Hemmingway her name was – for the first time on the train coming from Paris. She was going to Roville to wait there for a brother who was due to arrive from England. I had helped her with her baggage, got into conversation, had a bite of dinner with her in the restaurant-car, and the result was we had become remarkably chummy. I'm a bit apt, as a rule, to give the modern girl a miss, but there was something different about Aline Hemmingway.

I turned round, humming a blithe melody, and Jeeves shied like a startled mustang.

I had rather been expecting some such display of emotion on the man's part, for I was trying out a fairly fruity cummerbund that morning – one of those silk contrivances, you know, which you tie round your waist, something of the order of a sash, only more substantial. I had seen it in a shop the day before and hadn't been able to resist it, but I'd known all along that there might be trouble with Jeeves. It was a pretty brightish scarlet.

'I beg your pardon, sir,' he said, in a sort of hushed voice. 'You are surely not proposing to appear in public in that thing?'

'What, Cuthbert the Cummerbund?' I said in a careless, debonair way, passing it off. 'Rather!'

'I should not advise it, sir, really I shouldn't.'

'Why not?'

'The effect, sir, is loud in the extreme.'

I tackled the blighter squarely. I mean to say, nobody knows better than I do that Jeeves is a master-mind and all that, but, dash it, a fellow must call his soul his own. You can't be a serf to your valet.

'You know, the trouble with you, Jeeves,' I said, 'is that you're too – what's the word I want? – too bally insular. You can't realise that you aren't in Piccadilly all the time. In a place like this, simply dripping with the gaiety and *joie-de-vivre* of France, a bit of colour and a touch of the poetic is expected of you. Why, last night at the Casino I saw a fellow in a full evening suit of yellow velvet.'

'Nevertheless, sir—'

'Jeeves,' I said, firmly, 'my mind is made up. I'm in a foreign country; it's a corking day; God's in his heaven and all's right with the world and this cummerbund seems to me to be called for.'

'Very good, sir,' said Jeeves, coldly.

Dashed upsetting, this sort of thing. If there's one thing that gives me the pip, it's unpleasantness in the home; and I could see that relations were going to be pretty fairly strained for a while. I suppose the old brow must have been a bit furrowed or something, for Aline Hemmingway spotted that things were wrong directly we sat down to lunch.

'You seem depressed, Mr. Wooster,' she said. 'Have you been losing money at the Casino?'

'No,' I said. 'As a matter of fact, I won quite a goodish sum last night.'

'But something is the matter. What is it?'

'Well, to tell you the truth,' I said, 'I've just had rather a painful scene with my man, and it's shaken me a bit. He doesn't like this cummerbund.'

'Why, I've just been admiring it. I think it's very becoming.'

'No, really?'

'It has rather a Spanish effect.'

'Exactly what I thought myself. Extraordinary you should have said that. A touch of the hidalgo, what? Sort of Vincente y Blasco What's-his-name stuff. The jolly old hidalgo off to the bull-fight, what?'

'Yes. Or a corsair of the Spanish Main.'

'Absolutely! I say, you know, you have bucked me up. It's a rummy thing about you – how sympathetic you are, I mean. The ordinary girl you meet today is all bobbed hair and gaspers, but you—'

I was about to continue in this strain, when somebody halted at our table, and the girl jumped up.

'Sidney!' she cried.

The chappie who had anchored in our midst was a small, round cove with a face rather like a sheep. He wore pince-nez, his expression was benevolent, and he had on one of those collars which button at the back. A parson, in fact.

'Well, my dear,' he said, beaming pretty freely, 'here I am at last.'

'Are you very tired?'

'Not at all. A most enjoyable journey, in which tedium was rendered impossible by the beauty of the scenery through which we passed and the entertaining conversation of my fellow-travellers. But may I be presented to this gentleman?' he said, peering at me through the pince-nez.

'This is Mr. Wooster,' said the girl, 'who was very kind to me coming from Paris. Mr. Wooster, this is my brother.'

We shook hands, and the brother went off to get a wash.

'Sidney's such a dear,' said the girl. 'I know you'll like him.'

'Seems a topper.'

'I do hope he will enjoy his stay here: It's so seldom he gets a holiday. His vicar overworks him dreadfully.'

'Vicars are the devil, what?'

'I wonder if you will be able to spare any time to show him round the place? I can see he's taken such a fancy to you. But, of course, it would be a bother, I suppose, so—'

'Rather not. Only too delighted.' For half a second I thought of patting her hand, then I felt I'd better wait a bit. 'I'll do anything, absolutely anything.'

'It's awfully kind of you.'

'For you,' I said, 'I would—'

At this point the brother returned, and the conversation became what you might call general.

After lunch I fairly curvetted back to my suite, with a most extraordinary braced sensation going all over me like a rash.

'Jeeves,' I said, 'you were all wrong about that cummerbund. It went like a breeze from the start.'

'Indeed, sir?'

'Made an absolutely outstanding hit. The lady I was lunching with admired it. Her brother admired it. The waiter looked as if he admired it. Well, anything happened since I left?'

'Yes, sir. Mrs. Gregson has arrived at the hotel.'

A fellow I know who went shooting, and was potted by one

of his brother-sportsmen in mistake for a rabbit, once told me that it was several seconds before he realised that he had contributed to the day's bag. For about a tenth of a minute everything seemed quite O.K., and then suddenly he got it. It was just the same with me. It took about five seconds for this fearful bit of news to sink in.

'What!' I yelled. 'Aunt Agatha here?'

'Yes, sir.'

'She can't be.'

'I have seen her, sir.'

'But how did she get here?'

'The Express from Paris has just arrived, sir.'

'But, I mean, how the dickens did she know I was here?'

'You left a forwarding-address at the flat for your correspondence, sir. No doubt Mrs. Gregson obtained it from the hall-porter.'

'But I told the chump not to give it away to a soul.'

'That would hardly baffle a lady of Mrs. Gregson's forceful personality, sir.'

'Jeeves, I'm in the soup.'

'Yes, sir.'

'Right up to the hocks!'

'Yes, sir.'

'What shall I do?'

'I fear I have nothing to suggest, sir.'

I eyed the man narrowly. Dashed aloof his manner was. I saw what was the matter, of course. He was still brooding over that cummerbund.

'I shall go for a walk, Jeeves,' I said.

'Yes, sir?'

'A good long walk.'

'Very good, sir.'

'And if – er – if anybody asks for me, tell 'em you don't know when I'll be back.

*

To people who don't know my Aunt Agatha I find it extraordinarily difficult to explain why it is that she has always put the wind up me to such a frightful extent. I mean, I'm not dependent on her financially, or anything like that. It's simply personality, I've come to the conclusion. You see, all through my childhood and when I was a kid at school she was always able to turn me inside out with a single glance, and I haven't come out from under the 'fluence yet. We run to height a bit in our family, and there's about five-foot-nine of Aunt Agatha, topped off with a beaky nose, an eagle eye, and a lot of grey hair, and the general effect is pretty formidable.

Her arrival in Roville at this juncture had made things more than a bit complicated for me. What to do? Leg it quick before she could get hold of me, would no doubt have been the advice most fellows would have given me. But the situation wasn't as simple as that. I was in much the same position as the cat on the garden wall who, when on the point of becoming matey with the cat next door, observes the boot-jack sailing through the air. If he stays where he is, he gets it in the neck; if he biffs, he has to start all over again where he left off. I didn't like the prospect of being collared by Aunt Agatha, but on the other hand I simply barred the notion of leaving Roville by the night-train and parting from Aline Hemmingway. Absolutely a man's cross-roads, if you know what I mean.

I prowled about the neighbourhood all the afternoon and evening, then I had a bit of dinner at a quiet restaurant in the town and trickled cautiously back to the hotel. Jeeves was popping about in the suite.

'There is a note for you, sir,' he said, 'on the mantelpiece.'

The blighter's manner was still so cold and unchummy that I bit the bullet and had a dash at being airy.

'A note, eh?'

'Yes, sir. Mrs. Gregson's maid brought it shortly after you had left.'

'Tra-la-la!' I said.

'Precisely, sir.'

I opened the note.

'She wants me to look in on her after dinner some time.'

'Yes, sir?'

'Jeeves,' I said, 'mix me a stiffish brandy-and-soda.'

'Yes, sir.'

'Stiffish, Jeeves. Not too much soda, but splash the brandy about a bit.'

'Very good, sir.'

He shimmered off into the background to collect the materials, and just at that moment there was a knock at the door.

I'm bound to say it was a shock. My heart stood still, and I bit my tongue.

'Come in,' I bleated.

But it wasn't Aunt Agatha after all. It was Aline Hemmingway, looking rather rattled, and her brother, looking like a sheep with a secret sorrow.

'Oh, Mr. Wooster!' said the girl, in a sort of gasping way.

'Oh, what-ho!' I said. 'Won't you come in? Take a seat or two.'

'I don't know how to begin.'

'Eh?' I said. 'Is anything up?'

'Poor Sidney – it was my fault – I ought never to have let him go there alone.'

At this point the brother, who had been standing by wrapped in the silence, gave a little cough, like a sheep caught in the mist on a mountain-top.

'The fact is, Mr. Wooster,' he said. 'I have been gambling at the Casino.'

'Oh!' I said. 'Did you click?'

He sighed heavily.

'If you mean, was I successful, I must answer in the negative. I rashly persisted in the view that the colour red, having appeared no fewer than seven times in succession, must inevitably at no distant date give place to black. I was in error. I lost my little all, Mr. Wooster.'

'Tough luck,' I said.

'I left the Casino, and returned to the hotel. There I encountered one of my parishioners, a Colonel Musgrave, who chanced to be holiday-making over here. I – er – induced him to cash me a cheque for one hundred pounds on my bank in London.'

'Well, that was all to the good, what?' I said, hoping to induce the poor egg to look on the bright side. 'I mean bit of luck finding someone to slip it into, first crack out of the box.'

'On the contrary, Mr. Wooster, it did but make matters worse. I burn with shame as I make the confession, but I went back to the Casino and lost the entire sum.'

'I say!' I said. 'You *are* having a night out!'

'And,' concluded the chappie, 'the most lamentable feature of the whole affair is that I have no funds in the bank to meet the cheque, when presented.'

I'm free to confess that I gazed at him with no little interest and admiration. Never in my life before had I encountered a curate so genuinely all to the mustard. Little as he might look like one of the lads of the village, he certainly appeared to be the real tabasco.

'Colonel Musgrave,' he went on, gulping somewhat, 'is not a man who would be likely to overlook the matter. He is a hard man. He will expose me to my vic-ah. My vic-ah is a hard man. I shall be ruined if Colonel Musgrave presents that cheque, and he leaves for England tonight.'

'Mr. Wooster,' the girl burst out, 'won't you, won't you help us? Oh, do say you will. We must have the money to get back that cheque from Colonel Musgrave before nine o'clock – he leaves on the nine-twenty. I was at my wits' end what to do, when I remembered how kind you had always been and how you had told me at lunch that you had won some money at the Casino last night. Mr. Wooster, will you lend it to us, and take these as security?' And, before I knew what she was doing, she had dived into her bag, produced a case, and opened it. 'My pearls,' she said. 'I don't know what they are worth – they were a present from my poor father – but I know they must be worth ever so much more than the amount we want.'

Dashed embarrassing. Made me feel like a pawn-broker. More than a touch of popping the watch about the whole business.

'No, I say, really,' I protested, the haughty old spirit of the Woosters kicking like a mule at the idea. 'There's no need for any security, you know, or any rot of that kind. I mean to say, among pals, you know, what? Only too glad the money'll come in useful.'

And I fished it out and pushed it across. The brother shook his head.

'Mr. Wooster,' he said, 'we appreciate your generosity, your beautiful, heartening confidence in us, but we cannot permit this.'

'What Sidney means,' said the girl, 'is that you really don't know anything about us, when you come to think of it. You mustn't risk lending all this money without any security at all to two people who, after all, are almost strangers.'

'Oh, don't say that!'

'I do say it. If I hadn't thought that you would be quite businesslike about this, I would never have dared to come to you. If you will just give me a receipt, as a matter of form—'

'Oh, well.'

I wrote out the receipt and handed it over feeling more or less of an ass.

'Here you are,' I said.

The girl took the piece of paper, shoved it in her bag, grabbed the money and slipped it to brother Sidney, and then, before I knew what was happening, she had darted at me, kissed me, and legged it from the room.

I don't know when I've been so rattled. The whole thing was

95

so dashed sudden and unexpected. Through a sort of mist I could see that Jeeves had appeared from the background and was helping the brother on with his coat; and then the brother came up to me and grasped my hand.

'I can't thank you sufficiently, Mr. Wooster!'

'Oh, right-ho!'

'You have saved my good name. "Good name in man or woman, dear my lord",' he said, massaging the fin with some fervour, '"is the immediate jewel of their souls. Who steals my purse steals trash. 'Twas mine, 'tis his, and has been slave to thousands. But he that filches from me my good name robs me of that which not enriches him and makes me poor indeed". I thank you from the bottom of my heart. Good night, Mr. Wooster.'

'Good night, old thing,' I said.

'Your brandy-and-soda, sir,' said Jeeves, as the door shut.

I blinked at him.

'Oh, there you are!'

'Yes, sir.'

'Rather a sad affair, Jeeves.'

'Yes, sir.'

'Lucky I happened to have all that money handy.'

'Well – er – yes, sir.'

'You speak as though you didn't think much of it.'

'It is not my place to criticise your actions, sir, but I will venture to say that I think you behaved a little rashly.'

'What, lending that money?'

'Yes, sir. These fashionable French watering-places are notoriously infested by dishonest characters.'

This was a bit too thick.

'Now, look here, Jeeves,' I said, 'I can stand a lot, but when it comes to your casting asp-whatever-the-word-is on the sweetest girl in the world and a bird in Holy Orders—'

'Perhaps I am over-suspicious, sir. But I have seen a great deal of these resorts. When I was in the employment of Lord

Frederick Ranelagh, shortly before I entered your service, his lordship was very neatly swindled by a criminal known, I believe, by the sobriquet of Soapy Sid, who scraped acquaintance with us in Monte Carlo with the assistance of a female accomplice. I have never forgotten the circumstance.'

'I don't want to butt in on your reminiscences, Jeeves,' I said coldly, 'but you're talking through your hat. How can there have been anything fishy about this business? They've left me the pearls, haven't they? Very well, then, think before you speak. You had better be tooling down to the desk now and having these things shoved in the hotel safe.' I picked up the case and opened it. 'Oh, Great Scot!'

The bally thing was empty!

'Oh, my Lord!' I said, staring, 'don't tell me there's been dirty work at the cross-roads, after all!'

'Precisely, sir. It was in exactly the same manner that Lord Frederick was swindled on the occasion to which I have alluded. While his female accomplice was gratefully embracing his lordship, Soapy Sid substituted a duplicate case for the one containing the pearls, and went off with the jewels, the money, and the receipt. On the strength of the receipt he subsequently demanded from his lordship the return of the pearls, and his lordship, not being able to produce them, was obliged to pay a heavy sum in compensation. It is a simple but effective ruse.'

I felt as if the bottom had dropped out of things with a jerk. I mean to say, Aline Hemmingway, you know. What I mean is, if Love hadn't actually awakened in my heart, there's no doubt it was having a jolly good stab at it, and the thing was only a question of days. And all the time – well, I mean, dash it, you know.

'Soapy Sid? Sid! *Sidney*! Brother Sidney! Why, by Jove, Jeeves, do you think that parson was Soapy Sid?'

'Yes, sir.'

'But it seems so extraordinary. Why, his collar buttoned at the back – I mean, he would have deceived a bishop. Do you really think he was Soapy Sid?'

'Yes, sir. I recognised him directly he came into the room.'

I stared at the blighter.

'You recognised him?'

'Yes, sir.'

'Then, dash it all,' I said, deeply moved, 'I think you might have told me.'

'I thought it would save disturbance and unpleasantness if I merely abstracted the case from the man's pocket as I assisted him with his coat, sir. Here it is.'

He laid another case on the table beside the dud one, and, by Jove, you couldn't tell them apart. I opened it, and there were the good old pearls, as merry and bright as dammit, smiling up at me. I gazed feebly at the man. I was feeling a bit overwrought.

'Jeeves,' I said, 'you're an absolute genius!'

'Yes, sir.'

Relief was surging over me in great chunks by now. I'd almost forgotten that a woman had toyed with my heart and thrown it away like a worn-out tube of tooth-paste and all that sort of thing. What seemed to me the important item was the fact that, thanks to Jeeves, I was not going to be called on to cough up several thousand quid.

'It looks to me as though you had saved the old home. I mean, even a chappie endowed with the immortal rind of dear old Sid is hardly likely to have the nerve to come back and retrieve these little chaps.'

'I should imagine not, sir.'

'Well, then – Oh, I say, you don't think they are just paste or anything like that?'

'No, sir. These are genuine peals, and extremely valuable.'

'Well, then dash it, I'm on velvet. Absolutely reclining on the good old plush! I may be down a hundred quid, but I'm up a jolly good string of pearls. Am I right or wrong?'

'Hardly that, sir. I think that you will have to restore the pearls.'

'What! To Sid? Not while I have my physique!'

'No, sir. To their rightful owner.'

'But who is their rightful owner?'

'Mrs. Gregson, sir.'

'What! How do you know?'

'It was all over the hotel an hour ago that Mrs. Gregson's pearls had been abstracted. The man Sid travelled from Paris in the same train as Mrs. Gregson, and no doubt marked them down. I was speaking to Mrs. Gregson's maid shortly before you came in, and she informed me that the manager of the hotel is now in Mrs. Gregson's suite.'

'And having a devil of a time, what?'

'So I should be disposed to imagine, sir.'

The situation was beginning to unfold before me.

'I'll go and give them back to her, eh? It'll put me one up, what?'

'If I might make the suggestion, sir, I think it would strengthen your position if you were to affect to discover the pearls in Mrs. Gregson's suite – say, in a bureau drawer.'

'I don't see why.'

'I think I am right, sir.'

'Well, I stand on you. If you say so. I'll be popping, what?'

'The sooner the better, sir.'

Long before I reached Aunt Agatha's lair I could tell that the hunt was up. Divers chappies in hotel uniform and not a few chambermaids of sorts were hanging about in the corridor, and through the panels I could hear a mixed assortment of voices, with Aunt Agatha's topping the lot. I knocked, but no one took any notice, so I trickled in. Among those present I noticed a chambermaid in hysterics, Aunt Agatha with her hair bristling, and a whiskered cove who looked like a bandit, as no doubt he was, being the proprietor of the hotel.

'Oh, hallo,' I said. 'I got your note, Aunt Agatha.'

She waved me away. No welcoming smile for Bertram.

'Oh don't bother me now,' she snapped, looking at me as if I were more or less the last straw.

'Something up?'

'Yes, yes, yes! I've lost my pearls.'

'Pearls? Pearls? Pearls?' I said. 'No, really? Dashed annoying. Where did you see them last?'

'What *does* it matter where I saw them last? They have been stolen.'

Here Wilfred the Whisker-King, who seemed to have been taking a rest between rounds, stepped into the ring again and began to talk rapidly in French. Cut to the quick he seemed. The chambermaid whooped in the corner.

'Sure you've looked everywhere?' I asked.

'Of course I've looked everywhere.'

'Well, you know, I've often lost a collar-stud and—'

'Do try not to be so maddening, Bertie! I have enough to bear without your imbecilities. Oh, be quiet! Be quiet!' she shouted. And such was the magnetism of what Jeeves called her forceful personality that Wilfred subsided as though he had run into a wall. The chambermaid continued to go strong.

'I say,' I said, 'I think there's something the matter with this girl. Isn't she crying or something?'

'She stole my pearls! I am convinced of it.'

This started the whisker-specialist off again, and I left them at it and wandered off on a tour round the room. I slipped the pearls out of the case and decanted them into a drawer. By the time I'd done this and had leisure to observe the free-for-all once more, Aunt Agatha had reached the frozen grande-dame stage and was putting the Last of the Bandits through it in the voice she usually reserves for snubbing waiters in restaurants.

'I tell you, my good man, for the hundredth time, that I have searched thoroughly – everywhere. Why you should imagine that I have overlooked so elementary—'

'I say,' I said, 'don't want to interrupt you and all that sort of thing, but aren't these the little chaps?'

I pulled them out of the drawer and held them up.

'These look like pearls, what?'

I don't know when I've had a more juicy moment. It was one of those occasions about which I shall prattle to my grand-children – if I ever have any, which at the moment of going to press seems more or less of a hundred-to-one shot. Aunt Agatha simply deflated before my eyes. It reminded me of when I once saw some intrepid aeronauts letting the gas out of a balloon.

'Where – where – where?' she gurgled.

'In this drawer. They'd slid under some paper.'

'Oh!' said Aunt Agatha, and there was a bit of silence.

I dug out my entire stock of manly courage, breathed a short prayer, and let her have it right in the thorax.

'I must say, Aunt Agatha, dash it,' I said, crisply, 'I think you have been a little hasty, what? I mean to say, giving this poor man here so much anxiety and worry and generally biting him in the gizzard. You've been very, very unjust to this poor man!'

'Yes, yes,' chipped in the poor man.

'And this unfortunate girl, what about her? Where does she get off? You've accused her of pinching the things on absolutely no evidence. I think she would be jolly well advised to bring an action for – for whatever it is, and soak you for substantial damages.'

'Mais oui, mais oui, c'est trop fort!' shouted the Bandit Chief, backing me up like a good 'un. And the chambermaid looked up inquiringly, as if the sun was breaking the clouds.

'I shall recompense her,' said Aunt Agatha, feebly.

'If you take my tip, you jolly well will, and that eftsoones or right speedily. She's got a cast-iron case, and if I were her I wouldn't take a cent under twenty quid. But what gives me the pip most is the way you've abused this poor man and tried to give his hotel a bad name—'

'Yes, by damn! It's too bad!' cried the whiskered marvel. 'You careless old woman! You give my hotel bad names, would you or wasn't it? Tomorrow you leave my hotel.'

And more to the same effect, all good, ripe stuff. And presently, having said his say, he withdrew, taking the chambermaid with him, the latter with a crisp tenner clutched in a vicelike grip. I suppose she and the bandit split it outside. A French hotel-manager wouldn't be likely to let real money wander away from him without counting himself in on the division.

I turned to Aunt Agatha, whose demeanour was now rather like that of one who, picking daisies on the railway, has just caught the down-express in the small of the back.

'There was something you wished to speak to me about?' I said.

'No, no. Go away, go away.'

'You said in your note—'

'Yes, yes, never mind. Please go away, Bertie. I wish to be alone.'

'Oh, right-ho!' I said. 'Right-ho! right-ho!' And back to the good old suite.

'Ten o'clock, a clear night, and all's well, Jeeves,' I said, breezing in.

'I am gratified to hear it, sir.'

'If twenty quid would be any use to you, Jeeves—?'

'I am much obliged, sir.'

There was a pause. And then – well, it was a wrench, but I did it. I unstripped the cummerbund and handed it over.

'Do you wish me to press this, sir?'

I gave the thing one last longing look. It had been very dear to me.

'No,' I said, 'take it away; give it to the deserving poor. I shall never wear it again.'

'Thank you very much, sir,' said Jeeves.

You will notice, as you flit through these reminiscences of mine, that from time to time the scene of action is laid in and around the city of New York; and it is just possible that this may occasion the puzzled look and the start of surprise. 'What,' it is possible that you may ask yourselves, 'is Bertram doing so far from his beloved native land?'

Well, it's a fairly longish story; but, reefing it down a bit and turning it for the nonce into a two-reeler, what happened was that my Aunt Agatha on one occasion sent me over to America to try to stop young Gussie, my cousin, marrying a girl on the vaudeville stage, and I got the whole thing so mixed up that I decided it would be a sound scheme to stop on in New York for a bit instead of going back and having long, cosy chats with her about the affair.

So I sent Jeeves out to find a decent flat, and settled down for a spell of exile.

I'm bound to say New York's a most sprightly place to be exiled in. Everybody was awfully good to me, and there seemed to be plenty of things going on: so, take it for all in all, I didn't undergo any frightful hardships. Blokes introduced me to other blokes, and so on and so forth, and it wasn't long before I knew squads of the right sort, some who rolled in the stuff in houses up by the Park, and others who lived with the gas turned down mostly around Washington Square – artists and writers and so forth. Brainy coves.

Corky, the bird I am about to treat of, was one of the artists. A portrait-painter, he called himself, but as a matter of fact his score up to date had been nil. You see, the catch about portrait-painting – I've looked into the thing a bit – is that you can't start painting portraits till people come along and ask you to, and they won't come and ask you to until you've painted a lot first. This makes it kind of difficult, not to say tough, for the ambitious youngster.

Corky managed to get along by drawing an occasional picture for the comic papers – he had rather a gift for funny stuff when he got a good idea – and doing bedsteads and chairs and things for the advertisements. His principal source of income, however, was derived from biting the ear of a rich uncle – one Alexander Worple, who was in the jute business. I'm a bit foggy as to what jute is, but it's apparently something the populace is pretty keen on, for Mr. Worple had made quite an indecently large stack out of it.

Now, a great many fellows think that having a rich uncle is a pretty soft snap; but, according to Corky, such is not the case. Corky's uncle was a robust sort of cove, who looked like living for ever. He was fifty-one, and it seemed as if he might go to par. It was not this, however, that distressed poor Corky, for he was not bigoted and had no objection to the man going on living. What Corky kicked at was the way the above Worple used to harry him.

Corky's uncle, you see, didn't want him to be an artist. He didn't think he had any talent in that direction. He was always urging him to chuck Art and go into the jute business and start at the bottom and work his way up. And what Corky said was that, while he didn't know what they did at the bottom of a jute business, instinct told him that it was something too beastly for words. Corky, moreover, believed in his future as an artist. Some day, he said, he was going to make a hit. Meanwhile, by using the utmost tact and persuasiveness, he was inducing his uncle to cough up very grudgingly a small quarterly allowance.

He wouldn't have got this if his uncle hadn't had a hobby. Mr. Worple was peculiar in this respect. As a rule, from what I've observed, the American captain of industry doesn't do anything out of business hours. When he has put the cat out and locked up the office for the night, he just relapses into a state of coma from which he emerges only to start being a captain of industry again. But Mr. Worple in his spare time was what is known as an ornithologist. He had written a book called *American Birds*, and was writing another, to be called *More American Birds*. When he had finished that, the presumption was that he would begin a third, and keep on till the supply of American birds gave out. Corky used to go to him about once every three months and let him talk about American birds. Apparently you could do what you liked with old Worple if you gave him his head first on his pet subject, so these little chats used to make Corky's allowance all right for the time being. But it was pretty rotten for the poor chap. There was the frightful suspense, you see, and, apart from that, birds, except when broiled and in the society of a cold bottle, bored him stiff.

To complete the character-study of Mr. Worple, he was a man of extremely uncertain temper, and his general tendency was to think that Corky was a poor chump and that whatever step he took in any direction on his own account was just another proof of his innate idiocy. I should imagine Jeeves feels very much the same about me.

So when Corky trickled into my apartment one afternoon, shooing a girl in front of him, and said: 'Bertie, I want you to meet my *fiancée*, Miss Singer,' the aspect of the matter which hit me first was precisely the one which he had come to consult me about. The very first words I spoke were: 'Corky, how about your uncle?'

The poor chap gave one of those mirthless laughs. He was looking anxious and worried, like a man who has done the murder all right but can't think what the deuce to do with the body.

'We're so scared, Mr. Wooster,' said the girl. 'We were hoping that you might suggest a way of breaking it to him.'

Muriel Singer was one of those very quiet, appealing girls who have a way of looking at you with their big eyes as if they thought you were the greatest thing on earth and wondered that you hadn't got onto it yet yourself. She sat there in a sort of shrinking way, looking at me as if she were saying to herself, 'Oh, I do hope this great strong man isn't going to hurt me.' She gave a fellow a protective kind of feeling, made him want to stroke her hand and say: 'There, there, little one!' or words to that effect. She made me feel that there was nothing I wouldn't do for her. She was rather like one of those innocent-tasting American drinks which creep imperceptibly into your system so that, before you know what you're doing, you're starting out to reform the world by force if necessary and pausing on your way to tell the large man in the corner that, if he looks at you like that, you will knock his head off. What I mean is, she made me feel alert and dashing, like a knight-errant or something of that kind. I felt that I was with her in this thing to the limit.

'I don't see why your uncle shouldn't be most awfully bucked,' I said to Corky. 'He will think Miss Singer the ideal wife for you.'

Corky declined to cheer up.

'You don't know him. Even if he did like Muriel, he wouldn't admit it. That's the sort of pig-headed ass he is. It would be a matter of principle with him to kick. All he would consider would be that I had gone and taken an important step without asking his advice, and he would raise Cain automatically. He's always done it.'

I strained the old bean to meet this emergency.

'You want to work it so that he makes Miss Singer's acquaintance without knowing that you know her. Then you come along—'

'But how can I work it that way?'

I saw his point. That was the catch.

'There's only one thing to do,' I said.

'What's that?'

'Leave it to Jeeves.'

And I rang the bell.

'Sir?' said Jeeves, kind of manifesting himself. One of the rummy things about Jeeves is that, unless you watch like a hawk, you very seldom see him come into a room. He's like one of those weird birds in India who dissolve themselves into thin air and nip through space in a sort of disembodied way and assembled the parts again just where they want them. I've got a cousin who's what they call a Theosophist, and he says he's often nearly worked the thing himself, but couldn't quite bring it off, probably owing to having fed in his boyhood on the flesh of animals slain in anger and pie.

The moment I saw the man standing there, registering respectful attention, a weight seemed to roll off my mind. I felt like a lost child who spots his father in the offing.

'Jeeves,' I said, 'we want your advice.'

'Very good, sir.'

I boiled down Corky's painful case into a few well-chosen words.

'So you see what it amounts to, Jeeves. We want you to suggest some way by which Mr. Worple can make Miss Singer's acquaintance without getting on to the fact that Mr. Corcoran already knows her. Understand?'

'Perfectly, sir.'

'Well, try to think of something.'

'I have thought of something already, sir.'

'You have!'

'The scheme I would suggest cannot fail of success, but it has what may seem to you a drawback, sir, in that it requires a certain financial outlay.'

'He means,' I translated to Corky, 'that he has got a pippin of an idea, but it's going to cost a bit.'

Naturally the poor chap's face dropped, for this seemed to

dish the whole thing. But I was still under the influence of the girl's melting gaze, and I saw that this was where I started in as the knight-errant.

'You can count on me for all that sort of thing, Corky,' I said. 'Only too glad. Carry on, Jeeves.'

'I would suggest, sir, that Mr. Corcoran take advantage of Mr. Worple's attachment to ornithology.'

'How on earth did you know that he was fond of birds?'

'It is the way these New York apartments are constructed, sir. Quite unlike our London houses. The partitions between the rooms are of the flimsiest nature. With no wish to overhear, I have sometimes heard Mr. Corcoran expressing himself with a generous strength on the subject I have mentioned.'

'Oh! Well?'

'Why should not the young lady write a small volume, to be entitled – let us say – *The Children's Book of American Birds* and dedicate it to Mr. Worple? A limited edition could be published at your expense, sir, and a great deal of the book would, of course, be given over to eulogistic remarks concerning Mr. Worple's own larger treatise on the same subject. I should recommend the dispatching of a presentation copy to Mr. Worple, immediately on publication, accompanied by a letter in which the young lady asks to be allowed to make the acquaintance of one to whom she owes so much. This would, I fancy, produce the desired result, but as I say, the expense involved would be considerable.'

I felt like the proprietor of a performing dog on the vaudeville stage when the tyke has just pulled off his trick without a hitch. I had betted on Jeeves all along, and I had known that he wouldn't let me down. It beats me sometimes why a man with his genius is satisfied to hang around pressing my clothes and what not. If I had half Jeeves's brain I should have a stab at being Prime Minister or something.

'Jeeves,' I said, 'that is absolutely ripping! One of your very best efforts.'

'Thank you, sir.'

The girl made an objection.

'But I'm sure I couldn't write a book about anything. I can't even write good letters.'

'Muriel's talents,' said Corky, with a little cough, 'lie more in the direction of the drama, Bertie. I didn't mention it before, but one of our reasons for being a trifle nervous as to how Uncle Alexander will receive the news is that Muriel is in the chorus of that show "Choose your Exit" at the Manhattan. It's absurdly unreasonable, but we both feel that that fact might increase Uncle Alexander's natural tendency to kick like a steer.'

I saw what he meant. I don't know why it is – one of these psychology sharps could explain it, I suppose – but uncles and aunts, as a class, are always dead against the drama, legitimate or otherwise. They don't seem able to stick it at any price.

But Jeeves had a solution, of course.

'I fancy it would be a simple matter, sir, to find some impecunious author who would be glad to do the actual composition of the volume for a small fee. It is only necessary that the young lady's name should appear on the title page.'

'That's true,' said Corky. 'Sam Patterson would do it for a hundred dollars. He writes a novelette, three short stories, and ten thousand words of a serial for one of the all-fiction magazines under different names every month. A little thing like this would be nothing to him. I'll get after him right away.'

'Fine!'

'Will that be all, sir?' said Jeeves. 'Very good, sir. Thank you, sir.'

I always used to think that publishers had to be devilish intelligent fellows, loaded down with the grey matter; but I've got their number now. All a publisher has to do is to write cheques at intervals, while a lot of deserving and industrious chappies rally round and do the real work. I know, because I've been one myself. I simply sat tight in the old flat with a fountain-pen, and in due season a topping, shiny book came along.

I happened to be down at Corky's place when the first copies of *The Children's Book of American Birds* bobbed up. Muriel Singer was there, and we were talking of things in general when there was a bang at the door and the parcel was delivered.

It was certainly some book. It had a red cover with a fowl of some species on it, and underneath the girl's name in gold letters. I opened a copy at random.

'Often of a spring morning,' it said at the top of page twenty-one, 'as you wander through the fields, you will hear the sweet-toned, carelessly-flowing warble of the purple finch linnet. When you are older you must read all about him in Mr. Alexander Worple's wonderful book, *American Birds.*'

You see. A boost for the uncle right away. And only a few pages later there he was in the limelight again in connexion with the yellow-billed cuckoo. It was great stuff. The more I read, the more I admired the chap who had written it and Jeeves's genius in putting us on to the wheeze. I didn't see how the uncle could fail to drop. You can't call a chap the world's greatest authority on the yellow-billed cuckoo without rousing a certain disposition towards chumminess in him.

'It's a cert!' I said.

'An absolute cinch!' said Corky.

And a day or two later he meandered up the Avenue to my flat to tell me that all was well. The uncle had written Muriel a letter so dripping with the milk of human kindness that if he hadn't known Mr. Worple's handwriting Corky would have refused to believe him the author of it. Any time it suited Miss Singer to call, said the uncle, he would be delighted to make her acquaintance.

Shortly after this I had to go out of town. Divers sound sportsmen had invited me to pay visits to their country places, and it wasn't for several months that I settled down in the city again. I had been wondering a lot, of course, about Corky, whether it all turned out right, and so forth, and my first evening in New York, happening to pop into a quiet sort of little restaurant which I go to when I don't feel inclined for the bright lights, I found Muriel Singer there, sitting by herself at a table near the door. Corky, I took it, was out telephoning. I went up and passed the time of day.

'Well, well, well, what?' I said.

'Why, Mr. Wooster! How do you do?'

'Corky around?'

'I beg your pardon?'

'You're waiting for Corky, aren't you?'

'Oh, I didn't understand. No, I'm not waiting for him.'

It seemed to me that there was a sort of something in her voice, a kind of thingummy, you know.

'I say, you haven't had a row with Corky, have you?'

'A row?'

'A spat, don't you know – little misunderstanding – faults on both sides – er – and all that sort of thing.'

'Why, whatever makes you think that?'

'Oh, well, as it were, what? What I mean is – I thought you usually dined with him before you went to the theatre.'

'I've left the stage now.'

Suddenly the whole thing dawned on me. I had forgotten what a long time I had been away.

'Why, of course, I see now! You're married!'

'Yes.'

'How perfectly topping! I wish you all kinds of happiness.'

'Thank you so much. Oh, Alexander,' she said, looking past me, 'this is a friend of mine – Mr. Wooster.'

I spun round. A bloke with a lot of stiff grey hair and a red sort of healthy face was standing there. Rather a formidable Johnnie, he looked, though peaceful at the moment.

'I want you to meet my husband, Mr. Wooster. Mr. Wooster is a friend of Brace's, Alexander.'

The old boy grasped my hand warmly, and that was all that kept me from hitting the floor in a heap. The place was rocking. Absolutely.

'So you know my nephew, Mr. Wooster?' I heard him say. 'I wish you would try to knock a little sense into him and make him quit this playing at painting. But I have an idea that he is steadying down. I noticed it first that night he came to dinner with us, my dear, to be introduced to you. He seemed altogether quieter and more serious. Something seemed to have sobered him. Perhaps you will give us the pleasure of your company at dinner tonight, Mr. Wooster? Or have you dined?'

I said I had. What I needed then was air, not dinner. I felt that I wanted to get into the open and think this thing out.

When I reached my flat I heard Jeeves moving about in his lair. I called him.

'Jeeves,' I said, 'now is the time for all good men to come to the aid of the party. A stiff b.-and-s. first of all, and then I've a bit of news for you.'

He came back with a tray and a long glass.

'Better have one yourself, Jeeves. You'll need it.'

'Later on, perhaps, thank you, sir.'

'All right. Please yourself. But you're going to get a shock. You remember my friend, Mr. Corcoran?'

'Yes, sir.'

'And the girl who was to slide gracefully into his uncle's esteem by writing the book on birds?'

'Perfectly, sir.'

'Well, she's slid. She's married the uncle.'

He took it without blinking. You can't rattle Jeeves.

'That was always a development to be feared, sir.'

'You don't mean to tell me that you were expecting it?'

'It crossed my mind as a possibility.'

'Did it, by Jove! Well, I think you might have warned us!'

'I hardly liked to take the liberty, sir.'

*

Of course, as I saw after I had had a bite to eat and was in a calmer frame of mind, what had happened wasn't my fault, if you came down to it. I couldn't be expected to foresee that the scheme, in itself a cracker-jack, would skid into the ditch as it had done; but all the same I'm bound to admit that I didn't relish the idea of meeting Corky again until time, the great healer, had been able to get in a bit of soothing work. I cut Washington Square out absolutely for the next few months. I gave it the complete miss-in-baulk. And then, just when I was beginning to think I might safely pop down in that direction and gather up the dropped threads, so to speak, time, instead of working the healing wheeze, went and pulled the most awful boner and put the lid on it. Opening the paper one morning, I read that Mrs. Alexander Worple had presented her husband with a son and heir.

I was so dashed sorry for poor old Corky that I hadn't the heart to touch my breakfast. I was bowled over. Absolutely. It was the limit.

I hardly knew what to do. I wanted, of course, to rush down to Washington Square and grip the poor blighter silently by the hand; and then, thinking it over, I hadn't the nerve. Absent treatment seemed the touch. I gave it him in waves.

But after a month or so I began to hesitate again. It struck me that it was playing it a bit low-down on the poor chap, avoiding him like this just when he probably wanted his pals to surge round him most. I pictured him sitting in his lonely studio with no company but his bitter thoughts, and the pathos of it got me to such an extent that I bounded straight into a taxi and told the driver to go all out for the studio.

I rushed in, and there was Corky, hunched up at the easel, painting away, while on the model throne sat a severe-looking female of middle age, holding a baby.

A fellow has to be ready for that sort of thing.

'Oh, ah!' I said, and started to back out.

Corky looked over his shoulder.

'Hallo, Bertie. Don't go. We're just finishing for the day. That will be all this afternoon,' he said to the nurse, who got up with the baby and decanted it into a perambulator which was standing in the fairway.

'At the same hour tomorrow, Mr. Corcoran?'

'Yes, please.'

'Good afternoon.'

'Good afternoon.'

Corky stood there, looking at the door, and then he turned to me and began to get it off his chest. Fortunately, he seemed to take it for granted that I knew all about what had happened, so it wasn't as awkward as it might have been.

'It's my uncle's idea,' he said. 'Muriel doesn't know about it yet. The portrait's to be a surprise for her on her birthday. The nurse takes the kid out ostensibly to get a breather, and they beat it down here. If you want an instance of the irony of fate, Bertie, get acquainted with this. Here's the first commission I have ever had to paint a portrait, and the sitter is that human poached egg that has butted in and bounced me out of my inheritance. Can you beat it! I call it rubbing the thing in to expect me to spend my afternoons gazing into the ugly face of a little brat who to all intents and purposes has hit me behind the ear with a black-jack and swiped all I possess. I can't refuse to paint the portrait, because if I did my uncle would stop my allowance; yet every time I look up and catch that kid's vacant eye, I suffer agonies. I tell you, Bertie, sometimes when he gives me a patronising glance and then turns away and is sick, as if it revolted him to look at me, I come within an ace of occupying the entire front page of the evening papers as the latest murder sensation. There are moments when I can almost see the headlines: "Promising Young Artist Beans Baby With Axe".'

I patted his shoulder silently. My sympathy for the poor old scout was too deep for words.

I kept away from the studio for some time after that, because it didn't seem right to me to intrude on the poor chappie's sorrow. Besides, I'm bound to say that nurse intimidated me. She reminded me so infernally of Aunt Agatha. She was the same gimlet-eyed type.

But one afternoon Corky called me on the 'phone.

'Bertie!'

'Hallo?'

'Are you doing anything this afternoon?'

'Nothing special.'

'You couldn't come down here, could you?'

'What's the trouble? Anything up?'

'I've finished the portrait.'

'Good boy! Stout work!'

'Yes.' His voice sounded rather doubtful. 'The fact is, Bertie, it doesn't look quite right to me. There's something about it— My uncle's coming in half an hour to inspect it, and – I don't know why it is, but I kind of feel I'd like your moral support!'

I began to see that I was letting myself in for something. The sympathetic co-operation of Jeeves seemed to me to be indicated.

'You think he'll cut up rough?'

'He may.'

I threw my mind back to the red-faced chappie I had met at the restaurant, and tried to picture him cutting up rough. It was only too easy. I spoke to Corky firmly on the telephone.

'I'll come,' I said.

'Good!'

'But only if I may bring Jeeves.'

'Why Jeeves? What's Jeeves got to do with it? Who wants Jeeves? Jeeves is the fool who suggested the scheme that has led—'

'Listen, Corky, old top! If you think I am going to face that uncle of yours without Jeeves's support, you're mistaken. I'd sooner go into a den of wild beasts and bite a lion on the back of the neck.'

'Oh, all right,' said Corky. Not cordially, but he said it; so I rang for Jeeves, and explained the situation.

'Very good, sir,' said Jeeves.

We found Corky near the door, looking at the picture with one hand up in a defensive sort of way, as if he thought it might swing on him.

'Stand right where you are, Bertie,' he said, without moving. 'Now, tell me honestly, how does it strike you?'

The light from the big window fell right on the picture. I took a good look at it. Then I shifted a bit nearer and took another look. Then I went back to where I had been at first, because it hadn't seemed quite so bad from there.

'Well?' said Corky anxiously.

I hesitated a bit.

'Of course, old man, I only saw the kid once, and then only for a moment, but – but it *was* an ugly sort of kid, wasn't it, if I remember rightly?'

'As ugly as that?'

I looked again, and honesty compelled me to be frank.

'I don't see how it could have been, old chap.'

Poor old Corky ran his fingers through his hair in a temperamental sort of way. He groaned.

'You're quite right, Bertie. Something's gone wrong with the darned thing. My private impression is that, without knowing it, I've worked that stunt that Sargent used to pull – painting the soul of the sitter. I've got through the mere outward appearance, and have put the child's soul on canvas.'

'But could a child of that age have a soul like that? I don't see how he could have managed it in the time. What do you think, Jeeves?'

'I doubt it, sir.'

'It – it sort of leers at you, doesn't it?'

'You've noticed that, too?' said Corky.

'I don't see how one could help noticing.'

'All I tried to do was to give the little brute a cheerful expression. But, as it has worked out, he looks positively dissipated.'

'Just what I was going to suggest, old man. He looks as if he were in the middle of a colossal spree, and enjoying every minute of it. Don't you think so, Jeeves?'

'He has a decidedly inebriated air, sir.'

Corky was starting to say something, when the door opened and the uncle came in.

For about three seconds all was joy, jollity, and good will. The old boy shook hands with me, slapped Corky on the back, said he didn't think he had ever seen such a fine day, and whacked his leg with his stick. Jeeves had projected himself into the background, and he didn't notice him.

'Well, Bruce, my boy; so the portrait is really finished, is it – really finished? Well, bring it out. Let's have a look at it. This will be a wonderful surprise for your aunt. Where is it? Let's—'

And then he got it – suddenly, when he wasn't set for the punch; and he rocked back on his heels.

'Oosh!' he exclaimed. And for perhaps a minute there was one of the scaliest silences I've ever run up against.

'Is this a practical joke?' he said at last, in a way that set about sixteen draughts cutting through the room at once.

I thought it was up to me to rally round old Corky.

'You want to stand a bit farther away from it,' I said.

'You're perfectly right!' he snorted. 'I do! I want to stand so far away from it that I can't see the thing with a telescope!' He turned on Corky like an untamed tiger of the jungle who has just located a chunk of meat. 'And this – this – is what you have been wasting your time and my money for all these years! A painter! I wouldn't let you paint a house of mine. I gave you this commission, thinking that you were a competent worker, and this – this – this extract from a comic supplement is the result!' He swung towards the door, lashing his tail and growling to himself. 'This ends it. If you wish to continue this foolery of pretending to be an artist because you want an excuse for idleness, please yourself. But let me tell you this. Unless you report at my office on Monday morning, prepared to abandon all this idiocy and start in at the bottom of the business to work your way up, as you should have done half a dozen years ago, not another cent – not another cent – not another – Boosh!'

Then the door closed and he was no longer with us. And I crawled out of the bomb-proof shelter.

'Corky, old top!' I whispered faintly.

Corky was standing staring at the picture. His face was set. There was a hunted look in his eye.

'Well, that finishes it!' he muttered brokenly.

'What are you going to do?'

'Do? What can I do? I can't stick on here if he cuts off supplies. You heard what he said. I shall have to go to the office on Monday.'

I couldn't think of a thing to say. I knew exactly how he felt about the office. I don't know when I've been so infernally uncomfortable. It was like hanging round trying to make conversation to a pal who's just been sentenced to twenty years in quod.

And then a soothing voice broke the silence.

'If I might make a suggestion, sir!'

It was Jeeves. He had slid from the shadows and was gazing gravely at the picture. Upon my word, I can't give you a better idea of the shattering effect of Corky's Uncle Alexander when in action than by saying that he had absolutely made me forget for the moment that Jeeves was there.

'I wonder if I have ever happened to mention to you, sir, a Mr. Digby Thistleton, with whom I was once in service? Perhaps you have met him? He was a financier. He is now Lord Bridgworth. It was a favourite saying of his that there is always a way. The first time I heard him use the expression was after the failure of a patent depilatory which he promoted.'

'Jeeves,' I said, 'what on earth are you talking about?'

'I mentioned Mr. Thistleton, sir, because his was in some respects a parallel case to the present one. His depilatory failed, but he did not despair. He put it on the market again under the

name of Hair-o, guaranteed to produce a full crop of hair in a
few months. It was advertised, if you remember, sir, by a
humorous picture of a billiard ball, before and after taking, and
made such a substantial fortune that Mr. Thistleton was soon
afterwards elevated to the peerage for services to his Party. It
seems to me that, if Mr. Corcoran looks into the matter, he will
find, like Mr. Thistleton, that there is always a way. Mr. Worple
himself suggested the solution of the difficulty. In the heat of
the moment he compared the portrait to an extract from a
coloured comic supplement. I consider the suggestion a very
valuable one, sir. Mr. Corcoran's portrait may not have pleased
Mr. Worple as a likeness of his only child, but I have no doubt
that editors would gladly consider it as a foundation for a series
of humorous drawings. If Mr. Corcoran will allow me to make
the suggestion, his talent has always been for the humorous.
There is something about this picture – something bold and
vigorous, which arrests the attention. I feel sure it would be
highly popular.'

Corky was glaring at the picture, and making a sort of dry,
sucking noise with his mouth. He seemed completely
overwrought.

And then suddenly he began to laugh in a wild way.

'Corky, old man!' I said, massaging him tenderly. I feared the
poor blighter was hysterical.

He began to stagger about all over the floor.

'He's right! The man's absolutely right! Jeeves you're a life-
saver. You've hit on the greatest idea of the age. Report at the
office on Monday! Start at the bottom of the business! I'll buy
the business if I feel like it. I know the man who runs the comic
section of the *Sunday Star*. He'll eat this thing. He was telling
me only the other day how hard it was to get a good new series.
He'll give me anything I ask for a real winner like this. I've got
a gold-mine. Where's my hat? I've got an income for life!
Where's that confounded hat? Lend me a fiver, Bertie. I want to
take a taxi down to Park Row!'

Jeeves smiled paternally. Or, rather, he had a kind of paternal muscular spasm about the mouth, which is the nearest he ever gets to smiling.

'If I might make the suggestion, Mr. Corcoran – for a title of the series which you have in mind – "The Adventures of Baby Blobbs".'

Corky and I looked at the picture, then at each other in an awed way. Jeeves was right. There could be no other title.

'Jeeves,' I said. It was a few weeks later, and I had just finished looking at the comic section of the *Sunday Star*. 'I'm an optimist. I always have been. The older I get, the more I agree with Shakespeare and those poet Johnnies about it always being darkest before the dawn and there's a silver lining and what you lose on the swings you make up on the roundabouts. Look at Mr. Corcoran, for instance. There was a fellow, one would have said, clear up to the eyebrows in the soup. To all appearances he had got it right in the neck. Yet look at him now. Have you seen these pictures?'

'I took the liberty of glancing at them before bringing them to you, sir. Extremely diverting.'

'They have made a big hit, you know.'

'I anticipated it, sir.'

I leaned back against the pillows.

'You know, Jeeves, you're a genius. You ought to be drawing a commission on these things.'

'I have nothing to complain of in that respect, sir, Mr. Corcoran has been most generous. I am putting out the brown suit, sir.'

'No, I think I'll wear the blue with the faint red stripe.'

'Not the blue with the faint red stripe, sir.'

'But I rather fancy myself in it.'

'Not the blue with the faint red stripe, sir.'

'Oh, all right, have it your own way.'

'Very good, sir. Thank you, sir.'

You know, the longer I live in New York, the more clearly I see that half the trouble in this bally world is caused by the light-hearted and thoughtless way in which chappies dash off letters of introduction and hand them to other chappies to deliver to chappies of the third part. It's one of those things that make you wish you were living in the Stone Age. What I mean to say is, if a fellow in those days wanted to give anyone a letter of introduction, he had to spend a month or so carving it on a large-sized boulder, and the chances were that the other bird got so sick of lugging the thing round in the hot sun that he dropped it after the first mile. But nowadays it's so easy to write letters of introduction that everybody does it without a second thought, with the result that some perfectly harmless cove like myself gets in the soup. The last time that happened to me was when the chump Cyril Bassington-Bassington came over from England with a letter from my Aunt Agatha.

This chump Bassington-Bassington would seem from contemporary accounts to have blown in one morning at seven-forty-five. He was given the respectful raspberry by my man Jeeves, and told to try again about three hours later, when there would be a sporting chance of my having sprung from my bed with a glad cry to welcome another day and all that sort of thing. Which was rather decent of Jeeves, by the way, for it so happened that there was a slight estrangement, a touch of coldness, a bit of a row in other words, between us at the moment because of some rather priceless purple socks which I was wearing against his wishes: and a lesser man might easily have snatched at the chance of getting back at me a bit by loosing Cyril into my bedchamber at a moment when I couldn't have stood a two-minutes' conversation with my dearest pal. You know how it is. The fierce rush of modern life, the cheery supper-party, the wine when it is red, and so forth. Well, what I mean to say is, as far as I'm concerned, what with one thing and another, the old bean is a trifle slow at getting into its stride in the morning, and, until I have had my early cup of tea and brooded on life for a bit absolutely undisturbed, I'm not much of a lad for the merry chit-chat.

So Jeeves very sportingly shot Cyril out into the crisp morning air, and didn't let me know of his existence till he brought his card in with my tea.

'And what might all this be, Jeeves?' I said, giving the thing the glassy gaze.

'The gentleman called to see you earlier in the day, sir.'

'Good Lord, Jeeves! You don't mean to say the day starts earlier than this?'

'He desired me to say he would return later, sir.'

'I've never heard of him. Have *you* ever heard of him, Jeeves?'

'I am familiar with the name Bassington-Bassington, sir. There are three branches of the Bassington-Bassington family – the Shropshire Bassington-Bassingtons, the Hampshire Bassington-Bassingtons, and the Kent Bassington-Bassingtons.'

'England seems pretty well stocked up with Bassington-Bassingtons.'

'Tolerably so, sir.'

'No chance of a sudden shortage, I mean, what?'

'Presumably not, sir.'

'And what sort of a specimen is this one?'

'I could not say, sir, on such short acquaintance.'

'Will you give me a sporting two to one, Jeeves, judging from what you have seen of him, that this chappie is not a blighter or an excrescence?'

'No, sir. I should not care to venture such odds.'

'I knew it. Well, the only thing that remains to be discovered is what kind of a blighter he is.'

'Time will tell, sir. The gentleman brought this letter for you, sir.'

'What-ho! What-ho! What-ho! I say, Jeeves, this is from my Aunt Agatha!'

'Indeed, sir?'

I gave the thing the rapid eye. The wassail-bowl which had flowed overnight with a fairly steady gush into the small hours had left me rather pessimistic that morning, and the moment I saw Aunt Agatha's handwriting something seemed to tell me that Fate was about to let me have it in the lower ribs once again. It's a rummy thing. Aunt Agatha is the one person in the world I daren't offend, and it always happens that everyone she sends to me with letters of introduction gets into trouble of some sort. And she always seems to think that I ought to have watched over them while they were in New York like a blend of nursemaid and guardian angel. Which, of course, is a bit thick and pretty scaly.

There was only one gleam of comfort.

'He isn't going to stay in New York long, Jeeves. He's headed for Washington. Going to give the lads there the up-and-down before taking a whirl at the Diplomatic Service. So he ought to be leaving us pretty soon, thank goodness. I should say a lunch and a couple of dinners would about meet the case, what?'

'I fancy that should be entirely adequate, sir.'

He started to put out my things, and there was an awkward sort of silence.

'Not those socks, Jeeves,' I said, gulping a bit but having a dash at the careless, off-hand sort of tone. 'Give me the purple ones.'

'I beg your pardon, sir?' said Jeeves, coldly.

'Those jolly purple ones.'

'Very good, sir.'

He lugged them out of the drawer as if he were a vegetarian fishing a caterpillar out of his salad. You could see he was feeling deeply. Deuced painful and all that, this sort of thing, but a fellow has got to assert himself every now and then.

I was looking for Cyril to show up again any time after breakfast, but he didn't appear: so, towards one o'clock, I trickled out to the club, where I had a date to feed the Wooster face with a pal of mine of the name of Caffyn – George Caffyn, a fellow who writes plays and what not. He was a bit late, but bobbed up finally, saying that he had been kept at a rehearsal of his new piece, *Ask Dad,* and we started in. We had just reached the coffee, when the waiter came up and said that Jeeves wanted to see me.

Jeeves was in the waiting-room. He gave the socks one pained look as I came in, then averted his eyes.

'Mr. Bassington-Bassington has just telephoned, sir.'

'Why interrupt my lunch to tell me that, Jeeves? It means little or nothing in my young life.'

'He was somewhat insistent that I should inform you at the earliest possible moment, sir, as he had been arrested and would be glad if you could step around and bail him out.'

'Arrested!'

'Yes, sir.'

'What for?'

'He did not favour me with his confidence in that respect, sir.'

'This is a bit thick, Jeeves.'

'Precisely, sir.'

'I suppose I had better totter round, what?'

'That might be the judicious course, sir.'

So I collected old George, who very decently volunteered to stagger along with me, and we hopped into a taxi. We sat around at the police-station for a bit on a wooden bench in a sort of ante-room, and presently a policeman appeared, leading in Cyril.

'Halloa! Halloa! Halloa!' I said. 'What?'

My experience is that a fellow never really looks his best just after he's come out of a cell. When I was up at Oxford, I used to have a regular job bailing out a pal of mine who never failed to get pinched every Boat-race night, and he always looked like something that had been dug up by the roots. Cyril was in pretty much the same sort of shape. He had a black eye and a torn collar and altogether was nothing to write home about – especially if one was writing to Aunt Agatha. He was a thin, tall cove with a lot of light hair and pale-blue goggly eyes which made him look like one of the rarer kind of fish. He had just that expression of peeved surprise that one of those sheep's-head fish in Florida has when you haul it over the side of the boat.

'I got your message,' I said.

'Oh, are you Bertie Wooster?'

'Absolutely. And this is my pal George Caffyn. Writes plays and what not, don't you know.'

We all shook hands, and the policeman, having retrieved a piece of chewing-gum from the under-side of a chair, where he had parked it against a rainy day, went off into a corner and began to contemplate the infinite.

'This is a rotten country,' said Cyril.

'Oh, I don't know, you know, don't you know!' I said.

'We do our best,' said George.

'Old George is an American,' I explained. 'Writes plays, don't you know, and what not.'

'Of course, I didn't invent the country,' said George. 'That was Columbus. But I shall be delighted to consider any improvements you may suggest, and lay them before the proper authorities.'

'Well, why don't the policemen in New York dress properly?'

George took a look at the chewing officer across the room.

'I don't see anything missing,' he said.

'I mean to say, why don't they wear helmets like they do in London? Why do they look like postmen? It isn't fair on a fellow. Makes it dashed confusing. I was simply standing on the pavement, looking at things, when a fellow who looked like a postman prodded me in the ribs with a club. I didn't see why I should have postmen prodding me. Why the dickens should a fellow come three thousand miles to be prodded by postmen?'

'The point is well taken,' said George. 'What did you do?'

'I gave him a shove. And then he biffed me in the eye and lugged me off to this beastly place.'

'I'll fix it, old son,' I said. And I hauled out the bank-roll and went off to open negotiations, leaving Cyril to talk to George. I don't mind admitting that I was a bit perturbed. There were furrows in the old brow, and I had a kind of foreboding feeling. As long as this chump stayed in New York, I was sort of responsible for him: and he didn't give me the impression of being the species of cove a reasonable chappie would care to be responsible for for more than about three minutes.

I mused with a considerable amount of tensity over Cyril that night, when I had got home and Jeeves had brought me the final whisky. I couldn't help feeling that this visit of his to America was going to be one of those times that try men's souls. I hauled out Aunt Agatha's letter of introduction and re-read it, and there was no getting away from the fact that she undoubtedly appeared to be somewhat wrapped up in this blighter and to consider it my mission in life to shield him from harm while on the premises. I was deuced thankful that he had taken such a liking for George Caffyn, old George being a steady sort of cove. After I had got him out of his dungeon-cell, he and old George had gone off altogether, as chummy as brothers, to watch the afternoon rehearsal of *Ask Dad*. There was some talk, I gathered, of their dining together. I felt pretty easy in my mind while George had his eye on him.

I had got about as far as this in my meditations, when Jeeves came in with a telegram. At least, it wasn't a telegram: it was a cable – from Aunt Agatha, and this is what it said:

'Has Cyril Bassington-Bassington called yet? On no account introduce him into theatrical circles. Vitally important, letter follows.'

I read it a couple of times.

'This is rummy, Jeeves!'

'Yes, sir?'

'Very rummy and dashed disturbing!'

'Will there be anything further tonight, sir?'

Of course, if he was going to be as bally unsympathetic as that there was nothing to be done. My idea had been to show him the cable and ask his advice. But if he was letting those purple socks rankle to that extent, the good old *noblesse oblige* of the Woosters couldn't lower itself to the extent of pleading with the man. Absolutely not. So I gave it a miss.

'Nothing more, thanks.'

'Good night, sir.'

'Good night.'

He floated away, and I sat down to think the thing over. I had been directing the best efforts of the old bean to the problem for a matter of half an hour, when there was a ring at the bell. I went to the door, and there was Cyril, looking pretty festive.

'I'll come in for a bit if I may,' he said. 'Got something rather priceless to tell you.' He curveted past me into the sitting-room, and when I got there after shutting the front door I found him reading Aunt Agatha's cable and giggling in a rummy sort of manner. 'Oughtn't to have looked at this, I suppose. Caught sight of my name and read it without thinking. I say Wooster, old friend of my youth, this is rather funny. Do you mind if I have a drink? Thanks awfully and all that sort of rot. Yes, it's rather funny, considering what I came to tell you. Jolly old Caffyn has given me a small part in that musical comedy of his, *Ask Dad*. Only a bit, you know, but quite tolerably ripe. I'm feeling frightfully braced, don't you know!'

He drank his drink, and went on. He didn't seem to notice that I wasn't jumping about the room, yapping with joy.

'You know, I've always wanted to go on the stage, you know,' he said. 'But my old guv'nor wouldn't stick it at any price. Put the foot down with a bang, and turned bright purple whenever the subject was mentioned. That's the real reason why I came over here, if you want to know. I knew there wasn't a chance of my being able to work this stage wheeze in London without somebody getting on to it and tipping off the guv'nor, so I rather brainily sprang the scheme of popping over to Washington to broaden my mind. There's nobody to interfere on this side, you see, so I can go right ahead.'

I tried to reason with the poor chump.

'But your guv'nor will have to know sometime.'

'That'll be all right. I shall be a star by then, and he won't have a leg to stand on.'

'It seems to me he'll have one leg to stand on while he kicks me with the other.'

'Why, where do you come in? What have you got to do with it?'

'I introduced you to George Caffyn.'

'So you did, old top, so you did. I'd quite forgotten. I ought to have thanked you before. Well, so long. There's an early rehearsal of *Ask Dad* tomorrow morning, and I must be toddling. Rummy the thing should be called *Ask Dad*, when that's just what I'm not going to do. See what I mean, what, what? Well, pip-pip!'

'Toodle-oo!' I said, sadly, and the blighter scuddled off. I dived for the 'phone and called up George Caffyn.

'I say, George, what's all this about Cyril Bassington-Bassington?'

'What about him?'

'He tells me you've given him a part in your show.'

'Oh, yes. Just a few lines.'

'But I've just had fifty-seven cables from home telling me on no account to let him go on the stage.'

'I'm sorry. But Cyril is just the type I need for that part. He's simply got to be himself.'

'It's pretty tough on me, George, old man. My Aunt Agatha sent this blighter over with a letter of introduction to me, and she will hold me responsible.'

'She'll cut you out of her will?'

'It isn't a question of money. But – of course, you've never met my Aunt Agatha, so it's rather hard to explain. But she's a sort of human vampire-bat, and she'll make things most fearfully unpleasant for me when I go back to England. She's the kind of woman who comes and rags you before breakfast, don't you know.'

'Well, don't go back to England, then. Stick here and become president.'

'But, George, old top—!'

'Good night!'

'But, I say, George, old man!'

'You didn't get my last remark. It was "Good night!" You idle rich may not need sleep, but I've got to be bright and fresh in the morning. God bless you!'

I felt as if I hadn't a friend in the world. I was so jolly well worked up that I went and banged on Jeeves's door. It wasn't a thing I'd have cared to do as a rule, but it seemed to me that now was the time for all good men to come to the aid of the party, so to speak, and that it was up to Jeeves to rally round the young master, even if it broke up his beauty sleep.

Jeeves emerged in a brown dressing-gown.

'Sir?'

'Deuced sorry to wake you up, Jeeves, and so forth, but all sorts of dashed disturbing things have been happening.'

'I was not asleep, sir. It is my practice, on retiring, to read a few pages of some instructive book.'

'That's good! What I mean to say is, if you've just finished exercising the old bean, it's probably in mid-season form for tackling problems. Jeeves, Mr. Bassington-Bassington is going on the stage!'

'Indeed, sir?'

'Ah. The thing doesn't hit you. You don't get it properly. Here's the point. All his family are most fearfully dead against his going on the stage. There's going to be no end of trouble if he isn't headed off. And, what's worse, my Aunt Agatha will blame *me*, you see. And you know what *she* is!'

'Very much so, sir!'

'Well, can't you think of some way of stopping him?'

'Not, I confess, at the moment, sir.'

'Well, have a stab at it.'

'I will give the matter my best consideration, sir. Will there be anything further tonight?'

'I hope not. I've had all I can stand already.'

'Very good, sir.'

He popped off.

The part which old George had written for the chump Cyril took up about two pages of typescript: but it might have been Hamlet, the way that poor, misguided pinhead worked himself to the bone over it. I suppose, if I heard him say his lines once, I did it a dozen times in the first couple of days. He seemed to think that my only feeling about the whole affair was one of enthusiastic admiration, and that he could rely on my support and sympathy. What with trying to imagine how Aunt Agatha was going to take this thing and being woken up out of the dreamless in the small hours every other night to give my opinion of some new bit of business which Cyril had invented, I became more of less the good old shadow. And all the time Jeeves remained still pretty cold and distant about the purple socks. It's this sort of thing that ages a fellow, don't you know, and makes his youthful *joie-de-vivre* go a bit groggy at the knees.

In the middle of it Aunt Agatha's letter arrived. It took her about six pages to do justice to Cyril's father's feelings in regard to his going on the stage and about six more to give me a kind of sketch of what she would say, think, and do if I didn't keep him clear of injurious influences while he was in America. The letter came by the afternoon mail, and left me with a pretty firm conviction that it wasn't a thing I ought to keep to myself. I didn't even wait to ring the bell: I whizzed for the kitchen, bleating for Jeeves, and butted into the middle of a regular tea-party of sorts. Seated at the table were a depressed-looking cove who might have been a valet or something and a boy in a Norfolk suit. The valet-chappie was drinking a whisky-and-soda, and the boy was being tolerably rough with some jam and cake.

'Oh, I say, Jeeves!' I said. 'Sorry to interrupt but—'

At this juncture the small boy's eye hit me like a bullet and stopped me in my tracks. It was one of those cold, clammy, accusing sort of eyes – the kind that makes you reach up to see if your tie is straight: and he looked at me as if I were some sort of unnecessary product which the cat had brought in after a ramble among the local ash-cans. He was a stoutish infant with a lot of freckles and a good deal of jam on his face.

'Halloa! Halloa! Halloa!' I said. 'What?' There didn't seem much else to say.

The stripling stared at me in a nasty sort of way through the jam. He may have loved me at first sight but the impression he gave me was that he didn't think a lot of me and wasn't betting much that I would improve a great deal on acquaintance. I had a kind of feeling that I was about as popular with him as a cold Welsh rabbit.

'What's you name?' he asked.

'My name? Oh, Wooster, don't you know, and what not.'

'My pop's richer than you are!'

That seemed to be all about me. The child having said his say, started in on the jam again. I turned to Jeeves.

'I say, Jeeves, can you spare a moment? I want to show you something.'

'Very good, sir.'

We toddled into the sitting-room.

'Who is your little friend, Jeeves?'

'The young gentleman, sir?'

'It's a loose way of describing him, but I know what you mean.'

'I trust I was not taking a liberty in entertaining him, sir?'

'Not a bit. If that's you idea of a large afternoon, go ahead.'

'I happened to meet the young gentleman taking a walk with his father's valet, sir, whom I used to know somewhat intimately in London, and I ventured to invite them both to join me here.'

'Well, never mind about him, Jeeves. Read this letter.' He gave it the up-and-down.

'Very disturbing, sir!'

'What are we going to do about it?'

'Time may provide a solution, sir.'

'On the other hand, it mayn't, what?'

'Extremely true, sir.'

We'd got as far as this, when there was a ring at the door. Jeeves shimmered off, and Cyril blew in, full of good cheer and blitheringness.

'I say, Wooster, old thing,' he said. 'I want your advice. You know this part of mine. How ought I to dress it? What I mean is the first scene is laid in an hotel of sorts, at about three in the afternoon. What ought I to wear do you think?'

I wasn't feeling fit for a discussion of gent's suitings.

'You'd better consult Jeeves,' I said.

'A hot and by no means unripe idea! Where is he?'

'Gone back to the kitchen, I suppose.'

'I'll smite the good old bell, shall I? Yes? No?'

'Right-o.'

Jeeves poured silently in.

'Oh, I say, Jeeves,' began Cyril. 'I just wanted to have a syllable or two with you. It's this way – Halloa, who's this?'

I then perceived that the stout stripling had trickled into the room after Jeeves. He was standing near the door, looking at Cyril as if his worst fears had been realised. There was a bit of a silence. The child remained there, drinking Cyril in for about half a minute: then he gave his verdict: 'Fish-face!'

'Eh? What?' said Cyril.

The child, who had evidently been taught at his mother's knee to speak the truth, made his meaning a trifle clearer.

'You've a face like a fish!'

He spoke as if Cyril was more to be pitied than censured, which I'm bound to say I thought rather decent and broad-minded of him. I don't mind admitting that, whenever I looked at Cyril's face, I always had a feeling that he couldn't have got that way without its being mostly his own fault. I found myself warming to this child. Absolutely, don't you know. I liked his conversation.

It seemed to take Cyril a moment or two really to grasp the thing, and then you could hear the blood of the Bassington-Bassingtons begin to sizzle.

'Well, I'm dashed!' he said. 'I'm dashed if I'm not!'

'I wouldn't have a face like that,' proceeded the child, with a good deal of earnestness, 'not if you gave me a million dollars.' He thought for a moment, then corrected himself. 'Two million dollars!' he added.

Just what occurred then I couldn't exactly say, but the next few minutes were a bit exciting. I take it that Cyril must have made a dive for the infant. Anyway, the air seemed pretty well congested with arms and legs and things. Something bumped into the Wooster waistcoat just around the third button, and I collapsed on the settee and rather lost interest in things for the moment. When I had unscrambled myself, I found that Jeeves and the child had retired and Cyril was standing in the middle of the room snorting a bit.

'Who's that frightful little brute, Wooster?'

'I don't know. I never saw him before today.'

'I gave him a couple of tolerably juicy buffets before he legged it. I say, Wooster, that kid said a dashed odd thing. He yelled out something about Jeeves promising him a dollar if he called me – er – what he said.'

It sounded pretty unlikely to me.

'What would Jeeves do that for?'

'It struck me as rummy, too.'

'Where would be the sense of it?'

'That's what I can't see.'

'I mean to say, it's nothing to Jeeves what sort of a face you have.'

'No,' said Cyril. He spoke a little coldly, I fancied. I don't know why. 'Well, I'll be popping. Toodle-oo!'

It must have been about a week after this rummy little episode that George Caffyn called me up and asked me if I would care to go and see a run-through of his show. *Ask Dad*, it seemed, was to open out of town in Schenectady on the following Monday, and this was to be a sort of preliminary dress-rehearsal. A preliminary dress-rehearsal, old George explained, was the same as a regular dress-rehearsal inasmuch as it was apt to look like nothing on earth and last into the small hours, but more exciting because they wouldn't be timing the piece and consequently all the blighters who on these occasions let their angry passions rise would have plenty of scope for interruptions, with the result that a pleasant time would be had by all.

The thing was billed to start at eight o'clock, so I rolled up at ten-fifteen, so as not to have too long to wait before they began. The dress-parade was still going on. George was on the stage, talking to a cove in shirt-sleeves and an absolutely round chappie with big spectacles and a practically hairless dome. I had seen George with the latter merchant once or twice at the club, and I knew that he was Blumenfield, the manager. I waved to George, and slid into a seat at the back of the house, so as to be out of the way when the fighting started. Presently George hopped down off the stage and came and joined me, and fairly soon after that the curtain went down. The chappie at the piano whacked out a well-meant bar or two, and the curtain went up again.

I can't quite recall what the plot of *Ask Dad* was about, but I do know that it seemed able to jog along all right without much help from Cyril. I was rather puzzled at first. What I mean is, through brooding on Cyril and hearing him in his part and listening to his views on what ought and what ought not to be done, I suppose I had got a sort of impression rooted in the old bean that he was pretty well the backbone of the show, and that the rest of the company didn't do much except go on and fill in when he happened to be off the stage. I sat there for nearly half an hour, waiting for him to make his entrance, until I suddenly discovered he had been on from the start. He was, in fact, the rummy-looking plug-ugly who was now leaning against a potted palm a couple of feet from the O. P. side, trying to appear intelligent while the heroine sang a song about Love being like something which for the moment has slipped my memory. After the second refrain he began to dance in company with a dozen other equally weird birds, the whole platoon giving rather the impression of a bevy of car-conductors from Akron, Ohio, dressed up in their Sunday clothes for a swift visit to the city. A painful spectacle for one who could see a vision of Aunt Agatha reaching for the hatchet and old Bassington-Bassington senior putting on his strongest pair of hob-nailed boots. Absolutely!

The dance had just finished, and Cyril and his pals had shuffled off into the wings when a voice spoke from the darkness on my right.

'Pop!'

Old Blumenfield clapped his hands, and the hero, who had just been about to get the next line off his diaphragm, cheesed it. I peered into the shadows. Who should it be but Jeeves's little playmate with the freckles! He was now strolling down the aisle with his hands in his pockets as if the place belonged to him. An air of respectful attention seemed to pervade the building.

'Pop,' said the stripling, 'that number's no good.' Old Blumenfield beamed over his shoulder.

'Don't you like it, darling?'

'It gives me a pain.'

'You're dead right.'

'You want something zippy there. Something with a bit of jazz to it!'

'Quite right, my boy. I'll make a note of it. All right. Go on!'

I turned to George, who was muttering to himself in rather an overwrought way.

'I say, George, old man, who the dickens is that kid?'

Old George groaned a bit hollowly, as if things were a trifle thick.

'I didn't know he had crawled in. It's Blumenfield's son. Now we're going to have a hades of a time!'

'Does he always run things like this?'

'Always.'

'But why does old Blumenfield listen to him?'

'Nobody seems to know. It may be pure fatherly love, or he may regard him as a mascot. My own idea is that he thinks the kid has exactly the amount of intelligence of the average member of an audience, and that what makes a hit with him will please the general public. While, conversely, what he doesn't like will be too rotten for anyone. The kid is a pest, a wart, a pot of poison, and should be strangled!'

The rehearsal went on. The hero got off his lines. There was a slight outburst of frightfulness between the stage-manager and a Voice named Bill that came from somewhere near the roof, the subject under discussion being where the devil Bill's 'ambers' were at that particular juncture. Then things went on again until the moment arrived for Cyril's big scene.

I was still a trifle hazy about the plot, but I had got on to the fact that Cyril was some sort of an English peer who had come over to America doubtless for the best reasons. So far he had only had two lines to say. One was 'Oh, I say!' and the other was 'Yes, by Jove!': but I seemed to recollect from hearing him in his part, that pretty soon he was due rather to spread himself. I sat back in my seat and waited for him to bob up.

He bobbed up about five minutes later. Things had got a bit

stormy by that time. The Voice and the stage-director had had another of their love-feasts – this time something to do with why Bill's 'blues' weren't on the job or something. And, almost as soon as that was over, there was a bit of unpleasantness because a flower-pot fell off a window-ledge and nearly brained the hero. The atmosphere was consequently more or less hotted up when Cyril, who had been hanging about at the back of the stage with a squad of his Akron inseparables, breezed down centre and toed the mark for his most substantial chunk of entertainment. The heroine had been saying something about Love being something or not being something, if you follow me – and all the car-conductors, with Cyril at their head, had begun to surge round her in the restless sort of way those chappies do when there's a number coming along.

Cyril's first line was, 'Oh, I say, you know, you mustn't say that, really!' and it seemed to me he passed over the larynx with a goodish deal of vim and *je-ne-sais-quoi*. But, by Jove, before the heroine had time for the come-back, our little friend with the freckles had risen to lodge a protest.

'Pop!'

'Yes, sonny?'

'That one's no good!'

'Which one, darling?'

'The one with a face like a fish.'

'But they all have faces like fish.'

The child seemed to see the justice of this objection. He became more definite.

'The ugly one.'

'Which ugly one? That one?' said old Blumenfield, pointing to Cyril.

'Yep! He's rotten!'

'I thought so myself.'

'He's a pill!'

'You're dead right, my boy. I've noticed it for some time.'

Cyril had been gaping a bit while these few remarks were in

progress. He now shot down to the footlights. Even from where I was sitting, I could see that these harsh words had hit the old Bassington-Bassington family pride a frightful wallop. He started to get pink in the ears, and then in the nose, and then in the cheeks, till in about a quarter of a minute he looked pretty much like an explosion in a tomato cannery on a sunset evening.

'What the deuce do you mean?'

'What the deuce do *you* mean?' shouted old Blumenfield. 'Don't yell at me across the footlights!'

'I've a dashed good mind to come down and spank that little brute!'

'What!'

'A dashed good mind!'

Old Blumenfield swelled like a pumped-up tyre. He got rounder than ever.

'See here, Mister – I don't know your darn name—!'

'My name's Bassington-Bassington, and the jolly old Bassington-Bassingtons – I mean the Bassington-Bassingtons aren't accustomed—'

Old Blumenfield told him in a few brief words pretty much what he thought of the Bassington-Bassingtons and what they weren't accustomed to. The whole strength of the company rallied round to enjoy his remarks. You could see them jutting out from the wings and protruding from behind trees.

'You got to work good for my pop!' said the stout child, wagging his head reprovingly at Cyril.

'I don't want any bally cheek from you!' said Cyril gurgling a bit.

'What's that?' barked old Blumenfield. 'Do you understand that this boy is my son?'

'Yes, I do,' said Cyril. 'And you both have my sympathy!'

'You're fired!' bellowed old Blumenfield, swelling a good bit more. 'Get out of my theatre!'

About half-past ten next morning, just after I had finished

lubricating the good old interior with a soothing cup of Oolong, Jeeves filtered into my bedroom, and said that Cyril was waiting to see me in the sitting-room.

'How does he look, Jeeves?'

'Sir?'

'What does Mr. Bassington-Bassington look like?'

'It is hardly my place, sir, to criticize the facial peculiarities of your friends.'

'I don't meant that. I mean, does he appear peeved and what not?'

'Not noticeably, sir. His manner is tranquil.'

'That's rum!'

'Sir?'

'Nothing. Show him in, will you?'

I'm bound to say I had expected to see Cyril showing a few more traces of last night's battle. I was looking for a bit of the over-wrought soul and the quivering ganglions, if you know what I mean. He seemed pretty ordinary and quite fairly cheerful.

'Halloa, Wooster, old thing!'

'Hullo.'

'I just looked in to say good-bye.'

'Good-bye?'

'Yes. I'm off to Washington in an hour.' He sat down on the bed. 'You know, Wooster, old top,' he went on, 'I've been thinking it all over, and really it doesn't seem quite fair to the old guv'nor, my going on the stage and so forth. What do you think?'

'I see what you mean.'

'I mean to say, he sent me over here to broaden my jolly old mind and words to that effect, don't you know, and I can't help thinking it would be a bit of a jar for the old boy if I gave him the bird and went on the stage instead. I don't know if you understand me, but what I mean to say is, it's a sort of question of conscience.'

'Can you leave the show without upsetting everything?'

'Oh, that's all right. I've explained everything to old Blumenfield, and he quite sees my position. Of course, he's sorry to lose me – said he didn't see how he could fill my place and all that sort of thing – but, after all, even if it does land him in a bit of a hole, I think I'm right in resigning my part, don't you?'

'Oh, absolutely.'

'I thought you'd agree with me. Well, I ought to be shifting. Awfully glad to have seen something of you, and all that sort of rot. Pip-pip!'

'Toodle-oo!'

He sallied forth, having told all those bally lies with the clear, blue, pop-eyed gaze of a young child. I rang for Jeeves. You know, ever since last night I had been exercising the old bean to some extent, and a good deal of light had dawned upon me.

'Jeeves?'

'Sir?'

'Did you put that pie-faced infant up to bally-ragging Mr. Bassington-Bassington?'

'Sir?'

'Oh, you know what I mean. Did you tell him to get Mr. Bassington-Bassington sacked from the *Ask Dad* company?'

'I would not take such a liberty, sir.' He started to put out my clothes. 'It is possible that young Master Blumenfield may have gathered from casual remarks of mine that I did not consider the stage altogether a suitable sphere for Mr. Bassington-Bassington.'

'I say, Jeeves, you know, you're a bit of a marvel.'

'I endeavour to give satisfaction, sir.'

'And I'm frightfully obliged, if you know what I mean. Aunt Agatha would have had sixteen or seventeen fits if you hadn't headed him off.'

'I fancy there might have been some little friction and unpleasantness, sir. I am laying out the blue suit with the thin red stripe, sir. I fancy the effect will be pleasing.'

*

It's a rummy thing, but I had finished breakfast and gone out and got as far as the elevator before I remembered what it was that I had meant to do to reward Jeeves for his really sporting behaviour in this matter of the chump Cyril. My heart warmed to the man. Absolutely. It cut me to the heart to do it, but I had decided to give him his way and let those purple socks pass out of my life. After all, there are times when a cove must make sacrifices. I was just going to nip back and break the glad news to him, when the elevator came up, so I thought I would leave it till I got home.

The coloured chappie in charge of the elevator looked at me, as I hopped in, with a good deal of quiet devotion and what not.

'I wish to thank yo', suh,' he said, 'for yo' kindness.'

'Eh? What?'

'Misto' Jeeves done give me them purple socks, as you told him. Thank yo' very much, suh!'

I looked down. The blighter was a blaze of mauve from the ankle-bone southward. I don't know when I've seen anything so dressy.

'Oh, ah! Not at all! Right-o! Glad you like them!' I said.

Well, I mean to say, what? Absolutely!

I'm not absolutely certain of my facts, but I rather fancy it's Shakespeare who says that it's always just when a fellow is feeling particularly braced with things in general that Fate sneaks up behind him with the bit of lead piping. And what I'm driving at is that the man is perfectly right. Take, for instance, the business of Lady Malvern and her son Wilmot. That was one of the scaliest affairs I was ever mixed up with, and a moment before they came into my life I was just thinking how thoroughly all right everything was.

I was still in New York when the thing started, and it was about the time of year when New York is at its best. It was one of those topping mornings, and I had just climbed out from under the cold shower, feeling like a million dollars. As a matter of fact, what was bucking me up more than anything was the fact that the day before I had asserted myself with Jeeves – absolutely asserted myself, don't you know. You see, the way things had been going on I was rapidly becoming a dashed serf. The man had jolly well oppressed me. I didn't so much mind when he made me give up one of my new suits, because Jeeves's judgment about suits is sound and can generally be relied upon.

But I as near as a toucher rebelled when he wouldn't let me wear a pair of cloth-topped boots which I loved like a couple of brothers. And, finally, when he tried to tread on me like a worm in the matter of a hat, I put the Wooster foot down and showed him in no uncertain manner who was who.

It's a long story, and I haven't time to tell you now, but the nub of the thing was that he wanted me to wear the White House Wonder – as worn by President Coolidge – when I had set my heart on the Broadway Special, much patronised by the Younger Set; and the end of the matter was that, after a rather painful scene, I bought the Broadway Special. So that's how things were on this particular morning, and I was feeling pretty manly and independent.

Well, I was in the bathroom, wondering what there was going to be for breakfast while I massaged the spine with a rough towel and sang slightly, when there was a tap at the door. I stopped singing and opened the door an inch.

'What ho, without there!' I said.

'Lady Malvern has called, sir.'

'Eh?'

'Lady Malvern, sir. She is waiting in the sitting-room.'

'Pull yourself together, Jeeves, my man,' I said rather severely, for I bar practical jokes before breakfast. 'You know perfectly well there's no one waiting for me in the sitting-room. How could there be when it's barely ten o'clock yet?'

'I gathered from her ladyship, sir, that she had landed from an ocean liner at an early hour this morning.'

This made the thing a bit more plausible. I remembered that when I had arrived in America about a year before, the proceedings had begun at some ghastly hour like six, and that I had been shot out on to a foreign shore considerably before eight.

'Who the deuce is Lady Malvern, Jeeves?'

'Her ladyship did not confide in me, sir.'

'Is she alone?'

'Her ladyship is accompanied by a Lord Pershore, sir. I fancy that his lordship would be her ladyship's son.'

'Oh, well, put out rich raiment of sorts, and I'll be dressing.'

'The heather-mixture lounge is in readiness, sir.'

'Then lead me to it.'

While I was dressing I kept trying to think who on earth Lady Malvern could be. It wasn't till I had climbed through the top of my shirt and was reaching out for the studs that I remembered.

'I've placed her, Jeeves. She's a pal of my Aunt Agatha.'

'Indeed, sir?'

'Yes. I met her at lunch one Sunday before I left London. A very vicious specimen. Writes books. She wrote a book on social conditions in India when she came back from the Durbar.'

'Yes, sir? Pardon me, sir, but not that tie.'

'Eh?'

'Not that tie with the heather-mixture lounge, sir.'

It was a shock to me. I thought I had quelled the fellow. It was rather a solemn moment. What I mean is, if I weakened now, all my good work the night before would be thrown away. I braced myself.

'What's wrong with this tie? I've seen you give it a nasty look before. Speak out like a man! What's the matter with it?'

'Too ornate, sir.'

'Nonsense! A cheerful pink. Nothing more.'

'Unsuitable, sir.'

'Jeeves, this is the tie I wear!'

'Very good, sir.'

Dashed unpleasant. I could see that the man was wounded. But I was firm. I tied the tie, got into the coat and waistcoat, and went into the sitting-room.

'Hullo-ullo-ullo!' I said. 'What?'

'Ah! How do you do, Mr. Wooster? You have never met my son Wilmot, I think? Motty, darling, this is Mr. Wooster.'

Lady Malvern was a hearty, happy, healthy, overpowering sort of dashed female, not so very tall but making up for it by measuring about six feet from the O. P. to the Prompt Side. She fitted into my biggest arm-chair as if it had been built round her by someone who knew they were wearing arm-chairs tight about the hips that season. She had bright, bulging eyes and a lot of yellow hair, and when she spoke she showed about fifty-seven front teeth. She was one of those women who kind of numb a fellow's faculties. She made me feel as if I were ten years old and had been brought into the drawing-room in my Sunday clothes to say how-d'you-do. Altogether by no means the sort of thing a chappie would wish to find in his sitting-room before breakfast.

Motty, the son, was about twenty-three, tall and thin and meek-looking. He had the same yellow hair as his mother, but he wore it plastered down and parted in the middle. His eyes bulged, too, but they weren't bright. They were a dull grey with pink rims. His chin gave up the struggle about half-way down, and he didn't appear to have any eyelashes. A mild, furtive, sheepish sort of blighter, in short.

'Awfully glad to see you,' I said, though this was far from the case, for already I was beginning to have a sort of feeling that dirty work was threatening in the offing. 'So you've popped over, eh? Making a long stay in America?'

'About a month. Your aunt gave me your address and told me to be sure to call on you.'

I was glad to hear this, for it seemed to indicate that Aunt Agatha was beginning to come round a bit. As I believe I told you before, there had been some slight unpleasantness between us, arising from the occasion when she had sent me over to New York to disentangle my cousin Gussie from the clutches of a girl on the music-hall stage. When I tell you that by the time I had finished my operations Gussie had not only married the girl but had gone on the Halls himself and was doing well, you'll understand that relations were a trifle strained between aunt and nephew.

I simply hadn't dared go back and face her, and it was a relief to find that time had healed the wound enough to make her tell her pals to call on me. What I mean is, much as I liked America,

I didn't want to have England barred to me for the rest of my natural; and, believe me, England is a jolly sight too small for anyone to live in with Aunt Agatha, if she's really on the war-path. So I was braced at hearing these words and smiled genially on the assemblage.

'Your aunt said that you would do anything that was in your power to be of assistance to us.'

'Rather! Oh, rather. Absolutely.'

'Thank you so much. I want you to put dear Motty up for a little while.'

I didn't get this for a moment.

'Put him up? For my clubs?'

'No, no! Darling Motty is essentially a home bird. Aren't you, Motty, darling?' Motty, who was sucking the knob of his stick, uncorked himself.

'Yes, Mother,' he said, and corked himself up again.

'I should not like him to belong to clubs. I mean put him up here. Have him to live with you while I am away.'

These frightful words trickled out of her like honey. The woman simply didn't seem to understand the ghastly nature of her proposal. I gave Motty the swift east-to-west. He was sitting with his mouth nuzzling the stick, blinking at the wall. The thought of having this planted on me for an indefinite period appalled me. Absolutely appalled me, don't you know. I was just starting to say that the shot wasn't on the board at any price, and that the first sign Motty gave of trying to nestle into my little home I would yell for the police, when she went on, rolling placidly over me, as it were.

There was something about this woman that sapped one's will-power.

'I am leaving New York by the midday train, as I have to pay a visit to Sing-Sing prison. I am extremely interested in prison conditions in America. After that I work my way gradually across to the coast, visiting the points of interest on the journey. You see, Mr. Wooster, I am in America principally on business. No doubt you read my book, *India and the Indians*? My publishers are anxious for me to write a companion volume on the United States. I shall not be able to spend more than a month in the country, as I have to get back for the season, but a month should be ample. I was less than a month in India, and my dear friend Sir Roger Cremorne wrote his *America from Within* after a stay of only two weeks. I should love to take dear Motty with me, but the poor boy gets so sick when he travels by train. I shall have to pick him up on my return.'

From where I sat I could see Jeeves in the dining-room, laying the breakfast table. I wished I could have had a minute with him alone. I felt certain that he would have been able to think of some way of putting a stop to this woman.

'It will be such a relief to know that Motty is safe with you, Mr. Wooster. I know what the temptations of a great city are. Hitherto dear Motty has been sheltered from them. He has lived quietly with me in the country. I know that you will look after him carefully, Mr. Wooster. He will give very little trouble.' She talked about the poor blighter as if he wasn't there. Not that Motty seemed to mind. He had stopped chewing his walking-stick and was sitting there with his mouth open. 'He is a vegetarian and a teetotaller and is devoted to reading. Give him a nice book and he will be quite contented.' She got up. 'Thank you so much, Mr. Wooster. I don't know what I should have done without your help. Come, Motty. We have just time to see a few of the sights before my train goes. But I shall have to rely on you for most of my information about New York, darling. Be sure to keep your eyes open and take notes of your impressions. It will be such a help. Good-bye, Mr. Wooster. I will send Motty back early in the afternoon.'

They went out, and I howled for Jeeves.

'Jeeves!'

'Sir?'

'What's to be done? You heard it all, didn't you? You were in the dining-room most of the time. That pill is coming to stay here.'

'Pill, sir?'

'The excrescence.'

'I beg your pardon, sir?'

I looked at Jeeves sharply. This sort of thing wasn't like him. Then I understood.

'Lord Pershore will be staying here for tonight, Jeeves,' I said coldly.

'Very good, sir. Breakfast is ready, sir.'

I could have sobbed into the bacon and eggs. That there wasn't any sympathy to be got out of Jeeves was what put the lid on it. For a moment I almost weakened and told him to destroy the hat and tie if he didn't like them, but I pulled myself together again. I was dashed if I was going to let Jeeves treat me like a bally one-man chain-gang.

But, what with brooding on Jeeves and brooding on Motty, I was in a pretty reduced sort of state. The more I examined the situation, the more blighted it became. There was nothing I could do. If I slung Motty out, he would report to his mother, and she would pass it on to Aunt Agatha, and I didn't like to think what would happen then. Sooner or later I should be wanting to go back to England, and I didn't want to get there and find Aunt Agatha waiting on the quay for me with a sandbag. There was absolutely nothing for it but to put the fellow up and make the best of it.

About midday Motty's luggage arrived, and soon afterward a large parcel of what I took to be nice books. I brightened up a little when I saw it. It was one of those massive parcels and looked as if it had enough in it to keep him busy for a year. I felt a trifle more cheerful, and I got my Broadway Special and stuck it on my head, and gave the pink tie a twist, and reeled out to take a bite of lunch with one or two of the lads at a neighbouring hostelry; and what with excellent browsing and sluicing and cheery conversation and what-not, the afternoon passed quite happily. By dinner-time I had almost forgotten Motty's existence.

I dined at the club and looked in at a show afterward, and it wasn't till fairly late that I got back to the flat. There were no signs of Motty, and I took it that he had gone to bed.

It seemed rummy to me, though, that the parcel of nice books was still there with the string and paper on it. It looked as if Motty, after seeing mother off at the station, had decided to call it a day.

Jeeves came in with the nightly whisky-and-soda.

'Lord Pershore gone to bed, Jeeves?' I asked, with reserved hauteur and what-not.

'No, sir. His lordship has not yet returned.'

'Not returned? What do you mean?'

'His lordship came in shortly after six-thirty, and, having dressed, went out again.'

At this moment there was a noise outside the front door, a sort of scrabbling noise, as if somebody were trying to paw his way through the woodwork. Then a sort of thud.

'Better go and see what that is, Jeeves.'

'Very good, sir.'

He went out and came back again.

'If you would not mind stepping this way, sir, I think we might be able to carry him in.'

'Carry him in?'

'His lordship is lying on the mat, sir.'

I went to the front door. The man was right. There was Motty huddled up outside on the floor. He was moaning a bit.

'He's had some sort of dashed fit,' I said. I took another look. 'Jeeves! Someone's been feeding him meat!'

'Sir?'

'He's a vegetarian, you know. He must have been digging into a steak or something. Call up a doctor!'

'I hardly think it will be necessary, sir. If you would take his lordship's legs, while I—'

'Great Scott, Jeeves! You don't think – he can't be—'

'I am inclined to think so, sir.'

And, by Jove, he was right! Once on the right track, you

couldn't mistake it. Motty was under the surface. Completely sozzled.

It was the deuce of a shock.

'You never can tell, Jeeves!'

'Very seldom, sir.'

'Remove the eye of authority and where are you?'

'Precisely, sir.'

'Where is my wandering boy tonight and all that sort of thing, what?'

'It would seem so, sir.'

'Well, we had better bring him in, eh?'

'Yes, sir.'

So we lugged him in, and Jeeves put him to bed, and I lit a cigarette and sat down to think the thing over. I had a kind of foreboding. It seemed to me that I had let myself in for something pretty rocky.

Next morning, after I had sucked down a thoughtful cup of tea, I went into Motty's room to investigate. I expected to find the fellow a wreck, but there he was, sitting up in bed, quite chirpy, reading *Gingery Stories.*

'What ho!' I said.

'What ho!' said Motty.

'What ho! What ho!'

'What ho! What ho! What ho!'

After that it seemed rather difficult to go on with the conversation.

'How are you feeling this morning?' I asked.

'Topping!' replied Motty, blithely and with abandon. 'I say, you know, that fellow of yours – Jeeves, you know – is a corker. I had a most frightful headache when I woke up, and he brought me a sort of rummy dark drink, and it put me right again at once. Said it was his own invention. I must see more of that lad. He seems to me distinctly one of the ones.'

I couldn't believe that this was the same blighter who had sat and sucked his stick the day before.

'You ate something that disagreed with you last night, didn't you?' I said, by way of giving him a chance to slide out of it if he wanted to. But he wouldn't have it at any price.

'No!' he replied firmly. 'I didn't do anything of the kind. I drank too much. Much too much. Lots and lots too much. And, what's more, I'm going to do it again. I'm going to do it every night. If ever you see me sober, old top,' he said, with a kind of holy exaltation, 'tap me on the shoulder and say, "Tut! Tut!" and I'll apologise and remedy the defect.'

'But I say, you know, what about me?'

'What about you?'

'Well, I'm, so to speak, as it were, kind of responsible for you. What I mean to say is, if you go doing this sort of thing I'm apt to get in the soup somewhat.'

'I can't help your troubles,' said Motty firmly. 'Listen to me, old thing: this is the first time in my life that I've had a real chance to yield to the temptations of a great city. What's the use of a great city having temptations if fellows don't yield to them? Makes it so bally discouraging for the great city. Besides, mother told me to keep my eyes open and collect impressions.'

I sat on the edge of the bed. I felt dizzy.

'I know just how you feel, old dear,' said Motty consolingly. 'And, if my principles would permit it, I would simmer down for your sake. But duty first! This is the first time I've been let out alone, and I mean to make the most of it. We're only young once. Why interfere with life's morning? Young man, rejoice in thy youth! Tra-la! What ho!'

Put like that, it did seem reasonable.

'All my bally life, dear boy,' Motty went on, 'I've been cooped up in the ancestral home at Much Middlefold, in Shropshire, and till you've been cooped up in Much Middlefold you don't know what cooping is. The only time we get any excitement is when one of the choir-boys is caught sucking chocolate during the sermon. When that happens, we talk about it for days. I've got about a month of New York, and I mean to store up a few happy memories for the long winter evenings. This is my only chance to collect a past, and I'm going to do it. Now tell me, old sport, as man to man, how does one get in touch with that very decent bird Jeeves? Does one ring a bell or shout a bit? I should like to discuss the subject of a good stiff b.-and-s. with him.'

I had had a sort of vague idea, don't you know, that if I stuck close to Motty and went about the place with him, I might act as a bit of a damper on the gaiety. What I mean is, I thought that if, when he was being the life and soul of the party, he were to catch my reproving eye he might ease up a trifle on the revelry. So the next night I took him along to supper with me. It was the last time. I'm a quiet, peaceful sort of bloke who has lived all his life in London, and I can't stand the pace these swift sportsmen from the rural districts set. What I mean to say is, I'm all for rational enjoyment and so forth, but I think a fellow makes himself conspicuous when he throws soft-boiled eggs at the electric fan. And decent mirth and all that sort of thing are all right, but I do bar dancing on tables and having to dash all over the place dodging waiters, managers, and chuckers-out, just when you want to sit still and digest.

Directly I managed to tear myself away that night and get home, I made up my mind that this was jolly well the last time that I went about with Motty. The only time I met him late at night after that was once when I passed the door of a fairly low-down sort of restaurant and had to step aside to dodge him as he sailed through the air *en route* for the opposite pavement, with a muscular looking sort of fellow peering out after him with a kind of gloomy satisfaction.

In a way, I couldn't help sympathising with the chap. He had about four weeks to have the good time that ought to have been spread over about ten years, and I didn't wonder at his wanting to be pretty busy. I should have been just the same in his place. Still, there was no denying that it was a bit thick. If it hadn't been for the thought of Lady Malvern and Aunt Agatha in the background, I should have regarded Motty's rapid work with an indulgent smile. But I couldn't get rid of the feeling that, sooner or later, I was the lad who was scheduled to get it behind the ear. And what with brooding on this prospect, and sitting up in the old flat waiting for the familiar footstep, and putting it to bed when it got there, and stealing into the sick-chamber next morning to contemplate the wreckage, I was beginning to lose weight. Absolutely becoming the good old shadow, I give you my honest word. Starting at sudden noises and what-not.

And no sympathy from Jeeves. That was what cut me to the quick. The man was still thoroughly pipped about the hat and tie, and simply wouldn't rally round. One morning I wanted comforting so much that I sank the pride of the Woosters and appealed to the fellow direct.

'Jeeves,' I said, 'this is getting a bit thick!'

'Sir?'

'You know what I mean. This lad seems to have chucked all the principles of a well-spent boyhood. He has got it up his nose!'

'Yes, sir.'

'Well, I shall get blamed, don't you know. You know what my Aunt Agatha is.'

'Yes, sir.'

'Very well, then.'

I waited a moment, but he wouldn't unbend.

'Jeeves,' I said, 'haven't you any scheme up your sleeve for coping with this blighter?'

'No, sir.'

And he shimmered off to his lair. Obstinate devil! So dashed absurd, don't you know. It wasn't as if there was anything wrong with that Broadway Special hat. It was a remarkably priceless effort, and much admired by the lads. But, just because he preferred the White House Wonder, he left me flat.

It was shortly after this that young Motty got the idea of bringing pals back in the small hours to continue the gay revels in the home. This was where I began to crack under the strain. You see, the part of town where I was living wasn't the right place for that sort of thing. I knew lots of fellows down Washington Square way who started the evening at about two a.m. – artists and writers and so forth who frolicked considerably till checked by the arrival of the morning milk. That was all right. They like that sort of thing down there. The neighbours can't get to sleep unless there's someone dancing Hawaiian dances over their heads. But on Fifty-seventh Street the atmosphere wasn't right, and when Motty turned up at three in the morning with a collection of hearty lads, who only stopped singing their college song when they started singing "The Old Oaken Bucket", there was a marked peevishness among the old settlers in the flats. The management was extremely terse over the telephone at breakfast-time, and took a lot of soothing.

The next night I came home early, after a lonely dinner at a place which I'd chosen because there didn't seem any chance of meeting Motty there. The sitting-room was quite dark, and I was just moving to switch on the light, when there was a sort of explosion and something collared hold of my trouser-leg. Living with Motty had reduced me to such an extent that I was simply unable to cope with this thing. I jumped backward with a loud yell of anguish, and tumbled out into the hall just as Jeeves came out of his den to see what the matter was.

'Did you call, sir?'

'Jeeves! There's something in there that grabs you by the leg!'

'That would be Rollo, sir.'

'Eh?'

'I would have warned you of his presence, but I did not hear you come in. His temper is a little uncertain at present, as he has not yet settled down.'

'Who the deuce is Rollo?'

'His lordship's bull-terrier, sir. His lordship won him in a raffle, and tied him to the leg of the table. If you will allow me, sir, I will go in and switch on the light.'

There really is nobody like Jeeves. He walked straight into the sitting-room, the biggest feat since Daniel and the lions' den, without a quiver. What's more, his magnetism, or whatever they call it was such that the dashed animal, instead of pinning him by the leg, calmed down as if he had had a bromide, and rolled over on his back with all his paws in the air. If Jeeves had been his rich uncle he couldn't have been more chummy. Yet directly he caught sight of me again, he got all worked up and seemed to have only one idea in life – to start chewing me where he had left off.

'Rollo is not used to you yet, sir,' said Jeeves, regarding the bally quadruped in an admiring sort of way. 'He is an excellent watchdog.'

'I don't want a watchdog to keep me out of my rooms.'

'No, sir.'

'Well, what am I to do?'

'No doubt in time the animal will learn to discriminate, sir. He will learn to distinguish your peculiar scent.'

'What do you mean – my peculiar scent? Correct the impression that I intend to hang about in the hall while life slips by, in the hope that one of these days that dashed animal will decide that I smell all right.' I thought for a bit. 'Jeeves!'

'Sir?'

'I'm going away – tomorrow morning by the first train. I shall go and stop with Mr. Todd in the country.'

'Do you wish me to accompany you, sir?'

'No.'

'Very good, sir.'

'I don't know when I shall be back. Forward my letters.'

'Yes, sir.'

As a matter of fact, I was back within the week. Rocky Todd, the pal I went to stay with, is a rummy sort of a chap who lives all alone in the wilds of Long Island, and likes it; but a little of that sort of thing goes a long way with me. Dear old Rocky is one of the best, but after a few days in his cottage in the woods, miles away from anywhere, New York, even with Motty on the premises, began to look pretty good to me. The days down on Long Island have forty-eight hours in them; you can't get to sleep at night because of the bellowing of the crickets; and you have to walk two miles for a drink and six for an evening paper. I thanked Rocky for his kind hospitality, and caught the only train they have down in those parts. It landed me in New York about dinner-time. I went straight to the old flat. Jeeves came out of his lair. I looked cautiously for Rollo.

'Where's that dog, Jeeves? Have you got him tied up?'

'The animal is no longer here, sir. His lordship gave him to the porter, who sold him. His lordship took a prejudice against the animal on account of being bitten by him in the calf of the leg.'

I don't think I've ever been so bucked by a bit of news. I felt I had misjudged Rollo. Evidently, when you got to know him better, he had a lot of good in him.

'Fine!' I said. 'Is Lord Pershore in, Jeeves?'

'No, sir.'

'Do you expect him back to dinner?'

'No, sir.'

'Where is he?'

'In prison, sir.'

'In prison!'

'Yes, sir.'

'You don't mean – in prison?'

'Yes, sir.'

I lowered myself into a chair.

'Why?' I said.

'He assaulted a constable, sir.'

'Lord Pershore assaulted a constable!'

'Yes, sir.'

I digested this.

'But, Jeeves, I say! This is frightful!'

'Sir?'

'What will Lady Malvern say when she finds out?'

'I do not fancy that her ladyship will find out, sir.'

'But she'll come back and want to know where he is.'

'I rather fancy, sir, that his lordship's bit of time will have run out by then.'

'But supposing it hasn't?'

'In that event, sir, it may be judicious to prevaricate a little.'

'How?'

'If I might make the suggestion, sir, I should inform her ladyship that his lordship has left for a short visit to Boston.'

'Why Boston?'

'Very interesting and respectable centre, sir.'

'Jeeves, I believe you've hit it.'

'I fancy so, sir.'

'Why, this is really the best thing that could have happened. If this hadn't turned up to prevent him, young Motty would have been in a sanatorium by the time Lady Malvern got back.'

'Exactly, sir.'

The more I looked at it in that way, the sounder this prison wheeze seemed to me. There was no doubt in the world that prison was just what the doctor ordered for Motty. It was the only thing that could have pulled him up. I was sorry for the poor blighter, but after all, I reflected, a fellow who had lived all his life with Lady Malvern, in a small village in the interior of Shropshire, wouldn't have much to kick at in a prison. Altogether, I began to feel absolutely braced again. Life became like what the poet Johnnie says – one grand, sweet song. Things went on so comfortably and peacefully for a couple of weeks that I give you my word that I'd almost forgotten such a person as Motty existed. The only flaw in the scheme of things was that Jeeves was still pained and distant. It wasn't anything he said, or did, mind you, but there was a rummy something about him all the time. Once when I was tying the pink tie I caught sight of him in the looking-glass. There was a kind of grieved look in his eye.

And then Lady Malvern came back, a good bit ahead of schedule. I hadn't been expecting her for days. I'd forgotten how time had been slipping along. She turned up one morning while I was still in bed sipping tea and thinking of this and that. Jeeves flowed in with the announcement that he had just loosed her into the sitting-room. I draped a few garments round me and went in.

There she was, sitting in the same arm-chair, looking as massive as ever. The only difference was that she didn't uncover the teeth as she had done the first time.

'Good morning,' I said. 'So you've got back, what?'

'I have got back.'

There was something sort of bleak about her tone, rather as if she had swallowed an east wind. This I took to be due to the fact that she probably hadn't breakfasted. It's only after a bit of breakfast that I'm able to regard the world with that sunny cheeriness which makes a fellow the universal favourite. I'm never much of a lad till I've engulfed an egg or two and a beaker of coffee.

'I suppose you haven't breakfasted?'

'I have not yet breakfasted.'

'Won't you have an egg or something? Or a sausage or something? Or something?'

'No, thank you.'

She spoke as if she belonged to an anti-sausage society or a league for the suppression of eggs. There was a bit of a silence.

'I called on you last night,' she said, 'but you were out.'

'Awfully sorry. Had a pleasant trip?'

'Extremely, thank you.'

'See everything? Niagara Falls, Yellowstone Park, and the jolly old Grand Canyon, and what-not?'

'I saw a great deal.'

There was another slightly *frappé* silence. Jeeves floated silently into the dining-room and began to lay the breakfast-table.

'I hope Wilmot was not in your way, Mr. Wooster?'

I had been wondering when she was going to mention Motty.

'Rather not! Great pals. Hit it off splendidly.'

'You were his constant companion, then?'

'Absolutely. We were always together. Saw all the sights, don't you know. We'd take in the Museum of Art in the morning, and have a bit of lunch at some good vegetarian place, and then toddle along to a sacred concert in the afternoon, and home to an early dinner. We usually played dominoes after dinner. And then the early bed and the refreshing sleep. We had a great time. I was awfully sorry when he went away to Boston.'

'Oh! Wilmot is in Boston?'

'Yes. I ought to have let you know, but of course we didn't know where you were. You were dodging all over the place like a snipe – I mean, don't you know, dodging all over the place, and we couldn't get at you. Yes, Motty went off to Boston.'

'You're sure he went to Boston?'

'Oh, absolutely.' I called out to Jeeves, who was now messing about in the next room with forks and so forth: 'Jeeves, Lord Pershore didn't change his mind about going to Boston, did he?'

'No, sir.'

'I thought I was right. Yes, Motty went to Boston.'

'Then how do you account, Mr. Wooster, for the fact that when I went yesterday afternoon to Blackwell's Island prison, to secure material for my book, I saw poor, dear Wilmot there, dressed in a striped suit, seated beside a pile of stones with a hammer in his hands?'

I tried to think of something to say, but nothing came. A fellow has to be a lot broader about the forehead than I am to handle a jolt like this. I strained the old bean till it creaked, but between the collar and the hair parting nothing stirred. I was dumb. Which was lucky, because I wouldn't have had a chance to get any persiflage out of my system. Lady Malvern collared the conversation. She had been bottling it up, and now it came out with a rush.

'So this is how you have looked after my poor, dear boy, Mr. Wooster! So this is how you have abused my trust! I left him in your charge, thinking that I could rely on you to shield him from evil. He came to you innocent, unversed in the ways of the world, confiding, unused to the temptations of a large city, and you led him astray!'

I hadn't any remarks to make. All I could think of was the picture of Aunt Agatha drinking all this in and reaching out to sharpen the hatchet against my return.

'You deliberately—'

Far away in the misty distance a soft voice spoke:

'If I might explain, your ladyship.'

Jeeves had projected himself in from the dining-room and materialised on the rug. Lady Malvern tried to freeze him with a look, but you can't do that sort of thing to Jeeves. He is look-proof.

'I fancy, your ladyship, that you may have misunderstood Mr. Wooster, and that he may have given you the impression that he was in New York when his lordship was – removed. When Mr. Wooster informed your ladyship that his lordship had gone to Boston, he was relying on the version I had given him of his lordship's movements. Mr. Wooster was away, visiting a friend in the country, at the time, and knew nothing of the matter till your ladyship informed him.'

Lady Malvern gave a kind of grunt. It didn't rattle Jeeves.

'I feared Mr. Wooster might be disturbed if he knew the truth, as he is so attached to his lordship and has taken such pains to look after him, so I took the liberty of telling him that his lordship had gone away for a visit. It might have been hard for Mr. Wooster to believe that his lordship had gone to prison voluntarily and from the best motives, but your ladyship, knowing him better, will readily understand.'

'What!' Lady Malvern goggled at him. 'Did you say that Lord Pershore went to prison voluntarily?'

'If I might explain, your ladyship. I think that your ladyship's parting words made a deep impression on his lordship. I have frequently heard him speak to Mr. Wooster of his desire to do something to follow your ladyship's instructions and collect material for your ladyship's book on America. Mr. Wooster will bear me out when I say that his lordship was frequently extremely depressed at the thought that he was doing so little to help.'

'Absolutely, by Jove! Quite pipped about it!' I said.

'The idea of making a personal examination into the prison system of the country – from within – occurred to his lordship very suddenly one night. He embraced it eagerly. There was no restraining him.'

Lady Malvern looked at Jeeves, then at me, then at Jeeves again. I could see her struggling with the thing.

'Surely, your ladyship,' said Jeeves, 'it is more reasonable to suppose that a gentleman of his lordship's character went to prison of his own volition than that he committed some breach of the law which necessitated his arrest?'

Lady Malvern blinked. Then she got up.

'Mr. Wooster,' she said, 'I apologise. I have done you an injustice. I should have known Wilmot better. I should have had more faith in his pure, fine spirit.'

'Absolutely!' I said.

'Your breakfast is ready, sir,' said Jeeves.

I sat down and dallied in a dazed sort of way with a poached egg.

'Jeeves,' I said, 'you are certainly a life-saver.'

'Thank you, sir.'

'Nothing would have convinced my Aunt Agatha that I hadn't lured that blighter into riotous living.'

'I fancy you are right, sir.'

I champed my egg for a bit. I was most awfully moved, don't you know, by the way Jeeves had rallied round. Something seemed to tell me that this was an occasion that called for rich rewards. For a moment I hesitated. Then I made up my mind.

'Jeeves!'

'Sir?'

'That pink tie.'

'Yes, sir?'

'Burn it.'

'Thank you, sir.'

'And, Jeeves.'

'Yes, sir?'

'Take a taxi and get me that White House Wonder hat, as worn by President Coolidge.'

'Thank you very much, sir.'

I felt most awfully braced. I felt as if the clouds had rolled away and all was as it used to be. I felt like one of those birds in the novels who calls off the fight with his wife in the last chapter and decides to forget and forgive. I felt I wanted to do all sorts of other things to show Jeeves that I appreciated him.

'Jeeves,' I said, 'it isn't enough. Is there anything else you would like?'

'Yes, sir. If I may make the suggestion – fifty dollars.'

'Fifty dollars?'

'It will enable me to pay a debt of honour, sir. I owe it to his lordship.'

'You owe Lord Pershore fifty dollars?'

'Yes, sir. I happened to meet him in the street the night his lordship was arrested. I had been thinking a good deal about the most suitable method of inducing him to abandon his mode of living, sir. His lordship was a little overexcited at the time, and I fancy that he mistook me for a friend of his. At any rate, when I took the liberty of wagering him fifty dollars that he would not punch a passing policeman in the eye, he accepted the bet very cordially and won it.'

I produced my pocket-book and counted out a hundred.

'Take this, Jeeves,' I said; 'fifty isn't enough. Do you know, Jeeves, you're – well, you absolutely stand alone!'

'I endeavour to give satisfaction, sir,' said Jeeves.

Sometimes of a morning, as I've sat in bed sucking down the early cup of tea and watched Jeeves flitting about the room and putting out the raiment for the day, I've wondered what the deuce I should do if the fellow ever took it into his head to leave me. It's not so bad when I'm in New York, but in London the anxiety is frightful. There used to be all sorts of attempts on the part of low blighters to sneak him away from me. Young Reggie Foljambe to my certain knowledge offered him double what I was giving him, and Alistair Bingham-Reeves, who's got a man who had been known to press his trousers sideways, used to look at him, when he came to see me, with a kind of glittering, hungry eye which disturbed me deucedly. Bally pirates!

The thing, you see, is that Jeeves is so dashed competent. You can spot it even in the way he shoves studs into a shirt.

I rely on him absolutely in every crisis, and he never lets me down. And, what's more, he can always be counted on to extend himself on behalf of any pal of mine who happens to be to all appearances knee-deep in the bouillon. Take the rather rummy case, for instance, of dear old Bicky and his uncle, the hard-boiled egg.

It happened after I had been in America for a few months. I got back to the flat latish one night, and when Jeeves brought me the final drink he said:

'Mr. Bickersteth called to see you this evening, sir, while you were out.'

'Oh?' I said.

'Twice, sir. He appeared a trifle agitated.'

'What, pipped?'

'He gave that impression, sir.'

I sipped the whisky. I was sorry if Bicky was in trouble, but, as a matter of fact, I was rather glad to have something I could discuss freely with Jeeves just then, because things had been a bit strained between us for some time, and it had been rather difficult to hit on anything to talk about that wasn't apt to take a personal turn. You see, I had decided – rightly or wrongly – to grow a moustache, and this had cut Jeeves to the quick. He couldn't stick the thing at any price, and I had been living ever since in an atmosphere of bally disapproval till I was getting jolly well fed up with it. What I mean is, while there's no doubt that in certain matters of dress Jeeves's judgment is absolutely sound and should be followed, it seemed to me that it was getting a bit too thick if he was going to edit my face as well as my costume. No one can call me an unreasonable chappie, and many's the time I've given in like a lamb when Jeeves has voted against one of my pet suits or ties; but when it comes to a valet's staking out a claim on your upper lip you've simply got to have a bit of the good old bulldog pluck and defy the blighter.

'He said that he would call again later, sir.'

'Something must be up, Jeeves.'

'Yes, sir.'

I gave the moustache a thoughtful twirl. It seemed to hurt Jeeves a good deal, so I chucked it.

'I see by the paper, sir, that Mr. Bickersteth's uncle is arriving on the *Carmantic.*'

'Yes?'

'His Grace the Duke of Chiswick, sir.'

This was news to me, that Bicky's uncle was a duke. Rum, how little one knows about one's pals. I had met Bicky for the first time at a species of beano or jamboree down in Washington Square, not long after my arrival in New York. I suppose I was a bit homesick at the time, and I rather took to Bicky when I found that he was an Englishman and had, in fact, been up at Oxford with me. Besides, he was a frightful chump, so we naturally drifted together; and while we were taking a quiet snort in a corner that wasn't all cluttered up with artists and sculptors, he furthermore endeared himself to me by a most extraordinarily gifted imitation of a bull-terrier chasing a cat up a tree. But, though we had subsequently become extremely pally, all I really knew about him was that he was generally hard up, and had an uncle who relieved the strain a bit from time to time by sending him monthly remittances.

'If the Duke of Chiswick is his uncle,' I said, 'why hasn't he a title? Why isn't he Lord What-Not?'

'Mr. Bickersteth is the son of His Grace's late sister, sir, who married Captain Rollo Bickersteth of the Coldstream Guards.'

Jeeves knows everything.

'Is Mr. Bickersteth's father dead too?'

'Yes, sir.'

'Leave any money?'

'No, sir.'

I began to understand why poor old Bicky was always more or less on the rocks. To the casual and irreflective observer it may sound a pretty good wheeze having a duke for an uncle, but the trouble about old Chiswick was that, though an extremely wealthy old buster, owning half London and about five counties up north, he was notoriously the most prudent spender in England. He was what Americans call a hard-boiled egg. If Bicky's people hadn't left him anything and he depended on what he could prise out of the old duke, he was in a pretty bad way. Not that that explained why he was hunting me like this, because he was a chap who never borrowed money. He said he wanted to keep his pals, so never bit anyone's ear on principle.

At this juncture the door-bell rang. Jeeves floated out to answer it.

'Yes, sir. Mr. Wooster has just returned,' I heard him say.

And Bicky came beetling in, looking pretty sorry for himself.

'Hallo, Bicky,' I said. 'Jeeves told me you had been trying to get me. What's the trouble, Bicky?'

'I'm in a hole, Bertie. I want your advice.'

'Say on, old lad.'

'My uncle's turning up tomorrow, Bertie.'

'So Jeeves told me.'

'The Duke of Chiswick you know.'

'So Jeeves told me.'

Bicky seemed a bit surprised.

'Jeeves seems to know everything.'

'Rather rummily, that's exactly what I was thinking just now myself.'

'Well, I wish,' said Bicky, gloomily, 'that he knew a way to get me out of the hole I'm in.'

'Mr. Bickersteth is in a hole, Jeeves,' I said, 'and wants you to rally round.'

'Very good, sir.'

Bicky looked a bit doubtful.

'Well, of course, you know, Bertie, this thing is by way of being a bit private and all that.'

'I shouldn't worry about that, old top. I bet Jeeves knows all about it already. Don't you, Jeeves?'

'Yes, sir.'

'Eh?' said Bicky, rattled.

'I am open to correction, sir, but is not your dilemma due to the fact that you are at a loss to explain to His Grace why you are in New York instead of in Colorado?'

Bicky rocked like a jelly in a high wind.

'How the deuce do you know anything about it?'

'I chanced to meet His Grace's butler before we left England. He informed me that he happened to overhear His Grace speaking to you on the matter, sir, as he passed the library door.'

Bicky gave a hollow sort of laugh.

'Well, as everybody seems to know all about it, there's no

need to try to keep it dark. The old boy turfed me out, Bertie, because he said I was a brainless nincompoop. The idea was that he would give me a remittance on condition that I dashed out to some blighted locality of the name of Colorado and learned farming or ranching, or whatever they call it, at some bally ranch or farm, or whatever it's called. I didn't fancy the idea a bit. I should have had to ride horses and pursue cows, and so forth. At the same time, don't you know, I had to have that remittance.'

'I get you absolutely, old thing.'

'Well, when I got to New York it looked a decent sort of place to me, so I thought it would be a pretty sound notion to stop here. So I cabled to my uncle telling him that I had dropped into a good business wheeze in the city and wanted to chuck the ranch idea. He wrote back that it was all right, and here I've been ever since. He thinks I'm doing well at something or other over here. I never dreamed, don't you know, that he would ever come out here. What on earth am I to do?'

'Jeeves,' I said, 'what on earth is Mr. Bickersteth to do?'

'You see,' said Bicky, 'I had a wireless from him to say that he was coming to stay with me – to save hotel bills, I suppose. I've always given him the impression that I was living in pretty good style. I can't have him to stay at my boarding-house.'

'Thought of anything, Jeeves?' I said.

'To what extent, sir, if the question is not a delicate one, are you prepared to assist Mr. Bickersteth?'

'I'll do anything I can for you, of course, Bicky, old man.'

'Then if I might make the suggestion, sir, you might lend Mr. Bickersteth –'

'No, by Jove!' said Bicky firmly. 'I never have touched you, Bertie and I'm not going to start now. I may be a chump, but it's my boast that I don't owe a penny to a single soul – not counting tradesmen, of course.'

'I was about to suggest, sir, that you might lend Mr. Bickersteth this flat. Mr. Bickersteth could give His Grace the impression that he was the owner of it. With your permission I could convey the notion that I was in Mr. Bickersteth's employment and not in yours. You would be residing here temporarily as Mr. Bickersteth's guest. His Grace would occupy the second spare bedroom. I fancy that you would find this answer satisfactorily, sir.'

Bicky had stopped rocking himself and was staring at Jeeves in an awed sort of way.

'I would advocate the dispatching of a wireless message to His Grace on board the vessel, notifying him of the change of address. Mr. Bickersteth could meet His Grace at the dock and proceed directly here. Will that meet the situation, sir?'

'Absolutely.'

'Thank you, sir.'

Bicky followed him with his eye till the door closed.

'How does he do it, Bertie?' he said. 'I'll tell you what I think it is. I believe it's something to do with the shape of his head. Have you ever noticed his head, Bertie, old man? It sort of sticks out at the back!'

I hopped out of bed pretty early next morning, so as to be among those present when the old boy should arrive. I knew from experience that these ocean liners fetch up at the dock at a deucedly ungodly hour. It wasn't much after nine by the time I'd dressed and had my morning tea and was leaning out of the window, watching the street for Bicky and his uncle. It was one of those jolly, peaceful mornings that make a fellow wish he'd got a soul or something, and I was just brooding on life in general when I became aware of the dickens of a spat in progress down below. A taxi had driven up, and an old boy in a top hat had got out and was kicking up a frightful row about the fare. As far as I could make out, he was trying to get the cabby to switch from New York to London prices, and the cabby had apparently never heard of London before, and didn't seem to think a lot of it now. The old boy said that in London the trip would have set him back a shilling; and the cabby said he should worry. I called to Jeeves.

'The duke has arrived, Jeeves.'

'Yes, sir?'

'That'll be him at the door now.'

Jeeves made a long arm and opened the front door, and the old boy crawled in.

'How do you do, sir?' I said, bustling up and being the ray of sunshine. 'Your nephew went down to the dock to meet you, but you must have missed him. My name's Wooster, don't you know. Great pal of Bicky's, and all that sort of thing. I'm staying with him, you know. Would you like a cup of tea? Jeeves, bring a cup of tea.'

Old Chiswick had sunk into an arm-chair and was looking about the room.

'Does this luxurious flat belong to my nephew Francis?'

'Absolutely.'

'It must be terribly expensive.'

'Pretty well, of course. Everything costs a lot over here, you know.'

He moaned. Jeeves filtered in with the tea. Old Chiswick took a stab at it to restore his tissues, and nodded.

'A terrible country, Mr. Wooster! A terrible country. Nearly eight shillings for a short cab-drive. Iniquitous!' He took another look round the room. It seemed to fascinate him. 'Have you any idea how much my nephew pays for this flat, Mr. Wooster?'

'About five hundred dollars a month, I believe.'

'What! A hundred pounds a month!'

I began to see that, unless I made the thing a bit more plausible, the scheme might turn out a frost. I could guess what the old boy was thinking. He was trying to square all this prosperity with what he knew of poor old Bicky. And one had to admit that it took a lot of squaring, for dear old Bicky, though a stout fellow and absolutely unrivalled as an imitator of bull-terriers and cats, was in many ways one of the most pronounced fatheads that ever pulled on a suit of gents' underwear.

'I suppose it seems rummy to you,' I said, 'but the fact is New York often bucks fellows up and makes them show a flash of speed that you wouldn't have imagined them capable of. It sort of develops them. Something in the air, don't you know. I imagine that Bicky in the past, when you knew him, may have been something of a chump, but it's quite different now. Devilish efficient sort of bird, and looked on in commercial circles as quite the nib!'

'I am amazed! What is the nature of my nephew's business, Mr. Wooster?'

'Oh, just business, don't you know. The same sort of thing Rockefeller and all these coves do, you know.' I slid for the door. 'Awfully sorry to leave you, but I've got to meet some of the lads elsewhere.'

Coming out of the lift I met Bicky bustling in from the street.

'Hallo, Bertie. I missed him. Has he turned up?'

'He's upstairs now, having some tea.'

'What does he think of it all?'

'He's absolutely rattled.'

'Ripping! I'll be toddling up, then. Toodle-oo, Bertie, old man. See you later.'

'Pip-pip, Bicky, dear boy.'

He trotted off, full of merriment and good cheer, and I went off to the club to sit in the window and watch the traffic coming up one way and going down the other.

It was latish in the evening when I looked in at the flat to dress for dinner.

'Where's everybody, Jeeves?' I said, finding no little feet pattering about the place. 'Gone out?'

'His Grace desired to see some of the sights of the city, sir. Mr. Bickersteth is acting as his escort. I fancy their immediate objective was Grant's Tomb.'

'I suppose Mr. Bickersteth is a bit bucked at the way things are going – what?'

'Sir?'

'I say, I take it that Mr. Bickersteth is tolerably full of beans.'

'Not altogether, sir.'

'What's his trouble now?'

'The scheme which I took the liberty of suggesting to Mr. Bickersteth and yourself has, unfortunately, not answered entirely satisfactorily, sir.'

'Surely the duke believes that Mr. Bickersteth is doing well in business, and all that sort of thing?'

'Exactly, sir. With the result that he has decided to cancel Mr. Bickersteth's monthly allowance, on the ground that, as Mr. Bickersteth is doing so well on his own account, he no longer requires pecuniary assistance.'

'Great Scott, Jeeves! This is awful!'

'Somewhat disturbing, sir.'

'I never expected anything like this!'

'I confess I scarcely anticipated the contingency myself, sir.'

'I suppose it bowled the poor blighter over absolutely?'

'Mr. Bickersteth appeared somewhat taken aback, sir.'

My heart bled for Bicky.

'We must do something, Jeeves.'

'Yes, sir.'

'Can you think of anything?'

'Not at the moment, sir.'

'There must be something we can do.'

'It was a maxim of one of my former employers, sir – as I believe I mentioned to you once before – the present Lord Bridgworth, that there is always a way. No doubt we shall be able to discover some solution of Mr. Bickersteth's difficulty, sir.'

'Well, have a stab at it, Jeeves.'

'I will spare no pains, sir.'

I went and dressed sadly. It will show you pretty well how pipped I was when I tell you that I as near as a toucher put on a white tie with a dinner-jacket. I sallied out for a bit of food more to pass the time than because I wanted it. It seemed brutal to be wading into the bill of fare with poor old Bicky headed for the breadline.

When I got back old Chiswick had gone to bed, but Bicky was there, hunched up in an arm-chair, brooding pretty tensely, with a cigarette hanging out of the corner of his mouth and a more or less glassy stare in his eyes.

'This is a bit thick, old thing – what!' I said.

He picked up his glass and drained it feverishly, overlooking the fact that it hadn't anything in it.

'I'm done, Bertie!' he said.

He had another go at the glass. It didn't seem to do him any good.

'If only this had happened a week later, Bertie! My next month's money was due to roll in on Saturday. I could have worked a wheeze I've been reading about in the magazine advertisements. It seems that you can make a dashed amount of money if you can only collect a few dollars and start a chicken-farm. Jolly life, too, keeping hens!' He had begun to get quite worked up at the thought of it, but he slopped back in his chair at this juncture with a good deal of gloom. 'But, of course, it's no good,' he said, 'because I haven't the cash.'

'You've only to say the word, you know, Bicky, old top.'

'Thanks awfully, Bertie, but I'm not going to sponge on you.'

That's always the way in this world. The fellows you'd like to lend money to won't let you whereas the fellows you don't want to lend it to will do everything except actually stand you on your head and lift the specie out of your pockets. As a lad who has always rolled tolerably freely in the right stuff, I've had lots of experience of the second class. Many's the time, back in London, I've hurried along Piccadilly and felt the hot breath of the toucher on the back of my neck and heard his sharp, excited yapping as he closed in on me. I've simply spent my life scattering largesse to blighters I didn't care a hang for; yet here was I now, dripping doubloons and pieces of eight and longing to hand them over, and Bicky, poor fish, absolutely on his uppers, not taking any at any price.

'Well, there's only one hope then.'

'What's that?'

'Jeeves.'

'Sir?

There was Jeeves, standing behind me, full of zeal. In this matter of shimmering into rooms the man is rummy to a degree. You're sitting in the old armchair, thinking of this and that, and then suddenly you look up, and there he is. He moves from point to point with as little uproar as a jelly-fish. The thing startled poor old Bicky considerably. He rose from his seat like a rocketing pheasant. I'm used to Jeeves now, but often in the days when he first came to me I've bitten my tongue freely on finding him unexpectedly in my midst.

'Did you call, sir?'

'Oh, there you are, Jeeves!'

'Precisely, sir.'

'Any ideas, Jeeves?'

'Why, yes, sir. Since we had our recent conversation I fancy I have found what may prove a solution. I do not wish to appear to be taking a liberty, sir, but I think that we have overlooked His Grace's potentialities as a source of revenue.'

Bicky laughed what I have sometimes seen described as a hollow, mocking laugh, a sort of bitter cackle from the back of the throat, rather like a gargle.

'I do not allude, sir,' explained Jeeves, 'to the possibility of inducing His Grace to part with money. I am taking the liberty of regarding His Grace in the light of an at present – if I may say so – useless property, which is capable of being developed.'

Bicky looked at me in a helpless kind of way. I'm bound to say I didn't get it myself.

'Couldn't you make it a bit easier, Jeeves?'

'In a nutshell, sir, what I mean is this: His Grace is, in a sense, a prominent personage. The inhabitants of this country, as no doubt you are aware, sir, are peculiarly addicted to shaking hands with prominent personages. It occurred to me that Mr. Bickersteth or yourself might know of persons who would be willing to pay a small fee – let us say two dollars or three – for the privilege of an introduction, including handshake, to His Grace.'

Bicky didn't seem to think much of it.

'Do you mean to say that anyone would be mug enough to part with solid cash just to shake hands with my uncle?'

'I have an aunt, sir, who paid five shillings to a young fellow for bringing a moving-picture actor to tea at her house on Sunday. It gave her social standing among the neighbours.'

Bicky wavered.

'If you think it could be done—'

'I feel convinced of it, sir.'

'What do you think, Bertie?'

'I'm for it, old boy, absolutely. A very brainy wheeze.'

'Thank you, sir. Will there be anything further? Good night, sir.'

And he flitted out, leaving us to discuss details.

Until we started this business of floating old Chiswick as a money-making proposition I had never realised what a perfectly foul time those Stock Exchange fellows must have when the public isn't biting freely. Nowadays I read that bit they put in the financial reports about 'The market opened quietly' with a sympathetic eye, for, by Jove, it certainly opened quietly for us. You'd hardly believe how difficult it was to interest the public and make them take a flutter on the old boy. By the end of the week the only name we had on our list was a delicatessen-store keeper down in Bicky's part of the town, and as he wanted us to take it out in sliced ham instead of cash that didn't help much. There was a gleam of light when the brother of Bicky's pawnbroker offered ten dollars, money down, for an introduction to old Chiswick, but the deal fell through, owing to its turning out that the chap was an anarchist and intended to kick the old boy instead of shaking hands with him. At that, it took me the deuce of a time to persuade Bicky not to grab the cash and let things take their course. He seemed to regard the pawnbroker's brother rather as a sportsman and benefactor of his species than otherwise.

The whole thing, I'm inclined to think, would have been off if it hadn't been for Jeeves. He trickled into my room one morning with the good old cup of tea, and intimated that there was something doing.

'Might I speak to you with regard to that matter of His Grace, sir?'

'It's all off. We've decided to chuck it.'

'Sir?'

'It won't work. We can't get anybody to come.'

'I fancy I can arrange that aspect of the matter, sir.'

'Do you mean to say you've managed to get anybody?'

'Yes, sir. Eighty-seven gentlemen from Birdsburg, sir.'

I sat up in bed and spilt the tea.

'Birdsburg?'

'Birdsburg, Missouri, sir.'

'How did you get them?'

'I happened last night, sir, as you had intimated that you would be absent from home, to attend a theatrical performance, and entered into conversation between the acts with the occupant of the adjoining seat. I had observed that he was wearing a somewhat ornate decoration in his buttonhole, sir – a large blue button with the words "Boost for Birdsburg" upon it in red letters, scarcely a judicious addition to a gentleman's evening costume. To my surprise I noticed that the auditorium was full of persons similarly decorated. I ventured to inquire the explanation, and was informed that these gentlemen, forming a party of eighty-seven, are a convention from a town of the name of Birdsburg in the State of Missouri. Their visit, I gathered, was purely of a social and pleasurable nature, and my informant spoke at some length of the entertainments arranged for their stay in the city. It was when he related with a considerable amount of satisfaction and pride that a deputation of their number had been introduced to and had shaken hands with a well-known prize-fighter that it occurred to me to broach the subject of His Grace. To make a long story short, sir, I have arranged, subject to your approval, that the entire convention shall be presented to His Grace tomorrow afternoon.'

I was amazed.

'Eighty-seven, Jeeves! At how much a head?'

'I was obliged to agree to a reduction for quantity, sir. The terms finally arrived at were one hundred and fifty dollars for the party.'

I thought a bit.

'Payable in advance?'

'No, sir. I endeavoured to obtain payment in advance, but was not successful.'

'Well, anyway, when we get it I'll make it up to five hundred. Bicky'll never know. Do you suppose Mr. Bickersteth would suspect anything, Jeeves, if I made it up to five hundred?'

'I fancy not, sir. Mr. Bickersteth is an agreeable gentleman, but not bright.'

'All right, then. After breakfast run down to the bank and get me some money.'

'Yes, sir.'

'You know, you're a bit of a marvel, Jeeves.'

'Thank you, sir.'

'Right ho!'

'Very good, sir.'

When I took dear old Bicky aside in the course of the morning and told him what had happened he nearly broke down. He tottered into the sitting-room and buttonholed old Chiswick, who was reading the comic section of the morning paper with a kind of grim resolution.

'Uncle,' he said, 'are you doing anything special tomorrow

afternoon? I mean to say, I've asked a few of my pals in to meet you, don't you know.'

The old boy cocked a speculative eye at him.

'There will be no reporters among them?'

'Reporters? Rather not. Why?'

'I refuse to be badgered by reporters. There were a number of adhesive young men who endeavoured to elicit from me my views on America while the boat was approaching the dock. I will not be subjected to this persecution again.'

'That'll be absolutely all right, uncle. There won't be a newspaper man in the place.'

'In that case I shall be glad to make the acquaintance of your friends.'

'You'll shake hands with them, and so forth?'

'I shall naturally order my behaviour according to the accepted rules of civilised intercourse.'

Bicky thanked him heartily and came off to lunch with me at the club, where he babbled freely of hens, incubators, and other rotten things.

After mature consideration we had decided to unleash the Birdsburg contingent on the old boy ten at a time. Jeeves brought his theatre pal round to see us, and we arranged the whole thing with him. A very decent chappie, but rather inclined to collar the conversation and turn it in the direction of his home-town's new water-supply system. We settled that, as an hour was about all he would be likely to stand, each gang should consider itself entitled to seven minutes of the duke's society by Jeeves's stop-watch, and that when their time was up Jeeves should slide into the room and cough meaningly. Then we parted with what I believe are called mutual expressions of good-will, the Birdsburg chappie extending a cordial invitation to us all to pop out some day and take a look at the new water-supply system, for which we thanked him.

Next day the deputation rolled in. The first shift consisted of the cove we had met and nine others almost exactly like him in every respect. They all looked deuced keen and businesslike, as if from youth up they had been working in the office and catching the boss's eye and what not. They shook hands with the old boy with a good deal of apparent satisfaction – all except one bird, who seemed to be brooding about something – and then they stood off and became chatty.

'What message have you for Birdsburg, duke?' asked our pal.

The old boy seemed a bit rattled.

'I have never been to Birdsburg.'

The chappie seemed pained.

'You should pay it a visit,' he said. 'The most rapidly-growing city in the country. Boost for Birdsburg!'

'Boost for Birdsburg!' said the other chappies reverently.

The bird who had been brooding suddenly gave tongue.

'Say!'

He was a stout sort of well-fed cove with one of those determined chins and a cold eye.

The assemblage looked at him.

'As a matter of business,' said the bird – 'mind you, I'm not questioning anybody's good faith, but, as a matter of strict business – I think this gentleman here ought to put himself on record before witnesses as stating that he really is a duke.'

'What do you mean, sir?' cried the old boy, getting purple.

'No offence, simply business. I'm not saying anything, mind you, but there's one thing that seems kind of funny to me. This gentleman here says his name's Mr. Bickersteth, as I understand it. Well, if you're the Duke of Chiswick, why isn't he Lord Percy Something? I've read English novels, and I know all about it.'

'This is monstrous!'

'Now don't get hot under the collar. I'm only asking. I've a right to know. You're going to take our money, so it's only fair that we should see that we get our money's worth.'

The water-supply cove chipped in:

'You're quite right, Simms. I overlooked that when making

the agreement. You see, gentlemen, as business men we've a right to reasonable guarantees of good faith. We are paying Mr. Bickersteth here a hundred and fifty dollars for this reception, and we naturally want to know—'

Old Chiswick gave Bicky a searching look; then he turned to the water-supply chappie. He was frightfully calm.

'I can assure you that I know nothing of this,' he said quite politely. 'I should be grateful if you would explain.'

'Well, we arranged with Mr. Bickersteth that eighty-seven citizens of Birdsburg should have the privilege of meeting and shaking hands with you for a financial consideration mutually arranged, and what my friend Simms here means – and I'm with him – is that we have only Mr. Bickersteth's word for it – and he is a stranger to us – that you are the Duke of Chiswick at all.'

Old Chiswick gulped.

'Allow me to assure you, sir,' he said in a rummy kind of voice, 'that I am the Duke of Chiswick.'

'Then that's all right,' said the chappie heartily. 'That was all we wanted to know. Let the thing go on.'

'I am sorry to say,' said old Chiswick, 'that it cannot go on. I am feeling a little tired. I fear I must ask to be excused.'

'But there are seventy-seven of the boys waiting round the corner at this moment, duke, to be introduced to you.'

'I fear I must disappoint them.'

'But in that case the deal would have to be off.'

'That is a matter for you and my nephew to discuss.'

The chappie seemed troubled.

'You really won't meet the rest of them?'

'No!'

'Well, then, I guess we'll be going.'

They went out, and there was a pretty solid silence. Then old Chiswick turned to Bicky:

'Well?'

Bicky didn't seem to have anything to say.

'Was it true what that man said?'

'Yes, Uncle.'

'What do you mean by playing this trick?'

Bicky seemed pretty well knocked out, so I put in a word:

'I think you'd better explain the whole thing, Bicky, old top.'

Bicky's adam's-apple jumped about a bit; then he started.

'You see, you had cut off my allowance, Uncle, and I wanted a bit of money to start a chicken-farm. I mean to say it's an absolute cert if you once get a bit of capital. You buy a hen, and it lays an egg every day of the week, and you sell the eggs, say, seven for twenty-five cents. Keep of hen costs nothing. Profit practically—'

'What is all this nonsense about hens? You led me to suppose you were a substantial business man.'

'Old Bicky rather exaggerated, sir,' I said, helping the chappie out. 'The fact is, the poor old lad is absolutely dependent on that remittance of yours, and when you cut it off, don't you know, he was pretty solidly in the soup, and had to think of some way of closing in on a bit of the ready pretty quick. That's why we thought of this hand-shaking scheme.'

Old Chiswick foamed at the mouth.

'So you have lied to me! You have deliberately deceived me as to your financial status!'

'Poor old Bicky didn't want to go to that ranch,' I explained. 'He doesn't like cows and horses, but he rather thinks he would be hot stuff among the hens. All he wants is a bit of capital. Don't you think it would be rather a wheeze if you were to—'

'After what has happened? After this – this deceit and foolery? Not a penny!'

'But—'

'Not a penny!'

There was a respectful cough in the background.

'If I might make a suggestion, sir?'

Jeeves was standing on the horizon, looking devilish brainy.

'Go ahead, Jeeves!' I said.

'I would merely suggest, sir, that if Mr. Bickersteth is in need of a little ready money, and is at a loss to obtain it elsewhere, he might secure the sum he requires by describing the occurrences of this afternoon for the Sunday issue of one of the more spirited and enterprising newspapers.'

'By Jove!' I said.

'By George!' said Bicky.

'Great Heavens!' said old Chiswick.

'Very good, sir,' said Jeeves.

Bicky turned to old Chiswick with a gleaming eye.

'Jeeves is right! I'll do it! The *Chronicle* would jump at it. They eat that sort of stuff.'

Old Chiswick gave a kind of moaning howl.

'I absolutely forbid you, Francis, to do this thing!'

'That's all very well,' said Bicky, wonderfully braced, 'but if I can't get the money any other way—'

'Wait! Er – wait, my boy! You are so impetuous! We might arrange something.'

'I won't go to that bally ranch.'

'No, no! No, no, my boy! I would not suggest it. I would not for a moment suggest it. I – I think—' He seemed to have a bit of a struggle with himself. 'I – I think that, on the whole, it would be best if you returned with me to England. I – I might – in fact, I think I see my way to doing – to – I might be able to utilise your services in some secretarial position.'

'I shouldn't mind that.'

'I should not be able to offer you a salary, but, as you know, in English political life the unpaid secretary is a recognised figure—'

'The only figure I'll recognise,' said Bicky firmly, 'is five hundred quid a year, paid quarterly.'

'My dear boy!'

'Absolutely!'

'But your recompense, my dear Francis, would consist in the unrivalled opportunities you would have, as my secretary, to gain experience, to accustom yourself to the intricacies of political life, to – in fact, you would be in an exceedingly advantageous position.'

'Five hundred a year!' said Bicky, rolling it round his tongue. 'Why, that would be nothing to what I could make if I started a chicken-farm. It stands to reason. Suppose you have a dozen hens. Each of the hens has a dozen chickens. After a bit the chickens grow up and have a dozen chickens each themselves, and then they all start laying eggs! There's a fortune in it. You can get anything you like for eggs in America. Fellows keep them on ice for years and years, and don't sell them till they fetch about a dollar a whirl. You don't think I'm going to chuck a future like this for anything under five hundred o' goblins a year – what?'

A look of anguish passed over old Chiswick's face, then he seemed to be resigned to it. 'Very well, my boy,' he said.

'What ho!' said Bicky. 'All right, then.'

'Jeeves,' I said. Bicky had taken the old boy off to dinner to celebrate, and we were alone. 'Jeeves, this has been one of your best efforts.'

'Thank you, sir.'

'It beats me how you do it.'

'Yes, sir?'

'The only trouble is you haven't got much out of it yourself.'

'I fancy Mr. Bickersteth intends – I judge from his remarks – to signify his appreciation of anything I have been fortunate enough to do to assist him, at some later date when he is in a more favourable position to do so.'

'It isn't enough, Jeeves!'

'Sir?'

It was a wrench, but I felt it was the only possible thing to be done.

'Bring my shaving things.'

A gleam of hope shone in the man's eye, mixed with doubt.

'You mean, sir?'

'And shave off my moustache.'

There was a moment's silence. I could see the fellow was deeply moved.

'Thank you very much indeed, sir,' he said, in a low voice.

Now that it's all over, I may as well admit that there was a time during the affair of Rockmetteller Todd when I thought that Jeeves was going to let me down. Silly of me, of course, knowing him as I do, but that is what I thought. It seemed to me that the man had the appearance of being baffled.

The Rocky Todd business broke loose early one morning in spring. I was in bed, restoring the physique with my usual nine hours of the dreamless, when the door flew open and somebody prodded me in the lower ribs and began to shake the bedclothes in an unpleasant manner. And after blinking a bit and generally pulling myself together, I located Rocky, and my first impression was that it must be some horrid dream.

Rocky, you see, lived down on Long Island somewhere, miles away from New York; and not only that, but he had told me himself more than once that he never got up before twelve, and seldom earlier than one. Constitutionally the laziest young devil in America, he had hit on a walk in life which enabled him to go the limit in that direction. He was a poet. At least, he wrote poems when he did anything; but most of his time, as far as I could make out, he spent in a sort of trance. He told me once that he could sit on a fence, watching a worm and wondering what on earth it was up to, for hours at a stretch.

He had his scheme of life worked out to a fine point. About once a month he would take three days writing a few poems; the other three hundred and twenty-nine days of the year he rested. I didn't know there was enough money in poetry to support a fellow, even in the way in which Rocky lived; but it seems that, if you stick to exhortations to young men to lead the strenuous life and don't shove in any rhymes, American editors fight for the stuff. Rocky showed me one of his things once. It began:

> Be!
> Be!
> The past is dead,
> Tomorrow is not born.
>   Be today!
> Today!
>   Be with every nerve,
>   With every fibre,
>   With every drop of your red blood!
> Be!
> Be!

There were three more verses, and the thing was printed opposite the frontispiece of a magazine with a sort of scroll round it, and a picture in the middle of a fairly nude chappie with bulging muscles giving the rising sun the glad eye. Rocky said they gave him a hundred dollars for it, and he stayed in bed till four in the afternoon for over a month.

As regards the future he was pretty solid, owing to the fact that he had a moneyed aunt tucked away somewhere in Illinois. It's a curious thing how many of my pals seem to have aunts and uncles who are their main source of supply. There is Bicky, for one, with his uncle the Duke of Chiswick; Corky, who, until things went wrong, looked to Alexander Worple, the bird specialist, for sustenance. And I shall be telling you a story shortly of a dear old friend of mine, Oliver Sipperley, who had an aunt in Yorkshire. These things cannot be mere coincidence. They must be meant. What I'm driving at is that Providence seems to look after the chumps of this world; and, personally, I'm all for it. I suppose the fact is that, having been snootered from infancy upwards by my own aunts, I like to see that it is possible for these relatives to have a better and a softer side.

However, this is more or less of a side-track. Coming back to Rocky, what I was saying was that he had this aunt in Illinois; and, as he had been named Rockmetteller after her (which in itself, you might say, entitled him to substantial compensation) and was her only nephew, his position looked pretty sound. He told me that when he did come into the money he meant to do no work at all, except perhaps an occasional poem recommending the young man with life opening out before him with all its splendid possibilities to light a pipe and shove his feet up on the mantelpiece.

And this was the man who was prodding me in the ribs in the grey dawn!

'Read this, Bertie!' babbled old Rocky.

I could just see that he was waving a letter or something equally foul in my face. 'Wake up and read this!'

I can't read before I've had my morning tea and a cigarette. I groped for the bell.

Jeeves came in, looking as fresh as a dewy violet. It's a mystery to me how he does it.

'Tea, Jeeves.'

'Very good, sir.'

I found that Rocky was surging round with his beastly letter again.

'What is it?' I said. 'What on earth's the matter?'

'Read it!'

'I can't. I haven't had my tea.'

'Well, listen then.'

'Who's it from?'

'My aunt.'

At this point I fell asleep again. I woke to hear him saying: 'So what on earth am I to do?'

Jeeves flowed in with the tray, like some silent stream meandering over its mossy bed; and I saw daylight.

'Read it again, Rocky, old top,' I said. 'I want Jeeves to hear it. Mr. Todd's aunt has written him a rather rummy letter, Jeeves, and we want your advice.'

'Very good, sir.'

He stood in the middle of the room, registering devotion to the cause, and Rocky started again:

My dear Rockmetteller,

I have been thinking things over for a long while, and I have come to the conclusion that I have been very thoughtless to wait so long before doing what I have made up my mind to do now.

'What do you make of that, Jeeves?'

'It seems a little obscure at present, sir, but no doubt it becomes clearer at a later point in the communication.'

'Proceed, old scout,' I said, champing my bread and butter.

You know how all my life I have longed to visit New York and see for myself the wonderful gay life of which I have read so much. I fear that now it will be impossible for me to fulfil my dream. I am old and worn out. I seem to have no strength left in me.

'Sad, Jeeves, what?'

'Extremely, sir.'

'Sad nothing!' said Rocky. 'It's sheer laziness. I went to see her last Christmas and she was bursting with health. Her doctor told me himself that there was nothing wrong with her whatever. But she will insist that she's a hopeless invalid, so he has to agree with her. She's got a fixed idea that the trip to New York would kill her; so, though it's been her ambition all her life to come here, she stays where she is.'

'Rather like the chappie whose heart was "in the Highlands a-chasing of the deer", Jeeves?'

'The cases are in some respects parallel, sir,'

'Carry on, Rocky, dear boy.'

So I have decided that, if I cannot enjoy all the marvels of the city myself, I can at least enjoy them through you. I suddenly thought of this yesterday after reading a beautiful poem in the Sunday paper about a young man who had longed all his life for a certain thing and won it in the end only when he was too old to enjoy it. It was very sad, and it touched me.

'A thing,' interpolated Rocky bitterly, 'that I've not been able to do in ten years.'

As you know, you will have my money when I am gone; but until now I have never been able to see my way to giving you an allowance. I have now decided to do so — on one condition. I have written to a firm of lawyers in New York, giving them instructions to pay you quite a substantial sum each month. My one condition is that you live in New York and enjoy yourself as I have always wished to do. I want you to be my representative, to spend this money for me as I should do myself. I want you to plunge into the gay, prismatic life of New York. I want you to be the life and soul of brilliant supper parties.

Above all, I want you — indeed, I insist on this — to write me letters at least once a week, giving me a full description of all you are doing and all that is going on in the city, so that I may enjoy at second-hand what my wretched health prevents my enjoying for myself. Remember that I shall expect full details, and that no detail is too trivial to interest

Your affectionate Aunt,
Isabel Rockmetteller.

'What about it?' said Rocky.

'What about it?' I said.

'Yes. What on earth am I going to do?'

It was only then that I really got on to the extremely rummy attitude of the chappie, in view of the fact that a quite unexpected mess of good cash had suddenly descended on him from a blue sky. To my mind it was an occasion for the beaming smile and the joyous whoop; yet here the man was, looking and talking as if Fate had swung on his solar plexus. It amazed me.

'Aren't you bucked?' I said.

'Bucked!'

'If I were in your place I should be frightfully braced. I consider this pretty soft for you.'

He gave a kind of yelp, stared at me for a moment, and then began to talk of New York in a way that reminded me of Jimmy Munday, the reformer bloke. Jimmy had just come to New York on a hit-the-trail campaign, and I had popped in at Madison Square Garden a couple of days before, for half an hour or so, to hear him. He had certainly told New York some pretty straight things about itself, having apparently taken a dislike to the place, but, by Jove, you know, dear old Rocky made him look like a publicity agent for the old metrop!

'Pretty soft!' he cried. 'To have to come and live in New York! To have to leave my little cottage and take a stuffy, smelly, over-heated hole of an apartment in this Heaven-forsaken, festering Gehenna. To have to mix night after night with a mob who think that life is a sort of St. Vitus's dance, and imagine that they're having a good time because they're making enough noise for six and drinking too much for ten. I loathe New York, Bertie. I wouldn't come near the place if I hadn't got to see editors occasionally. There's a blight on it. It's got moral delirium tremens. It's the limit. The very thought of staying more than a day in it makes me sick. And you call this thing pretty soft for me!'

I felt rather like Lot's friends must have done when they

dropped in for a quiet chat and their genial host began to criticise the Cities of the Plain. I had no idea old Rocky could be so eloquent.

'It would kill me to have to live in New York,' he went on. 'To have to share the air with six million people! To have to wear stiff collars and decent clothes all the time! To – ' He started. 'Good Lord! I suppose I should have to dress for dinner in the evenings. What a ghastly notion!'

I was shocked, absolutely shocked.

'My dear chap!' I said, reproachfully.

'Do you dress for dinner every night, Bertie?'

'Jeeves,' I said coldly. 'How many suits of evening clothes have we?'

'We have three suits full of evening dress, sir; two dinner jackets—'

'Three.'

'For practical purposes two only, sir. If you remember, we cannot wear the third. We have also seven white waistcoats.'

'And shirts?'

'Four dozen, sir.'

'And white ties?'

'The first two shallow shelves in the chest of drawers are completely filled with our white ties, sir.'

I turned to Rocky.

'You see?'

He writhed like an electric fan.

'I won't do it! I can't do it! I'll be hanged if I'll do it! How on earth can I dress up like that? Do you realise that most days I don't get out of my pyjamas till five in the afternoon, and then I just put on an old sweater?'

I saw Jeeves wince, poor chap. This sort of revelation shocked his finest feelings.

'Then, what are you going to do about it?' I said.

'That's what I want to know.'

'You might write and explain to your aunt.'

'I might – if I wanted her to get round to her lawyer's in two rapid leaps and cut me out of her will.'

I saw his point.

'What do you suggest, Jeeves?' I said.

Jeeves cleared his throat respectfully.

'The crux of the matter would appear to be, sir, that Mr. Todd is obliged by the conditions under which the money is delivered into his possession to write Miss Rockmetteller long and detailed letters relating to his movements, and the only method by which this can be accomplished, if Mr. Todd adheres to his expressed intention of remaining in the country, is for Mr. Todd to induce some second party to gather the actual experiences which Miss Rockmetteller wishes reported to her, and to convey these to him in the shape of a careful report, on which it would be possible for him, with the aid of his imagination, to base the suggested correspondence.'

Having got which off the old diaphragm, Jeeves was silent. Rocky looked at me in a helpless sort of way. He hasn't been brought up on Jeeves as I have, and he isn't on to his curves.

'Could he put it a little clearer, Bertie?' he said. 'I thought at the start it was going to make sense, but it kind of nickered. What's the idea?'

'My dear old man, perfectly simple. I knew we could stand on Jeeves. All you've got to do is to get somebody to go round the town for you and take a few notes, and then you work the notes up into letters. That's it, isn't it, Jeeves?'

'Precisely, sir.'

The light of hope gleamed in Rocky's eyes. He looked at Jeeves in a startled way, dazed by the man's vast intellect.

'But who would do it?' he said. 'It would have to be a pretty smart sort of man, a man who would notice things.'

'Jeeves!' I said. 'Let Jeeves do it.'

'But would he?'

'You would do it, wouldn't you, Jeeves?'

For the first time in our long connexion I observed Jeeves

almost smile. The corner of his mouth curved quite a quarter of an inch, and for a moment his eye ceased to look like a meditative fish's.

'I should be delighted to oblige, sir. As a matter of fact, I have already visited some of New York's places of interest on my evening out, and it would be most enjoyable to make a practice of the pursuit.'

'Fine! I know exactly what your aunt wants to hear about, Rocky. She wants an earful of cabaret stuff. The place you ought to go to first, Jeeves, is Reigelheimer's. It's on Forty-second Street. Anybody will show you the way.'

Jeeves shook his head.

'Pardon me, sir. People are no longer going to Reigelheimer's. The place at the moment is Frolics on the Roof.'

'You see?' I said to Rocky. 'Leave it to Jeeves. He knows.'

It isn't often that you find an entire group of your fellow-humans happy in this world; but our little circle was certainly an example of the fact that it can be done. We were all full of beans. Everything went absolutely right from the start.

Jeeves was happy, partly because he loves to exercise his giant brain, and partly because he was having a corking time among the bright lights. I saw him one night at the Midnight Revels. He was sitting at a table on the edge of the dancing floor, doing himself remarkably well with a fat cigar. His face wore an expression of austere benevolence, and he was making notes in a small book.

As for the rest of us, I was feeling pretty good, because I was fond of old Rocky and glad to be able to do him a good turn. Rocky was perfectly contented, because he was still able to sit on fences in his pyjamas and watch worms. And as for the aunt, she seemed tickled to death. She was getting Broadway at pretty long range, but it seemed to be hitting her just right. I read one of her letters to Rocky, and it was full of life.

But then Rocky's letters, based on Jeeves's notes, were enough to buck anybody up. It was rummy when you came to think of it. There was I, loving the life, while the mere mention of it gave Rocky a tired feeling; yet here is a letter I wrote home to a pal of mine in London:

Dear Freddie, –
Well, here I am in New York. It's not a bad place. I'm not having a bad time. Everything's not bad. The cabarets aren't bad. Don't know when I shall be back. How's everybody ? Cheerio! –

Yours,
Bertie.

P.S. – Seen old Ted lately?

Not that I cared about old Ted; but if I hadn't dragged him in I couldn't have got the confounded thing on to the second page. Now here's old Rocky on exactly the same subject:

Dearest Aunt Isabel, –
How can I ever thank you enough for giving me the opportunity to live in this astounding city! New York seems more wonderful every day.
Fifth Avenue is at its best, of course, just now. The dresses are magnificent!

Wads of stuff about the dresses. I didn't know Jeeves was such an authority.

I was out with some of the crowd at the Midnight Revels the other night. We took in a show first, after a little dinner at a new place on Forty-third Street. We were quite a gay party. Georgie Cohan looked in about midnight and got off a good story about Willie Collier. Fred Stone could only stay a minute, but Doug. Fairbanks did all sorts of stunts and made us roar. Ed. Wynn was there, and Laurette Taylor showed up with a

*party. The show at the Revels is quite good. I am enclosing a
programme.*

Last night a few of us went round to Frolics on the Roof—

And so on and so forth, yards of it. I suppose it's the artistic
temperament or something. What I mean is, it's easier for a bird
who's used to writing poems and that sort of tosh to put a bit of
a punch into a letter than it is for a fellow like me. Anyway,
there's no doubt that Rocky's correspondence was hot stuff. I
called Jeeves in and congratulated him.

'Jeeves, you're a wonder!'

'Thank you, sir.'

'How you notice everything at these places beats me. I
couldn't tell you a thing about them, except that I've had a good
time.'

'It's just a knack, sir.'

'Well, Mr. Todd's letters ought to brace Miss Rockmetteller
all right, what?'

'Undoubtedly, sir,' agreed Jeeves.

And, by Jove, they did! They certainly did, by George! What
I mean to say is, I was sitting in the apartment one afternoon,
about a month after the thing had started, smoking a cigarette
and resting the old bean, when the door opened and the voice of
Jeeves burst the silence like a bomb.

It wasn't that he spoke loud. He has one of those soft,
soothing voices that slide through the atmosphere like the note
of a far-off sheep. It was what he said that made me leap like a
young gazelle.

'Miss Rockmetteller!'

And in came a large, solid female.

The situation floored me. I'm not denying it. Hamlet must
have felt much as I did when his father's ghost bobbed up in the
fairway. I'd come to look on Rocky's aunt as such a permanency
at her own home that it didn't seem possible that she could really
be here in New York. I stared at her. Then I looked at Jeeves.

He was standing there in an attitude of dignified detachment, the chump, when, if ever he should have been rallying round the young master, it was now.

Rocky's aunt looked less like an invalid than anyone I've ever seen, except my Aunt Agatha. She had a good deal of Aunt Agatha about her, as a matter of fact. She looked as if she might be deucedly dangerous if put upon; and something seemed to tell me that she would certainly regard herself as put upon if she ever found out the game which poor old Rocky had been pulling on her.

'Good afternoon,' I managed to say.

'How do you do?' she said. 'Mr. Cohan?'

Er – no.

'Mr. Fred Stone?'

'Not absolutely. As a matter of fact, my name's Wooster – Bertie Wooster.'

She seemed disappointed. The fine old name of Wooster appeared to mean nothing in her life.

'Isn't Rockmetteller home?' she said. 'Where is he?'

She had me with the first shot. I couldn't think of anything to say. I couldn't tell her that Rocky was down in the country, watching worms.

There was the faintest flutter of sound in the background. It was the respectful cough with which Jeeves·announces that he is about to speak without having been spoken to.

'If you remember, sir, Mr. Todd went out in the automobile with a party earlier in the afternoon.'

'So he did, Jeeves; so he did,' I said, looking at my watch. 'Did he say when he would be back?'

'He gave me to understand, sir, that he would be somewhat late in returning.'

He vanished; and the aunt took the chair which I'd forgotten to offer her. She looked at me in rather a rummy way. It was a nasty look. It made me feel as if I were something the dog had brought in and intended to bury later on, when he had time. My own Aunt

Agatha, back in England, has looked at me in exactly the same way many a time, and it never fails to make my spine curl.

'You seem very much at home here, young man. Are you a great friend of Rockmetteller's?'

'Oh, yes, rather!'

She frowned as if she had expected better things of old Rocky.

'Well, you need to be,' she said, 'the way you treat his flat as your own!'

I give you my word, this quite unforeseen slam simply robbed me of the power of speech. I'd been looking on myself in the light of the dashing host, and suddenly to be treated as an intruder jarred me. It wasn't, mark you, as if she had spoken in a way to suggest that she considered my presence in the place as an ordinary social call. She obviously looked on me as a cross between a burglar and the plumber's man come to fix the leak in the bathroom. It hurt her – my being there.

At this juncture, with the conversation showing every sign of being about to die in awful agonies, an idea came to me. Tea – the good old stand-by.

'Would you care for a cup of tea?' I said.

'Tea?'

She spoke as if she had never heard of the stuff.

'Nothing like a cup after a journey,' I said. 'Buck you up! Puts a bit of zip into you. What I mean is, restores you, and so on, don't you know. I'll go and tell Jeeves.'

I tottered down the passage to Jeeves's lair. The man was reading the evening paper as if he hadn't a care in the world.

'Jeeves,' I said, 'we want some tea.'

'Very good, sir.'

'I say, Jeeves, this is a bit thick, what?'

I wanted sympathy, don't you know – sympathy and kindness. The old nerve centres had had the deuce of a shock.

'She's got the idea this place belongs to Mr. Todd. What on earth put that into her head?'

Jeeves filled the kettle with a restrained dignity.

'No doubt because of Mr. Todd's letters, sir,' he said. 'It was my suggestion, sir, if you remember, that they should be addressed from this apartment in order that Mr. Todd should appear to possess a good central residence in the city.'

I remembered. We had thought it a brainy scheme at the time.

'Well, it's dashed awkward, you know, Jeeves. She looks on me as an intruder. By Jove! I suppose she thinks I'm someone who hangs about here, touching Mr. Todd for free meals and borrowing his shirts.'

'Extremely probable, sir.'

'It's pretty rotten, you know.'

'Most disturbing, sir.'

'And there's another thing: What are we to do about Mr. Todd? We've got to get him up here as soon as ever we can. When you have brought the tea you had better go out and send him a telegram, telling him to come up by the next train.'

'I have already done so, sir. I took the liberty of writing the message and dispatching it by the lift attendant.'

'By Jove, you think of everything, Jeeves!'

'Thank you, sir. A little buttered toast with the tea? Just so, sir. Thank you.'

I went back to the sitting-room. She hadn't moved an inch. She was still bolt upright on the edge of her chair, gripping her umbrella like a hammer-thrower. She gave me another of those looks as I came in. There was no doubt about it; for some reason she had taken a dislike to me. I suppose because I wasn't George M. Cohan. It was a bit hard on a chap.

'This is a surprise, what?' I said, after about five minutes' restful silence, trying to crank the conversation up again.

'What is a surprise?'

'Your coming here, don't you know, and so on.'

She raised her eyebrows and drank me in a bit more through her glasses.

'Why is it surprising that I should visit my only nephew?' she said.

'Oh, rather,' I said. 'Of course! Certainly. What I mean is—'

Jeeves projected himself into the room with the tea. I was jolly glad to see him. There's nothing like having a bit of business arranged for one when one isn't certain of one's lines. With the teapot to fool about with I felt happier.

'Tea, tea, tea – what? What?' I said.

It wasn't what I had meant to say. My idea had been to be a good deal more formal, and so on. Still, it covered the situation. I poured her out a cup. She sipped it and put the cup down with a shudder.

'Do you mean to say, young man,' she said, frostily, 'that you expect me to drink this stuff?'

'Rather! Bucks you up, you know.'

'What do you mean by the expression "Bucks you up"?'

'Well, makes you full of beans, you know. Makes you fizz.'

'I don't understand a word you say. You're English, aren't you?'

I admitted it. She didn't say a word. And she did it in a way that made it worse than if she had spoken for hours. Somehow it was brought home to me that she didn't like Englishmen, and that if she had had to meet an Englishman I was the one she'd have chosen last.

Conversation languished once more after that.

Then I tried again. I was becoming more convinced every moment that you can't make a real lively *salon* with a couple of people, especially if one of them lets it go a word at a time.

'Are you comfortable at your hotel?' I said.

'At which hotel?'

'The hotel you're staying at.'

'I am not staying at an hotel.'

'Stopping with friends – what?'

'I am naturally stopping with my nephew.'

I didn't get it for the moment; then it hit me.

'What! Here?' I gurgled.

'Certainly! Where else should I go?'

The full horror of the situation rolled over me like a wave. I couldn't see what on earth I was to do. I couldn't explain that this wasn't Rocky's flat without giving the poor old chap away hopelessly, because she would then ask me where he did live, and then he would be right in the soup. I was trying to recover from the shock when she spoke again.

'Will you kindly tell my nephew's manservant to prepare my room? I wish to lie down.'

'Your nephew's manservant?'

'The man you call Jeeves. If Rockmetteller has gone for an automobile ride there is no need for you to wait for him. He will naturally wish to be alone with me when he returns.'

I found myself tottering out of the room. The thing was too much for me. I crept into Jeeves's den.

'Jeeves!' I whispered.

'Sir?'

'Mix me a b.-and-s., Jeeves. I feel weak.'

'Very good, sir.'

'This is getting thicker every minute, Jeeves.'

'Sir?'

'She thinks you're Mr. Todd's man. She thinks the whole place is his, and everything in it. I don't see what you're to do, except stay on and keep it up. We can't say anything or she'll get on to the whole thing, and I don't want to let Mr. Todd down. By the way, Jeeves, she wants you to prepare her bed.'

He looked wounded.

'It is hardly my place, sir—'

'I know – I know. But do it as a personal favour to me. If you come to that, it's hardly my place to be flung out of the flat like this and have to go to an hotel, what?'

'Is it your intention to go to an hotel, sir? What will you do for clothes?'

'Good Lord! I hadn't thought of that. Can you put a few

things in a bag when she isn't looking, and sneak them down to me at the St. Aurea?'

'I will endeavour to do so, sir.'

'Well, I don't think there's anything more, is there? Tell Mr. Todd where I am when he gets here.'

'Very good, sir.'

I looked round the place. The moment of parting had come. I felt sad. The whole thing reminded me of one of those melodramas where they drive chappies out of the old homestead into the snow.

'Good-bye, Jeeves,' I said.

'Good-bye, sir.' And I staggered out.

You know, I rather think I agree with those poet-and-philosopher Johnnies who insist that a fellow ought to be devilish pleased if he has a bit of trouble. All that stuff about being refined by suffering, you know. Suffering does give a chap a sort of broader and more sympathetic outlook. It helps you to understand other people's misfortunes if you've been through the same thing yourself.

As I stood in my lonely bedroom at the hotel, trying to tie my white tie myself, it struck me for the first time that there must be whole squads of chappies in the world who had to get along without a man to look after them. I'd always thought of Jeeves as a kind of natural phenomenon; but, by Jove! of course, when you come to think of it, there must be quite a lot of fellows who have to press their own clothes themselves, and haven't got anybody to bring them tea in the morning, and so on. It was rather a solemn thought, don't you know. I mean to say, ever since then I've been able to appreciate the frightful privations the poor have to stick.

I got dressed somehow. Jeeves hadn't forgotten a thing in his packing. Everything was there, down to the final stud. I'm not sure this didn't make me feel worse. It kind of deepened the pathos. It was like what somebody or other wrote about the touch of a vanished hand.

I had a bit of dinner somewhere and went to a show of some

kind; but nothing seemed to make any difference. I simply hadn't the heart to go on to supper anywhere. I just went straight up to bed. I don't know when I've felt so rotten. Somehow I found myself moving about the room softly, as if there had been a death in the family. If I had had anybody to talk to I should have talked in a whisper; in fact, when the telephone-bell rang I answered in such a sad, hushed voice that the fellow at the other end of the wire said 'Hallo!' five times, thinking he hadn't got me.

It was Rocky. The poor old scout was deeply agitated.

'Bertie! Is that you, Bertie? Oh, gosh! I'm having a time!'

'Where are you speaking from?'

'The Midnight Revels. We've been here an hour, and I think we're a fixture for the night. I've told Aunt Isabel I've gone out to call up a friend to join us. She's glued to a chair, with this-is-the-life written all over her, taking it in through the pores. She loves it, and I'm nearly crazy.'

'Tell me all, old top,' I said.

'A little more of this,' he said, 'and I shall sneak quietly off to the river and end it all. Do you mean to say you go through this sort of thing every night, Bertie, and enjoy it? It's simply infernal! I was just snatching a wink of sleep behind the bill of fare just now when about a million yelling girls swooped down, with toy balloons. There are two orchestras here, each trying to see if it can't play louder than the other. I'm a mental and physical wreck. When your telegram arrived I was just lying down for a quiet pipe, with a sense of absolute peace stealing over me. I had to get dressed and sprint two miles to catch the train. It nearly gave me heart-failure; and on top of that I almost got brain fever inventing lies to tell Aunt Isabel. And then I had to cram myself into these confounded evening clothes of yours.'

I gave a sharp wail of agony. It hadn't struck me till then that Rocky was depending on my wardrobe to see him through.

'You'll ruin them!'

'I hope so,' said Rocky in the most unpleasant way. His

troubles seemed to have had the worst effect on his character. 'I should like to get back at them somehow; they've given me a bad enough time. They're about three sizes too small, and something's apt to give at any moment. I wish to goodness it would, and give me a chance to breathe. I haven't breathed since half-past seven. Thank heaven, Jeeves managed to get out and buy me a collar that fitted, or I should be a strangled corpse by now! It was touch and go till the stud broke. Bertie, this is pure Hades! Aunt Isabel keeps on urging me to dance. How on earth can I dance when I don't know a soul to dance with? And how the deuce could I, even if I knew every girl in the place? It's taking big chances even to move in these trousers. I had to tell her I've hurt my ankle. She keeps asking me when Cohan and Stone are going to turn up; and it's simply a question of time before she discovers that Stone is sitting two tables away. Something's got to be done, Bertie! You've got to think up some way of getting me out of this mess. It was you who got me into it.'

'Me! What do you mean?'

'Well, Jeeves, then. It's all the same. It was you who suggested leaving it to Jeeves. It was those letters I wrote from his notes that did the mischief. I made them too good. My aunt's just been telling me about it. She says she had resigned herself to ending her life where she was, and then my letters began to arrive, describing the joys of New York; and they stimulated her to such an extent that she pulled herself together and made the trip. She seems to think she's had some miraculous kind of faith cure. I tell you I can't stand it, Bertie! It's got to end!'

'Can't Jeeves think of anything?'

'No. He just hangs round, saying: "Most disturbing, sir!" A fat lot of help that is!'

'Well, old lad,' I said, 'after all, it's far worse for me than it is for you. You've got a comfortable home and Jeeves. And you're saving a lot of money.'

'Saving money? What do you mean – saving money?'

'Why, the allowance your aunt was giving you. I suppose she's paying all the expenses now, isn't she?'

'Certainly she is; but she's stopped the allowance. She wrote the lawyers tonight. She says that, now she's in New York, there is no necessity for it to go on, as we shall always be together, and it's simpler for her to look after that end of it. I tell you, Bertie, I've examined the darned cloud with a miscroscope, and if it's got a silver lining it's some little dissembler!'

'But, Rocky, old top, it's too bally awful! You've no notion of what I'm going through in this beastly hotel, without Jeeves. I must get back to the flat.'

'Don't come near the flat!'

'But it's my own flat.'

'I can't help that. Aunt Isabel doesn't like you. She asked me what you did for a living. And when I told her you didn't do anything she said she thought as much, and that you were a typical specimen of a useless and decaying aristocracy. So if you think you have made a hit, forget it. Now I must be going back, or she'll be coming out here after me. Good-bye.'

Next morning Jeeves came round. It was all so home-like when he floated noiselessly into the room that I nearly broke down.

'Good morning, sir,' he said. 'I have brought a few more of your personal belongings.'

He began to unstrap the suit-case he was carrying.

'Did you have any trouble sneaking them away?'

'It was not easy, sir. I had to watch my chance. Miss Rockmetteller is a remarkably alert lady.'

'You know, Jeeves, say what you like – this *is* a bit thick, isn't it?'

'The situation is certainly one that has never before come under my notice, sir. I have brought the heather-mixture suit, as the climatic conditions are congenial. Tomorrow, if not prevented, I will endeavour to add the brown lounge with the faint green twill.'

'It can't go on – this sort of thing – Jeeves.'

'We must hope for the best, sir.'

'Can't you think of anything to do?'

'I have been giving the matter considerable thought, sir, but so far without success. I am placing three silk shirts – the dove-coloured, the light blue, and the mauve – in the first long drawer, sir.'

'You don't mean to say you can't think of anything, Jeeves?'

'For the moment, sir, no. You will find a dozen handkerchiefs and the tan socks in the upper drawer on the left.' He strapped the suit-case and put it on a chair. 'A curious lady, Miss Rockmetteller, sir.'

'You understate it, Jeeves.'

He gazed meditatively out of the window.

'In many ways, sir, Miss Rockmetteller reminds me of an aunt of mine who resides in the south-east portion of London. Their temperaments are much alike. My aunt has the same taste for the pleasures of the great city. It is a passion with her to ride in taxi-cabs, sir. Whenever the family take their eyes off her she escapes from the house and spends the day riding about in cabs. On several occasions she has broken into the children's savings bank to secure the means to enable her to gratify this desire.'

'I love to have these little chats with you about your female relatives, Jeeves,' I said coldly, for I felt that the man had let me down, and I was fed up with him. 'But I don't see what all this has got to do with my trouble.'

'I beg your pardon, sir. I am leaving a small assortment of our neckties on the mantelpiece, sir, for you to select according to your preference. I should recommend the blue with the red domino pattern, sir.'

Then he streamed imperceptibly toward the door and flowed silently out.

I've often heard that fellows after some great shock or loss, have a habit, after they've been on the floor for a while wondering what hit them, of picking themselves up and pieceing themselves together, and sort of taking a whirl at beginning a new life. Nature adjusting itself and so on and so forth. There's a lot in it. I know, because in my own case, after a day or two of what you might call prostration, I began to recover. The frightful loss of Jeeves made any thought of pleasure more or less a mockery, but at least I found that I was able to have a dash at enjoying life again. What I mean is, I braced up to the extent of going round the cabarets once more, so as to try to forget, if only for the moment.

New York's a small place when it comes to the part of it that wakes up just as the rest is going to bed, and it wash't long before my tracks began to cross old Rocky's. I saw him once at Peak's, and again at Frolics on the Roof. There wasn't anybody with him either time except the aunt, and, though he was trying to look as if he had struck the ideal life, it wasn't difficult for me, knowing the circumstances, to see that beneath the mask the poor chap was suffering. My heart bled for the fellow. At least, what there was of it that wasn't bleeding for myself bled for him. He had the air of one who was about to crack under the strain.

It seemed to me that the aunt was looking slightly upset also. I took it that she was beginning to wonder when the celebrities were going to surge round, and what had suddenly become of all those wild, careless spirits Rocky used to mix with in his letters. I didn't blame her. I had only read a couple of his letters, but they certainly gave the impression that poor old Rocky was by way of being the hub of New York night life, and that, if by any chance he failed to show up at a cabaret, the management said, 'What's the use?' and put up the shutters.

The next two nights I didn't come across them, but the night after that I was sitting by myself at the Maison Pierre when somebody tapped me on the shoulder-blade, and I found Rocky standing beside me, with a sort of mixed expression of wistfulness and apoplexy on his face. How the man had contrived to wear my evening clothes so many times without disaster was a mystery to me. He confided later that early in the proceedings he had slit the waist-coat up the back and that that had helped a lot.

For a moment I had the idea that he had managed to get away from his aunt for the evening; but, looking past him, I saw that she was in again. She was at a table over by the wall, looking at me as if I were something the management ought to be complained to about.

'Bertie, old scout,' said Rocky, in a quiet sort of crushed voice, 'we've always been pals, haven't we? I mean, you know I'd do you a good turn if you asked me.'

'My dear old lad,' I said. The man had moved me.

'Then, for Heaven's sake, come over and sit at our table for the rest of the evening.'

Well, you know, there are limits to the sacred claims of friendship.

'My dear chap,' I said, 'you know I'd do anything in reason; but—'

'You must come, Bertie. You've got to. Something's got to be done to divert her mind. She's brooding about something. She's been like that for the last two days. I think she's beginning to suspect. She can't understand why we never seem to meet anyone I know at these joints. A few nights ago I happened to run into two newspaper men I used to know fairly well. That kept me going for a while. I introduced them to Aunt Isabel as Ed. Wynn and Jim Corbett, and it went well. But the effect has worn off now, and she's beginning to wonder again. Something's got to be done, or she will find out everything, and if she does I'd take a nickel for my chance of getting a cent from her later on. So, for the love of Mike, come across to our table and help things along.'

I went along. One has to rally round a pal in distress. Aunt Isabel was sitting bolt upright, as usual. It certainly did seem as if she had lost a bit of the zest with which she had started out to explore Broadway. She looked as if she had been thinking a good deal about rather unpleasant things.

'You've met Bertie Wooster, Aunt Isabel?' said Rocky.

'I have.'

'Take a seat, Bertie,' said Rocky.

And so the merry party began. It was one of those jolly, happy, bread-crumbling parties where you cough twice before you speak, and then decide not to say it after all. After we had had an hour of this wild dissipation, Aunt Isabel said she wanted to go home. In the light of what Rocky had been telling me, this struck me as sinister. I had gathered that at the beginning of her visit she had had to be dragged home with ropes.

It must have hit Rocky the same way, for he gave me a pleading look.

'You'll come along, won't you, Bertie, and have a drink at the flat?'

I had a feeling that this wasn't in the contract, but there wasn't anything to be done. It seemed brutal to leave the poor chap alone with the woman, so I went along.

Right from the start, from the moment we stepped into the taxi, the feeling began to grow that something was about to break loose. A massive silence prevailed in the corner where the aunt sat, and though Rocky, balancing himself on the little seat in front, did his best to supply dialogue, we weren't a chatty party.

I had a glimpse of Jeeves as we went into the flat, sitting in his lair, and I wished I could have called to him to rally round. Something told me that I was about to need him.

The stuff was on the table in the sitting-room. Rocky took up the decanter.

'Say when, Bertie.'

'Stop!' barked the aunt, and he dropped it.

I caught Rocky's eye as he stooped to pick up the ruins. It was the eye of one who sees it coming.

'Leave it there, Rockmetteller!' said Aunt Isabel; and Rocky left it there.

'The time has come to speak,' she said. 'I cannot stand idly by and see a young man going to perdition!'

Poor old Rocky gave a sort of gurgle, a kind of sound rather like the whisky had made running out of the decanter on to my carpet.

'Eh?' he said, blinking.

The aunt proceeded.

'The fault,' she said, 'was mine. I had not then seen the light. But now my eyes are open. I see the hideous mistake I have made. I shudder at the thought of the wrong I did you, Rockmetteller, by urging you into contact with this wicked city.'

I saw Rocky grope feebly for the table. His fingers touched it, and a look of relief came into the poor chappie's face. I understood his feelings.

'But when I wrote you that letter, Rockmetteller, instructing you to go to the city and live its life, I had not had the privilege of hearing Mr. Mundy speak on the subject of New York.'

'Jimmy Mundy!' I cried.

You know how it is sometimes when everything seems all mixed up and you suddenly get a clue. When she mentioned Jimmy Munday I began to understand more or less what had happened. I'd seen it happen before. I remember, back in England, the man I had before Jeeves sneaked off to a meeting on his evening out, and came back and denounced me in front of a crowd of chappies I was giving a bit of supper to as a useless blot on the fabric of Society.

The aunt gave me a withering up and down.

'Yes; Jimmy Mundy!' she said. 'I am surprised at a man of your stamp having heard of him. There is no music, there are no drunken, dancing men, no shameless, flaunting women at his meetings; so for you they would have no attraction. But for others, less dead in sin, he has his message. He has come to save New York from itself; to force it – in his picturesque phrase – to hit the trail. It was three days ago, Rockmetteller, that I first heard him. It was an accident that took me to his meeting. How often in this life a mere accident may shape our whole future!

'You had been called away by that telephone message from

Mr. Durante; so you could not take me to the Hippodrome, as we had arranged. I asked your man-servant, Jeeves, to take me there. The man has very little intelligence. He seems to have misunderstood me. I am thankful that he did. He took me to what I subsequently learned was Madison Square Garden, where Mr. Mundy is holding his meetings. He escorted me to a seat and then left me. And it was not till the meeting had begun that I discovered the mistake which had been made. My seat was in the middle of a row. I could not leave without inconveniencing a great many people, so I remained.'

She gulped.

'Rockmetteller, I have never been so thankful for anything else. Mr. Mundy was wonderful! He was like some prophet of old, scourging the sins of the people. He leaped about in a frenzy of inspiration till I feared he would do himself an injury. Sometimes he expressed himself in a somewhat odd manner, but every word carried conviction. He showed me New York in its true colours. He showed me the vanity and wickedness of sitting in gilded haunts of vice, eating lobster when decent people should be in bed.

'He said that the tango and the fox-trot were devices of the devil to drag people down into the Bottomless Pit. He said that there was more sin in ten minutes with a negro banjo orchestra than in all the ancient revels of Nineveh and Babylon. And when he stood on one leg and pointed right at where I was sitting and shouted "This means you!" I could have sunk through the floor. I came away a changed woman. Surely you must have noticed the change in me, Rockmetteller? You must have seen that I was no longer the careless, thoughtless person who had urged you to dance in those places of wickedness?'

Rocky was holding on to the table as if it was his only friend.

'Y-yes,' he stammered; 'I – I thought something was wrong.'

'Wrong? Something was right! Everything was right! Rockmetteller, it is not too late for you to be saved. You have only sipped of the evil cup. You have not drained it. It will be hard at first, but you will find that you can do it if you fight with a stout heart against the glamour and fascination of this dreadful city. Won't you, for my sake, try, Rockmetteller? Won't you go to the country tomorrow and begin the struggle? Little by little, if you use your will—'

I can't help thinking it must have been that word 'will' that roused dear old Rocky like a trumpet call. It must have brought home to him the realisation that a miracle had come off and saved him from being cut out of Aunt Isabel's. At any rate, as she said it he perked up, let go of the table, and faced her with gleaming eyes.

'Do you want me to go to the country, Aunt Isabel?'

'Yes.'

'To live in the country?'

'Yes, Rockmetteller.'

'Stay in the country all the time? Never come to New York?'

'Yes, Rockmetteller; I mean just that. It is the only way. Only there can you be safe from temptation. Will you do it, Rockmetteller? Will you – for my sake?'

Rocky grabbed the table again. He seemed to draw a lot of encouragement from that table.

'I will!' he said.

'Jeeves,' I said. It was next day, and I was back in the old flat, lying in the old arm-chair, with my feet upon the good old table. I had just come from seeing dear old Rocky off to his country cottage, and an hour before he had seen his aunt off to whatever hamlet it was that she was the curse of; so we were alone at last. 'Jeeves, there's no place like home – what?'

'Very true, sir.'

'The jolly old roof-tree, and all that sort of thing – what?'

'Precisely, sir.'

I lit another cigarette.

'Jeeves.'

'Sir?'

'Do you know, at one point in the business I really thought you were baffled.'

'Indeed, sir?'

'When did you get the idea of taking Miss Rockmetteller to the meeting? It was pure genius!'

'Thank you, sir. It came to me a little suddenly, one morning when I was thinking of my aunt, sir.'

'Your aunt? The hansom cab one?'

'Yes, sir. I recollected that, whenever we observed one of her attacks coming on, we used to send for the clergymen of the parish. We always found that if he talked to her a while of higher things it diverted her mind from hansom cabs. It occurred to me that the same treatment might prove efficacious in the case of Miss Rockmetteller.'

I was stunned by the man's resource.

'It's brain,' I said; 'pure brain! What do you do to get like that, Jeeves? I believe you must eat a lot of fish, or something. Do you eat a lot of fish, Jeeves?'

'No, sir.'

'Oh, well, then, it's just a gift, I take it; and if you aren't born that way there's no use worrying.'

'Precisely, sir,' said Jeeves. 'If I might make the suggestion, sir, I should not continue to wear your present tie. The green shade gives you a slightly bilious air. I should strongly advocate the blue with the red domino pattern, instead, sir.

'All right, Jeeves,' I said humbly. 'You know!'

The thing really started in the Park – at the Marble Arch end, where blighters of every description collect on Sunday afternoons and stand on soap-boxes and make speeches. It isn't often you'll find me there, but it so happened that on this particular Sabbath, having a call to pay in Manchester Square, I had taken a short cut through and found myself right in the middle of it. On the prompt side a gang of top-hatted birds were starting an open-air missionary service; on the O.P. side an atheist was hauling up his slacks with a good deal of vim, though handicapped a bit by having no roof to his mouth; a chappie who wanted a hundred million quid to finance him in a scheme for solving the problem of perpetual motion was playing to a thin house up left centre; while in front of me there stood a little group of serious thinkers with a banner labelled 'Heralds Of the Red Dawn'; and as I came up one of the Heralds, a bearded egg in a slouch hat and a tweed suit, was slipping it into the Idle Rich with such breadth and vigour that I paused for a moment to get an earful. While I was standing there somebody spoke to me.

'Mr. Wooster, surely?'

Stout chappie. Couldn't place him for a second. Then I got him. Bingo Little's uncle, the one I had lunch with at the time when young Bingo was in love with that waitress at the Piccadilly bun-shop. No wonder I hadn't recognised him at first. When I had seen him last he had been a rather sloppy old gentleman – coming down to lunch, I remember, in carpet slippers and a velvet smoking-jacket; whereas now dapper simply wasn't the word. He absolutely gleamed in the sunlight in a silk hat, morning coat, lavender spats, and sponge-bag trousers, as now worn. Dressy to a degree.

'Oh, hallo!' I said. 'Going strong?'

'I am in excellent health, I thank you. And you?'

'In the pink. Just been over in France for a change of air. Got back the day before yesterday. Seen anything of Bingo lately?'

'Bingo?'

'Your nephew.'

'Oh, Richard? No, not very recently. Since my marriage a little coolness seems to have sprung up.'

'Sorry to hear that. So you've married since I saw you, what? Mrs. Little all right?'

'My wife is happily robust. But – er – *not* Mrs. Little. Since we last met a gracious Sovereign has been pleased to bestow on me a signal mark of his favour in the shape of – ah – a peerage. On the publication of the last Honours List I became Lord Bittlesham.'

'By Jove! Really? I say, heartiest congratulations. Lord Bittlesham?' I said. 'Why, you're the owner of Ocean Breeze.'

'Yes. Marriage has enlarged my horizon in many directions. My wife is interested in horse-racing, and I now maintain a small stable. I understand that Ocean Breeze is fancied, as I am told the expression is, for a race which will take place at the end of the month at Goodwood, the Duke of Richmond's seat in Sussex.'

'The Goodwood Cup. Rather! I've got my chemise on it for one.'

'Indeed? Well, I trust the animal will justify your confidence. I know little of these matters myself, but my wife tells me that it is regarded in knowledgeable circles as what I believe is termed a snip.'

At this moment I suddenly noticed that the audience was gazing in our direction with a good deal of interest, and I saw that the bearded chappie was pointing at us.

'Yes, look at them! Drink them in!' he was yelling, his voice rising above the perpetual-motion fellow's and beating the missionary service all to nothing. 'There you see two typical members of the class which has down-trodden the poor for centuries. Idlers! Non-producers! Look at the tall, thin one with the face like a motor-mascot. Has he ever done an honest day's work in his life? No! A prowler, a trifler, and a blood-sucker! And I bet he still owes his tailor for those trousers!'

He seemed to me to be verging on the personal, and I didn't think a lot of it. Old Bittlesham, on the other hand, was pleased and amused.

'A great gift of expression these fellows have,' he chuckled. 'Very trenchant.'

'And the fat one!' proceeded the chappie. 'Don't miss him. Do you know who that is? That's Lord Bittlesham. One of the worst. What has he ever done except eat four square meals a day? His god is his belly, and he sacrifices burnt-offerings to it till his eyes bubble. If you opened that man now you would find enough lunch to support ten working-class families for a week.'

'You know, that's rather well put,' I said, but the old boy didn't seem to see it. He had turned a brightish magenta and was bubbling like a kettle on the boil.

'Come away, Mr. Wooster,' he said. 'I am the last man to oppose the right of free speech, but I refuse to listen to this vulgar abuse any longer.'

We legged it with quiet dignity, the chappie pursuing us with his foul innuendoes to the last. Dashed embarrassing.

Next day I looked in at the club, and found young Bingo in the smoking-room.

'Hallo, Bingo,' I said, toddling over to his corner full of bonhomie, for I was glad to see the chump. 'How's the boy?'

'Jogging along.'

'I saw your uncle yesterday.'

Young Bingo unleased a grin that split his face in half.

'I know you did, you trifler. Well, sit down, old thing, and suck a bit of blood. How's the prowling these days?'

'Good Lord! You weren't there!'

'Yes, I was.'

'I didn't see you.'

'Yes, you did. But perhaps you didn't recognise me in the shrubbery.'

'The shrubbery?'

'The beard, my boy. Worth every penny I paid for it. Defies detection.'

I goggled at him.

'I don't understand.'

'It's a long story. Have a martini or a small gore-and-soda, and I'll tell you all about it. Before we start, give me your honest opinion. Isn't she the most wonderful girl you ever saw in your puff?'

He had produced a photograph from somewhere, like a conjuror taking a rabbit out of a hat, and was waving it in front of me. It appeared to be a female of sorts, all eyes and teeth.

'Oh, great Scott!' I said. 'Don't tell me you're in love again.'

He seemed aggrieved.

'What do you mean – again?'

'Well, to my certain knowledge you've been in love with at least half-a-dozen girls since the Spring, and it's only July now. There was that waitress and Honoria Glossop and—'

'Oh, tush! Not to say pish! Those girls? Mere passing fancies. This is the real thing.'

'Where did you meet her?'

'On top of a bus. Her name is Charlotte Corday Rowbotham.'

'My God!'

'It's not her fault, poor child. Her father had her christened that because he's all for the Revolution, and it seems that the original Charlotte Corday used to go about stabbing oppressors in their baths, which entitles her to consideration and respect. You must meet old Rowbotham, Bertie. A delightful chap. Wants to massacre the bourgeoisie, sack Park Lane, and disembowel the hereditary aristocracy. Well, nothing could be fairer than that, what? But about Charlotte. We were on top of the bus and it started to rain. I offered her my umbrella, and we chatted of this and that. I fell in love and got her address, and a couple of days later I bought the beard and toddled round and met the family.'

'But why the beard?'

'Well, she had told me all about her father on the bus, and I saw that to get any footing at all in the home I should have to join these Red Dawn blighters; and naturally, if I was to make speeches in the Park, where at any moment I might run into a dozen people I knew, something in the nature of a disguise was indicated. So I bought the beard, and, by Jove, old boy, I've become dashed attached to the thing. When I take it off to come in here, for instance, I feel absolutely nude. It's done me a lot of good with old Rowbotham. He thinks I'm a Bolshevist of sorts who has to go about disguised because of the police. You really must meet old Rowbotham, Bertie. I tell you what, are you doing anything tomorrow afternoon?'

'Nothing special. Why?'

'Good! Then you can have us all to tea at your flat. I had promised to take the crowd to Lyon's Popular Café after a meeting we're holding down in Lambeth, but I can save money this way; and, believe me laddie, nowadays, as far as I'm concerned, a penny saved is a penny earned. My uncle told you he'd got married?'

'Yes. And he said there was a coolness between you.'

'Coolness? I'm down to zero. Ever since he married he's been launching out in every direction and economising on *me*. I suppose that peerage cost the old devil the deuce of a sum. Even baronetcies have gone up frightfully nowadays, I'm told. And he's started a racing-stable. By the way, put your last collar-stud on Ocean Breeze for the Goodwood Cup. It's a cert.'

'I'm going to.'

'It can't lose. I mean to win enough on it to marry Charlotte with. You're going to Goodwood of course?'

'Rather!'

'So are we. We're holding a meeting on Cup day just outside the paddock.'

'But, I say, aren't you taking frightful risks? Your uncle's sure to be at Goodwood. Suppose he spots you? He'll be fed to the gills if he finds out that you're the fellow who ragged him in the Park.'

'How the deuce is he to find out? Use your intelligence, you prowling inhaler of red corpuscles. If he didn't spot me yesterday, why should he spot me at Goodwood? Well, thanks for your cordial invitation for tomorrow, old thing. We shall be delighted to accept. Do us well, laddie, and blessings shall reward you. By the way, I may have misled you by using the word "tea". None of your wafer slices of bread-and-butter. We're good trenchermen, we of the Revolution. What we shall require will be something in the order of scrambled eggs, muffins, jam, ham, cake, and sardines. Expect us at five sharp.'

'But, I say, I'm not quite sure—'

'Yes, you are. Silly ass, don't you see that this is going to do you a bit of good when the Revolution breaks loose? When you see old Rowbotham sprinting up Piccadilly with a dripping knife in each hand, you'll be jolly thankful to be able to remind him that he once ate your tea and shrimps. There will be four of us – Charlotte, self, the old man, and Comrade Butt. I suppose he will insist on coming along.'

'Who the devil's Comrade Butt?'

'Did you notice a fellow standing on my left in our little troupe yesterday? Small, shrivelled chap. Looks like a haddock with lung-trouble. That's Butt. My rival, dash him. He's sort of semi-engaged to Charlotte at the moment. Till I came along he was the blue-eyed boy. He's got a voice like a fog-horn, and old Rowbotham thinks a lot of him. But, hang it, if I can't thoroughly encompass this Butt and cut him out and put him where he belongs among the discards – well, I'm not the man I was, that's all. He may have a big voice, but he hasn't my gift of expression. Thank heaven I was once cox of my college boat. Well, I must be pushing now. I say, you don't know how I could raise fifty quid somehow, do you?'

'Why don't you work?'

'Work?' said young Bingo, surprised. 'What, me? No, I shall have to think of some way. I must put at least fifty on Ocean Breeze. Well, see you tomorrow. God bless you, old sport, and don't forget the muffins.'

I don't know why, ever since I first knew him at school, I should have felt a rummy feeling of responsibility for young Bingo. I mean to say, he's not my son (thank goodness) or my brother or anything like that. He's got absolutely no claim on me at all, and yet a large-sized chunk of my existence seems to be spent in fussing over him like a bally old hen and hauling him out of the soup. I suppose it must be some rare beauty in my nature or something. At any rate, this latest affair of his worried me. He seemed to be doing his best to marry into a family of pronounced loonies, and how the deuce he thought he was going to support even a mentally afflicted wife on nothing a year beat me. Old Bittlesham was bound to knock off his allowance if he did anything of the sort; and, with a fellow like young Bingo, if you knocked off his allowance, you might just as well hit him on the head with an axe and make a clean job of it.

'Jeeves,' I said, when I got home, 'I'm worried.'

'Sir?'

'About Mr. Little. I won't tell you about it now, because he's bringing some friends of his to tea tomorrow, and then you will be able to judge for yourself. I want you to observe closely, Jeeves, and form your decision.'

'Very good, sir.'

'And about the tea. Get in muffins.'

'Yes, sir.'

'And some jam, ham, cake, scrambled eggs, and five or six wagonloads of sardines.'

'Sardines, sir?' said Jeeves, with a shudder.

'Sardines.'

There was an awkward pause.

'Don't blame me, Jeeves,' I said. 'It isn't my fault.'

'No, sir.'

'Well, that's that.'

'Yes, sir.'

I could see the man was brooding tensely.

I've found, as a general rule in life, that the things you think are going to be the scaliest nearly always turn out not so bad after all; but it wasn't that way with Bingo's tea-party. From the moment he invited himself I felt that the thing was going to be blue round the edges, and it was. And I think the most gruesome part of the whole affair was the fact that, for the first time since I'd known him, I saw Jeeves come very near to being rattled. I suppose there's a chink in everyone's armour, and young Bingo found Jeeves's right at the drop of the flag when he breezed in with six inches or so of brown beard hanging on to his chin. I had forgotten to warn Jeeves about the beard, and it came on him absolutely out of a blue sky. I saw the man's jaw drop, and he clutched at the table for support. I don't blame him, mind you. Few people have ever looked fouler than young Bingo in the fungus. Jeeves paled a little; then the weakness passed and he was himself again. But I could see that he had been shaken.

Young Bingo was too busy introducing the mob to take much notice. They were a very C_3 collection. Comrade Butt looked like one of the things that come out of dead trees after the rain; moth-eaten was the word I should have used to describe old Rowbotham; and as for Charlotte, she seemed to take me straight into another and a dreadful world. It wasn't that she was exactly bad-looking. In fact, if she had knocked off starchy foods and done Swedish exercises for a bit, she might have been quite tolerable. But there was too much of her. Billowy curves. Well-nourished perhaps expresses it best. And, while she may have had a heart of gold, the thing you noticed about her first was that she had a tooth of gold. I knew that young Bingo, when in form, could fall in love with practically anything of the other sex; but this time I couldn't see any excuse for him at all.

'My friend Mr. Wooster,' said Bingo, completing the ceremonial.

Old Rowbotham looked at me and then he looked round the room, and I could see he wasn't particularly braced. There's nothing of absolutely Oriental luxury about the old flat, but I have managed to make myself fairly comfortable, and I suppose the surroundings jarred him a bit.

'Mr. Wooster?' said old Rowbotham. 'May I say Comrade Wooster?'

'I beg your pardon?'

'Are you of the movement?'

'Well – er—'

'Do you yearn for the Revolution?'

'Well, I don't know that I exactly yearn. I mean to say, as far as I can make out, the whole nub of the scheme seems to be to massacre coves like me; and I don't mind owning I'm not frightfully keen on the idea.'

'But I'm talking him round,' said Bingo. 'I'm wrestling with him. A few more treatments ought to do the trick.'

Old Rowbotham looked at me a bit doubtfully.

'Comrade Little has great eloquence,' he admitted.

'I think he talks something wonderful,' said the girl, and young Bingo shot a glance of such succulent devotion at her that

I reeled in my tracks. It seemed to depress Comrade Butt a good deal too. He scowled at the carpet and said something about dancing on volcanoes.

'Tea is served, sir,' said Jeeves.

'Tea, pa!' said Charlotte, starting at the word like the old war-horse who hears the bugle; and we got down to it.

Funny how one changes as the years roll on. At school, I remember, I would cheerfully have sold my soul for scrambled eggs and sardines at five in the afternoon; but somehow, since reaching man's estate, I had rather dropped out of the habit; and I'm bound to admit I was appalled to a goodish extent at the way the sons and daughter of the Revolution shoved their heads down and went for the foodstuffs. Even Comrade Butt cast off his gloom for a space and immersed his whole being in scrambled eggs, only coming to the surface at intervals to grab another cup of tea. Presently the hot water gave out, and I turned to Jeeves.

'More hot water.'

'Very good, sir.'

'Hey! what's this? What's this?' Old Rowbotham had lowered his cup and was eyeing us sternly. He tapped Jeeves on the shoulder. 'No servility, my lad; no servility!'

'I beg your pardon, sir?'

'Don't call me "sir". Call me Comrade. Do you know what you are, my lad? You're an obsolete relic of an exploded feudal system.'

'Very good, sir.'

'If there's one thing that makes the blood boil in my veins—'

'Have another sardine,' chipped in young Bingo – the first sensible thing he'd done since I had known him. Old Rowbotham took three and dropped the subject, and Jeeves drifted away. I could see by the look of his back what he felt.

At last, just as I was beginning to feel that it was going on for ever, the thing finished. I woke up to find the party getting ready to leave.

Sardines and about three quarts of tea had mellowed old Rowbotham. There was quite a genial look in his eye as he shook my hand.

'I must thank you for your hospitality, Comrade Wooster,' he said.

'Oh, not at all! Only too glad—'

'Hospitality!' snorted the man Butt, going off in my ear like a depth-charge. He was scowling in a morose sort of manner at young Bingo and the girl, who were giggling together by the window. 'I wonder the food didn't turn to ashes in our mouths! Eggs! Muffins! Sardines! All wrung from the bleeding lips of the starving poor!'

'Oh, I say! What a beastly idea!'

'I will send you some literature on the subject of the Cause,' said old Rowbotham. 'And soon, I hope, we shall see you at one of our little meetings.'

Jeeves came in to clear away, and found me sitting among the ruins. It was all very well for Comrade Butt to knock the food, but he had pretty well finished the ham; and if you had shoved the remainder of the jam into the bleeding lips of the starving poor it would hardly have made them sticky.

'Well, Jeeves,' I said, 'how about it?'

'I would prefer to express no opinion, sir.'

'Jeeves, Mr. Little is in love with that female.'

'So I gathered, sir. She was slapping him in the passage.'

I clutched the brow.

'Slapping him?'

'Yes, sir. Roguishly.'

'Great Scott! I didn't know it had got as far as that. How did Comrade Butt seem to be taking it? Or perhaps he didn't see?'

'Yes, sir, he observed the entire proceedings. He struck me as extremely jealous.'

'I don't blame him. Jeeves, what are we to do?'

'I could not say, sir.'

'It's a bit thick.'

'Very much so, sir.'

And that was all the consolation I got from Jeeves.

I had promised to meet young Bingo next day, to tell him what I thought of his infernal Charlotte, and I was mooching slowly up St. James's Street, trying to think how the dickens I could explain to him, without hurting his feelings, that I considered her one of the world's foulest, when who should come toddling out of the Devonshire Club but old Bittlesham and Bingo himself. I hurried on and overtook them.

'What-ho!' I said.

The result of this simple greeting was a bit of a shock. Old Bittlesham quivered from head to foot like a pole-axed blanc-mange. His eyes were popping and his face had gone sort of greenish.

'Mr. Wooster!' He seemed to recover somewhat, as if I wasn't the worst thing that could have happened to him. 'You gave me a severe start.'

'Oh, sorry!'

'My uncle,' said young Bingo in a hushed, bedside sort of voice, 'isn't feeling quite himself this morning. He's had a threatening letter.'

'I go in fear of my life,' said old Bittlesham.

'Threatening letter?'

'Written,' said old Bittlesham, 'in an uneducated hand and couched in terms of uncompromising menace. Mr. Wooster, do you recall a sinister, bearded man who assailed me in no measured terms in Hyde Park last Sunday?'

I jumped, and shot a look at young Bingo. The only expression on his face was one of grave, kindly concern.

'Why – ah – yes,' I said. 'Bearded man. Chap with a beard.'

'Could you identify him, if necessary?'

'Well, I – er – how do you mean?'

'The fact is, Bertie,' said Bingo, 'we think this man with the beard is at the bottom of all this business. I happened to be walking late last night through Pounceby Gardens, where Uncle Mortimer lives, and as I was passing the house a fellow came hurrying down the steps in a furtive sort of way. Probably he had just been shoving the letter in at the front door. I noticed that he had a beard. I didn't think any more of it, however, until this morning, when Uncle Mortimer showed me the letter he had received and told me about the chap in the Park. I'm going to make inquiries.'

'The police should be informed,' said Lord Bittlesham.

'No,' said young Bingo, firmly, 'not at this stage of the proceedings. It would hamper me. Don't you worry, Uncle; I think I can track this fellow down. You leave it all to me. I'll pop you into a taxi now, and go and talk it over with Bertie.'

'You're a good boy, Richard,' said old Bittlesham and we put him in a passing cab and pushed off. I turned and looked young Bingo squarely in the eye ball.

'Did you send that letter?' I said.

'Rather! You ought to have seen it, Bertie! One of the best gent's ordinary threatening letters I ever wrote.'

'But where's the sense of it?'

'Bertie, my lad,' said Bingo, taking me earnestly by the coat-sleeve, 'I had an excellent reason. Posterity may say of me what it will, but one thing it can never say – that I have not a good solid business head. Look here!' He waved a bit of paper in front of my eyes.

'Great Scott!' It was a cheque – an absolute, dashed cheque for fifty of the best, signed Bittlesham and made out to the order of R. Little. 'What's that for?'

'Expenses,' said Bingo, pouching it. 'You don't suppose an investigation like this can be carried on for nothing, do you? I now proceed to the bank and startle them into a fit with it. Later I edge round to my bookie and put the entire sum on Ocean Breeze. What you want in situations of this kind, Bertie, is tact. If I had gone to my uncle and asked him for fifty quid, would I have got it? No! But by exercising tact – Oh! by the way, what do you think of Charlotte?'

'Well-er—'

Young Bingo massaged my sleeve affectionately.

'I know, old man, I know. Don't try to find words. She bowled you over, eh? Left you speechless, what? I know! That's the effect she has on everybody. Well, I leave you here, laddie. Oh, before we part – Butt! What of Butt? Nature's worst blunder, don't you think?'

'I must say I've seen cheerier souls.'

'I think I've got him licked, Bertie. Charlotte is coming to the Zoo with me this afternoon. Alone. And later on to the pictures. That looks like the beginning of the end, what? Well, toodle-oo, friend of my youth. If you've nothing better to do this morning, you might take a stroll along Bond Street, and be picking out a wedding present.'

I lost sight of Bingo after that. I left messages a couple of times at the club, asking him to ring me up, but they didn't have any effect. I took it that he was too busy to respond. The Sons of the Red Dawn also passed out of my life, though Jeeves told me he had met Comrade Butt one evening and had a brief chat with him. He reported Butt as gloomier than ever. In the competition for the bulging Charlotte, Butt had apparently gone right back in the betting.

'Mr. Little would appear to have eclipsed him entirely, sir,' said Jeeves.

'Bad news, Jeeves; bad news!'

'Yes, sir.'

'I suppose what it amounts to, Jeeves, is that, when young Bingo really takes his coat off and starts in, there is no power of God or man that can prevent him making a chump of himself.'

'It would seem so, sir,' said Jeeves.

Then Goodwood came along, and I dug out the best suit and popped down.

I never know, when I'm telling a story, whether to cut the thing down to plain facts or whether to drool and shove in a lot of atmosphere and all that. I mean, many a cove would no doubt edge into the final spasm of this narrative with a long description of Goodwood, featuring the blue sky, the rolling prospects, the joyous crowds of pickpockets, and the parties of the second part who were having their pockets picked, and – in a word, what not. But better give it a miss, I think. Even if I wanted to go into details about the bally meeting I don't think I'd have the heart to. The thing's too recent. The anguish hasn't had time to pass. You see, what happened was that Ocean Breeze (curse him!) finished absolutely nowhere for the Cup. Believe me, nowhere.

These are the times that try men's souls. It's never pleasant to be caught in the machinery when a favourite comes unstitched and in the case of this particular dashed animal, one had come to look on the running of the race as a pure formality, a sort of quaint, old-world ceremony to be gone through before one sauntered up to the bookie and collected. I had wandered out of the paddock to try and forget, when I bumped into old Bittlesham; and he looked so rattled and purple, and his eyes were standing out of his head at such an angle, that I simply pushed my hand out and shook his in silence.

'Me, too,' I said. 'Me, too. How much did *you* drop?'

'Drop?'

'On Ocean Breeze.'

'I did not bet on Ocean Breeze.'

'What! You owned the favourite for the Cup, and didn't back it!'

'I never bet on horse-racing. It is against my principles. I am told that the animal failed to win the contest.'

'Failed to win! Why, he was so far behind that he nearly came in first in the next race.'

'Tut!' said old Bittlesham.

'Tut is right,' I agreed. Then the rumminess of the thing struck me. 'But if you haven't dropped a parcel over the race,' I said, 'why are you looking so rattled?'

'That fellow is here!'

'What fellow is here!'

'That bearded man.'

It will show you to what an extent the iron had entered into my soul when I say that this was the first time I had given a thought to young Bingo. I suddenly remembered now that he had told me he would be at Goodwood.

'He is making an inflammatory speech at this very moment, specifically directed at me. Come! Where that crowd is.' He lugged me along and, by using his weight scientifically, got us into the front rank. 'Look! Listen!'

Young Bingo was certainly tearing off some ripe stuff. Inspired by the agony of having put his little all on a stumer that hadn't finished in the first six, he was fairly letting himself go on the subject of the blackness of the hearts of plutocratic owners who allowed a trusting public to imagine a horse was the real goods when it couldn't trot the length of its stable without getting its legs crossed and sitting down to rest. He then went on to draw what I'm bound to say was a most moving picture of the ruin of a working-man's home, due to this dishonesty. He showed us the working-man, all optimism and simple trust, believing every word he read in the papers about Ocean Breeze's form; depriving his wife and children of food in order to back the brute; going without beer so as to be able to cram an extra bob on; robbing the baby's money-box with a hatpin on the eve of the race; and finally getting let down with a thud. Dashed impressive it was. I could see old Rowbotham nodding his head gently, while poor old Butt glowered at the speaker with ill-concealed jealousy. The audience ate it.

'But what does Lord Bittlesham care,' shouted Bingo, 'if the poor working-man loses his hard-earned savings? I tell you, friends and comrades, you may talk, and you may argue, and you may cheer, and you may pass resolutions, but what you need is Action! Action! The world won't be a fit place for honest men to live in till the blood of Lord Bittlesham and his kind flows in rivers down the gutters of Park Lane!'

Roars of approval from the populace, most of whom, I suppose, had had their little bit on blighted Ocean Breeze, and were feeling it deeply. Old Bittlesham bounded over to a large, sad policeman who was watching the proceedings, and appeared to be urging him to rally round. The policeman pulled at his moustache, and smiled gently, but that was as far as he seemed inclined to go; and old Bittlesham came back to me, puffing not a little.

'It's monstrous! The man definitely threatens my personal safety, and that policeman declines to interefere. Said it was just talk. Talk! It's monstrous!'

'Absolutely,' I said, but I can't say it seemed to cheer him up much.

Comrade Butt had taken the centre of the stage now. He had a voice like the Last Trump, and you could hear every word he said, but somehow he didn't seem to be clicking. I suppose the fact was he was too impersonal, if that's the word I want. After Bingo's speech the audience was in the mood for something a good deal snappier than just general remarks about the Cause. They had started to heckle the poor blighter pretty freely when he stopped in the middle of a sentence, and I saw that he was staring at old Bittlesham.

The crowd thought he had dried up.

'Suck a lozenge,' shouted someone.

Comrade Butt pulled himself together with a jerk, and even from where I stood I could see the nasty gleam in his eye.

'Ah,' he yelled, 'you may mock, comrades; you may jeer and sneer; and you may scoff; but let me tell you that the movement is spreading every day and every hour. Yes, even amongst the so-called upper classes it's spreading. Perhaps you'll believe me when I tell you that here today on this very spot we have in our little band one of our most earnest workers, the nephew of that very Lord Bittlesham whose name you were hooting but a moment ago.'

And before poor old Bingo had a notion of what was up, he had reached out a hand and grabbed the beard. It came off all in one piece, and, well as Bingo's speech had gone, it was simply nothing compared with the hit made by this bit of business. I heard old Bittlesham give one short, sharp snort of amazement at my side, and then any remarks he may have made were drowned in thunders of applause.

I'm bound to say that in this crisis young Bingo acted with a good deal of decision and character. To grab Comrade Butt by the neck and try to twist his head off was with him the work of a moment. But before he could get any results the sad policeman, brightening up like magic, had charged in, and the next minute he was shoving his way back through the crowd, with Bingo in his right hand and Comrade Butt in his left.

'Let me pass, sir, please,' he said, civilly, as he came up against old Bittlesham, who was blocking the gangway.

'Eh?' said old Bittlesham, still dazed.

At the sound of his voice young Bingo looked up quickly from under the shadow of the policeman's right hand, and as he did so all the stuffing seemed to go out of him with a rush. For an instant he drooped like a bally lily, and then shuffled brokenly on. His air was the air of a man who has got it in the neck properly.

Sometimes when Jeeves has brought in my morning tea and shoved it on the table beside my bed, he drifts silently from the room, and leaves me to go to it; at other times he sort of shimmies respectfully in the middle of the carpet, and then I know that he wants a word or two. On the day after I had got back from Goodwood I was lying on my back, staring at the ceiling, when I noticed that he was still in my midst.

'Oh, hallo,' I said. 'Yes?'

'Mr. Little called earlier in the morning, sir.'

'Oh, by Jove, what? Did he tell you about what happened?'

'Yes, sir. It was in connexion with that that he wished to see you. He proposes to retire to the country and remain there for some little while.'

'Dashed sensible.'

'That was my opinion also, sir. There was, however, a slight financial difficulty to be overcome. I took the liberty of advancing him ten pounds on your behalf to meet current expenses. I trust that meets with your approval, sir?'

'Oh, of course. Take a tenner off the dressing-table.'

'Very good, sir.'

'Jeeves,' I said.

'Sir?'

'What beats me is how the dickens the thing happened. I mean, how did the chappie Butt ever get to know who he was?'

Jeeves coughed.

'There, sir, I fear I may have been somewhat to blame.'

'You? How?'

'I fear I may carelessly have disclosed Mr. Little's identity to Mr. Butt on the occasion when I had that conversation with him.'

I sat up.

'What!'

'Indeed, now that I recall the incident, sir, I distinctly remember saying that Mr. Little's work for the Cause really seemed to me to deserve something in the nature of public recognition. I greatly regret having been the means of bringing about a temporary estrangement between Mr. Little and his lordship. And I am afraid there is another aspect to the matter. I am also responsible for the breaking-off of relations between Mr. Little and the young lady who came to tea here.'

I sat up again. It's a rummy thing, but the silver lining had absolutely escaped my notice till then.

'Do you mean to say it's off?'

'Completely, sir. I gathered from Mr. Little's remarks that his hopes in the direction may now be looked on as definitely quenched. If there were no other obstacle, the young lady's father, I am informed by Mr. Little, now regards him as a spy and a deceiver.'

'Well, I'm dashed!'

'I appear inadvertently to have caused much trouble, sir.'

'Jeeves!' I said.

'Sir?'

'How much money is there on the dressing-table?'

'In addition to the ten-pound note which you instructed me to take, sir, there are two five-pound notes, three one-pounds, a ten-shillings, two half-crowns, a florin, four shillings, a sixpence, and a halfpenny, sir.'

'Collar it all,' I said. 'You've earned it.'

You can always rely on Jeeves. Just as I was wiping the brow and gasping like a stranded goldfish, in he drifted, merry and bright, with the good old tissue-restorers on a tray.

'Jeeves,' I said, 'it's beastly hot.'

'The weather *is* oppressive, sir.'

'Not all the soda, Jeeves.'

'No, sir.'

'London in August,' I said, quaffing deeply of the flowing b., 'rather tends to give me the pip. All my pals are away, most of the theatres are shut, and they're taking up Piccadilly in large spadefuls. The world is empty and smells of burning asphalt. Shift-ho, I think, Jeeves, what?'

'Just as you say, sir. There is a letter on the tray, sir.'

'By Jove, Jeeves, that was practically poetry. Rhymed, did you notice?' I opened the letter. 'I say, this is rather extraordinary.'

'Sir?'

'You know Twing Hall?'

'Yes, sir.'

'Well, Mr. Little is there.'

'Indeed, sir?'

'Absolutely in the flesh. He's had to take another of those tutoring jobs.'

I don't know if you remember, but immediately after that

fearful mix-up at Goodwood, young Bingo Little, a broken man, had touched me for a tenner and whizzed silently off into the unknown. I had been all over the place ever since, asking mutual friends if they had heard anything of him, but nobody had. And all the time he had been at Twing Hall. Rummy. And I'll tell you why it was rummy. Twing Hall belongs to old Lord Wickhammersley, a great pal of my guv'nor's when he was alive, and I have a standing invitation to pop down there when I like. I generally put in a week or two some time in the summer, and I was thinking of going there before I read the letter.

'And, what's more, Jeeves, my cousin Claude and my cousin Eustace – you remember them?'

'Very vividly, sir.'

'Well, they're down there, too, reading for some exam, or other with the vicar. I used to read with him myself at one time. He's known far and wide as a pretty hot coach for those of fairly feeble intellect. Well, when I tell you he got *me* through Smalls, you'll gather that he's a bit of a hummer. I call this most extraordinary.'

I read the letter again. It was from Eustace. Claude and Eustace are twins, and more or less generally admitted to be the curse of the human race.

'The Vicarage,
'Twing, Glos.

'Dear Bertie,

'Do you want to make a bit of money? I hear you had a bad Goodwood, so you probably do. Well, come down here quick and get in on the biggest sporting event of the season. I'll explain when I see you, but you can take it from me it's all right.

'Claude and I are with a reading-party at old Heppenstall's. There are nine of us, not counting your pal Bingo Little, who is tutoring the kid up at the Hall.

'Don't miss this golden opportunity, which may never occur again. Come and join us.

'Yours,

'Eustace.'

I handed this to Jeeves. He studied it thoughtfully. 'What do you make of it? A rummy communication, what?'

'Very high-spirited young gentlemen, sir, Mr. Claude and Mr. Eustace. Up to some game, I should be disposed to imagine.'

'Yes. But what game, do you think?'

'It is impossible to say, sir. Did you observe that the letter continues over the page?'

'Eh, what?' I grabbed the thing. This was what was on the other side of the last page:

SERMON HANDICAP
RUNNERS AND BETTING
PROBABLE STARTERS.

Rev. Joseph Tucker (Badgwick), scratch.

Rev. Leonard Starkie (Stapleton), scratch.

Rev. Alexander Jones (Upper Bingley), receives three minutes.

Rev. W. Dix (Little Clickton-in-the-Wold), receives five minutes.

Rev. Francis Heppenstall (Twing), receives eight minutes.

Rev. Cuthbert Dibble (Boustead Parva), receives nine minutes.

Rev. Orlo Hough (Boustead Magna), receives nine minutes.

Rev. J. J. Roberts (Fale-by-the-Water), receives ten minutes.

Rev. G. Hayward (Lower Bingley), receives twelve minutes.

Rev. James Bates (Gandle-by-the-Hill), receives fifteen minutes.

The above have arrived.

Prices: 5-2, Tucker, Starkie; 3-1, Jones; 9-2, Dix; 6-1, Heppenstall, Dibble, Hough; 100-8 any other.

*

It baffled me.

'Do you understand it, Jeeves?'

'No, sir.'

'Well, I think we ought to have a look into it, anyway, what?'

'Undoubtedly, sir.'

'Right-o, then. Pack our spare dickey and a toothbrush in a neat brown-paper parcel, send a wire to Lord Wickhammersley to say we're coming, and buy two tickets on the five-ten at Paddington tomorrow.'

The five-ten was late as usual, and everybody was dressing for dinner when I arrived at the Hall. It was only by getting into my evening things in record time and taking the stairs to the dining-room in a couple of bounds that I managed to dead-heat with the soup. I slid into the vacant chair, and found that I was sitting next to old Wickhammersley's youngest daughter, Cynthia.

'Oh, hallo, old thing,' I said.

Great pals we've always been. In fact there was a time when I had an idea I was in love with Cynthia. However, it blew over. A dashed pretty and lively and attractive girl, mind you, but full of ideals and all that. I may be wronging her, but I have an idea that she's the sort of girl who would want a fellow to carve out a career and what not. I know I've heard her speak favourably of Napoleon. So what with one thing and another the jolly old frenzy sort of petered out, and now we're just pals. I think she's a topper, and she thinks me next door to a looney, so everything's nice and matey.

'Well, Bertie, so you've arrived?'

'Oh, yes, I've arrived. Yes, here I am. I say, I seem to have plunged into the middle of quite a young dinner-party. Who are all these coves?'

'Oh, just people from round about. You know most of them. You remember Colonel Willis, and the Spencers—'

'Of course, yes. And there's old Heppenstall. Who's the other clergyman next to Mrs. Spencer?'

'Mr. Hayward, from Lower Bingley.'

'What an amazing lot of clergymen there are round here. Why, there's another, next to Mrs. Willis.'

'That's Mr. Bates, Mr. Heppenstall's nephew. He's an assistant-master at Eton. He's down here during the summer holidays, acting as locum tenens for Mr. Spettigue, the rector of Gandle-by-the-Hill.'

'I thought I knew his face. He was in his fourth year at Oxford when I was a fresher. Rather a blood. Got his rowing-blue and all that.'

I took another look round the table, and spotted young Bingo.

'Ah, there he is,' I said. 'There's the old egg.'

'There's who?'

'Young Bingo Little. Great pal of mine. He's tutoring your brother, you know.'

'Good gracious! Is he a friend of yours?'

'Rather! Known him all my life.'

'Then tell me, Bertie, is he at all weak in the head?'

'Weak in the head?'

'I don't mean simply because he's a friend of yours. But he's so strange in his manner.'

'How do you mean?'

'Well, he keeps looking at me so oddly.'

'Oddly, How? Give an imitation.'

'I can't in front of all these people.'

'Yes, you can. I'll hold my napkin up.'

'All right, then. Quick. There!'

Considering that she had only about a second and half to do it in, I must say it was a jolly fine exhibition. She opened her mouth and eyes pretty wide and let her jaw drop sideways, and managed to look so like a dyspeptic calf that I recognised the symptoms immediately.

'Oh, that's all right,' I said. 'No need to be alarmed. He's simply in love with you.'

'In love with me? Don't be absurd.'

'My dear old thing, you don't know young Bingo. He can fall in love with *anybody*.'

'Thank you!'

'Oh, I didn't mean it that way, you know. I don't wonder at his taking to you. Why, I was in love with you myself once.'

'Once? Ah! And all that remains now are the cold ashes? This isn't one of your tactful evenings, Bertie.'

'Well, my dear sweet thing, dash it all, considering that you gave me the bird and nearly laughed yourself into a permanent state of hiccoughs when I asked you—'

'Oh, I'm not reproaching you. No doubt there were faults on both sides. He's very good-looking, isn't he?'

'Good-looking? Bingo? Bingo good-looking? No, I say, come now, really!'

'I mean, compared with some people,' said Cynthia.

Some time after this, Lady Wickhammersley gave the signal for the females of the species to leg it, and they duly stampeded. I didn't get a chance of talking to young Bingo when they'd gone, and later, in the drawing-room, he didn't show up. I found him eventually in his room, lying on the bed with his feet on the rail, smoking a toofah. There was a notebook on the counterpane beside him.

'Hallo, old scream,' I said.

'Hallo, Bertie,' he replied, in what seemed to me rather a moody, distrait sort of manner.

'Rummy finding you down here. I take it your uncle cut off your allowance after that Goodwood binge and you had to take this tutoring job to keep the wolf from the door?'

'Correct,' said young Bingo, tersely.

'Well, you might have let your pals know where you were.'

He frowned darkly.

'I didn't want them to know where I was. I wanted to creep

away and hide myself. I've been through a bad time, Bertie, these last weeks. The sun ceased to shine—'

'That's curious. We've had gorgeous weather in London.'

'The birds ceased to sing—'

'What birds?'

'What the devil does it matter what birds?' said young Bingo, with some asperity. 'Any birds. The birds round about here. You don't expect me to specify them by their pet names, do you? I tell you, Bertie, it hit me hard at first, very hard.'

'What hit you?' I simply couldn't follow the blighter.

'Charlotte's calculated callousness.'

'Oh, ah!' I've seen poor old Bingo through so many unsuccessful love-affairs that I'd almost forgotten there was a girl mixed up with that Goodwood business. Of course! Charlotte Corday Rowbotham. And she had given him the raspberry, I remembered now, and gone off with Comrade Butt.

'I went through torments. Recently, however, I've – er – bucked up a bit. Tell me, Bertie, what are you doing down here? I didn't know you knew these people.'

'Me? Why, I've known them since I was a kid.'

Young Bingo put his feet down with a thud.

'Do you mean to say you've known Lady Cynthia all that time?'

'Rather! She can't have been seven when I met her first.'

'Good Lord!' said young Bingo. He looked at me for the first time as though I amounted to something, and swallowed a mouthful of smoke the wrong way. 'I love that girl, Bertie,' he went on, when he'd finished coughing.

'Yes? Nice girl, of course.'

He eyed me with pretty deep loathing.

'Don't speak of her in that horrible casual way. She's an angel. An angel! Was she talking about me at all at dinner, Bertie?'

'Oh, yes.'

'What did she say?'

'I remember one thing. She said she thought you good-looking.'

Young Bingo closed his eyes in a sort of ecstasy. Then he picked up the notebook.

'Pop off now, old man, there's a good chap,' he said, in a hushed, far-away voice. 'I've got a bit of writing to do.'

'Writing?'

'Poetry, if you must know. I wish the dickens,' said young Bingo, not without some bitterness, 'she had been christened something except Cynthia. There isn't a dam word in the language it rhymes with. Ye gods, how I could have spread myself if she had only been called Jane!'

Bright and early next morning, as I lay in bed blinking at the sunlight on the dressing-table and wondering when Jeeves was going to show up with the cup of tea, a heavy weight descended on my toes, and the voice of young Bingo polluted the air. The blighter had apparently risen with the lark.

'Leave me,' I said, 'I would be alone. I can't see anybody till I've had my tea.'

'When Cynthia smiles,' said young Bingo, 'the skies are blue; the world takes on a roseate hue; birds in the garden trill and sing, and Joy is king of everything, when Cynthia smiles.' He coughed, changing gears. 'When Cynthia frowns—'

'What the devil are you talking about?'

'I'm reading you my poem. The one I wrote to Cynthia last night. I'll go on, shall I?'

'No!'

'No?'

'No. I haven't had my tea.'

At this moment Jeeves came in with the good old beverage, and I sprang on it with a glad cry. After a couple of sips things looked a bit brighter. Even young Bingo didn't offend the eye to quite such an extent. By the time I'd finished the first cup I was a new man, so much so that I not only permitted but encouraged the poor fish to read the rest of the bally as to criticise the scansion of the fourth line of the fifth verse. We were arguing the point when the door burst open and in blew Claude and Eustace. One of the things which discourage me about rural life is the frightful earliness with which events begin to break loose. I've stayed at places in the country where they've jerked me out of the dreamless at about six-thirty to go for a jolly swim in the lake. At Twing, thank heaven, they know me, and let me breakfast in bed.

The twins seemed pleased to see me.

'Good old Bertie!' said Claude.

'Stout fellow!' said Eustace. 'The Rev. told us you had arrived. I thought that letter of mine would fetch you.'

'You can always bank on Bertie,' said Claude. 'A sportsman to the fingertips. Well, has Bingo told you about it?'

'Not a word. He's been—'

'We've been talking,' said Bingo, hastily, 'of other matters.'

Claude pinched the last slice of thin bread-and-butter, and Eustace poured himself out a cup of tea.

'It's like this, Bertie,' said Eustace, settling down cosily. 'As I told you in my letter, there are nine of us marooned in this desert spot, reading with old Heppenstall. Well, of course, nothing is jollier than sweating up the Classics when it's a hundred in the shade, but there does come a time when you begin to feel the need of a little relaxation; and, by Jove, there are absolutely no facilities for relaxation in this place whatever. And then Steggles got this idea. Steggles is one of our reading-party, and, between ourselves, rather a worm as a general thing. Still, you have to give him credit for getting this idea.'

'What idea?'

'Well, you know how many parsons there are round about here. There are about a dozen hamlets within a radius of six miles, and each hamlet has a church and each church has a parson and each parson preaches a sermon every Sunday. Tomorrow week – Sunday the twenty-third – we're running off the great Sermon Handicap. Steggles is making the book. Each parson is to be clocked by a reliable steward of the course, and the one that preaches the longest sermon wins. Did you study the race-card I sent you?'

'I couldn't understand what it was all about.'

'Why, you chump, it gives the handicaps and the current odds on each starter. I've got another one here, in case you've lost yours. Take a careful look at it. It gives you the thing in a nutshell. Jeeves, old son, do you want a sporting flutter?'

'Sir?' said Jeeves, who had just meandered in with my breakfast.

Claude explained the scheme. Amazing the way Jeeves grasped it right off. But he merely smiled in a paternal sort of way.

'Thank you, sir, I think not.'

'Well, you're with us, Bertie, aren't you?' said Claude, sneaking a roll and a slice of bacon. 'Have you studied that card? Well, tell me, does anything strike you about it?'

Of course it did. It had struck me the moment I looked at it.

'Why, it's a sitter for old Heppenstall,' I said. 'He's got the event sewed up in a parcel. There isn't a parson in the land who could give him eight minutes. Your pal Steggles must be an ass, giving him a handicap like that. Why, in the days when I was with him, old Heppenstall never used to preach under half an hour, and there was one sermon of his on Brotherly Love which lasted forty-five minutes if it lasted a second. Has he lost his vim lately, or what is it?'

'Not a bit of it,' said Eustace. 'Tell him what happened, Claude.'

'Why,' said Claude, 'the first Sunday we were here, we all went to Twing church, and old Heppenstall preached a sermon that was well under twenty minutes. This is what happened. Steggles didn't notice it, and the Rev. didn't notice it himself, but Eustace and I both spotted that he had dropped a chunk of at least half-a-dozen pages out of his sermon-case as he was walking up to the pulpit. He sort of nickered when he got to the gap in the manuscript, but carried on all right, and Steggles went away with the impression that twenty minutes or a bit under was his usual form. The next Sunday we heard Tucker and Starkie, and they both went well over the thirty-five minutes, so Steggles arranged the handicapping as you see on the card. You must come into this, Bertie. You see, the trouble is that I haven't a bean, and Eustace hasn't a bean, and Bingo Little hasn't a bean, so you'll have to finance the syndicate. Don't weaken! It's just putting money in all our pockets. Well, we'll have to be getting back now. Think the thing over, and 'phone me later in the day. And, if you let us down, Bertie, may a cousin's curse – Come on, Claude, old thing.'

The more I studied the scheme, the better it looked.

'How about it, Jeeves?' I said.

Jeeves smiled gently, and drifted out.

'Jeeves has no sporting blood,' said Bingo.

'Well, I have. I'm coming into this. Claude's quite right. It's like finding money by the wayside.'

'Good man!' said Bingo. 'Now I can see daylight. Say I have a tenner on Heppenstall, and cop; that'll give me a bit in hand to back Pink Pill with in the two o'clock at Gatwick the week after next: cop on that, put the pile on Musk-Rat for the one-thirty at Lewes, and there I am with a nice little sum to take to Alexandra Park on September the tenth, when I've got a tip straight from the stable.'

It sounded like a bit out of 'Smiles's Self-Help'.

'And then,' said young Bingo, 'I'll be in a position to go to my uncle and beard him in his lair somewhat. He's quite a bit of a snob, you know, and when he hears that I'm going to marry the daughter of an earl—'

'I say, old man,' I couldn't help saying, 'aren't you looking ahead rather far?'

'Oh, that's all right. It's true nothing's actually settled yet, but she practically told me the other day she was fond of me.'

'What!'

'Well she said that the sort of man she liked was the self-reliant, manly man with strength, good looks, character, ambition, and initiative.'

'Leave me, laddie,' I said. 'Leave me to my fried egg.'

Directly I'd got up I went to the 'phone, snatched Eustace away from his morning's work, and instructed him to put a tenner on the Twing flier at current odds for each of the syndicate; and after lunch Eustace rang me up to say that he had done business at a snappy seven-to-one, the odds having lengthened owing to a rumour in knowledgeable circles that the Rev. was subject to hay-fever and was taking big chances strolling in the paddock behind the Vicarage in the early mornings. And it was dashed lucky, I thought next day, that we had managed to get the money on in time, for on the Sunday morning old Heppenstall fairly took the bit between his teeth, and gave us thirty-six solid minutes on Certain Popular Superstitions. I was sitting next to Steggles in the pew, and I saw him blench visibly. He was a little, rat-faced fellow, with shifty eyes and a suspicious nature. The first thing he did when we emerged into the open air was to announce, formally, that anyone who fancied the Rev. could now be accommodated at fifteen-to-eight on, and he added, in a rather nasty manner, that if he had his way, this sort of in-and-out running would be brought to the attention of the Jockey Club, but that he supposed that there was nothing to be done about it. This ruinous price checked the punters at once, and there was little money in sight. And so matters stood till just after lunch on Tuesday afternoon, when, as I was strolling up and down in front of the house with a cigarette, Claude and Eustace came bursting up the drive on bicycles, dripping with momentous news.

'Bertie,' said Claude, deeply agitated, 'unless we take immediate action and do a bit of quick thinking, we're in the cart.'

'What's the matter?'

'G. Hayward's the matter,' said Eustace, morosely. 'The Lower Bingley starter.'

'We never even considered him,' said Claude. 'Somehow or other, he got overlooked. It's always the way. Steggles overlooked him. We all overlooked him. But Eustace and I happened by the merest fluke to be riding through Lower Bingley this morning, and there was a wedding on at the church, and it suddenly struck us that it wouldn't be a bad move to get a line on G. Hayward's form, in case he might be a dark horse.'

'And it was jolly lucky we did,' said Eustace. 'He delivered an address of twenty-six minutes by Claude's stop-watch. At a village wedding, mark you! What'll he do when he really extends himself!'

'There's only one thing to be done, Bertie,' said Claude. 'You must spring some more funds, so that we can hedge on Hayward and save ourselves.'

'But—'

'Well, it's the only way out.'

'But I say, you know, I hate the idea of all that money we put on Heppenstall being chucked away.'

'What else can you suggest? You don't suppose the Rev. can give this absolute marvel a handicap and win, do you?'

'I've got it!' I said.

'What?'

'I see a way by which we can make it safe for our nominee. I'll pop over this afternoon, and ask him as a personal favour to preach that sermon of his on Brotherly Love on Sunday.'

Claude and Eustace looked at each other, like those chappies in the poem, with a wild surmise.

'It's a scheme,' said Claude.

'A jolly brainy scheme,' said Eustace. 'I didn't think you had it in you, Bertie.'

'But even so,' said Claude, 'fizzer as that sermon no doubt is, will it be good enough in the face of a four-minute handicap?'

'Rather!' I said. 'When I told you it lasted forty-five minutes, I was probably understating it. I should call it – from my recollection of the thing – nearer fifty.'

'Then carry on,' said Claude.

I toddled over in the evening and fixed the thing up. Old Heppenstall was most decent about the whole affair. He seemed pleased and touched that I should have remembered the sermon all these years, and said he had once or twice had an idea of preaching it again, only it had seemed to him, on reflection, that it was perhaps a trifle long for a rustic congregation.

'And in these restless times, my dear Wooster,' he said, 'I fear that brevity in the pulpit is becoming more and more desiderated by even the bucolic churchgoer, who one might have supposed would be less afflicted with the spirit of hurry and impatience than his metropolitan brother. I have had many arguments on the subject with my nephew, young Bates, who is taking my old friend Spettigue's cure over at Gandle-by-the-Hill. His view is that a sermon nowadays should be a bright, brisk, straight-from-the-shoulder address, never lasting more than ten or twelve minutes.'

'Long?' I said. 'Why, my goodness! you don't call that Brotherly Love sermon of yours *long*, do you?'

"It takes fully fifty minutes to deliver.'

'Surely not?'

'Your incredulity, my dear Wooster, is extremely flattering – far more flattering, of course, than I deserve. Nevertheless, the facts are as I have stated. You are sure that I would not be well advised to make certain excisions and eliminations? You do not think it would be a good thing to cut, to prune? I might, for example, delete the rather exhaustive excursus into the family life of the early Assyrians?'

'Don't touch a word of it, or you'll spoil the whole thing,' I said earnestly.

'I am delighted to hear you say so, and I shall preach the sermon without fail next Sunday morning.'

What I have always said, and what I always shall say, is that this ante-post betting is a mistake, an error, and a mug's game. You never can tell what's going to happen. If fellows would only stick to the good old S.P. there would be fewer young men go wrong. I'd hardly finished my breakfast on the Saturday morning, when Jeeves came to my bedside to say that Eustace wanted me on the telephone.

'Good Lord, Jeeves, what's the matter, do you think?'

I'm bound to say I was beginning to get a bit jumpy by this time.

'Mr. Eustace did not confide in me, sir.'

'Has he got the wind up?'

'Somewhat vertically, sir, to judge by his voice.'

'Do you know what I think, Jeeves? Something's gone wrong with the favourite.'

'Which is the favourite, sir?'

'Mr. Heppenstall. He's gone to odds on. He was intending to preach a sermon on Brotherly Love which would have brought him home by lengths. I wonder if anything's happened to him.'

'You could ascertain, sir, by speaking to Mr. Eustace on the telephone. He is holding the wire.'

'By Jove, yes!'

I shoved on a dressing-gown, and flew downstairs like a mighty, rushing wind. The moment I heard Eustace's voice I knew we were for it. It had a croak of agony in it.

'Bertie?'

'Here I am.'

'Deuce of a time you've been. Bertie, we're sunk. The favourite's blown up.'

'No!'

'Yes. Coughing in his stable all last night.'

'What!'

'Absolutely! Hay-fever.'

'Oh, my sainted aunt!'

'The doctor is with him now, and it's only a question of minutes before he's officially scratched. That means the curate will show up at the post instead, and he's no good at all. He is being offered at a hundred-to-six, but no takers. What shall we do?'

I had to grapple with the thing for a moment in silence.

'Eustace.'

'Hallo?'

'What can you get on G. Hayward?'

'Only four-to-one now. I think there's been a leak, and Steggles has heard something. The odds shortened late last night in a significant manner.'

'Well, four-to-one will clear us. Put another fiver all round on G. Hayward for the syndicate. That'll bring us out on the right side of the ledger.'

'If he wins.'

'What do you mean? I thought you considered him a cert., bar Heppenstall.'

'I'm beginning to wonder,' said Eustace, gloomily, 'if there's such a thing as a cert, in this world. I'm told the Rev. Joseph Tucker did an extraordinarily fine trial gallop at a mothers' meeting over at Badgwick yesterday. However, it seems our only chance. So-long.'

Not being one of the official stewards, I had my choice of churches next morning, and naturally I didn't hesitate. The only drawback to going to Lower Bingley was that it was ten miles away, which meant an early start, but I borrowed a bicycle from one of the grooms and tooled off. I had only Eustace's word for it that G. Hayward was such a stayer, and it might have been that he had showed too flattering form at that wedding where the twins had heard him preach; but any misgivings I may have had disappeared the moment he got into the pulpit. Eustace had been right. The man was a trier. He was a tall, rangy-looking greybeard, and he went off from the start with a nice, easy action, pausing and clearing his throat at the end of each sentence, and it wasn't five minutes before I realised that here was the winner. His habit of stopping dead and looking round the church at intervals was worth minutes to us, and in the home stretch we gained no little advantage owing to his dropping his pince-nez and having to grope for them. At the twenty-minute mark he had merely settled down. Twenty-five minutes saw him going strong. And when he finally finished with a good burst, the clock showed thirty-five minutes fourteen seconds. With the handicap which he had been given, this seemed to me to make the event easy for him, and it was with much *bonhomie* and goodwill to all men that I hopped on to the old bike and started back to the Hall for lunch.

Bingo was talking on the 'phone when I arrived.

'Fine! Splendid! Topping!' he was saying. 'Eh? Oh, we needn't worry about him. Right-o, I'll tell Bertie.' He hung up the receiver and caught sight of me. 'Oh, hallo, Bertie; I was just talking to Eustace. It's all right, old man. The report from Lower Bingley has just got in. G. Hayward romps home.'

'I knew he would. I've just come from there.'

'Oh, were you there? I went to Badgwick. Tucker ran a splendid race, but the handicap was too much for him. Starkie had a sore throat and was nowhere. Roberts, of Fale-by-the-Water, ran third. Good old G. Hayward!' said Bingo, affectionately, and we strolled out on to the terrace.

'Are all the returns in, then?' I asked.

'All except Gandle-by-the-Hill. But we needn't worry about Bates. He never had a chance. By the way, poor old Jeeves loses his tenner. Silly ass!'

'Jeeves? How do you mean?'

'He came to me this morning, just after you had left, and asked me to put a tenner on Bates for him. I told him he was a chump and begged him not to throw his money away, but he would do it.'

'I beg your pardon, sir. This note arrived for you just after you had left the house this morning.'

Jeeves had materialised from nowhere, and was standing at my elbow.

'Eh? What? Note?'

'The Reverend Mr. Heppenstall's butler brought it over from

the Vicarage, sir. It came too late to be delivered to you at the moment.'

Young Bingo was talking to Jeeves like a father on the subject of betting against the form-book. The yell I gave made him bite his tongue in the middle of a sentence.

'What the dickens is the matter?' he asked, not a little peeved.

'We're dished! Listen to this!'

I read him the note:

> 'The Vicarage,
> 'Twing, Glos.

'Mr dear Wooster,

'As you may have heard, circumstances over which I have no control will prevent my preaching the sermon on Brotherly Love for which you made such a flattering request. I am unwilling, however, that you shall be disappointed, so, if you will attend divine service at Gandle-by-the-Hill this morning, you will hear my sermon preached by young Bates, my nephew. I have lent him the manuscript at his urgent desire, for, between ourselves, there are wheels within wheels. My nephew is one of the candidates for the headmastership of a well-known public school, and the choice has narrowed down between him and one rival.

'Late yesterday evening James received private information that the head of the Board of Governors of the school proposed to sit under him this Sunday in order to judge of the merits of his preaching, a most important item in swaying the Board's choice. I acceded to his plea that I lend him my sermon on Brotherly Love, of which, like you, he apparently retains a vivid recollection. It would have been too late for him to compose a sermon of suitable length in place of the brief address which – mistakenly, in my opinion – he had designed to deliver to his rustic flock, and I wished to help the boy.

'Trusting that his preaching of the sermon will supply you with as pleasant memories as you say you have of mine, I remain,

'Cordially yours,
'F. Heppenstall.

'P.S. The hay-fever has rendered my eyes unpleasantly weak for the time being, so I am dictating this letter to my butler, Brookfield, who will convey it to you.'

I don't know when I've experienced a more massive silence than the one that followed my reading of this cheery epistle. Young Bingo gulped once or twice, and practically every known emotion came and went on his face. Jeeves coughed one soft, low, gentle cough like a sheep with a blade of grass stuck in its throat, and then stood gazing serenely at the landscape. Finally young Bingo spoke.

'Great Scot!' he whispered, hoarsely. 'An S.P. job!'

'I believe that is the technical term, sir,' said Jeeves.

'So you had inside information, dash it!' said young Bingo.

'Why, yes, sir,' said Jeeves. 'Brookfield happened to mention the contents of the note to me when he brought it. We are old friends.'

Bingo registered grief, anguish, rage, despair, and resentment.

'Well, all I can say,' he cried, 'is that it's a bit thick! Preaching another man's sermon! Do you call that honest? Do you call that playing the game?'

'Well, my dear old thing,' I said, 'be fair. It's quite within the rules. Clergymen do it all the time. They aren't expected always to make up the sermons they preach.'

Jeeves coughed again, and fixed me with an expressionless eye.

'And in the present case, sir, if I may be permitted to take the liberty of making the observation, I think we should make allowances. We should remember that the securing of this headmastership meant everything to the young couple.'

'Young couple! What young couple?'

'The Reverend James Bates, sir, and Lady Cynthia. I am informed by her ladyship's maid that they have been engaged to be married for some weeks – provisionally, so to speak; and his lordship made his consent conditional on Mr. Bates securing a really important and remunerative position.'

Young Bingo turned a light green.

'Engaged to be married!'

'Yes, sir.'

There was a silence.

'I think I'll go for a walk,' said Bingo.

'But, my dear old thing,' I said, 'it's just lunchtime. The gong will be going any minute now.'

'I don't want any lunch!' said Bingo.

When the thing was over, I made my mind up.

'Jeeves,' I said.

'Sir?'

'Never again! The strain is too great. I don't say I shall chuck betting altogether: if I get hold of a good thing for one of the big races no doubt I shall have my bit on as aforetime: but you won't catch me mixing myself up with one of these minor country meetings again. They're too hot.'

'I think perhaps you are right, sir,' said Jeeves.

It was young Bingo Little who lured me into the thing. About the third week of my visit at Twing Hall he blew into my bedroom one morning while I was toying with a bit of breakfast and thinking of this and that.

'Bertie!' he said, in an earnest kind of voice.

I decided to take a firm line from the start. Young Bingo, if you remember, was at a pretty low ebb at about this juncture. He had not only failed to put his finances on a sound basis over the recent Sermon Handicap, but had also discovered that Lady Cynthia Wickhammersley loved another. These things had jarred the unfortunate mutt, and he had developed a habit of dropping in on me at all hours and decanting his anguished soul on me. I could stand this all right after dinner, and even after lunch; but before breakfast, no. We Woosters are amiability itself, but there is a limit.

'Now look here, old friend,' I said. 'I know your bally heart is broken and all that, and at some future time I shall be delighted to hear all about it, but—'

'I didn't come to talk about that.'

'No? Good egg!'

'The past,' said young Bingo, 'is dead. Let us say no more about it.'

'Right-o!'

'I have been wounded to the very depths of my soul, but don't speak about it.'

'I won't.'

'Ignore it. Forget it.'

'Absolutely!'

I hadn't seen him so dashed reasonable for weeks.

'What I came to see you about this morning, Bertie,' he said, fishing a sheet of paper out of his pocket, 'was to ask if you would care to come in on another little flutter.'

If there is one thing we Woosters are simply dripping with, it is sporting blood. I bolted the rest of my sausage, and sat up and took notice.

'Proceed,' I said. 'You interest me strangely, old bird.'

Bingo laid the paper on the bed.

'On Monday week,' he said, 'you may or may not know, the annual village school-treat takes place. Lord Wickhammersley lends the Hall grounds for the purpose. There will be games, and a conjuror, and coconut shies, and tea in a tent. And also sports.'

'I know. Cynthia was telling me.'

Young Bingo winced.

'Would you mind not mentioning that name? I am not made of marble.'

'Sorry!'

'Well, as I was saying, this jamboree is slated for Monday week. The question is, Are we on?'

'How do you mean, "Are we on"?'

'I am referring to the sports. Steggles did so well out of the

Sermon Handicap that he has decided to make a book on these sports. Punters can be accommodated at ante-post odds or starting price, according to their preference.'

Steggles, I don't know if you remember, was one of the gang of youths who were reading for some examination or other with old Heppenstall down at the Vicarage. He was the fellow who had promoted the Sermon Handicap. A bird of considerable enterprise and vast riches, being the only son of one of the biggest bookies in London, but no pal of mine. I never liked the chap. He was a ferret-faced egg with a shifty eye and not a few pimples. On the whole, a nasty growth.

'I think we ought to look into it,' said young Bingo.

I pressed the bell.

'I'll consult Jeeves. I don't touch any sporting proposition without his advice. Jeeves,' I said, as he drifted in, 'rally round.'

'Sir?'

'Stand by. We want your advice.'

'Very good, sir.'

'State your case, Bingo.'

Bingo stated his case.

'What about it, Jeeves?' I said. 'Do we go in?'

Jeeves pondered to some extent.

'I am inclined to favour the idea, sir.'

That was good enough for me. 'Right,' I said. 'Then we will form a syndicate and bust the Ring. I supply the money, you supply the brains, and Bingo – what do you supply, Bingo?'

'If you will carry me, and let me settle up later,' said young Bingo, 'I think I can put you in the way of winning a parcel on the Mothers' Sack Race.'

'All right. We will put you down as Inside Information. Now, what are the events?'

Bingo reached for his paper and consulted it.

'Girls' Under Fourteen Fifty-Yard Dash seems to open the proceedings.'

'Anything to say about that, Jeeves?'

'No, sir. I have no information.'

'What's the next?'

'Boys' and Girls' Mixed Animal Potato Race, All Ages.'

This was a new one to me. I had never heard of it at any of the big meetings.

'What's that?'

'Rather sporting,' said young Bingo. 'The competitors enter in couples, each couple being assigned an animal cry and a potato. For instance, let's suppose that you and Jeeves entered. Jeeves would stand at a fixed point holding a potato. You would have your head in a sack, and you would grope about trying to find Jeeves and making a noise like a cat; Jeeves also making a noise like a cat. Other competitors would be making noises like cows and pigs and dogs, and so on, and groping about for *their* potato-holders, who would also be making noises like cows and pigs and dogs and so on—'

I stopped the poor fish.

'Jolly if you're fond of animals,' I said, 'but on the whole—'

'Precisely, sir,' said Jeeves. 'I wouldn't touch it.'

'Too open, what?'

'Exactly, sir. Very hard to estimate form.'

'Carry on, Bingo. Where do we go from there?'

'Mothers' Sack Race.'

'Ah! that's better. This is where you know something.'

'A gift for Mrs. Penworthy, the tobacconist's wife,' said Bingo, confidently. 'I was in at her shop yesterday, buying cigarettes, and she told me she had won three times at fairs in Worcestershire. She only moved to these parts a short time ago, so nobody knows about her. She promised me she would keep herself dark, and I think we could get a good price.'

'Risk a tenner each way, Jeeves, what?'

'I think so, sir.'

'Girls' Open Egg and Spoon Race,' read Bingo.

'How about that?'

'I doubt if it would be worth while to invest, sir,' said Jeeves. 'I am told it is a certainty for last year's winner, Sarah Mills, who will doubtless start an odds-on favourite.'

'Good, is she?'

'They tell me in the village that she carries a beautiful egg, sir.'

'Then there's the Obstacle Race,' said Bingo. 'Risky, in my opinion. Like betting on the Grand National. Father's Hat-Trimming Contest – another speculative event. That's all, except the Choir Boys' Hundred Yards Handicap, for a pewter mug presented by the vicar – open to all whose voices have not broken before the second Sunday in Epiphany. Willie Chambers won last year, in a canter, receiving fifteen yards. This time he will probably be handicapped out of the race. I don't know what to advise.'

'If I might make a suggestion, sir.'

I eyed Jeeves with interest. I don't know that I'd ever seen him look so nearly excited.

'You've got something up your sleeve?'

'I have, sir.'

'Red-hot?'

'That precisely describes it, sir. I think I may confidently assert that we have the winner of the Choir Boys' Handicap under this very roof, sir. Harold, the page-boy.'

'Page-boy? Do you mean the tubby little chap in buttons one sees bobbing about here and there? Why, dash it, Jeeves, nobody has a greater respect for your knowledge of form than I have, but I'm hanged if I can see Harold catching the judge's eye. He's practically circular, and every time I've seen him he's been leaning up against something half-asleep.'

'He receives thirty yards, sir, and could win from scratch. The boy is a flier.'

'How do you know?'

Jeeves coughed, and there was a dreamy look in his eye.

'I was as much astonished as yourself, sir, when I first became aware of the lad's capabilities. I happened to pursue him one morning with the intention of fetching him a clip on the side of the head—'

'Great Scott, Jeeves! You!'

'Yes, sir. The boy is of an outspoken disposition, and had made an opprobrious remark respecting my personal appearance.'

'What did he say about your appearance?'

'I have forgotten, sir,' said Jeeves, with a touch of austerity. 'But it was opprobrious. I endeavoured to correct him, but he out-distanced me by yards, and made good his escape.'

'But, I say, Jeeves, this is sensational. And yet – if he's such a sprinter, why hasn't anybody in the village found it out? Surely he plays with the other boys?'

'No, sir. As his lordship's page-boy, Harold does not mix with the village lads.'

'Bit of a snob, what?'

'He is somewhat acutely alive to the existence of class distinctions, sir.'

'You're absolutely certain he's such a wonder?' said Bingo. 'I mean, it wouldn't do to plunge unless you're sure.'

'If you desire to ascertain the boy's form by personal inspection, sir, it will be a simple matter to arrange a secret trial.'

'I'm bound to say I should feel easier in my mind,' I said.

'Then if I may take a shilling from the money on your dressing-table—'

'What for?'

'I propose to bribe the lad to speak slightingly of the second footman's squint, sir. Charles is somewhat sensitive on the point, and should undoubtedly make the lad extend himself. If you will be at the first-floor passage-window, overlooking the back-door, in half an hour's time—'

I don't know when I've dressed in such a hurry. As a rule, I'm what you might call a slow and careful dresser: I like to linger over the tie and see that the trousers are just so; but this morning I was all worked up. I just shoved on my things anyhow, and joined Bingo at the window with a quarter of an hour to spare.

The passage-window looked down on to a broad sort of paved courtyard, which ended after about twenty yards in an archway through a high wall. Beyond this archway you got on to a strip of the drive, which curved round for another thirty yards or so till it was lost behind a thick shrubbery. I put myself in the stripling's place and thought what steps I would take with a second footman after me. There was only one thing to do – leg it for the shrubbery and take cover; which meant that at least fifty yards would have to be covered – an excellent test. If good old Harold could fight off the second footman's challenge long enough to allow him to reach the bushes, there wasn't a choirboy in England who could give him thirty yards in the hundred. I waited, all of a twitter, for what seemed hours, and then suddenly there was a confused noise without and something round and blue and buttony shot through the back-door and buzzed for the archway like a mustang. And about two seconds later out came the second footman, going his hardest.

There was nothing to it. Absolutely nothing. The field never had a chance. Long before the footman reached the half-way mark, Harold was in the bushes, throwing stones. I came away from the window thrilled to the marrow; and when I met Jeeves on the stairs I was so moved that I nearly grasped his hand.

'Jeeves,' I said, 'no discussion! The Wooster shirt goes on this boy!'

'Very good, sir,' said Jeeves.

The worst of these country meetings is that you can't plunge as heavily as you would like when you get a good thing, because it alarms the Ring. Steggles, though pimpled, was, as I have indicated, no chump, and if I had invested all I wanted to he would have put two and two together. I managed to get a good solid bet down for the syndicate, however, though it did make him look thoughtful. I heard in the next few days that he had been making searching inquiries in the village concerning Harold; but nobody could tell him anything, and eventually he came to the conclusion, I suppose, that I must be having a long shot on the strength of that thirty yards start. Public opinion wavered between Jimmy Goode, receiving ten yards, at seven-to-two, and Alexander Bartlett, with six yards start, at eleven-to-four. Willie Chambers, scratch, was offered to the public at two-to-one, but found no takers.

We were taking no chances on the big event, and directly we had got our money on at a nice hundred-to-twelve Harold was put into strict training. It was a wearing business, and I can understand now why most of the big trainers are grim, silent men, who look as though they had suffered. The kid wanted constant watching. It was no good talking to him about honour and glory and how proud his mother would be when he wrote and told her he had won a real cup – the moment blighted Harold discovered that training meant knocking off pastry, taking exercise, and keeping away from the cigarettes, he was all against it, and it was only by unceasing vigilance that we managed to keep him in any shape at all. It was the diet that was the stumbling block. As far as exercise went, we could generally arrange for a sharp dash every morning with the assistance of the second footman. It ran into money, of course, but that couldn't be helped. Still, when a kid has simply to wait till the butler's back is turned to have the run of the pantry and has only to nip into the smoking-room to collect a handful of the best Turkish, training becomes a rocky job. We could only hope that on the day his natural stamina would pull him through.

And then one evening young Bingo came back from the links with a disturbing story. He had been in the habit of giving Harold mild exercise in the afternoons by taking him out as a caddie.

At first he seemed to think it humorous, the poor chump! He bubbled over with merry mirth as he began his tale.

'I say, rather funny this afternoon,' he said. 'You ought to have seen Steggles's face!'

'Seen Steggles's face? What for?'

'When he saw young Harold sprint, I mean.'

I was filled with a grim foreboding of an awful doom.

'Good heavens! You didn't let Harold sprint in front of Steggles?'

Young Bingo's jaw dropped.

'I never thought of that,' he said gloomily. 'It wasn't my fault. I was playing a round with Steggles, and after we'd finished we went into the clubhouse for a drink, leaving Harold with the clubs outside. In about five minutes we came out, and there was the kid on the gravel practising swings with Steggles's driver and a stone. When he saw us coming, the kid dropped the club and was over the horizon like a streak. Steggles was absolutely dumbfounded. And I must say it was a revelation even to me. The kid certainly gave of his best. Of course, it's a nuisance in a way; but I don't see, on second thoughts,' said Bingo, brightening up, 'that it matters. We're on at a good price. We've nothing to lose by the kid's form becoming known. I take it he will start odds on, but that doesn't affect us.'

I looked at Jeeves. Jeeves looked at me.

'It affects us all right if he doesn't start at all.'

'Precisely, sir.'

'What do you mean?' asked Bingo.

'If you ask me,' I said, 'I think Steggles will try to nobble him before the race.'

'Good Lord! I never thought of that.' Bingo blenched. 'You don't think he would really do it?'

'I think he would have a jolly good try. Steggles is a bad man. From now on, Jeeves, we must watch Harold like hawks.'

'Undoubtedly, sir.'

'Ceaseless vigilance, what?'

'Precisely, sir.'

'You wouldn't care to sleep in his room, Jeeves?'

'No, sir, I should not.'

'No, nor would I, if it comes to that. But dash it all,' I said, 'we're letting ourselves get rattled! We're losing our nerve. This won't do. How can Steggles possibly get at Harold, even if he wants to?'

There was no cheering young Bingo up. He's one of those birds who simply leap at the morbid view, if you give them half a chance.

'There are all sorts of ways of nobbling favourites,' he said, in a sort of death-bed voice. 'You ought to read some of these racing novels. In *Pipped on the Post*, Lord Jasper Mauleverer as near as a toucher outed Bonny Betsy by bribing the head-lad to slip a cobra into her stable the night before the Derby!'

'What are the chances of a cobra biting Harold, Jeeves?'

'Slight, I should imagine, sir. And in such an event, knowing the boy as intimately as I do, my anxiety would be entirely for the snake.'

'Still, unceasing vigilance, Jeeves.'

'Most certainly, sir.'

I must say I got a bit fed with young Bingo in the next few days. It's all very well for a fellow with a big winner in his stable to exercise proper care, but in my opinion Bingo overdid it. The blighter's mind appeared to be absolutely saturated with racing fiction; and in stories of that kind, as far as I could make out, no horse is ever allowed to start in a race without at least a dozen attempts to put it out of action. He stuck to Harold like a plaster. Never let the unfortunate kid out of his sight. Of course, it meant a lot to the poor old egg if he could collect on this race, because it would give him enough money to chuck his tutoring job and get back to London; but all the same, he needn't have woken me up at three in the morning twice running – once to tell me we ought to cook Harold's food ourselves to prevent doping: the other time to say that he had heard mysterious noises in the shrubbery. But he reached the limit, in my opinion, when he insisted on my going to evening service on Sunday, the day before the sports.

'Why on earth?' I said, never being much of a lad for evensong.

'Well, I can't go myself. I shan't be here. I've got to go to London to-day with young Egbert.' Egbert was Lord Wickhammersley's son, the one Bingo was tutoring. 'He's going for a visit down in Kent, and I've got to see him off at Charing Cross. It's an infernal nuisance. I shan't be back till Monday afternoon. In fact, I shall miss most of the sports, I expect. Everything, therefore, depends on you, Bertie.'

'But why should either of us go to evening service?'

'Ass! Harold sings in the choir, doesn't he?'

'What about it? I can't stop him dislocating his neck over a high note, if that's what you're afraid of.'

'Fool! Steggles sings in the choir, too. There may be dirty work after the service.'

'What absolute rot!'

'Is it?' said young Bingo. 'Well, let me tell you that in *Jenny, the Girl Jockey,* the villain kidnapped the boy who was to ride the favourite the night before the big race, and he was the only one who understood and could control the horse, and if the heroine hadn't dressed up in riding things and—'

'Oh, all right, all right. But, if there's any danger, it seems to me the simplest thing would be for Harold not to turn out on Sunday evening.'

'He must turn out. You seem to think the infernal kid is a monument of rectitude, beloved by all. He's got the shakiest reputation of any kid in the village. His name is as near being mud as it can jolly well stick. He's played hookey from the choir so often that the vicar told him, if one more thing happened, he would fire him out. Nice chumps we should look if he was scratched the night before the race!'

Well, of course, that being so, there was nothing for it but to toddle along.

There's something about evening service in a country church

that makes a fellow feel drowsy and peaceful. Sort of end-of-a-perfect-day feeling. Old Heppenstall, the vicar, was up in the pulpit, and he has a kind of regular, bleating delivery that assists thought. They had left the door open, and the air was full of a mixed scent of trees and honeysuckle and mildew and villagers' Sunday clothes. As far as the eye could reach, you could see farmers propped up in restful attitudes, breathing heavily; and the children in the congregation who had fidgeted during the earlier part of the proceedings were now lying back in a surfeited sort of coma. The last rays of the setting sun shone through the stained-glass windows, birds were twittering in the trees, the women's dresses crackled gently in the stillness. Peaceful. That's what I'm driving at. I felt peaceful. Everybody felt peaceful. And that is why the explosion, when it came, sounded like the end of all things.

I call it an explosion, because that was what it seemed like when it broke loose. One moment a dreamy hush was all over the place, broken only by old Heppenstall talking about our duty to our neighbours; and then, suddenly, a sort of piercing, shrieking squeal that got you right between the eyes and ran all the way down your spine and out at the soles of the feet.

'EE-ee-ee-ee-ee! Oo-ee! Ee-ee-ee-ee!'

It sounded like about six hundred pigs having their tails twisted simultaneously, but it was simply the kid Harold, who appeared to be having some species of fit. He was jumping up and down and slapping at the back of his neck. And about every other second he would take a deep breath and give out another of the squeals.

Well, I mean, you can't do that sort of thing in the middle of the sermon during evening service without exciting remark. The congregation came out of its trance with a jerk, and climbed on the pews to get a better view. Old Heppenstall stopped in the middle of a sentence and spun round. And a couple of vergers with great presence of mind bounded up the aisle like leopards, collected Harold, still squealing, and marched him out. They disappeared into the vestry, and I grabbed my hat and legged it round to the stage-door, full of apprehension and what not. I couldn't think what the deuce could have happened, but somewhere dimly behind the proceedings there seemed to me to lurk the hand of the blighter Steggles.

By the time I got there and managed to get someone to open the door, which was locked, the service seemed to be over. Old Heppenstall was standing in the middle of a crowd of choir-boys and vergers and sextons and what not, putting the wretched Harold through it with no little vim. I had come in at the tail-end of what must have been a fairly fruity oration.

'Wretched boy! How dare you—'

'I got a sensitive skin!'

'This is no time to talk about your—skin.'

'Somebody put a beetle down my back!'

'Absurd!'

'I felt it wriggling—'

'Nonsense!'

'Sounds pretty thin, doesn't it?' said someone at my side.

It was Steggles, dash him. Clad in a snowy surplice or cassock, or whatever they call it, and wearing an expression of grave concern, the blighter had the cold, cynical crust to look me in the eyeball without a blink.

'Did you put a beetle down his neck?' I cried.

'Me!' said Steggles. 'Me!'

Old Heppenstall was putting on the black cap.

'I do not credit a word of your story, wretched boy! I have warned you before, and now the time has come to act. You cease from this moment to be a member of my choir. Go, miserable child!'

Steggles plucked at my sleeve.

'In that case,' he said, 'those bets, you know – I'm afraid you lose your money, dear old boy. It's a pity you didn't put it on S.P. I always think S.P.'s the only safe way.'

I gave him one look. Not a bit of good, of course.

'And they talk about the Purity of the Turf!' I said. And I meant it to sting, by Jove!

Jeeves received the news bravely, but I think the man was a bit rattled beneath the surface.

'An ingenious young gentleman, Mr. Steggles, sir.'

'A bally swindler, you mean.'

'Perhaps that would be a more exact description. However, these things will happen on the Turf, and it is useless to complain.'

'I wish I had your sunny disposition, Jeeves!'

Jeeves bowed.

'We now rely, then, it would seem, sir, almost entirely on Mrs. Penworthy. Should she justify Mr. Little's encomiums and show real class in the Mothers' Sack Race, our gains will just balance our losses.'

'Yes; but that's not much consolation when you've been looking forward to a big win.'

'It is just possible that we may still find ourselves on the right side of the ledger after all, sir. Before Mr. Little left, I persuaded him to invest a small sum for the syndicate of which you were kind enough to make me a member, sir, on the Girls' Egg and Spoon Race.'

'On Sarah Mills?'

'No, sir. On a long-priced outsider. Little Prudence Baxter, sir, the child of his lordship's head gardener. Her father assures me she has a very steady hand. She is accustomed to bring him his mug of beer from the cottage each afternoon, and he informs me she has never spilled a drop.'

Well, that sounded as though young Prudence's control was good. But how about speed? With seasoned performers like Sarah Mills entered, the thing practically amounted to a classic race, and in these big events you must have speed.

'I am aware that it is what is termed a long shot, sir. Still, I thought it judicious.'

'You backed her for a place, too, of course?'

'Yes, sir. Each way.'

'Well, I suppose it's all right. I've never known you make a bloomer yet.'

'Thank you very much, sir.'

I'm bound to say that, as a general rule, my idea of a large afternoon would be to keep as far away from a village school-treat as possible. A sticky business. But with such grave issues toward, if you know what I mean, I sank my prejudices on this occasion and rolled up. I found the proceedings about as scaly as I had expected. It was a warm day, and the Hall grounds were a dense, practically liquid mass of peasantry. Kids seethed to and fro. One of them, a small girl of sorts, grabbed my hand and hung on to it as I clove my way through the jam to where the Mothers' Sack Race was to finish. We hadn't been introduced, but she seemed to think I would do as well as anyone else to talk to about the rag-doll she had won in the Lucky Dip, and she rather spread herself on the topic.

'I'm going to call it Gertrude,' she said. 'And I shall undress it every night and put it to bed, and wake it up in the morning and dress it, and put it to bed at night, and wake it up next morning and dress it—'

'I say, old thing,' I said. 'I don't want to hurry you and all that, but you couldn't condense it a bit, could you? I'm rather anxious to see the finish of this race. The Wooster fortunes are by way of hanging on it.'

'I'm going to run in a race soon,' she said, shelving the doll for the nonce and descending to ordinary chit-chat.

'Yes?' I said. Distrait, if you know what I mean, and trying to peer through the chinks in the crowd.

'What race is that?'

'Egg'n Spoon.'

'No, really? Are you Sarah Mills?'

'Na-ow!' Registering scorn. 'I'm Prudence Baxter.'

Naturally this put our relations on a different footing. I gazed at her with considerable interest. One of the stable. I must say she didn't look much of a flier. She was short and round. Bit out of condition, I thought.

'I say,' I said, 'that being so, you mustn't dash about in the hot sun and take the edge off yourself. You must conserve your energies, old friend. Sit down here in the shade.'

'Don't want to sit down.'

'Well, take it easy, anyhow.'

The kid flitted to another topic like a butterfly hovering from flower to flower.

'I'm a good girl,' she said.

'I bet your are. I hope you're a good egg-and-spoon racer, too.'

'Harold's a bad boy. Harold squealed in church and isn't allowed to come to the treat. I'm glad,' continued this ornament of her sex, wrinkling her nose virtuously, 'because he's a bad boy. He pulled my hair Friday. Harold isn't coming to the treat! Harold isn't coming to the treat! Harold isn't coming to the treat!' she chanted, making a regular song of it.

'Don't rub it in, my dear old gardener's daughter,' I pleaded. 'You don't know it, but you've hit on rather a painful subject.'

'Ah, Wooster, my dear fellow! So you have made friends with this little lady?'

It was old Heppenstall, beaming pretty profusely. Life and soul of the party.

'I am delighted, my dear Wooster,' he went on, 'quite delighted at the way you young men are throwing yourselves into the spirit of this little festivity of ours.'

'Oh, yes?' I said.

'Oh, yes! Even Rupert Steggles. I must confess that my opinion of Rupert Steggles has materially altered for the better this afternoon.'

Mine hadn't. But I didn't say so.

'I had always considered Rupert Steggles, between ourselves, a rather self-centred youth, by no means the kind who would put himself out to further the enjoyment of his fellows. And yet twice within the last half-hour I have observed him escorting Mrs. Penworthy, our worthy tobacconist's wife, to the refreshment tent.'

I left him standing. I shook off the clutching hand of the Baxter kid and hared it rapidly to the spot where the Mothers' Sack Race was just finishing. I had a horrid presentiment that there had been more dirty work at the cross-roads. The first person I ran into was young Bingo. I grabbed him by the arm.

'Who won?'

'I don't know. I didn't notice.' There was bitterness in the chappie's voice. 'It wasn't Mrs. Penworthy, dash her! Bertie, that hound Steggles is nothing more nor less than one of our leading snakes. I don't know how he heard about her, but he must have got on to it that she was dangerous. Do you know what he did? He lured that miserable woman into the refreshment-tent five minutes before the race, and brought her out so weighed down with cake and tea that she blew up in the first twenty yards. Just rolled over and lay there! Well, thank goodness we still have Harold!'

I gaped at the poor chump.

'Harold! Haven't you heard?'

'Heard?' Bingo turned a delicate green. 'Heard what? I haven't heard anything. I only arrived five minutes ago. Came here straight from the station. What has happened? Tell me!'

I slipped him the information. He stared at me for a moment in a ghastly sort of way, then with a hollow groan tottered away and was lost in the crowd. A nasty knock, poor chap. I didn't blame him for being upset.

They were clearing the decks now for the Egg and Spoon Race, and I thought I might as well stay where I was and watch the finish. Not that I had much hope. Young Prudence was a good conversationalist, but she didn't seem to me to be the build for a winner.

As far as I could see through the mob, they got off to a good start. A short, red-haired child was making the running, with a freckled blonde second and Sarah Mills lying up an easy third. Our nominee was straggling along with the field, well behind the leaders. It was not hard even as early as this to spot the winner. There was a grace, a practised precision, in the way Sarah Mills held her spoon that told its own story. She was cutting out a good pace, but her egg didn't even wobble, a natural egg-and-spooner, if ever there was one.

Class will tell. Thirty yards from the tape, the red-haired kid tripped over her feet and shot her egg on to the turf. The freckled blonde fought gamely, but she had run herself out halfway down the straight, and Sarah Mills came past home on a tight rein by several lengths, a popular winner. The blonde was second. A sniffing female in blue gingham beat a pie-faced kid in pink for the place-money, and Prudence Baxter, Jeeves's long shot, was either fifth or sixth, I couldn't see which.

And then I was carried along with the crowd to where old Heppenstall was going to present the prizes. I found myself standing next to the man Steggles.

'Hallo, old chap!' he said, very bright and cheery. 'You've had a bad day, I'm afraid.'

I looked at him with silent scorn. Lost on the blighter, of course.

'It's not been a good meeting for any of the big punters,' he went on. 'Poor old Bingo Little went down badly over that Egg and Spoon Race.'

I hadn't been meaning to chat with the fellow, but I was startled.

'How do you mean badly?' I said. 'We – he only had a small bet on.'

'I don't know what you call small. He had thirty quid each way on the Baxter kid.'

The landscape reeled before me.

'What!'

'Thirty quid at ten to one. I thought he must have heard something, but apparently not. The race went by the form-book all right.'

I was trying to do sums in my head. I was just in the middle of working out the syndicate's losses, when old Heppenstall's voice came sort of faintly to me out of the distance. He had been pretty fatherly and debonair when ladling out the prizes for the other events, but now he had suddenly grown all pained and grieved. He peered sorrowfully at the multitude.

'With regard to the Girls' Egg and Spoon Race, which has just concluded,' he said, 'I have a painful duty to perform. Circumstances have arisen which it is impossible to ignore. It is not too much to say that I am stunned.'

He gave the populace about five seconds to wonder why he was stunned, then went on.

'Three years ago, as you are aware, I was compelled to expunge from the list of events at this annual festival the Fathers' Quarter-Mile, owing to reports coming to my ears of wagers taken and given on the result at the village inn and a strong suspicion that on at least one occasion the race had actually been sold by the speediest runner. That unfortunate occurrence shook my faith in human nature, I admit – but still there was one event at least which I confidently expected to remain untainted by the miasma of Professionalism. I allude to the Girls' Egg and Spoon Race. It seems, alas, that I was too sanguine.'

He stopped again, and wrestled with his feelings.

'I will not weary you with the unpleasant details. I will merely say that before the race was run a stranger in our midst, the manservant of one of the guests at the Hall – I will not specify with more particularity – approached several of the competitors and presented each of them with five shillings on condition that they – er – finished. A belated sense of remorse has led him to confess to me what he did, but it is too late. The evil is accomplished, and retribution must take its course. It is no time for half-measures. I must be firm. I rule that Sarah Mills, Jane Parker, Bessie Clay, and Rosie Jukes, the first four to pass the winning-post, have forfeited their amateur status and are disqualified, and this handsome work-bag, presented by Lord Wickhammersley, goes, in consequence, to Prudence Baxter. Prudence, step forward!'

Nobody is more alive than I am to the fact that young Bingo Little is in many respects a sound old egg; but I must say there are things about him that could be improved. The man's too expansive altogether. When it comes to letting the world in on the secrets of his heart, he has about as much shrinking reticence as a steam calliope. Well, for instance, here's the telegram I got from him one evening in November:

'I say Bertie old man I am in love at last. She is the most wonderful girl Bertie old man. This is the real thing at last Bertie. Come here at once and bring Jeeves. Oh I say you know that tobacco shop in Bond Street on the left side as you go up. Will you get me a hundred of their special cigarettes and send them to me here. I have run out. I know when you see her you will think she is the most wonderful girl. Mind you bring Jeeves. Don't forget the cigarettes. – BINGO.'

It had been handed in at Twing Post Office. In other words, he had submitted that frightful rot to the goggling eye of a village post-mistress who was probably the mainspring of local gossip and would have the place ringing with the news before nightfall. He couldn't have given himself away more completely if he had hired the town-crier. When I was a kid, I used to read stories about Knights and Vikings and that species of chappie who would get up without a blush in the middle of a crowded banquet and loose off a song about how perfectly priceless they thought their best girl. I've often felt that those days would have suited young Bingo down to the ground.

Jeeves had brought the thing in with the evening drink, and I slung it to him.

'It's about due, of course,' I said. 'Young Bingo hasn't been in love for at least a couple of months. I wonder who it is this time?'

'Miss Mary Burgess, sir,' said Jeeves, 'the niece of the Reverend Mr. Heppenstall. She is staying at Twing Vicarage.'

'Great Scott!' I knew that Jeeves knew practically everything in the world, but this sounded like second-sight. 'How do you know that?'

'When we were visiting Twing Hall in the summer, sir, I formed a somewhat close friendship with Mr. Heppenstall's butler. He is good enough to keep me abreast of the local news from time to time. From this account, sir, the young lady appears to be a very estimable young lady. Of a somewhat serious nature, I understand. Mr. Little is very *épris*, sir. Brookfield, my correspondent, writes that last week he observed him in the moonlight at an advanced hour gazing up at his window.'

'Whose window? Brookfield's?'

'Yes, sir. Presumably under the impression that it was the young lady's.'

'But what the deuce is he doing at Twing at all?'

'Mr. Little was compelled to resume his old position as tutor to Lord Wickhammersley's son at Twing Hall, sir. Owing to having been unsuccessful in some speculations at Hurst Park at the end of October.'

'Good Lord, Jeeves! Is there anything you don't know?'

'I could not say, sir.'

I picked up the telegram.

'I suppose he wants us to go down and help him out a bit?'

'That would appear to be his motive in dispatching the message, sir.'

'Well, what shall we do? Go?'

'I would advocate it, sir. If I may say so, I think that Mr. Little should be encouraged in this particular matter.'

'You think he's picked a winner this time?'

'I hear nothing but excellent reports of the young lady, sir. I think it is beyond question that she would be an admirable influence for Mr. Little, should the affair come to a happy conclusion. Such a union would also, I fancy, go far to restore Mr. Little to the good graces of his uncle, the young lady being well connected and possessing private means. In short, sir, I think that if there is anything that we can do we should do it.'

'Well, with you behind him,' I said, 'I don't see how he can fail to click.'

'You are very good, sir,' said Jeeves. 'The tribute is much appreciated.'

Bingo met us at Twing station next day, and insisted on my sending Jeeves on in the car with the bags while he and I walked. He started in about the female the moment we had begun to hoof it.

'She is very wonderful, Bertie. She is not one of these flippant, shallow-minded modern girls. She is sweetly grave and beautifully earnest. She reminds me of – what is the name I want?'

'Clara Bow?'

'Saint Cecilia,' said young Bingo, eyeing me with a great deal of loathing. 'She reminds me of Saint Cecilia. She makes me yearn to be a better, nobler, deeper, broader man.'

'What beats me,' I said, following up a train of thought, 'is what principle you pick them on. The girls you fall in love with, I mean. I mean to say, what's your system? As far as I can see, no two of them are alike. First it was Mabel the waitress, then Honoria Glossop, then that fearful blister Charlotte Corday Rowbotham—'

I own that Bingo had the decency to shudder. Thinking of Charlotte always made me shudder, too.

'You don't seriously mean, Bertie, that you are intending to compare the feeling I have for Mary Burgess, the holy devotion, the spiritual—'

'Oh, all right, let it go,' I said. 'I say, old lad, aren't we going rather a long way round?'

Considering that we were supposed to be heading for Twing Hall, it seemed to me that we were making a longish job of it. The Hall is about two miles from the station by the main road, and we had cut off down a lane, gone across country for a bit, climbed a stile or two, and were now working our way across a field that ended in another lane.

'She sometimes takes her little brother for a walk round this way,' explained Bingo. 'I thought we would meet her and bow, and you could see her, you know, and then we would walk on.'

'Of course,' I said, 'that's enough excitement for anyone, and undoubtedly a corking reward for tramping three miles out of one's way over ploughed fields with tight boots, but don't we do anything else? Don't we tack on to the girl and buzz along with her?'

'Good Lord!' said Bingo, honestly amazed. 'You don't suppose I've got nerve enough for that, do you? I just look at her from afar and all that sort of thing. Quick! Here she comes! No, I'm wrong!'

It was like that song of Harry Lauder's where he's waiting for the girl and says: 'This is her-r-r. No, it's a rabbut.' Young Bingo made me stand there in the teeth of a nor'-east half-gale for ten minutes, keeping me on my toes with a series of false alarms, and I was thinking of suggesting that we should lay off and give the rest of the proceedings a miss, when round the corner there came a fox-terrier, and Bingo quivered like an aspen. Then there hove in sight a small boy, and he shook like a jelly. Finally, like a star whose entrance has been worked up by the *personnel* of the *ensemble*, a girl appeared, and his emotion was painful to witness. His face got so red that, what with his white collar and the fact that the wind had turned his nose blue, he looked more like a French flag than anything else. He sagged from the waist upwards, as if he had been filleted.

He was just raising his fingers limply to his cap when he saw that the girl wasn't alone. A bloke in clerical costume was also among those present, and the sight of him didn't seem to do Bingo a bit of good. His face got redder and his nose bluer, and it wasn't till they had nearly passed that he managed to get hold of his cap.

The girl bowed, the curate said: 'Ah, Little. Rough weather,' the dog barked, and then they toddled on and the entertainment was over.

The curate was a new factor in the situation to me. I reported his movements to Jeeves when I got to the Hall. Of course, Jeeves knew all about it already.

'That is the Reverend Mr. Wingham, Mr. Heppenstall's new curate, sir. I gather from Brookfield that he is Mr. Little's rival, and that at the moment the young lady appears to favour him. Mr. Wingham has the advantage of being on the premises. He and the young lady play duets after dinner, which acts as a bond. Mr. Little on these occasions, I understand, prowls about in the road, chafing visibly.'

'That seems to be all the poor fish is able to do, dash it. He can chafe all right, but there he stops. He's lost his pep. He's got no dash. Why, when we met her just now, he hadn't even the common manly courage to say "Good evening"!'

'I gather that Mr. Little's affection is not unmingled with awe, sir.'

'Well, how are we to help a man when he's such a rabbit as that? Have you anything to suggest? I shall be seeing him after dinner, and he's sure to ask first thing what you advise.'

'In my opinion, sir, the most judicious course for Mr. Little to pursue would be to concentrate on the young gentleman.'

'The small brother? How do you mean?'

'Make a friend of him, sir – take him for walks and so forth.'

'It doesn't sound one of your red-hottest ideas. I must say I expected something fruitier than that.'

'It would be a beginning, sir, and might lead to better things.'

'Well, I'll tell him. I liked the look of her, Jeeves.'

'A thoroughly estimable young lady, sir.'

I slipped Bingo the tip from the stable that night, and was glad to observe that it seemed to cheer him up.

'Jeeves is always right,' he said. 'I ought to have thought of it myself. I'll start in tomorrow.'

It was amazing how the chappie bucked up. Long before I left for town it had become a mere commonplace for him to speak to the girl. I mean, he didn't simply look stuffed when they met. The brother was forming a bond that was a dashed sight stronger than the curate's duets. She and Bingo used to take him for walks together. I asked Bingo what they talked about on these occasions, and he said Wilfred's future. The girl hoped that Wilfred would one day become a curate, but Bingo said no, there was something about curates he didn't quite like.

The day we left, Bingo came to see us off with Wilfred frisking about him like an old college chum. The last I saw of them, Bingo was standing him chocolates out of the slot-machine. A scene of peace and cheery good-will. Dashed promising, I thought.

Which made it all the more of a jar, about a fortnight later, when his telegram arrived. As follows:

'Bertie old man I say Bertie could you possibly come down here at once. Everything gone wrong bang it all. Dash it Bertie you simply must come, I am in a state of absolute despair and heart-broken. Would you mind sending another hundred of those cigarettes. Bring Jeeves when you come Bertie. You simply must come Bertie. I rely on you. Don't forget to bring Jeeves. – BINGO.'

For a chap who's perpetually hard-up, I must say that young Bingo is the most wasteful telegraphist I ever struck. He's got no notion of condensing. The silly ass simply pours out his wounded soul at twopence a word, or whatever it is, without a thought.

'How about it, Jeeves?' I said. 'I'm getting a bit fed. I can't go chucking all my engagements every second week in order to biff down to Twing and rally round young Bingo. Send him a wire telling him to end it all in the village pond.'

'If you could spare me for the night, sir, I should be glad to run down and investigate.'

'Oh, dash it! Well, I suppose there's nothing else to be done. After all, you're the fellow he wants. All right, carry on.'

Jeeves got back late the next day.

'Well?' I said.

Jeeves appeared perturbed. He allowed his left eyebrow to flicker upwards in a concerned sort of manner.

'I have done what I could, sir,' he said, 'but I fear Mr. Little's chances do not appear bright. Since our last visit, sir, there has been a decidedly sinister and disquieting development.'

'Oh, what's that?'

'You may remember Mr. Steggles, sir – the young gentleman who was studying for an examination with Mr. Heppenstall at the Vicarage?'

Of course I remembered Steggles. You'll place him if you throw your mind back. Recollect the rat-faced chappie of sporting tastes who made the book on the Sermon Handicap and then made another on the Choir Boys' Sports? That's the fellow. A blighter of infinite guile and up to every shady scheme on the list. Though, thanks to Jeeves, we had let him in pretty badly on the Girls' Egg-and-Spoon Race and collected a parcel off him in spite of his villainies.

'What's Steggles got to do with it?' I asked.

'I gather from Brookfield, sir, who chanced to overhear a conversation, that Mr. Steggles is interesting himself in the affair.'

'Good Lord! What, making a book on it?'

'I understand that he is accepting wagers from those in his immediate circle, sir. Against Mr. Little, whose chances he does not seem to fancy.'

'I don't like that, Jeeves.'

'No, sir. It is sinister.'

'From what I know of Steggles there will be dirty work.'

'It has already occurred, sir.'

'Already?'

'Yes, sir. It seems that, in pursuance of the policy which he had been good enough to allow me to suggest to him, Mr. Little escorted Master Burgess to the church bazaar, and there met Mr. Steggles, who was in the company of young Master Heppenstall, the Reverend Mr. Heppenstall's second son, who is home from Rugby just now, having recently recovered from an attack of mumps. The encounter took place in the refreshment-room, where Mr. Steggles was at that moment entertaining Master Heppenstall. To cut a long story short, sir, the two gentlemen became extremely interested in the hearty manner in which the lads were fortifying themselves; and Mr. Steggles offered to back his nominee in a weight-for-age eating contest against Master Burgess for a pound a side. Mr. Little admitted to me that he was conscious of a certain hesitation as to what the upshot might be, should Miss Burgess get to hear of the matter, but his sporting blood was too much for him and he agreed to the contest. This was duly carried out, both lads exhibiting the utmost willingness and enthusiasm, and eventually Master Burgess justified Mr. Little's confidence by winning, but only after a bitter struggle. Next day both contestants were in considerable pain; inquiries were made and confessions extorted, and Mr. Little – I learn from Brookfield, who happened to be near the door of the drawing-room at the moment – had an extremely unpleasant interview with the young lady, which ended in her desiring him never to speak to her again.'

There's no getting away from the fact that, if ever a man required watching, it's Steggles. Machiavelli could have taken his correspondence course.

'It was a put-up job, Jeeves!' I said. 'I mean, Steggles worked the whole thing on purpose. It's his old nobbling game.'

'There would seem to be no doubt about that, sir.'

'Well, he seems to have dished poor old Bingo all right.'

'That is the prevalent opinion, sir. Brookfield tells me that down in the village at the Cow and Horses seven to one is being freely offered on Mr. Wingham and finding no takers.'

'Good Lord! Are they betting about it down in the village, too?'

'Yes, sir. And in adjoining hamlets also. The affair has caused widespread interest. I am told that there is a certain sporting reaction in even so distant a spot as Lower Bingley.'

'Well, I don't see what there is to do. If Bingo is such a chump—'

'One is fighting a losing battle, I fear, sir, but I did venture to indicate to Mr. Little a course of action which might prove of advantage. I recommended him to busy himself with good works.'

'Good works?'

'About the village, sir. Reading to the bed-ridden – chatting with the sick – that sort of thing, sir. We can but trust that good results will ensue.'

'Yes, I suppose so,' I said, doubtfully. 'But, by gosh, if I was a sick man I'd hate to have a looney like young Bingo coming and gibbering at my bedside.'

'There *is* that aspect of the matter, sir,' said Jeeves.

I didn't hear a word from Bingo for a couple of weeks, and I took it after a while that he had found the going too hard and had chucked in the towel. And then, one night not long before Christmas, I came back to the flat pretty latish, having been out dancing at the Embassy. I was fairly tired, having swung a practically non-stop shoe from shortly after dinner till two a.m., and bed seemed to be indicated. Judge of my chagrin and all that sort of thing, therefore, when, tottering to my room and switching on the light, I observed the foul features of young Bingo all over the pillow. The blighter had appeared from nowhere and was in my bed, sleeping like an infant with a sort of happy dreamy smile on his map.

A bit thick, I mean to say! We Woosters are all for the good old mediaeval hosp. and all that, but when it comes to finding chappies collaring your bed, the thing becomes a trifle too mouldy. I hove a shoe, and Bingo sat up, gurgling.

''S matter? 's matter?' said young Bingo.

'What the deuce are you doing in my bed?' I said.

'Oh, hallo, Bertie! So there you are!'

'Yes, here I am. What are you doing in my bed?'

'I came up to town for the night on business.'

'Yes, but what are you doing in my bed?'

'Dash it all, Bertie,' said young Bingo, querulously, 'don't keep harping on your beastly bed. There's another made up in the spare room. I saw Jeeves make it with my own eyes. I believe he meant it for me, but I knew what a perfect host you were, so I just turned in here. I say, Bertie, old man,' said Bingo, apparently fed up with the discussion about sleeping-quarters, 'I see daylight.'

'Well, it's getting on for three in the morning.'

'I was speaking figuratively, you ass. I meant that hope has begun to dawn. About Mary Burgess, you know. Sit down and I'll tell you all about it.'

'I won't. I'm going to sleep.'

'To begin with,' said young Bingo, settling himself comfortably against the pillows and helping himself to a cigarette from my special private box, 'I must once again pay a marked tribute to good old Jeeves. A modern Solomon. I was badly up against it when I came to him for advice, but he rolled up with a tip which has put me – I use the term advisedly and in a conservative spirit – on velvet. He may have told you that he recommended me to win back the lost ground by busying myself with good works? Bertie, old man,' said young Bingo, earnestly, 'for the last two weeks I've been comforting the sick to such an extent that, if I had a brother and you brought him to me on a sickbed at this moment, by Jove, old man, I'd heave a brick at him. However, though it took it out of me like the deuce, the scheme worked splendidly. She softened visibly before I'd been at it a week. Started to bow again when we met in the street, and so forth. About a couple of days ago she distinctly smiled – in a sort of faint, saint-like kind of way, you know – when I ran into her outside the Vicarage. And yesterday – I say, you remember that curate chap, Wingham? Fellow with a long nose and a sort of goofy expression?'

'Of course I remember him. Your rival.'

'Rival?' Bingo raised his eyebrows. 'Oh, well, I suppose you could have called him that at one time. Though it sounds a little far-fetched.'

'Does it?' I said, stung by the sickening complacency of the chump's manner. 'Well, let me tell you that the last I heard was that at the Cow and Horses in Twing village and all over the place as far as Lower Bingley they were offering seven to one on the curate and finding no takers.'

Bingo started violently, and sprayed cigarette-ash all over my bed.

'Betting!' he gargled. 'Betting! You don't mean that they're betting on this holy, sacred – Oh, I say, dash it all! Haven't people any sense of decency and reverence? Is nothing safe from their beastly, sordid graspingness? I wonder,' said young Bingo, thoughtfully, 'if there's a chance of my getting any of that seven-to-one money? Seven to one! What a price! Who's offering it, do you know? Oh, well, I suppose it wouldn't do. No, I suppose it wouldn't be quite the thing.'

'You seem dashed confident,' I said. 'I'd always thought that Wingham—'

'Oh, I'm not worried about him,' said Bingo. 'I was just going to tell you. Wingham's got the mumps, and won't be out and about for weeks. And, jolly as that is in itself, it's not all. You see, he was producing the Village School Christmas Entertainment, and now I've taken over the job. I went to old Heppenstall last night and clinched the contract. Well, you see what that means. It means that I shall be absolutely the centre of the village life and thought for three solid weeks, with a terrific triumph to wind up with. Everybody looking up to me and fawning on me, don't you see, and all that. It's bound to have a powerful effect on Mary's mind. It will show her that I am capable of serious effort; that there is a solid foundation of worth in me; that, mere butterfly as she may once have thought me, I am in reality—'

'Oh, all right, let it go!'

'It's a big thing, you know, this Christmas Entertainment. Old Heppenstall's very much wrapped up in it. Nibs from all over the countryside rolling up. The Squire present, with family. A big chance for me, Bertie, my boy, and I mean to make the most of it. Of course, I'm handicapped a bit by not having been in on the thing from the start. Will you credit it that that uninspired doughnut of a curate wanted to give the public some rotten little fairy play out of a book for children published about fifty years ago, without one good laugh or the semblance of a gag in it? It's too late to alter the thing entirely, but at least I can jazz it up. I'm going to write them in something zippy to brighten the thing up a bit.'

'You can't write.'

'Well, when I say write, I mean pinch. That's why I've popped up to town. I've been to see that revue, *Cuddle Up!* at the Palladium, tonight. Full of good stuff. Of course, it's rather hard to get anything in the nature of a big spectacular effect in the Twing Village Hall, with no scenery to speak of and a chorus of practically imbecile kids of ages ranging from nine to fourteen, but I think I see my way. Have you seen *Cuddle Up?*'

'Yes. Twice.'

'Well, there's some good stuff in the first act, and I can lift practically all the numbers. Then there's that show at the Palace. I can see the *matinee* of that tomorrow before I leave. There's sure to be some decent bits in that. Don't you worry about my not being able to write a hit. Leave it to me, laddie, leave it to me. And now, my dear old chap,' said young Bingo, snuggling down cosily, 'you mustn't keep me up talking all night. It's all right for you fellows who have nothing to do, but I'm a busy man. Good night, old thing. Close the door quietly after you and switch out the light. Breakfast about ten tomorrow, I suppose, what? Right-ho. Good night.'

For the next three weeks I didn't see Bingo. He became a sort of Voice Heard Off, developing a habit of ringing me up on long-distance and consulting me on various points arising at rehearsal, until the day when he got me out of bed at eight in the morning to ask whether I thought 'Merry Christmas!' was a good title. I told him then that this nuisance must now cease, and after that he cheesed it, and practically passed out of my life till one afternoon when I got back to the flat to dress for dinner and found Jeeves inspecting a whacking big poster sort of thing which he had draped over the back of an armchair.

'Good Lord, Jeeves!' I said. I was feeling rather weak that day, and the thing shook me. 'What on earth's that?'

'Mr. Little sent it to me, sir, and desired me to bring it to your notice.'

'Well, you've certainly done it!'

I took another look at the object. There was no doubt about it, it caught the eye. It was about seven feet long, and most of the lettering in about as bright red as I ever struck.

This was how it ran:

TWING VILLAGE HALL
Friday, December 23rd
RICHARD LITTLE
presents
New and Original Revue
Entitled
WHAT HO, TWING! !
Book by
RICHARD LITTLE
Lyrics by
RICHARD LITTLE
Music by
RICHARD LITTLE
With the Full Twing Juvenile
Company and Chorus
Scenic effects by
RICHARD LITTLE
Produced by
RICHARD LITTLE
A RICHARD LITTLE PRODUCTION

'What do you make of it, Jeeves?' I said.

'I confess I am a little doubtful, sir. I think Mr. Little would have done better to follow my advice and confine himself to good works about the village.'

'You think the thing will be a frost?'

'I could not hazard a conjecture, sir. But my experience has been that what pleases the London public is not always so acceptable to the rural mind. The metropolitan touch sometimes proves a trifle too exotic for the provinces.'

'I suppose I ought to go down and see the dashed thing?'

'I think Mr. Little would be wounded were you not present, sir.'

The Village Hall at Twing is a smallish building, smelling of apples. It was full when I turned up on the evening of the twenty-third, for I had purposely timed myself to arrive not long before the kick-off. I had had experience of one or two of these binges, and didn't want to run any risk of coming early and finding myself shoved into a seat in one of the front rows where I wouldn't be able to execute a quiet sneak into the open air half-way through the proceedings, if the occasion seemed to demand it. I secured a nice strategic position near the door at the back of the Hall.

From where I stood I had a good view of the audience. As always on these occasions, the first few rows were occupied by the Nibs – consisting of the Squire, a fairly mauve old sportsman with white whiskers, his family, a platoon of local parsons, and perhaps a couple of dozen of prominent pew-holders. Then came a dense squash of what you might call the lower middle classes. And at the back, where I was, we came down with a jerk in the social scale, this end of the hall being given up almost entirely to a collection of frankly Tough Eggs, who had rolled up not so much for any love of the drama as because there was a free tea after the show. Take it for all in all, a representative gathering of Twing life and thought. The Nibs were whispering in a pleased manner to each other, the Lower Middles were sitting up very straight as if they'd been bleached, and the Tough Eggs whiled away the time by cracking nuts and exchanging low rustic wheezes. The girl, Mary Burgess, was at the piano, playing a waltz. Beside her stood the curate, Wingham, apparently recovered. The temperature, I should think, was about a hundred and twenty-seven.

Somebody jabbed me heartily in the lower ribs, and I perceived the man Steggles.

'Hallo!' he said. 'I didn't know you were coming down.'

I didn't like the chap, but we Woosters can wear the mask. I beamed a bit.

'Oh, yes,' I said. 'Bingo wanted me to roll up and see his show.'

'I hear he's giving us something pretty ambitious,' said the man Steggles. 'Big effects and all that sort of thing.'

'I believe so.'

'Of course, it means a lot to him, doesn't it? He's told you about the girl, of course?'

'Yes. And I hear you're laying seven to one against him,' I said, eyeing the blighter a trifle austerely.

He didn't even quiver.

'Just a little flutter to relieve the monotony of country life,' he said. 'But you've got the facts a bit wrong. It's down in the village that they're laying seven to one. I can do you better than that, if you feel in a speculative mood. How about a tenner at a hundred to eight?'

'Good Lord! Are you giving that?'

'Yes. Somehow,' said Steggles, meditatively, 'I have a sort of feeling, a kind of premonition, that something's going to go wrong tonight. You know what Little is. A bungler if ever there was one. Something tells me that this show of his is going to be a frost. And if it is, of course I should think it would prejudice the girl against him pretty badly. His standing always was rather shaky.'

'Are you going to try and smash up the show?' I said sternly.

'Me!' said Steggles. 'Why, what could I do? Half a minute, I want to go and speak to a man.'

He buzzed off, leaving me distinctly disturbed. I could see from the fellow's eye that he was meditating some of his customary rough stuff, and I thought Bingo ought to be warned. But there wasn't time and I couldn't get at him. Almost immediately after Steggles had left me the curtain went up.

Except as a prompter, Bingo wasn't much in evidence in the early part of the performance. The thing at the outset was merely one of those weird dramas which you dig out of books published around Christmas time and entitled 'Twelve Little Plays for the Tots', or something like that. The kids drooled on in the usual manner, the booming voice of Bingo ringing out from time to time behind the scenes when the fat-heads forgot their lines; and the audience was settling down into the sort of torpor usual on these occasions, when the first of Bingo's interpolated bits occurred. It was that number which What's-her-name sings in the revue at the Palace – you would recognise the tune if I hummed it, but I never can get hold of the dashed thing. It always got three encores at the Palace, and it went well now, even with a squeaky-voiced child jumping on and off the key like a chamois of the Alps leaping from crag to crag. Even the Tough Eggs liked it. At the end of the second refrain the entire house was shouting for an encore, and the kid with the voice like a slate-pencil took a deep breath and started to let it go once more.

At this point all the lights went out.

I don't know when I've had anything so sudden and devastating happen to me before. They didn't flicker. They just went out. The Hall was in complete darkness.

Well, of course, that sort of broke the spell, as you might put it. People started to shout directions, and the Tough Eggs stamped their feet and settled down for a pleasant time. And of course, young Bingo had to make an ass of himself. His voice suddenly shot at us out of the darkness.

'Ladies and gentlemen, something has gone wrong with the lights—'

The Tough Eggs were tickled by this bit of information straight from the stable. They took it up as a sort of battlecry. Then, after about five minutes, the lights went up again, and the show was resumed.

It took ten minutes after that to get the audience back into its state of coma, but eventually they began to settle down, and everything was going nicely when a small boy with a face like a turbot edged out in front of the curtain, which had been lowered after a pretty painful scene about a wishing ring or a fairy's curse or something of that sort, and started to sing that song of

George Thingummy's out of *Cuddle Up*. You know the one I mean. 'Always Listen to Mother, Girls!' it's called, and he gets the audience to join in and sing the refrain. Quite a ripeish ballad, and one which I myself have frequently sung in my bath with not a little vim; but by no means – as anyone but a perfect sap-headed prune like young Bingo would have known – by no means the sort of thing for a children's Christmas entertainment in the old Village Hall. Right from the start of the first refrain the bulk of the audience had begun to stiffen in their seats and fan themselves, and the Burgess girl at the piano was accompanying in a stunned, mechanical sort of way, while the curate at her side averted his gaze in a pained manner. The Tough Eggs, however, were all for it.

At the end of the second refrain the kid stopped and began to sidle towards the wings. Upon which the following brief duologue took place:

YOUNG BINGO *(Voice heard off, ringing against the rafters):* 'Go on!'
THE KID *(Coyly):* 'I don't like to.'
YOUNG BINGO *(Still louder):* 'Go on, you little blighter, or I'll slay you!'

I suppose the kid thought it over swiftly and realised that Bingo, being in a position to get at him, had better be conciliated whatever the harvest might be; for he shuffled down to the front and, having shut his eyes and giggled hysterically, said: 'Ladies and gentlemen, I will now call upon Squire Tressidder to oblige by singing the refrain!'

You know, with the most charitable feelings towards him, there are moments when you can't help thinking that young Bingo ought to be in some sort of a home. I suppose, poor fish, he had pictured this as the big punch of the evening. He had imagined, I take it, that the Squire would spring jovially to his feet, rip the song off his chest, and all would be gaiety and mirth.

Well, what happened was simply that old Tressidder – and, mark you, I'm not blaming him – just sat where he was, swelling and turning a brighter purple every second. The lower middle classes remained in frozen silence, waiting for the roof to fall. The only section of the audience that really seemed to enjoy the idea was the Tough Eggs, who yelled with enthusiasm. It was jam for the Tough Eggs.

And then the lights went out again.

When they went up, some minutes later, they disclosed the Squire marching stiffly out at the head of his family, fed up to the eyebrows; the Burgess girl at the piano with a pale, set look; and the curate gazing at her with something in his expression that seemed to suggest that, though all this was no doubt deplorable, he had spotted the silver lining.

The show went on once more. There were great chunks of Plays-for-the-Tots dialogue, and then the girl at the piano struck up the prelude to that Orange-Girl number that's the big hit of the Palace revue. I took it that this was to be Bingo's smashing act one finale. The entire company was on the stage, and a clutching hand had appeared round the edge of the curtain, ready to pull at the right moment. It looked like the finale all right. It wasn't long before I realised that it was something more. It was the finish.

I take it you know that Orange number at the Palace? It goes

Oh, won't you something something oranges,
  My something oranges,
  My something oranges;
Oh, won't you something something something I forget,
Something something something tumty tumty yet:
                                Oh—

or words to that effect. It's a dashed clever lyric, and the tune's good, too; but the thing that made the number was the business where the girls take oranges out of their baskets, you know, and toss them lightly to the audience. I don't know if you've ever noticed it, but it always seems to tickle an audience to bits when they get things thrown at them from the stage. Every time I've been to the Palace the customers have simply gone wild over this number.

But at the Palace, of course, the oranges are made of yellow wool and the girls don't so much chuck them as drop them limply into the first and second rows. I began to gather that the business was going to be treated rather differently tonight, when a dashed great chunk of pips and mildew sailed past my ear and burst on the wall behind me. Another landed with a squelch on the neck of one of the Nibs in the third row. And then a third took me right on the tip of the nose, and I kind of lost interest in the proceedings for awhile.

When I had scrubbed my face and got my eyes to stop watering for a moment, I saw that the evening's entertainment had begun to resemble one of Belfast's livelier nights. The air was thick with shrieks and fruit. The kids on the stage, with Bingo buzzing distractedly to and fro in their midst, were having the time of their lives. I suppose they realised that this couldn't go on for ever, and were making the most of their chances. The Tough Eggs had begun to pick up all the oranges that hadn't burst and were shooting them back, so that the audience got it both coming and going. In fact, take it all round, there was a certain amount of confusion; and, just as things had begun really to hot up, out went the lights again.

It seemed to me about my time for leaving, so I slid for the door. I was hardly outside when the audience began to stream out. They surged about me in twos and threes, and I've never seen a public body so dashed unanimous on any point. To a man – and to a woman – they were cursing poor old Bingo; and there was a large and rapidly growing school of thought which held that the best thing to do would be to waylay him as he emerged and splash him about in the village pond a bit.

There were such a dickens of a lot of these enthusiasts and they looked so jolly determined that it seemed to me that the only matey thing to do was to go behind and warn young Bingo to turn his coat-collar up and breeze off shakily by some side-exit. I went behind, and found him sitting on a box in the wings, perspiring pretty freely and looking more or less like the spot marked with a cross where the accident happened. His hair was standing up and his ears were hanging down, and one harsh word would undoubtedly have made him burst into tears.

'Bertie,' he said hollowly, as he saw me, 'it was that blighter Steggles! I caught one of the kids before he could get away and got it all out of him. Steggles substituted real oranges for the balls of wool which with infinite sweat and at a cost of nearly a quid I had specially prepared. Well, I will now proceed to tear him limb from limb. It'll be something to do.'

I hated to spoil his day-dreams, but it had to be. 'Good heavens, man,' I said, 'you haven't time for frivolous amusements now. You've got to get out. And quick!'

'Bertie,' said Bingo in a dull voice, 'she was here just now. She said it was all my fault and that she would never speak to me again. She said she had always suspected me of being a heartless practical joker, and now she knew. She said – Oh, well, she ticked me off properly.'

'That's the least of your troubles,' I said. It seemed impossible to rouse the poor zib to a sense of his position. 'Do you realise that about two hundred of Twing's heftiest are waiting for you outside to chuck you into the pond?'

'No!'

'Absolutely!'

For a moment the poor chap seemed crushed. But only for a moment. There has always been something of the good old English bulldog breed about Bingo. A strange, sweet smile flickered for an instant over his face.

'It's all right,' he said. 'I can sneak out through the cellar and climb over the wall at the back. They can't intimidate *me*!'

*

It couldn't have been more than a week later when Jeeves, after he had brought me my tea, gently steered me away from the sporting page of the *Morning Post* and directed my attention to an announcement in the engagements and marriages column.

It was a brief statement that a marriage had been arranged and would shortly take place between the Hon. and Rev. Hubert Wingham, third son of the Right Hon. the Earl of Sturridge, and Mary, only daughter of the late Matthew Burgess, of Weatherly Court, Hants.

'Of course,' I said, after I had given it the east-to-west, 'I expected this, Jeeves.'

'Yes, sir.'

'She would never forgive him what happened that night.'

'No, sir.'

'Well,' I said, as I took a sip of the fragrant and steaming, 'I don't suppose it will take old Bingo long to get over it. It's about the hundred and eleventh time this sort of thing has happened to him. You're the man I'm sorry for.'

'Me, sir?'

'Well, dash it all, you can't have forgotten what a deuce of a lot of trouble you took to bring the thing off for Bingo. It's too bad that all your work should have been wasted.'

'Not entirely wasted, sir.'

'Eh?'

'It is true that my efforts to bring about the match between Mr. Little and the young lady were not successful, but still I look back upon the matter with a certain satisfaction.'

'Because you did your best, you mean?'

'Not entirely, sir, though of course that thought also gives me pleasure. I was alluding more particularly to the fact that I found the affair financially remunerative.'

'Financially remunerative? What do you mean?'

'When I learned that Mr. Steggles had interested himself in the contest, sir, I went shares with my friend Brookfield and bought the book which had been made on the issue by the landlord of the Cow and Horses. It has proved a highly profitable investment. Your breakfast will be ready almost immediately, sir. Kidneys on toast and mushrooms. I will bring it when you ring.'

The feeling I had when Aunt Agatha trapped me in my lair that morning and spilled the bad news was that my luck had broken at last. As a rule, you see, I'm not lugged into family rows. On the occasions when Aunt is calling to Aunt like mastodons bellowing across primeval swamps and Uncle James's letter about Cousin Mabel's peculiar behaviour is being shot round the family circle ('Please read this carefully and send it on to Jane,') the clan has a tendency to ignore me. It's one of the advantages I get from being a bachelor – and, according to my nearest and dearest, practically a half-witted bachelor at that. 'It's no good trying to get Bertie to take the slightest interest' is more or less the slogan, and I'm bound to say I'm all for it. A quiet life is what I like. And that's why I felt that the curse had come upon me, so to speak, when Aunt Agatha sailed into my sitting-room while I was having a placid cigarette and started to tell me about Claude and Eustace.

I rather fancy I've touched on Claude and Eustace before in these little reminiscences of mine. My cousins, if you remember. Was at school with them when they were kids, and saved them from being sacked on no fewer than three separate occasions. Since they've been up at Oxford I haven't seen so much of them, but what I have seen has been quite tolerably sufficient. Bright lads, mind you, but a trifle too much for a fellow like me who wants to jog along peacefully through life.

'Thank goodness,' said Aunt Agatha, 'arrangements have at last been made about Eustace and Claude.'

'Arrangements?' I said, not having the foggiest.

'They sail on Friday for South Africa. Mr. Van Alstyne, a friend of poor Emily's, has given them berths in his firm at Johannesburg, and we are hoping that they will settle down there and do well.'

I didn't get the thing at all.

'Friday? The day after tomorrow, do you mean?'

'Yes.'

'For South Africa?'

'Yes. They leave on the *Edinburgh Castle*.'

'But what's the idea? I mean, aren't they in the middle of their term at Oxford?'

Aunt Agatha looked at me coldly.

'Do you positively mean to tell me, Bertie, that you take so little interest in the affairs of your nearest relatives that you are not aware that Claude and Eustace were expelled from Oxford over a fortnight ago?'

'No, really?'

'You are hopeless, Bertie. I should have thought that even you—'

'Why were they sent down?'

'They poured lemonade on the Junior Dean of their college ... I see nothing amusing in the outrage, Bertie.'

'No, no, rather not,' I said, hurriedly. 'I wasn't laughing. Choking. Got something stuck in my throat, you know.'

'Poor Emily,' went on Aunt Agatha, 'being one of those doting mothers who are the ruin of their children, wished to keep the boys in London. She suggested that they might cram for the Army. But I was firm. The Colonies are the only place for wild youths like Eustace and Claude. So they sail on Friday. They have been staying for the last two weeks with your Uncle Clive in Worcestershire. They will spend tomorrow night in London and catch the boat-train on Friday morning.'

'Bit risky, isn't it? I mean, aren't they apt to cut loose a bit tomorrow night if they're left all alone in London?'

'They will not be alone. They will be in your charge.'

'Mine!'

'Yes. I wish you to put them up in your flat for the night, and see that they do not miss the train in the morning.'

'Oh, I say, no!'

'Bertie!'

'Well, I mean, quite jolly coves both of them, but I don't know – They're rather nuts, you know. Always glad to see them, of course, but when it comes to putting them up for the night—'

'Bertie, if you are so sunk in callous self-indulgence that you cannot even put yourself to this trifling inconvenience for the sake of—'

'Oh, all right,' I said. 'All right.'

It was no good arguing, of course. Aunt Agatha always makes me feel as if I had gelatine where my spine ought to be. When she holds me with her glittering eye and says, 'Jump to it, my lad,' or words to that effect, I make it so without further discussion.

When she had gone I rang for Jeeves to break the news to him.

'Oh, Jeeves,' I said, 'Mr. Claude and Mr. Eustace will be staying here tomorrow night.'

'Very good, sir.'

'I'm glad you think so. To me the outlook seems black and scaly. You know what those two lads are!'

'Very high-spirited young gentlemen, sir.'

'Blisters, Jeeves. Undeniable blisters. It's a bit thick!'

'Would there be anything further, sir?'

At that, I'm bound to say, I drew myself up a trifle haughtily. We Woosters freeze like the dickens when we seek sympathy and meet with cold reserve. I knew what was up, of course. For the last day or so there had been a certain amount of coolness in the home over a pair of jazz spats which I had dug up while exploring in the Burlington Arcade. Some dashed brainy cove, probably the chap who invented those coloured cigarette-cases, had recently had the rather topping idea of putting out a line of spats on the same system. I mean to say, instead of the ordinary grey and white, you can now get them in your regimental or school colours. And, believe me, it would have taken a man of stronger fibre than I am to resist the pair of Old Etonian spats which had smiled up at me from inside the window. I was inside the shop, opening negotiations, before it had even occurred to me that Jeeves might not approve. And I must say he had taken the thing a bit hardly. The fact of the matter is, Jeeves, though in many ways the best valet in London is too conservative. Hidebound, if you know what I mean, and an enemy to Progress.

'Nothing further, Jeeves,' I said, with quiet dignity.

'Very good, sir.'

He gave one frosty look at the spats and biffed off. Dash him!

Anything merrier and brighter than the twins, when they curveted into the old flat while I was dressing for dinner the next night, I have never struck in my whole puff. I'm only about four years older than Claude and Eustace, but in some rummy manner they always make me feel as if I were well on in the grandfather class and just waiting for the end. Almost before I realised they were in the place they had collared the best chairs, pinched a couple of my special cigarettes, poured themselves out a whisky-and-soda apiece, and started to prattle with the gaiety and abandon of two birds who had achieved their life's ambition instead of having come a most frightful purler and being under sentence of exile.

'Hallo, Bertie, old thing!' said Claude. 'Jolly decent of you to put us up.'

'Oh, no,' I said. (Always the gentleman.) 'Only wish you were staying a good long time.'

'Hear that, Eustace? He wishes we were staying a good long time.'

'I expect it will seem a good long time,' said Eustace, philosophically.

'You heard about the binge, Bertie? Our little bit of trouble, I mean?'

'Oh, yes. Aunt Agatha was telling me.'

'We leave our country for our country's good,' said Eustace.

'And let there be no moaning at the bar,' said Claude, 'when I put out to sea. What did Aunt Agatha tell you?'

'She said you poured lemonade on the Junior Dean.'

'I wish the deuce,' said Claude, annoyed, 'that people would get these things right. It wasn't the Junior Dean. It was the Senior Tutor.'

'And it wasn't lemonade,' said Eustace. 'It was soda-water. The dear old thing happened to be standing just under our window while I was leaning out with a siphon in my hand. He looked up, and – well, it would have been chucking away the opportunity of a lifetime if I hadn't let him have it in the eyeball.'

'Simply chucking it away,' agreed Claude.

'Might never have occurred again,' said Eustace.

'Hundred to one against it,' said Claude.

'Now what,' said Eustace, 'do you propose to do, Bertie, in the way of entertaining the handsome guests tonight?'

'My idea was to have a bite of dinner in the flat,' I said. 'Jeeves is getting it ready now.'

'And afterwards?'

'Well, I thought we might chat of this and that, and then it struck me that you would probably like to turn in early, as your train goes about ten or something, doesn't it?'

The twins gazed at each other in a pitying sort of way.

'Bertie,' said Eustace, 'you've got the programme nearly right, but not quite. I envisage the evening's events thus. We will toddle along to Ciro's after dinner. It's an extension night, isn't it? Well, that will see us through till about two-thirty or three.'

'After which, no doubt,' said Claude, 'the Lord will provide.'

'But I thought you would want to get a good night's rest.'

'Good night's rest!' said Eustace. 'My dear old chap, you don't for a moment imagine that we are dreaming of going to *bed* tonight, do you?'

I suppose the fact of the matter is, I'm not the man I was. I mean, these all-night vigils don't seem to fascinate me as they used to a few years ago. Nowadays two o'clock is about my limit; and by two o'clock the twins were just settling down and beginning to go nicely. As far as I can remember, we went on from Ciro's to play chemmy with some fellows I don't recall having met before, and it must have been about nine in the morning when we fetched up again at the flat. By which time, I'm bound to admit, as far as I was concerned, the first careless freshness was beginning to wear off a bit. In fact, I'd got just enough strength to say good-bye to the twins, wish them a pleasant voyage and a happy and successful career in South Africa, and stagger into bed. The last I remember was hearing the blighters chanting like larks under the cold shower, breaking off from time to time to shout to Jeeves to rush along the eggs and bacon.

It must have been about one in the afternoon when I woke. I was feeling more or less like something the Pure Food Committee had rejected, but there was one bright thought which cheered me up, and that was that about now the twins would be leaning on the rail of the liner, taking their last glimpse of the dear old homeland. Which made it all the more of a shock when the door opened and Claude walked in.

'Hallo, Bertie!' said Claude. 'Had a nice refreshing sleep? Now, what about a good old bite of lunch?'

I'd been having so many distorted nightmares since I had dropped off to sleep that for half a minute I thought this was simply one more of them, and the worst of the lot. It was only when Claude sat down on my feet that I got on to the fact that this was stern reality.

'Great Scott! What on earth are you doing here?' I gurgled.

Claude looked at me reproachfully.

'Hardly the tone I like to hear in a host, Bertie,' he said, reprovingly. 'Why, it was only last night that you were saying you wished I was stopping a good long time. Your dream has come true. I am!'

'But why aren't you on your way to South Africa?'

'Now that,' said Claude, 'is a point I rather thought you would want to have explained. It's like this, old man. You remember that girl you introduced me to at Ciro's last night?'

'Which girl?'

'There was only one,' said Claude, coldly. 'Only one that counted, that is to say. Her name was Marion Wardour. I danced with her a good deal, if you remember.'

I began to recollect in a hazy sort of way. Marion Wardour has been a pal of mine for some time. A very good sort. She's playing in that show at the Apollo at the moment. I remembered now that she had been at Ciro's with a party the night before, and the twins had insisted on being introduced.

'We are soul-mates, Bertie,' said Claude. 'I found it out quite early in the p.m., and the more thought I've given to the matter the more convinced I've become. It happens like that now and then, you know. Two hearts that beat as one, I mean, and all that sort of thing. So the long and the short of it is that I gave old Eustace the slip at Waterloo and slid back here. The idea of going to South Africa and leaving a girl like that in England doesn't appeal to me a bit. I'm all for thinking imperially and giving the Colonies a leg-up and all that sort of thing; but it can't be done. After all,' said Claude, reasonably, 'South Africa has got along all right without me up till now, so why shouldn't it stick it?'

'But what about Van Alstyne, or whatever his name is? He'll be expecting you to turn up.'

'Oh, he'll have Eustace. That'll satisfy him. Very sound fellow, Eustace. Probably end up by being a magnate of some kind. I shall watch his future progress with considerable interest.

And now you must excuse me for a moment, Bertie. I want to go and hunt up Jeeves and get him to mix me one of those pick-me-ups of his. For some reason which I can't explain, I've got a slight headache this morning.'

And, believe me or believe me not, the door had hardly closed behind him when in blew Eustace with a shining morning face that made me ill to look at.

'Oh, my aunt!' I said.

Eustace started to giggle pretty freely.

'Smooth work, Bertie, smooth work!' he said. 'I'm sorry for poor old Claude, but there was no alternative. I eluded his vigilance at Waterloo and snaked off in a taxi. I suppose the poor old ass is wondering where the deuce I've got to. But it couldn't be helped. If you really seriously expected me to go slogging off to South Africa, you shouldn't have introduced me to Miss Wardour last night. I want to tell you all about that, Bertie. I'm not a man,' said Eustace, sitting down on the bed, 'who falls in love with every girl he sees. I suppose "strong, silent" would be the best description you could find for me. But when I do meet my affinity I don't waste time. I—'

'Oh, heavens! Are you in love with Marion Wardour, too?'

'Too? What do you mean, "too"?'

I was going to tell him about Claude, when the blighter came in in person, looking like a giant refreshed. There's no doubt that Jeeves's pick-me-ups will produce immediate results in anything short of an Egyptian mummy. It's something he puts in them – the Worcester sauce or something. Claude had revived like a watered flower, but he nearly had a relapse when he saw his bally brother goggling at him over the bedrail.

'What on earth are you doing here?' he said.

'What on earth are *you* doing here?' said Eustace.

'Have you come back to inflict your beastly society upon Miss Wardour?'

'Is that why you've come back?'

They thrashed the subject out a bit further.

'Well,' said Claude, at last, 'I suppose it can't be helped. If you're here, you're here. May the best man win!'

'Yes, but dash it all!' I managed to put in at this point. 'What's the idea? Where do you think you're going to stay if you stick on in London?'

'Why, here,' said Eustace, surprised.

'Where else?' said Claude, raising his eyebrows.

'You won't object to putting us up, Bertie?' said Eustace.

'Not a sportsman like you,' said Claude.

'But, you silly asses, suppose Aunt Agatha finds out that I'm hiding you when you ought to be in South Africa? Where do I get off?'

'Where *does* he get off?' Claude asked Eustace.

'Oh, I expect he'll manage somehow,' said Eustace to Claude.

'Of course,' said Claude, quite cheered up. 'He'll manage.'

'Rather!' said Eustace. 'A resourceful chap like Bertie! Of course he will.'

'And now,' said Claude, shelving the subject, 'what about that bite of lunch we were discussing a moment ago, Bertie? That stuff good old Jeeves slipped into me just now has given me what you might call an appetite. Something in the nature of six chops and a batter pudding would about meet the case, I think.'

I suppose every fellow in the world has black periods in his life to which he can't look back without the smouldering eye and the silent shudder. Some coves, if you can judge by the novels you read nowadays, have them practically all the time; but, what with enjoying a sizable private income and a topping digestion, I'm bound to say it isn't very often I find my own existence getting a flat tyre. That's why this particular epoch is one that I don't think about more often than I can help. For the days that followed the unexpected resurrection of the blighted twins were so absolutely foul that the old nerves began to stick out of my body a foot long and curling at the ends. All of a twitter, believe me. I imagine the fact of the matter is that we Woosters are so frightfully honest and open and all that, that it gives us the pip to have to deceive.

All was quiet along the Potomac for about twenty-four hours, and then Aunt Agatha trickled in to have a chat. Twenty minutes earlier and she would have found the twins gaily shoving themselves outside a couple of rashers and an egg. She sank into a chair, and I could see that she was not in her usual sunny spirits.

'Bertie,' she said, 'I am uneasy.'

So was I. I didn't know how long she intended to stop, or when the twins were coming back.

'I wonder,' she said, 'if I took too harsh a view towards Claude and Eustace.'

'You couldn't.'

'What do you mean?'

'I – er – mean it would be so unlike you to be harsh to anybody, Aunt Agatha.' And not bad, either. I mean, quick – like that – without thinking. It pleased the old relative, and she looked at me with slightly less loathing than she usually does.

'It is nice of you to say that, Bertie, but what I was thinking was, are they *safe*?'

'Are they *what*?'

It seemed such a rummy adjective to apply to the twins, they being about as innocuous as a couple of sprightly young tarantulas.

'Do you think all is well with them?'

'How do you mean?'

Aunt Agatha eyed me almost wistfully.

'Has it ever occurred to you, Bertie,' she said, 'that your Uncle George may be psychic?'

She seemed to me to be changing the subject.

'Psychic?'

'Do you think it is possible that he could *see* things not visible to the normal eye?'

I thought it dashed possible, if not probable. I don't know if you've ever met my Uncle George. He's a festive old egg who wanders from club to club continually having a couple with other festive old eggs. When he heaves in sight, waiters brace themselves up and the wine-steward toys with his corkscrew. It was my Uncle George who discovered that alcohol was a food well in advance of modern medical thought.

'Your Uncle George was dining with me last night, and he was quite shaken. He declares that, while on his way from the Devonshire Club to Boodle's, he suddenly saw the phantasm of Eustace.'

'The what of Eustace?'

'The phantasm. The wraith. It was so clear that he thought for an instant that it was Eustace himself. The figure vanished round a corner, and when Uncle George got there nothing was to be seen. It is all very queer and disturbing. It had a marked effect on poor George. All through dinner he touched nothing but barley-water, and his manner was quite disturbed. You do think those poor, dear boys are safe, Bertie? They have not met with some horrible accident?'

It made my mouth water to think of it, but I said no, I didn't think they had met with any horrible accident. I thought Eustace was a horrible accident, and Claude about the same, but I didn't say so. And presently she biffed off, still worried.

When the twins came in, I put it squarely to the blighters. Jolly as it was to give Uncle George shocks, they must not wander at large about the metrop.

'But, my dear old soul,' said Claude, 'be reasonable. We can't have our movements hampered.'

'Out of the question,' said Eustace.

'The whole essence of the thing, if you understand me,' said Claude, 'is that we should be at liberty to flit hither and thither.'

'Exactly,' said Eustace. 'Now hither, now thither.'

'But, damn it—'

'Bertie!!' said Eustace, reprovingly. 'Not before the boy!'

'Of course, in a way I see his point,' said Claude. 'I suppose the solution of the problem would be to buy a couple of disguises.'

'My dear old chap!' said Eustace, looking at him with admiration. 'The brightest idea on record. Not your own, surely?'

'Well, as a matter of fact, it was Bertie who put it into my head.'

'Me!'

'You were telling me the other day about old Bingo Little and the beard he bought when he didn't want his uncle to recognise him.'

'If you think I'm going to have you two excrescences popping in and out of my flat in beards—'

'Something in that,' agreed Eustace. 'We'll make it whiskers, then.'

'And false noses,' said Claude.

'And, as you say, false noses. Right-o, then, Bertie, old chap, that's a load off your mind. We don't want to be any trouble to you while we're paying you this little visit.'

And when I went buzzing round to Jeeves for consolation, all he would say was something about Young Blood. No sympathy.

'Very good, Jeeves,' I said. 'I shall go for a walk in the Park. Kindly put me out the Old Etonian spats.'

'Very good, sir.'

It must have been a couple of days after that that Marion Wardour rolled in at about the hour of tea. She looked warily round the room before sitting down.

'Your cousins not at home, Bertie?' she said.

'No, thank goodness!'

'Then I'll tell you where they are. They're in my sitting-room, glaring at each other from opposite corners, waiting for me to come in. Bertie, this has got to stop.'

'You're seeing a good deal of them, are you?'

Jeeves came in with the tea, but the poor girl was so worked up that she didn't wait for him to pop off before going on with her complaint. She had an absolutely hunted air, poor thing.

'I can't move a step without tripping over one or both of them,' she said. 'Generally both. They've taken to calling together, and they just settle down grimly and try to sit each other out. It's wearing me to a shadow.'

'I know,' I said, sympathetically. 'I know.'

'Well, what's to be done?'

'It beats me. Couldn't you tell your maid to say you are not at home?'

She shuddered slightly.

'I tried that once. They camped on the stairs, and I couldn't get out all the afternoon. And I had a lot of particularly important engagements. I wish you would persuade them to go to South Africa, where they seem to be wanted.'

'You must have made the dickens of an impression on them!'

'I should say I have. They've started giving me presents now. At least, Claude has. He insisted on my accepting this cigarette-case last night. Came round to the theatre and wouldn't go away till I took it. It's not a bad one, I must say.'

It wasn't. It was a distinctly fruity concern in gold with a diamond stuck in the middle. And the rummy thing was that I had a notion I'd seen something very like it before somewhere. How the deuce Claude had been able to dig up the cash to buy a thing like that was more than I could imagine.

Next day was a Wednesday, and as the object of their devotion had a *matinée*, the twins were, so to speak, off duty. Claude had gone with his whiskers on to Hurst Park, and Eustace and I were in the flat, talking. At least, he was talking and I was wishing he would go.

'The love of a good woman, Bertie,' he was saying, 'must be a wonderful thing. Sometimes – Good Lord! what's that?'

The front door had opened, and from out in the hall there came the sound of Aunt Agatha's voice asking if I was in. Aunt Agatha has one of those high, penetrating voices, but this was the first time I'd ever been thankful for it. There was just about two seconds to clear the way for her, but it was long enough for Eustace to dive under the sofa. His last shoe had just disappeared when she came in.

She had a worried look. It seemed to me about this time that everybody had.

'Bertie,' she said, 'what are your immediate plans?'

'How do you mean? I'm dining tonight with—'

'No, no. I don't mean tonight. Are you busy for the next few days? But of course you are not,' she went on, not waiting for me to answer. 'You never have anything to do. Your whole life is spent in idle – but we can got into that later. What I came for this afternoon was to tell you that I wish you to go with your poor Uncle George to Harrogate for a few weeks. The sooner you can start the better.'

This appeared to me to approximate so closely to the frozen limit that I uttered a yelp of protest. Uncle George is all right, but he won't do. I was trying to say as much when she waved me down.

'If you are not entirely heartless, Bertie, you will do as I ask you. Your poor Uncle George has had a severe shock.'

'What, another!'

'He feels that only complete rest and careful medical attendance can restore his nervous system to its normal poise. It seems that in the past he has derived benefit from taking the waters at Harrogate, and he wishes to go there now. We do not think he ought to be alone, so I wish you to accompany him.'

'But, I say!'

'Bertie!'

There was a lull in the conversation.

'What shock has he had?' I said.

'Between ourselves,' said Aunt Agatha, lowering her voice in an impressive manner, 'I incline to think that the whole affair was the outcome of an overexcited imagination. You are one of the family, Bertie, and I can speak freely to you. You know as well as I do that your poor Uncle George has for many years *not* been a – he has – er – developed a habit of – how shall I put it?'

'Shifting it a bit?'

'I beg your pardon?'

'Mopping up the stuff to some extent?'

'I dislike your way of putting it exceedingly, but I must confess that he has not been, perhaps, as temperate as he should. He is highly strung, and – Well, the fact is that he has had a shock.'

'Yes, but what?'

'That is what it is so hard to induce him to explain with any precision. With all his good points, your poor Uncle George is apt to become incoherent when strongly moved. As far as I could gather, he appears to have been the victim of a burglary.'

'Burglary!'

'He says that a strange man with whiskers and a peculiar nose entered his rooms in Jermyn Street during his absence and stole some of his property. He says that he came back and found the man in his sitting-room. He immediately rushed out of the room and disappeared.'

'Uncle George?'

'No, the man. And, according to your Uncle George, he had stolen a valuable cigarette-case. But, as I say, I am inclined to think that the whole thing was imagination. He has not been himself since the day when he fancied that he saw Eustace in the street. So I should like you, Bertie, to be prepared to start for Harrogate with him not later than Saturday.'

She popped off, and Eustace crawled out from under the sofa. The blighter was strongly moved. So was I, for the matter of that. The idea of several weeks with Uncle George at Harrogate seemed to make everything go black.

'So that's where he got that cigarette-case, dash him!' said Eustace, bitterly. 'Of all the dirty tricks! Robbing his own flesh and blood! The fellow ought to be in chokey.'

'He ought to be in South Africa,' I said. 'And so ought you.'

And with an eloquence which rather surprised me, I hauled up my slacks for perhaps ten minutes on the subject of his duty to his family and what not. I appealed to his sense of decency. I boosted South Africa with vim. I said everything I could think of, much of it twice over. But all the blighter did was to babble about his dashed brother's baseness in putting one over on him in the matter of the cigarette-case. He seemed to think that Claude, by slinging in the handsome gift, had got right ahead of him; and there was a painful scene when the latter came back from Hurst Park. I could hear them talking half the night, long after I had tottered off to bed. I don't know when I've met fellows who could do with less sleep than those two.

After this things became a bit strained at the flat, owing to Claude and Eustace not being on speaking terms. I'm all for a certain chumminess in the home, and it was wearing to have to live with two fellows who wouldn't admit that the other one was on the map at all.

One felt the thing couldn't go on like that for long, and, by Jove, it didn't. But, if anyone had come to me the day before and told me what was going to happen, I should simply have smiled wanly. I mean, I'd got so accustomed to thinking that nothing short of a dynamite explosion could ever dislodge those two nestlers from my midst that, when Claude sidled up to me on the Friday morning and told me his bit of news, I could hardly believe I was hearing right.

'Bertie,' he said, 'I've been thinking it over.'

'What over?' I said.

'The whole thing. This business of staying in London when I ought to be in South Africa. It isn't fair,' said Claude, warmly. 'It isn't right. And the long and the short of it is, Bertie, old man, I'm leaving tomorrow.'

I reeled in my tracks.

'You are?' I gasped.

'Yes. If,' said Claude, 'you won't mind sending old Jeeves out to buy a ticket for me. I'm afraid I'll have to stick you for the passage money, old man. You don't mind?'

'Mind!' I said, clutching his hand fervently.

'That's all right, then. Oh, I say, you won't say a word to Eustace about this, will you?'

'But isn't he going, too?'

Claude shuddered.

'No, thank Heaven! The idea of being cooped up on board a ship with that blighter gives me the pip just to think of it. No, not a word to Eustace. I say, I suppose you can get me a berth all right at such short notice?'

'Rather!' I said. Sooner than let this opportunity slip, I would have bought the bally boat.

'Jeeves,' I said, breezing into the kitchen, 'go out on first speed to the Union-Castle offices and book a berth on tomorrow's boat for Mr. Claude. He is leaving us, Jeeves.'

'Yes, sir.'

'Mr. Claude does not wish any mention of this to be made to Mr. Eustace.'

'No, sir. Mr. Eustace made the same proviso when he desired me to obtain a berth on tomorrow's boat for himself.'

I gaped at the man.

'Is he going, too?'

'Yes, sir.'

'This is rummy.'

'Yes, sir.'

Had circumstances been other than they were, I would at this juncture have unbent considerably towards Jeeves. Frisked round him a bit and whooped to a certain extent and what not. But those spats still formed a barrier, and I regret to say that I took the opportunity of rather rubbing it in a bit on the man. I mean, he'd been so dashed aloof and unsympathetic, though perfectly aware that the young master was in the soup and that it was up to him to rally round, that I couldn't help pointing out how the happy ending had been snaffled without any help from him.

'So that's that, Jeeves,' I said. 'The episode is concluded. I knew things would sort themselves out if one gave them time and didn't get rattled. Many chaps in my place would have got rattled, Jeeves.'

'Yes, sir.'

'Gone rushing about, I mean, asking people for help and advice and so forth.'

'Very possibly, sir.'

'But not me, Jeeves.'

'No, sir.'

I left him to brood on it.

Even the thought that I'd got to go to Harrogate with Uncle George couldn't depress me that Saturday when I gazed about the old flat and realised that Claude and Eustace weren't in it. They had slunk off stealthily and separately immediately after breakfast, Eustace to catch the boat-train at Waterloo, Claude to go round to the garage where I kept my car. I didn't want any chance of the two meeting at Waterloo and changing their minds, so I had suggested to Claude that he might find it pleasanter to drive down to Southampton.

I was lying back on the old settee, gazing peacefully up at the flies on the ceiling and feeling what a wonderful world this was, when Jeeves came in with a letter. 'A messenger-boy has brought this, sir.'

I opened the envelope, and the first thing that fell out was a five-pound note.

'Great Scott!' I said. 'What's all this?'

The letter was scribbled in pencil, and was quite brief:

'Dear Bertie. – Will you give enclosed to your man, and tell him I wish I could make it more. He has saved my life. This is the first happy day I've had for a week.

'Yours,

'M.W.'

Jeeves was standing holding out the fiver, which had fluttered to the floor.

'You'd better stick to it,' I said. 'It seems to be for you.'

'Sir?'

'I say that fiver is for you, apparently. Miss Wardour sent it.'

'That was extremely kind of her, sir.'

'What the dickens is she sending you fivers for? She says you saved her life.'

Jeeves smiled gently.

'She over-estimates my services, sir.'

'But what *were* your services, dash it?'

'It was in the matter of Mr. Claude and Mr. Eustace, sir. I was hoping that she would not refer to the matter, as I did not wish you to think that I had been taking a liberty.'

'What do you mean?'

'I chanced to be in the room while Miss Wardour was complaining with some warmth of the manner in which Mr. Claude and Mr. Eustace were thrusting their society upon her. I felt that in the circumstances it might be excusable if I suggested a slight ruse to enable her to dispense with their attentions.'

'Good Lord! You don't mean to say you were at the bottom of their popping off, after all?'

Silly ass it made me feel. I mean, after rubbing it into him like that about having clicked without his assistance.

'It occurred to me that, were Miss Wardour to inform Mr. Claude and Mr. Eustace independently that she proposed sailing for South Africa to take up a theatrical engagement, the desired effect might be produced. It appears that my anticipations were correct, sir. The young gentlemen ate it, if I may use the expression.'

'Jeeves,' I said – we Woosters may make bloomers, but we are never too proud to admit it – 'you stand alone!'

'Thank you very much, sir.'

'Oh, but I say!' A ghastly thought had struck me. 'When they get on the boat and find she isn't there, won't they come buzzing back?'

'I anticipated that possibility, sir. At my suggestion, Miss Wardour informed the young gentlemen that she proposed to travel by another boat to Madeira and join the vessel there.'

'And where do they touch after Madeira?'

'Nowhere, sir.'

For a moment I just lay back, letting the idea of the thing soak in. There seemed to me to be only one flaw.

'The only pity is,' I said, 'that on a large boat like that they will be able to avoid each other. I mean, I should have liked to feel that Claude was having a good deal of Eustace's society, and *vice versa*.'

'I fancy that that will be so, sir. I secured a two-berth stateroom. Mr. Claude will occupy one berth, Mr. Eustace the other.'

I sighed with pure ecstasy. It seemed a dashed shame that on this joyful occasion I should have to go off to Harrogate with my Uncle George.

'Have you started packing yet, Jeeves?' I asked.

'Packing sir?'

'For Harrogate. I've got to go there today with my Uncle George.'

'Of course, yes, sir. I forgot to mention it. His lordship rang up on the telephone this morning while you were still asleep, and said that he had changed his plans. He does not intend to go to Harrogate.'

'Oh, I say, how absolutely topping!'

'I thought you might be pleased, sir.'

'What made him change his plans? Did he say?'

'No, sir. But I gather from his man, Stevens, that he is feeling much better and does not now require a rest-cure. I took the liberty of giving Stevens the recipe for that pick-me-up of mine, of which you have always approved so much. Stevens tells me that His lordship informed him this morning that he is feeling a new man.'

Well, there was only one thing to do, and I did it. I'm not saying it didn't hurt, but there was no alternative.

'Jeeves,' I said, 'those spats.'

'Yes, sir?'

'You really dislike them?'

'Intensely, sir.'

'You don't think time might induce you to change your views?'

'No, sir.'

'All right, then. Very well. Say no more. You may burn them.'

'Thank you very much, sir. I have already done so. Before breakfast this morning. A quiet grey is far more suitable, sir. Thank you, sir.'

I ran into young Bingo Little in the smoking-room of the Senior Liberal Club. He was lying back in an arm-chair with his mouth open and a sort of goofy expression in his eyes, while a grey-bearded cove in the middle distance watched him with so much dislike that I concluded that Bingo had pinched his favourite seat. That's the worst of being in a strange club – absolutely without intending it, you find yourself constantly trampling upon the vested interests of the Oldest Inhabitants.

'Hallo, face!' I said.

'Cheerio, ugly!' said young Bingo, and we settled down to have a small one before lunch.

Once a year the committee of the Drones decides that the old club could do with a wash and brush-up, so they shoo us out, and dump us down for a few weeks at some other institution. This time we were roosting at the Senior Liberal, and, personally, I had found the strain pretty fearful. I mean, when you've got used to a club where everything's nice and cheery, and where, if you want to attract a fellow's attention, you heave a bit of bread at him, it kind of damps you to come to a place where the youngest member is about eighty-seven, and it isn't considered good form to talk to anyone unless you and he were through the Peninsular War together. It was a relief to come across Bingo. We started to talk in hushed voices.

'This club,' I said, 'is the limit.'

'It is the eel's eyebrows,' agreed young Bingo. 'I believe that old boy over by the window has been dead three days, but I don't like to mention it to anyone.'

'Have you lunched here yet?'

'No. Why?'

'They have waitresses instead of waiters.'

'Good Lord! I thought that went out with the Armistice.' Bingo mused a moment, straightening his tie absently. 'Er – pretty girls?' he said.

'No.'

He seemed disappointed, but pulled round.

'Well, I've heard that the cooking's the best in London.'

'So they say. Shall we be going in?'

'All right. I expect,' said young Bingo, 'that at the end of the meal – or possibly at the beginning – the waitress will say: "Both together, sir?" Reply in the affirmative. I haven't a bean.'

'Hasn't your uncle forgiven you yet?'

'Not yet, confound him!'

You see, young Bingo had had a bit of a dust-up with Lord Bittlesham, his uncle, some time earlier, resulting in his allowance being knocked off. I was sorry to hear the row was still on. I resolved to do the poor old thing well at the festive board, and I scanned the menu with some intentness when the girl rolled up with it.

'How would this do you, Bingo?' I said at length. 'A few hors d'oeuvres to weigh in with, a cup of soup, a touch of cold salmon, some cold curry, and a splash of gooseberry tart and cream, with a bite of cheese to finish?'

I don't know that I had expected the man actually to scream with delight, though I had picked the items from my knowledge of his pet dishes, but I had expected him to say something. I looked up, and found that his attention was elsewhere. He was gazing at the waitress with the look of a dog that's just remembered where its bone was buried.

She was a tallish girl with sort of soft, soulful brown eyes. Nice figure and all that. Rather decent hands, too. I didn't remember having seen her about before, and I must say she raised the standard of the place quite a bit.

'How about it, laddie?' I said, being all for getting the order booked and going on to the serious knife-and-fork work.

'Eh?' said young Bingo, absently.

I recited the programme once more.

'Oh, yes, fine,' said Bingo. 'Anything, anything!' The girl pushed off, and he turned to me with protruding eyes. 'I thought you said they weren't pretty, Bertie?' he said, reproachfully.

'Oh, my heavens!' I said. 'You surely haven't fallen in love again – and with a girl you've only just seen?'

'There are times, Bertie,' said young Bingo, 'when a look is enough – when, passing through a crowd, we meet somebody's eye and something seems to whisper—'

At this point the hors d'oeuvres arrived, and he suspended his remarks in order to swoop on them with some vigour.

'Jeeves,' I said that night when I got home, 'stand by.'

'Sir?'

'Burnish the old brain, and be alert and vigilant. I suspect that Mr. Little will be calling round shortly for sympathy and assistance.'

'Is Mr. Little in trouble, sir?'

'Well, you might call it that. He's in love. For about the fifty-third time. I ask you, Jeeves, as man to man, did you ever see such a chap?'

'Mr. Little is certainly warm-hearted, sir.'

'Warm-hearted! I should think he has to wear asbestos vests. Well, stand by, Jeeves.'

'Very good, sir.'

And, sure enough, it wasn't ten days before in rolled the old ass, bleating for volunteers to step one pace forward and come to the aid of the party.

'Bertie,' he said, 'if you are a pal of mine, now is the time to show it.'

'Proceed, old gargoyle,' I replied. 'You have our ear.'

'You remember giving me lunch at the Senior Liberal some days ago. We were waited on by a—'

'I remember. Tall, lissom female.'

He shuddered somewhat.

'I wish you wouldn't talk of her like that, dash it all! She's an angel.'

'All right. Carry on.'

'I love her.'

'Right-o! Push along.'

'For goodness' sake don't bustle me. Let me tell the story in my own way. I love her, as I was saying, and I want you, Bertie, old boy, to pop round to my uncle and do a bit of diplomatic work. That allowance of mine must be restored, and dashed quick, too. What's more, it must be increased.'

'But look here,' I said, being far from keen on the bally business, 'why not wait a while?'

'Wait? What's the good of waiting?'

'Well, you know what generally happens when you fall in love. Something goes wrong with the works and you get left. Much better tackle your uncle after the whole thing's fixed and settled.'

'It *is* fixed and settled. She accepted me this morning.'

'Good Lord! That's quick work. You haven't known her two weeks!'

'Not in this life, no,' said young Bingo. 'But she has a sort of idea that we must have met in some previous existence. She thinks I must have been a king in Babylon when she was a Christian slave. I can't say I remember it myself, but there may be something in it.'

'Great Scott!' I said. 'Do waitresses really talk like that?'

'How should I know how waitresses talk?'

'Well, you ought to by now. The first time I ever met your uncle was when you hounded me on to ask him if he would rally round to help you marry that girl Mabel in the Piccadilly bunshop.'

Bingo started violently. A wild gleam came into his eyes. And before I knew what he was up to he had brought down his hand with a most frightful whack on my summer trousering, causing me to leap like a young ram.

'Here!' I said.

'Sorry,' said Bingo. 'Excited. Carried away. You've given me an idea, Bertie.' He waited till I had finished massaging the limb, and resumed his remarks. 'Can you throw your mind back to that occasion, Bertie? Do you remember the frightfully subtle scheme I worked? Telling him you were what's-her-name – the woman who wrote those books, I mean?'

It wasn't likely I'd forget. The ghastly thing was absolutely seared into my memory. What had happened – stop me if I've told you this before – was that, in order to induce his dashed uncle to look on me as a chum and hang upon my words, and all that, the ass Bingo had told him that I was the author of a lot of mushy novels of which he was particularly fond. All that series by Rosie M. Banks, you know. Said that I had written them, and that Rosie's name on the title-page was simply my what-d'you-call-it. Lord Bittlesham, the uncle, had lapped it up without the slightest hesitation, and had treated me both then and on the other occasions on which we had met with the dickens of a lot of reverence.

'That is the line of attack,' said Bingo. 'That is the scheme. Rosie M. Banks forward once more.'

'It can't be done, old thing. Sorry, but it's out of the ques. I couldn't go through all that again.'

'Not for me?'

'Not for a dozen more like you.'

'I never thought,' said Bingo, sorrowfully, 'to hear those words from Bertie Wooster!'

'Well, you've heard them now,' I said. 'Paste them in your hat.'

'Bertie, we were at school together.'

'It wasn't my fault.'

'We've been pals for fifteen years.'

'I know. It's going to take me the rest of my life to live it down.'

'Bertie, old man,' said Bingo, drawing up his chair closer and starting to knead my shoulder-blade, 'listen. Be reasonable!'

And, of course, dash it! at the end of ten minutes I'd allowed the blighter to talk me round. It's always the way. Anyone can talk me round. If I were in a Trappist monastery, the first thing that would happen would be that some smooth performer would lure me into some frightful idiocy against my better judgment by means of the deaf-and-dumb language.

'Well, what do you want me to do?' I said, realising that it was hopeless to struggle.

'Start off by sending the old boy an autographed copy of your latest effort, with a flattering inscription. That will tickle him to death. Then you pop round and put it across him.'

'What *is* my latest?'

'*The Woman Who Braved All*,' said young Bingo. 'I've seen it all over the place. The shop windows and bookstalls are full of nothing but. It looks to me from the picture on the jacket the sort of book any bloke would be proud to have written. Of course, he will want to discuss it with you.'

'Ah!' I said, cheering up. 'That dishes the scheme, doesn't it? I don't know what the bally thing is about.'

'You will have to read it, naturally.'

'Read it! No, I say—'

'Bertie, we were at school together.'

'Oh, right-o! Right-o!' I said.

'I knew I could rely on you. You have a heart of gold. Jeeves,' said young Bingo, as the faithful servitor rolled in, 'Mr. Wooster has a heart of gold.'

'Very good, sir,' said Jeeves.

*

Bar a weekly wrestle with the *Pink 'Un* and an occasional dip into the form-book, I'm not much of a lad for reading, and my sufferings as I tackled *The Woman* – curse her! – *Who Braved All* were pretty fearful. But I managed to get through it, and only just in time, as it happened, for I'd hardly reached the bit where their lips met in one long, slow kiss, and everything was still but for the gentle sighing of the breeze in the laburnum, when a messenger-boy brought a note from old Bittlesham asking me to trickle round to lunch.

I found the old boy in a mood you could only describe as melting. He had a copy of the book on the table beside him, and kept turning the pages in the intervals of dealing with things in aspic and what not.

'Mr. Wooster,' he said, swallowing a chunk of trout, 'I wish to congratulate you. I wish to thank you. You go from strength to strength. I have read *All for Love,* I have read *Only a Factory Girl,* I know *Madcap Myrtle* by heart. But this – this is your bravest and best. It tears the heart-strings.'

'Yes?'

'Indeed yes! I have read it three times since you most kindly sent me the volume – I wish to thank you once more for the charming inscription – and I think I may say that I am a better, sweeter, deeper man. I am full of human charity and kindliness towards my species.'

'No, really?'

'Indeed, indeed I am.'

'Towards the whole species?'

'Towards the whole species.'

'Even young Bingo?' I said, trying him pretty high.

'My nephew? Richard?' He looked a bit thoughtful, but stuck it like a man and refused to hedge. 'Yes, even towards Richard. Well – that is to say – perhaps – yes, even towards Richard.'

'That's good, because I wanted to talk about him. He's pretty hard up, you know.'

'In straitened circumstances?'

'Stoney. And he could use a bit of the right stuff paid every quarter, if you felt like unbelting.'

He mused awhile, and got through a slab of cold guinea-hen before replying. He toyed with the book, and it fell open at page two hundred and fifteen. I couldn't remember what was on page two hundred and fifteen, but it must have been something tolerably zippy, for his expression changed and he gazed at me with misty eyes, as if he'd taken a shade too much mustard with his last bite of ham.

'Very well, Mr. Wooster,' he said. 'Fresh from a perusal of this noble work of yours, I cannot harden my heart. Richard shall have his allowance.'

'Stout fellow!' I said. Then it occurred to me that the expression might strike a bird who weighed seventeen stone as a bit personal. 'Good egg, I mean. That'll take a weight off his mind. He wants to get married, you know.'

'I did not know. And I am not sure that I altogether approve. Who is the lady?'

'Well, as a matter of fact, she's a waitress.'

He leaped in his seat.

'You don't say so, Mr. Wooster! This is remarkable. This is most cheering. I had not given the boy credit for such tenacity of purpose. An excellent trait in him which I had not hitherto suspected. I recollect clearly that, on the occasion when I first had the pleasure of making your acquaintance, nearly eighteen months ago, Richard was desirous of marrying this same waitress.'

I had to break it to him.

'Well, not absolutely this same waitress. In fact, quite a different waitress. Still, a waitress, you know.'

The light of avuncular affection died out of the old boy's eyes.

'H'm!' he said, a bit dubiously. 'I had supposed that Richard was displaying the quality of constancy which is so rare in the modern young man. I – I must think it over.'

So we left it at that, and I came away and told Bingo the position of affairs.

'Allowance O.K.,' I said. 'Uncle's blessing a trifle wobbly.'

'Doesn't he seem to want the wedding-bells to ring out?'

'I left him thinking it over. If I were a bookie, I should feel justified in offering a hundred to eight against.'

'You can't have approached him properly. I might have known you would muck it up,' said young Bingo. Which, considering what I had been through for his sake, struck me as a good bit sharper than a serpent's tooth.

'It's awkward,' said young Bingo, 'It's infernally awkward. I can't tell you all the details at the moment, but – yes, it's awkward.'

He helped himself absently to a handful of my cigars, and pushed off.

I didn't see him again for three days. Early in the afternoon of the third day he blew in with a flower in his buttonhole and a look on his face as if someone had hit him behind the ear with a stuffed eel-skin.

'Hallo, Bertie!'

'Hallo, old turnip! Where have you been all this while?'

'Oh, here and there. Ripping weather we're having, Bertie!'

'Not bad.'

'I see the Bank Rate is down again.'

'No, really?'

'Disturbing news from Lower Silesia, what?'

'Oh, dashed.'

He pottered about the room for a bit, babbling at intervals. The boy seemed cuckoo.

'Oh, I say, Bertie,' he said, suddenly, 'I know what it was I wanted to tell you. I'm married.'

I stared at him. That flower in his buttonhole. That dazed look. Yes, he had all the symptoms; and yet the thing seemed incredible. The fact is, I suppose, I'd seen so many of young Bingo's love-affairs start off with a whoop and a rattle and poof themselves out half-way down the straight that I couldn't believe he had actually brought it off at last.

'Married!'

'Yes. This morning, at a registrar's in Holborn. I've just come from the wedding-breakfast.'

I sat up in my chair. Alert. The man of affairs. It seemed to me that this thing wanted threshing out in all its aspects.

'Let's get this straight,' I said. 'You're really married?'

'Yes.'

'The same girl you were in love with the day before yesterday?'

'What do you mean?'

'Well, you know what you're like. Tell me, what made you commit this rash act?'

'I wish the deuce you wouldn't talk like that. I married her because I love her, dash it. The best little woman,' said young Bingo, 'in the world.'

'That's all right, and deuced creditable, I'm sure. But have you reflected what your uncle's going to say? The last I saw of him, he was by no means in a confetti-scattering mood.'

'Bertie,' said Bingo, 'I'll be frank with you. The little woman rather put it up to me, if you know what I mean. I told her how my uncle felt about it, and she said that we must part unless I loved her enough to brave the old boy's wrath and marry her right away. So I had no alternative. I bought a buttonhole and went to it.'

'And what do you propose to do now?'

'Oh, I've got it all planned out. After you've seen my uncle and broken the news—'

'What!'

'After you've—'

'You don't mean to say you think you're going to lug *me* into it?'

He looked at me like Greta Garbo coming out of a swoon.

'Is this Bertie Wooster talking?' he said, pained.

'Yes, it jolly well is.'

'Bertie, old man,' said Bingo, patting me gently here and there, 'reflect! We were at sch—'

'Oh, all right!'

'Good man! I knew I could rely on you. She's waiting down below in the hall. We'll pick her up and dash round to Pounceby Gardens right away.'

I had only seen the bride before in her waitress kit, and I was rather expecting that on her wedding day she would have launched out into something fairly zippy in the way of upholstery. The first gleam of hope I had felt since the start of this black business came to me when I saw that, instead of being all velvet and scent and flowery hat, she was dressed in dashed good taste. Quiet. Nothing loud. As far as looks went she might have stepped straight out of Berkeley Square.

'This is my old pal Bertie Wooster, darling,' said Bingo. 'We were at school together, weren't we, Bertie?'

'We were!' I said. 'How do you do? I think we – er – met at lunch the other day, didn't we?'

'Oh, yes. How do you do?'

'My uncle eats out of Bertie's hand,' explained Bingo. 'So he's coming round with us to start things off and kind of pave the way. Hi, taxi!'

We didn't talk much on the journey. Kind of tense feeling. I was glad when the cab stopped at old Bittlesham's wigwam and we all hopped out. I left Bingo and wife in the hall, while I went upstairs to the drawing-room, and the butler toddled off to dig out the big chief.

While I was prowling about the room, waiting for him to show up, I suddenly caught sight of that bally *Woman Who Braved All* lying on one of the tables. It was open at page two hundred and fifteen, and a passage heavily marked in pencil caught my eye. And directly I read it, I saw that it was all to the mustard and was going to help me in my business.

This was the passage:

'What can prevail' – Millicent's eyes flashed as she faced the stern old man – 'what can prevail against a pure and all-consuming love? Neither principalities nor powers, my lord, nor all the puny prohibitions of guardians and parents. I love your son, Lord Windermere, and nothing can keep us apart. Since time first began, this love of ours was fated, and who are you to pit yourself against the decrees of Fate?'

THE EARL LOOKED AT HER KEENLY FROM BENEATH HIS BUSHY EYEBROWS.

'HUMPH!' HE SAID.

Before I had time to refresh my memory as to what Millicent's come-back had been to that remark, the door opened and old Bittlesham rolled in. All over me, as usual.

'My dear Mr. Wooster, this is an unexpected pleasure. Pray take a seat. What can I do for you?'

'Well, the fact is, I'm more or less in the capacity of a jolly old ambassador at the moment. Representing young Bingo, you know.'

His geniality sagged a trifle, I thought, but he didn't heave me out, so I pushed on.

'The way I've always looked at it,' I said, 'is that it's dashed difficult for anything to prevail against what you might call a pure and all-consuming love. I mean, can it be done? I doubt it.'

My eyes didn't exactly flash as I faced the stern old man, but I sort of waggled my eyebrows. He puffed a bit, and looked doubtful.

'We discussed this matter at our last meeting, Mr. Wooster. And on that occasion—'

'Yes. But there have been developments, as it were, since then. The fact of the matter is,' I said, coming to the point, 'this morning young Bingo went and jumped off the dock.'

'Good heavens!' he jerked himself to his feet with his mouth open. 'Why? Where? Which dock?'

I saw that he wasn't quite on.

'I was speaking metaphorically,' I explained, 'if that's the word I want. I mean he got married.'

'Married!'

'Absolutely hitched up. I hope you aren't ratty about it, what? Young blood, you know. Two loving hearts, and all that.'

He panted in a rather overwrought way.

'I am greatly disturbed by your news. I – I consider that I have been – er – defied. Yes, defied.'

'But who are you to pit yourself against the decrees of Fate?' I said, taking a look at the prompt-book out of the corner of my eye.

'Eh?'

'You see, this love of theirs was fated. Since time began, you know.'

I'm bound to admit that if he'd said 'Humph!' at this juncture, he would have had me stymied. Luckily, it didn't occur to him. There was a silence, during which he appeared to brood a bit. Then his eye fell on the book, and he gave a sort of start.

'Why, bless my soul, Mr. Wooster, you have been quoting!'

'More or less.'

'I thought your words sounded familiar.' His whole appearance changed, and he gave a sort of gurgling chuckle. 'Dear me, dear me, you know my weak spot!' He picked up the book, and buried himself in it for quite a while. I began to think he had forgotten I was there. After a bit, however, he put it down again, and wiped his eyes. 'Ah, well!' he said.

I shuffled my feet and hoped for the best.

'Ah, well!' he said again. 'I must not be like Lord Windermere, must I, Mr. Wooster? Tell me, did you draw that haughty old man from a living model?'

'Oh, no. Just thought of him and bunged him down, you know.'

'Genius!' murmured old Bittlesham. 'Genius! Well, Mr. Wooster, you have won me over. Who, as you say, am I to pit myself against the decrees of Fate? I will write to Richard tonight and inform him of my consent to his marriage.'

'You can slip him the glad news in person,' I said. 'He's waiting downstairs, with wife complete. I'll pop down and send them up. Cheerio, and thanks very much. Bingo will be most awfully bucked.'

I shot out and went downstairs. Bingo and Mrs. were sitting on a couple of chairs like patients in a dentist's waiting-room.

'Well?' said Bingo, eagerly.

'All over except the hand-clasping,' I replied, slapping the old crumpet on the back. 'Charge up and get matey. Toodle-oo, old things. You know where to find me, if wanted. A thousand congratulations, and all that sort of rot.'

And I pipped, not wishing to be fawned upon.

You never can tell in this world. If ever I felt that something attempted, something done, had earned a night's repose, it was when I got back to the flat and shoved my feet up on the mantelpiece and started to absorb the cup of tea which Jeeves had brought in. Used as I am to seeing Life's sitters blow up in the home-stretch and finish nowhere, I couldn't see any cause for alarm in this affair of young Bingo's. All he had to do when I left him in Pounceby Gardens was to walk upstairs with the little missus and collect the blessing. I was so convinced of this that when, about half an hour later, he came galloping into my sitting-room, all I thought was that he wanted to thank me in broken accents and tell me what a good chap I had been. I merely beamed benevolently on the old creature as he entered, and was just going to offer him a cigarette when I observed that he seemed to have something on his mind. In fact, he looked as if something solid had hit him in the solar plexus.

'My dear old soul,' I said, 'what's up?'

Bingo plunged about the room.

'I *will* be calm!' he said, knocking over an occasional table. 'Calm, dammit!' He upset a chair.

'Surely nothing has gone wrong?'

Bingo uttered one of those hollow, mirthless yelps.

'Only every bally thing that could go wrong. What do you

think happened after you left us? You know that beastly book you insisted on sending my uncle?'

It wasn't the way I should have put it myself, but I saw the poor old lizard was upset for some reason or other, so I didn't correct him.

'*The Woman Who Braved All?*' I said. 'It came in dashed useful. It was by quoting bits out of it that I managed to talk him round.'

'Well, it didn't come in useful when we got into the room. It was lying on the table, and, after we had started to chat a bit, and everything was going along nicely, the little woman spotted it. "Oh, have you read this, Lord Bittlesham?" she said. "Three times, already," said my uncle. "I'm so glad," said the little woman. "Why, are you also an admirer of Rosie M. Banks?" asked the old boy, beaming. "I *am* Rosie M. Banks!" said the little woman.'

'Oh, my aunt! Not really?'

'Yes.'

'But how could she be? I mean, dash it, she was slinging the foodstuffs at the Senior Liberal Club.'

Bingo gave the settee a moody kick.

'She took the job to collect material for a book she's writing called *Mervyn Keene, Clubman.*'

'She might have told you.'

'It made such a hit with her when she found that I loved her for herself alone, despite her humble station, that she kept it under her hat. She meant to spring it on me later on, she said.'

'Well, what happened then?'

'There was the dickens of a painful scene. The old boy nearly got apoplexy. Called her an impostor. They both started talking at once at the top of their voices, and the thing ended with the little woman buzzing off to her publishers to collect proofs as a preliminary to getting a written apology from the old boy. What's going to happen now, I don't know. Apart from the fact that my uncle will be as mad as a wet hen when he finds out that he has been fooled, there's going to be a lot of trouble when the little woman discovers that we worked the Rosie M. Banks wheeze with a view to trying to get me married to somebody else. You see, one of the things that first attracted her to me was the fact that I had never been in love before.'

'Did you tell her that?'

'Yes.'

'Great Scott!'

'Well, I hadn't been – not really in love. There's all the difference in the world between – Well, never mind that. What am I going to do? That's the point.'

'I don't know.'

'Thanks,' said young Bingo. 'That's a lot of help.'

Next morning he rang me up on the 'phone just after I'd got the bacon and eggs into my system – the one moment of the day, in short, when a fellow wishes to muse on life absolutely undisturbed.

'Bertie!'

'Hallo!'

'Things are hotting up.'

'What's happened now?'

'My uncle has given the little woman's proofs the once-over and admits her claim. I've just been having five snappy minutes with him on the telephone. He says that you and I made a fool of him, and he could hardly speak, he was so shirty. Still, he made it clear all right that my allowance has gone phut again.'

'I'm sorry.'

'Don't waste time being sorry for me,' said young Bingo, grimly. 'He's coming to call on you today to demand a personal explanation.'

'Great Scott!'

'And the little woman is coming to call on you to demand a personal explanation.'

'Good Lord!'

'I shall watch your future career with considerable interest,' said young Bingo.

I bellowed for Jeeves.

'Jeeves!'

'Sir?'

'I'm in the soup.'

'Indeed, sir?'

I sketched out the scenario for him.

'What would you advise?'

'I think, if I were you, sir, I would accept Mr. Pitt-Waley's invitation immediately. If you remember, sir, he invited you to shoot with him in Norfolk this week.'

'So he did! By Jove, Jeeves, you're always right. Meet me at the station with my things the first train after lunch. I'll go and lie low at the club for the rest of the morning.'

'Would you require my company on this visit, sir?'

'Do you want to come?'

'If I might suggest it, sir, I think it would be better if I remained here and kept in touch with Mr. Little. I might possibly hit upon some method of pacifying the various parties, sir.'

'Right-o! But, if you do, you're a marvel.'

I didn't enjoy myself much in Norfolk. It rained most of the time, and, when it wasn't raining, I was so dashed jumpy I couldn't hit a thing. By the end of the week I couldn't stand it any longer. Too bally absurd, I mean, being marooned miles away in the country just because young Bingo's uncle and wife wanted to have a few words with me. I made up my mind that I would pop back and do the strong, manly thing by lying low in my flat and telling Jeeves to inform everybody who called that I wasn't at home.

I sent Jeeves a telegram, saying I was coming, and drove straight to Bingo's place when I reached town. I wanted to find out the general posish of affairs. But apparently the man was out. I rang a couple of times, but nothing happened, and I was just going to leg it when I heard the sound of footsteps inside, and the door opened. It wasn't one of the cheeriest moments of my career when I found myself peering into the globular face of Lord Bittlesham.

'Oh, er – hallo!' I said. And there was a bit of a pause.

I don't quite know what I had been expecting the old boy to do if by bad luck we should ever meet again, but I had a sort of general idea that he would turn fairly purple and start almost immediately to let me have it in the gizzard. It struck me as somewhat rummy, therefore, when he simply smiled weakly. A sort of frozen smile it was. His eyes kind of bulged, and he swallowed once or twice.

'Er—' he said.

I waited for him to continue, but apparently that was all there was.

'Bingo in?' I said, after a rather embarrassing pause.

He shook his head, and smiled again. And then, suddenly, just as the flow of conversation had begun to slacken once more, I'm dashed if he didn't make a sort of lumbering leap back into the flat and bang the door.

I couldn't understand it. But, as it seemed that the interview, such as it was, was over, I thought I might as well be shifting. I had just started down the stairs when I met young Bingo, charging up three steps at a time.

'Hallo, Bertie!' he said. 'Where did you spring from? I thought you were out of town.'

'I've just got back. I looked in on you to see how the land lay.'

'How do you mean?'

'Why, all that business, you know.'

'Oh, that,' said young Bingo, airily. 'That was all settled days ago. The dove of peace is flapping its wings all over the place. Everything's as right as it can be. Jeeves fixed it all up. He's a marvel, that man, Bertie, I've always said so. Put the whole thing straight in half a minute with one of those brilliant ideas of his.'

'This is topping!'

'I knew you'd be pleased.'

'Congratulate you.'

'Thanks.'

'What did Jeeves do? I couldn't think of any solution of the bally thing myself.'

'Oh, he took the matter in hand and smoothed it all out in a second. My uncle and the little woman are tremendous pals now. They gas away by the hour together about literature and all that. He's always dropping in for a chat.'

This reminded me.

'He's in there now,' I said. 'I say, Bingo, how *is* your uncle these days?'

'Much as usual. How do you mean?'

'I mean he hasn't been feeling the strain of things a bit, has he? He seemed rather strange in his manner just now.'

'Why, have you met him?'

'He opened the door when I rang. And then, after he had stood goggling at me for a bit, he suddenly banged the door in my face. Puzzled me, you know. I mean, I could have understood it if he'd ticked me off and all that, but, dash it, the man seemed absolutely scared.'

Young Bingo laughed a care-free laugh.

'Oh, that's all right,' he said. 'I forgot to tell you about that. Meant to write, but kept putting it off. He thinks you're a loony.'

'He – what?'

'Yes. That was Jeeves's idea, you know. It's solved the whole problem splendidly. He suggested that I should tell my uncle that I had acted in perfect good faith in introducing you to him as Rosie M. Banks; that I had repeatedly had it from your own lips that you were, and that I didn't see any reason why you shouldn't be. The idea being that you were subject to hallucinations and generally potty. And then we got hold of Sir Roderick Glossop – you remember, the old boy whose kid you pushed into the lake that day down at Ditteredge Hall – and he rallied round with his story of how he had come to lunch with you once and found your bedroom full up with cats and fish, and how you had pinched his hat while you were driving past his car in a taxi, and all that, you know. It just rounded the whole thing off nicely. I always say, and I always shall say, that you've only got to stand on Jeeves and Fate can't touch you.'

I can put up with a good deal, but there are limits.

'Well, of all the dashed bits of nerve I ever—'

Bingo looked at me, astonished.

'You aren't *annoyed?*' he said.

'Annoyed! At having half London going about under the impression that I'm off my chump? Dash it all—'

'Bertie,' said Bingo, 'you amaze and wound me. If I had dreamed that you would object to doing a trifling good turn to a fellow who's been a pal of yours for fifteen years—'

'Yes, but look here—'

'Have you forgotten,' said young Bingo, 'that we were at school together?'

I pushed on to the old flat, seething like the dickens. One thing I was jolly certain of, and that was that this was where Jeeves and I parted company. A topping valet, of course, none better in London, but I wasn't going to allow that to weaken me. I buzzed into the flat like an east wind – and there was the box of cigarettes on the small table and the illustrated weekly papers on the big table, and my slippers on the floor, and every dashed thing so bally *right,* if you know what I mean, that I started to calm down in the first two seconds. It was like one of those moments in a play where the chappie, about to steep himself in crime, suddenly hears the soft, appealing strains of the old melody he learned at his mother's knee. Softened, I mean to say. That's the word I want, I was softened.

And then through the doorway there shimmered good old Jeeves in the wake of a tray full of the necessary ingredients, and there was something about the mere look of the man—

However, I steeled the old heart and had a stab at it.

'I have just met Mr. Little, Jeeves,' I said.

'Indeed, sir?'

'He – er – he told me you had been helping him.'

'I did my best, sir. And I am happy to say that matters now appear to be proceeding smoothly. Whisky, sir?'

'Thanks. Er – Jeeves.'

'Sir?'

'Another time—'

'Sir?'

'Oh, nothing – Not all the soda, Jeeves.'

'Very good, sir.'

He started to drift out.

'Oh, Jeeves!'

'Sir?'

'I wish – that is – I think – I mean – oh, nothing.'

'Very good, sir. The cigarettes are at your elbow, sir. Dinner will be ready at a quarter to eight precisely, unless you desire to dine out?'

'No. I'll dine in.'

'Yes, sir.'

'Jeeves!'

'Sir?'

'Oh, nothing,' I said.

'Very good, sir,' said Jeeves.

'Jeeves,' I said, emerging from the old tub, 'rally round.'

'Yes, sir.'

I beamed on the man with no little geniality. I was putting in a week or two in Paris at the moment, and there's something about Paris that always makes me feel fairly full of *espièglerie* and *joie de vivre*.

'Lay out our gent's medium-smart raiment, suitable for Bohemian revels,' I said. 'I am lunching with an artist bloke on the other side of the river.'

'Very good, sir.'

'And if anybody calls for me, Jeeves, say that I shall be back towards the quiet evenfall.'

'Yes, sir. Mr. Biffen rang up on the telephone while you were in your bath.'

'Mr. Biffen? Good heavens!'

Amazing how one's always running across fellows in foreign cities – coves, I mean, whom you haven't seen for ages and would have betted weren't anywhere in the neighbourhood. Paris was the last place where I should have expected to find old Biffy popping up. There was a time when he and I had been lads about town together, lunching and dining together practically every day; but some eighteen months back his old godmother had died and left him that place in Herefordshire, and he had retired there to wear gaiters and prod cows in the ribs and generally be the country gentleman and landed proprietor. Since then I had hardly seen him.

'Old Biffy in Paris? What's he doing here?'

'He did not confide in me, sir,' said Jeeves – a trifle frostily, I thought. It sounded somehow as if he didn't like Biffy. And yet they had always been matey enough in the old days.

'Where's he staying?'

'At the Hotel Avenida, Rue du Colisée, sir. He informed me that he was about to take a walk and would call this afternoon.'

'Well, if he comes when I'm out, tell him to wait. And now, Jeeves, *mes gants, mon chapeau, et le whangee de monsieur*. I must be popping.'

It was such a corking day and I had so much time in hand that near the Sorbonne I stopped my cab, deciding to walk the rest of the way. And I had hardly gone three steps and a half when there on the pavement before me stood old Biffy in person. If I had completed the last step I should have rammed him.

'Biffy!' I cried. 'Well, well, well!'

He peered at me in a blinking kind of way, rather like one of his Herefordshire cows prodded unexpectedly while lunching.

'Bertie!' he gurgled, in a devout sort of tone. 'Thank God!' He clutched my arm. 'Don't leave me, Bertie. I'm lost.'

'What do you mean, lost?'

'I came out for a walk and suddenly discovered after a mile or two that I didn't know where on earth I was. I've been wandering round in circles for hours.'

'Why didn't you ask the way?'

'I can't speak a word of French.'

'Well, why didn't you call a taxi?'

'I suddenly discovered I'd left all my money at my hotel.'

'You could have taken a cab and paid it when you got to the hotel.'

'Yes, but I suddenly discovered, dash it, that I'd forgotten its name.'

And there in a nutshell you have Charles Edward Biffen. As

vague and woollen-headed a blighter as ever bit a sandwich. Goodness knows – and my Aunt Agatha will bear me out in this – I'm no master-mind myself; but compared with Biffy I'm one of the great thinkers of all time.

'I'd give a shilling,' said Biffy wistfully, 'to know the name of that hotel.'

'You can owe it to me. Hotel Avenida, Rue du Colisée.'

'Bertie! This is uncanny. How the deuce did you know?'

'That was the address you left with Jeeves this morning.'

'So it was. I had forgotten.'

'Well, come along and have a drink, and then I'll put you in a cab and send you home. I'm engaged for lunch, but I've plenty of time.'

We drifted to one of the eleven cafés which jostled each other along the street and I ordered restoratives.

'What on earth are you doing in Paris?' I asked.

'Bertie, old man,' said Biffy solemnly, 'I came here to try and forget.'

'Well, you've certainly succeeded.'

'You don't understand. The fact is, Bertie, old lad, my heart is broken. I'll tell you the whole story.'

'No, I say!' I protested. But he was off.

'Last year,' said Biffy, 'I buzzed over to Canada to do a bit of salmon fishing.'

I ordered another. If this was going to be a fish-story, I needed stimulants.

'On the liner going to New York I met a girl.' Biffy made a sort of curious gulping noise not unlike a bulldog trying to swallow half a cutlet in a hurry so as to be ready for the other half. 'Bertie, old man, I can't describe her. I simply can't describe her.'

This was all to the good.

'She was wonderful! We used to walk on the boat-deck after dinner. She was on the stage. At least, sort of.'

'How do you mean, sort of?'

'Well, she had posed for artists and been a mannequin in a big dressmaker's and all that sort of thing, don't you know. Anyway, she had saved up a few pounds and was on her way to see if she could get a job in New York. She told me all about herself. Her father ran a milk-walk in Clapham. Or it may have been Cricklewood. At least, it was either a milk-walk or a boot-shop.'

'Easily confused.'

'What I'm trying to make you understand,' said Biffy, 'is that she came of good, sturdy, respectable middle-class stock. Nothing flashy about her. The sort of wife any man might have been proud of.'

'Well, whose wife was she?'

'Nobody's. That's the whole point of the story. I wanted her to be mine, and I lost her.'

'Had a quarrel, you mean?'

'No, I don't mean we had a quarrel. I mean I literally lost her. The last I ever saw of her was in the Customs sheds at New York. We were behind a pile of trunks, and I had just asked her to be my wife, and she had just said she would and everything was perfectly splendid, when a most offensive blighter in a peaked cap came up to talk about some cigarettes which he had found at the bottom of my trunk and which I had forgotten to declare. It was getting pretty late by then, for we hadn't docked till about ten-thirty, so I told Mabel to go on to her hotel and I would come round next day and take her to lunch. And since then I haven't set eyes on her.'

'You mean she wasn't at the hotel?'

'Probably she was. But—'

'You don't mean you never turned up?'

'Bertie, old man,' said Biffy, in an overwrought kind of way, 'for Heaven's sake don't keep trying to tell me what I mean and what I don't mean! Let me tell this my own way, or I shall get all mixed up and have to go back to the beginning.'

'Tell it your own way,' I said hastily.

'Well, then, to put it in a word, Bertie, I forgot the name of the hotel. By the time I'd done half an hour's heavy explaining about those cigarettes my mind was a blank. I had an idea I had written the name down somewhere, but I couldn't have done, for it wasn't on any of the papers in my pocket. No, it was no good. She was gone.'

'Why didn't you make inquiries?'

'Well, the fact is, Bertie, I had forgotten her name.'

'Oh, no, dash it!' I said. This seemed a bit too thick even for Biffy. 'How could you forget her name? Besides, you told it me a moment ago. Muriel or something.'

'Mabel,' corrected Biffy coldly. 'It was her surname I'd forgotten. So I gave it up and went to Canada.'

'But half a second,' I said. 'You must have told her your name. I mean, if you couldn't trace her, she could trace you.'

'Exactly. That's what makes it all seem so infernally hopeless. She knows my name and where I live and everything, but I haven't heard a word from her. I suppose, when I didn't turn up at the hotel, she took it that that was my way of hinting delicately that I had changed my mind and wanted to call the thing off.'

'I suppose so,' I said. There didn't seem anything else to suppose. 'Well, the only thing to do is to whizz around and try to heal the wound, what? How about dinner tonight, winding up at the Abbaye or one of those places?'

Biffy shook his head.

'It wouldn't be any good. I've tried it. Besides, I'm leaving on the four o'clock train. I have a dinner engagement tomorrow with a man who's nibbling at that house of mine in Herefordshire.'

'Oh, are you trying to sell that place? I thought you liked it.'

'I did. But the idea of going on living in that great, lonely barn of a house after what has happened appals me, Bertie. So when Sir Roderick Glossop came along—'

'Sir Roderick Glossop! You don't mean the loony-doctor?'

'The great nerve specialist, yes. Why, do you know him?'

It was a warm day, but I shivered.

'I was engaged to his daughter for a week or two,' I said, in a hushed voice. The memory of that narrow squeak always made me feel faint.

'Has he a daughter?' said Biffy absently.

'He has. Let me tell you all about—'

'Not just now, old man,' said Biffy, getting up. 'I ought to be going back to my hotel to see about my packing.'

Which, after I had listened to his story, struck me as pretty low-down. However, the longer you live, the more you realise that the good old sporting spirit of give-and-take has practically died out in our midst. So I boosted him into a cab and went off to lunch.

It can't have been more than ten days after this that I received a nasty shock while getting outside my morning tea and toast. The English papers had arrived, and Jeeves was just drifting out of the room after depositing *The Times* by my bed-side, when, as I idly turned the pages in search of the sporting section, a paragraph leaped out and hit me squarely in the eyeball.

As follows:

FORTHCOMING MARRIAGES
Mr. C. E. Biffen and Miss Glossop

'The engagement is announced between Charles Edward, only son of the late Mr. E. C. Biffen, and Mrs. Biffen, of 11, Penslow Square, Mayfair, and Honoria Jane Louise, only daughter of Sir Roderick and Lady Glossop, of 6b, Harley Street, W.'

'Great Scott!' I exclaimed.

'Sir?' said Jeeves, turning at the door.

'Jeeves, you remember Miss Glossop?'

'Very vividly, sir.'

'She's engaged to Mr. Biffen!'

'Indeed, sir?' said Jeeves. And, with not another word, he slid out. The blighter's calm amazed and shocked me. It seemed to indicate that there must be a horrible streak of callousness in him. I mean to say, it wasn't as if he didn't know Honoria Glossop.

I read the paragraph again. A peculiar feeling it gave me. I don't know if you have ever experienced the sensation of seeing the announcement of the engagement of a pal of yours to a girl whom you were only saved from marrying yourself by the skin of your teeth. It induces a sort of – well, it's difficult to describe it exactly; but I should imagine a fellow would feel much the same if he happened to be strolling through the jungle with a boyhood chum and met a tigress or a jaguar, or what not, and managed to shin up a tree and looked down and saw the friend of his youth vanishing into the undergrowth in the animal's slavering jaws. A sort of profound, prayerful relief, if you know what I mean, blended at the same time with a pang of pity. What I'm driving at is that, thankful as I was that I hadn't had to marry Honoria myself, I was sorry to see a real good chap like old Biffy copping it. I sucked down a spot of tea and began to brood over the business.

Of course, there are probably fellows in the world – tough, hardy blokes with strong chins and glittering eyes – who could get engaged to this Glossop menace and like it; but I knew perfectly well that Biffy was not one of them. Honoria, you see, is one of those robust, dynamic girls with the muscles of a welter-weight and a laugh like a squadron of cavalry charging over a tin bridge. A beastly thing to have to face over the breakfast table. Brainy, moreover. The sort of girl who reduces you to pulp with sixteen sets of tennis and a few rounds of golf, and then comes down to dinner as fresh as a daisy, expecting you to take an intelligent interest in Freud. If I had been engaged to her another week, her old father would have had one more patient on his books; and Biffy is much the same quiet sort of peaceful, inoffensive bird as me. I was shocked, I tell you, shocked.

And, as I was saying, the thing that shocked me most was Jeeves's frightful lack of proper emotion. The man happening to float in at this juncture, I gave him one more chance to show some human sympathy.

'You got the name correctly, didn't you, Jeeves?' I said. 'Mr. Biffen is going to marry Honoria Glossop, the daughter of the old boy with the egg-like head and the eyebrows.'

'Yes, sir. Which suit would you wish me to lay out this morning?'

And this, mark you, from the man who, when I was engaged to the Glossop, strained every fibre in his brain to extricate me. It beat me. I couldn't understand it.

'The blue with the red twill,' I said coldly. My manner was marked, and I meant him to see that he had disappointed me sorely.

About a week later I went back to London, and scarcely had I got settled in the old flat when Biffy blew in. One glance was enough to tell me that the poisoned wound had begun to fester. The man did not look bright. No, there was no getting away from it, not bright. He had that kind of stunned, glassy expression which I used to see on my own face in the shaving-mirror during my brief engagement to the Glossop pestilence. However, if you don't want to be one of the What is Wrong Within This Picture brigade, you must observe the conventions, so I shook his hand as warmly as I could.

'Well, well, old man,' I said. 'Congratulations.'

'Thanks,' said Biffy wanly, and there was rather a weighty silence.

'Bertie,' said Biffy, after the silence had lasted about three minutes.

'Hallo?'

'Is it really true—?'

'What?'

'Oh, nothing,' said Biffy, and conversation languished again.

After about a minute and a half he came to the surface once more.

'Bertie.'

'Still here, old thing. What is it?'

'I say, Bertie, is it really true that you were once engaged to Honoria?'

'It is.'

Biffy coughed.

'How did you get out – I mean, what was the nature of the tragedy that prevented the marriage?'

'Jeeves worked it. He thought out the entire scheme.'

'I think, before I go,' said Biffy thoughtfully, 'I'll just step into the kitchen and have a word with Jeeves.'

I felt that the situation called for complete candour.

'Biffy, old egg,' I said, 'as man to man, do you want to oil out of this thing?'

'Bertie, old cork,' said Biffy earnestly, 'as one friend to another, I do.'

'Then why the dickens did you ever get into it?'

'I don't know. Why did you?'

'I – well, it sort of happened.'

'And it sort of happened with me. You know how it is when your heart's broken. A kind of lethargy comes over you. You get absent-minded and cease to exercise proper precautions, and the first thing you know you're for it. I don't know how it happened, old man, but there it is. And what I want you to tell me is, what's the procedure?'

'You mean, how does a fellow edge out?'

'Exactly. I don't want to hurt anybody's feelings, Bertie, but I can't go through with this thing. The shot is not on the board. For about a day and a half I thought it might be all right, but now— You remember that laugh of hers?'

'I do.'

'Well, there's that, and then all this business of never letting a fellow alone – improving his mind and so forth—'

'I know. I know.'

'Very well, then. What do you recommend? What did you mean when you said that Jeeves worked a scheme?'

'Well, you see, old Sir Roderick, who's a loony-doctor and nothing but a loony-doctor, however much you may call him a nerve specialist, discovered that there was a modicum of insanity in my family. Nothing serious. Just one of my uncles. Used to keep rabbits in his bedroom. And the old boy came to lunch here to give me the once-over, and Jeeves arranged matters so that he went away firmly convinced that I was off my onion.'

'I see,' said Biffy thoughtfully. 'The trouble is there isn't any insanity in my family.'

'None?'

It seemed to me almost incredible that a fellow could be such a perfect chump as dear old Biffy without a bit of assistance.

'Not a loony on the list,' he said gloomily. 'It's just like my luck. The old boy's coming to lunch with me tomorrow, no doubt to test me as he did you. And I never felt saner in my life.'

I thought for a moment. The idea of meeting Sir Roderick again gave me a cold shivery feeling; but when there is a chance of helping a pal we Woosters have no thought of self.

'Look here, Biffy,' I said, 'I'll tell you what. I'll roll up for that lunch. It may easily happen that when he finds you are a pal of mine he will forbid the banns right away and no more questions asked.'

'Something in that,' said Biffy, brightening. 'Awfully sporting of you, Bertie.'

'Oh, not at all,' I said. 'And meanwhile I'll consult Jeeves. Put the whole thing up to him and ask his advice. He's never failed me yet.'

Biffy pushed off, a good deal braced, and I went into the kitchen.

'Jeeves,' I said, 'I want your help once more. I've just been having a painful interview with Mr. Biffen.'

'Indeed, sir?'

'It's like this,' I said, and told him the whole thing.

It was rummy, but I could feel him freezing from the start. As a rule, when I call Jeeves into conference on one of these little problems, he's all sympathy and bright ideas; but not today.

'I fear, sir,' he said, when I had finished, 'it is hardly my place to intervene in a private matter affecting—'

'Oh, come!'

'No, sir. It would be taking a liberty.'

'Jeeves,' I said, tackling the blighter squarely, 'what have you got against old Biffy?'

'I, sir?'

'Yes, you.'

'I assure you, sir!'

'Oh, well, if you don't want to chip in and save a fellow-creature, I suppose I can't make you. But let me tell you this. I am now going back to the sitting-room, and I am going to put in some very tense thinking. You'll look pretty silly when I come and tell you that I've got Mr. Biffen out of the soup without your assistance. Extremely silly you'll look.'

'Yes, sir. Shall I bring you a whisky-and-soda, sir?'

'No. Coffee! Strong and black. And if anybody wants to see me, tell 'em that I'm busy and can't be disturbed.'

An hour later I rang the bell.

'Jeeves,' I said with hauteur.

'Yes, sir?'

'Kindly ring Mr. Biffen up on the 'phone and say that Mr. Wooster presents his compliments and that he has got it.'

I was feeling more than a little pleased with myself next morning as I strolled round to Biffy's. As a rule the bright ideas you get overnight have a trick of not seeming quite so frightfully fruity when you examine them by the light of day; but this one looked as good at breakfast as it had done before dinner. I examined it narrowly from every angle, and I didn't see how it could fail.

A few days before, my Aunt Emily's son Harold had

celebrated his sixth birthday; and, being up against the necessity of weighing in with a present of some kind, I had happened to see in a shop in the Strand a rather sprightly little gadget, well calculated in my opinion to amuse the child and endear him to one and all. It was a bunch of flowers in a sort of holder ending in an ingenious bulb attachment which, when pressed, shot about a pint and a half of pure spring water into the face of anyone who was ass enough to sniff at it. It seemed to me just the thing to please the growing mind of a kid of six, and I had rolled round with it.

But when I got to the house I found Harold sitting in the midst of a mass of gifts so luxurious and costly that I simply hadn't the crust to contribute a thing that had set me back a mere elevenpence-ha'penny; so with rare presence of mind – for we Woosters can think quick on occasion – I wrenched my Uncle James's card off a toy aeroplane, substituted my own, and trousered the squirt, which I took away with me. It had been lying around in my flat ever since, and it seemed to me that the time had come to send it into action.

'Well?' said Biffy anxiously, as I curveted into his sitting-room.

The poor old bird was looking pretty green about the gills. I recognised the symptoms. I had felt much the same myself when waiting for Sir Roderick to turn up and lunch with me. How the deuce people who have anything wrong with their nerves can bring themselves to chat with that man, I can't imagine; and yet he has the largest practice in London. Scarcely a day passes without his having to sit on somebody's head and ring for the attendant to bring the strait-waistcoat: and his outlook on life has become so jaundiced through constant association with coves who are picking straws out of their hair that I was convinced that Biffy had merely got to press the bulb and nature would do the rest.

So I patted him on the shoulder and said: 'It's all right, old man!'

'What does Jeeves suggest?' asked Biffy eagerly.

'Jeeves doesn't suggest anything.'

'But you said it was all right.'

'Jeeves isn't the only thinker in the Wooster home, my lad. I have taken over your little problem, and I can tell you at once that I have the situation well in hand.'

'You?' said Biffy.

His tone was far from flattering. It suggested a lack of faith in my abilities, and my view was that an ounce of demonstration would be worth a ton of explanation. I shoved the bouquet at him.

'Are you fond of flowers, Biffy?' I said.

'Eh?'

'Smell these.'

Biffy extended the old beak in a careworn sort of way, and I pressed the bulb as per printed instructions on the label.

I do like getting my money's-worth. Elevenpence-ha'penny the thing had cost me, and it would have been cheap at double. The advertisement on the outside of the box had said that its effects were 'indescribably ludicrous', and I can testify that it was no over-statement. Poor old Biffy leaped three feet in the air and overturned a small table.

'There!' I said.

The old egg was a trifle incoherent at first, but he found words fairly soon, and began to express himself with a good deal of warmth.

'Calm yourself, laddie,' I said, as he paused for breath. 'It was no mere jest to pass an idle hour. It was a demonstration. Take this, Biffy, with an old friend's blessing, refill the bulb, shove it into Sir Roderick's face, press firmly, and leave the rest to him. I'll guarantee that in something under three seconds the idea will have dawned on him that you are not required in his family.'

Biffy stared at me.

'Are you suggesting that I squirt Sir Roderick?'

'Absolutely. Squirt him good. Squirt as you have never squirted before.'

'But—'

He was still yammering at me in a feverish sort of way when there was a ring at the front-door bell.

'Good Lord!' cried Biffy, quivering like a jelly. 'There he is. Talk to him while I go and change my shirt.'

I had just time to refill the bulb and shove it beside Biffy's plate, when the door opened and Sir Roderick came in. I was picking up the fallen table at the moment, and he started talking brightly to my back.

'Good afternoon. I trust I am not— Mr. Wooster!'

I'm bound to say I was not feeling entirely at my ease. There is something about the man that is calculated to strike terror into the stoutest heart. If ever there was a bloke at the very mention of whose name it would be excusable for people to tremble like aspens, that bloke is Sir Roderick Glossop. He has an enormous bald head, all the hair which ought to be on it seeming to have run into his eyebrows, and his eyes go through you like a couple of Death Rays.

'How are you, how are you, how are you?' I said, overcoming a slight desire to leap backwards out of the window. 'Long time since we met, what?'

'Nevertheless, I remember you most distinctly, Mr. Wooster.'

'That's fine,' I said. 'Old Biffy asked me to come and join you in mangling a bit of lunch.'

He waggled the eyebrows at me.

'Are you a friend of Charles Biffen?'

'Oh, rather. Been friends for years and years.'

He drew in his breath sharply, and I could see that Biffy's stock had dropped several points. His eye fell on the floor, which was strewn with things that had tumbled off the upset table.

'Have you had an accident?' he said.

'Nothing serious,' I explained. 'Old Biffy had some sort of fit or seizure just now and knocked over the table.'

'A fit!'

'Or seizure.'

'Is he subject to fits?'

I was about to answer, when Biffy hurried in. He had forgotten to brush his hair, which gave him a wild look, and I saw the old boy direct a keen glance at him. It seemed to me that what you might call the preliminary spade-work had been most satisfactorily attended to and that the success of the good old bulb could be in no doubt whatever.

Biffy's man came in with the nose-bags and we sat down to lunch.

It looked at first as though the meal was going to be one of those complete frosts which occur from, time to time in the career of a constant luncher-out. Biffy, a very C_3 host, contributed nothing to the feast of reason and flow of soul beyond an occasional hiccup, and every time I started to pull a nifty, Sir Roderick swung round on me with such a piercing stare that it stopped me in my tracks. Fortunately, however, the second course consisted of a chicken fricassée of such outstanding excellence that the old boy, after wolfing a plateful, handed up his dinner-pail for a second instalment and became almost genial.

'I am here this afternoon, Charles,' he said, with what practically amounted to bonhomie, 'on what I might describe as a mission. Yes, a mission. This is most excellent chicken.'

'Glad you like it,' mumbled old Biffy.

'Singularly toothsome,' said Sir Roderick, pronging another half ounce. 'Yes, as I was saying, a mission. You young fellows nowadays are, I know, content to live in the centre of the most wonderful metropolis the world has seen, blind and indifferent to its many marvels. I should be prepared – were I a betting man, which I am not – to wager a considerable sum that you have never in your life visited even so historic a spot as Westminster Abbey. Am I right?'

Biffy gurgled something about always having meant to.

'Nor the Tower of London?'

No, nor the Tower of London.

'And there exists at this very moment, not twenty minutes by cab from Hyde Park Corner, the most supremely absorbing and educational collection of objects, both animate and inanimate, gathered from the four corners of the Empire, that has ever been assembled in England's history. I allude to the British Empire Exhibition now situated at Wembley.'

'A fellow told me one about Wembley yesterday,' I said, to help on the cheery flow of conversation. 'Stop me if you've heard it before. Chap goes up to deaf chap outside the exhibition and says, "Is this Wembley?" "Hey?" says deaf chap. "Is this Wembley?" says chap. "Hey?" says deaf chap. "Is this Wembley?" says chap. "No, Thursday," says deaf chap. Ha, ha, I mean, what?'

The merry laughter froze on my lips. Sir Roderick sort of just waggled an eyebrow in my direction and I saw that it was back to the basket for Bertram. I never met a man who had such a knack of making a fellow feel like a waste-product.

'Have you yet paid a visit to Wembley, Charles?' he asked. 'No? Precisely as I suspected. Well, that is the mission on which I am here this afternoon. Honoria wishes me to take you to Wembley. She says it will broaden your mind, in which view I am at one with her. We will start immediately after luncheon.'

Biffy cast an imploring look at me.

'You'll come too, Bertie?'

There was such agony in his eyes that I only hesitated for a second. A pal is a pal. Besides, I felt that, if only the bulb fulfilled the high expectations I had formed of it, the merry expedition would be cancelled in no uncertain manner.

'Oh, rather,' I said.

'We must not trespass on Mr. Wooster's good nature,' said Sir Roderick, looking pretty puff-faced.

'Oh, that's all right,' I said. 'I've been meaning to go to the good old exhibish for a long time. I'll slip home and change my clothes and pick you up here in my car.'

There was a silence. Biffy seemed too relieved at the thought of not having to spend the afternoon alone with Sir Roderick to be capable of speech, and Sir Roderick was registering silent disapproval. And then he caught sight of the bouquet by Biffy's plate.

'Ah, flowers,' he said. 'Sweet peas, if I am not in error. A charming plant, pleasing alike to the eye and the nose.'

I caught Biffy's eye across the table. It was bulging, and a strange light shone in it.

'Are you fond of flowers, Sir Roderick?' he croaked.

'Extremely.'

'Smell these.'

Sir Roderick dipped his head and sniffed. Biffy's fingers closed slowly over the bulb. I shut my eyes and clutched the table.

'Very pleasant,' I heard Sir Roderick say. 'Very pleasant indeed.'

I opened my eyes, and there was Biffy leaning back in his chair with a ghastly look, and the bouquet on the cloth beside him. I realised what had happened. In that supreme crisis of his life, with his whole happiness depending on a mere pressure of the fingers, Biffy, the poor spineless fish, had lost his nerve. My closely-reasoned scheme had gone phut.

Jeeves was fooling about with the geraniums in the sitting-room window-box when I got home.

'They make a very nice display, sir,' he said, cocking a paternal eye at the things.

'Don't talk to me about flowers,' I said. 'Jeeves, I know now how a general feels when he plans out some great scientific movement and his troops let him down at the eleventh hour.'

'Indeed, sir?'

'Yes,' I said, and told him what had happened.

He listened thoughtfully.

'A somewhat vacillating and changeable young gentleman, Mr. Biffen,' was his comment when I had finished. 'Would you be requiring me for the remainder of the afternoon, sir?'

'No. I'm going to Wembley. I just came back to change and

get the car. Produce some fairly durable garments which can stand getting squashed by the many-headed, Jeeves, and then 'phone to the garage.'

'Very good, sir. The grey cheviot lounge will, I fancy, be suitable. Would it be too much if I asked you to give me a seat in the car, sir? I had thought of going to Wembley myself this afternoon.'

'Eh? Oh, all right.'

'Thank you very much, sir.'

I got dressed, and we drove round to Biffy's flat. Biffy and Sir Roderick got in at the back and Jeeves climbed into the front seat next to me. Biffy looked so ill-attuned to an afternoon's pleasure that my heart bled for the blighter and I made one last attempt to appeal to Jeeves's better feelings.

'I must say, Jeeves,' I said, 'I'm dashed disappointed in you.'

'I am sorry to hear that, sir.'

'Well, I am. Dashed disappointed. I do think you might rally round. Did you see Mr. Biffen's face?'

'Yes, sir.'

'Well, then.'

'If you will pardon my saying so, sir, Mr. Biffen has surely only himself to thank if he has entered upon matrimonial obligations which do not please him.'

'You're talking absolute rot, Jeeves. You know as well as I do that Honoria Glossop is an Act of God. You might just as well blame a fellow for getting run over by a truck.'

'Yes, sir?'

'Absolutely yes. Besides, the poor ass wasn't in a condition to resist. He told me all about it. He had lost the only girl he had ever loved, and you know what a man's like when that happens to him.'

'How was that, sir?'

'Apparently he fell in love with some girl on the boat going over to New York, and they parted at the Customs sheds, arranging to meet next day at her hotel. Well, you know what

Biffy's like. He forgets his own name half the time. He never made a note of the address, and it passed clean out of his mind. He went about in a sort of trance, and suddenly woke up to find that he was engaged to Honoria Glossop.'

'I did not know of this, sir.'

'I don't suppose anybody knows of it except me. He told me when I was in Paris.'

'I should have supposed it would have been feasible to make inquiries, sir.'

'That's what I said. But he had forgotten her name.'

'That sounds remarkable, sir.'

'I said that, too. But it's a fact. All he remembered was that her Christian name was Mabel. Well, you can't go scouring New York for a girl named Mabel, what?'

'I appreciate the difficulty, sir.'

'Well, there it is, then.'

'I see, sir.'

We had got into a mob of vehicles outside the Exhibition by this time, and, some tricky driving being indicated, I had to suspend the conversation. We parked ourselves eventually and went in. Jeeves drifted away, and Sir Roderick took charge of the expedition. He headed for the Palace of Industry, with Biffy and myself trailing behind.

Well, you know, I have never been much of a lad for exhibitions. The citizenry in the mass always rather puts me off, and after I have been shuffling along with the multitude for a quarter of an hour or so I feel as if I were walking on hot bricks. About this particular binge, too, there seemed to me a lack of what you might call human interest. I mean to say, millions of people, no doubt, are so constituted that they scream with joy and excitement at the spectacle of a stuffed porcupine-fish or a glass jar of seeds from Western Australia – but not Bertram. No; if you will take the word of one who would not deceive you, not Bertram. By the time we had tottered out of the Gold Coast village and were working towards the Palace of Machinery, everything pointed to my shortly executing a quiet sneak in the direction of that rather jolly Planters' Bar in the West Indian section. Sir Roderick had whizzed us past this at a high rate of speed, it touching no chord in him; but I had been able to observe that there was a sprightly sportsman behind the counter mixing things out of bottles and stirring them up with a stick in long glasses that seemed to have ice in them, and the urge came upon me to see more of this man. I was about to drop away from the main body and become a straggler, when something pawed at my coat-sleeve. It was Biffy, and he had the air of one who has had about sufficient.

There are certain moments in life when words are not needed. I looked at Biffy, Biffy looked at me. A perfect understanding linked our two souls.

'?'

'!'

Three minutes later we had joined the Planters.

I have never been in the West Indies, but I am in a position to state that in certain of the fundamentals of life they are streets ahead of our European civilisation. The man behind the counter, as kindly a bloke as I ever wish to meet, seemed to guess our requirements the moment we hove in view. Scarcely had our elbows touched the wood before he was leaping to and fro, bringing down a new bottle with each leap. A planter, apparently, does not consider he has had a drink unless it contains at least seven ingredients, and I'm not saying, mind you, that he isn't right. The man behind the bar told us the things were called Green Swizzles; and, if ever I marry and have a son, Green Swizzle Wooster is the name that will go down on the register, in memory of the day his father's life was saved at Wembley.

After the third, Biffy breathed a contented sigh.

'Where do you think Sir Roderick is?' he said.

'Biffy, old thing,' I replied frankly, 'I'm not worrying.'

'Bertie, old bird,' said Biffy, 'nor am I.'

He sighed again, and broke a long silence by asking the man for a straw.

'Bertie,' he said, 'I've just remembered something rather rummy. You know Jeeves?'

I said I knew Jeeves.

'Well, a rather rummy incident occurred as we were going into this place. Old Jeeves sidled up to me and said something rather rummy. You'll never guess what it was.'

'No. I don't believe I ever shall.'

'Jeeves said,' proceeded Biffy earnestly, 'and I am quoting his very words – Jeeves said, "Mr. Biffen" – addressing me, you understand—'

'I understand.'

'"Mr. Biffen," he said, "I strongly advise you to visit the—"'

'The what?' I asked as he paused.

'Bertie, old man,' said Biffy, deeply concerned, 'I've absolutely forgotten!'

I stared at the man.

'What I can't understand,' I said, 'is how you manage to run that Herefordshire place of yours for a day. How on earth do you remember to milk the cows and give the pigs their dinner?'

'Oh, that's all right. There are divers blokes about the places – hirelings and menials, you know – who look after all that.

'Ah!' I said. 'Well, that being so, let us have one more Green Swizzle, and then hey for the Amusement Park.'

When I indulged in those few rather bitter words about exhibitions, it must be distinctly understood that I was not alluding to what you might call the more earthy portion of these curious places. I yield to no man in my approval of those institutions where on payment of a shilling you are permitted to slide down a slippery run-way sitting on a mat. I love the Jiggle-Joggle, and I am prepared to take on all and sundry at Skee Ball for money, stamps, or Brazil nuts.

But, joyous reveller as I am on these occasions, I was simply not in it with old Biffy. Whether it was the Green Swizzles or merely the relief of being parted from Sir Roderick. I don't know, but Biffy flung himself into the pastimes of the proletariat with a zest that was almost frightening. I could hardly drag him away from the Whip, and as for the Switchback, he looked like spending the rest of his life on it. I managed to remove him at last, and he was wandering through the crowd at my side with gleaming eyes, hesitating between having his fortune told and taking a whirl at the Wheel of Joy, when he suddenly grabbed my arm and uttered a sharp animal cry.

'Bertie!'

'Now what?'

He was pointing at a large sign over a building.

'Look! Palace of Beauty!'

I tried to choke him off. I was getting a bit weary by this time. Not so young as I was.

'You don't want to go in there,' I said. 'A fellow at the club was telling me about that. It's only a lot of girls. You don't want to see a lot of girls.'

'I do want to see a lot of girls,' said Biffy firmly. 'Dozens of girls, and the more unlike Honoria they are, the better. Besides, I've suddenly remembered that that's the place Jeeves told me to be sure and visit. It all comes back to me. "Mr. Biffen," he said, "I strongly advise you to visit the Palace of Beauty." Now, what the man was driving at or what his motive was, I don't know; but I ask you, Bertie, is it wise, is it safe, is it judicious ever to ignore Jeeves's lightest word? We enter by the door on the left.'

I don't know if you know this Palace of Beauty place? It's a sort of aquarium full of the delicately-nurtured instead of fishes. You go in, and there is a kind of cage with a female goggling out at you through a sheet of plate glass. She's dressed in some weird kind of costume, and over the cage is written 'Helen of Troy'. You pass on to the next, and there's another one doing jiu-jitsu with a snake. Sub-title, Cleopatra. You get the idea – Famous Women Through the Ages and all that. I can't say it fascinated me to any great extent. I maintain that a lovely woman loses a lot of her charm if you have to stare at her in a tank. Moreover, it gave me a rummy sort of feeling of having wandered into the wrong bedroom at a country house, and I was flying past at a fair rate of speed, anxious to get it over, when Biffy suddenly went off his rocker.

At least, it looked like that. He let out a piercing yell, grabbed my arm with a sudden clutch that felt like the bite of a crocodile, and stood there gibbering.

'Wuk!' ejaculated Biffy, or words to that general import.

A large and interested crowd had gathered round. I think they thought the girls were going to be fed or something. But Biffy paid no attention to them. He was pointing in a loony manner at one of the cages. I forget which it was, but the female inside wore a ruff, so it may have been Queen Elizabeth or Boadicea or someone of that period. She was rather a nice-looking girl, and she was staring at Biffy in much the same pop-eyed way as he was staring at her.

'Mabel!' yelled Biffy, going off in my ear like a bomb.

I can't say I was feeling my chirpiest. Drama is all very well, but I hate getting mixed up in it in a public spot; and I had not realised before how dashed public this spot was. The crowd seemed to have doubled itself in the last five seconds, and, while most of them had their eye on Biffy, quite a goodish few were looking at me as if they thought I was an important principal in the scene and might be expected at any moment to give of my best in the way of wholesome entertainment for the masses.

Biffy was jumping about like a lamb in the springtime – and, what is more, a feeble-minded lamb.

'Bertie! It's her! It's she!' He looked about him wildly. 'Where the deuce is the stage-door?' he cried. 'Where's the manager? I want to see the house-manager immediately.'

And then he suddenly bounded forward and began hammering on the glass with his stick.

'I say, old lad!' I began, but he shook me off.

These fellows who live in the country are apt to go in for fairly sizable clubs instead of the light canes which your well-dressed man about town considers suitable for metropolitan use; and down in Herefordshire, apparently, something in the nature of a knobkerrie is *de rigueur*. Biffy's first slosh smashed the glass all to a hash. Three more cleared the way for him to go into the cage without cutting himself. And, before the crowd had time to realise what a wonderful bob's-worth it was getting in exchange for its entrance-fee, he was inside, engaging the girl in earnest conversation. And at the same moment two large policemen rolled up.

You can't make policemen take the romantic view. Not a tear did these two blighters stop to brush away. They were inside the cage and out of it and marching Biffy through the crowd before you had time to blink. I hurried after them, to do what I could in the way of soothing Biffy's last moments, and the poor old lad turned a glowing face in my direction.

'Chiswick, 60873,' he bellowed in a voice charged with emotion. 'Write it down, Bertie, or I shall forget it. Chiswick, 60873. Her telephone number.'

And then he disappeared, accompanied by about eleven thousand sightseers, and a voice spoke at my elbow.

'Mr. Wooster! What – what – what is the meaning of this?'

Sir Roderick, with bigger eyebrows than ever, was standing at my side.

'It's all right,' I said. 'Poor old Biffy's only gone off his crumpet.'

He tottered.

'What?'

'Had a sort of fit or seizure, you know.'

'Another!' Sir Roderick drew a deep breath. 'And this is the man I was about to allow my daughter to marry!' I heard him mutter.

I tapped him in a kindly spirit on the shoulder. It took some doing, mark you, but I did it.

'If I were you,' I said, 'I should call that off. Scratch the fixture. Wash it out absolutely, is my advice.'

He gave me a nasty look.

'I do not require your advice, Mr. Wooster! I had already arrived independently at the decision of which you speak. Mr. Wooster, you are a friend of this man – a fact which should in itself have been sufficient warning to me. You will – unlike myself – be seeing him again. Kindly inform him, when you do see him, that he may consider his engagement at an end.'

'Right-ho,' I said, and hurried off after the crowd. It seemed to me that a little bailing-out might be in order.

It was about an hour later that I shoved my way out to where I had parked the car. Jeeves was sitting in the front seat, brooding over the cosmos. He rose courteously as I approached.

'You are leaving, sir?'

'I am.'

'And Sir Roderick, sir?'

'Not coming. I am revealing no secrets, Jeeves, when I inform you that he and I have parted brass-rags. Not on speaking terms now.'

'Indeed, sir? And Mr. Biffen? Will you wait for him?'

'No. He's in prison.'

'Really, sir?'

'Yes. I tried to bail him out, but they decided on second thoughts to coop him up for the night.'

'What was his offence, sir?'

'You remember that girl of his I was telling you about? He found her in a tank at the Palace of Beauty and went after her by the quickest route, which was *via* a plate-glass window. He was then scooped up and borne off in irons by the constabulary.' I gazed sideways at him. It is difficult to bring off a penetrating glance out of the corner of your eye, but I managed it. 'Jeeves,' I said, 'there is more in this than the casual observer would suppose. You told Mr. Biffen to go to the Palace of Beauty. Did you know the girl would be there?'

'Yes, sir.'

This was most remarkable and rummy to a degree.

'Dash it, do you know everything?'

'Oh, no, sir,' said Jeeves with an indulgent smile. Humouring the young master.

'Well, how did you know that?'

'I happen to be acquainted with the future Mrs. Biffen, sir.'

'I see. Then you knew all about that business in New York?'

'Yes, sir. And it was for that reason that I was not altogether favourably disposed towards Mr. Biffen when you were first kind enough to suggest that I might be able to offer some slight assistance. I mistakenly supposed that he had been trifling with the girl's affections, sir. But when you told me the true facts of the case I appreciated the injustice I had done to Mr. Biffen and endeavoured to make amends.'

'Well, he certainly owes you a lot. He's crazy about her.'

'That is very gratifying, sir.'

'And she ought to be pretty grateful to you, too. Old Biffy's got fifteen thousand a year, not to mention more cows, pigs, hens, and ducks than he knows what to do with. A dashed useful bird to have in any family.'

'Yes, sir.'

'Tell me, Jeeves,' I said, 'how did you happen to know the girl in the first place?'

Jeeves looked dreamily out into the traffic.

'She is my niece, sir. If I might make the suggestion, sir, I should not jerk the steering-wheel with quite such suddenness. We very nearly collided with that omnibus.'

The evidence was all in. The machinery of the law had worked without a hitch. And the beak, having adjusted a pair of pince-nez which looked as though they were going to do a nose dive any moment, coughed like a pained sheep and slipped us the bad news.

'The prisoner, Wooster,' he said – and who can paint the shame and agony of Bertram at hearing himself so described? – 'will pay a fine of five pounds.'

'Oh, rather!' I said. 'Absolutely! Like a shot!'

I was dashed glad to get the thing settled at such a reasonable figure. I gazed across what they call the sea of faces till I picked up Jeeves, sitting at the back. Stout fellow, he had come to see the young master through his hour of trial.

'I say, Jeeves,' I sang out, 'have you got a fiver? I'm a bit short.'

'Silence!' bellowed some officious blighter.

'It's all right,' I said; 'just arranging the financial details. Got the stuff, Jeeves?'

'Yes, sir.'

'Good egg!'

'Are you a friend of the prisoner?' asked the beak.

'I am in Mr. Wooster's employment, Your Worship, in the capacity of gentleman's personal gentleman.'

'Then pay the fine to the clerk.'

'Very good, Your Worship.'

The beak gave a coldish nod in my direction, as much as to say that they might now strike the fetters from my wrists; and having hitched up the pince-nez once more, proceeded to hand poor old Sippy one of the nastiest looks ever seen in Bosher Street Police Court.

'The case of the prisoner Leon Trotzky – which,' he said, giving Sippy the eye again, 'I am strongly inclined to think an assumed and fictitious name – is more serious. He has been convicted of a wanton and violent assault upon the police. The evidence of the officer has proved that the prisoner struck him in the abdomen, causing severe internal pain, and in other ways interfered with him in the execution of his duties. I am aware that on the night following the annual aquatic contest between the Universities of Oxford and Cambridge a certain licence is traditionally granted by the authorities, but aggravated acts of ruffianly hooliganism like that of the prisoner Trotzky cannot be overlooked or palliated. He will serve a sentence of thirty days in the Second Division without the option of a fine.'

'No, I say – here – hi – dash it all!' protested poor old Sippy.

'Silence!' bellowed the officious blighter.

'Next case,' said the beak. And that was that.

The whole affair was most unfortunate. Memory is a trifle blurred; but as far as I can piece together the facts, what happened was more or less this:

Abstemious cove though I am as a general thing, there is one night in the year when, putting all other engagements aside, I am rather apt to let myself go a bit and renew my lost youth, as it were. The night to which I allude is the one following the annual aquatic contest between the Universities of Oxford and Cambridge; or, putting it another way, Boat-Race Night. Then, if ever, you will see Bertram under the influence. And on this occasion, I freely admit, I had been doing myself rather juicily, with the result that when I ran into old Sippy opposite the Empire I was in quite fairly bonhomous mood. This being so, it cut me to the quick to perceive that Sippy, generally the brightest of revellers, was far from being his usual sunny self. He had the air of a man with a secret sorrow.

'Bertie,' he said as we strolled along toward Piccadilly Circus, 'the heart bowed down by weight of woe to weakest hope will cling.' Sippy is by way of being an author, though mainly dependent for the necessaries of life on subsidies from an old aunt who lives in the country, and his conversation often takes a literary turn. 'But the trouble is that I have no hope to cling to, weak or otherwise. I am up against it, Bertie.'

'In what way, laddie?'

'I've got to go tomorrow and spend three weeks with some absolutely dud – I will go further – some positively scaly friends of my Aunt Vera. She has fixed the thing up, and may a nephew's curse blister every bulb in her garden.'

'Who are these hounds of hell?' I asked.

'Some people named Pringle. I haven't seen them since I was ten, but I remember them at that time striking me as England's premier warts.'

'Tough luck. No wonder you've lost your morale.'

'The world,' said Sippy, 'is very grey. How can I shake off this awful depression?'

It was then that I got one of those bright ideas one does get round about 11.30 on Boat-Race Night.

'What you want, old man,' I said, 'is a policeman's helmet.'

'Do I, Bertie?'

'If I were you, I'd just step straight across the street and get that one over there.'

'But there's a policeman inside it. You can see him distinctly.'

'What does that matter?' I said. I simply couldn't follow his reasoning.

Sippy stood for a moment in thought.

'I believe you're absolutely right,' he said at last. 'Funny I never thought of it before. You really recommend me to get that helmet?'

'I do, indeed.'

'Then I will,' said Sippy, brightening up in the most remarkable manner.

So there you have the posish, and you can see why, as I left the dock a free man, remorse gnawed at my vitals. In his twenty-fifth year, with life opening out before him and all that sort of thing, Oliver Randolph Sipperley had become a jailbird, and it was all my fault. It was I who had dragged that fine spirit down into the mire, so to speak, and the question now arose: What could I do to atone?

Obviously the first move must be to get in touch with Sippy and see if he had any last messages and what not. I pushed about a bit, making inquiries, and presently found myself in a little dark room with whitewashed walls and a wooden bench. Sippy was sitting on the bench with his head in his hands.

'How are you, old lad?' I asked in a hushed bedside voice.

'I'm a ruined man,' said Sippy, looking like a poached egg.

'Oh, come,' I said, 'it's not so bad as all that. I mean to say, you had the swift intelligence to give a false name. There won't be anything about you in the papers.'

'I'm not worrying about the papers. What's bothering me is, how can I go and spend three weeks with the Pringles, starting today, when I've got to sit in a prison cell with a ball and chain on my ankle?'

'But you said you didn't want to go.'

'It isn't a question of wanting, fathead. I've got to go. If I don't my aunt will find out where I am. And if she finds out that I am doing thirty days, without the option, in the lowest dungeon beneath the castle moat – well, where shall I get off?'

I saw his point.

'This is not a thing we can settle for ourselves,' I said gravely. 'We must put our trust in a higher power. Jeeves is the man we must consult.'

And having collected a few of the necessary data, I shook his hand, patted him on the back and tooled off home to Jeeves.

'Jeeves,' I said, when I had climbed outside the pick-me-up which he had thoughtfully prepared against my coming, 'I've got something to tell you; something important; something that vitally affects one whom you have always regarded with – one whom you have always looked upon – one whom you have – well, to cut a long story short, as I'm not feeling quite myself – Mr. Sipperley.'

'Yes, sir?'

'Jeeves, Mr. Souperley is in the sip.'

'Sir?'

'I mean, Mr. Sipperley is in the soup.'

'Indeed, sir?'

'And all owing to me. It was I who, in a moment of mistaken kindness, wishing only to cheer him up and give him something to occupy his mind, recommended him to pinch that policeman's helmet.'

'Is that so, sir?'

'Do you mind not intoning the responses, Jeeves?' I said. 'This is a most complicated story for a man with a headache to have to tell, and if you interrupt you'll make me lose the thread. As a favour to me, therefore, don't do it. Just nod every now and then to show that you're following me.'

I closed my eyes and marshalled the facts.

'To start with then, Jeeves, you may or may not know that Mr. Sipperley is practically dependent on his Aunt Vera.'

'Would that be Miss Sipperley of the Paddock, Beckley-on-the-Moor, in Yorkshire, sir?'

'Yes. Don't tell me you know her!'

'Not personally, sir. But I have a cousin residing in the village who has some slight acquaintance with Miss Sipperley. He has described her to me as an imperious and quick-tempered old lady . . . But I beg your pardon, sir, I should have nodded.'

'Quite right, you should have nodded. Yes, Jeeves, you should have nodded. But it's too late now.'

I nodded myself. I hadn't had my eight hours the night before, and what you might call a lethargy was showing a tendency to steal over me from time to time.

'Yes, sir?' said Jeeves.

'Oh – ah – yes,' I said, giving myself a bit of a hitch up. 'Where had I got to?'

'You were saying that Mr. Sipperley is practically dependent upon Miss Sipperley, sir.'

'Was I?'

'You were, sir.'

'You're perfectly right; so I was. Well, then, you can readily understand, Jeeves, that he has got to take jolly good care to keep in with her. You get that?'

Jeeves nodded.

'Now mark this closely: The other day she wrote to old Sippy, telling him to come down and sing at her village concert. It was equivalent to a royal command, if you see what I mean, so Sippy couldn't refuse in so many words. But he had sung at her village concert once before and had got the bird in no uncertain manner, so he wasn't playing any return dates. You follow so far, Jeeves?'

Jeeves nodded.

'So what did he do, Jeeves? He did what seemed to him at the moment a rather brainy thing. He told her that, though he would have been delighted to sing at her village concert, by a most unfortunate chance an editor had commissioned him to write a series of articles on the colleges of Cambridge and he was obliged to pop down there at once and would be away for quite three weeks. All clear up to now?'

Jeeves inclined the coco-nut.

'Whereupon, Jeeves, Miss Sipperley wrote back, saying that she quite realised that work must come before pleasure – pleasure being her loose way of describing the act of singing songs at the Beckley-on-the-Moor concert and getting the laugh from the local toughs; but that, if he was going to

Cambridge, he must certainly stay with her friends, the Pringles, at their house just outside the town. And she dropped them a line telling them to expect him on the twenty-eighth, and they dropped another line saying right-ho, and the thing was settled. And now Mr. Sipperley is in the jug, and what will be the ultimate outcome or upshot? Jeeves, it is a problem worthy of your great intellect. I rely on you.'

'I will do my best to justify your confidence, sir.'

'Carry on, then. And meanwhile pull down the blinds and bring a couple more cushions and heave that small chair this way so that I can put my feet up, and then go away and brood and let me hear from you in – say, a couple of hours, or maybe three. And if anybody calls and wants to see me, inform them that I am dead.'

'Dead, sir?'

'Dead. You won't be so far wrong.'

It must have been well toward evening when I woke up with a crick in my neck but otherwise somewhat refreshed. I pressed the bell.

'I looked in twice, sir,' said Jeeves, 'but on each occasion you were asleep and I did not like to disturb you.'

'The right spirit, Jeeves. . . . Well?'

'I have been giving close thought to the little problem which you indicated, sir, and I can see only one solution.'

'One is enough. What do you suggest?'

'That you go to Cambridge in Mr. Sipperley's place, sir.'

I stared at the man. Certainly I was feeling a good deal better than I had been a few hours before; but I was far from being in a fit condition to have rot like this talked to me.

'Jeeves,' I said sternly, 'pull yourself together. This is mere babble from the sickbed.'

'I fear I can suggest no other plan of action, sir, which will extricate Mr. Sipperley from his dilemma.'

'But think! Reflect! Why, even I, in spite of having had a disturbed night and a most painful morning with the minions of the law, can see that the scheme is a loony one. To put the finger on only one leak in the thing, it isn't me these people want to see; it's Mr. Sipperley. They don't know me from Adam.'

'So much the better, sir. For what I am suggesting is that you go to Cambridge, affecting actually to be Mr. Sipperley.'

This was too much.

'Jeeves,' I said, and I'm not half sure there weren't tears in my eyes, 'surely you can see for yourself that this is pure banana-oil. It is not like you to come into the presence of a sick man and gibber.'

'I think the plan I have suggested would be practicable, sir. While you were sleeping, I was able to have a few words with Mr. Sipperley, and he informed me that Professor and Mrs. Pringle have not set eyes upon him since he was a lad of ten.'

'No, that's true. He told me that. But even so, they would be sure to ask him questions about my aunt – or rather his aunt. Where would I be then?'

'Mr. Sipperley was kind enough to give me a few facts respecting Miss Sipperley, sir, which I jotted down. With these, added to what my cousin has told me of the lady's habits, I think you would be in a position to answer any ordinary question.'

There is something dashed insidious about Jeeves. Time and again since we first came together he has stunned me with some apparently drivelling suggestion or scheme or ruse or plan of campaign, and after about five minutes has convinced me that it is not only sound but fruity. It took nearly a quarter of an hour to reason me into this particular one, it being considerably the weirdest to date; but he did it. I was holding out pretty firmly, when he suddenly clinched the thing.

'I would certainly suggest, sir,' he said, 'that you left London as soon as possible and remained hid for some little time in some retreat where you would not be likely to be found.'

'Eh? Why?'

'During the last hour Mrs. Spenser Gregson has been on the telephone three times, sir, endeavouring to get into communication with you.'

'Aunt Agatha!' I cried, paling beneath my tan.

'Yes, sir. I gathered from her remarks that she had been reading in the evening paper a report of this morning's proceedings in the police court.'

I hopped from the chair like a jack rabbit of the prairie. If Aunt Agatha was out with her hatchet, a move was most certainly indicated.

'Jeeves,' I said, 'this is a time for deeds, not words. Pack – and that right speedily.'

'I have packed, sir.'

'Find out when there is a train for Cambridge.'

'There is one in forty minutes, sir.'

'Call a taxi.'

'A taxi is at the door, sir.'

'Good!' I said. 'Then lead me to it.'

The Maison Pringle was quite a bit of way out of Cambridge, a mile or two down the Trumpington Road; and when I arrived everybody was dressing for dinner. So it wasn't till I had shoved on the evening raiment and got down to the drawing-room that I met the gang.

'Hullo-ullo!' I said, taking a deep breath and floating in.

I tried to speak in a clear and ringing voice, but I wasn't feeling my chirpiest. It is always a nervous job for a diffident and unassuming bloke to visit a strange house for the first time; and it doesn't make the thing any better when he goes there pretending to be another fellow. I was conscious of a rather pronounced sinking feeling, which the appearance of the Pringles did nothing to allay.

Sippy had described them as England's premier warts, and it looked to me as if he might be about right. Professor Pringle was a thinnish, baldish, dyspeptic-lookingish cove with an eye like a haddock, while Mrs. Pringle's aspect was that of one who had had bad news round about the year 1900 and never really got over it. And I was just staggering under the impact of these two when I was introduced to a couple of ancient females with shawls all over them.

'No doubt you remember my mother?' said Professor Pringle mournfully, indicating Exhibit A.

'Oh – ah!' I said, achieving a bit of a beam.

'And my aunt,' sighed the prof, as if things were getting worse and worse.

'Well, well, well!' I said shooting another beam in the direction of Exhibit B.

'They were saying only this morning that they remembered you,' groaned the prof, abandoning all hope.

There was a pause. The whole strength of the company gazed at me like a family group out of one of Edgar Allan Poe's less cheery yarns, and I felt my *joie de vivre* dying at the roots.

'I remember Oliver,' said Exhibit A. She heaved a sigh. 'He was such a pretty child. What a pity! What a pity!'

Tactful, of course, and calculated to put the guest completely at his ease.

'I remember Oliver,' said Exhibit B. looking at me in much the same way as the Bosher Street beak had looked at Sippy before putting on the black cap. 'Nasty little boy! He teased my cat.'

'Aunt Jane's memory is wonderful, considering that she will be eighty-seven next birthday,' whispered Mrs. Pringle with mournful pride.

'What did you say?' asked the Exhibit suspiciously.

'I said your memory was wonderful.'

'Ah!' The dear old creature gave me another glare. I could see that no beautiful friendship was to be looked for by Bertram in this quarter. 'He chased my Tibby all over the garden, shooting arrows at her from a bow.'

At this moment a cat strolled out from under the sofa and made for me with its tail up. Cats always do take to me, which made it all the sadder that I should be saddled with Sippy's criminal record. I stooped to tickle it under the ear, such being my invariable policy, and the Exhibit uttered a piercing cry.

'Stop him! Stop him!'

She leaped forward, moving uncommonly well for one of her years, and having scooped up the cat, stood eyeing me with bitter defiance, as if daring me to start anything. Most unpleasant.

'I like cats,' I said feebly.

It didn't go. The sympathy of the audience was not with me. And conversation was at what you might call a low ebb, when the door opened and a girl came in.

'My daughter Heloise,' said the prof moodily, as if he hated to admit it.

I turned to mitt the female, and stood there with my hand out, gaping. I can't remember when I've had such a nasty shock.

I suppose everybody has had the experience of suddenly meeting somebody who reminded them frightfully of some fearful person. I mean to say, by way of an example, once when I was golfing in Scotland I saw a woman come into the hotel who was the living image of my Aunt Agatha. Probably a very decent sort, if I had only waited to see, but I didn't wait. I legged it that evening, utterly unable to stand the spectacle. And on another occasion I was driven out of a thoroughly festive night club because the head waiter reminded me of my Uncle Percy.

Well, Heloise Pringle, in the most ghastly way, resembled Honoria Glossop.

I think I may have told you before about this Glossop scourge. She was the daughter of Sir Roderick Glossop, the loony doctor, and I had been engaged to her for about three weeks, much against my wishes, when the old boy most fortunately got the idea that I was off my rocker and put the bee on the proceedings. Since then the mere thought of her had been enough to make me start out of my sleep with a loud cry. And this girl was exactly like her.

'Er – how are you?' I said.

'How do you do?'

Her voice put the lid on it. It might have been Honoria

herself talking. Honoria Glossop has a voice like a lion tamer making some authoritative announcement to one of the troupe, and so had this girl. I backed away convulsively and sprang into the air as my foot stubbed itself against something squashy. A sharp yowl rent the air, followed by an indignant cry, and I turned to see Aunt Jane, on all fours, trying to put things right with the cat, which had gone to earth under the sofa. She gave me a look, and I could see that her worst fears had been realised.

At this juncture dinner was announced – not before I was ready for it.

'Jeeves,' I said, when I got him alone that night, 'I am no faint-heart, but I am inclined to think that this binge is going to prove a shade above the odds.'

'You are not enjoying your visit, sir?'

'I am not, Jeeves. Have you seen Miss Pringle?'

'Yes, sir, from a distance.'

'The best way to see her. Did you observe her keenly?'

'Yes, sir.'

'Did she remind you of anybody?'

'She appeared to me to bear a remarkable likeness to her cousin, Miss Glossop, sir.'

'Her cousin! You don't mean to say she's Honoria Glossop's cousin!'

'Yes, sir. Mrs. Pringle was a Miss Blatherwick – the younger of two sisters, the elder of whom married Sir Roderick Glossop.'

'Great Scott! That accounts for the resemblance.'

'Yes, sir.'

'And what a resemblance, Jeeves! She even talks like Miss Glossop.'

'Indeed, sir? I have not yet heard Miss Pringle speak.'

'You have missed little. And what it amounts to, Jeeves, is that, though nothing will induce me to let old Sippy down, I can see that this visit is going to try me high. At a pinch, I could stand the prof and wife. I could even make the effort of a lifetime and bear up against Aunt Jane. But to expect a man to mix daily with the girl Heloise – and to do it, what is more, on lemonade, which is all there was to drink at dinner – is to ask too much of him. What shall I do, Jeeves?'

'I think that you should avoid Miss Pringle's society as much as possible.'

'The same great thought had occurred to me,' I said.

It is all very well, though, to talk airily about avoiding a female's society; but when you are living in the same house with her, and she doesn't want to avoid you, it takes a bit of doing. It is a peculiar thing in life that the people you most particularly want to edge away from always seem to cluster round like a poultice. I hadn't been twenty-four hours in the place before I perceived that I was going to see a lot of this pestilence.

She was one of those girls you're always meeting on the stairs and in passages. I couldn't go into a room without seeing her drift in a minute later. And if I walked in the garden she was sure to leap out at me from a laurel bush or the onion bed or something. By about the tenth day I had begun to feel absolutely haunted.

'Jeeves,' I said, 'I have begun to feel absolutely haunted.'

'Sir?'

'This woman dogs me. I never seem to get a moment to myself. Old Sippy was supposed to come here to make a study of the Cambridge colleges, and she took me round about fifty-seven this morning. This afternoon I went to sit in the garden, and she popped up through a trap and was in my midst. This evening she cornered me in the morning-room. It's getting so that, when I have a bath, I wouldn't be a bit surprised to find her nestling in the soap dish.'

'Extremely trying, sir.'

'Dashed so. Have you any remedy to suggest?'

'Not at the moment, sir. Miss Pringle does appear to be distinctly interested in you, sir. She was asking me questions this morning respecting your mode of life in London.'

'What?'

'Yes, sir.'

I stared at the man in horror. A ghastly thought had struck me. I quivered like an aspen.

At lunch that day a curious thing had happened. We had just finished mangling the cutlets and I was sitting back in my chair, taking a bit of an easy before being allotted my slab of boiled pudding, when, happening to look up, I caught the girl Heloise's eye fixed on me in what seemed to me a rather rummy manner. I didn't think much about it at the time, because boiled pudding is a thing you have to give your undivided attention to if you want to do yourself justice; but now, recalling the episode in the light of Jeeves's words, the full sinister meaning of the thing seemed to come home to me.

Even at the moment, something about that look had struck me as oddly familiar, and now I suddenly saw why. It had been the identical look which I had observed in the eye of Honoria Glossop in the days immediately preceding our engagement – the look of a tigress that has marked down its prey.

'Jeeves, do you know what I think?'

'Sir?'

I gulped slightly.

'Jeeves,' I said, 'listen attentively. I don't want to give the impression that I consider myself one of those deadly coves who exercise an irresistible fascination over one and all and can't meet a girl without wrecking her peace of mind in the first half-minute. As a matter of fact, it's rather the other way with me, for girls on entering my presence are mostly inclined to give me the raised eyebrow and the twitching upper lip. Nobody, therefore, can say that I am a man who's likely to take alarm unnecessarily. You admit that, don't you?'

'Yes, sir.'

'Nevertheless, Jeeves, it is a known scientific fact that there is a particular style of female that does seem strangely attracted to the sort of fellow I am.'

'Very true, sir.'

'I mean to say, I know perfectly well that I've got, roughly speaking, half the amount of brain a normal bloke ought to possess. And when a girl comes along who has about twice the regular allowance, she too often makes a bee line for me with the love light in her eyes. I don't know how to account for it, but it is so.'

'It may be Nature's provision for maintaining the balance of the species, sir.'

'Very possibly. Anyway, it has happened to me over and over again. It was what happened in the case of Honoria Glossop. She was notoriously one of the brainiest women of her year at Girton, and she just gathered me in like a bull pup swallowing a piece of steak.'

'Miss Pringle, I am informed, sir, was an even more brilliant scholar than Miss Glossop.'

'Well, there you are! Jeeves, she looks at me.'

'Yes, sir?'

'I keep meeting her on the stairs and in passages.'

'Indeed, sir?'

'She recommends me books to read, to improve my mind.'

'Highly suggestive, sir.'

'And at breakfast this morning, when I was eating a sausage, she told me I shouldn't, as modern medical science held that a four-inch sausage contained as many germs as a dead rat. The maternal touch, you understand; fussing over my health.'

'I think we may regard that, sir, as practically conclusive.'

I sank into a chair, thoroughly pipped.

'What's to be done, Jeeves?'

'We must think, sir.'

'You think. I haven't the machinery.'

'I will most certainly devote my very best attention to the matter, sir, and will endeavour to give satisfaction.'

Well, that was something. But I was ill at ease. Yes, there is no getting away from it, Bertram was ill at ease.

*

Next morning we visited sixty-three more Cambridge colleges, and after lunch I said I was going to my room to lie down. After staying there for half an hour to give the coast time to clear, I shoved a book and smoking materials in my pocket, and climbing out of a window, shinned down a convenient water-pipe into the garden. My objective was the summer-house, where it seemed to me that a man might put in a quiet hour or so without interruption.

It was extremely jolly in the garden. The sun was shining, the crocuses were all to the mustard and there wasn't a sign of Heloise Pringle anywhere. The cat was fooling about on the lawn, so I chirruped to it and it gave a low gargle and came trotting up. I had just got it in my arms and was scratching it under the ear when there was a loud shriek from above, and there was Aunt Jane half out of the window. Dashed disturbing.

'Oh, right-ho,' I said.

I dropped the cat, which galloped off into the bushes, and dismissing the idea of bunging a brick at the aged relative, went on my way, heading for the shrubbery. Once safely hidden there, I worked round till I got to the summer-house. And, believe me, I had hardly got my first cigarette nicely under way when a shadow fell on my book and there was young Sticketh-Closer-Than-a-Brother in person.

'So there you are,' she said.

She seated herself by my side, and with a sort of gruesome playfulness jerked the gasper out of the holder and heaved it through the door.

'You're always smoking,' she said, a lot too much like a lovingly chiding young bride for my comfort. 'I wish you wouldn't. It's so bad for you. And you ought not to be sitting out here without your light overcoat. You want someone to look after you.'

'I've got Jeeves.'

She frowned a bit.

'I don't like him,' she said.

'Eh? Why not?'

'I don't know. I wish you would get rid of him.'

My flesh absolutely crept. And I'll tell you why. One of the first things Honoria Glossop had done after we had become engaged was to tell me she didn't like Jeeves and wanted him shot out. The realisation that this girl resembled Honoria not only in body but in blackness of soul made me go all faint.

'What are you reading?'

She picked up my book and frowned again. The thing was one I had brought down from the old flat in London, to glance at in the train – a fairly zippy effort in the detective line called *The Trail of Blood*. She turned the pages with a nasty sneer.

'I can't understand you liking nonsense of this—' She stopped suddenly. 'Good gracious!'

'What's the matter?'

'Do you know Bertie Wooster?'

And then I saw that my name was scrawled right across the title page, and my heart did three back somersaults.

'Oh – er – well – that is to say – well, slightly.'

'He must be a perfect horror. I'm surprised that you can make a friend of him. Apart from anything else, the man is practically an imbecile. He was engaged to my Cousin Honoria at one time, and it was broken off because he was next door to insane. You should hear my Uncle Roderick talk about him!'

I wasn't keen.

'Do you see much of him?'

'A goodish bit.'

'I saw in the paper the other day that he was fined for making a disgraceful disturbance in the street.'

'Yes, I saw that.'

She gazed at me in a foul, motherly way.

'He can't be a good influence for you,' she said. 'I do wish you would drop him. Will you?'

'Well—' I began. And at this point old Cuthbert, the cat,

having presumably found it a bit slow by himself in the bushes, wandered in with a matey expression on his face and jumped on my lap. I welcomed him with a good deal of cordiality. Though but a cat, he did make a sort of third at this party; and he afforded a good excuse for changing the conversation.

'Jolly birds, cats,' I said.

She wasn't having any.

'Will you drop Bertie Wooster?' she said, absolutely ignoring the cat *motif*.

'It would be so difficult.'

'Nonsense! It only needs a little will power. The man surely can't be so interesting a companion as all that. Uncle Roderick says he is an invertebrate waster.'

I could have mentioned a few things that I thought Uncle Roderick was, but my lips were sealed, so to speak.

'You have changed a great deal since we last met,' said the Pringle disease reproachfully. She bent forward and began to scratch the cat under the other ear. 'Do you remember, when we were children together, you used to say that you would do anything for me?'

'Did I?'

'I remember once you cried because I was cross and wouldn't let you kiss me.'

I didn't believe it at the time, and I don't believe it now. Sippy is in many ways a good deal of a chump, but surely even at the age of ten he cannot have been such a priceless ass as that. I think the girl was lying, but that didn't make the position of affairs any better. I edged away a couple of inches and sat staring before me, the old brow beginning to get slightly bedewed.

And then suddenly – well, you know how it is, I mean. I suppose everyone has had that ghastly feeling at one time or another of being urged by some overwhelming force to do some absolutely blithering act. You get it every now and then when you're in a crowded theatre, and something seems to be egging you on to shout 'Fire!' and see what happens. Or you're talking to someone and all at once you feel, 'Now, suppose I suddenly biffed this bird in the eye!'

Well, what I'm driving at is this, at this juncture, with her shoulder squashing against mine and her back hair tickling my nose, a perfectly loony impulse came sweeping over me to kiss her.

'No, really?' I croaked.

'Have you forgotten?'

She lifted the old onion and her eyes looked straight into mine. I could feel myself skidding. I shut my eyes. And then from the doorway there spoke the most beautiful voice I had ever heard in my life:

'Give me that cat!'

I opened my eyes. There was good old Aunt Jane, that queen of her sex, standing before me, glaring at me as if I were a vivisectionist and she had surprised me in the middle of an experiment. How this pearl among women had tracked me down I don't know, but there she stood, bless her dear, intelligent old soul, like the rescue party in the last reel of a motion picture.

I didn't wait. The spell was broken and I legged it. As I went, I heard that lovely voice again.

'He shot arrows at my Tibby from a bow,' said this most deserving and excellent octogenarian.

For the next few days all was peace. I saw comparatively little of Heloise. I found the strategic value of that water-pipe outside my window beyond praise. I seldom left the house now by any other route. It seemed to me that, if only the luck held like this, I might after all be able to stick this visit out for the full term of the sentence.

But meanwhile, as they used to say in the movies—

The whole family appeared to be present and correct as I came down to the drawing-room a couple of nights later. The Prof, Mrs. Prof, the two Exhibits and the girl Heloise were scattered about at intervals. The cat slept on the rug, the canary in its cage. There was nothing, in short, to indicate that this was not just one of our ordinary evenings.

'Well, well, well!' I said cheerily. 'Hullo-ullo-ullo!'

I always like to make something in the nature of an entrance speech, it seeming to me to lend a chummy tone to the proceedings.

The girl Heloise looked at me reproachfully.

'Where have you been all day?' she asked.

'I went to my room after lunch.'

'You weren't there at five.'

'No. After putting in a spell of work on the good old colleges I went for a stroll. Fellow must have exercise if he means to keep fit.'

'*Mens sana in corpore sano,*' observed the prof.

'I shouldn't wonder,' I said cordially.

At this point, when everything was going as sweet as a nut and I was feeling on top of my form, Mrs. Pringle suddenly soaked me on the base of the skull with a sandbag. Not actually, I don't mean. No, no. I speak figuratively, as it were.

'Roderick is very late,' she said.

You may think it strange that the sound of that name should have sloshed into my nerve centres like a half-brick. But, take it from me, to a man who has had any dealings with Sir Roderick Glossop there is only one Roderick in the world – and that is one too many.

'Roderick?' I gurgled.

'My brother-in-law, Sir Roderick Glossop, comes to Cambridge tonight,' said the prof. 'He lectures at St. Luke's tomorrow. He is coming here to dinner.'

And while I stood there, feeling like the hero when he discovers that he is trapped in the den of the Secret Nine, the door opened.

'Sir Roderick Glossop,' announced the maid or some such person, and in he came.

One of the things that get this old crumb so generally disliked among the better element of the community is the fact that he has a head like the dome of St. Paul's and eyebrows that want bobbing or shingling to reduce them to anything like reasonable size. It is a nasty experience to see this bald and bushy bloke advancing on you when you haven't prepared the strategic railways in your rear.

As he came into the room I backed behind a sofa and commended my soul to God. I didn't need to have my hand read to know that trouble was coming to me through a dark man.

He didn't spot me at first. He shook hands with the prof and wife, kissed Heloise and waggled his head at the Exhibits.

'I fear I am somewhat late,' he said. 'A slight accident on the road, affecting what my chauffeur termed the—'

And then he saw me lurking on the outskirts and gave a startled grunt, as if I hurt him a good deal internally.

'This—' began the prof, waving in my direction.

'I am already acquainted with Mr. Wooster.'

'This,' went on the prof, 'is Miss Sipperley's nephew, Oliver. You remember Miss Sipperley?'

'What do you mean?' barked Sir Roderick. Having had so much to do with loonies has given him a rather sharp and authoritative manner on occasion. 'This is that wretched young man, Bertram Wooster. What is all this nonsense about Olivers and Sipperleys?'

The prof was eyeing me with some natural surprise. So were the others. I beamed a bit weakly.

'Well, as a matter of fact—' I said.

The prof was wrestling with the situation. You could hear his brain buzzing.

'He said he was Oliver Sipperley,' he moaned.

'Come here!' bellowed Sir Roderick. 'Am I to understand that you have inflicted yourself on this household under the pretence of being the nephew of an old friend?'

It seemed a pretty accurate description of the facts.

'Well – er – yes,' I said.

Sir Roderick shot an eye at me. It entered the body somewhere about the top stud, roamed around inside for a bit and went out at the back.

'Insane! Quite insane, as I knew from the first moment I saw him.'

'What did he say?' asked Aunt Jane.

'Roderick says this young man is insane,' roared the prof.

'Ah!' said Aunt Jane, nodding. 'I thought so. He climbs down water-pipes.'

'Does what?'

'I've seen him – ah, many a time!'

Sir Roderick snorted violently.

'He ought to be under proper restraint. It is abominable that a person in his mental condition should be permitted to roam the world at large. The next stage may quite easily be homicidal.'

It seemed to me that, even at the expense of giving old Sippy away, I must be cleared of this frightful charge. After all, Sippy's number was up anyway.

'Let me explain,' I said. 'Sippy asked me to come here.'

'What do you mean?'

'He couldn't come himself, because he was jugged for biffing a cop on Boat-Race Night.'

Well, it wasn't easy to make them get the hang of the story, and even when I'd done it it didn't seem to make them any chummier towards me. A certain coldness about expresses it, and when dinner was announced I counted myself out and pushed off rapidly to my room. I could have done with a bit of dinner, but the atmosphere didn't seem just right.

'Jeeves,' I said, having shot in and pressed the bell, 'we're sunk.'

'Sir?'

'Hell's foundations are quivering and the game is up.'

He listened attentively.

'The contingency was one always to have been anticipated as a possibility, sir. It only remains to take the obvious step.'

'What's that?'

'Go and see Miss Sipperley, sir.'

'What on earth for?'

'I think it would be judicious to apprise her of the facts yourself, sir, instead of allowing her to hear of them through the medium of a letter from Professor Pringle. That is to say, if you are still anxious to do all in your power to assist Mr. Sipperley.'

'I can't let Sippy down. If you think it's any good—'

'We can but try it, sir. I have an idea, sir, that we may find Miss Sipperley disposed to look leniently upon Mr. Sipperley's misdemeanour.'

'What makes you think that?'

'It is just a feeling that I have, sir.'

'Well, if you think it would be worth trying— How do we get there?'

'The distance is about a hundred and fifty miles, sir. Our best plan would be to hire a car.'

'Get it at once,' I said.

The idea of being a hundred and fifty miles away from Heloise Pringle, not to mention Aunt Jane and Sir Roderick Glossop, sounded about as good to me as anything I had ever heard.

The Paddock, Beckley-on-the-Moor, was about a couple of parasangs from the village, and I set out for it next morning, after partaking of a hearty breakfast at the local inn, practically without a tremor. I suppose when a fellow has been through it as I had in the last two weeks his system becomes hardened. After all, I felt, whatever this aunt of Sippy's might be like, she wasn't Sir Roderick Glossop, so I was that much on velvet from the start.

The Paddock was one of those medium-sized houses with a goodish bit of very tidy garden and a carefully rolled gravel drive curving past a shrubbery that looked as if it had just come back from the dry cleaner – the sort of house you take one look at and say to yourself, 'Somebody's aunt lives there.' I pushed on up the drive, and as I turned the bend I observed in the middle distance a woman messing about by a flower-bed with a trowel in her hand. If this wasn't the female I was after, I was very much mistaken, so I halted, cleared the throat and gave tongue.

'Miss Sipperley?'

She had had her back to me, and at the sound of my voice she executed a sort of leap or bound, not unlike a barefoot dancer who steps on a tin-tack halfway through the Vision of Salome. She came to earth and goggled at me in a rather goofy manner. A large stout female with a reddish face.

'Hope I didn't startle you,' I said.

'Who are you?'

'My name's Wooster. I'm a pal of your nephew, Oliver.'

Her breathing had become more regular.

'Oh?' she said. 'When I heard your voice I thought you were someone else.'

'No, that's who I am. I came up here to tell you about Oliver.'

'What about him?'

I hesitated. Now that we were approaching what you might call the nub, or crux, of the situation, a good deal of my breezy confidence seemed to have slipped from me.

'Well, it's rather a painful tale, I must warn you.'

'Oliver isn't ill? He hasn't had an accident?'

She spoke anxiously, and I was pleased at this evidence of human feeling. I decided to shoot the works with no more delay.

'Oh, no, he isn't ill,' I said; 'and as regards having accidents, it depends on what you call an accident. He's in chokey.'

'In what?'

'In prison.'

'In prison!'

'It was entirely my fault. We were strolling along on Boat-Race Night and I advised him to pinch a policeman's helmet.'

'I don't understand.'

'Well, he seemed depressed, don't you know; and rightly or wrongly, I thought it might cheer him up if he stepped across the street and collared a policeman's helmet. He thought it a good idea, too, so he started doing it, and the man made a fuss and Oliver sloshed him.'

'Sloshed him?'

'Biffed him – smote him a blow – in the stomach.'

'My nephew Oliver hit a policeman in the stomach?'

'Absolutely in the stomach. And next morning the beak sent him to the bastille for thirty days without the option.'

I was looking at her a bit anxiously all this while to see how she was taking the thing, and at this moment her face seemed suddenly to split in half. For an instant she appeared to be all mouth, and then she was staggering about the grass, shouting with laughter and waving the trowel madly.

It seemed to me a bit of luck for her that Sir Roderick Glossop wasn't on the spot. He would have been calling for the strait-waistcoat in the first half-minute.

'You aren't annoyed?' I said.

'Annoyed?' She chuckled happily. 'I've never heard such a splendid thing in my life.'

I was pleased and relieved. I had hoped the news wouldn't upset her too much, but I had never expected it to go with such a roar as this.

'I'm proud of him,' she said.

'That's fine.'

'If every young man in England went about hitting policemen in the stomach, it would be a better country to live in.'

I couldn't follow her reasoning, but everything seemed to be all right; so after a few more cheery words I said good-bye and legged it.

'Jeeves,' I said when I got back to the inn, 'everything's fine. But I am far from understanding why.'

'What actually occurred when you met Miss Sipperley, sir?'

'I told her Sippy was in the jug for assaulting the police. Upon which she burst into hearty laughter, waved her trowel in a pleased manner and said she was proud of him.'

'I think I can explain her apparently eccentric behaviour, sir. I am informed that Miss Sipperley has had a good deal of annoyance at the hands of the local constable during the past two weeks. This has doubtless resulted in a prejudice on her part against the force as a whole.'

'Really? How was that?'

'The constable has been somewhat over-zealous in the performance of his duties, sir. On no fewer than three occasions in the last ten days he has served summonses upon Miss Sipperley – for exceeding the speed limit in her car; for allowing her dog to appear in public without a collar; and for failing to abate a smoky chimney. Being in the nature of an autocrat, if I may use the term, in the village, Miss Sipperley has been accustomed to do these things in the past with impunity, and the constable's unexpected zeal has made her somewhat ill-disposed to policemen as a class and consequently disposed to look upon such assaults as Mr. Sipperley's in a kindly and broad minded spirit.'

I saw his point.

'What an amazing bit of luck, Jeeves!'

'Yes, sir.'

'Where did you hear all this?'

'My informant was the constable himself, sir. He is my cousin.'

I gaped at the man. I saw, so to speak, all.

'Good Lord, Jeeves! You didn't bribe him?'

'Oh, no, sir. But it was his birthday last week, and I gave him a little present, I have always been fond of Egbert, sir.'

'How much?'

'A matter of five pounds, sir.'

I felt in my pocket.

'Here you are,' I said. 'And another fiver for luck.'

'Thank you very much, sir.'

'Jeeves,' I said, 'you move in a mysterious way your wonders to perform. You don't mind if I sing a bit, do you?'

'Not at all, sir,' said Jeeves.

'Jeeves,' I said looking in on him one afternoon on my return from the club, 'I don't want to interrupt you.'

'No, sir?'

'But I would like a word with you.'

'Yes, sir?'

He had been packing a few of the Wooster necessaries in the old kit-bag against our approaching visit to the seaside, and he now rose and stood bursting with courteous zeal.

'Jeeves,' I said, 'a somewhat disturbing situation has arisen with regard to a pal of mine.'

'Indeed, sir?'

'You know Mr. Bullivant?'

'Yes, sir.'

'Well, I slid into the Drones this morning for a bite of lunch, and found him in a dark corner of the smoking-room looking like the last rose of summer. Naturally I was surprised. You know what a bright lad he is as a rule. The life and soul of every gathering he attends.'

'Yes, sir.'

'Quite the little lump of fun, in fact.'

'Precisely, sir.'

'Well, I made inquiries, and he told me that he had had a quarrel with the girl he's engaged to. You knew he was engaged to Miss Elizabeth Vickers?'

'Yes, sir. I recall reading the announcement in the *Morning Post*.'

'Well, he isn't any longer. What the row was about he didn't say, but the broad facts, Jeeves, are that she has scratched the fixture. She won't let him come near her, refuses to talk on the 'phone, and sends back his letters unopened.'

'Extremely trying, sir.'

'We ought to do something, Jeeves. But what?'

'It is somewhat difficult to make a suggestion, sir.'

'Well, what I'm going to do for a start is to take him down to Marvis Bay with me. I know these birds who have been handed their hat by the girl of their dreams, Jeeves. What they want is complete change of scene.'

'There is much in what you say, sir.'

'Yes. Change of scene is the thing. I heard of a man. Girl refused him. Man went abroad. Two months later girl wired him "Come back, Muriel." Man started to write out a reply; suddenly found that he couldn't remember girl's surname; so never answered at all, and lived happily ever after. It may well be, Jeeves, that after Freddie Bullivant has had a few weeks of Marvis Bay he will get completely over it.'

'Very possibly, sir.'

'And, if not, it is quite likely that, refreshed by sea air and good simple food, you will get a brainwave and think up some scheme for bringing these two misguided blighters together again.'

'I will do my best, sir.'

'I knew it, Jeeves, I knew it. Don't forget to put in plenty of socks.'

'No, sir.'

'Also of tennis shirts not a few.'

'Very good, sir.'

I left him to his packing, and a couple of days later we started off for Marvis Bay, where I had taken a cottage for July and August.

I don't know if you know Marvis Bay? It's in Dorsetshire; and, while not what you would call a fiercely exciting spot, has many good points. You spend the day there bathing and sitting on the sands, and in the evening you stroll out on the shore with the mosquitoes. At nine p.m. you rub ointment on the wounds and go to bed. It was a simple, healthy life, and it seemed to suit poor old Freddie absolutely. Once the moon was up and the breeze sighing in the trees, you couldn't drag him from that beach with ropes. He became quite a popular pet with the mosquitoes. They would hang round waiting for him to come out, and would give a miss to perfectly good strollers just so as to be in good condition for him.

It was during the day that I found Freddie, poor old chap, a trifle heavy as a guest. I suppose you can't blame a bloke whose heart is broken, but it required a good deal of fortitude to bear up against this gloom-crushed exhibit during the early days of our little holiday. When he wasn't chewing a pipe and scowling at the carpet, he was sitting at the piano, playing 'The Rosary' with one finger. He couldn't play anything except 'The Rosary', and he couldn't play much of that. However firmly and confidently he started off, somewhere around the third bar a fuse would blow out and he would have to start all over again.

He was playing it as usual one morning when I came in from bathing: and it seemed to me that he was extracting more hideous melancholy from it even than usual. Nor had my senses deceived me.

'Bertie,' he said in a hollow voice, skidding on the fourth crotchet from the left as you enter the second bar and producing a distressing sound like the death-rattle of a sand-eel, 'I've seen her!'

'Seen her?' I said. 'What, Elizabeth Vickers? How do you mean, you've seen her? She isn't down here.'

'Yes, she is. I suppose she's staying with relations or something. I was down at the post office, seeing if there were any letters, and we met in the doorway.'

'What happened?'

'She cut me dead.'

He started 'The Rosary' again, and stubbed his finger on a semi-quaver.

'Bertie,' he said, 'you ought never to have brought me here. I must go away.'

'Go away? Don't talk such rot. This is the best thing that could have happened. It's a most amazing bit of luck, her being down here. This is where you come out strong.'

'She cut me.'

'Never mind. Be a sportsman. Have another dash at her.'

'She looked clean through me.'

'Well, don't mind that. Stick at it. Now, having got her down here, what you want,' I said, 'is to place her under some obligation to you. What you want is to get her timidly thanking you. What you want—'

'What's she going to thank me timidly for?'

I thought for a while. Undoubtedly he had put his finger on the nub of the problem. For some moments I was at a loss, not to say nonplussed. Then I saw the way.

'What you want,' I said, 'is to look out for a chance and save her from drowning.'

'I can't swim.'

That was Freddie Bullivant all over. A dear old chap in a thousand ways, but no help to a fellow, if you know what I mean.

He cranked up the piano once more, and I legged it for the open.

I strolled out on the beach and began to think this thing over. I would have liked to consult Jeeves, of course, but Jeeves had disappeared for the morning. There was no doubt that it was hopeless expecting Freddie to do anything for himself in this crisis. I'm not saying that dear old Freddie hasn't got his strong qualities. He is good at polo, and I have heard him spoken of as a coming man at snookerpool. But apart from this you couldn't call him a man of enterprise.

Well, I was rounding some rocks, thinking pretty tensely, when I caught sight of a blue dress, and there was the girl in person. I had never met her, but Freddie had sixteen photographs of her sprinkled round his bedroom, and I knew I couldn't be mistaken. She was sitting on the sand, helping a small, fat child to build a castle. On a chair close by was an elderly female reading a novel. I heard the girl call her 'aunt'. So, getting the reasoning faculties to work, I deduced that the fat child must be her cousin. It struck me that if Freddie had been there he would probably have tried to work up some sentiment about the kid on the strength of it. I couldn't manage this. I don't think I ever saw a kid who made me feel less sentimental. He was one of those round, bulging kids.

After he had finished his castle he seemed to get bored with life and began to cry. The girl, who seemed to read him like a book, took him off to where a fellow was selling sweets at a stall. And I walked on.

Now, those who know me, if you ask them, will tell you that I'm a chump. My Aunt Agatha would testify to this effect. So would my Uncle Percy and many more of my nearest and – if you like to use the expression – dearest. Well, I don't mind. I admit it. I *am* a chump. But what I do say – and I should like to lay the greatest possible stress on this – is that every now and then, just when the populace has given up hope that I will ever show any real human intelligence – I get what it is idle to pretend is not an inspiration. And that's what happened now. I doubt if the idea that came to me at this juncture would have occurred to a single one of any dozen of the largest-brained blokes in history. Napoleon might have got it, but I'll bet Darwin and Shakespeare and Marcus Aurelius wouldn't have thought of it in a thousand years.

It came to me on my return journey. I was walking back along the shore, exercising the old bean fiercely, when I saw the fat child meditatively smacking a jelly-fish with a spade. The girl wasn't with him. The aunt wasn't with him. In fact, there wasn't anybody else in sight. And the solution of the whole trouble between Freddie and his Elizabeth suddenly came to me in a flash.

From what I had seen of the two, the girl was evidently fond of this kid: and, anyhow, he was her cousin, so what I said to myself was this: 'If I kidnap this young heavyweight for a brief space of time: and if, when the girl has got frightfully anxious about where he can have got to, dear old Freddie suddenly appears leading the infant by the hand and telling a story to the effect that he had found him wandering at large about the country and practically saved his life, the girl's gratitude is bound to make her chuck hostilities and be friends again.'

So I gathered up the kid and made off with him.

Freddie, dear old chap, was rather slow at first in getting on to the fine points of the idea. When I appeared at the cottage, carrying the child, and dumped him down in the sitting-room, he showed no joy whatever. The child had started to bellow by this time, not thinking much of the thing, and Freddie seemed to find it rather trying.

'What the devil's all this?' he asked, regarding the little visitor with a good deal of loathing.

The kid loosed off a yell that made the windows rattle, and I saw that this was a time for strategy. I raced to the kitchen and fetched a pot of honey. It was the right idea. The kid stopped bellowing and began to smear his face with the stuff.

'Well?' said Freddie, when silence had set in.

I explained the scheme. After a while it began to strike him. The careworn look faded from his face, and for the first time since his arrival at Marvis Bay he smiled almost happily.

'There's something in this, Bertie.'

'It's the goods.

'I think it will work,' said Freddie.

And, disentangling the child from the honey, he led him out.

'I expect Elizabeth will be on the beach somewhere,' he said.

What you might call a quiet happiness suffused me, if that's the word I want. I was very fond of old Freddie, and it was jolly to think that he was shortly about to click once more. I was leaning back in a chair on the veranda, smoking a peaceful cigarette, when down the road I saw the old boy returning, and, by George, the kid was still with him.

'Hallo!' I said. 'Couldn't you find her?'

I then perceived that Freddie was looking as if he had been kicked in the stomach.

'Yes, I found her,' he replied, with one of those bitter, mirthless laughs you read about.

'Well, then—?'

He sank into a chair and groaned.

'This isn't her cousin, you idiot,' he said. 'He's no relation at all – just a kid she met on the beach. She had never seen him before in her life.'

'But she was helping him build a sand-castle.'

'I don't care. He's a perfect stranger.'

It seemed to me that, if the modern girl goes about building sand-castles with kids she has only known for five minutes and probably without a proper introduction at that, then all that has been written about her is perfectly true. Brazen is the word that seems to meet the case.

I said as much to Freddie, but he wasn't listening.

'Well, who is this ghastly child, then?' I said.

'I don't know. O Lord, I've had a time! Thank goodness you will probably spend the next few years of your life in Dartmoor for kidnapping. That's my only consolation. I'll come and jeer at you through the bars on visiting days.'

'Tell me all, old man,' I said.

He told me all. It took him a good long time to do it, for he broke off in the middle of nearly every sentence to call me names, but I gradually gathered what had happened. The girl Elizabeth had listened like an iceberg while he worked off the story he had prepared, and then – well, she didn't actually call him a liar in so many words, but she gave him to understand in a general sort of way that he was a worm and an outcast. And then he crawled off with the kid, licked to a splinter.

'And mind,' he concluded, 'this is your affair. I'm not mixed up in it at all. If you want to escape your sentence – or anyway get a portion of it remitted – you'd better go and find the child's parents and return him before the police come for you.'

'Who are his parents?'

'I don't know.'

'Where do they live?'

'I don't know.'

The kid didn't seem to know, either. A thoroughly vapid and uninformed infant. I got out of him the fact that he had a father, but that was as far as he went. It didn't seem ever to have occurred to him, chatting of an evening with the old man, to ask him his name and address. So, after a wasted ten minutes, out we went into the great world, more or less what you might call at random.

I give you my word that, until I started to tramp the place with this child, I never had a notion that it was such a difficult job restoring a son to his parents. How kidnappers ever get caught is a mystery to me. I searched Marvis Bay like a bloodhound, but nobody came forward to claim the infant. You would have thought, from the lack of interest in him, that he was stopping there all by himself in a cottage of his own. It wasn't till, by another inspiration, I thought to ask the sweet-stall man that I got on the track. The sweet-stall man, who seemed to have seen a lot of him, said that the child's name was Kegworthy, and that his parents lived at a place called Ocean Rest.

It then remained to find Ocean Rest. And eventually, after visiting Ocean View, Ocean Prospect, Ocean Breeze, Ocean Cottage, Ocean Bungalow, Ocean Nook and Ocean Homestead, I trailed it down.

I knocked at the door. Nobody answered. I knocked again. I could hear movements inside, but nobody appeared. I was just going to get to work with that knocker in such a way that it would filter through the people's heads that I wasn't standing there just for the fun of the thing, when a voice from somewhere above shouted 'Hi!'

I looked up and saw a round, pink face, with grey whiskers east and west of it, staring down at me from an upper window.

'Hi!' it shouted again. 'You can't come in.'

'I don't want to come in.'

'Because— Oh, is that Tootles?'

'My name is not Tootles. Are you Mr. Kegworthy? I've brought back your son.'

'I see him. Peep-bo, Tootles, Dadda can see 'oo.'

The face disappeared with a jerk. I could hear voices. The face reappeared.

'Hi!'

I churned the gravel madly. This blighter was giving me the pip.

'Do you live here?' asked the face.

'I have taken a cottage here for a few weeks.'

'What's your name?'

'Wooster.'

'Fancy that! Do you spell it W-o-r-c-e-s-t-e-r or W-o-o-s-t-e-r?'

'W-o-o—'

'I asked because I once knew a Miss Wooster, spelled W-o-o—'

I had had about enough of this spelling-bee.

'Will you open the door and take this child in?'

'I mustn't open the door. This Miss Wooster that I knew married a man named Spenser Gregson. Was she any relation?'

'She is my Aunt Agatha,' I replied, and I spoke with a good deal of bitterness, trying to suggest by my manner that he was exactly the sort of man, in my opinion, who would know my Aunt Agatha.

He beamed down at me.

'This is most fortunate. We were wondering what to do with Tootles. You see, we have mumps here. My daughter Bootles has just developed mumps. Tootles must not be exposed to the risk of infection. We could not think what to do with him. It was most fortunate, your finding the dear child. He strayed from his nurse. I would hesitate to trust him to a stranger, but you are different. Any nephew of Mrs. Gregson's has my complete confidence. You must take Tootles into your house. It will be an ideal arrangement. I have written to my brother in London to come and fetch him. He may be here in a few days.'

'May!'

'He is a busy man, of course; but he should certainly be here within a week. Till then Tootles can stop with you. It is an excellent plan. Very much obliged to you. Your wife will like Tootles.'

'I haven't got a wife!' I yelled; but the window had closed with a bang, as if the man with the whiskers had found a germ trying to escape and had headed it off just in time.

I breathed a deep breath and wiped the old forehead.

The window flew up again.

'Hi!'

A package weighing about a ton hit me on the head and burst like a bomb.

'Did you catch it?' said the face, reappearing. 'Dear me, you missed it. Never mind. You can get it at the grocer's. Ask for Bailey's Granulated Breakfast Chips. Tootles takes them for breakfast with a little milk. Not cream. Milk. Be sure to get Bailey's.'

'Yes, but—'

The face disappeared, and the window was banged down again. I lingered a while, but nothing else happened, so, taking Tootles by the hand, I walked slowly away.

And as we turned up the road we met Freddie's Elizabeth.

'Well, baby?' she said, sighting the kid. 'So daddy found you again, did he? Your little son and I made great friends on the beach this morning,' she said to me.

This was the limit. Coming on top of that interview with the whiskered lunatic, it so utterly unnerved me that she had nodded good-bye and was half-way down the road before I caught up with my breath enough to deny the charge of being the infant's father.

I hadn't expected Freddie to sing with joy when he saw me looming up with child complete, but I did think he might have shown a little more manly fortitude, a little more of the old British bull-dog spirit. He leaped up when we came in, glared at the kid and clutched his head. He didn't speak for a long time; but, to make up for it, when he began he did not leave off for a long time.

'Well,' he said, when he had finished the body of his remarks, 'say something! Heavens, man, why don't you say something?'

'If you'll give me a chance, I will,' I said, and shot the bad news.

'What are you going to do about it?' he asked. And it would be idle to deny that his manner was peevish.

'What can we do about it?'

'We? What do you mean, we? I'm not going to spend my time taking turns as a nursemaid to this excrescence. I'm going back to London.'

'Freddie!' I cried. 'Freddie, old man!' My voice shook. 'Would you desert a pal at a time like this?'

'Yes, I would.'

'Freddie,' I said, 'you've got to stand by me. You must. Do you realise that this child has to be undressed, and bathed, and dressed again? You wouldn't leave me to do all that single-handed?'

'Jeeves can help you.'

'No, sir,' said Jeeves, who had just rolled in with lunch; 'I must, I fear, disassociate myself completely from the matter.' He spoke respectfully but firmly. 'I have had little or no experience with children.'

'Now's the time to start,' I urged.

'No, sir; I am sorry to say that I can't involve myself in any way.'

'Then you must stand by me, Freddie.'

'I won't.'

'You must. Reflect, old man! We have been pals for years. Your mother likes me.'

'No, she doesn't.'

'Well, anyway, we were at school together and you owe me a tenner.'

'Oh, well,' he said in a resigned sort of voice.

'Besides, old thing,' I said, 'I did it all for your sake, you know.'

He looked at me in a curious way, and breathed rather hard for some moments.

'Bertie,' he said, 'one moment. I will stand a good deal, but I will not stand being expected to be grateful.'

Looking back at it, I can see that what saved me from Colney Hatch in this crisis was my bright idea in buying up most of the contents of the local sweetshop. By serving out sweets to the kid practically incessantly we managed to get through the rest of that day pretty satisfactorily. At eight o'clock he fell asleep in a chair; and, having undressed him by unbuttoning every button in sight and, where there were no buttons, pulling till something gave, we carried him up to bed.

Freddie stood looking at the pile of clothes on the floor with a sort of careworn wrinkle between his eyes, and I knew what he was thinking. To get the kid undressed had been simple – a mere matter of muscle. But how were we to get him into his clothes again? I stirred the heap with my foot. There was a long linen arrangement which might have been anything. Also a strip of pink flannel which was like nothing on earth. All most unpleasant.

But in the morning I remembered that there were children in the next bungalow but one, and I went there before breakfast and borrowed their nurse. Women are wonderful, by Jove they are! This nurse had all the spare parts assembled and in the right places in about eight minutes, and there was the kid dressed and looking fit to go to a garden party at Buckingham Palace. I showered wealth upon her, and she promised to come in morning and evening. I sat down to breakfast almost cheerful again. It was the first bit of silver lining that had presented itself to date.

'And, after all,' I said, 'there's lots to be argued in favour of having a child about the place, if you know what I mean. Kind of cosy and domestic, what?'

Just then the kid upset the milk over Freddie's trousers, and when he had come back after changing he lacked sparkle.

It was shortl y after breakfast that Jeeves asked if he could have a word in my ear.

Now, though in the anguish of recent events I had rather tended to forget what had been the original idea in bringing Freddie down to this place, I hadn't forgotten it altogether; and I'm bound to say that, as the days went by, I had found myself a little disappointed in Jeeves. The scheme had been, if you recall, that he should refresh himself with sea-air and simple food and, having thus got his brain into prime working order, evolve some means of bringing Freddie and his Elizabeth together again.

And what had happened? The man had eaten well and he had slept well, but not a step did he appear to have taken towards bringing about the happy ending. The only move that had been made in that direction had been made by me, alone and unaided; and, though I freely admit that it had turned out a good deal of a bloomer, still the fact remains that I had shown zeal and enterprise. Consequently I received him with a bit of hauteur when he blew in. Slightly cold. A trifle frosty.

'Yes, Jeeves?' I said. 'You wished to speak to me?'

'Yes, sir.'

'Say on, Jeeves,' I said.

'Thank you, sir. What I desired to say, sir, was this: I attended a performance at the local cinema last night.'

I raised the eyebrows. I was surprised at the man. With life in the home so frightfully tense and the young master up against it to such a fearful extent, I disapproved of him coming toddling in and prattling about his amusements.

'I hope you enjoyed yourself,' I said in rather a nasty manner.

'Yes, sir, thank you. The management was presenting a super-super-film in seven reels, dealing with life in the wilder and more feverish strata of New York Society, featuring Bertha Blevitch, Orlando Murphy and Baby Bobbie. I found it most entertaining, sir.'

'That's good,' I said. 'And if you have a nice time this morning on the sands with your spade and bucket, you will come and tell me all about it, won't you? I have so little on my mind just now that it's a treat to hear all about your happy holiday.'

Satirical, if you see what I mean. Sarcastic. Almost bitter, as a matter of fact, if you come right down to it.

'The title of the film was "Tiny Hands", sir. And the father and mother of the character played by Baby Bobbie had unfortunately drifted apart—'

'Too bad,' I said.

'Although at heart they loved each other still, sir.'

'Did they really? I'm glad you told me that.'

'And so matters went on, sir, till came a day when—'

'Jeeves,' I said, fixing him with a dashed unpleasant eye, 'what the dickens do you think you're talking about? Do you suppose that, with this infernal child landed on me and the peace of the home practically shattered into a million bits, I want to hear—'

'I beg your pardon, sir. I would not have mentioned this cinema performance were it not for the fact that it gave me an idea, sir.'

'An idea!'

'An idea that will, I fancy, sir, prove of value in straightening out the matrimonial future of Mr. Bullivant. To which end, if you recollect, sir, you desired me to—'

I snorted with remorse.

'Jeeves,' I said, 'I wronged you.'

'Not at all, sir.'

'Yes, I did. I wronged you. I had a notion that you had given yourself up entirely to the pleasures of the seaside and had chucked that business altogether. I might have known better. Tell me all, Jeeves.'

He bowed in a gratified manner. I beamed. And, while we didn't actually fall on each other's necks, we gave each other to understand that all was well once more.

'In this super-super-film, "Tiny Hands", sir,' said Jeeves, 'the parents of the child had, as I say, drifted apart.'

'Drifted apart,' I said, nodding. 'Right! And then?'

'Came a day, sir, when their little child brought them together again.'

'How?'

'If I remember rightly, sir, he said, "Dadda, doesn't 'oo love mummie no more?"'

'And then?'

'They exhibited a good deal of emotion. There was what I believe is termed a cut-back, showing scenes from their courtship and early married life and some glimpses of Lovers Through the Ages, and the picture concluded with a close-up of the pair in an embrace, with the child looking on with natural gratification and an organ playing "Hearts and Flowers" in the distance.'

'Proceed, Jeeves,' I said. 'You interest me strangely. I begin to grasp the idea. You mean—?'

'I mean, sir, that, with this young gentleman on the premises, it might be possible to arrange a *dénouement* of a somewhat similar nature in regard to Mr. Bullivant and Miss Vickers.'

'Aren't you overlooking the fact that this kid is no relation of Mr. Bullivant or Miss Vickers?'

'Even with this handicap, sir, I fancy that good results might ensue. I think that, if it were possible to bring Mr. Bullivant and Miss Vickers together for a short space of time in the presence of the child, sir, and if the child were to say something of a touching nature—'

'I follow you absolutely, Jeeves,' I cried with enthusiasm. 'It's big. This is the way I see it. We lay the scene in this room. Child, centre. Girl, l.c. Freddie up stage, playing the piano. No, that won't do. He can only play a little of "The Rosary" with one finger, so we'll have to cut out the soft music. But the rest's all right. Look here,' I said. 'This inkpot is Miss Vickers. This mug with "A Present from Marvis Bay" on it is the child. This pen-wiper is Mr. Bullivant. Start with dialogue leading up to child's line. Child speaks line, let us say "Boofer lady, does 'oo love dadda?" Business of outstretched hands. Hold picture for a moment. Freddie crosses l. takes girl's hand. Business of swallowing lump in throat. Then big speech: "Ah, Elizabeth, has not this misunderstanding of ours gone on too long? See! A little child rebukes us!" And so on. I'm just giving you the general outline. Freddie must work up his own part. And we must get a good line for the child. "Boofer lady, does 'oo love dadda?" isn't definite enough. We want something more—'

'If I might make the suggestion, sir—?'

'Yes?'

'I would advocate the words "Kiss Freddie!" It is short, readily memorised, and has what I believe is technically termed the punch.'

'Genius, Jeeves!'

'Thank you very much, sir.'

'"Kiss Freddie!" it is then. But, I say, Jeeves, how the deuce are we to get them together in here? Miss Vickers cuts Mr. Bullivant. She wouldn't come within a mile of him.'

'It is awkward, sir.'

'It doesn't matter. We shall have to make it an exterior set instead of an interior. We can easily corner her on the beach somewhere, when we're ready. Meanwhile, we must get the kid word-perfect.'

'Yes, sir.'

'Right! First rehearsal for lines and business at eleven sharp tomorrow morning.'

Poor old Freddie was in such a gloomy frame of mind that I decided not to tell him the idea till we had finished coaching the child. He wasn't in the mood to have a thing like that hanging over him. So we concentrated on Tootles. And pretty early in the proceedings we saw that the only way to get Tootles worked up to the spirit of the thing was to introduce sweets of some sort as a sub-motive, so to speak.

'The chief difficulty, sir,' said Jeeves, at the end of the first rehearsal, 'is, as I envisage it, to establish in the young gentleman's mind a connexion between the words we desire him to say and the refreshment.'

'Exactly,' I said. 'Once the blighter has grasped the basic fact that those two words, clearly spoken, result automatically in chocolate nougat, we have got a success.'

I've often thought how interesting it must be to be one of those animal-trainer blokes – to stimulate the dawning intelligence and all that. Well, this was every bit as exciting. Some days success seemed to be staring us in the eyeball, and the kid got out the line as if he had been an old professional. And then he would go all to pieces again. And time was flying.

'We must hurry up, Jeeves,' I said. 'The kid's uncle may arrive any day now and take him away.'

'Exactly, sir.'

'And we have no understudy.'

'Very true, sir.'

'We must work! I must say this child is a bit discouraging at times. I should have thought a deaf-mute would have learned his part by now.'

I will say this for the kid, though: he was a trier. Failure didn't damp him. Whenever there was any kind of sweet in sight he had a dash at his line, and kept saying something till he had got what he was after. His chief fault was his uncertainty. Personally, I would have been prepared to risk opening in the act and was ready to start the public performance at the first opportunity, but Jeeves said no.

'I would not advocate undue haste, sir,' he said. 'As long as the young gentleman's memory refuses to act with any certainty, we are running grave risks of failure. Today, if you recollect, sir, he said "Kick Freddie!" That is not a speech to win a young lady's heart, sir.'

'No. And she might do it, too. You're right. We must postpone production.'

But, by Jove, we didn't! The curtain went up the very next afternoon.

It was nobody's fault – certainly not mine. It was just fate. Jeeves was out, and I was alone in the house with Freddie and the child. Freddie had just settled down at the piano, and I was leading the kid out of the place for a bit of exercise, when, just as we'd got on to the veranda, along came the girl Elizabeth on her way to the beach. And at the sight of her the kid set up a matey yell, and she stopped at the foot of the steps.

'Hallo, baby,' she said. 'Good morning,' she said to me. 'May I come up?'

She didn't wait for an answer. She just hopped on to the veranda. She seemed to be that sort of girl. She started fussing over the child. And six feet away, mind you, Freddie smiting the piano in the sitting-room. It was a dashed disturbing situation, take it from Bertram. At any minute Freddie might take it into his head to come out on the veranda, and I hadn't even begun to rehearse him in his part.

I tried to break up the scene.

'We were just going down to the beach,' I said.

'Yes?' said the girl. She listened for a moment. 'So you're having your piano tuned?' she said. 'My aunt has been trying to find a tuner for ours. Do you mind if I go in and tell this man to come on to us when he has finished here?'

I mopped the brow.

'Er – I shouldn't go in just now,' I said. 'Not just now, while he's working, if you don't mind. These fellows can't bear to be disturbed when they're at work. It's the artistic temperament. I'll tell him later.'

'Very well. Ask him to call at Pine Bungalow. Vickers is the name. . . . Oh, he seems to have stopped. I suppose he will be out in a minute now. I'll wait.'

'Don't you think – shouldn't you be getting on to the beach?' I said.

She had started talking to the kid and didn't hear. She was feeling in her bag for something.

'The beach,' I babbled.

'See what I've got for you, baby,' said the girl. 'I thought I might meet you somewhere, so I brought some of your favourite sweets.'

And, by Jove, she held up in front of the kid's bulging eyes a chunk of toffee about the size of the Albert Memorial!

That finished it. We had just been having a long rehearsal, and the kid was all worked up in his part. He got it right first time.

'Kiss Fweddie!' he shouted.

And the French windows opened and Freddie came out on to the veranda, for all the world as if he had been taking a cue.

'Kiss Fweddie!' shrieked the child.

Freddie looked at the girl, and the girl looked at him. I looked at the ground, and the kid looked at the toffee.

'Kiss Fweddie!' he yelled. 'Kiss Fweddie!'

'What does this mean?' said the girl, turning on me.

'You'd better give it him,' I said. 'He'll go on till you do, you know.'

She gave the kid the toffee and he subsided. Freddie, poor ass, still stood there gaping, without a word.

'What does it mean?' said the girl again. Her face was pink, and her eyes were sparkling in the sort of way, don't you know, that makes a fellow feel as if he hadn't any bones in him, if you know what I mean. Yes, Bertram felt filleted. Did you ever tread on your partner's dress at a dance – I'm speaking now of the days when women wore dresses long enough to be trodden on – and hear it rip and see her smile at you like an angel and say, '*Please* don't apologise. It's nothing,' and then suddenly meet her clear blue eyes and feel as if you had stepped on the teeth of a rake and had the handle jump up and hit you in the face? Well, that's how Freddie's Elizabeth looked.

'*Well*?' she said, and her teeth gave a little click.

I gulped. Then I said it was nothing. Then I said it was nothing much. Then I said, 'Oh, well, it was this way.' And I told her all about it. And all the while Idiot Freddie stood there gaping, without a word. Not one solitary yip had he let out of himself from the start.

And the girl didn't speak, either. She just stood listening.

And then she began to laugh. I never heard a girl laugh so much. She leaned against the side of the veranda and shrieked. And all the while Freddie, the World's Champion Dumb Brick, standing there, saying nothing.

Well, I finished my story and sidled to the steps. I had said all I had to say, and it seemed to me that about here the stage-direction 'exit cautiously' was written in my part. I gave poor old Freddie up in despair. If only he had said a word it might have been all right. But there he stood, speechless.

Just out of sight of the house I met Jeeves, returning from his stroll.

'Jeeves,' I said, 'all is over. The thing's finished. Poor dear old Freddie has made a complete ass of himself and killed the whole show.'

'Indeed, sir? What has actually happened?'

I told him.

'He fluffed in his lines,' I concluded. 'Just stood there saying nothing, when if ever there was a time for eloquence, this was it. He . . . Great Scott! Look!'

We had come back within view of the cottage, and there in front of it stood six children, a nurse, two loafers, another nurse, and the fellow from the grocer's. They were all staring. Down the road came galloping five more children, a dog, three men and a boy, all about to stare. And on our porch, as unconscious of the spectators as if they had been alone in the Sahara, stood Freddie and his Elizabeth, clasped in each other's arms.

'Great Scott!' I said.

'It would appear, sir,' said Jeeves, 'that everything has concluded most satisfactorily, after all.'

'Yes. Dear old Freddie may have been fluffy in his lines,' I said, 'but his business certainly seems to have gone with a bang.'

'Very true, sir,' said Jeeves.

I blotted the last page of my manuscript and sank back, feeling more or less of a spent force. After incredible sweat of the old brow the thing seemed to be in pretty fair shape, and I was just reading it through and debating whether to bung in another paragraph at the end, when there was a tap at the door and Jeeves appeared.

'Mrs. Travers, sir, on the telephone.'

'Oh?' I said. Preoccupied, don't you know.

'Yes, sir. She presents her compliments and would be glad to know what progress you have made with the article which you are writing for her.'

'Jeeves, can I mention men's knee-length under-clothing in a woman's paper?'

'No, sir.'

'Then tell her it's finished.'

'Very good, sir.'

'And, Jeeves, when you're through, come back. I want you to cast your eye over this effort and give it the O.K.'

My Aunt Dahlia, who runs a woman's paper called *Milady's Boudoir,* had recently backed me into a corner and made me promise to write her a few authoritative words for her 'Husbands and Brothers' page on 'What the Well-Dressed Man is Wearing'. I believe in encouraging aunts, when deserving; and, as there are many worse eggs than her knocking about the metrop. I had consented blithely. But I give you my honest word that if I had had the foggiest notion of what I was letting myself in for, not even a nephew's devotion would have kept me from giving her the raspberry. A deuce of a job it had been, taxing the physique to the utmost. I don't wonder now that all these author blokes have bald heads and faces like birds who have suffered.

'Jeeves,' I said, when he came back, 'you don't read a paper called *Milady's Boudoir* by any chance, do you?'

'No, sir. The periodical has not come to my notice.'

'Well, spring sixpence on it next week, because this article will appear in it. Wooster on the well-dressed man, don't you know.'

'Indeed, sir?'

'Yes, indeed, Jeeves. I've rather extended myself over this little bijou. There's a bit about socks that I think you will like.'

He took the manuscript, brooded over it, and smiled a gentle, approving smile.

'The sock passage is quite in the proper vein, sir,' he said.

'Well expressed, what?'

'Extremely, sir.'

I watched him narrowly as he read on, and, as I was expecting, what you might call the love-light suddenly died out of his eyes. I braced myself for an unpleasant scene.

'Come to the bit about soft silk shirts for evening wear?' I asked carelessly.

'Yes, sir,' said Jeeves, in a low, cold voice, as if he had been bitten in the leg by a personal friend.

'And if I may be pardoned for saying so—'

'You don't like it?'

'No, sir. I do not. Soft silk shirts with evening costume are not worn, sir.'

'Jeeves,' I said, looking the blighter diametrically in the centre of the eyeball, 'they're dashed well going to be. I may as well tell you now that I have ordered a dozen of those shirtings from

Peabody and Simms, and it's no good looking like that, because I am jolly well adamant.'

'If I might—'

'No, Jeeves,' I said, raising my hand, 'argument is useless. Nobody has a greater respect than I have for your judgment in socks, in ties, and – I will go farther – in spats; but when it comes to evening shirts your nerve seems to fail you. You have no vision. You are prejudiced and reactionary. Hidebound is the word that suggests itself. It may interest you to learn that when I was at Le Touquet the Prince of Wales buzzed into the Casino one night with soft silk shirt complete.'

'His Royal Highness, sir, may permit himself a certain licence which in your own case—'

'No, Jeeves,' I said firmly, 'it's no use. When we Woosters are adamant, we are – well, adamant, if you know what I mean.'

'Very good, sir.'

I could see the man was wounded, and, of course, the whole episode had been extremely jarring and unpleasant; but these things have to be gone through. Is one a serf or isn't one? That's what it all boils down to. Having made my point, I changed the subject.

'Well, that's that,' I said. 'We now approach another topic. Do you know any housemaids, Jeeves?'

'Housemaids, sir?'

'Come, come, Jeeves, you know what housemaids are.'

'Are you requiring a housemaid, sir?'

'No, but Mr. Little is. I met him at the club a couple of days ago, and he told me that Mrs. Little is offering rich rewards to anybody who will find her one guaranteed to go light on the china.'

'Indeed, sir?'

'Yes. The one now in office apparently runs through the *objets d'art* like a typhoon, simoon, or sirocco. So if you know any—'

'I know a great many, sir. Some intimately, others mere acquaintances.'

'Well, start digging round among the old pals. And now the hat, the stick, and other necessaries. I must be getting along and handing in this article.'

The offices of *Milady's Boudoir* were in one of those rummy streets in the Covent Garden neighbourhood; and I had just got to the door, after wading through a deep top-dressing of old cabbages and tomatoes, when who should come out but Mrs. Little. She greeted me with the warmth due to the old family friend, in spite of the fact that I hadn't been round to the house for a goodish while.

'Whatever are you doing in these parts, Bertie? I thought you never came east of Leicester Square.'

'I've come to deliver an article of sorts which my Aunt Dahlia asked me to write. She edits a species of journal up those stairs. *Milady's Boudoir.*'

'What a coincidence! I have just promised to write an article for her, too.'

'Don't you do it,' I said earnestly. 'You've simply no notion what a ghastly labour— Oh, but, of course, I was forgetting. You're used to it, what?'

Silly of me to have talked like that. Young Bingo Little, if you remember, had married the famous female novelist, Rosie M. Banks, author of some of the most pronounced and widely-read tripe ever put on the market. Naturally a mere article would be pie for her.

'No, I don't think it will give me much trouble,' she said. 'Your aunt has suggested a most delightful subject.'

'That's good. By the way, I spoke to my man Jeeves about getting you a housemaid. He knows all the hummers.'

'Thank you so much. Oh, are you doing anything tomorrow night?'

'Not a thing.'

'Then do come and dine with us. Your aunt is coming, and hopes to bring your uncle. I am looking forward to meeting him.'

'Thanks. Delighted.'

I meant it, too. The Little household may be weak on housemaids, but it is right there when it comes to cooks. Somewhere or other some time ago Bingo's missus managed to dig up a Frenchman of the most extraordinary vim and skill. A most amazing Johnnie who dishes a wicked *ragout*. Old Bingo has put on at least ten pounds in weight since this fellow Anatole arrived in the home.

'At eight, then.'

'Right. Thanks ever so much.'

She popped off, and I went upstairs to hand in my copy, as we boys of the Press call it. I found Aunt Dahlia immersed to the gills in papers of all descriptions.

I am not much of a lad for my relatives as a general thing, but I've always been very pally with Aunt Dahlia. She married my Uncle Thomas – between ourselves a bit of a squirt – the year Bluebottle won the Cambridgeshire; and they hadn't got half-way down the aisle before I was saying to myself, 'That woman is much too good for the old bird.' Aunt Dahlia is a large, genial soul, the sort you see in dozens on the hunting-field. As a matter of fact, until she married Uncle Thomas, she put in most of her time on horseback; but he won't live in the country, so nowadays she expends her energy on this paper of hers.

She came to the surface as I entered, and flung a cheery book at my head.

'Hullo, Bertie! I say, have you really finished that article?'

'To the last comma.'

'Good boy! My gosh, I'll bet it's rotten.'

'On the contrary, it is extremely hot stuff, and most of it approved by Jeeves, what's more. The bit about soft silk shirts got in amongst him a trifle; but you can take it from me, Aunt Dahlia, that they are the latest yodel and will be much seen at first nights and other occasions where Society assembles.'

'Your man Jeeves,' said Aunt Dahlia, flinging the article into a basket and skewering a few loose pieces of paper on a sort of meat-hook, 'is a wash-out, and you can tell him I said so.'

'Oh, come,' I said. 'He may not be sound on shirtings—'

'I'm not referring to that. As long as a week ago I asked him to get me a cook, and he hasn't found one yet.'

'Great Scott! Is Jeeves a domestic employment agency? Mrs. Little wants him to find her a housemaid. I met her outside. She tells me she's doing something for you.'

'Yes, thank goodness. I'm relying on it to bump the circulation up a bit. I can't read her stuff myself, but women love it. Her name on the cover will mean a lot. And we need it.'

'Paper not doing well?'

'It's doing all right really, but it's got to be a slow job building up a circulation.'

'I suppose so.'

'I can get Tom to see that in his lucid moments,' said Aunt Dahlia, skewering a few more papers. 'But just at present the poor fathead has got one of his pessimistic spells. It's entirely due to that mechanic who calls herself a cook. A few more of her alleged dinners, and Tom will refuse to go on paying the printers' bills.'

'You don't mean that!'

'I do mean it. There was what she called a *ris de veau à la financière* last night which made him talk for three-quarters of an hour about good money going to waste and nothing to show for it.'

I quite understood, and I was dashed sorry for her. My Uncle Thomas is a cove who made a colossal pile of money out in the East, but in doing so put his digestion on the blink. This has made him a tricky proposition to handle. Many a time I've lunched with him and found him perfectly chirpy up to the fish, only to have him turn blue on me well before the cheese.

Who was that lad they used to try to make me read at Oxford? Ship – Shop – Schopenhauer. That's the name. A grouch of the most pronounced description. Well, Uncle Thomas, when his gastric juices have been giving him the elbow, can make

Schopenhauer look like Pollyanna. And the worst of it is, from Aunt Dahlia's point of view, that on these occasions he always seems to think he's on the brink of ruin and wants to start to economise.

'Pretty tough,' I said. 'Well, anyway, he'll get one good dinner tomorrow night at the Littles'.'

'Can you guarantee that, Bertie?' asked Aunt Dahlia earnestly. 'I simply daren't risk unleashing him on anything at all wonky.'

'They've got a marvellous cook. I haven't been round there for some time, but unless he's lost his form of two months ago Uncle Thomas is going to have the treat of a lifetime.'

'It'll only make it all the worse for him, coming back to our steak-incinerator,' said Aunt Dahlia, a bit on the Schopenhauer side herself.

The little nest where Bingo and his bride had settled themselves was up in St. John's Wood; one of those rather jolly houses with a bit of garden. When I got there on the following night, I found that I was the last to weigh in. Aunt Dahlia was chatting with Rosie in a corner, while Uncle Thomas, standing by the mantelpiece with Bingo, sucked down a cocktail in a frowning, suspicious sort of manner, rather like a chappie having a short snort before dining with the Borgias: as if he were saying to himself that, even if this particular cocktail wasn't poisoned, he was bound to cop it later on.

Well, I hadn't expected anything in the nature of beaming *joie de vivre* from Uncle Thomas, so I didn't pay much attention to him. What did surprise me was the extraordinary gloom of young Bingo. You may say what you like against Bingo, but nobody has ever found him a depressing host. Why, many a time in the days of his bachelorhood I've known him to start throwing bread before the soup course. Yet now he and Uncle Thomas were a pair. He looked haggard and careworn, like a Borgia who has suddenly remembered that he has forgotten to shove cyanide in the *consommé*, and the dinner-gong due any moment.

And the mystery wasn't helped at all by the one remark he made to me before conversation became general. As he poured out my cocktail, he suddenly bent forward.

'Bertie,' he whispered, in a nasty, feverish manner, 'I want to see you. Life and death matter. Be in tomorrow morning.'

That was all. Immediately after that the starting-gun went and we toddled down to the festive. And from that moment, I'm bound to say, in the superior interest of the proceedings he rather faded out of my mind. For good old Anatole, braced presumably by the fact of there being guests, had absolutely surpassed himself.

I am not a man who speaks hastily in these matters. I weigh my words. And I say again that Anatole had surpassed himself. It was as good a dinner as I have ever absorbed, and it revived Uncle Thomas like a watered flower. As we sat down he was saying some things about the Government which they wouldn't have cared to hear. With the *consommé pâté d'Italie* he said but what could you expect nowadays? With the *paupiettes de sole à la princesse* he admitted rather decently that the Government couldn't be held responsible for the rotten weather, anyway. And shortly after the *caneton Aylesbury à la broche* he was practically giving the lads the benefit of his whole-hearted support.

And all the time young Bingo looking like an owl with a secret sorrow. Rummy!

I thought about it a good deal as I walked home, and I was hoping he wouldn't roll round with his hard-luck story too early in the morning. He had the air of one who intends to charge in at about six-thirty.

Jeeves was waiting up for me when I got back.

'A pleasant dinner, sir?' he said.

'Magnificent, Jeeves.'

'I am glad to hear that, sir. Lord Yaxley rang up on the

telephone shortly after you had left. He was extremely desirous that you should join him at Harrogate, sir. He leaves for that town by an early train tomorrow.'

My Uncle George is a festive old bird who had made a habit for years of doing himself a dashed sight too well, with the result that he's always got Harrogate or Buxton hanging over him like the sword of what's-his-name. And he hates going there alone.

'It can't be done,' I said. Uncle George is bad enough in London, and I wasn't going to let myself be cooped up with him in one of these cure-places.

'He was extremely urgent, sir.'

'No, Jeeves,' I said firmly. 'I am always anxious to oblige, but Uncle George – no, no! I mean to say, what?'

'Very good, sir,' said Jeeves.

It was a pleasure to hear the way he said it. Docile the man was becoming, absolutely docile. It just showed that I had been right in putting my foot down about those shirts.

When Bingo showed up next morning I had had breakfast and was all ready for him. Jeeves shot him into the presence, and he sat down on the bed.

'Good morning, Bertie,' said young Bingo.

'Good morning, old thing,' I replied courteously.

'Don't go, Jeeves,' said young Bingo hollowly. 'Wait.'

'Sir?'

'Remain. Stay. Cluster round. I shall need you.'

'Very good, sir.'

Bingo lit a cigarette and frowned bleakly at the wallpaper.

'Bertie,' he said, 'the most frightful calamity has occurred. Unless something is done, and done right speedily, my social prestige is doomed, my self-respect will be obliterated, my name will be mud, and I shall not dare to show my face in the West End of London again.'

'My aunt!' I cried, deeply impressed.

'Exactly,' said young Bingo, with a hollow laugh. 'You have

put it in a nutshell. The whole trouble is due to your blasted aunt.'

'Which blasted aunt? Specify, old thing. I have so many.'

'Mrs. Travers. The one who runs that infernal paper.'

'Oh, no, dash it, old man,' I protested. 'She's the only decent aunt I've got. Jeeves, you will bear me out in this?'

'Such has always been my impression, I must confess, sir.'

'Well, get rid of it, then,' said young Bingo. 'The woman is a menace to society, a home-wrecker, and a pest. Do you know what's she's done? She's got Rosie to write an article for that rag of hers.'

'I know that.'

'Yes, but you don't know what it's about.'

'No. She only told me Aunt Dahlia had given her a splendid idea for the thing.'

'It's about me!'

'You?'

'Yes, me! Me! And do you know what it's called? It is called "How I Keep the Love of My Husband-Baby".'

'My what?'

'Husband-baby!'

'What's a husband-baby?'

'I am, apparently,' said young Bingo, with much bitterness. 'I am also, according to this article, a lot of other things which I have too much sense of decency to repeat even to an old friend. This beastly composition, in short, is one of those things they call "human interest stories"; one of those intimate revelations of married life over which the female public loves to gloat; all about Rosie and me and what she does when I come home cross, and so on. I tell you, Bertie, I am still blushing all over at the recollection of something she says in paragraph two.'

'What?'

'I decline to tell you. But you can take it from me that it's the edge. Nobody could be fonder of Rosie than I am, but – dear, sensible girl as she is in ordinary life – the moment she gets in front of a dictating-machine she becomes absolutely maudlin. Bertie, that article must not appear!'

'But—'

'If it does I shall have to resign from my clubs, grow a beard, and become a hermit. I shall not be able to face the world.'

'Aren't you pitching it a bit strong, old lad?' I said. 'Jeeves, don't you think he's pitching it a bit strong?'

'Well, sir—'

'I am pitching it feebly,' said young Bingo earnestly. 'You haven't heard the thing. I have. Rosie shoved the cylinder on the dictating-machine last night before dinner, and it was grisly to hear the instrument croaking out those awful sentences. If that article appears I shall be kidded to death by every pal I've got. Bertie,' he said, his voice sinking to a hoarse whisper, 'you have about as much imagination as a warthog, but surely even you can picture to yourself what Jimmy Bowles and Tuppy Glossop, to name only two, will say when they see me referred to in print as "half god, half prattling, mischievous child"?'

I jolly well could.

'She doesn't say that?' I gasped.

'She certainly does. And when I tell you that I selected that particular quotation because it's about the only one I can stand hearing spoken, you will realise what I'm up against.'

I picked at the coverlet. I had been a pal of Bingo's for many years, and we Woosters stand by our pals. 'Jeeves,' I said, 'you have heard?'

'Yes, sir.'

'The position is serious.'

'Yes, sir.'

'We must cluster round.'

'Yes, sir.'

'Does anything suggest itself to you?'

'Yes, sir.'

'What! You don't really mean that?'

'Yes, sir.'

'Bingo,' I said, 'the sun is still shining. Something suggests itself to Jeeves.'

'Jeeves,' said young Bingo in a quivering voice, 'if you see me through this fearful crisis, ask of me what you will even unto half my kingdom.'

'The matter,' said Jeeves, 'fits in very nicely, sir, with another mission which was entrusted to me this morning.'

'What do you mean?'

'Mrs. Travers rang me up on the telephone shortly before I brought you your tea, sir, and was most urgent that I should endeavour to persuade Mr. Little's cook to leave Mr. Little's service and join her staff. It appears that Mr. Travers was fascinated by the man's ability, sir, and talked far into the night of his astonishing gifts.'

Young Bingo uttered a frightful cry of agony.

'What! Is that – that buzzard trying to pinch our cook?'

'Yes, sir.'

'After eating our bread and salt, dammit?'

'I fear, sir,' sighed Jeeves, 'that when it comes to a matter of cooks, ladies have but a rudimentary sense of morality.'

'Half a second, Bingo,' I said, as the fellow seemed about to plunge into something of an oration. 'How does this fit in with the other thing, Jeeves?'

'Well, sir, it has been my experience that no lady can ever forgive another lady for taking a really good cook away from her. I am convinced that, if I am able to accomplish the mission which Mrs. Travers entrusted to me, an instant breach of cordial relations must inevitably ensue. Mrs. Little will, I feel certain, be so aggrieved with Mrs. Travers that she will decline to contribute to her paper. We shall therefore not only bring happiness to Mr. Travers, but also suppress the article. Thus killing two birds with one stone, if I may use the expression, sir.'

'Certainly you may use the expression, Jeeves,' I said cordially.

'And I may add that in my opinion this is one of your best and ripest.'

'Yes, but I say, you know,' bleated young Bingo. 'I mean to say – old Anatole, I mean – what I'm driving at is that he's a cook in a million.'

'You poor chump, if he wasn't there would be no point in the scheme.'

'Yes, but what I mean – I shall miss him, you know. Miss him fearfully.'

'Good heavens!' I cried. 'Don't tell me that you are thinking of your tummy in a crisis like this?'

Bingo sighed heavily.

'Oh, all right,' he said. 'I suppose it's a case of the surgeon's knife. All right, Jeeves, you may carry on. Yes, carry on, Jeeves. Yes, yes, Jeeves, carry on. I'll look in tomorrow morning and hear what you have to report.'

And with bowed head young Bingo biffed off.

He was bright and early next morning. In fact, he turned up at such an indecent hour that Jeeves very properly refused to allow him to break in on my slumbers.

By the time I was awake and receiving, he and Jeeves had had a heart-to-heart chat in the kitchen; and when Bingo eventually crept into my room I could see by the look on his face that something had gone wrong.

'It's all off,' he said, slumping down on the bed.

'Off?'

'Yes; that cook-pinching business. Jeeves tells me he saw Anatole last night, and Anatole refused to leave.'

'But surely Aunt Dahlia had the sense to offer him more than he was getting with you?'

'The sky was the limit, as far as she was concerned. Nevertheless, he refused to skid. It seems he's in love with our parlourmaid.'

'But you haven't got a parlourmaid.'

'We have got a parlourmaid.'

'I've never seen her. A sort of bloke who looked like a provincial undertaker waited at table the night before last.'

'That was the local greengrocer, who comes to help out when desired. The parlourmaid is away on her holiday – or was still last night. She returned about ten minutes before Jeeves made his call, and Anatole, I take it, was in such a state of elation and devotion and what-not on seeing her again that the contents of the Mint wouldn't have bribed him to part from her.'

'But look here, Bingo,' I said, 'this is all rot. I see the solution right off. I'm surprised that a bloke of Jeeves's mentality overlooked it. Aunt Dahlia must engage the parlourmaid as well as Anatole. Then they won't be parted.'

'I thought of that, too. Naturally.'

'I bet you didn't.'

'I certainly did.'

'Well, what's wrong with the scheme?'

'It can't be worked. If your aunt engaged our parlourmaid she would have to sack her own, wouldn't she?'

'Well?'

'Well, if she sacks her parlourmaid, it will mean that the chauffeur will quit. He's in love with her.'

'With my aunt?'

'No, with the parlourmaid. And apparently he's the only chauffeur your uncle has ever found who drives carefully enough for him.'

I gave it up. I had never imagined before that life below stairs was so frightfully mixed up with what these coves call the sex complex. The *personnel* of domestic staffs seemed to pair off like characters in a musical comedy.

'Oh!' I said. 'Well, that being so, we do seem to be more or less stymied. That article will have to appear after all, what?'

'No, it won't.'

'Has Jeeves thought of another scheme?'

'No, but I have.' Bingo bent forward and patted my knee

affectionately. 'Look here, Bertie,' he said, 'you and I were at school together. You'll admit that?'

'Yes, but—'

'And you're a fellow who never lets a pal down. That's well known, isn't it?'

'Yes, but listen—'

'You'll cluster round. Of course you will. As if,' said Bingo with a scornful laugh, 'I ever doubted it! You won't let an old school-friend down in his hour of need. Not you. Not Bertie Wooster. No, no!'

'Yes, but just one moment. What is this scheme of yours?'

Bingo massaged my shoulder soothingly.

'It's something right in your line, Bertie, old man; something that'll come as easy as pie to you. As a matter of fact, you've done very much the same thing before – that time you were telling me about when you pinched your uncle's Memoirs at Easeby. I suddenly remembered that, and it gave me the idea. It's—'

'Here! Listen!'

'It's all settled, Bertie. Nothing for you to worry about. Nothing whatever. I see now that we made a big mistake in ever trying to tackle this job in Jeeves's silly, roundabout way. Much better to charge straight ahead without any of that finesse and fooling about. And so—'

'Yes, but listen—'

'And so this afternoon I'm going to take Rosie to a *matinée*. I shall leave the window of her study open, and when we have got well away you will climb in, pinch the cylinder and pop off again. It's absurdly simple—'

'Yes, but half a second—'

'I know what you are going to say,' said Bingo, raising his hand. 'How are you to find the cylinder? That's what is bothering you, isn't it? Well, it will be quite easy. Not a chance of a mistake. The thing is in the top left-hand drawer of the desk, and the drawer will be left unlocked because Rosie's stenographer is to come round at four o'clock and type the article.'

'Now listen, Bingo,' I said. 'I'm frightfully sorry for you and all that, but I must firmly draw the line at burglary.'

'But, dash it, I'm only asking you to do what you did at Easeby.'

'No, you aren't. I was staying at Easeby. It was simply a case of having to lift a parcel off the hall table. I hadn't got to break into a house. I'm sorry, but I simply will not break into your beastly house on any consideration whatever.'

He gazed at me, astonished and hurt.

'Is this Bertie Wooster speaking?' he said in a low voice.

'Yes, it is!'

'But, Bertie,' he said gently, 'we agreed that you were at school with me.'

'I don't care.'

'At school, Bertie. The dear old school.'

'I don't care. I will not—'

'Bertie!'

'I will not—'

'Bertie!'

'No!'

'Bertie!'

'Oh, all right,' I said.

'There,' said young Bingo, patting me on the shoulder, 'spoke the true Bertram Wooster!'

I don't know if it has ever occurred to you, but to the thoughtful cove there is something dashed reassuring in all the reports of burglaries you read in the papers. I mean, if you're keen on Great Britain maintaining her prestige and all that. I mean, there can't be much wrong with the *morale* of a country whose sons go in to such a large extent for housebreaking, because you can take it from me that the job requires a nerve of the most cast-iron description. I suppose I was walking up and down in front of that house for half an hour before I could bring myself to dash in at the front gate and slide round to the side where the study window was. And even then I stood for about ten minutes cowering against the wall and listening for police-whistles.

Eventually, however, I braced myself up and got to business. The study was on the ground floor and the window was nice and large, and, what is more, wide open. I got the old knee over the sill, gave a jerk which took an inch of skin off my ankle, and hopped down into the room. And there I was, if you follow me.

I stood for a moment, listening. Everything seemed to be all right. I was apparently alone in the world.

In fact, I was so much alone that the atmosphere seemed positively creepy. You know how it is on these occasions. There was a clock on the mantelpiece that ticked in a slow, shocked sort of way that was dashed unpleasant. And over the clock a large portrait stared at me with a good deal of dislike and suspicion. It was a portrait of somebody's grandfather. Whether he was Rosie's or Bingo's I didn't know, but he was certainly a grandfather. In fact, I wouldn't be prepared to swear that he wasn't a great-grandfather. He was a big, stout old buffer in a high collar that seemed to hurt his neck, for he had drawn his chin back a goodish way and was looking down his nose as much as to say, '*You* made me put this dam' thing on!'

Well, it was only a step to the desk, and nothing between me and it but a brown shaggy rug; so I avoided grandfather's eye and, summoning up the good old bulldog courage of the Woosters, moved forward and started to navigate the rug. And I had hardly taken a step when the south-east corner of it suddenly detached itself from the rest and sat up with a snuffle.

Well, I mean to say, to bear yourself fittingly in the face of an occurrence of this sort you want to be one of those strong, silent, phlegmatic birds who are ready for anything. This type of bloke, I imagine, would simply have cocked an eye at the rug, said to himself, 'Ah, a Pekingese dog, and quite a good one, too!' and started at once to make cordial overtures to the animal in order to win its sympathy and moral support. I suppose I must be one of the neurotic younger generation you read about in the papers nowadays, because it was pretty plain within half a second that I wasn't strong and I wasn't phlegmatic. This wouldn't have mattered so much, but I wasn't silent either. In the emotion of the moment I let out a sort of sharp yowl and leaped about four feet in a north-westerly direction. And there was a crash that sounded as though somebody had touched off a bomb.

What a female novelist wants with an occasional table in her study containing a vase, two framed photographs, a saucer, a lacquer box, and a jar of potpourri, I don't know; but that was what Bingo's Rosie had, and I caught it squarely with my right hip and knocked it endways. It seemed to me for a moment as if the whole world had dissolved into a kind of cataract of glass and china. A few years ago, when I legged it to America to elude my Aunt Agatha, who was out with her hatchet, I remember going to Niagara and listening to the Falls. They made much the same sort of row, but not so loud.

And at the same instant the dog began to bark.

It was a small dog – the sort of animal from which you would have expected a noise like a squeaking slate-pencil; but it was simply baying. It had retired into a corner, and was leaning against the wall with bulging eyes; and every two seconds it chucked its head back in a kind of pained way and let out another terrific bellow.

Well, I know when I'm licked. I was sorry for Bingo and regretted the necessity of having to let him down; but the time had come, I felt, to shift. 'Outside for Bertram!' was the slogan, and I took a running leap at the window and scrambled through.

And there on the path, as if they had been waiting for me by appointment, stood a policeman and a parlourmaid.

It was an embarrassing moment.

'Oh – er – there you are!' I said. And there was what you might call a contemplative silence for a moment.

'I told you I heard something,' said the parlourmaid.

The policeman was regarding me in a boiled way.

'What's all this?' he asked.

I smiled in a sort of saint-like manner.

'It's a little hard to explain,' I said.

'Yes, it is!' said the policeman.

'I was just – er – just having a look round, you know. Old friend of the family, you understand.'

'How did you get in?'

'Through the window. Being an old friend of the family, if you follow me.'

'Old friend of the family, are you?'

'Oh, very. Very. Very old. Oh, a very old friend of the family.'

'I've never seen him before,' said the parlourmaid.

I looked at the girl with positive loathing. How she could have inspired affection in anyone, even a French cook, beat me. Not that she was a bad-looking girl, mind you. Not at all. On another and happier occasion I might even have thought her rather pretty. But now she seemed one of the most unpleasant females I had ever encountered.

'No,' I said. 'You have never seen me before. But I'm an old friend of the family.'

'Then why didn't you ring at the front door?'

'I didn't want to give any trouble.'

'It's no trouble answering front doors, that being what you're paid for,' said the parlourmaid virtuously. 'I've never seen him before in my life,' she added, perfectly gratuitously. A horrid girl.

'Well, look here,' I said, with an inspiration, 'the undertaker knows me.'

'What undertaker?'

'The cove who was waiting at table when I dined here the night before last.'

'Did the undertaker wait at table on the sixteenth instant?' asked the policeman.

'Of course he didn't,' said the parlourmaid.

'Well, he looked like— By Jove, no. I remember now. He was the greengrocer.'

428

'On the sixteenth instant,' said the policeman – pompous ass! – 'did the greengrocer—?'

'Yes, he did, if you want to know,' said the parlourmaid. She seemed disappointed and baffled, like a tigress that sees its prey being sneaked away from it. Then she brightened. 'But this fellow could easily have found that out by asking round about.'

A perfectly poisonous girl.

'What's your name?' asked the policeman.

'Well, I say, do you mind awfully if I don't give my name, because—'

'Suit yourself. You'll have to tell it to the magistrate.'

'Oh, no, I say, dash it!'

'I think you'd better come along.'

'But I say, really, you know, I am an old friend of the family. Why, by Jove, now I remember, there's a photograph of me in the drawing-room. Well, I mean, that shows you!'

'If there is,' said the policeman.

'I've never seen it,' said the parlourmaid.

I absolutely hated this girl.

'You would have seen it if you had done your dusting more conscientiously,' I said severely. And I meant it to sting, by Jove!

'It is not a parlourmaid's place to dust the drawing-room,' she sniffed haughtily.

'No,' I said bitterly. 'It seems to be a parlourmaid's place to lurk about and hang about and – er – waste her time fooling about in the garden with policemen who ought to be busy about their duties elsewhere.'

'It's a parlourmaid's place to open the front door to visitors. Them that don't come in through windows.'

I perceived that I was getting the loser's end of the thing. I tried to be conciliatory.

'My dear old parlourmaid,' I said, 'don't let us descend to vulgar wrangling. All I'm driving at is that there is a photograph of me in the drawing-room, cared for and dusted by whom I know not; and this photograph will, I think, prove to you that I am an old friend of the family. I fancy so, officer?'

'If it's there,' said the man in a grudging way.

'Oh, it's there all right. Oh, yes, it's there.'

'Well, we'll go to the drawing-room and see.'

'Spoken like a man, my dear old policeman,' I said.

The drawing-room was on the first floor, and the photograph was on the table by the fire-place. Only, if you understand me, it wasn't. What I mean is, there was the fire-place, and there was the table by the fire-place, but, by Jove, not a sign of any photograph of me whatsoever. A photograph of Bingo, yes. A photograph of Bingo's uncle, Lord Bittlesham, right. A photograph of Mrs. Bingo, three-quarter face, with a tender smile on her lips, all present and correct. But of anything resembling Bertram Wooster, not a trace.

'Ho!' said the policeman.

'But, dash it, it was there the night before last.'

'Ho!' he said again. 'Ho! Ho!' As if he were starting a drinking-chorus in a comic opera, confound him.

Then I got what amounted to the brain-wave of a lifetime.

'Who dusts these things?' I said, turning on the parlourmaid.

'I don't.'

'I didn't say you did. I said who did.'

'Mary. The housemaid, of course.'

'Exactly. As I suspected. As I foresaw. Mary, officer, is notoriously the worst smasher in London. There have been complaints about her on all sides. You see what has happened? The wretched girl has broken the glass of my photograph, and, not being willing to come forward and admit it in an honest, manly way, has taken the thing off and concealed it somewhere.'

'Ho!' said the policeman, still working through the drinking-chorus.

'Well, ask her. Go down and ask her.'

'You go down and ask her,' said the policeman to the parlourmaid. 'If it's going to make him any happier.'

The parlourmaid left the room, casting a pestilential glance at me over her shoulder as she went. I'm not sure she didn't say 'Ho!' too. And then there was a bit of a lull. The policeman took up a position with a large beefy back against the door, and I wandered to and fro and hither and yonder.

'What are you playing at?' demanded the policeman.

'Just looking round. They may have moved the thing.'

'Ho!'

And then there was another bit of a lull. And suddenly I found myself by the window, and, by Jove, it was six inches open at the bottom. And the world beyond looked so bright and sunny and— Well, I don't claim that I am a particularly swift thinker, but once more something seemed to whisper 'Outside for Bertram!' I slid my fingers nonchalantly under the sash, gave a hefty heave, and up she came. And the next moment I was in a laurel bush, feeling like the cross which marks the spot where the accident occurred.

A large red face appeared in the window. I got up and skipped lightly to the gate.

'Hi!' shouted the policeman.

'Ho!' I replied, and went forth, moving well.

'This,' I said to myself, as I hailed a passing cab and sank back on the cushions, 'is the last time I try to do anything for young Bingo!'

These sentiments I expressed in no guarded language to Jeeves when I was back in the old flat with my feet on the mantelpiece, pushing down a soothing whisky-and.

'Never again, Jeeves!' I said. 'Never again!'

'Well, sir—'

'No, never again!'

'Well, sir—'

'What do you mean, "Well, sir"? What are you driving at?'

'Well, sir, Mr. Little is an extremely persistent young gentleman, and yours, if I may say so, sir, is a yielding and obliging nature—'

'You don't think that young Bingo would have the immortal rind to try to get me into some other foul enterprise?'

'I should say that it was more than probable, sir.'

I removed the dogs swiftly from the mantelpiece, and jumped up, all of a twitter.

'Jeeves, what would you advise?'

'Well, sir, I think a little change of scene would be judicious.'

'Do a bolt?'

'Precisely, sir. If I might suggest it, sir, why not change your mind and join Lord Yaxley at Harrogate?'

'Oh, I say, Jeeves!'

'You would be out of what I might describe as the danger zone, there, sir.'

'Perhaps you're right, Jeeves,' I said thoughtfully. 'Yes, possibly you're right. How far is Harrogate from London?'

'Two hundred and six miles, sir.'

'Yes, I think you're right. Is there a train this afternoon?'

'Yes, sir. You could catch it quite easily.'

'All right, then. Bung a few necessaries in a bag.'

'I have already done so, sir.'

'Ho!' I said.

It's a rummy thing, but when you come down to it Jeeves is always right. He had tried to cheer me up at the station by saying that I would not find Harrogate unpleasant, and, by Jove, he was perfectly correct. What I had overlooked, when examining the project, was the fact that I should be in the middle of a bevy of blokes who were taking the cure and I shouldn't be taking it myself. You've no notion what a dashed cosy, satisfying feeling that gives a fellow.

I mean to say, there was old Uncle George, for instance. The medicine-man, having given him the once-over, had ordered him to abstain from all alcoholic liquids, and in addition to tool down the hill to the Royal Pump-Room each morning at eight-thirty and imbibe twelve ounces of warm crescent saline and magnesia. It doesn't sound much, put that way, but I gather from contemporary accounts that it's practically equivalent to getting outside a couple of little old last year's eggs beaten up in sea-water. And the thought of Uncle George, who had oppressed me sorely in my childhood, sucking down that stuff and having to hop out of bed at eight-fifteen to do so was extremely grateful and comforting of a morning.

At four in the afternoon he would toddle down the hill again and repeat the process, and at night we would dine together and I would loll back in my chair, sipping my wine, and listen to him telling me what the stuff had tasted like. In many ways the ideal existence.

I generally managed to fit it in with my engagements to go down and watch him tackle his afternoon dose, for we Woosters are as fond of a laugh as anyone. And it was while I was enjoying the performance in the middle of the second week that I heard my name spoken. And there was Aunt Dahlia.

'Hallo!' I said. 'What are you doing here?'

'I came down yesterday with Tom.'

'Is Tom taking the cure?' asked Uncle George, looking up hopefully from the hell-brew.

'Yes.'

'Are you taking the cure?'

'Yes.'

'Ah!' said Uncle George, looking happier than I had seen him for days. He swallowed the last drops, and then, the programme calling for a brisk walk before his massage, left us.

'I shouldn't have thought you would have been able to get away from the paper,' I said. 'I say,' I went on, struck by a pleasing idea. 'It hasn't bust up, has it?'

'Bust up? I should say not. A pal of mine is looking after it for me while I'm here. It's right on its feet now. Tom has given me a couple of thousand and says there's more if I want it, and I've been able to buy the serial rights of Lady Bablockhythe's *Frank Recollections of a Long Life*. The hottest stuff, Bertie. Certain to double the circulation and send half the best-known people in London into hysterics for a year.'

'Oh!' I said. 'Then you're pretty well fixed, what? I mean, what with the Frank Recollections and that article of Mrs. Little's.'

Aunt Dahlia was drinking something that smelled like a leak in the gas-pipe, and I thought for a moment that it was that that made her twist up her face. But I was wrong.

'Don't mention that woman to me, Bertie!' she said. 'One of the worst.'

'But I thought you were rather pally.'

'No longer. Will you credit it that she positively refuses to let me have that article—'

'What!'

'— purely and simply on account of some fancied grievance she thinks she has against me because her cook left her and came to me.'

I couldn't follow this at all.

'Anatole left her?' I said. 'But what about the parlourmaid?'

'Pull yourself together, Bertie. You're babbling. What do you mean?'

'Why, I understood—'

'I'll bet you never understood anything in your life.' She laid down her empty glass. 'Well, that's done!' she said with relief. 'Thank goodness, I'll be able to watch Tom drinking his in a few minutes. It's the only thing that enables me to bear up. Poor old chap, he does hate it so! But I cheer him by telling him it's going to put him in shape for Anatole's cooking. And that, Bertie, is something worth going into training for. A master of his art, that man. Sometimes I'm not altogether surprised that Mrs. Little made such a fuss when he went. But, really, you know, she ought not to mix sentiment with business. She has no right to refuse to let me have that article just because of a private difference. Well, she jolly well can't use it anywhere else, because it was my idea and I have witnesses to prove it. If she tries to sell it to another paper, I'll sue her. And, talking of sewers, it's high time Tom was here to drink his sulphur-water.'

'But look here—'

'Oh, by the way, Bertie,' said Aunt Dahlia, 'I withdraw any harsh expressions I may have used about your man Jeeves. A most capable feller!'

'Jeeves?'

'Yes; he attended to the negotiations. And very well he did it, too. And he hasn't lost by it, you can bet. I saw to that. I'm grateful to him. Why, if Tom gives up a couple of thousand now, practically without a murmur, the imagination reels at what he'll do with Anatole cooking regularly for him. He'll be signing cheques in his sleep.'

I got up. Aunt Dahlia pleaded with me to stick around and watch Uncle Tom in action, claiming it to be a sight nobody should miss, but I couldn't wait. I rushed up the hill, left a farewell note for Uncle George, and caught the next train for London.

'Jeeves,' I said, when I had washed off the stains of travel, 'tell me frankly all about it. Be as frank as Lady Bablockhythe.'

'Sir?'

'Never mind, if you've not heard of her. Tell me how you worked this binge. The last I heard was that Anatole loved that parlourmaid – goodness knows why! – so much that he refused to leave her. Well, then?'

'I was somewhat baffled for a while, I must confess, sir. Then I was materially assisted by a fortunate discovery.'

'What was that?'

'I chanced to be chatting with Mrs. Travers's housemaid, sir, and, remembering that Mrs. Little was anxious to obtain a domestic of that description, I asked her if she would consent to leave Mrs. Travers and go at an advanced wage to Mrs. Little. To this she assented, and I saw Mrs. Little and arranged the matter.'

'Well? What was the fortunate discovery?'

'That the girl, in a previous situation some little time back, had been a colleague of Anatole, sir. And Anatole, as is the too frequent practice of these Frenchmen, had made love to her. In fact, they were, so I understood it, sir, formally affianced until Anatole disappeared one morning, leaving no address, and passed out of the poor girl's life. You will readily appreciate that this discovery simplified matters considerably. The girl no longer had any affection for Anatole, but the prospect of being under the same roof with two young persons, both of whom he had led to assume—'

'Great Scott! Yes, I see! It was rather like putting in a ferret to start a rabbit.'

'The principle was much the same, sir. Anatole was out of the house and in Mrs. Travers's service within half an hour of the receipt of the information that the young person was about to arrive. A volatile man, sir. Like so many of these Frenchmen.'

'Jeeves,' I said, 'this is genius of a high order.'

'It is very good of you to say so, sir.'

'What did Mr. Little say about it?'

'He appeared gratified, sir.'

'To go into sordid figures, did he—'

'Yes, sir. Twenty pounds. Having been fortunate in his selections at Hurst Park on the previous Saturday.'

'My aunt told me that she—'

'Yes, sir. Most generous. Twenty-five pounds.'

'Good Lord, Jeeves! You've been coining the stuff!'

'I have added appreciably to my savings, yes sir. Mrs. Little was good enough to present me with ten pounds for finding her such a satisfactory housemaid. And then there was Mr. Travers—'

'Uncle Thomas?'

Yes, sir. He also behaved most handsomely, quite independently of Mrs. Travers. Another twenty-five pounds. And his lordship—'

'Don't tell me that Uncle George gave you something, too! What on earth for?'

'Well, really, sir, I do not quite understand myself. But I received a cheque for ten pounds from him. He seemed to be under the impression that I had been in some way responsible for your joining him at Harrogate, sir.'

I gaped at the fellow.

'Well, everybody seems to be doing it,' I said, 'so I suppose I had better make the thing unanimous. Here's a fiver.'

'Why, thank you, sir. This is extremely—'

'It won't seem much compared with these vast sums you've been acquiring.'

'Oh, I assure you, sir.'

'And I don't know why I'm giving it to you.'

'No, sir.'

'Still, there it is.'

'Thank you very much, sir.'

I got up.

'It's pretty late,' I said, 'but I think I'll dress and go out and have a bite somewhere. I feel like having a whirl of some kind after two weeks at Harrogate.'

'Yes, sir. I will unpack your clothes.'

'Oh, Jeeves,' I said, 'did Peabody and Simms send those soft silk shirts?'

'Yes, sir. I sent them back.'

'Sent them back!'

'Yes, sir.'

I eyed him for a moment. But I mean to say. I mean, what's the use?

'Oh, all right,' I said. 'Then lay out one of the gents' stiff-bosomed.'

'Very good, sir,' said Jeeves.

It was the morning of the day on which I was slated to pop down to my Aunt Agatha's place at Woollam Chersey in the county of Herts for a visit of three solid weeks; and, as I seated myself at the breakfast table, I don't mind confessing that the heart was singularly heavy. We Woosters are men of iron, but beneath my intrepid exterior at that moment there lurked a nameless dread.

'Jeeves,' I said. 'I am not the old merry self this morning.'

'Indeed, sir?'

'No, Jeeves. Far from it. Far from the old merry self.'

'I am sorry to hear that, sir.'

He uncovered the fragrant eggs and b., and I pronged a moody forkful.

'Why – this is what I keep asking myself, Jeeves – why has my Aunt Agatha invited me to her country seat?'

'I could not say, sir.'

'Not because she is fond of me.'

'No, sir.'

'It is a well-established fact that I give her a pain in the neck. How it happens I cannot say, but every time our paths cross, so to speak, it seems to be a mere matter of time before I perpetrate some ghastly floater and have her hopping after me with her hatchet. The result being that she regards me as a worm and an outcast. Am I right or wrong, Jeeves?'

'Perfectly correct, sir.'

'And yet now she has absolutely insisted on my scratching all previous engagements and buzzing down to Woollam Chersey. She must have some sinister reason of which we know nothing. Can you blame me, Jeeves, if the heart is heavy?'

'No, sir. Excuse me, sir, I fancy I heard the front-door bell.'

He shimmered out, and I took another listless stab at the e. and bacon.

'A telegram, sir,' said Jeeves, re-entering the presence.

'Open it, Jeeves, and read contents. Who is it from?'

'It is unsigned, sir.'

'You mean there's no name at the end of it?'

'That is precisely what I was endeavouring to convey, sir.'

'Let's have a look.'

I scanned the thing. It was a rummy communication. Rummy. No other word. As follows:

Remember when you come here absolutely vital meet perfect strangers.

We Woosters are not very strong in the head, particularly at breakfast-time; and I was conscious of a dull ache between the eyebrows.

'What does it mean, Jeeves?'

'I could not say, sir.'

'It says "come here". Where's here?'

'You will notice that the message was handed in at Woollam Chersey, sir.'

'You're absolutely right. At Woollam, as you very cleverly spotted, Chersey. This tells us something, Jeeves.'

'What, sir?'

'I don't know. It couldn't be from my Aunt Agatha, do you think?'

'Hardly, sir.'

'No; you're right again. Then all we can say is that some

person unknown, resident at Woollam Chersey, considers it absolutely vital for me to meet perfect strangers. But why should I meet perfect strangers, Jeeves?'

'I could not say, sir.'

'And yet, looking at it from another angle, why shouldn't I?'

'Precisely, sir.'

'Then what it comes to is that the thing is a mystery which time alone can solve. We must wait and see, Jeeves.'

'The very expression I was about to employ, sir.'

I hit Woollam Chersey at about four o'clock, and found Aunt Agatha in her lair, writing letters. And, from what I know of her, probably offensive letters, with nasty postscripts. She regarded me with not a fearful lot of joy.

'Oh, there you are, Bertie.'

'Yes, here I am.'

'There's a smut on your nose.'

I plied the handkerchief.

'I am glad you have arrived so early. I want to have a word with you before you meet Mr. Filmer.'

'Who?'

'Mr. Filmer, the Cabinet Minister. He is staying in the house. Surely even you must have heard of Mr. Filmer?'

'Oh, rather,' I said, though as a matter of fact the bird was completely unknown to me. What with one thing and another, I'm not frightfully up in the *personnel* of the political world.

'I particularly wish you to make a good impression on Mr. Filmer.'

'Right-ho.'

'Don't speak in that casual way, as if you supposed that it was perfectly natural that you would make a good impression upon him. Mr. Filmer is a serious-minded man of high character and purpose, and you are just the type of vapid and frivolous wastrel against which he is most likely to be prejudiced.'

Hard words, of course, from one's own flesh and blood, but well in keeping with past form.

'You will endeavour, therefore, while you are here not to display yourself in the *role* of a vapid and frivolous wastrel. In the first place, you will give up smoking during your visit.'

'Oh, I say!'

'Mr. Filmer is president of the Anti-Tobacco League. Nor will you drink alcoholic stimulants.'

'Oh, dash it!'

'And you will kindly exclude from your conversation all that is suggestive of the bar, the billiard-room, and the stage-door. Mr. Filmer will judge you largely by your conversation.'

I rose to a point of order.

'Yes, but why have I got to make an impression on this – on Mr. Filmer?'

'Because,' said the old relative, giving me the eye, 'I particularly wish it.'

Not, perhaps, a notably snappy come-back as come-backs go; but it was enough to show me that that was more or less that; and I beetled out with an aching heart.

I headed for the garden, and I'm dashed if the first person I saw wasn't young Bingo Little.

Bingo Little and I have been pals practically from birth. Born in the same village within a couple of days of one another, we went through kindergarten, Eton, and Oxford together; and, grown to riper years we have enjoyed in the old metrop full many a first-class binge in each other's society. If there was one fellow in the world, I felt, who could alleviate the horrors of this blighted visit of mine, that bloke was young Bingo Little.

But how he came to be there was more than I could understand. Some time before, you see, he had married the celebrated authoress, Rosie M. Banks; and the last I had seen of him he had been on the point of accompanying her to America on a lecture tour. I distinctly remembered him cursing rather freely because the trip would mean his missing Ascot.

Still, rummy as it might seem, here he was. And aching for the sight of a friendly face, I gave tongue like a bloodhound.

'Bingo!'

He spun round; and, by Jove, his face wasn't friendly after all. It was what they call contorted. He waved his arms at me like a semaphore.

' 'Ssh!' he hissed. 'Would you ruin me?'

'Eh?'

'Didn't you get my telegram?'

'Was that *your* telegram?'

'Of course it was my telegram.'

'Then why didn't you sign it?'

'I did sign it.'

'No, you didn't. I couldn't make out what it was all about.'

'Well, you got my letter.'

'What letter?'

'My letter.'

'I didn't get any letter.'

'Then I must have forgotten to post it. It was to tell you that I was down here tutoring your Cousin Thomas, and that it was essential that, when we met, you should treat me as a perfect stranger.'

'But why?'

'Because, if your aunt supposed that I was a pal of yours, she would naturally sack me on the spot.'

'Why?'

Bingo raised his eyebrows.

'Why? Be reasonable, Bertie. If you were your aunt, and you knew the sort of chap you were, would you let a fellow you knew to be your best pal tutor your son?'

This made the old head swim a bit, but I got his meaning after a while, and I had to admit that there was much rugged good sense in what he said. Still, he hadn't explained what you might call the nub or gist of the mystery.

'I thought you were in America,' I said.

442

'Well, I'm not.'

'Why not?'

'Never mind why not. I'm not.'

'But why have you taken a tutoring job?'

'Never mind why. I have my reasons. And I want you to get it into your head, Bertie – to get it right through the concrete – that you and I must not be seen hobnobbing. Your foul cousin was caught smoking in the shrubbery the day before yesterday, and that has made my position pretty tottery, because your aunt said that, if I had exercised an adequate surveillance over him, it couldn't have happened. If, after that, she finds out I'm a friend of yours, nothing can save me from being shot out. And it is vital that I am not shot out.'

'Why?'

'Never mind why.'

At this point he seemed to think he heard somebody coming, for he suddenly leaped with incredible agility into a laurel bush. And I toddled along to consult Jeeves about these rummy happenings.

'Jeeves,' I said, repairing to the bedroom, where he was unpacking my things, 'you remember that telegram?'

'Yes, sir.'

'It was from Mr. Little. He's here, tutoring my young Cousin Thomas.'

'Indeed, sir?'

'I can't understand it. He appears to be a free agent, if you know what I mean; and yet would any man who was a free agent wantonly come to a house which contained my Aunt Agatha?'

'It seems peculiar, sir.'

'Moreover, would anybody of his own free-will and as a mere pleasure-seeker tutor my Cousin Thomas, who is notoriously a tough egg and a fiend in human shape?'

'Most improbable, sir.'

'These are deep waters, Jeeves.'

'Precisely, sir.'

'And the ghastly part of it all is that he seems to consider it necessary, in order to keep his job, to treat me like a long-lost leper. Thus killing my only chance of having anything approaching a decent time in this abode of desolation. For do you realise, Jeeves, that my aunt says I mustn't smoke while I'm here?'

'Indeed, sir?'

'Nor drink.'

'Why is this, sir?'

'Because she wants me – for some dark and furtive reason which she will not explain – to impress a fellow named Filmer.'

'Too bad, sir. However, many doctors, I understand, advocate such abstinence as the secret of health. They say it promotes a freer circulation of the blood and insures the arteries against premature hardening.'

'Oh, do they? Well, you can tell them next time you see them that they are silly asses.'

'Very good, sir.'

And so began what, looking back along a fairly eventful career, I think I can confidently say was the scaliest visit I have ever experienced in the course of my life. What with the agony of missing the life-giving cocktail before dinner; the painful necessity of being obliged, every time I wanted a quiet cigarette, to lie on the floor in my bedroom and puff the smoke up the chimney; the constant discomfort of meeting Aunt Agatha round unexpected corners; and the fearful strain on the *morale* of having to chum with the Right Hon. A. B. Filmer, it was not long before Bertram was up against it to an extent hitherto undreamed of.

I played golf with the Right Hon. every day, and it was only by biting the Wooster lip and clenching the fists till the knuckles stood out white under the strain that I managed to pull through. The Right Hon. punctuated some of the ghastliest golf I have ever seen with a flow of conversation which, as far as I was concerned, went completely over the top; and, all in all, I was beginning to feel pretty sorry for myself when, one night as I was in my room listlessly donning the soup-and-fish in preparation for the evening meal, in trickled young Bingo and took my mind off my own troubles.

For when it is a question of a pal being in the soup, we Woosters no longer think of self; and that poor old Bingo was knee-deep in the bisque was made plain by his mere appearance – which was that of a cat which has just been struck by a half-brick and is expecting another shortly.

'Bertie,' said Bingo, having sat down on the bed and diffused silent gloom for a moment, 'how is Jeeves's brain these days?'

'Fairly strong on the wing, I fancy. How is the grey matter, Jeeves? Surging about pretty freely?'

'Yes, sir.'

'Thank Heaven for that,' said young Bingo, 'for I require your soundest counsel. Unless right-thinking people take strong steps through the proper channels, my name will be mud.'

'What's wrong, old thing?' I asked, sympathetically.

Bingo plucked at the coverlet.

'I will tell you,' he said. 'I will also now reveal why I am staying in this pest-house, tutoring a kid who requires not education in the Greek and Latin languages but a swift slosh on the base of the skull with a black-jack. I came here, Bertie, because it was the only thing I could do. At the last moment before she sailed to America, Rosie decided that I had better stay behind and look after the Peke. She left me a couple of hundred quid to see me through till her return. This sum, judiciously expended over the period of her absence, would have been enough to keep Peke and self in moderate affluence. But you know how it is.'

'How what is?'

'When someone comes slinking up to you in the club and tells you that some cripple of a horse can't help winning even if it develops lumbago and the botts ten yards from the starting-post. I tell you, I regarded the thing as a cautious and conservative investment.'

'You mean you planked the entire capital on a horse?'

Bingo laughed bitterly.

'If you could call the thing a horse. If it hadn't shown a flash of speed in the straight, it would have got mixed up with the next race. It came in last, putting me in a dashed delicate position. Somehow or other I had to find the funds to keep me going, so that I could win through till Rosie's return without her knowing what had occurred. Rosie is the dearest girl in the world; but if you were a married man, Bertie, you would be aware that the best of wives is apt to cut up rough if she finds that her husband has dropped six weeks' housekeeping money on a single race. Isn't that so, Jeeves?'

'Yes, sir. Women are odd in that respect.'

'It was a moment for swift thinking. There was enough left from the wreck to board the Peke out at a comfortable home. I signed him up for six weeks at the Kosy Komfort Kennels at Kingsbridge, Kent, and tottered out, a broken man, to get a tutoring job. I landed the kid Thomas. And here I am.'

It was a sad story, of course, but it seemed to me that, awful as it might be to be in constant association with my Aunt Agatha and young Thos, he had got rather well out of a tight place.

'All you have to do,' I said, 'is to carry on here for a few weeks more, and everything will be oojah-cum-spiff.'

Bingo barked bleakly.

'A few weeks more! I shall be lucky if I stay two days. You remember I told you that your aunt's faith in me as a guardian of her blighted son was shaken a few days ago by the fact that he was caught smoking. I now find that the person who caught him smoking was the man Filmer. And ten minutes ago young Thomas told me that he was proposing to inflict some hideous revenge on Filmer for having reported him to your aunt. I don't know what he is going to do, but if he does it, out I inevitably go on my left ear. Your aunt thinks the world of Filmer, and would sack me on the spot. And three weeks before Rosie gets back!'

I saw all.

'Jeeves,' I said.

'Sir?'

'I see all. Do you see all?'

'Yes, sir.'

'Then flock round.'

'I fear, sir—'

Bingo gave a low moan.

'Don't tell me, Jeeves,' he said, brokenly, 'that nothing suggests itself.'

'Nothing at the moment, I regret to say, sir.'

Bingo uttered a stricken woofle like a bull-dog that has been refused cake.

'Well, then, the only thing I can do, I suppose,' he said sombrely, 'is not to let the pie-faced little thug out of my sight for a second.'

'Absolutely,' I said. 'Ceaseless vigilance, eh, Jeeves?'

'Precisely, sir.'

'But meanwhile, Jeeves,' said Bingo in a low, earnest voice, 'you will be devoting your best thought to the matter, won't you?'

'Most certainly, sir.'

'Thank you, Jeeves.'

'Not at all, sir.'

I will say for young Bingo that, once the need for action arrived, he behaved with an energy and determination which compelled respect. I suppose there was not a minute during the next two days when the kid Thos was able to say to himself: 'Alone at last!' But on the evening of the second day Aunt Agatha announced that some people were coming over on the morrow for a spot of tennis, and I feared that the worst must now befall.

Young Bingo, you see, is one of those fellows who, once their fingers close over the handle of a tennis racket, fall into a sort of trance in which nothing outside the radius of the lawn exists for them. If you came up to Bingo in the middle of a set and told him that panthers were devouring his best friend in the kitchen garden, he would look at you and say: 'Oh, ah?' or words to that effect. I knew that he would not give a thought to young Thomas and the Right Hon. till the last ball had bounced, and, as I dressed for dinner that night, I was conscious of an impending doom.

'Jeeves,' I said, 'have you ever pondered on Life?'

'From time to time, sir, in my leisure moments.'

'Grim, isn't it, what?'

'Grim, sir?'

'I mean to say, the difference between things as they look and things as they are.

'The trousers perhaps a half-inch higher, sir. A very slight adjustment of the braces will effect the necessary alteration. You were saying, sir?'

'I mean, here at Woollam Chersey we have apparently a happy, care-free country-house party. But beneath the glittering surface, Jeeves, dark currents are running. One gazes at the Right Hon. wrapping himself round the salmon mayonnaise at lunch, and he seems a man without a care in the world. Yet all the while a dreadful fate is hanging over him, creeping nearer and nearer. What exact steps do you think the kid Thomas intends to take?'

'In the course of an informal conversation which I had with the young gentleman this afternoon, sir, he informed me that he had been reading a romance entitled *Treasure Island*, and had been much struck by the character and actions of a certain Captain Flint. I gathered that he was weighing the advisability of modelling his own conduct on that of the Captain.'

'But, good heavens, Jeeves! If I remember *Treasure Island*, Flint was the bird who went about hitting people with a cutlass. You don't think young Thomas would bean Mr. Filmer with a cutlass?'

'Possibly he does not possess a cutlass, sir.'

'Well, with anything.'

'We can but wait and see, sir. The tie, if I might suggest it, sir, a shade more tightly knotted. One aims at the perfect butterfly effect. If you will permit me—'

'What do ties matter, Jeeves, at a time like this? Do you realise that Mr. Little's domestic happiness is hanging in the scale?'

'There is no time, sir, at which ties do not matter.'

I could see the man was pained, but I did not try to heal the wound. What's the word I want? Preoccupied. I was too preoccupied, don't you know. And distrait. Not to say careworn.

I was still careworn when, next day at half-past two, the revels commenced on the tennis lawn. It was one of those close, baking days, with thunder rumbling just round the corner; and it seemed to me that there was a brooding menace in the air.

'Bingo,' I said, as we pushed forth to do our bit in the first doubles, 'I wonder what young Thos will be up to this afternoon, with the eye of authority no longer on him?'

'Eh?' said Bingo, absently. Already the tennis look had come into his face, and his eye was glazed. He swung his racket and snorted a little.

'I don't see him anywhere,' I said.

'You don't what?'

'See him.'

'Who?'

'Young Thos.'

'What about him?'

I let it go.

The only consolation I had in the black period of the opening of the tourney was the fact that the Right Hon. had taken a seat among the spectators and was wedged in between a couple of females with parasols. Reason told me that even a kid so steeped in sin as young Thomas would hardly perpetrate any outrage on a man in such a strong strategic position. Considerably relieved, I gave myself up to the game; and was in the act of putting it across the local curate with a good deal of vim when there was a roll of thunder and the rain started to come down in buckets.

We all stampeded for the house, and had gathered in the drawing-room for tea, when suddenly Aunt Agatha, looking up from the cucumber-sandwich, said:

'Has anybody seen Mr. Filmer?'

It was one of the nastiest jars I have ever experienced.

What with my fast serve zipping sweetly over the net and the man of God utterly unable to cope with my slow bending return down the centre-line, I had for some little rime been living, as it were, in another world. I now came down to earth with a bang: and my slice of cake, slipping from my nerveless fingers, fell to the ground and was wolfed by Aunt Agatha's spaniel, Robert. Once more I seemed to become conscious of an impending doom.

For this man Filmer, you must understand, was not one of those men who are lightly kept from the tea-table. A hearty trencherman, and particularly fond of his five o'clock couple of cups and bite of muffin, he had until this afternoon always been well up among the leaders in the race for the food-trough. If one thing was certain, it was that only the machinations of some enemy could be keeping him from being in the drawing-room now, complete with nose-bag.

'He must have got caught in the rain and be sheltering somewhere in the grounds,' said Aunt Agatha. 'Bertie, go out and find him. Take a raincoat to him.'

'Right-ho!' I said. My only desire in life now was to find the Right Hon. And I hoped it wouldn't be merely his body.

I put on a raincoat and tucked another under my arm, and was sallying forth, when in the hall I ran into Jeeves.

'Jeeves,' I said, 'I fear the worst. Mr. Filmer is misssing.'

'Yes, sir.'

'I am about to scour the grounds in search of him.'

'I can save you the trouble, sir. Mr. Filmer is on the island in the middle of the lake.'

'In this rain? Why doesn't the chump row back?'

'He has no boat, sir.'

'Then how can he be on the island?'

'He rowed there, sir. But Master Thomas rowed after him and set his boat adrift. He was informing me of the circumstances a moment ago, sir. It appears that Captain Flint was in the habit of marooning people on islands, and Master Thomas felt that he could pursue no more judicious course than to follow his example.'

'But, good Lord, Jeeves! The man must be getting soaked.'

'Yes, sir. Master Thomas commented upon that aspect of the matter.'

It was a time for action.

'Come with me, Jeeves!'

'Very good, sir.'

I buzzed for the boathouse.

My Aunt Agatha's husband, Spenser Gregson, who is on the Stock Exchange, had recently cleaned up to an amazing extent in Sumatra Rubber; and Aunt Agatha, in selecting a country estate, had lashed out on an impressive scale. There were miles of what they call rolling parkland, trees in considerable profusion well provided with doves and what not cooing in no uncertain voice, gardens full of roses, and also stables, out-houses, and messuages, the whole forming a rather fruity *tout ensemble*. But the feature of the place was the lake.

It stood to the east of the house, beyond the rose garden, and covered several acres. In the middle of it was an island. In the middle of the island was a building known as the Octagon. And in the middle of the Octagon, seated on the roof and spouting water like a public fountain, was the Right Hon. A. B. Filmer. As we drew nearer, striking a fast clip with self at the oars and Jeeves handling the tiller-ropes, we heard cries of gradually increasing volume, if that's the expression I want; and presently, up aloft, looking from a distance as if he were perched on top of the bushes, I located the Right Hon. It seemed to me that even a Cabinet Minister ought to have more sense than to stay right out in the open like that when there were trees to shelter under.

'A little more to the right, Jeeves.'

'Very good, sir.'

I made a neat landing.

'Wait here, Jeeves.'

'Very good, sir. The head gardener was informing me this morning, sir, that one of the swans had recently nested on this island.'

'This is no time for natural history gossip, Jeeves,' I said, a little severely, for the rain was coming down harder than ever and the Wooster trouser-legs were already considerably moistened.

'Very good, sir.'

I pushed my way through the bushes. The going was sticky and took about eight and elevenpence off the value of my Sure-Grip tennis shoes in the first two yards: but I persevered, and presently came out in the open and found myself in a sort of clearing facing the Octagon.

This building was run up somewhere in the last century, I have been told, to enable the grandfather of the late owner to have some quiet place out of earshot of the house where he could practise the fiddle. From what I know of fiddlers, I should imagine that he had produced some fairly frightful sounds there in his time: but they can have been nothing to the ones that were coming from the roof of the place now. The Right Hon., not having spotted the arrival of the rescue-party, was apparently trying to make his voice carry across the waste of waters to the house; and I'm not saying it was not a good sporting effort. He had one of those highish tenors, and his yowls seemed to screech over my head like shells.

I thought it about time to slip him the glad news that assistance had arrived, before he strained a vocal cord.

'Hi!' I shouted, waiting for a lull.

He poked his head over the edge.

'Hi!' he bellowed, looking in every direction but the right one, of course.

'Hi!'

'Hi!'

'Hi!'

'Hi!'

'Oh!' he said, spotting me at last.

'What-ho!' I replied, sort of clinching the thing.

I suppose the conversation can't be said to have touched a frightfully high level up to this moment; but probably we should have got a good deal brainier very shortly – only just then, at the very instant when I was getting ready to say something good, there was a hissing noise like a tyre bursting in a nest of cobras, and out of the bushes to my left there popped something so large and white and active that, thinking quicker than I have ever done in my puff, I rose like a rocketing pheasant, and, before I knew what I was doing, had begun the climb for life. Something slapped against the wall about an inch below my right ankle, and any doubts I may have had about remaining below vanished. The lad who bore 'mid snow and ice the banner with the strange device 'Excelsior!' was the model for Bertram.

'Be careful!' yipped the Right Hon.

I was.

Whoever built the Octagon might have constructed it especially for this sort of crisis. Its walls had grooves at regular intervals which were just right for the hands and feet, and it wasn't very long before I was parked up on the roof beside the Right Hon., gazing down at one of the largest and shortest-tempered swans I had ever seen. It was standing below, stretching up a neck like a hose-pipe, just where a bit of brick, judiciously bunged, would catch it amidships.

I bunged the brick and scored a bull's eye.

The Right Hon. didn't seem any too well pleased.

'Don't tease it!' he said.

'It teased me,' I said.

The swan extended another eight feet of neck and gave an imitation of steam escaping from a leaky pipe. The rain continued to lash down with what you might call indescribable fury, and I was sorry that in the agitation inseparable from shinning up a stone wall at practically a second's notice I had dropped the raincoat which I had been bringing with me for my fellow-rooster. For a moment I thought of offering him mine, but wiser counsels prevailed.

'How near did it come to getting you?' I asked.

'Within an ace,' replied my companion, gazing down with a look of marked dislike. 'I had to make a very rapid spring.'

The Right Hon. was a tubby little chap who looked as if he had been poured into his clothes and had forgotten to say 'When!' and the picture he conjured up, if you know what I mean, was rather pleasing.

'It is no laughing matter,' he said, shifting the look of dislike to me.

'Sorry.'

'I might have been seriously injured.'

'Would you consider bunging another brick at the bird?'

'Do nothing of the sort. It will only annoy him.'

'Well, why not annoy him? He hasn't shown such a dashed lot of consideration for our feelings.'

The Right Hon. now turned to another aspect of the matter.

'I cannot understand how my boat, which I fastened securely to the stump of a willow-tree, can have drifted away.'

'Dashed mysterious.'

'I begin to suspect that it was deliberately set loose by some mischievous person.'

'Oh, I say, no, hardly likely, that. You'd have seen them doing it.'

'No, Mr. Wooster. For the bushes form an effective screen. Moreover, rendered drowsy by the unusual warmth of the afternoon, I dozed off for some little time almost immediately I reached the island.'

This wasn't the sort of thing I wanted his mind dwelling on, so I changed the subject.

'Wet, isn't it, what?' I said.

'I had already observed it,' said the Right Hon. in one of those nasty, bitter voices. 'I thank you, however, for drawing the matter to my attention.'

Chit-chat about the weather hadn't gone with much of a bang, I perceived. I had a shot at Bird Life in the Home Counties.

'Have you ever noticed,' I said, 'how a swan's eyebrows sort of meet in the middle?'

'I have had every opportunity of observing all that there is to observe about swans.'

'Gives them a sort of peevish look, what?'

'The look to which you allude has not escaped me.'

'Rummy,' I said, rather warming to my subject, 'how bad an effect family life has on a swan's disposition.'

'I wish you would select some other topic of conversation than swans.'

'No, but really, it's rather interesting. I mean to say, our old pal down there is probably a perfect ray of sunshine in normal circumstances. Quite the domestic pet, don't you know. But purely and simply because the little woman happens to be nesting—'

I paused. You will scarcely believe me, but until this moment, what with all the recent bustle and activity, I had clean forgotten that, while we were treed up on the roof like this, there lurked all the time in the background one whose giant brain, if notified of the emergency and requested to flock round, would probably be able to think up half-a-dozen schemes for solving our little difficulties in a couple of minutes.

'Jeeves!' I shouted.

'Sir?' came a faint respectful voice from the great open spaces.

'My man,' I explained to the Right Hon. 'A fellow of infinite resource and sagacity. He'll have us out of this in a minute. Jeeves!'

'Sir?'

'I'm sitting on the roof.'

'Very good, sir.'

'Don't say "Very good". Come and help us. Mr. Filmer and I are treed, Jeeves.'

'Very good, sir.'

'Don't keep saying "Very good". It's nothing of the kind. The place is alive with swans.'

'I will attend to the matter immediately, sir.'

I turned to the Right Hon. I even went so far as to pat him on the back. It was like slapping a wet sponge.

'All is well,' I said. 'Jeeves is coming.'

'What can he do?'

I frowned a trifle. The man's tone had been peevish, and I didn't like it.

'That,' I replied with a touch of stiffness, 'we cannot say until we see him in action. He may pursue one course, or he may pursue another. But on one thing you can rely with the utmost confidence – Jeeves will find a way. See, here he comes stealing through the undergrowth, his face shining with the light of pure intelligence. There are no limits to Jeeves's brain-power. He virtually lives on fish.'

I bent over the edge and peered into the abyss.

'Look out for the swan, Jeeves.'

'I have the bird under close observation, sir.'

The swan had been uncoiling a further supply of neck in our direction; but now he whipped round. The sound of a voice speaking in his rear seemed to affect him powerfully. He subjected Jeeves to a short, keen scrutiny; and then, taking in some breath for hissing purposes, gave a sort of jump and charged ahead.

'Look out, Jeeves!'

'Very good, sir.'

Well, I could have told that swan it was no use. As swans go, he may have been well up in the ranks of the intelligentsia; but, when it came to pitting his brains against Jeeves, he was simply wasting his time. He might just as well have gone home at once.

Every young man starting life ought to know how to cope with an angry swan, so I will briefly relate the proper procedure. You begin by picking up the raincoat which somebody has dropped; and then, judging the distance to a nicety, you simply shove the raincoat over the bird's head; and, taking the boat-hook which you have prudently brought with you, you insert it underneath the swan and heave. The swan goes into a bush and starts trying to unscramble itself; and you saunter back to your boat, taking with you any friends who may happen at the moment to be sitting on roofs in the vicinity. That was Jeeves's method, and I cannot see how it could have been improved upon.

The Right Hon. showing a turn of speed of which I would not have believed him capable, we were in the boat in considerably under two ticks.

'You behaved very intelligently, my man,' said the Right Hon. as we pushed away from the shore.

'I endeavour to give satisfaction, sir.'

The Right Hon. appeared to have said his say for the time being. From that moment he seemed to sort of huddle up and meditate. Dashed absorbed he was. Even when I caught a crab and shot about a pint of water down his neck he didn't seem to notice it.

It was only when we were landing that he came to life again.

'Mr. Wooster.'

'Oh, ah?'

'I have been thinking of that matter of which I spoke to you some time back – the problem of how my boat can have got adrift.'

I didn't like this.

'The dickens of a problem,' I said. 'Better not bother about it any more. You'll never solve it.'

'On the contrary, I have arrived at a solution, and one which I think is the only feasible solution. I am convinced that my boat was set adrift by the boy Thomas, my hostess's son.'

'Oh, I say, no! Why?'

'He had a grudge against me. And it is the sort of thing only a boy, or one who is practically an imbecile, would have thought of doing.'

He legged it for the house; and I turned to Jeeves, aghast. Yes, you might say aghast.

'You heard, Jeeves?'

'Yes, sir.'

'What's to be done?'

'Perhaps Mr. Filmer, on thinking the matter over, will decide that his suspicions are unjust.'

'But they aren't unjust.'

'No, sir.'

'Then what's to be done?'

'I could not say, sir.'

I pushed off rather smartly to the house and reported to Aunt Agatha that the Right Hon. had been saved; and then I toddled upstairs to have a hot bath, being considerably soaked from stem to stern as the result of my rambles. While I was enjoying the grateful warmth, a knock came at the door.

It was Benson, Aunt Agatha's butler.

'Mrs. Gregson desires me to say, sir, that she would be glad to see you as soon as you are ready.'

'But she has seen me.'

'I gather that she wishes to see you again, sir.'

'Oh, right-ho.'

I lay beneath the surface for another few minutes; then, having dried the frame, went along the corridor to my room. Jeeves was there, fiddling about with underclothing.

'Oh, Jeeves,' I said, 'I've just been thinking. Oughtn't somebody to go and give Mr. Filmer a spot of quinine or something? Errand of mercy, what?'

'I have already done so, sir.'

'Good. I wouldn't say I like the man frightfully, but I don't want him to get a cold in the head.' I shoved on a sock. 'Jeeves,' I said, 'I suppose you know that we've got to think of something pretty quick? I mean to say, you realise the position? Mr. Filmer suspects young Thomas of doing exactly what he did do, and if he brings home the charge Aunt Agatha will undoubtedly fire Mr. Little, and then Mrs. Little will find out what Mr. Little has been up to, and what will be the upshot and outcome, Jeeves? I will tell you. It will mean that Mrs. Little will get the goods on Mr. Little to an extent to which, though only a bachelor myself, I should say that no wife ought to get the goods on her husband if the proper give and take of married life – what you might call the essential balance, as it were – is to be preserved. Women bring these things up, Jeeves. They do not forget and forgive.'

'Very true, sir.'

'Then how about it?'

'I have already attended to the matter, sir.'

'You have?'

'Yes, sir. I had scarcely left you when the solution of the affair presented itself to me. It was a remark of Mr. Filmer's that gave me the idea.'

'Jeeves, you're a marvel!'

'Thank you very much, sir.'

'What was the solution?'

'I conceived the notion of going to Mr. Filmer and saying that it was you who had stolen his boat, sir.'

The man flickered before me. I clutched a sock in a feverish grip.

'Saying – what?'

'At first Mr. Filmer was reluctant to credit my statement. But I pointed out to him that you had certainly known that he was on the island – a fact which he agreed was highly significant. I pointed out, furthermore, that you were a light-hearted young gentleman, sir, who might well do such a thing as a practical joke. I left him quite convinced, and there is now no danger of his attributing the action to Master Thomas.'

I gazed at the blighter spellbound.

'And that's what you consider a neat solution?' I said.

'Yes, sir. Mr. Little will now retain his position as desired.'

'And what about me?'

'You are also benefited, sir.'

'Oh, I am, am I?'

'Yes, sir. I have ascertained that Mrs. Gregson's motive in inviting you to this house was that she might present you to Mr. Filmer with a view to your becoming his private secretary.'

'What!'

'Yes, sir. Benson, the butler, chanced to overhear Mrs. Gregson in conversation with Mr. Filmer on the matter.'

'Secretary to that superfatted bore! Jeeves, I could never have survived it.'

'No, sir. I fancy you would not have found it agreeable. Mr. Filmer is scarcely a congenial companion for you. Yet, had Mrs. Gregson secured the position for you, you might have found it embarrassing to decline to accept it.'

'Embarrassing is right!'

'Yes, sir.'

'But I say, Jeeves, there's just one point which you seem to have overlooked. Where exactly do I get off?'

'Sir?'

'I mean to say, Aunt Agatha sent word by Purvis just now that she wanted to see me. Probably she's polishing up her hatchet at this very moment.'

'It might be the most judicious plan not to meet her, sir.'

'But how can I help it?'

'There is a good, stout waterpipe running down the wall immediately outside this window, sir. And I could have the two-seater waiting outside the park gates in twenty minutes.'

I eyed him with reverence.

'Jeeves,' I said, 'you are always right. You couldn't make it five, could you?'

'Let us say ten, sir.'

'Ten it is. Lay out some raiment suitable for travel, and leave the rest to me. Where is this waterpipe of which you speak so highly?'

I checked the man with one of my glances. I was astounded and shocked.

'Not another word, Jeeves,' I said. 'You have gone too far. Hats, yes. Socks, yes. Coats, trousers, shirts, ties, and spats, absolutely. On all these things I defer to your judgment. But when it comes to vases, no.'

'Very good, sir.'

'You say that this vase is not in harmony with the appointments of the room – whatever that means, if anything. I deny this, Jeeves, *in toto*. I like this vase. I call it decorative, striking, and, all in all, an exceedingly good fifteen bob's worth.'

'Very good, sir.'

'That's that, then. If anybody rings up, I shall be closeted during the next hour with Mr. Sipperley at the offices of *The Mayfair Gazette*.'

I beetled off with a fairish amount of restrained hauteur, for I was displeased with the man. On the previous afternoon, while sauntering along the Strand, I had found myself wedged into one of those sort of alcove places where fellows with voices like fog-horns stand all day selling things by auction. And, though I was still vague as to how exactly it had happened, I had somehow become the possessor of a large china vase with crimson dragons on it. And not only dragons, but birds, dogs, snakes, and a thing that looked like a leopard. This menagerie was now stationed on a bracket over the door of my sitting-room.

I liked the thing. It was bright and cheerful. It caught the eye. And that was why, when Jeeves, wincing a bit, had weighed in with some perfectly gratuitous art-criticism, I ticked him off with no little vim. *Ne sutor ultra* whatever-it-is, I would have said to him, if I'd thought of it. I mean to say, where does a valet get off, censoring vases? Does it fall within his province to knock the young master's chinaware? Absolutely not, and so I told him.

I was still pretty heartily hipped when I reached the office of *The Mayfair Gazette,* and it would have been a relief to my feelings to have decanted my troubles on to old Sippy, who, being a very dear old pal of mine, would no doubt have understood and sympathised. But when the office-boy had slipped me through into the inner cubbyhole where the old lad performed his editorial duties, he seemed so preoccupied that I hadn't the heart.

All these editor blokes, I understand, get pretty careworn after they've been at the job for a while. Six months before, Sippy had been a cheery cove, full of happy laughter; but at that time he was what they call a free-lance, bunging in a short story here and a set of verses there and generally enjoying himself. Ever since he had become editor of this rag, I had sensed a change, so to speak.

Today he looked more editorial than ever; so, shelving my own worries for the nonce, I endeavoured to cheer him up by telling him how much I had enjoyed his last issue. As a matter of fact, I hadn't read it, but we Woosters do not shrink from subterfuge when it is a question of bracing up a buddy.

The treatment was effective. He showed animation and verve.

'You really liked it?'

'Red-hot, old thing.'

'Full of good stuff, eh?'

'Packed.'

'That poem – Solitude?'

'What a gem!'

'A genuine masterpiece.'

'Pure tabasco. Who wrote it?'

'It was signed,' said Sippy, a little coldly.

'I keep forgetting names.'

'It was written,' said Sippy, 'by Miss Gwendolen Moon. Have you ever met Miss Moon, Bertie?'

'Not to my knowledge. Nice girl?'

'My God!' said Sippy.

I looked at him keenly. If you ask my Aunt Agatha she will tell you – in fact, she is quite likely to tell you even if you don't ask her – that I am a vapid and irreflective chump. Barely sentient, was the way she once described me: and I'm not saying that in a broad, general sense she isn't right. But there is one department of life in which I am Hawkshaw the detective in person. I can recognise Love's Young Dream more quickly than any other bloke of my weight and age in the Metropolis. So many of my pals have copped it in the past few years that now I can spot it a mile off on a foggy day. Sippy was leaning back in his chair, chewing a piece of indiarubber with a far-off look in his eyes, and I formed my diagnosis instantly.

'Tell me all, laddie,' I said.

'Bertie, I love her.'

'Have you told her so?'

'How can I?'

'I don't see why not. Quite easy to bring into the general conversation.'

Sippy groaned hollowly.

'Do you know what it is, Bertie, to feel the humility of a worm?'

'Rather! I do sometimes with Jeeves. But today he went too far. You will scarcely credit, old man, but he had the crust to criticise a vase which—'

'She is so far above me.'

'Tall girl?'

'Spiritually. She is all soul. And what am I? Earthy.'

'Would you say that?'

'I would. Have you forgotten that a year ago I did thirty days without the option for punching a policeman in the stomach on Boat-Race Night?'

'But you were whiffled at the time.'

'Exactly. What right has an inebriated jail-bird to aspire to a goddess?'

My heart bled for the poor old chap.

'Aren't you exaggerating things a trifle, old lad?' I said. 'Everybody who has had a gentle upbringing gets a bit sozzled on Boat-Race Night, and the better element nearly always have trouble with the gendarmes.'

He shook his head.

'It's no good, Bertie. You mean well, but words are useless. No, I can but worship from afar. When I am in her presence a strange dumbness comes over me. My tongue seems to get entangled with my tonsils. I could no more muster up the nerve to propose to her than . . . Come in!' he shouted.

For, just as he was beginning to go nicely and display a bit of eloquence, a knock had sounded on the door. In fact, not so much a knock as a bang – or even a slosh. And there now entered a large, important-looking bird with penetrating eyes, a Roman nose, and high cheek-bones. Authoritative. That's the word I want. I didn't like his collar, and Jeeves would have had a thing or two to say about the sit of his trousers; but, nevertheless, he was authoritative. There was something compelling about the man. He looked like a traffic-policeman.

'Ah, Sipperley!' he said.

Old Sippy displayed a good deal of agitation. He had leaped from his chair, and was now standing in a constrained attitude, with a sort of pop-eyed expression on his face.

'Pray be seated, Sipperley,' said the cove. He took no notice of me. After one keen glance and a brief waggle of the nose in my direction, he had washed Bertram out of his life. 'I have brought you another little offering – ha! Look it over at your leisure, my dear fellow.'

'Yes, sir,' said Sippy.

'I think you will enjoy it. But there is just one thing. I should be glad, Sipperley, if you would give it a leetle better display, a rather more prominent position in the paper than you accorded to my "Landmarks of Old Tuscany". I am quite aware that in a weekly journal space is a desideratum, but one does not like one's efforts to be – I can only say pushed away in a back corner among advertisements of bespoke tailors and places of amusement.' He paused, and a nasty gleam came into his eyes. 'You will bear this in mind, Sipperley?'

'Yes, sir,' said Sippy.

'I am greatly obliged, my dear fellow,' said the cove, becoming genial again. 'You must forgive my mentioning it. I would be the last person to attempt to dictate the – ha! – editorial policy, but— Well, good afternoon, Sipperley. I will call for your decision at three o'clock tomorrow.'

He withdrew, leaving a gap in the atmosphere about ten feet by six. When this had closed in, I sat up.

'What was it?' I said.

I was startled to observe poor old Sippy apparently go off his onion. He raised his hands over his head, clutched his hair, wrenched it about for a while, kicked a table with great violence, and then flung himself into his chair.

'Curse him!' said Sippy. 'May he tread on a banana-skin on his way to chapel and sprain both ankles!'

'Who was he?'

'May he get frog-in-the-throat and be unable to deliver the end-of-term sermon!'

'Yes, but who was he?'

'My old head master, Bertie,' said Sippy.

'Yes, but, my dear old soul—'

'Head master of my old school.' He gazed at me in a distraught sort of way. 'Good Lord! Can't you understand the position?'

'Not by a jugful, laddie.'

Sippy sprang from his chair and took a turn or two up and down the carpet.

'How do you feel,' he said, 'when you meet the head master of your old school?'

'I never do. He's dead.'

'Well, I'll tell you how I feel. I feel as if I were in the Lower Fourth again, and had been sent up by my form-master for creating a disturbance in school. That happened once, Bertie, and the memory still lingers. I can recall as if it were yesterday knocking at old Waterbury's door and hearing him say: "Come in!" like a lion roaring at an early Christian, and going in and shuffling my feet on the mat and him looking at me and me explaining – and then, after what seemed a lifetime, bending over and receiving six of the juiciest on the old spot with a cane that bit like an adder. And whenever he comes into my office now the old wound begins to trouble me, and I just say: "Yes, sir," and "No, sir," and feel like a kid of fourteen.'

I began to grasp the posish. The whole trouble with these fellows like Sippy, who go in for writing, is that they develop the artistic temperament, and you never know when it is going to break out.

'He comes in here with his pockets full of articles on "The Old School Cloisters" and "Some Little-Known Aspects of Tacitus", and muck like that, and I haven't the nerve to refuse them. And this is supposed to be a paper devoted to the lighter interests of Society.'

'You must be firm, Sippy. Firm, old thing.'

'How can I, when the sight of him makes me feel like a piece of chewed blotting-paper? When he looks at me over that nose, my *morale* goes blue at the roots and I am back at school again. It's persecution, Bertie. And the next thing that'll happen is that my proprietor will spot one of those articles, assume with perfect justice that, if I can print that sort of thing, I must be going off my chump, and fire me.'

I pondered. It was a tough problem.

'How would it be——?' I said.

'That's no good.'

'Only a suggestion,' I said.

'Jeeves,' I said, when I got home, 'surge round!'

'Sir?'

'Burnish the old bean. I have a case that calls for one of your best efforts. Have you ever heard of a Miss Gwendolen Moon?'

'Authoress of *Autumn Leaves*, *'Twas on an English June*, and other works. Yes, sir.'

'Great Scott, Jeeves, you seem to know everything.'

'Thank you very much, sir.'

'Well, Mr. Sipperley is in love with Miss Moon.'

'Yes, sir.'

'But fears to speak.'

'It is often the way, sir.'

'Deeming himself unworthy.'

'Precisely, sir.'

'Right! But that is not all. Tuck that away in a corner of the mind, Jeeves, and absorb the rest of the facts. Mr. Sipperley, as you are aware, is the editor of a weekly paper devoted to the interests of the lighter Society. And now the head master of his old school has started calling at the office and unloading on him junk entirely unsuited to the lighter Society. All clear?'

'I follow you perfectly, sir.'

'And this drip Mr. Sipperley is compelled to publish, much against his own wishes, purely because he lacks the nerve to tell the man to go to blazes. The whole trouble being, Jeeves, that he has got one of those things that fellows do get – it's on the tip of my tongue.'

'An inferiority complex, sir?'

'Exactly. An inferiority complex. I have one myself with regard to my Aunt Agatha. You know me, Jeeves. You know that if it were a question of volunteers to man the lifeboat, I would spring to the task. If anyone said: "Don't go down the coal-mine, daddy," it would have not the slightest effect on my resolution—'

'Undoubtedly, sir.'

'And yet – and this is where I want you to follow me very closely, Jeeves – when I hear that my Aunt Agatha is out with her hatchet and moving in my direction, I run like a rabbit. Why? Because she gives me an inferiority complex. And so it is with Mr. Sipperley. He would, if called upon, mount the deadly breach, and do it without a tremor; but he cannot bring himself to propose to Miss Moon, and he cannot kick his old head master in the stomach and tell him to take his beastly essays on "The Old School Cloisters" elsewhere, because he has an inferiority complex. So what about it, Jeeves?'

'I fear I have no plan which I could advance with any confidence on the spur of the moment, sir.'

'You want time to think, eh?'

'Yes, sir.'

'Take it, Jeeves, take it. You may feel brainier after a night's sleep. What is it the poet calls sleep, Jeeves?'

'Tired Nature's sweet restorer, sir.'

'Exactly. Well, there you are, then.'

You know, there's nothing like sleeping on a thing. Scarcely had I woken up next morning when I discovered that, while I slept, I had got the whole binge neatly into order and worked out a plan Foch might have been proud of. I rang the bell for Jeeves to bring me my tea.

I rang again. But it must have been five minutes before the man showed up with the steaming.

'I beg your pardon, sir,' he said, when I reproached him. 'I did not hear the bell. I was in the sitting-room sir.'

'Ah?' I said, sucking down a spot of the mixture, 'Doing this and that, no doubt?'

'Dusting your new vase, sir.'

My heart warmed to the fellow. If there's one person I like, it's the chap who is not too proud to admit it when he's in the wrong. No actual statement to that effect had passed his lips, of course, but we Woosters can read between the lines. I could see that he was learning to love the vase.

'How does it look?'

'Yes, sir.'

A bit cryptic, but I let it go.

'Jeeves,' I said.

'Sir?'

'That matter we were in conference about yestereen.'

'The matter of Mr. Sipperley, sir?'

'Precisely. Don't worry yourself any further. Stop the brain working. I shall not require your services. I have found the solution. It came on me like a flash.'

'Indeed, sir?'

'Just like a flash. In a matter of this kind, Jeeves, the first thing to do is to study – what's the word I want?'

'I could not say, sir.'

'Quite a common word – though long.'

'Psychology, sir?'

'The exact noun. It is a noun?'

'Yes, sir.'

'Spoken like a man! Well, Jeeves, direct your attention to the psychology of old Sippy. Mr. Sipperley, if you follow me, is in the position of a man from whose eyes the scales have not fallen. The task that faced me, Jeeves, was to discover some scheme which would cause those scales to fall. You get me?

'Not entirely, sir.'

'Well, what I'm driving at is this. At present this head master bloke, this Waterbury, is trampling all over Mr. Sipperly because he is hedged about with dignity, if you understand what

I mean. Years have passed; Mr. Sipperley now shaves daily and is in an important editorial position; but he can never forget that this bird once gave him six of the juiciest. Result: an inferiority complex. The only way to remove that complex, Jeeves, is to arrange that Mr. Sipperley shall see this Waterbury in a thoroughly undignified position. This done, the scales will fall from his eyes. You must see that for yourself, Jeeves. Take your own case. No doubt there are a number of your friends and relations who look up to you and respect you greatly. But suppose one night they were to see you, in an advanced state of intoxication, dancing the Charleston in your underwear in the middle of Piccadilly Circus?'

'The contingency is remote, sir.'

'Ah, but suppose they did. The scales would fall from their eyes, what?'

'Very possibly, sir.'

'Take another case. Do you remember a year or so ago the occasion when my Aunt Agatha accused the maid at that French hotel of pinching her pearls, only to discover that they were still in her drawer?'

'Yes, sir.'

'Whereupon she looked the most priceless ass. You'll admit that.'

'Certainly I have seen Mrs. Spenser Gregson appear to greater advantage than at that moment, sir.'

'Exactly. Now follow me like a leopard. Observing my Aunt Agatha in her downfall; watching her turn bright mauve and listening to her being told off in liquid French by a whiskered hotel proprietor without coming back with so much as a single lift of the eyebrows, I felt as if the scales had fallen from my eyes. For the first time in my life, Jeeves, the awe with which this woman had inspired me from childhood's days left me. It came back later, I'll admit; but at the moment I saw my Aunt Agatha for what she was – not, as I had long imagined, a sort of man-eating fish at the very mention of whose name strong men quivered like aspens, but a poor goop who had just dropped a very serious brick. At that moment, Jeeves, I could have told her precisely where she got off; and only a too chivalrous regard for the sex kept me from doing so. You won't dispute that?'

'No, sir.'

'Well, then, my firm conviction is that the scales will fall from Mr. Sipperley's eyes when he sees this Waterbury, this old head master, stagger into his office covered from head to foot with flour.'

'Flour, sir?'

'Flour, Jeeves.'

'But why should he pursue such a course, sir?'

'Because he won't be able to help it. The stuff will be balanced on top of the door, and the force of gravity will do the rest. I propose to set a booby-trap for this Waterbury, Jeeves.'

'Really, sir, I would scarcely advocate—'

I raised my hand.

'Peace, Jeeves! There is more to come. You have not forgotten that Mr. Sipperley loves Miss Gwendolen Moon, but fears to speak. I bet you'd forgotten that.'

'No, sir.'

'Well, then, my belief is that, once he finds he has lost his awe of this Waterbury, he will be so supremely braced that there will be no holding him. He will rush right off and bung his heart at her feet, Jeeves.'

'Well, sir—'

'Jeeves,' I said, a little severely, 'whenever I suggest a plan or scheme or course of action, you are too apt to say "Well, sir," in a nasty tone of voice. I do not like it, and it is a habit you should check. The plan or scheme or course of action which I have outlined contains no flaw. If it does, I should like to hear it.'

'Well, sir—'

'Jeeves!'

'I beg your pardon, sir. I was about to remark that, in my

opinion, you are approaching Mr. Sipperley's problems in the wrong order.'

'How do you mean, the wrong order?'

'Well, I fancy, sir, that better results would be obtained by first inducing Mr. Sipperley to offer marriage to Miss Moon. In the event of the .young lady proving agreeable, I think that Mr. Sipperley would be in such an elevated frame of mind that he would have no difficulty in asserting himself with Mr. Waterbury.'

'Ah, but you are then stymied by the question – How is he to be induced?'

'It had occurred to me, sir, that, as Miss Moon is a poetess and of a romantic nature, it might have weight with her if she heard that Mr. Sipperley had met with a serious injury and was mentioning her name.'

'Calling for her brokenly, you mean?'

'Calling for her, as you say, sir, brokenly.'

I sat up in bed, and pointed at him rather coldly with the teaspoon.

'Jeeves,' I said, 'I would be the last man to accuse you of dithering, but this is not like you. It is not the old form, Jeeves. You are losing your grip. It might be years before Mr. Sipperley had a serious injury.'

'There is that to be considered, sir.'

'I cannot believe that it is you, Jeeves, who are meekly suggesting that we should suspend all activities in this matter year after year, on the chance that some day Mr. Sipperley may fall under a truck or something. No! The programme will be as I have sketched it out, Jeeves. After breakfast, kindly step out, and purchase about a pound and a half of the best flour. The rest you may leave to me.'

'Very good, sir.'

The first thing you need in matters of this kind, as every general knows, is a thorough knowledge of the terrain. Not know the terrain, and where are you? Look at Napoleon and that sunken road at Waterloo. Silly ass!

I had a thorough knowledge of the terrain of Sippy's office, and it ran as follows. I won't draw a plan, because my experience is that, when you're reading one of those detective stories and come to the bit where the author draws a plan of the Manor, showing room where body was found, stairs leading to passageway, and all the rest of it, one just skips. I'll simply explain in a few brief words.

The offices of *The Mayfair Gazette* were on the first floor of a mouldy old building off Covent Garden. You went in at a front door and ahead of you was a passage leading to the premises of Bellamy Bros., dealers in seeds and garden produce. Ignoring the Bros. Bellamy, you proceeded upstairs and found two doors opposite you. One, marked Private, opened into Sippy's editorial sanctum. The other – sub-title: Inquiries – shot you into a small room where an office-boy sat, eating peppermints and reading the adventures of Tarzan. If you got past the office-boy, you went through another door and there you were in Sippy's room, just as if you had nipped through the door marked Private. Perfectly simple.

It was over the door marked Inquiries that I proposed to suspend the flour.

Now, setting a booby-trap for a respectable citizen like a head master (even of an inferior school to your own) is not a matter to be approached lightly and without careful preparation. I don't suppose I've ever selected a lunch with more thought than I did that day. And after a nicely-balanced meal, preceded by a couple of dry Martinis, washed down with half a bot. of nice light, dry champagne, and followed by a spot of brandy, I could have set a booby-trap for a bishop.

The only really difficult part of the campaign was to get rid of the office-boy; for naturally you don't want witnesses when you're shoving bags of flour on doors. Fortunately, every man has his price, and it wasn't long before I contrived to persuade the lad that there was sickness at home and he was needed at Cricklewood. This done, I mounted a chair and got to work.

It was many, many years since I had tackled this kind of job, but the old skill came back as good as ever. Having got the bag so nicely poised that a touch on the door would do all that was necessary, I skipped down from my chair, popped off through Sippy's room, and went into the street. Sippy had not shown up yet, which was all to the good, but I knew he usually trickled in at about five to three. I hung about in the street, and presently round the corner came the bloke Waterbury. He went in at the front door, and I started off for a short stroll. It was no part of my policy to be in the offing when things began to happen.

It seemed to me that, allowing for wind and weather, the scales should have fallen from old Sippy's eyes by about three-fifteen, Greenwich mean time; so, having prowled around Covent Garden among the spuds and cabbages for twenty minutes or so, I retraced my steps and pushed up the stairs. I went in at the door marked Private, fully expecting to see old Sippy, and conceive of my astonishment and chagrin when I found on entering only the bloke Waterbury. He was seated at Sippy's desk, reading a paper, as if the place belonged to him.

And, moreover, there was of flour on his person not a trace.

'Great Scott!' I said.

It was a case of the sunken road, after all. But, dash it, how could I have been expected to take into consideration the possibility that this cove, head master though he was, would have had the cold nerve to walk into Sippy's private office instead of pushing in a normal and orderly manner through the public door?

He raised the nose, and focused me over it.

'Yes?'

'I was looking for old Sippy.'

'Mr. Sipperley has not yet arrived.'

He spoke with a good deal of pique, seeming to be a man who was not used to being kept waiting.

'Well, how is everything?' I said, to ease things along.

He started reading again. He looked up as if he found me pretty superfluous.

'I beg your pardon?'

'Oh, nothing.'

'You spoke.'

'I only said "How is everything?" don't you know.'

'How is what?'

'Everything.'

'I fail to understand you.'

'Let it go,' I said.

I found a certain difficulty in boosting along the chit-chat. He was not a responsive cove.

'Nice day,' I said.

'Quite.'

'But they say the crops need rain.'

He had buried himself in his paper once more, and seemed peeved this time on being lugged to the surface.

'What?' The crops.

'The crops?'

'Crops.'

'What crops?'

'Oh, just crops.'

He laid down his paper.

'You appear to be desirous of giving me some information about crops. What is it?'

'I hear they need rain.'

'Indeed?'

That concluded the small-talk. He went on reading, and I found a chair and sat down and sucked the handle of my stick. And so the long day wore on.

It may have been some two hours later, or it may have been about five minutes, when there became audible in the passage outside a strange wailing sound, as of some creature in pain. The bloke Waterbury looked up. I looked up.

The wailing came closer. It came into the room. It was Sippy, singing.

'—I love you. That's all that I can say. I love you, I lo-o-ve you. The same old—'

He suspended the chant, not too soon for me.

'Oh, hullo!' he said.

I was amazed. The last time I had seen old Sippy, you must remember, he had had all the appearance of a man who didn't know it was loaded. Haggard. Drawn face. Circles under the eyes. All that sort of thing. And now, not much more than twenty-four hours later, he was simply radiant. His eyes sparkled. His mobile lips were curbed in a happy smile. He looked as if he had been taking as much as will cover a sixpence every morning before breakfast for years.

'Hullo, Bertie!' he said. 'Hullo, Waterbury old man! Sorry I'm late.'

The bloke Waterbury seemed by no means pleased at this cordial form of address. He froze visibly.

'You are exceedingly late. I may mention that I have been waiting for upwards of half an hour, and my time is not without its value.'

'Sorry, sorry, sorry, sorry, sorry,' said Sippy, jovially. 'You wanted to see me about that article on the Elizabethan dramatists you left here yesterday, didn't you? Well, I've read it, and I'm sorry to say, Waterbury, my dear chap, that it's N.G.'

'I beg your pardon?'

'No earthly use to us. Quite the wrong sort of stuff. This paper is supposed to be all light Society interest. What the *debutante* will wear for Goodwood, you know, and I saw Lady Betty Bootle in the Park yesterday – she is, of course, the sister-in-law of the Duchess of Peebles, "Cuckoo" to her intimates – all that kind of rot. My readers don't want stuff about Elizabethan dramatists.'

'Sipperley—!'

Old Sippy reached out and patted him in a paternal manner on the back.

'Now listen, Waterbury,' he said, kindly. 'You know as well as I do that I hate to turn down an old pal. But I have my duty to the paper. Still, don't be discouraged. Keep trying, and you'll do fine. There is a lot of promise in your stuff, but you want to study your market. Keep your eyes open and see what editors need. Now, just as a suggestion, why not have a dash at a light, breezy article on pet dogs. You've probably noticed that the pug, once so fashionable, has been superseded by the Peke, the griffon, and the Sealyham. Work on that line and—'

The bloke Waterbury navigated towards the door.

'I have no desire to work on that line, as you put it,' he said, stiffly. 'If you do not require my paper on the Elizabethan dramatists I shall no doubt be able to find another editor whose tastes are more in accord with my work.'

'The right spirit absolutely, Waterbury,' said Sippy, cordially. 'Never give in. Perseverance brings home the gravy. If you get an article accepted, send another article to that editor. If you get an article refused, send that article to another editor. Carry on, Waterbury. I shall watch your future progress with considerable interest.'

'Thank you,' said the bloke Waterbury, bitterly. 'This expert advice should prove most useful.'

He biffed off, banging the door behind him, and I turned to Sippy, who was swerving about the room like an exuberant snipe.

'Sippy—'

'Eh? What? Can't stop, Bertie, can't stop. Only looked in to tell you the news. I'm taking Gwendolen to tea at the Carlton. I'm the happiest man in the world, Bertie. Engaged, you know. Betrothed. All washed up and signed on the dotted line. Wedding, June the first, at eleven a.m. sharp, at St. Peter's, Eaton Square. Presents should be delivered before the end of May.'

'But, Sippy! Come to roost for a second. How did this happen? I thought—'

'Well, it's a long story. Much too long to tell you now. Ask Jeeves. He came along with me, and is waiting outside. But when I found her bending over me weeping, I knew that a word from me was all that was needed. I took her little hand in mine and—'

'What do you mean, bending over you? Where?'

'In your sitting-room.'

'Why?'

'Why what?'

'Why was she bending over you?'

'Because I was on the floor, ass. Naturally a girl would bend over a fellow who was on the floor. Good-bye, Bertie, I must rush.'

He was out of the room before I knew he had started. I followed at a high rate of speed, but he was down the stairs before I reached the passage. I legged it after him, but when I got into the street it was empty.

No, not absolutely empty. Jeeves was standing on the pavement, gazing dreamily at a brussels sprout which lay in the fairway.

'Mr. Sipperley has this moment gone, sir,' he said, as I came charging out.

I halted and mopped the brow.

'Jeeves,' I said, 'what has been happening?'

'As far as Mr. Sipperley's romance is concerned, sir, all, I am happy to report, is well. He and Miss Moon have arrived at a satisfactory settlement.'

'I know. They're engaged. But how did it happen?'

'I took the liberty of telephoning to Mr. Sipperley in your name, asking him to come immediately to the flat, sir.'

'Oh, that's how he came to be at the flat? Well?'

'I then took the liberty of telephoning to Miss Moon and informing her that Mr. Sipperley had met with a nasty accident. As I anticipated, the young lady was strongly moved and announced her intention of coming to see Mr. Sipperley immediately. When she arrived, it required only a few moments to arrange the matter. It seems that Miss Moon has long loved Mr. Sipperley, sir, and—'

'I should have thought that, when she turned up and found he hadn't had a nasty accident, she would have been thoroughly pipped at being fooled.'

'Mr. Sipperley had had a nasty accident, sir.'

'He had?'

'Yes, sir.'

'Rummy coincidence. I mean, after what you were saying this morning.'

'Not altogether, sir. Before telephoning to Miss Moon, I took the further liberty of striking Mr. Sipperley a sharp blow on the head with one of your golf-clubs, which was fortunately lying in a corner of the room. The putter, I believe, sir. If you recollect, you were practising with it this morning before you left.'

I gaped at the blighter. I had always known Jeeves for a man of infinite sagacity, sound beyond belief on any question of ties or spats; but never before had I suspected him capable of strong-arm work like this. It seemed to open up an entirely new aspect of the fellow. I can't put it better than by saying that, as I gazed at him, the scales seemed to fall from my eyes.

'Good heavens, Jeeves!'

'I did it with the utmost regret, sir. It appeared to me the only course.'

'But look here, Jeeves. I don't get this. Wasn't Mr. Sipperley pretty shirty when he came to and found that you had been soaking him with putters?'

'He was not aware that I had done so, sir. I took the precaution of waiting until his back was momentarily turned.'

'But how did you explain the bump on his head?'

'I informed him that your new vase had fallen on him, sir.'

'Why on earth would he believe that? The vase would have been smashed.'

'The vase was smashed, sir.'

'What!'

'In order to achieve verisimilitude, I was reluctantly compelled to break it, sir. And in my excitement, sir, I am sorry to say I broke it beyond repair.'

I drew myself up.

'Jeeves!' I said.

'Pardon me, sir, but would it not be wiser to wear a hat? There is a keen wind.'

I blinked.

'Aren't I wearing a hat?'

'No, sir.'

I put up a hand and felt the lemon. He was perfectly right.

'Nor I am! I must have left it in Sippy's office. Wait here, Jeeves, while I fetch it.'

'Very good, sir.'

'I have much to say to you.'

'Thank you, sir.'

I galloped up the stairs and dashed in at the door. And something squashy fell on my neck, and the next minute the whole world was a solid mass of flour. In the agitation of the moment I had gone in at the wrong door; and what it all boils down to is that, if any more of my pals get inferiority complexes, they can jolly well get rid of them for themselves. Bertram is through.

The letter arrived on the morning of the sixteenth. I was pushing a bit of breakfast into the Wooster face at the moment and, feeling fairly well-fortified with coffee and kippers, I decided to break the news to Jeeves without delay. As Shakespeare says, if you're going to do a thing you might just as well pop right at it and get it over. The man would be disappointed, of course, and possibly even chagrined: but, dash it all, a splash of disappointment here and there does a fellow good. Makes him realise that life is stern and life is earnest.

'Oh, Jeeves,' I said.

'Sir?'

'We have here a communication from Lady Wickham. She has written inviting me to Skeldings for Christmas. So you will see about bunging the necessaries together. We repair thither on the twenty-third. Plenty of white ties, Jeeves, also a few hearty country suits for use in the daytime. We shall be there some little time, I expect.'

There was a pause. I could feel he was directing a frosty gaze at me, but I dug into the marmalade and refused to meet it.

'I thought I understood you to say, sir, that you proposed to visit Monte Carlo immediately after Christmas.'

'I know. But that's all off. Plans changed.'

'Very good, sir.'

At this point the telephone bell rang, tiding over very nicely what had threatened to be an awkward moment. Jeeves unhooked the receiver.

'Yes? . . . Yes, madam . . . Very good, madam. Here is Mr. Wooster.' He handed me the instrument. 'Mrs. Spenser Gregson, sir.'

You know, every now and then I can't help feeling that Jeeves is losing his grip. In his prime it would have been with him the work of a moment to have told Aunt Agatha that I was not at home. I gave him one of those reproachful glances, and took the machine.

'Hullo?' I said. 'Yes? Hullo? Hullo? Bertie speaking. Hullo? Hullo? Hullo?'

'Don't keep on saying Hullo,' yipped the old relative in her customary curt manner. 'You're not a parrot. Sometimes I wish you were, because then you might have a little sense.'

Quite the wrong sort of tone to adopt towards a fellow in the early morning, of course, but what can one do?

'Bertie, Lady Wickham tells me she has invited you to Skeldings for Christmas. Are you going?'

'Rather!'

'Well, mind you behave yourself. Lady Wickham is an old friend of mine.'

I was in no mood for this sort of thing over the telephone. Face to face, I'm not saying, but at the end of a wire, no.

'I shall naturally endeavour, Aunt Agatha,' I replied stiffly, 'to conduct myself in a manner befitting an English gentleman paying a visit—'

'What did you say? Speak up. I can't hear.'

'I said Right-ho.'

'Oh? Well, mind you do. And there's another reason why I particularly wish you to be as little of an imbecile as you can manage while at Skeldings. Sir Roderick Glossop will be there.'

'What!'

'Don't bellow like that. You nearly deafened me.'

'Did you say Sir Roderick Glossop?'

'I did.'

'You don't mean Tuppy Glossop?'

'I mean Sir Roderick Glossop. Which was my reason for saying Sir Roderick Glossop. Now, Bertie, I want you to listen to me attentively. Are you there?'

'Yes. Still here.'

'Well, then, listen. I have at last succeeded, after incredible difficulty, and in face of all the evidence, in almost persuading Sir Roderick that you are not actually insane. He is prepared to suspend judgment until he has seen you once more. On your behaviour at Skeldings, there—'

But I had hung up the receiver. Shaken. That's what I was. S. to the core.

Stop me if I've told you this before: but, in case you don't know, let me just mention the facts in the matter of this Glossop. He was a formidable old bird with a bald head and out-size eyebrows, by profession a loony-doctor. How it happened, I couldn't tell you to this day, but I once got engaged to his daughter, Honoria, a ghastly dynamic exhibit who read Nietzsche and had a laugh like waves breaking on a stern and rock-bound coast. The fixture was scratched owing to events occurring which convinced the old boy that I was off my napper; and since then he has always had my name at the top of his list of 'Loonies I have Lunched With'.

It seemed to me that even at Christmas time, with all the peace on earth and goodwill towards men that there is knocking about at that season, a reunion with this bloke was likely to be tough going. If I hadn't had more than one particularly good reason for wanting to go to Skeldings, I'd have called the thing off.

'Jeeves,' I said, all of a twitter: 'Do you know what? Sir Roderick Glossop is going to be at Lady Wickham's.'

'Very good, sir. If you have finished breakfast, I will clear away.'

Cold and haughty. No symp. None of the rallying-round

spirit which one likes to see. As I had anticipated, the information that we were not going to Monte Carlo had got in amongst him. There is a keen sporting streak in Jeeves and I knew he had been looking forward to a little flutter at the tables.

We Woosters can wear the mask. I ignored his lack of decent feeling.

'Do so, Jeeves,' I said proudly, 'and with all convenient speed.'

Relations continued pretty fairly strained all through the rest of the week. There was a frigid detachment in the way the man brought me my dollop of tea in the mornings. Going down to Skeldings in the car on the afternoon of the twenty-third, he was aloof and reserved. And before dinner on the first night of my visit he put the studs in my dress-shirt in what I can only call a marked manner. The whole thing was extremely painful, and it seemed to me, as I lay in bed on the morning of the twenty-fourth, that the only step to take was to put the whole facts of the case before him and trust to his native good sense to effect an understanding. I was feeling considerably in the pink that morning. Everything had gone like a breeze. My hostess, Lady Wickham, was a beaky female built far too closely on the lines of my Aunt Agatha for comfort, but she had seemed matey enough on my arrival. Her daughter, Roberta, had welcomed me with a warmth which, I'm bound to say, had set the old heart-strings fluttering a bit. And Sir Roderick, in the brief moment we had had together, appeared to have let the Yule-tide spirit soak into him to the most amazing extent. When he saw me, his mouth sort of flickered at one corner, which I took to be his idea of smiling, and he said 'Ha, young man!' Not particularly chummily, but he said it: and my view was that it practically amounted to the lion lying down with the lamb.

So, all in all, life at this juncture seemed pretty well all to the mustard, and I decided to tell Jeeves exactly how matters stood.

'Jeeves,' I said, as he appeared with the steaming.

'Sir?'

'Touching on this business of our being here, I would like to say a few words of explanation. I consider that you have a right to the facts.'

'Sir?'

'I'm afraid scratching that Monte Carlo trip has been a bit of a jar for you, Jeeves.'

'Not at all, sir.'

'Oh, yes, it has. The heart was set on wintering in the world's good old Plague Spot, I know. I saw your eye light up when I said we were due for a visit there. You snorted a bit and your fingers twitched. I know, I know. And now that there has been a change of programme the iron has entered into your soul.'

'Not at all, sir.'

'Oh, yes, it has. I've seen it. Very well, then, what I wish to impress upon you, Jeeves, is that I have not been actuated in this matter by any mere idle whim. It was through no light and airy caprice that I accepted this invitation to Lady Wickham's. I have been angling for it for weeks, prompted by many considerations. In the first place, does one get the Yule-tide spirit at a spot like Monte Carlo?'

'Does one desire the Yule-tide spirit, sir?'

'Certainly one does. I am all for it. Well, that's one thing. Now here's another. It was imperative that I should come to Skeldings for Christmas, Jeeves, because I knew that young Tuppy Glossop was going to be here.'

'Sir Roderick Glossop, sir?'

'His nephew. You may have observed hanging about the place a fellow with light hair and a Cheshire-cat grin. That is Tuppy, and I have been anxious for some time to get to grips with him. I have it in for that man of wrath. Listen to the facts, Jeeves, and tell me if I am not justified in planning a hideous vengeance.' I took a sip of tea, for the mere memory of my wrongs had shaken me. 'In spite of the fact that young Tuppy is the nephew of Sir Roderick Glossop, at whose hands, Jeeves, as you are aware, I have suffered much, I fraternised with him freely, both at the Drones Club and elsewhere. I said to myself that a man is not to be blamed for his relations, and that I would hate to have my pals hold my Aunt Agatha, for instance, against me. Broad-minded, Jeeves, I think?'

'Extremely, sir.'

'Well, then, as I say, I sought this Tuppy out, Jeeves, and hobnobbed, and what do you think he did?'

'I could not say, sir.'

'I will tell you. One night after dinner at the Drones he betted me I wouldn't swing myself across the swimming-bath by the ropes and rings. I took him on and was buzzing along in great style until I came to the last ring. And then I found that this fiend in human shape had looped it back against the rail, thus leaving me hanging in the void with no means of getting ashore to my home and loved ones. There was nothing for it but to drop into the water. He told me that he had often caught fellows that way: and what I maintain, Jeeves, is that, if I can't get back at him somehow at Skeldings – with all the vast resources which a country house affords at my disposal – I am not the man I was.'

'I see, sir.'

There was still something in his manner which told me that even now he lacked complete sympathy and understanding, so, delicate though the subject was, I decided to put all my cards on the table.

'And now, Jeeves, we come to the most important reason why I had to spend Christmas at Skeldings. Jeeves,' I said, diving into the old cup once more for a moment and bringing myself out wreathed in blushes, 'the fact of the matter is, I'm in love.'

'Indeed, sir?'

'You've seen Miss Roberta Wickham?'

'Yes, sir.'

'Very well, then.'

There was a pause, while I let it sink in.

'During your stay here, Jeeves,' I said, 'you will, no doubt, be thrown a good deal together with Miss Wickham's maid. On such occasions, pitch it strong.'

'Sir?'

'You know what I mean. Tell her I'm rather a good chap. Mention my hidden depths. These things get round. Dwell on the fact that I had a kind heart and was runner-up in the Squash Handicap at the Drones this year. A boost is never wasted, Jeeves.'

'Very good, sir. But—'

'But what?'

'Well, sir—'

'I wish you wouldn't say "Well, sir" in that soupy tone of voice. I have had to speak of this before. The habit is one that is growing upon you. Check it. What's on your mind?'

'I hardly like to take the liberty—'

'Carry on, Jeeves. We are always glad to hear from you, always.'

'What I was about to remark, if you will excuse me, sir, was that I would scarcely have thought Miss Wickham a suitable—'

'Jeeves,' I said coldly, 'if you have anything to say against that lady, it had better not be said in my presence.'

'Very good, sir.'

'Or anywhere else, for that matter. What is your kick against Miss Wickham?'

'Oh, really, sir!'

'Jeeves, I insist. This is a time for plain speaking. You have beefed about Miss Wickham. I wish to know why.'

'It merely crossed my mind, sir, that for a gentleman of your description Miss Wickham is not a suitable mate.'

'What do you mean by a gentleman of my description?'

'Well, sir—'

'Jeeves!'

'I beg your pardon, sir. The expression escaped me inadvertently. I was about to observe that I can only asseverate—'

'Only what?'

'I can only say that, as you have invited my opinion—'

'But I didn't.'

'I was under the impression that you desired to canvass my views on the matter, sir.'

'Oh? Well, let's have them, anyway.'

'Very good, sir. Then briefly, if I may say so, sir, though Miss Wickham is a charming young lady—'

'There, Jeeves, you spoke an imperial quart. What eyes!'

'Yes, sir.'

'What hair!'

'Very true, sir.'

'And what *espièglerie*, if that's the word I want.'

'The exact word, sir.'

'All right, then. Carry on.'

'I grant Miss Wickham the possession of all these desirable qualities, sir. Nevertheless, considered as a matrimonial prospect for a gentleman of your description, I cannot look upon her as suitable. In my opinion Miss Wickham lacks seriousness, sir. She is too volatile and frivolous. To qualify as Miss Wickham's husband, a gentleman would need to possess a commanding personality and considerable strength of character.'

'Exactly!'

'I would always hesitate to recommend as a life's companion a young lady with quite such a vivid shade of red hair. Red hair, sir, in my opinion, is dangerous.'

I eyed the blighter squarely.

'Jeeves,' I said, 'you're talking rot.'

'Very good, sir.'

'Absolute drivel.'

'Very good, sir.'

'Pure mashed potatoes.'

'Very good, sir.'

'Very good, sir – I mean very good Jeeves, that will be all,' I said.

And I drank a modicum of tea, with a good deal of hauteur.

It isn't often that I find myself able to prove Jeeves in the wrong, but by dinner-time that night I was in a position to do so, and I did it without delay.

'Touching on that matter we were touching on, Jeeves,' I said, coming in from the bath and tackling him as he studded the shirt, 'I should be glad if you would give me your careful attention for a moment. I warn you that what I am about to say is going to make you look pretty silly.'

'Indeed, sir?'

'Yes, Jeeves. Pretty dashed silly it's going to make you look. It may lead you to be rather more careful in future about broadcasting these estimates of yours of people's characters. This morning, if I remember rightly, you stated that Miss Wickham was volatile, frivolous and lacking in seriousness. Am I correct?'

'Quite correct, sir.'

'Then what I have to tell you may cause you to alter that opinion. I went for a walk with Miss Wickham this afternoon; and, as we walked, I told her about what young Tuppy Glossop did to me in the swimming-bath at the Drones. She hung upon my words, Jeeves, and was full of sympathy.'

'Indeed, sir?'

'Dripping with it. And that's not all. Almost before I had finished, she was suggesting the ripest, fruitiest, brainiest scheme for bringing young Tuppy's grey hairs in sorrow to the grave that anyone could possibly imagine.'

'That is very gratifying, sir.'

'Gratifying is the word. It appears that at the girls' school where Miss Wickham was educated, Jeeves, it used to become necessary from time to time for the right-thinking element of the community to slip it across certain of the baser sort. Do you know what they did, Jeeves?'

'No, sir.'

'They took a long stick, Jeeves, and – follow me closely here – they tied a darning-needle to the end of it. Then at dead of night, it appears, they sneaked privily into the party of the second part's cubicle and shoved the needle through the bed-clothes and punctured her hot-water bottle. Girls are much subtler in these matters than boys, Jeeves. At my old school one would occasionally heave a jug of water over another bloke during the night-watches, but we never thought of effecting the same result in this particularly neat and scientific manner. Well, Jeeves, that was the scheme which Miss Wickham suggested I should work on young Tuppy, and that is the girl you call frivolous and lacking in seriousness. Any girl who can think up a wheeze like that is my idea of a helpmeet. I shall be glad, Jeeves, if by the time I come to bed tonight you have waiting for me in this room a stout stick with a good sharp darning needle attached.'

'Well, sir—'

I raised my hand.

'Jeeves,' I said. 'Not another word. Stick, one, and needle, darning, good, sharp, one, without fail in this room at eleven-thirty tonight.'

'Very good, sir.'

'Have you any idea where young Tuppy sleeps?'

'I could ascertain, sir.'

'Do so, Jeeves.

In a few minutes he was back with the necessary informash.

'Mr. Glossop is established in the Moat Room, sir.'

'Where's that?'

'The second door on the floor below this, sir.'

'Right-ho, Jeeves. Are the studs in my shirt?'

'Yes, sir.'

'And the links also?'

'Yes, sir.'

'Then push me into it.'

*

The more I thought about this enterprise which a sense of duty and good citizenship had thrust upon me, the better it seemed to me. I am not a vindictive man, but I felt, as anybody would have felt in my place, that if fellows like young Tuppy are allowed to get away with it the whole fabric of Society and Civilisation must inevitably crumble. The task to which I had set myself was one that involved hardship and discomfort, for it meant sitting up till well into the small hours and then padding down a cold corridor, but I did not shrink from it. After all, there is a lot to be said for family tradition. We Woosters did our bit in the Crusades.

It being Christmas Eve, there was, as I had foreseen, a good deal of revelry and what not. First, the village choir surged round and sang carols outside the front door, and then somebody suggested a dance, and after that we hung around chatting of this and that, so that it wasn't till past one that I got to my room. Allowing for everything, it didn't seem that it was going to be safe to start my little expedition till half-past two at the earliest: and I'm bound to say that it was only the utmost resolution that kept me from snuggling into the sheets and calling it a day. I'm not much of a lad now for late hours.

However, by half-past two everything appeared to be quiet. I shook off the mists of sleep, grabbed the good old stick-and-needle, and off along the corridor. And presently, pausing outside the Moat Room, I turned the handle, found the door wasn't locked, and went in.

I suppose a burglar – I mean a real professional who works at the job six nights a week all the year round – gets so that finding himself standing in the dark in somebody else's bedroom means absolutely nothing to him. But for a bird like me, who has had no previous experience, there's a lot to be said in favour of washing the whole thing out and closing the door gently and popping back to bed again. It was only by summoning up all the old bull-dog courage of the Woosters, and reminding myself that, if I let this opportunity slip another might never occur, that

I managed to stick out what you might call the initial minute of the binge. Then the weakness passed, and Bertram was himself again.

At first when I beetled in, the room had seemed as black as a coal-cellar: but after a bit things began to lighten. The curtains weren't quite drawn over the window and I could see a trifle of the scenery here and there. The bed was opposite the window, with the head against the wall and the end where the feet were jutting out towards where I stood, thus rendering it possible after one had sown the seed, so to speak, to make a quick getaway. There only remained now the rather tricky problem of locating the old hot-water bottle. I mean to say, the one thing you can't do if you want to carry a job like this through with secrecy and dispatch is to stand at the end of a fellow's bed, jabbing the blankets at random with a darning-needle. Before proceeding to anything in the nature of definite steps, it is imperative that you locate the bot.

I was a good deal cheered at this juncture to hear a fruity snore from the direction of the pillows. Reason told me that a bloke who could snore like that wasn't going to be awakened by a trifle. I edged forward and ran a hand in a gingerly sort of way over the coverlet. A moment later I had found the bulge. I steered the good old darning-needle on to it, gripped the stick, and shoved. Then, pulling out the weapon, I sidled towards the door, and in another moment would have been outside, buzzing for home and the good night's rest, when suddenly there was a crash that sent my spine shooting up through the top of my head and the contents of the bed sat up like a jack-in-the-box and said:

'Who's that?'

It just shows how your most careful strategic moves can be the very ones that dish your campaign. In order to facilitate the orderly retreat according to plan I had left the door open, and the beastly thing had slammed like a bomb.

But I wasn't giving much thought to the causes of the

explosion, having other things to occupy my mind. What was disturbing me was the discovery that, whoever else the bloke in the bed might be, he was not young Tuppy. Tuppy has one of those high, squeaky voices that sound like the tenor of the village choir failing to hit a high note. This one was something in between the Last Trump and a tiger calling for breakfast after being on a diet for a day or two. It was the sort of nasty, rasping voice you hear shouting 'Fore!' when you're one of a slow foursome on the links and are holding up a couple of retired colonels. Among the qualities it lacked were kindliness, suavity and that sort of dove-like cooing note which makes a fellow feel he has found a friend.

I did not linger. Getting swiftly off the mark, I dived for the door-handle and was off and away, banging the door behind me. I may be a chump in many ways, as my Aunt Agatha will freely attest, but I know when and when not to be among those present.

And I was just about to do the stretch of corridor leading to the stairs in a split second under the record time for the course, when something brought me up with a sudden jar. One moment, I was all dash and fire and speed; the next, an irresistible force had checked me in my stride and was holding me straining at the leash, as it were.

You know, sometimes it seems to me as if Fate were going out of its way to such an extent to snooter you that you wonder if it's worth while continuing to struggle. The night being a trifle chillier than the dickens, I had donned for this expedition a dressing-gown. It was the tail of this infernal garment that had caught in the door and pipped me at the eleventh hour.

The next moment the door had opened, light was streaming through it, and the bloke with the voice had grabbed me by the arm.

It was Sir Roderick Glossop.

The next thing that happened was a bit of a lull in the proceedings.

For about three and a quarter seconds or possibly more we just stood there, drinking each other in, so to speak, the old boy still attached with a limpet-like grip to my elbow. If I hadn't been in a dressing-gown and he in pink pyjamas with a blue stripe, and if he hadn't been glaring quite so much as if he were shortly going to commit a murder, the tableau would have looked rather like one of those advertisements you see in the magazines, where the experienced elder is patting the young man's arm, and saying to him: 'My boy, if you subscribe to the Mutt-Jeff Correspondence School of Oswego, Kan., as I did, you may some day, like me, become Third Assistant Vice-President of the Schenectady Consolidated Nail-File and Eyebrow Tweezer Corporation'.

'You!' said Sir Roderick finally. And in this connection I want to state that it's all rot to say you can't hiss a word that hasn't an 's' in it. The way he pushed out that 'You!' sounded like an angry cobra, and I am betraying no secrets when I mention that it did me no good whatsoever.

By rights, I suppose, at this point I ought to have said something. The best I could manage, however, was a faint, soft bleating sound. Even on ordinary social occasions, when meeting this bloke as man to man and with a clear conscience, I could never be completely at my ease: and now those eyebrows seemed to pierce me like a knife.

'Come in here,' he said, lugging me into the room. 'We don't want to wake the whole house. Now,' he said, depositing me on the carpet, and closing the door and doing a bit of eyebrow work, 'kindly inform me what is this latest manifestation of insanity?'

It seemed to me that a light and cheery laugh might help the thing along. So I had a pop at one.

'Don't gibber!' said my genial host. And I'm bound to admit that the light and cheery hadn't come out quite as I'd intended.

I pulled myself together with a strong effort.

'Awfully sorry about all this,' I said in a hearty sort of voice. 'The fact is, I thought you were Tuppy.'

'Kindly refrain from inflicting your idiotic slang on me. What do you mean by the adjective "tuppy"?'

'It isn't so much an adjective, don't you know. More of a noun, I should think, if you examine it squarely. What I mean to say is, I thought you were your nephew.'

'You thought I was my nephew? Why should I be my nephew?'

'What I'm driving at is, I thought this was his room.'

'My nephew and I changed rooms. I have a great dislike for sleeping on an upper floor. I am nervous about fire.'

For the first time since this interview had started, I braced up a trifle. The injustice of the whole thing stirred me to such an extent that for a moment I lost that sense of being a toad under the harrow which had been cramping my style up till now. I even went so far as to eye this pink-pyjamaed poltroon with a good deal of contempt and loathing. Just because he had this craven fear of fire and this selfish preference for letting Tuppy be cooked instead of himself should the emergency occur, my nicely-reasoned plans had gone up the spout. I gave him a look, and I think I may even have snorted a bit.

'I should have thought that your man-servant would have informed you,' said Sir Roderick, 'that we contemplated making this change. I met him shortly before luncheon and told him to tell you.'

I reeled. Yes, it is not too much to say that I reeled. This extraordinary statement had taken me amidships without any preparation, and it staggered me. That Jeeves had been aware all along that this old crumb would be the occupant of the bed which I was proposing to prod with darning-needles and had let me rush upon my doom without a word of warning was almost beyond belief. You might say I was aghast. Yes, practically aghast.

'You told Jeeves that you were going to sleep in this room?' I gasped.

'I did. I was aware that you and my nephew were on terms of

intimacy, and I wished to spare myself the possibility of a visit from you. I confess that it never occurred to me that such a visit was to be anticipated at three o'clock in the morning. What the devil do you mean,' he barked, suddenly hotting up, 'by prowling about the house at this hour? And what is that thing in your hand?'

I looked down, and found that I was still grasping the stick. I give you my honest word that, what with the maelstrom of emotions into which his revelation about Jeeves had cast me, the discovery came as an absolute surprise.

'This?' I said, 'Oh, yes.'

'What do you mean, Oh yes? What is it?'

'Well, it's a long story—'

'We have the night before us.'

'It's this way. I will ask you to picture me some weeks ago, perfectly peaceful and inoffensive, after dinner at the Drones, smoking a thoughtful cigarette and—'

I broke off. The man wasn't listening. He was goggling in a rapt sort of way at the end of the bed, from which there had now begun to drip on to the carpet a series of drops.

'Good heavens!'

'—thoughtful cigarette and chatting pleasantly of this and that—'

I broke off again. He had lifted the sheets and was gazing at the corpse of the hot-water bottle.

'Did you do this?' he said in a low, strangled sort of voice.

'Er – yes. As a matter of fact, yes. I was just going to tell you—'

'And your aunt tried to persuade me that you were not insane!'

'I'm not. Absolutely not. If you'll just let me explain.'

'I will do nothing of the kind.'

'It all began—'

'Silence!'

'Right-ho.'

He did some deep-breathing exercises through the nose.

'My bed is drenched!'

'The way it all began—'

'Be quiet!' He heaved somewhat for awhile. 'You wretched, miserable idiot,' he said, 'kindly inform me which bedroom you are supposed to be occupying?'

'It's on the floor above. The Clock Room.'

'Thank you. I will find it.'

'Eh?'

He gave me the eyebrow.

'I propose,' he said, 'to pass the remainder of the night in your room where, I presume, there is a bed in a condition to be slept in. You may bestow yourself as comfortably as you can here. I will wish you good night.'

He buzzed off, leaving me flat.

Well, we Woosters are old campaigners. We can take the rough with the smooth. But to say that I liked the prospect now before me would be paltering with the truth. One glance at the bed told me that any idea of sleeping there was out. A goldfish could have done it, but not Bertram. After a bit of a look round, I decided that the best chance of getting a sort of night's rest was to doss as well as I could in the arm-chair. I pinched a couple of pillows off the bed, shoved the hearth-rug over my knees, and sat down and started counting sheep.

But it wasn't any good. The old lemon was sizzling much too much to admit of anything in the nature of slumber. This hideous revelation of the blackness of Jeeves's treachery kept coming back to me every time I nearly succeeded in dropping off: and, what's more it seemed to get colder and colder as the long night wore on. I was just wondering if I would ever get to sleep again in this world when a voice at my elbow said 'Good morning, sir,' and I sat up with a jerk.

I could have sworn I hadn't so much as dozed off for even a minute, but apparently I had. For the curtains were drawn back and daylight was coming in through the window and there was Jeeves standing beside me with a cup of tea on a tray.

'Merry Christmas, sir!'

I reached out a feeble hand for the restoring brew. I swallowed a mouthful or two, and felt a little better. I was aching in every limb and the dome felt like lead, but I was now able to think with a certain amount of clearness, and I fixed the man with a stony eye and prepared to let him have it.

'You think so, do you?' I said. 'Much, let me tell you, depends on what you mean by the adjective "merry". If, moreover, you suppose that it is going to be merry for you, correct that impression. Jeeves,' I said, taking another half-oz. of tea and speaking in a cold, measured voice, 'I wish to ask you one question. Did you or did you not know that Sir Roderick Glossop was sleeping in this room last night?'

'Yes, sir.'

'You admit it!'

'Yes, sir.'

'And you didn't tell me!'

'No, sir. I thought it would be more judicious not to do so.'

'Jeeves—'

'If you will allow me to explain, sir.'

'Explain!'

'I was aware that my silence might lead to something in the nature of an embarrassing contretemps, sir—'

'You thought that, did you?'

'Yes, sir.'

'You were a good guesser,' I said, sucking down further Bohea.

'But it seemed to me, sir, that whatever might occur was all for the best.'

I would have put in a crisp word or two here, but he carried on without giving me the opp.

'I thought that possibly, on reflection, sir, your views being what they are, you would prefer your relations with Sir Roderick Glossop and his family to be distant rather than cordial.'

'My views? What do you mean, my views?'

'As regards a matrimonial alliance with Miss Honoria Glossop, sir.'

Something like an electric shock seemed to zip through me. The man had opened up a new line of thought. I suddenly saw what he was driving at, and realised all in a flash that I had been wronging this faithful fellow. All the while I supposed he had been landing me in the soup, he had really been steering me away from it. It was like those stories one used to read as a kid about the traveller going along on a dark night and his dog grabs him by the leg of his trousers and he says 'Down, sir! What are you doing, Rover?' and the dog hangs on and he gets rather hot under the collar and curses a bit but the dog won't let him go and then suddenly the moon shines through the clouds and he finds he's been standing on the edge of a precipice and one more step would have well, anyway, you get the idea: and what I'm driving at is that much the same sort of thing seemed to have been happening now.

It's perfectly amazing how a fellow will let himself get off his guard and ignore the perils which surround him. I give you my honest word, it had never struck me till this moment that my Aunt Agatha had been scheming to get me in right with Sir Roderick so that I should eventually be received back into the fold, if you see what I mean, and subsequently pushed off on Honoria.

'My God, Jeeves!' I said, paling.

'Precisely, sir.'

'You think there was a risk?'

'I do, sir. A very grave risk.'

A disturbing thought struck me.

'But, Jeeves, on calm reflection, won't Sir Roderick have gathered by now that my objective was young Tuppy and that puncturing his hot-water bottle was just one of those things that occur when the Yule-tide spirit is abroad – one of those things that have to be overlooked and taken with the indulgent smile and the fatherly shake of the head? I mean to say, Young Blood and all that sort of thing? What I mean is he'll realise that I wasn't trying to snooter him, and then all the good work will have been wasted.'

'No, sir. I fancy not. That might possibly have been Sir Roderick's mental reaction, had it not been for the second incident.'

'The second incident?'

'During the night, sir, while Sir Roderick was occupying your bed, somebody entered the room, pierced his hot-water bottle with some sharp instrument, and vanished in the darkness.'

I could make nothing of this.

'What! Do you think I walked in my sleep?'

'No, sir. It was young Mr. Glossop who did it. I encountered him this morning, sir, shortly before I came here. He was in cheerful spirits and inquired of me how you were feeling about the incident. Not being aware that his victim had been Sir Roderick.'

'But, Jeeves, what an amazing coincidence!'

'Sir?'

'Why, young Tuppy getting exactly the same idea as I did. Or, rather, as Miss Wickham did. You can't say that's not rummy. A miracle, I call it.'

'Not altogether, sir. It appears that he received the suggestion from the young lady.'

'From Miss Wickham?'

'Yes, sir.'

'You mean to say that, after she had put me up to the scheme of puncturing Tuppy's hot-water bottle, she went away and tipped Tuppy off to puncturing mine?'

'Precisely, sir. She is a young lady with a keen sense of humour, sir.'

I sat there, you might say stunned. When I thought how near I had come to offering the heart and hand to a girl capable of double-crossing a strong man's honest love like that, I shivered.

'Are you cold, sir?'

'No, Jeeves. Just shuddering.'

'The occurrence, if I may take the liberty of saying so, sir, will perhaps lend colour to the view which I put forward yesterday that Miss Wickham, though in many respects a charming young lady—'

I raised the hand.

'Say no more, Jeeves,' I replied. 'Love is dead.'

'Very good, sir.'

I brooded for a while.

'You've seen Sir Roderick this morning, then?'

'Yes, sir.'

'How did he seem?'

'A trifle feverish, sir.'

'Feverish?'

'A little emotional, sir. He expressed a strong desire to meet you, sir.'

'What would you advise?'

'If you were to slip out by the back entrance as soon as you are dressed, sir, it would be possible for you to make your way across the field without being observed and reach the village, where you could hire an automobile to take you to London. I could bring on your effects later in your own car.'

'But London, Jeeves? Is any man safe? My Aunt Agatha is in London.'

'Yes, sir.'

'Well, then?'

He regarded me for a moment with a fathomless eye.

'I think the best plan, sir, would be for you to leave England, which is not pleasant at this time of the year, for some little while. I would not take the liberty of dictating your movements, sir, but as you already have accommodation engaged on the Blue Train for Monte Carlo for the day after tomorrow—'

'But you cancelled the booking?'

'No, sir.

'I thought you had.'

'No, sir.'

'I told you to.'

'Yes, sir. It was remiss of me, but the matter slipped my mind.'

'Oh?'

'Yes, sir.'

'All right, Jeeves. Monte Carlo ho, then.'

'Very good, sir.'

'It's lucky, as things have turned out, that you forgot to cancel that booking.'

'Very fortunate indeed, sir. If you will wait here, sir, I will return to your room and procure a suit of clothes.'

Another day had dawned all hot and fresh and, in pursuance of my unswerving policy at that time, I was singing 'Sonny Boy' in my bath, when there was a soft step without and Jeeves's voice came filtering through the woodwork.

'I beg your pardon, sir.'

I had just got to that bit about the Angels being lonely, where you need every ounce of concentration in order to make the spectacular finish, but I signed off courteously.

'Yes, Jeeves? Say on.'

'Mr. Glossop, sir.'

'What about him?'

'He is in the sitting-room, sir.'

'Young Tuppy Glossop?'

'Yes, sir.'

'In the sitting-room?'

'Yes, sir.'

'Desiring speech with me?'

'Yes, sir.'

'H'm!'

'Sir?'

'I only said H'm.'

And I'll tell you why I said H'm. It was because the man's story had interested me strangely. The news that Tuppy was visiting me at my flat, at an hour when he must have known that

I would be in my bath and consequently in a strong strategic position to heave a wet sponge at him, surprised me considerably.

I hopped out with some briskness and, slipping a couple of towels about the limbs and torso, made for the sitting-room. I found young Tuppy at the piano, playing 'Sonny Boy' with one finger.

'What ho!' I said, not without a certain hauteur.

'Oh, hullo, Bertie,' said young Tuppy. 'I say, Bertie, I want to see you about something important.'

It seemed to me that the bloke was embarrassed. He had moved to the mantelpiece, and now he broke a vase in rather a constrained way.

'The fact is, Bertie, I'm engaged.'

'Engaged?'

'Engaged,' said young Tuppy, coyly dropping a photograph frame into the fender. 'Practically, that is.'

'Practically?'

'Yes. You'll like her, Bertie. Her name is Cora Bellinger. She's studying for Opera. Wonderful voice she has. Also dark, flashing eyes and a great soul.'

'How do you mean, practically?'

'Well, it's this way. Before ordering the trousseau, there is one little point she wants cleared up. You see, what with her great soul and all that, she has a rather serious outlook on life: and the one thing she absolutely bars is anything in the shape of hearty humour. You know, practical joking and so forth. She said if she thought I was a practical joker she would never speak to me again. And unfortunately she appears to have heard about that little affair at the Drones – I expect you have forgotten all about that, Bertie?'

'I have not!'

'No, no, not forgotten exactly. What I mean is, nobody laughs more heartily at the recollection than you. And what I want you to do, old man, is to seize an early opportunity of taking Cora aside and categorically denying that there is any truth in the story. My happiness, Bertie, is in your hands, if you know what I mean.'

Well, of course, if he put it like that, what could I do? We Woosters have our code.

'Oh, all right,' I said, but far from brightly.

'Splendid fellow!'

'When do I meet this blighted female?'

'Don't call her "this blighted female", Bertie, old man. I have planned all that out. I will bring her round here today for a spot of lunch.'

'What!'

'At one-thirty. Right. Good. Fine. Thanks. I knew I could rely on you.'

He pushed off, and I turned to Jeeves, who had shimmered in with the morning meal.

'Lunch for three today, Jeeves,' I said.

'Very good, sir.'

'You know, Jeeves, it's a bit thick. You remember my telling you about what Mr. Glossop did to me that night at the Drones?'

'Yes, sir.'

'For months I have been cherishing dreams of getting a bit of my own back. And now, so far from crushing him into the dust, I've got to fill him and fiancée with rich food and generally rally round and be the good angel.'

'Life is like that, sir.'

'True, Jeeves. What have we here?' I asked, inspecting the tray.

'Kippered herrings, sir.'

'And I shouldn't wonder,' I said, for I was in thoughtful mood, 'if even herrings haven't troubles of their own.'

'Quite possibly, sir.'

'I mean, apart from getting kippered.'

'Yes, sir.'

'And so it goes on, Jeeves, so it goes on.'

*

I can't say I exactly saw eye to eye with young Tuppy in his admiration for the Bellinger female. Delivered on the mat at one-twenty-five, she proved to be an upstanding light-heavyweight of some thirty summers, with a commanding eye and a square chin which I, personally, would have steered clear of. She seemed to me a good deal like what Cleopatra would have been after going in too freely for the starches and cereals. I don't know why it is, but women who have anything to do with Opera, even if they're only studying for it, always appear to run to surplus poundage.

Tuppy, however, was obviously all for her. His whole demeanour, both before and during lunch, was that of one striving to be worthy of a noble soul. When Jeeves offered him a cocktail, he practically recoiled as from a serpent. It was terrible to see the change which love had effected in the man. The spectacle put me off my food.

At half-past two, the Bellinger left to go to a singing lesson. Tuppy trotted after her to the door, bleating and frisking a goodish bit, and then came back and looked at me in a goofy sort of way.

'Well, Bertie?'

'Well, what?'

'I mean, isn't she?'

'Oh, rather,' I said, humouring the poor fish.

'Wonderful eyes?'

'Oh, rather.'

'Wonderful figure?'

'Oh, quite.'

'Wonderful voice?'

Here I was able to intone the response with a little more heartiness. The Bellinger, at Tuppy's request, had sung us a few songs before digging in at the trough, and nobody could have denied that her pipes were in great shape. Plaster was still falling from the ceiling.

'Terrific,' I said.

Tuppy sighed, and, having helped himself to about four inches of whisky and one of soda, took a deep, refreshing draught.

'Ah!' he said. 'I needed that.'

'Why didn't you have it at lunch?'

'Well, it's this way,' said Tuppy. 'I have not actually ascertained what Cora's opinions are on the subject of the taking of slight snorts from time to time, but I thought it more prudent to lay off. The view I took was that laying off would seem to indicate the serious mind. It is touch-and-go, as you might say, at the moment, and the smallest thing may turn the scale.'

'What beats me is how on earth you expect to make her think you've got a mind at all – let alone a serious one.'

'I have my methods.'

'I bet they're rotten.'

'You do, do you?' said Tuppy warmly. 'Well, let me tell you, my lad, that that's exactly what they're anything but. I am handling this affair with consummate generalship. Do you remember Beefy Bingham who was at Oxford with us?'

'I ran into him only the other day. He's a parson now.'

'Yes. Down in the East End. Well, he runs a Lads' Club for the local toughs – you know the sort of thing – cocoa and back-gammon in the reading-room and occasional clean, bright entertainments in the Oddfellows' Hall: and I've been helping him. I don't suppose I've passed an evening away from the back-gammon board for weeks. Cora is extremely pleased. I've got her to promise to sing on Tuesday at Beefy's next clean, bright entertainment.'

'You have?'

'I absolutely have. And now mark my devilish ingenuity, Bertie. I'm going to sing, too.'

'Why do you suppose that's going to get you anywhere?'

'Because the way I intend to sing the song I intend to sing will prove to her that there are great deeps in my nature, whose existence she has not suspected. She will see that rough, unlettered audience wiping the tears out of its bally eyes and she will say to herself "What ho! The old egg really has a soul!" For it is not one of your mouldy comic songs, Bertie. No low buffoonery of that sort for me. It is all about Angels being lonely and what not—'

I uttered a sharp cry.

'You don't mean you're going to sing "Sonny Boy"?'

'I jolly well do.'

I was shocked. Yes, dash it, I was shocked. You see, I held strong views on 'Sonny Boy'. I considered it a song only to be attempted by a few of the elect in the privacy of the bathroom. And the thought of it being murdered in open Oddfellows' Hall by a man who could treat a pal as young Tuppy had treated me that night at the Drones sickened me. Yes, sickened me.

I hadn't time, however, to express my horror and disgust, for at this juncture Jeeves came in.

'Mrs. Travers had just rung up on the telephone, sir. She desired me to say that she will be calling to see you in a few minutes.'

'Contents noted, Jeeves,' I said. 'Now listen, Tuppy—'

I stopped. The fellow wasn't there.

'What have you done with him, Jeeves?' I asked.

'Mr. Glossop has left, sir.'

'Left? How can he have left? He was sitting there—'

'That is the front door closing now, sir.'

'But what made him shoot off like that?'

'Possibly Mr. Glossop did not wish to meet Mrs. Travers, sir.'

'Why not?'

'I could not say, sir. But undoubtedly at the mention of Mrs. Travers' name he rose very swiftly.'

'Strange, Jeeves.'

'Yes, sir.'

I turned to a subject of more moment.

'Jeeves,' I said. 'Mr. Glossop proposes to sing "Sonny Boy" at an entertainment down in the East End next Tuesday.'

'Indeed, sir?'

'Before an audience consisting mainly of coster-mongers, with a sprinkling of whelk-stall owners, purveyors of blood-oranges, and minor pugilists.'

'Indeed, sir?'

'Make a note to remind me to be there. He will infallibly get the bird, and I want to witness his downfall.'

'Very good, sir.'

'And when Mrs. Travers arrives, I shall be in the sitting-room.'

Those who know Bertram Wooster best are aware that in his journey through life he is impeded and generally snootered by about as scaly a platoon of aunts as was ever assembled. But there is one exception to the general ghastliness – viz., my Aunt Dahlia. She married old Tom Travers the year Bluebottle won the Cambridgeshire, and is one of the best. It is always a pleasure to me to chat with her, and it was with a courtly geniality that I rose to receive her as she sailed over the threshold at about two fifty-five.

She seemed somewhat perturbed, and snapped into the agenda without delay. Aunt Dahlia is one of those big, hearty women. She used to go in a lot for hunting, and she generally speaks as if she had just sighted a fox on a hillside half a mile away.

'Bertie,' she cried, in the manner of one encouraging a bevy of hounds to renewed efforts. 'I want your help.'

'And you shall have it, Aunt Dahlia,' I replied suavely. 'I can honestly say that there is no one to whom I would more readily do a good turn than yourself; no one to whom I am more delighted to be—'

'Less of it,' she begged, 'less of it. You know that friend of yours, young Glossop?'

'He's just been lunching here.'

'He has, has he? Well, I wish you'd poisoned his soup.'

'We didn't have soup. And, when you describe him as a friend of mine, I wouldn't quite say the term absolutely squared with the facts. Some time ago, one night when we had been dining together at the Drones—'

At this point Aunt Dahlia – a little brusquely, it seemed to me – said that she would rather wait for the story of my life till she could get it in book-form. I could see now that she was definitely not her usual sunny self, so I shelved my personal grievances and asked what was biting her.

'It's that young hound Glossop,' she said.

'What's he been doing?'

'Breaking Angela's heart.' (Angela. Daughter of above. My cousin. Quite a good egg.)

'Breaking Angela's heart?'

'Yes. . . Breaking . . . Angela's . . . HEART!'

'You say he's breaking Angela's heart?'

She begged me in rather a feverish way to suspend the vaudeville cross-talk stuff.

'How's he doing that?' I asked.

'With his neglect. With his low, callous, double-crossing duplicity.'

'Duplicity is the word, Aunt Dahlia,' I said. 'In treating of young Tuppy Glossop, it springs naturally to the lips. Let me just tell you what he did to me one night at the Drones. We had finished dinner—'

'Ever since the beginning of the season, up till about three weeks ago, he was all over Angela. The sort of thing which, when I was a girl, we should have described as courting—'

'Or wooing?'

'Wooing or courting, whichever you like.'

'Whichever *you* like, Aunt Dahlia,' I said courteously.

'Well, anyway, he haunted the house, lapped up daily lunches, danced with her half the night, and so on, till naturally the poor kid, who's quite off her oats about him, took it for granted that it was only a question of time before he suggested that they should feed for life out of the same crib. And now he's gone and dropped her like a hot brick, and I hear he's infatuated with some girl he met at a Chelsea tea-party – a girl named – now, what was it?'

'Cora Bellinger.'

'How do you know?'

'She was lunching here today.'

'He brought her?'

'Yes.'

'What's she like?'

'Pretty massive. In shape, a bit on the lines of the Albert Hall.'

'Did he seem very fond of her?'

'Couldn't take his eyes off the chassis.'

'The modern young man,' said Aunt Dahlia, 'is a congenital idiot and wants a nurse to lead him by the hand and some strong attendant to kick him regularly at intervals of a quarter of an hour.'

I tried to point out the silver lining.

'If you ask me, Aunt Dahlia,' I said, 'I think Angela is well out of it. This Glossop is a tough baby. One of London's toughest. I was trying to tell you just now what he did to me one night at the Drones. First having got me in sporting mood with a bottle of the ripest, he betted I wouldn't swing myself across the swimming-bath by the ropes and rings. I knew I could do it on my head, so I took him on, exulting in the fun, so to speak. And when I'd done half the trip and was going as strong as dammit, I found he had looped the last rope back against the rail, leaving me no alternative but to drop into the depths and swim ashore in correct evening costume.'

'He did?'

'He certainly did. It was months ago, and I haven't got really dry yet. You wouldn't want your daughter to marry a man capable of a thing like that?'

'On the contrary, you restore my faith in the young hound. I see that there must be lots of good in him, after all. And I want this Bellinger business broken up, Bertie.'

'How?'

'I don't care how. Any way you please.'

'But what can I do?'

'Do? Why, put the whole thing before your man Jeeves. Jeeves will find a way. One of the most capable fellers I ever met. Put the thing squarely up to Jeeves and tell him to let his mind play round the topic.'

'There may be something in what you say, Aunt Dahlia,' I said thoughtfully.

'Of course there is,' said Aunt Dahlia. 'A little thing like this will be child's play to Jeeves. Get him working on it, and I'll look in tomorrow to hear the result.'

With which, she biffed off, and I summoned Jeeves to the presence.

'Jeeves,' I said, 'you have heard all?'

'Yes, sir.'

'I thought you would. My Aunt Dahlia has what you might call a carrying voice. Has it ever occurred to you that, if all other sources of income failed, she could make a good living calling the cattle home across the Sands of Dee?'

'I had not considered the point, sir, but no doubt you are right.'

'Well, how do we go? What is your reaction? I think we should do our best to help and assist.'

'Yes, sir.'

'I am fond of my Aunt Dahlia and I am fond of my cousin Angela. Fond of them both, if you get my drift. What the misguided girl finds to attract her in young Tuppy, I cannot say, Jeeves, and you cannot say. But apparently she loves the man – which shows it can be done, a thing I wouldn't have believed myself – and is pining away like—'

'Patience on a monument, sir.'

513

'Like Patience, as you very shrewdly remark, on a monument. So we must cluster round. Bend your brain to the problem, Jeeves. It is one that will tax you to the uttermost.'

Aunt Dahlia blew in on the morrow, and I rang the bell for Jeeves. He appeared looking brainier than one could have believed possible – sheer intellect shining from every feature – and I could see at once that the engine had been turning over.

'Speak, Jeeves,' I said.

'Very good, sir.'

'You have brooded?'

'Yes, sir.'

'With what success?'

'I have a plan, sir, which I fancy may produce satisfactory results.'

'In affairs of this description, madam, the first essential is to study the psychology of the individual.'

'The what of the individual?'

'The psychology, madam.'

'He means, the psychology,' I said. 'And by psychology, Jeeves, you imply—?'

'The natures and dispositions of the principals in the matter, sir.'

'You mean, what they're like?'

'Precisely, sir.'

'Does he talk like this to you when you're alone, Bertie?' asked Aunt Dahlia.

'Sometimes. Occasionally. And, on the other hand, some-times not. Proceed, Jeeves.

'Well, sir, if I may say so, the thing that struck me most forcibly about Miss Bellinger when she was under my observation was that hers was a somewhat hard and intolerant nature. I could envisage Miss Bellinger applauding success. I could not so easily see her pitying and sympathising with failure. Possibly you will recall, sir, her attitude when Mr. Glossop endeavoured to light her cigarette with his automatic lighter? I thought I detected a certain impatience at his inability to produce the necessary flame.'

'True, Jeeves. She ticked him off.'

'Precisely, sir.'

'Let me get this straight,' said Aunt Dahlia, looking a bit fogged. 'You think that, if he goes on trying to light her cigarettes with his automatic lighter long enough, she will eventually get fed up and hand him the mitten? Is that the idea?'

'I merely mentioned the episode, madam, as an indication of Miss Bellinger's somewhat ruthless nature.'

'Ruthless,' I said, 'is right. The Bellinger is hard-boiled. Those eyes. That chin. I could read them. A woman of blood and iron, if ever there was one.'

'Precisely, sir. I think, therefore, that, should Miss Bellinger be a witness of Mr. Glossop appearing to disadvantage in public, she would cease to entertain affection for him. In the event, for instance, of his failing to please the audience on Tuesday with his singing—'

I saw daylight.

'By Jove, Jeeves! You mean if he gets the bird, all will be off?'

'I shall be greatly surprised if such is not the case, sir.'

I shook my head.

'We cannot leave this thing to chance, Jeeves. Young Tuppy, singing "Sonny Boy", is the likeliest prospect for the bird that I can think of – but, no – you must see for yourself that we can't simply trust to luck.'

'We need not trust to luck, sir. I would suggest that you approach your friend, Mr. Bingham, and volunteer your services as a performer at his forthcoming entertainment. It could readily be arranged that you sang immediately before Mr. Glossop. I fancy, sir, that, if Mr. Glossop were to sing "Sonny Boy" directly after you, too, had sung "Sonny Boy", the audience would respond satisfactorily. By the time Mr. Glossop began to sing, they would have lost their taste for that particular song and would express their feelings warmly.'

'Jeeves,' said Aunt Dahlia, 'you're a marvel!'

'Thank you, madam.'

'Jeeves,' I said, 'you're an ass!'

'What do you mean, he's an ass?' said Aunt Dahlia hotly. 'I think it's the greatest scheme I ever heard.'

'Me sing "Sonny Boy" at Beefy Bingham's clean, bright entertainment? I can see myself!'

'You sing it daily in your bath, sir. Mr. Wooster,' said Jeeves, turning to Aunt Dahlia, 'has a pleasant, light baritone—'

'I bet he has,' said Aunt Dahlia.

I froze the man with a look.

'Between singing "Sonny Boy" in one's bath, Jeeves, and singing it before a hall full of assorted blood-orange merchants and their young, there is a substantial difference.'

'Bertie,' said Aunt Dahlia, 'you'll sing, and like it!'

'I will not.'

'Bertie!'

'Nothing will induce—'

'Bertie,' said Aunt Dahlia firmly, 'you will sing "Sonny Boy" on Tuesday, the third *prox.*, and sing it like a lark at sunrise, or may an aunt's curse—'

'I won't!'

'Think of Angela!'

'Dash Angela!'

'Bertie!'

'No, I mean, hang it all!'

'You won't?'

'No, I won't.'

'That is your last word, is it?'

'It is. Once and for all, Aunt Dahlia, nothing will induce me to let out so much as a single note.'

And so that afternoon I sent a pre-paid wire to Beefy Bingham, offering my services in the cause, and by nightfall the thing was fixed up. I was billed to perform next but one after the intermission. Following me, came Tuppy. And, immediately after him, Miss Cora Bellinger, the well-known operatic soprano.

'Jeeves,' I said that evening – and I said it coldly – 'I shall be obliged if you will pop round to the nearest music-shop and procure me a copy of "Sonny Boy". It will now be necessary for me to learn both verse and refrain. Of the trouble and nervous strain which this will involve, I say nothing.'

'Very good, sir.'

'But this I do say—'

'I had better be starting immediately, sir, or the shop will be closed.'

'Ha!' I said.

And I meant it to sting.

Although I had steeled myself to the ordeal before me and had set out full of the calm, quiet courage which makes men do desperate deeds with careless smiles, I must admit that there was a moment, just after I had entered the Oddfellows' Hall at Bermondsey East and run an eye over the assembled pleasure-seekers, when it needed all the bull-dog pluck of the Woosters to keep me from calling it a day and taking a cab back to civilisation. The clean, bright entertainment was in full swing when I arrived, and somebody who looked as if he might be the local undertaker was reciting 'Gunga Din'. And the audience, though not actually chi-yiking in the full technical sense of the term, had a grim look which I didn't like at all. The mere sight of them gave me the sort of feeling Shadrach, Meshach and Abednego must have had when preparing to enter the burning, fiery furnace.

Scanning the multitude, it seemed to me that they were for the nonce suspending judgment. Did you ever tap on the door of one of those New York speakeasy places and see the grille snap back and a Face appear? There is one long, silent moment when its eyes are fixed on yours and all your past life seems to rise up before you. Then you say that you are a friend of Mr. Zinzinheimer and he told you they would treat you right if you mentioned his name, and the strain relaxes. Well, these costermongers and whelkstallers appeared to me to be looking just like that Face. Start something, they seemed to say, and they would know what to do about it. And I couldn't help feeling that my singing 'Sonny Boy' would come, in their opinion, under the head of starting something.

'A nice, full house, sir,' said a voice at my elbow. It was Jeeves, watching the proceedings with an indulgent eye.

'You here, Jeeves?' I said, coldly.

'Yes, sir. I have been present since the commencement.'

'Oh?' I said. 'Any casualties yet?'

'Sir?'

'You know what I mean, Jeeves,' I said sternly, 'and don't pretend you don't. Anybody got the bird yet?'

'Oh, no, sir.'

'I shall be the first, you think?'

'No, sir. I see no reason to expect such a misfortune. I anticipate that you will be well received.'

A sudden thought struck me.

'And you think everything will go according to plan?'

'Yes, sir.'

'Well, I don't,' I said. 'And I'll tell you why I don't. I've spotted a flaw in your beastly scheme.'

'A flaw, sir?'

'Yes. Do you suppose for a moment that, when Mr. Glossop hears me singing that dashed song, he'll come calmly on a minute after and sing it too? Use your intelligence, Jeeves. He will perceive the chasm in his path and pause in time. He will back out and refuse to go on at all.'

'Mr. Glossop will not hear you sing, sir. At my advice, he has stepped across the road to the Jug and Bottle, an establishment immediately opposite the hall, and he intends to remain there until it is time for him to appear on the platform.'

'Oh?' I said.

'If I might suggest it, sir, there is another house named the Goat and Grapes only a short distance down the street. I think it might be a judicious move—'

'If I were to put a bit of custom in their way?'

'It would ease the nervous strain of waiting, sir.'

I had not been feeling any too pleased with the man for having let me in for this ghastly binge, but at these words, I'm bound to say, my austerity softened a trifle. He was undoubtedly right. He had studied the psychology of the individual, and it had not led him astray. A quiet ten minutes at the Goat and Grapes was exactly what my system required. To buzz off there and inhale a couple of swift whisky-and-sodas was with Bertram Wooster the work of a moment.

The treatment worked like magic. What they had put into the stuff, besides vitriol, I could not have said; but it completely altered my outlook on life. That curious, gulpy feeling passed. I was no longer conscious of the sagging sensation at the knees. The limbs ceased to quiver gently, the tongue became loosened in its socket, and the backbone stiffened. Pausing merely to order and swallow another of the same, I bade the barmaid a cheery good night, nodded affably to one or two fellows in the bar whose faces I liked, and came prancing back to the hall, ready for anything.

And shortly afterwards I was on the platform with about a million bulging eyes goggling up at me. There was a rummy sort of buzzing in my ears, and then through the buzzing I heard the sound of a piano starting to tinkle: and, commending my soul to God, I took a good, long breath and charged in.

Well, it was a close thing. The whole incident is a bit blurred, but I seem to recollect a kind of murmur as I hit the refrain. I thought at the time it was an attempt on the part of the many-headed to join in the chorus, and at the moment it rather encouraged me. I passed the thing over the larynx with all the vim at my disposal, hit the high note, and off gracefully into the wings. I didn't come on again to take a bow. I just receded and oiled round to where Jeeves awaited me among the standees at the back.

'Well, Jeeves,' I said, anchoring myself at his side and brushing the honest sweat from the brow, 'they didn't rush the platform.'

'No, sir.'

'But you can spread it about that that's the last time I perform outside my bath. My swan-song, Jeeves. Anybody who wants to hear me in future must present himself at the bathroom door and shove his ear against the keyhole. I may be wrong, but it seemed to me that towards the end they were hotting up a trifle. The bird was hovering in the air. I could hear the beating of its wings.'

'I did detect a certain restlessness, sir, in the audience. I fancy they had lost their taste for that particular melody.'

'Eh?'

'I should have informed you earlier, sir, that the song had already been sung twice before you arrived.'

'What!'

'Yes, sir. Once by a lady and once by a gentleman. It is a very popular song, sir.'

I gaped at the man. That, with this knowledge, he could calmly have allowed the young master to step straight into the jaws of death, so to speak, paralysed me. It seemed to show that the old feudal spirit had passed away altogether. I was about to give him my views on the matter in no uncertain fashion, when I was stopped by the spectacle of young Tuppy lurching on to the platform.

Young Tuppy had the unmistakable air of a man who has recently been round to the Jug and Bottle. A few cheery cries of welcome, presumably from some of his backgammon-playing pals who felt that blood was thicker than water, had the effect of causing the genial smile on his face to widen till it nearly met at the back. He was plainly feeling about as good as a man can feel and still remain on his feet. He waved a kindly hand to his supporters, and bowed in a regal sort of manner, rather like an Eastern monarch acknowledging the plaudits of the mob.

Then the female at the piano struck up the opening bars of 'Sonny Boy', and Tuppy swelled like a balloon, clasped his hands together, rolled his eyes up at the ceiling and began.

I think the populace was too stunned for the moment to take immediate steps. It may seem incredible, but I give you my word that young Tuppy got right through the verse without so much as a murmur. Then they all seemed to pull themselves together.

A costermonger, roused, is a terrible thing. I had never seen the proletariat really stirred before, and I'm bound to say it rather awed me. I mean, it gave you some idea of what it must have been like during the French Revolution. From every corner of the hall there proceeded simultaneously the sort of noise which you hear, they tell me, at one of those East End boxing places where the referee disqualifies the popular favourite and makes the quick dash for life. And then they passed beyond mere words and began to introduce the vegetable motive.

I don't know why, but somehow I had got it into my head that the first thing thrown at Tuppy would be a potato. One gets these fancies. It was, however, as a matter of fact, a banana, and I saw in an instant that the choice had been made by wiser heads than mine. These blokes who have grown up from childhood in the knowledge of how to treat a dramatic entertainment that doesn't please them are aware by a sort of instinct just what to do for the best, and the moment I saw that banana splash on Tuppy's shirt-front I realised how infinitely more effective and artistic it was than any potato could have been.

Not that the potato school of thought had not also its supporters. As the proceedings warmed up, I noticed several intelligent-looking fellows who threw nothing else.

The effect on young Tuppy was rather remarkable. His eyes bulged and his hair seemed to stand up, and yet his mouth went on opening and shutting, and you could see that in a dazed, automatic way he was still singing 'Sonny Boy'. Then, coming out of his trance, he began to pull for the shore with some rapidity. The last seen of him, he was beating a tomato to the exit by a short head.

Presently the tumult and the shouting died. I turned to Jeeves.

'Painful, Jeeves,' I said. 'But what would you?'

'Yes, sir.'

'The surgeon's knife, what?'

'Precisely, sir.'

'Well, with this happening beneath her eyes, I think we may definitely consider the Glossop-Bellinger romance off.'

'Yes, sir.'

At this point old Beefy Bingham came out on to the platform.

'Ladies and gentlemen,' said old Beefy.

I supposed that he was about to rebuke his flock for the recent expression of feeling. But such was not the case. No doubt he was accustomed by now to the wholesome give-and-take of these clean, bright entertainments and had ceased to think it worth while to make any comment when there was a certain liveliness.

'Ladies and gentlemen,' said old Beefy, 'the next item on the programme was to have been Songs by Miss Cora Bellinger, the well-known operatic soprano. I have just received a telephone-message from Miss Bellinger, saying that her car has broken down. She is, however, on her way here in a cab and will arrive shortly. Meanwhile, our friend Mr. Enoch Simpson will recite "Dangerous Dan McGrew".'

I clutched at Jeeves.

'Jeeves! You heard?'

'Yes, sir.'

'She wasn't there!'

'No, sir.'

'She saw nothing of Tuppy's Waterloo.'

'No, sir.'

'The whole bally scheme has blown a fuse.'

'Yes, sir.'

'Come, Jeeves,' I said, and those standing by wondered, no doubt, what had caused that clean-cut face to grow so pale and set. 'I have been subjected to a nervous strain unparalleled since the days of the early Martyrs. I have lost pounds in weight and permanently injured my entire system. I have gone through an ordeal, the recollection of which will make me wake up screaming in the night for months to come. And all for nothing. Let us go.'

'If you have no objection, sir, I would like to witness the remainder of the entertainment.'

'Suit yourself, Jeeves,' I said moodily. 'Personally, my heart is dead and I am going to look in at the Goat and Grapes for another of their cyanide specials and then home.'

It must have been about half-past ten, and I was in the old sitting-room sombrely sucking down a more or less final restorative, when the front door bell rang, and there on the mat was young Tuppy. He looked like a man who passed through some great experience and stood face to face with his soul. He had the beginnings of a black eye.

'Oh, hullo, Bertie,' said young Tuppy.

He came in, and hovered about the mantelpiece as if he were looking for things to fiddle with and break.

'I've just been singing at Beefy Bingham's entertainment,' he said after a pause.

'Oh?' I said. 'How did you go?'

'Like a breeze,' said young Tuppy. 'Held them spellbound.'

'Knocked 'em, eh?'

'Cold,' said young Tuppy. 'Not a dry eye.'

And this, mark you, a man who had had a good upbringing and had, no doubt, spent years at his mother's knee being taught to tell the truth.

'I suppose Miss Bellinger is pleased?'

'Oh, yes. Delighted.'

'So now everything's all right?'

'Oh, quite.'

Tuppy paused.

'On the other hand, Bertie—'

'Yes?'

'Well, I've been thinking things over. Somehow I don't believe Miss Bellinger is the mate for me, after all.'

'You don't?'

'No, I don't.'

'Why don't you?'

'Oh, I don't know. These things sort of flash on you. I respect Miss Bellinger, Bertie. I admire her. But – er – well, I can't help feeling now that a sweet, gentle girl— er – like your cousin Angela, for instance, Bertie— would – er – in fact— well, what I came round for was to ask if you would 'phone Angela and find out how she reacts to the idea of coming out with me tonight to the Berkeley for a segment of supper and a spot of dancing.'

'Go ahead. There's the 'phone.'

'No, I'd rather you asked her, Bertie. What with one thing and another, if you paved the way— You see, there's just a chance that she may be— I mean, you know how mis-understandings occur— and— well, what I'm driving at, Bertie, old man, is that I'd rather you surged round and did a bit of paving, if you don't mind.'

I went to the 'phone and called up Aunt Dahlia's.

'She says come right along,' I said.

'Tell her,' said Tuppy in a devout sort of voice, 'that I will be with her in something under a couple of ticks.'

He had barely biffed, when I heard a click in the keyhole and a soft padding in the passage without.

'Jeeves,' I called.

'Sir?' said Jeeves, manifesting himself.

'Jeeves, a remarkably rummy thing has happened. Mr. Glossop has just been here. He tells me that it is all off between him and Miss Bellinger.'

'Yes, sir.'

'You don't seem surprised.'

'No, sir. I confess I had anticipated some such eventuality.'

'Eh? What gave you that idea?'

'It came to me, sir, when I observed Miss Bellinger strike Mr. Glossop in the eye.

'Strike him!'

'Yes, sir.'

'In the eye?'

'The right eye, sir.'

I clutched the brow.

'What on earth made her do that?'

'I fancy she was a little upset, sir, at the reception accorded to her singing.'

'Great Scott! Don't tell me she got the bird, too?'

'Yes, sir.'

'But why? She's got a red-hot voice.'

'Yes, sir. But I think the audience resented her choice of a song.'

'Jeeves!' Reason was beginning to do a bit of tottering on its throne. 'You aren't going to stand there and tell me that Miss Bellinger sang "Sonny Boy", too!'

'Yes, sir. And – rashly, in my opinion – brought a large doll on to the platform to sing it to. The audience affected to mistake it for a ventriloquist's dummy, and there was some little disturbance.'

'But, Jeeves, what a coincidence!'

'Not altogether, sir. I ventured to take the liberty of accosting Miss Bellinger on her arrival at the hall and recalling myself to her recollection. I then said that Mr. Glossop had asked me to request her that as a particular favour to him – the song being a favourite of his – she would sing "Sonny Boy". And when she found that you and Mr. Glossop had also sung the song immediately before her, I rather fancy that she supposed that she had been made the victim of a practical pleasantry by Mr. Glossop. Will there be anything further, sir?'

'No, thanks.'

'Good night, sir.'

'Good night, Jeeves,' I said reverently.

I was jerked from the dreamless by a sound like the rolling of distant thunder; and, the mists of sleep clearing away, was enabled to diagnose this and trace it to its source. It was my Aunt Agatha's dog, Mcintosh, scratching at the door. The above, an Aberdeen terrier of weak intellect, had been left in my charge by the old relative while she went off to Aix-les-Bains to take the cure, and I had never been able to make it see eye to eye with me on the subject of early rising. Although a glance at my watch informed me that it was barely ten, here was the animal absolutely up and about.

I pressed the bell, and presently in shimmered Jeeves, complete with tea-tray and preceded by dog, which leaped upon the bed, licked me smartly in the right eye, and immediately curled up and fell into a deep slumber. And where the sense is in getting up at some ungodly hour of the morning and coming scratching at people's doors, when you intend at the first opportunity to go to sleep again, beats me. Nevertheless, every day for the last five weeks this loony hound had pursued the same policy, and I confess I was getting a bit fed.

There were one or two letters on the tray; and, having slipped a refreshing half-cupful into the abyss, I felt equal to dealing with them. The one on top was from my Aunt Agatha.

'Ha!' I said.

'Sir?'

'I said "Ha!" Jeeves. And I meant "Ha!" I was registering relief. My Aunt Agatha returns this evening. She will be at her town residence between the hours of six and seven, and she expects to find Mcintosh waiting for her on the mat.'

'Indeed, sir? I shall miss the little fellow.'

'I, too, Jeeves. Despite his habit of rising with the milk and being hearty before breakfast, there is sterling stuff in Mcintosh. Nevertheless, I cannot but feel relieved at the prospect of shooting him back to the old home. It has been a guardianship fraught with anxiety. You know what my Aunt Agatha is. She lavishes on that dog a love which might better be bestowed on a nephew: and if the slightest thing had gone wrong with him while I was *in loco parentis*; if, while in my charge, he had developed rabies or staggers or the botts, I should have been blamed.'

'Very true, sir.'

'And, as you are aware, London is not big enough to hold Aunt Agatha and anybody she happens to be blaming.'

I had opened the second letter, and was giving it the eye.

'Ha!' I said.

'Sir?'

'Once again "Ha!" Jeeves, but this time signifying mild surprise. This letter is from Miss Wickham.'

'Indeed, sir?'

I sensed – if that is the word I want – the note of concern in the man's voice, and I knew he was saying to himself 'Is the young master about to slip?' You see, there was a time when the Wooster heart was to some extent what you might call ensnared by this Roberta Wickham, and Jeeves had never approved of her. He considered her volatile and frivolous and more or less of a menace to man and beast. And events, I'm bound to say, had rather borne out his view.

'She wants me to give her lunch today.'

'Indeed, sir?'

'And two friends of hers.'

'Indeed, sir?'

'Here. At one-thirty.'

'Indeed, sir?'

I was piqued.

'Correct this parrot-complex, Jeeves,' I said, waving a slice of bread-and-butter rather sternly at the man. 'There is no need for you to stand there saying "Indeed, sir?" I know what you're thinking, and you're wrong. As far as Miss Wickham is concerned, Bertram Wooster is chilled steel. I see no earthly reason why I should not comply with this request. A Wooster may have ceased to love, but he can still be civil.'

'Very good, sir.'

'Employ the rest of the morning, then, in buzzing to and fro and collecting provender. The old King Wenceslas touch, Jeeves. You remember? Bring me fish and bring me fowl—'

'Bring me flesh and bring me wine, sir.'

'Just as you say. You know best. Oh, and roly-poly pudding, Jeeves.'

'Sir?'

'Roly-poly pudding with lots of jam in it. Miss Wickham specifically mentions this. Mysterious, what?'

'Extremely, sir.'

'Also oysters, ice-cream, and plenty of chocolates with the goo-ey, slithery stuff in the middle. Makes you sick to think of it, eh?'

'Yes, sir.'

'Me, too. But that's what she says. I think she must be on some kind of diet. Well, be that as it may, see to it, Jeeves, will you?'

'Yes, sir.'

'At one-thirty of the clock.'

'Very good, sir.'

'Very good, Jeeves.'

At half past twelve I took the dog McIntosh for his morning

saunter in the Park; and, returning at about one-ten, found young Bobbie Wickham in the sitting-room, smoking a cigarette and chatting to Jeeves, who seemed a bit distant, I thought.

I have an idea I've told you about this Bobbie Wickham. She was the red-haired girl who let me down so disgracefully in the sinister affair of Tuppy Glossop and the hot-water bottle, that Christmas when I went to stay at Skeldings Hall, her mother's place in Hertfordshire. Her mother is Lady Wickham, who writes novels which, I believe, command a ready sale among those who like their literature pretty sloppy. A formidable old bird, rather like my Aunt Agatha in appearance. Bobbie does not resemble her, being constructed more on the lines of Clara Bow. She greeted me cordially as I entered – in fact, so cordially that I saw Jeeves pause at the door before biffing off to mix the cocktails and shoot me the sort of grave, warning look a wise old father might pass out to the effervescent son on seeing him going fairly strong with the local vamp. I nodded back, as much as to say 'Chilled steel!' and he oozed out, leaving me to play the sparkling host.

'It was awfully sporting of you to give us this lunch, Bertie,' said Bobbie.

'Don't mention it, my dear old thing,' I said. 'Always a pleasure.'

'You got all the stuff I told you about?'

'The garbage, as specified, is in the kitchen. But since when have you become a roly-poly pudding addict?'

'That isn't for me. There's a small boy coming.'

'What!'

'I'm awfully sorry,' she said, noting my agitation. 'I know just how you feel, and I'm not going to pretend that this child isn't pretty near the edge. In fact, he has to be seen to be believed. But it's simply vital that he be cosseted and sucked up to and generally treated as the guest of honour, because everything depends on him.'

'How do you mean?'

'I'll tell you. You know mother?'

'Whose mother?'

'My mother.'

'Oh, yes. I thought you meant the kid's mother.'

'He hasn't got a mother. Only a father, who is a big theatrical manager in America. I met him at a party the other night.'

'The father?'

'Yes, the father.'

'Not the kid?'

'No, not the kid.'

'Right. All clear so far. Proceed.'

'Well, mother – my mother – has dramatised one of her novels, and when I met this father, this theatrical manager father, and, between ourselves, made rather a hit with him, I said to myself, "Why not?" '

'Why not what?'

'Why not plant mother's play on him.'

'Your mother's play?'

'Yes, not his mother's play. He is like his son, he hasn't got a mother, either.'

'These things run in families, don't they?'

'You see, Bertie, what with one thing and another, my stock isn't very high with mother just now. There was that matter of my smashing up the car – oh, and several things. So I thought, here is where I get a chance to put myself right. I cooed to old Blumenfield—'

'Name sounds familiar.'

'Oh, yes, he's a big man over in America. He has come to London to see if there's anything in the play line worth buying. So I cooed to him a goodish bit and then asked him if he would listen to mother's play. He said he would, so I asked him to come to lunch and I'd read it to him.'

'You're going to read your mother's play – here?' I said, paling.

'Yes.'

'My God!'

'I know what you mean,' she said. 'I admit its pretty sticky stuff. But I have an idea that I shall put it over. It all depends on how the kid likes it. You see, old Blumenfield, for some reason, always banks on his verdict. I suppose he thinks the child's intelligence is exactly the same as an average audience's and—'

I uttered a slight yelp, causing Jeeves, who had entered with cocktails, to look at me in a pained sort of way. I had remembered.

'Jeeves!'

'Sir?'

'Do you recollect, when we were in New York, a dish-faced kid of the name of Blumenfield who on a memorable occasion snootered Cyril Bassington-Bassington when the latter tried to go on the stage?'

'Very vividly, sir.'

'Well, prepare yourself for a shock. He's coming to lunch.'

'Indeed, sir?'

'I'm glad you can speak in that light, careless way. I only met the young stoup of arsenic for a few brief minutes, but I don't mind telling you the prospect of hob-nobbing with him again makes me tremble like a leaf.'

'Indeed, sir?'

'Don't keep saying "Indeed, sir?" You have seen this kid in action and you know what he's like. He told Cyril Bassington-Bassington, a fellow to whom he had never been formally introduced, that he had a face like a fish. And this not thirty seconds after their initial meeting. I give you fair warning that, if he tells me I have a face like a fish, I shall clump his head.'

'Bertie!' cried the Wickham, contorted with anguish and apprehension and what not.

'Yes, I shall.'

'Then you'll simply ruin the whole thing.'

'I don't care. We Woosters have our pride.'

'Perhaps the young gentleman will not notice that you have a face like a fish, sir,' suggested Jeeves.

'Ah! There's that, of course.'

'But we can't just trust to luck,' said Bobbie. 'It's probably the first thing he will notice.'

'In that case, miss,' said Jeeves, 'it might be the best plan if Mr. Wooster did not attend the luncheon.'

I beamed on the man. As always, he had found the way.

'But Mr. Blumenfield will think it so odd.'

'Well, tell him I'm eccentric. Tell him I have these moods, which come upon me quite suddenly, when I can't stand the sight of people. Tell him what you like.'

'He'll be offended.'

'Not half so offended as if I socked his son on the upper maxillary bone.'

'I really think it would be the best plan, miss.'

'Oh, all right,' said Bobbie. 'Push off, then. But I wanted you to be here to listen to the play and laugh in the proper places.'

'I don't suppose there are any proper places,' I said. And with these words I reached the hall in two bounds, grabbed a hat, and made for the street. A cab was just pulling up at the door as I reached it, and inside it were Pop Blumenfield and his foul son. With a slight sinking of the old heart, I saw that the kid had recognised me.

'Hullo!' he said.

'Hullo!' I said.

'Where are you off to?' said the kid.

'Ha, ha!' I said, and legged it for the great open spaces.

I lunched at the Drones, doing myself fairly well and lingering pretty considerably over the coffee and cigarettes. At four o'clock I thought it would be safe to think about getting back; but, not wishing to take any chances, I went to the 'phone and rang up the flat.

'All clear, Jeeves?'

'Yes, sir.'

'Blumenfield junior nowhere about?'

'No, sir.'

'Not hiding in any nook or cranny, what?'

'No, sir.'

'How did everything go off?'

'Quite satisfactorily, I fancy, sir.'

'Was I missed?'

'I think Mr. Blumenfield and young Master Blumenfield were somewhat surprised at your absence, sir. Apparently they encountered you as you were leaving the building.'

'They did. An awkward moment, Jeeves. The kid appeared to desire speech with me, but I laughed hollowly and passed on. Did they comment on this at all?'

'Yes, sir. Indeed, young Master Blumenfield was somewhat outspoken.'

'What did he say?'

'I cannot recall his exact words, sir, but he drew a comparison between your mentality and that of a cuckoo.'

'A cuckoo, eh?'

'Yes, sir. To the bird's advantage.'

'He did, did he? Now you see how right I was to come away. Just one crack like that out of him face to face, and I should infallibly have done his upper maxillary a bit of no good. It was wise of you to suggest that I should lunch out.'

'Thank you, sir.'

'Well, the coast being clear, I will now return home.'

'Before you start, sir, perhaps you would ring Miss Wickham up. She instructed me to desire you to do so.'

'You mean she asked you to ask me?'

'Precisely, sir.'

'Right ho. And the number?'

'Sloane 8090. I fancy it is the residence of Miss Wickham's aunt, in Eaton Square.'

I got the number. And presently young Bobbie's voice came

floating over the wire. From the *timbre* I gathered that she was extremely bucked.

'Hullo? Is that you, Bertie?'

'In person. What's the news?'

'Wonderful. Everything went off splendidly. The lunch was just right. The child stuffed himself to the eyebrows and got more and more amiable, till by the time he had had his third go of ice-cream, he was ready to say that any play – even one of mother's – was the goods. I fired it at him before he could come out from under the influence, and he sat there absorbing it in a sort of gorged way, and at the end old Blumenfield said "Well, sonny, how about it?" and the child gave a sort of faint smile, as if he was thinking about roly-poly pudding, and said "O.K., pop," and that's all there was to it. Old Blumenfield has taken him off to the movies, and I'm to look in at the Savoy at five-thirty to sign the contract. I've just been talking to mother on the 'phone, and she's quite consumedly braced.'

'Terrific!'

'I knew you'd be pleased. Oh, Bertie, there's just one other thing. You remember saying to me once that there wasn't anything in the world you wouldn't do for me?'

I paused a trifle warily. It is true that I had expressed myself in some such terms as she had indicated, but that was before the affair of Tuppy and the hot-water bottle, and in the calmer frame of mind induced by that episode I wasn't feeling quite so spacious. You know how it is. Love's flame flickers and dies, Reason returns to her throne, and you aren't nearly as ready to hop about and jump through hoops as in the first pristine glow of the divine passion.

'What do you want me to do?'

'Well, it's nothing I actually want you to do. It's something I've done that I hope you won't be sticky about. Just before I began reading the play, that dog of yours, the Aberdeen terrier, came into the room. The child Blumenfield was very much taken with it and said he wished he had a dog like that, looking at me in a meaning sort of way. So naturally, I had to say "Oh, I'll give you this one!"'

I swayed somewhat.

'You . . . You . . . What was that?'

'I gave him the dog. I knew you wouldn't mind. You see, it was vital to keep cosseting him. If I'd refused, he would have cut up rough and all that roly-poly pudding and stuff would have been thrown away. You see—'

I hung up. The jaw had fallen, the eyes were protruding. I tottered from the booth and, reeling out of the club, hailed a taxi. I got to the flat and yelled for Jeeves.

'Jeeves!'

'Sir?'

'Do you know what?'

'No, sir.'

'The dog . . . my Aunt Agatha's dog . . . Mcintosh . . .'

'I have not seen him for some little while, sir. He left me after the conclusion of luncheon. Possibly he is in your bedroom.'

'Yes, and possibly he jolly dashed well isn't. If you want to know where he is, he's in a suite at the Savoy.'

'Sir?'

'Miss Wickham has just told me she gave him to Blumenfield junior.'

'Sir?'

'Gave him to Jumenfield blunior, I tell you. As a present. As a gift. With warm personal regards.'

'What was her motive in doing that, sir?'

I explained the circs. Jeeves did a bit of respectful tongue-clicking.

'I have always maintained, if you will remember, sir,' he said, when I had finished, 'that Miss Wickham, though a charming young lady—'

'Yes, yes, never mind about that. What are we going to do? That's the point. Aunt Agatha is due back between the hours of six and seven. She will find herself short of one Aberdeen terrier.

And, as she will probably have been considerably sea-sick all the way over, you will readily perceive, Jeeves, that, when I break the news that her dog has been given away to a total stranger, I shall find her in no mood of gentle charity.'

'I see, sir. Most disturbing.'

'What did you say it was?'

'Most disturbing, sir.'

I snorted a trifle.

'Oh?' I said. 'And I suppose, if you had been in San Francisco when the earthquake started, you would just have lifted up your finger and said "Tweet, tweet! Shush, shush! Now, now! Come, come!" The English language, they used to tell me at school, is the richest in the world, crammed full from end to end with about a million red-hot adjectives. Yet the only one you can find to describe this ghastly business is the adjective "disturbing". It is not disturbing, Jeeves. It is . . . what's the word I want?'

'Cataclysmal, sir?'

'I shouldn't wonder. Well, what's to be done?'

'I will bring you a whisky-and-soda, sir.'

'What's the good of that?'

'It will refresh you, sir. And in the meantime, if it is your wish, I will give the matter consideration.'

'Carry on.'

'Very good, sir. I assume that it is not your desire to do anything that may in any way jeopardise the cordial relations which now exist between Miss Wickham and Mr. and Master Blumenfield?'

'Eh?'

'You would not, for example, contemplate proceeding to the Savoy Hotel and demanding the return of the dog?'

It was a tempting thought, but I shook the old onion firmly. There are things which a Wooster can do and things which, if you follow me, a Wooster cannot do. The procedure which he had indicated would undoubtedly have brought home the bacon, but the thwarted kid would have been bound to turn nasty and change his mind about the play. And, while I didn't think that any drama written by Bobbie's mother was likely to do the theatre-going public much good, I couldn't dash the cup of happiness, so to speak, from the blighted girl's lips, as it were. *Noblesse oblige* about sums the thing up.

'No, Jeeves,' I said. 'But if you can think of some way by which I can oil privily into the suite and sneak the animal out of it without causing any hard feelings, spill it.'

'I will endeavour to do so, sir.'

'Snap into it, then, without delay. They say fish are good for the brain. Have a go at the sardines and come back and report.'

'Very good, sir.'

It was about ten minutes later that he entered the presence once more.

'I fancy, sir—'

'Yes, Jeeves?'

'I rather fancy, sir, that I have discovered a plan of action.'

'Or scheme.'

'Or scheme, sir. A plan of action or scheme which will meet the situation. If I understood you rightly, sir, Mr. and Master Blumenfield have attended a motion-picture performance?'

'Correct.'

'In which case, they should not return to the hotel before five-fifteen?'

'Correct once more. Miss Wickham is scheduled to blow in at five-thirty to sign the contract.'

'The suite, therefore, is at present unoccupied.'

'Except for Mcintosh.'

'Except for Mcintosh, sir. Everything, accordingly, must depend on whether Mr. Blumenfield left instructions that, in the event of her arriving before he did, Miss Wickham was to be shown straight up to the suite, to await his return.'

'Why does everything depend on that?'

'Should he have done so, the matter becomes quite simple. All that is necessary is that Miss Wickham shall present herself at the hotel at five o'clock. She will go up to the suite. You will also have arrived at the hotel at five, sir, and will have made your way to the corridor outside the suite. If Mr. and Master Blumenfield have not returned, Miss Wickham will open the door and come out and you will go in, secure the dog, and take your departure.'

I stared at the man.

'How many tins of sardines did you eat, Jeeves?'

'None, sir. I am not fond of sardines.'

'You mean, you thought of this great, this ripe, this amazing scheme entirely without the impetus given to the brain by fish?'

'Yes, sir.'

'You stand alone, Jeeves.'

'Thank you, sir.'

'But I say!'

'Sir?'

'Suppose the dog won't come away with me? You know how meagre his intelligence is. By this time, especially when he's got used to a new place, he may have forgotten me completely and will look on me as a perfect stranger.'

'I had thought of that, sir. The most judicious move will be for you to sprinkle your trousers with aniseed.'

'Aniseed?'

'Yes, sir. It is extensively used in the dog-stealing industry.'

'But, Jeeves . . . dash it . . . aniseed?'

'I consider it essential, sir.'

'But where do you get the stuff?'

'At any chemist's, sir. If you will go out now and procure a small bottle, I will be telephoning to Miss Wickham to apprise her of the contemplated arrangements and ascertain whether she is to be admitted to the suite.'

I don't know what the record is for popping out and buying aniseed, but I should think I hold it. The thought of Aunt Agatha getting nearer and nearer to the Metropolis every minute induced a rare burst of speed. I was back at the flat so quick that I nearly met myself coming out.

Jeeves had good news.

'Everything is perfectly satisfactory, sir. Mr. Blumenfield did leave instructions that Miss Wickham was to be admitted to his suite. The young lady is now on her way to the hotel. By the time you reach it, you will find her there.'

You know, whatever you may say against old Jeeves – and I, for one, have never wavered in my opinion that his views on shirts for evening wear are hidebound and reactionary to a degree – you've got to admit that the man can plan a campaign. Napoleon could have taken his correspondence course. When he sketches out a scheme, all you have to do is to follow it in every detail, and there you are.

On the present occasion everything went absolutely according to plan. I had never realised before that dog-stealing could be so simple, having always regarded it rather as something that called for the ice-cool brain and the nerve of iron. I see now that a child can do it, if directed by Jeeves. I got to the hotel, sneaked up the stairs, hung about in the corridor trying to look like a potted palm in case anybody came along, and presently the door of the suite opened and Bobbie appeared, and suddenly, as I approached, out shot Mcintosh, sniffing passionately, and the next moment his nose was up against my Spring trouserings and he was drinking me in with every evidence of enjoyment. If I had been a bird that had been dead about five days, he could not have nuzzled me more heartily. Aniseed isn't a scent that I care for particularly myself, but it seemed to speak straight to the deeps in Mcintosh's soul.

The connexion, as it were, having been established in this manner, the rest was simple. I merely withdrew, followed by the animal in the order named. We passed down the stairs in good shape, self reeking to heaven and animal inhaling the bouquet, and after a few anxious moments were safe in a cab, homeward bound. As smooth a bit of work as London had seen that day.

Arrived at the flat, I handed Mcintosh to Jeeves and instructed him to shut him up in the bathroom or somewhere where the spell cast by my trousers would cease to operate. This done, I again paid the man a marked tribute.

'Jeeves,' I said, 'I have had occasion to express the view before, and I now express it again fearlessly – you stand in a class of your own.'

'Thank you very much, sir. I am glad that everything proceeded satisfactorily.'

'The festivities went like a breeze from start to finish. Tell me, were you always like this, or did it come on suddenly?'

'Sir?'

'The brain. The grey matter. Were you an outstandingly brilliant boy?'

'My mother thought me intelligent, sir.'

'You can't go by that. My mother thought *me* intelligent. Anyway, setting that aside for the moment, would a fiver be any use to you?'

'Thank you very much, sir.'

'Not that a fiver begins to cover it. Figure to yourself, Jeeves – try to envisage, if you follow what I mean, the probable behaviour of my Aunt Agatha if I had gone to her between the hours of six and seven and told her that Mcintosh had passed out of the picture. I should have had to leave London and grow a beard.'

'I can readily imagine, sir, that she would have been somewhat perturbed.'

'She would. And on the occasions when my Aunt Agatha is perturbed heroes dive down drain-pipes to get out of her way. However, as it is, all has ended happily. . . . Oh, great Scott!'

'Sir?'

I hesitated. It seemed a shame to cast a damper on the man just when he had extended himself so notably in the cause, but it had to be done.

'You've overlooked something, Jeeves.'

'Surely not, sir?'

'Yes, Jeeves, I regret to say that the late scheme or plan of action, while gilt-edged as far as I am concerned, has rather landed Miss Wickham in the cart.'

'In what way, sir?'

'Why, don't you see that, if they know that she was in the suite at the time of the outrage, the Blumenfields, father and son, will instantly assume that she was mixed up in Mcintosh's disappearance, with the result that in their pique and chagrin they will call off the deal about the play? I'm surprised at you not spotting that, Jeeves. You'd have done much better to eat those sardines, as I advised.'

I waggled the head rather sadly, and at this moment there was a ring at the front door bell. And not an ordinary ring, mind you, but one of those resounding peals that suggest that somebody with a high blood-pressure and a grievance stands without. I leaped in my tracks. My busy afternoon had left the old nervous system not quite in mid-season form.

'Good Lord, Jeeves!'

'Somebody at the door, sir.'

'Yes.'

'Probably Mr. Blumenfield, senior, sir.'

'What!'

'He rang up on the telephone, sir, shortly before you returned, to say that he was about to pay you a call.'

'You don't mean that?'

'Yes, sir.'

'Advise me, Jeeves.'

'I fancy the most judicious procedure would be for you to conceal yourself behind the settee, sir.'

I saw that his advice was good. I had never met this Blumenfield socially, but I had seen him from afar on the occasion when he and Cyril Bassington-Bassington had had their falling out, and he hadn't struck me then as a bloke with whom, if in one of his emotional moods, it would be at all agreeable to be shut up in a small room. A large, round, flat, overflowing bird, who might quite easily, if stirred, fall on a fellow and flatten him to the carpet.

So I nestled behind the settee, and in about five seconds there was a sound like a mighty, rushing wind and something extraordinarily substantial bounded into the sitting-room.

'This guy Wooster,' bellowed a voice that had been strengthened by a lifetime of ticking actors off at dress-rehearsals from the back of the theatre. 'Where is he?'

Jeeves continued suave.

'I could not say, sir.'

'He's sneaked my son's dog.'

'Indeed, sir?'

'Walked into my suite as cool as dammit and took the animal away.'

'Most disturbing, sir.'

'And you don't know where he is?'

'Mr. Wooster may be anywhere, sir. He is uncertain in his movements.'

The bloke Blumenfield gave a loud sniff.

'Odd smell here!'

'Yes, sir?'

'What is it?'

'Aniseed, sir.'

'Aniseed?'

'Yes, sir. Mr. Wooster sprinkles it on his trousers.'

'Sprinkles it on his trousers?'

'Yes, sir.'

'What on earth does he do that for?'

'I could not say, sir. Mr. Wooster's motives are always somewhat hard to follow. He is eccentric.'

'Eccentric? He must be a loony.'

'Yes, sir.'

'You mean he is?'

'Yes, sir!'

There was a pause. A long one.

'Oh?' said old Blumenfield, and it seemed to me that a good deal of what you might call the vim had gone out of his voice.

He paused again.

'Not *dangerous*?'

'Yes, sir, when roused.'

'Er – what rouses him chiefly?'

'One of Mr. Wooster's peculiarities is that he does not like the sight of gentlemen of full habit, sir. They seem to infuriate him.'

'You mean, fat men?'

'Yes, sir.'

'Why?'

'One cannot say, sir.'

There was another pause.

'*I'm* fat!' said old Blumenfield in a rather pensive sort of voice.

'I would not have ventured to suggest it myself, sir, but as you say so. . . . You may recollect that, on being informed that you were to be a member of the luncheon party, Mr. Wooster, doubting his power of self-control, refused to be present.'

'That's right. He went rushing out just as I arrived. I thought it odd at the time. My son thought it odd. We both thought it odd.'

'Yes, sir. Mr. Wooster, I imagine, wished to avoid any possible unpleasantness, such as has occurred before. . . . With regard to the smell of aniseed, sir, I fancy I have now located it. Unless I am mistaken it proceeds from behind the settee. No doubt Mr. Wooster is sleeping there.'

'Doing what?'

'Sleeping, sir.'

'Does he often sleep on the floor?'

'Most afternoons, sir. Would you desire me to wake him?'

'No!'

'I thought you had something that you wished to say to Mr. Wooster, sir.'

Old Blumenfield drew a deep breath. 'So did I,' he said. 'But I find I haven't. Just get me alive out of here, that's all I ask.'

I heard the door close, and a little while later the front door banged. I crawled out. It hadn't been any too cosy behind the settee, and I was glad to be elsewhere. Jeeves came trickling back.

'Gone, Jeeves?'

'Yes, sir.'

I bestowed an approving look on him.

'One of your best efforts, Jeeves.'

'Thank you, sir.'

'But what beats me is why he ever came here. What made him think that I had sneaked Mcintosh away?'

'I took the liberty of recommending Miss Wickham to tell Mr. Blumenfield that she had observed you removing the animal from his suite, sir. The point which you raised regarding the possibility of her being suspected of complicity in the affair, had not escaped me. It seemed to me that this would establish her solidly in Mr. Blumenfield's good opinion.'

'I see. Risky, of course, but possibly justified. Yes, on the whole, justified. What's that you've got there?'

'A five pound note, sir.'

'Ah, the one I gave you?'

'No, sir. The one Mr. Blumenfield gave me.'

'Eh? Why did he give you a fiver?'

'He very kindly presented it to me on my handing him the dog, sir.'

I gaped at the man.

'You don't mean to say—?'

'Not Mcintosh, sir. Mcintosh is at present in my bedroom. This was another animal of the same species which I purchased at the shop in Bond Street during your absence. Except to the eye of love, one Aberdeen terrier looks very much like another Aberdeen terrier, sir. Mr. Blumenfield, I am happy to say, did not detect the innocent subterfuge.'

'Jeeves,' I said – and I am not ashamed to confess that there was a spot of chokiness in the voice – 'there is none like you, none.'

'Thank you very much, sir.'

'Owing solely to the fact that your head bulges in unexpected spots, thus enabling you to do about twice as much bright thinking in any given time as any other two men in existence, happiness, you might say, reigns supreme. Aunt Agatha is on velvet, I am on velvet, the Wickhams, mother and daughter, are on velvet, the Blumenfields, father and son, are on velvet. As far as the eye can reach, a solid mass of humanity, owing to you, all on velvet. A fiver is not sufficient, Jeeves. If I thought the world thought that Bertram Wooster thought a measly five pounds an adequate reward for such services as yours, I should never hold my head up again. Have another?'

'Thank you, sir.'

'And one more?'

'Thank you very much, sir.'

'And a third for luck?'

'Really, sir, I am exceedingly obliged. Excuse me, sir, I fancy I heard the telephone.'

He pushed out into the hall, and I heard him doing a good deal of the 'Yes, madam,' 'Certainly, madam!' stuff. Then he came back.

'Mrs. Spenser Gregson on the telephone, sir.'

'Aunt Agatha?'

'Yes, sir. Speaking from Victoria Station. She desires to communicate with you with reference to the dog Mcintosh. I gather that she wishes to hear from your own lips that all is well with the little fellow, sir.'

I straightened the tie. I pulled down the waistcoat. I shot the cuffs. I felt absolutely all-righto.

'Lead me to her,' I said.

I was lunching at my Aunt Dahlia's, and despite the fact that Anatole, her outstanding cook, had rather excelled himself in the matter of the bill-of-fare, I'm bound to say the food was more or less turning to ashes in my mouth. You see, I had some bad news to break to her – always a prospect that takes the edge off the appetite. She wouldn't be pleased, I knew, and when not pleased Aunt Dahlia, having spent most of her youth in the hunting-field, has a crispish way of expressing herself.

However, I supposed I had better have a dash at it and get it over.

'Aunt Dahlia,' I said, facing the issue squarely.

'Hullo?'

'You know that cruise of yours?'

'Yes.'

'That yachting-cruise you are planning?'

'Yes.'

'That jolly cruise in your yacht in the Mediterranean to which you so kindly invited me and to which I have been looking forward with such keen anticipation?'

'Get on, fathead, what about it?'

I swallowed a chunk of *côtelette-suprème-aux-choux-fleurs* and slipped her the distressing info'.

'I'm frightfully sorry, Aunt Dahlia,' I said, 'but I shan't be able to come.'

As I had foreseen, she goggled.

'What!'

'I'm afraid not.'

'You poor, miserable hell-hound, what do you mean, you won't be able to come?

'Well, I won't.'

'Why not?'

'Matters of the most extreme urgency render my presence in the Metropolis imperative.'

She sniffed.

'I suppose what you really mean is that you're hanging round some unfortunate girl again?'

I didn't like the way she put it, but I admit I was stunned by her penetration, if that's the word I want. I mean the sort of thing detectives have.

'Yes, Aunt Dahlia,' I said, 'you have guessed my secret. I do indeed love.'

'Who is she?'

'A Miss Pendlebury. Christian name, Gwladys. She spells it with a "w".'

'With a "g", you mean.'

'With a "w" *and* a "g".'

'Not Gwladys?'

'That's it.'

The relative uttered a yowl.

'You sit there and tell me you haven't enough sense to steer clear of a girl who calls herself Gwladys? Listen, Bertie,' said Aunt Dahlia earnestly, 'I'm an older woman than you are – well, you know what I mean – and I can tell you a thing or two. And one of them is that no good can come of association with anything labelled Gwladys or Ysobel or Ethyl or Mabelle or Kathryn. But particularly Gwladys. What sort of girl is she?'

'Slightly divine.'

'She isn't that female I saw driving you at sixty miles p.h. in the Park the other day. In a red two-seater?'

'She did drive me in the Park the other day. I thought it

rather a hopeful sign. And her Widgeon Seven is red.'

Aunt Dahlia looked relieved.

'Oh well, then, she'll probably break your silly fat neck before she can get you to the altar. That's some consolation. Where did you meet her?'

'At a party in Chelsea. She's an artist.'

'Ye gods!'

'And swings a jolly fine brush, let me tell you. She's painted a portrait of me. Jeeves and I hung it up in the flat this morning. I have an idea Jeeves doesn't like it.'

'Well, if it's anything like you I don't see why he should. An artist! Calls herself Gwladys! And drives a car in the sort of way Campbell would if he were pressed for time.' She brooded awhile. 'Well, it's all very sad, but I can't see why you won't come on the yacht.'

I explained.

'It would be madness to leave the metrop. at this juncture,' I said. 'You know what girls are. They forget the absent face. And I'm not at all easy in my mind about a certain cove of the name of Lucius Pim. Apart from the fact that he's an artist, too, which forms a bond, his hair waves. One must never discount wavy hair, Aunt Dahlia. Moreover, this bloke is one of those strong, masterful men. He treats Gwladys as if she were less than the dust beneath his taxi wheels. He criticises her hats and says nasty things about her chiaroscuro. For some reason, I've often noticed, this always seems to fascinate girls, and it has some-times occurred to me that, being myself more the parfait gentle knight, if you know what I mean, I am in grave danger of getting the short end. Taking all these things into consideration, then, I cannot breeze off to the Mediterranean, leaving this Pim a clear field. You must see that?'

Aunt Dahlia laughed. Rather a nasty laugh. Scorn in its *timbre*, or so it seemed to me.

'I shouldn't worry,' she said. 'You don't suppose for a moment that Jeeves will sanction the match?'

I was stung.

'Do you imply, Aunt Dahlia,' I said – and I can't remember if I rapped the table with the handle of my fork or not, but I rather think I did – 'that I allow Jeeves to boss me to the extent of stopping me marrying somebody I want to marry?'

'Well, he stopped you wearing a moustache, didn't he? And purple socks. And soft-fronted shirts with dress-clothes.'

'That is a different matter altogether.'

'Well, I'm prepared to make a small bet with you, Bertie. Jeeves will stop this match.'

'What absolute rot!'

'And if he doesn't like that portrait, he will get rid of it.'

'I never heard such dashed nonsense in my life.'

'And, finally, you wretched, pie-faced wambler, he will present you on board my yacht at the appointed hour. I don't know how he will do it, but you will be there, all complete with yachting-cap and spare pair of socks.'

'Let us change the subject, Aunt Dahlia,' I said coldly.

Being a good deal stirred up by the attitude of the flesh-and-blood at the luncheon-table, I had to go for a bit of a walk in the Park after leaving, to soothe the nervous system. By about four-thirty the ganglions had ceased to vibrate, and I returned to the flat. Jeeves was in the sitting-room, looking at the portrait.

I felt a trifle embarrassed in the man's presence, because just before leaving I had informed him of my intention to scratch the yacht-trip, and he had taken it on the chin a bit. You see, he had been looking forward to it rather. From the moment I had accepted the invitation, there had been a sort of nautical glitter in his eye, and I'm not sure I hadn't heard him trolling chanties in the kitchen. I think some ancestor of his must have been one of Nelson's tars or something, for he has always had the urge of the salt sea in his blood. I have noticed him on liners, when we were going to America, striding the deck with a sailorly roll and giving the distinct impression of being just about to heave the main-brace or splice the binnacle.

So, though I had explained my reasons, taking the man fully into my confidence and concealing nothing, I knew that he was distinctly peeved; and my first act, on entering, was to do the cheery a bit. I joined him in front of the portrait.

'Looks good, Jeeves, what?'

'Yes, sir.'

'Nothing like a spot of art for brightening the home.'

'No, sir.'

'Seems to lend the room a certain – what shall I say—'

'Yes, sir.'

The responses were all right, but his manner was far from hearty, and I decided to tackle him squarely. I mean, dash it. I mean, I don't know if you have ever had your portrait painted, but if you have you will understand my feelings. The spectacle of one's portrait hanging on the wall creates in one a sort of paternal fondness for the thing: and what you demand from the outside public is approval and enthusiasm – not the curling lip, the twitching nostril, and the kind of supercilious look which you see in the eye of a dead mackerel. Especially is this so when the artist is a girl for whom you have conceived sentiments deeper and warmer than those of ordinary friendship.

'Jeeves,' I said, 'you don't like this spot of art.'

'Oh, yes, sir.'

'No. Subterfuge is useless. I can read you like a book. For some reason this spot of art fails to appeal to you. What do you object to about it?'

'Is not the colour-scheme a trifle bright, sir?'

'I had not observed it, Jeeves. Anything else?'

'Well, in my opinion, sir, Miss Pendlebury has given you a somewhat too hungry expression.'

'Hungry?'

'A little like that of a dog regarding a distant bone, sir.'

I checked the fellow.

'There is no resemblance whatever, Jeeves, to a dog regarding a distant bone. The look to which you allude is wistful and denotes Soul.'

'I see, sir.'

I proceeded to another subject.

'Miss Pendlebury said she might look in this afternoon to inspect the portrait. Did she turn up?'

'Yes, sir.'

'But has left?'

'Yes, sir.'

'You mean she's gone, what?'

'Precisely, sir.'

'She didn't say anything about coming back, I suppose?'

'No, sir. I received the impression that it was not Miss Pendlebury's intention to return. She was a little upset, sir, and expressed a desire to go to her studio and rest.'

'Upset? What was she upset about?'

'The accident, sir.'

I didn't actually clutch the brow, but I did a bit of mental brow-clutching, as it were.

'Don't tell me she had an accident!'

'Yes, sir.'

'What sort of accident?'

'Automobile, sir.'

'Was she hurt?'

'No, sir. Only the gentleman.'

'What gentleman?'

'Miss Pendlebury had the misfortune to run over a gentleman in her car almost immediately opposite this building. He sustained a slight fracture of the leg.'

'Too bad! But Miss Pendlebury is all right?'

'Physically, sir, her condition appeared to be satisfactory. She was suffering a certain distress of mind.'

'Of course, with her beautiful, sympathetic nature. Naturally. It's a hard world for a girl, Jeeves, with fellows flinging themselves under the wheels of her car in a long, unending stream. It must have been a great shock to her. What became of the chump?'

'The gentleman, sir?'

'Yes.'

'He is in your spare bedroom, sir.'

'What!'

'Yes, sir.'

'In my spare bedroom?'

'Yes, sir. It was Miss Pendlebury's desire that he should be taken there. She instructed me to telegraph to the gentleman's sister, sir, who is in Paris, advising her of the accident. I also summoned a medical man, who gave it as his opinion that the patient should remain for the time being *in statu quo*.'

'You mean, the corpse is on the premises for an indefinite visit?'

'Yes, sir.'

'Jeeves, this is a bit thick!'

'Yes, sir.'

And I meant it, dash it. I mean to say, a girl can be pretty heftily divine and ensnare the heart and what not, but she's no right to turn a fellow's flat into a morgue. I'm bound to say that for a moment passion ebbed a trifle.

'Well, I suppose I'd better go and introduce myself to the blighter. After all, I am his host. Has he a name?'

'Mr. Pim, sir.'

'Pim!'

'Yes, sir. And the young lady addressed him as Lucius. It was owing to the fact that he was on his way here to examine the portrait which she had painted that Mr. Pim happened to be in the roadway at the moment when Miss Pendlebury turned the corner.'

I headed for the spare bedroom. I was perturbed to a degree. I don't know if you have ever loved and been handicapped in your wooing by a wavy-haired rival, but one of the things you don't want in such circs, is the rival parking himself on the premises with a broken leg. Apart from anything else, the advantage the position gives him is obviously terrific. There he is, sitting up and toying with a grape, and looking pale and interesting, the object of the girl's pity and concern, and where do you get off, bounding about the place in morning costume and spats and with the rude flush of health on the cheek? It seemed to me that things were beginning to look pretty mouldy.

I found Lucius Pim lying in bed, draped in a suit of my pyjamas, smoking one of my cigarettes, and reading a detective story. He waved the cigarette at me in what I considered a dashed patronising manner.

'Ah, Wooster!' he said.

'Not so much of the "Ah, Wooster!"' I replied brusquely. 'How soon can you be moved?'

'In a week or so, I fancy.'

'In a week!'

'Or so. For the moment, the doctor insists on perfect quiet and repose. So forgive me, old man, for asking you not to raise your voice. A hushed whisper is the stuff to give the troops. And now, Wooster, about this accident. We must come to an understanding.'

'Are you sure you can't be moved?'

'Quite. The doctor said so.'

'I think we ought to get a second opinion.'

'Useless, my dear fellow. He was most emphatic, and evidently a man who knew his job. Don't worry about my not being comfortable here. I shall be quite all right. I like this bed. And now, to return to the subject of this accident. My sister will be arriving tomorrow. She will be greatly upset. I am her favourite brother.'

'You are?'

'I am.'

'How many of you are there?'

'Six.'

'And you're her favourite?'

'I am.'

It seemed to me that the other five must be pretty fairly sub-human, but I didn't say so. We Woosters can curb the tongue.

'She married a bird named Slingsby. Slingsby's Superb Soups. He rolls in money. But do you think I can get him to lend a trifle from time to time to a needy brother-in-law?' said Lucius Pim bitterly. 'No, sir! However, that is neither here nor there. The point is that my sister loves me devotedly, and, this being the case, she might try to prosecute and persecute and generally bite pieces out of poor little Gwladys if she knew that it was she who was driving the car that laid me out. She must never know, Wooster. I appeal to you as a man of honour to keep your mouth shut.'

'Naturally.'

'I'm glad you grasp the point so readily, Wooster. You are not the fool people take you for.'

'Who takes me for a fool?'

The Pim raised his eyebrows slightly.

'Don't people?' he said. 'Well, well. Anyway, that's settled. Unless I can think of something better I shall tell my sister that I was knocked down by a car which drove on without stopping and I didn't get its number. And now perhaps you had better leave me. The doctor made a point of quiet and repose. Moreover, I want to go on with this story. The villain has just dropped a cobra down the heroine's chimney, and I must be at her side. It is impossible not to be thrilled by Edgar Wallace. I'll ring if I want anything.'

I headed for the sitting-room. I found Jeeves there, staring at the portrait in rather a marked manner, as if it hurt him.

'Jeeves,' I said, 'Mr. Pim appears to be a fixture.'

'Yes, sir.'

'For the nonce, at any rate. And tomorrow we shall have his sister, Mrs. Slingsby, of Slingsby's Superb Soups, in our midst.'

'Yes, sir. I telegraphed to Mrs. Slingsby shortly before four. Assuming her to have been at her hotel in Paris at the moment of the telegram's delivery, she will no doubt take a boat early tomorrow afternoon, reaching Dover – or, should she prefer the alternative route, Folkestone – in time to begin the railway journey at an hour which will enable her to arrive in London at about seven. She will possibly proceed first to her London residence—'

'Yes, Jeeves,' I said, 'Yes. A gripping story, full of action and human interest. You must have it set to music some time and sing it. Meanwhile, get this into your head. It is imperative that Mrs. Slingsby does not learn that it was Miss Pendlebury who broke her brother in two places. I shall require you, therefore, to approach Mr. Pim before she arrives, ascertain exactly what tale he intends to tell, and be prepared to back it up in every particular.'

'Very good, sir.'

'And now, Jeeves, what of Miss Pendlebury?'

'Sir?'

'She's sure to call to make inquiries.'

'Yes, sir.'

'Well, she mustn't find me here. You know all about women, Jeeves?'

'Yes, sir.'

'Then tell me this. Am I not right in supposing that if Miss Pendlebury is in a position to go into the sick-room, take a long look at the interesting invalid, and then pop out, with the memory of that look fresh in her mind, and get a square sight of me lounging about in sponge-bag trousers, she will draw damaging comparisons? You see what I mean? Look on this picture and on that – the one romantic, the other not . . . Eh?'

'Very true, sir. It is a point which I had intended to bring to your attention. An invalid undoubtedly exercises a powerful appeal to the motherliness which exists in every woman's heart, sir. Invalids seem to stir their deepest feelings. The poet Scott has put the matter neatly in the lines – "Oh, Woman in our hours of ease uncertain, coy, and hard to please. . . . When pain and anguish rack the brow—"'

I held up a hand.

'At some other time, Jeeves,' I said, 'I shall be delighted to hear you say your piece, but just now I am not in the mood. The position being as I have outlined, I propose to clear out early tomorrow morning and not to reappear until nightfall. I shall take the car and dash down to Brighton for the day.'

'Very good, sir.'

'It is better so, is it not, Jeeves?'

'Indubitably, sir.'

'I think so, too. The sea breezes will tone up my system, which sadly needs a dollop of toning. I leave you in charge of the old home.'

'Very good, sir.'

'Convey my regrets and sympathy to Miss Pendlebury and tell her I have been called away on business.'

'Yes, sir.'

'Should the Slingsby require refreshment, feed her in moderation.'

'Very good, sir.'

'And, in poisoning Mr. Pim's soup, don't use arsenic, which is readily detected. Go to a good chemist and get something that leaves no traces.' I sighed, and cocked an eye at the portrait.

'All this is very wonky, Jeeves.'

'Yes, sir.'

'When that portrait was painted, I was a happy man.'

'Yes, sir.'

'Ah, well, Jeeves!'

'Very true, sir.' And we left it at that.

It was latish when I got back on the following evening. What with a bit of ozone-sniffing, a good dinner, and a nice run home in the moonlight with the old car going as sweet as a nut, I was feeling in pretty good shape once more. In fact, coming through

Purley, I went so far as to sing a trifle. The spirit of the Woosters is a buoyant spirit, and optimism had begun to reign again in the W. bosom.

The way I looked at it was, I saw I had been mistaken in assuming that a girl must necessarily love a fellow just because he has broken a leg. At first, no doubt, Gwladys Pendlebury would feel strangely drawn to the Pim when she saw him lying there a more or less total loss. But it would not be long before other reflections crept in. She would ask herself if she were wise in trusting her life's happiness to a man who hadn't enough sense to leap out of the way when he saw a car coming. She would tell herself that, if this sort of thing had happened once, who knew that it might not go on happening again and again all down the long years. And she would recoil from a married life which consisted entirely of going to hospitals and taking her husband fruit. She would realise how much better off she would be, teamed up with a fellow like Bertram Wooster, who, whatever his faults, at least walked on the pavement and looked up and down a street before he crossed it.

It was in excellent spirits, accordingly, that I put the car in the garage, and it was with a merry Tra-la on my lips that I let myself into the flat as Big Ben began to strike eleven. I rang the bell and presently, as if he had divined my wishes, Jeeves came in with siphon and decanter.

'Home again, Jeeves,' I said, mixing a spot.

'Yes, sir.'

'What has been happening in my absence? Did Miss Pendlebury call?'

'Yes, sir. At about two o'clock.'

'And left?'

'At about six, sir.'

I didn't like this so much. A four-hour visit struck me as a bit sinister. However, there was nothing to be done about it.

'And Mrs. Slingsby?'

'She arrived shortly after eight and left at ten, sir.'

'Ah? Agitated?'

'Yes, sir. Particularly when she left. She was very desirous of seeing you, sir.'

'Seeing me?'

'Yes, sir.'

'Wanted to thank me brokenly I suppose, for so courteously allowing her favourite brother a place to have his game legs in. Eh?'

'Possibly, sir. On the other hand, she alluded to you in terms suggestive of disapprobation, sir.'

'She – what?'

'"Feckless idiot" was one of the expressions she employed, sir.'

'Feckless idiot?'

'Yes, sir.'

I couldn't make it out. I simply couldn't see what the woman had based her judgment on. My Aunt Agatha has frequently said that sort of thing about me, but she has known me from a boy.

'I must look into this, Jeeves. Is Mr. Pim asleep?'

'No, sir. He rang the bell a moment ago to inquire if we had not a better brand of cigarette in the flat.'

'He did, did he?'

'Yes, sir.'

'The accident doesn't seem to have affected his nerve.'

'No, sir.'

I found Lucius Pim sitting propped up among the pillows, reading his detective story.

'Ah, Wooster,' he said. 'Welcome home. I say, in case you were worrying, it's all right about that cobra. The hero had got at it without the villain's knowledge and extracted its poison-fangs. With the result that when it fell down the chimney and started trying to bite the heroine its efforts were null and void. I doubt if a cobra has ever felt so silly.'

'Never mind about cobras.'

'It's no good saying Never mind about cobras,' said Lucius Pim in a gentle, rebuking sort of voice. 'You've jolly well *got* to mind about cobras, if they haven't had their poison-fangs extracted. Ask anyone. By the way, my sister looked in. She wants to have a word with you.'

'And I want to have a word with her.'

'"Two minds with but a single thought". What she wants to talk to you about is this accident of mine. You remember that story I was to tell her? About the car driving on? Well, the understanding was, if you recollect, that I was only to tell it if I couldn't think of something better. Fortunately, I thought of something much better. It came to me in a flash as I lay in bed looking at the ceiling. You see, that driving-on story was thin. People don't knock fellows down and break their legs and go driving on. The thing wouldn't have held water for a minute. So I told her you did it.'

'What!'

'I said it was you who did it in your car. Much more likely. Makes the whole thing neat and well-rounded. I knew you would approve. At all costs we have got to keep it from her that I was outed by Gwladys. I made it as easy for you as I could, saying that you were a bit pickled at the time and so not to be blamed for what you did. Some fellows wouldn't have thought of that. Still,' said Lucius Pim with a sigh, 'I'm afraid she's not any too pleased with you.'

'She isn't, isn't she?'

'No, she is not. And I strongly recommend you, if you want anything like a pleasant interview tomorrow, to sweeten her a bit overnight.'

'How do you mean, sweeten her?'

'I'd suggest you sent her some flowers. It would be a graceful gesture. Roses are her favourites. Shoot her in a few roses – Number Three, Hill Street, is the address – and it may make all the difference. I think it my duty to inform you, old man, that my sister Beatrice is rather a tough egg, when roused. My brother-in-law is due back from New York at any moment and the danger, as I see it, is that Beatrice, unless sweetened, will get at him and make him bring actions against you for torts and malfeasances and what not and get thumping damages. He isn't overfond of me and, left to himself, would rather approve than otherwise of people who broke my legs: but he's crazy about Beatrice and will do anything she asks him to. So my advice is, Gather ye rose-buds while ye may and bung them in to Number Three, Hill Street. Otherwise, the case of Slingsby *v.* Wooster will be on the calendar before you can say What-ho.'

I gave the fellow a look. Lost on him, of course.

'It's a pity you didn't think of all that before,' I said. And it wasn't so much the actual words, if you know what I mean, as the way I said it.

'I thought of it all right,' said Lucius Pim. 'But, as we were both agreed that at all costs—'

'Oh, all right,' I said. 'All right, all right.'

'You aren't annoyed ?' said Lucius Pim, looking at me with a touch of surprise.

'Oh, no!'

'Splendid,' said Lucius Pim, relieved. 'I knew you would feel that I had done the only possible thing. It would have been awful if Beatrice had found out about Gwladys. I daresay you have noticed, Wooster, that when women find themselves in a position to take a running kick at one of their own sex they are twice as rough on her as they would be on a man. Now, you, being of the male persuasion, will find everything made nice and smooth for you. A quart of assorted roses, a few smiles, tactful word or two, and she'll have melted before you know where you are. Play your cards properly, and you and Beatrice will be laughing merrily and having a game of Round and Round the Mulberry Bush together in about five minutes. Better not let Slingsby's Soups catch you at it, however. He's very jealous where Beatrice is concerned. And now you'll forgive me, old chap, if I send you away. The doctor says I ought not to talk too much for a day or two. Besides, it's time for bye-bye.'

The more I thought it over, the better that idea of sending those roses looked. Lucius Pim was not a man I was fond of – in fact, if I had had to choose between him and a cockroach as a companion for a walking-tour, the cockroach would have had it by a short head – but there was no doubt that he had outlined the right policy. His advice was good, and I decided to follow it. Rising next morning at ten-fifteen, I swallowed a strengthening breakfast and legged it off to that flower-shop in Piccadilly. I couldn't leave the thing to Jeeves. It was essentially a mission that demanded the personal touch. I laid out a couple of quid on a sizable bouquet, sent it with my card to Hill Street, and then looked in at the Drones for a brief refresher. It is a thing I don't often do in the morning, but this threatened to be rather a special morning.

It was about noon when I got back to the flat. I went into the sitting-room and tried to adjust the mind to the coming interview. It had to be faced, of course, but it wasn't any good my telling myself that it was going to be one of those jolly scenes the memory of which cheer you up as you sit toasting your toes at the fire in your old age. I stood or fell by the roses. If they sweetened the Slingsby, all would be well. If they failed to sweeten her, Bertram was undoubtedly for it.

The clock ticked on, but she did not come. A late riser, I took it, and was slightly encouraged by the reflection. My experience of women has been that the earlier they leave the hay the more vicious specimens they are apt to be. My Aunt Agatha, for instance, is always up with the lark, and look at her.

Still, you couldn't be sure that this rule always worked, and after a while the suspense began to get in amongst me a bit. To divert the mind, I fetched the old putter out of its bag and began to practise putts into a glass. After all, even if the Slingsby turned out to be all that I had pictured her in my gloomier moments, I should have improved my close-to-the-hole work on the green and be that much up, at any rate.

It was while I was shaping for a rather tricky shot that the front door bell went.

I picked up the glass and shoved the putter behind the settee. It struck me that if the woman found me engaged on what you might call a frivolous pursuit she might take it to indicate lack of remorse and proper feeling. I straightened the collar, pulled down the waistcoat, and managed to fasten on the face a sort of sad half-smile which was welcoming without being actually jovial. It looked all right in the mirror, and I held it as the door opened.

'Mr. Slingsby,' announced Jeeves.

And, having spoken these words, he closed the door and left us alone together.

For quite a time there wasn't anything in the way of chit-chat. The shock of expecting Mrs. Slingsby and finding myself confronted by something entirely different – in fact, not the same thing at all – seemed to have affected the vocal chords. And the visitor didn't appear to be disposed to make light conversation himself. He stood there looking strong and silent. I suppose you have to be like that if you want to manufacture anything in the nature of a really convincing soup.

Slingsby's Superb Soups was a Roman Emperor-looking sort of bird, with keen, penetrating eyes and one of those jutting chins. The eyes seemed to be fixed on me in a dashed unpleasant stare and, unless I was mistaken, he was grinding his teeth a trifle. For some reason he appeared to have taken a strong dislike to me at sight, and I'm bound to say this rather puzzled me. I don't pretend to have one of those Fascinating Personalities which you get from studying the booklets advertised in the back pages of the magazines, but I couldn't recall another case in the whole of my career where a single glimpse of the old map had been enough to make anyone look as if he wanted to foam at the mouth. Usually, when people meet me for the first time, they don't seem to know I'm there.

However, I exerted myself to play the host.

'Mr. Slingsby?'

'That is my name.'

'Just got back from America?'

'I landed this morning.'

'Sooner than you were expected, what?'

'So I imagine.'

'Very glad to see you.'

'You will not be long.'

I took time off to do a bit of gulping. I saw now what had happened. This bloke had been home, seen his wife, heard the story of the accident, and had hastened round to the flat to slip it across me. Evidently those roses had not sweetened the female of the species. The only thing to do now seemed to be to take a stab at sweetening the male.

'Have a drink?' I said.

'No!'

'A cigarette?'

'No!'

'A chair?'

'No!'

I went into the silence once more. These non-drinking, non-smoking, non-sitters are hard birds to handle.

'Don't grin at me, sir!'

I shot a glance at myself in the mirror, and saw what he meant. The sad half-smile *had* slopped over a bit. I adjusted it, and there was another pause.

'Now, sir,' said the Superb Souper. 'To business. I think I need scarcely tell you why I am here.'

'No. Of course. Absolutely. It's about that little matter—'

He gave a snort which nearly upset a vase on the mantelpiece.

'Little matter? So you consider it a little matter, do you?'

'Well—'

'Let me tell you, sir, that when I find that during my absence from the country a man has been annoying my wife with his importunities I regard it as anything but a little matter. And I shall endeavour,' said the Souper, the eyes gleaming a trifle brighter as he rubbed his hands together in a hideous, menacing way, 'to make you see the thing in the same light.'

I couldn't make head or tail of this. I simply couldn't follow him. The lemon began to swim.

'Eh?' I said. 'Your wife?'

'You heard me.'

'There must be some mistake.'

'There is. You made it.'

'But I don't know your wife.'

'Ha!'

'I've never even met her.'

'Tchah!'

'Honestly, I haven't.'

'Bah!'

He drank me in for a moment.

'Do you deny you sent her flowers?'

I felt the heart turn a double somersault. I began to catch his drift.

'Flowers!' he proceeded. 'Roses, sir. Great, fat, beastly roses. Enough of them to sink a ship. Your card was attached to them by a small pin—'

His voice died away in a sort of gurgle, and I saw that he was staring at something behind me. I spun round, and there, in the doorway – I hadn't seen it open, because during the last spasm of dialogue I had been backing cautiously towards it – there in the doorway stood a female. One glance was enough to tell me who she was. No woman could look so like Lucius Pi Pim who hadn't the misfortune to be related to him. It was Sister Beatrice, the tough egg. I saw all. She had left home before the flowers had arrived: she had sneaked, unsweetened, into the flat, while I was fortifying the system at the Drones; and here she was.

'Er—' I said.

'Alexander!' said the female.

'Goo!' said the Souper. Or it may have been Coo!

Whatever it was, it was in the nature of a battlecry or slogan of war. The Souper's worst suspicions had obviously been confirmed. His eyes shone with a strange light. His chin pushed itself out another couple of inches. He clenched and unclenched his fingers once or twice, as if to make sure that they were working properly and could be relied on to do a good, clean job of strangling. Then, once more observing 'Coo!' (or 'Goo!'), he sprang forward, trod on the golf-ball I had been practising putting with, and took one of the finest tosses I have ever witnessed. The purler of a lifetime. For a moment the air seemed to be full of arms and legs, and then, with a thud that nearly dislocated the flat, he made a forced landing against the wall.

And, feeling I had had about all I wanted, I oiled from the room and was in the act of grabbing my hat from the rack in the hall, when Jeeves appeared.

'I fancied I heard a noise, sir,' said Jeeves.

'Quite possibly,' I said. 'It was Mr. Slingsby.'

'Sir?'

'Mr. Slingsby practising Russian dances,' I explained. 'I rather think he has fractured an assortment of limbs. Better go in and see.'

'Very good, sir.'

'If he is the wreck I imagine, put him in my room and send for the doctor. The flat is filling up nicely with the various units of the Pim family and its connexions, eh, Jeeves?'

'Yes, sir.'

'I think the supply is about exhausted, but should any aunts or uncles by marriage come along and break their limbs, bed them out on the Chesterfield.'

'Very good, sir.'

'I, personally, Jeeves,' I said, opening the front door and

pausing on the threshold, 'am off to Paris. I will wire you the address. Notify me in due course when the place is free from Pims and completely purged of Slingsbys, and I will return. Oh, and Jeeves.'

'Sir?'

'Spare no effort to mollify these birds. They think – at least, Slingsby (female) thinks, and what she thinks today he will think tomorrow – that it was I who ran over Mr. Pim in my car. Endeavour during my absence to sweeten them.'

'Very good, sir.'

'And now perhaps you had better be going in and viewing the body. I shall proceed to the Drones, where I shall lunch, subsequently catching the two o'clock train at Charing Cross. Meet me there with an assortment of luggage.'

It was a matter of three weeks or so before Jeeves sent me the 'All clear' signal. I spent the time pottering pretty perturbedly about Paris and environs. It is a city I am fairly fond of, but I was glad to be able to return to the old home. I hopped on to a passing aeroplane and a couple of hours later was bowling through Croydon on my way to the centre of things. It was somewhere down in the Sloane Square neighbourhood that I first caught sight of the posters.

A traffic block had occurred, and I was glancing idly this way and that, when suddenly my eye was caught by something that looked familiar. And then I saw what it was.

Pasted on a blank wall and measuring about a hundred feet each way was an enormous poster, mostly red and blue. At the top of it were the words:

SLINGSBY'S SUPERB SOUPS

and at the bottom:

SUCCULENT AND STRENGTHENING

And, in between me. Yes, dash it. Bertram Wooster in person. A reproduction of the Pendlebury portrait, perfect in every detail.

It was the sort of thing to make a fellow's eyes flicker, and mine flickered. You might say a mist seemed to roll before them. Then it lifted, and I was able to get a good long look before the traffic moved on.

Of all the absolutely foul sights I have ever seen, this took the biscuit with ridiculous ease. The thing was a bally libel on the Wooster face, and yet it was as unmistakable as if it had had my name under it. I saw now what Jeeves had meant when he said that the portrait had given me a hungry look. In the poster this look had become one of bestial greed. There I sat absolutely slavering through a monocle about six inches in circumference at a plateful of soup, looking as if I hadn't had a meal for weeks. The whole thing seemed to take one straight away into a different and a dreadful world.

I woke from a species of trance or coma to find myself at the door of the block of flats. To buzz upstairs and charge into the home was with me the work of a moment.

Jeeves came shimmering down the hall, the respectful beam of welcome on his face.

'I am glad to see you back, sir.'

'Never mind about that,' I yipped. 'What about—?'

'The posters, sir? I was wondering if you might have observed them.'

'I observed them!'

'Striking, sir?'

'Very striking. Now, perhaps you'll kindly explain—'

'You instructed me, if you recollect, sir, to spare no effort to mollify Mr. Slingsby.'

'Yes, but—'

'It proved a somewhat difficult task, sir. For some time Mr. Slingsby, on the advice and owing to the persuasion of Mrs. Slingsby, appeared to be resolved to institute an action in law against you – a procedure which I knew you would find most distasteful.'

'Yes, but—'

'And then, the first day he was able to leave his bed, he observed the portrait, and it seemed to me judicious to point out to him its possibilities as an advertising medium. He readily fell in with the suggestion and, on my assurance that, should he abandon the projected action in law, you would willingly permit the use of the portrait, he entered into negotiations with Miss Pendlebury for the purchase of the copyright.'

'Oh? Well, I hope she's got something out of it, at any rate?'

'Yes, sir. Mr. Pim, acting as Miss Pendlebury's agent, drove, I understand, an extremely satisfactory bargain.'

'He acted as her agent, eh?'

'Yes, sir. In his capacity as fiancé to the young lady, sir.'

'Fiancé!'

'Yes, sir.'

It shows how the sight of that poster had got into my ribs when I state that, instead of being laid out cold by this announcement, I merely said 'Ha!' or 'Ho!' or it may have been 'H'm'. After the poster, nothing seemed to matter.

'After that poster, Jeeves,' I said, 'nothing seems to matter.'

'No, sir?'

'No, Jeeves. A woman has tossed my heart lightly away, but what of it?'

'Exactly, sir.'

'The voice of Love seemed to call to me, but it was a wrong number. Is that going to crush me?'

'No, sir.'

'No, Jeeves. It is not. But what does matter is this ghastly business of my face being spread from end to end of the Metropolis with the eyes fixed on a plate of Slingsby's Superb Soup. I must leave London. The lads at the Drones will kid me without ceasing.'

'Yes, sir. And Mrs. Spenser Gregson—'

I paled visibly. I hadn't thought of Aunt Agatha and what she might have to say about letting down the family prestige.

'You don't mean to say she has been ringing up?'

'Several times daily, sir.'

'Jeeves, flight is the only resource.'

'Yes, sir.'

'Back to Paris, what?'

'I should not recommend the move, sir. The posters are, I understand, shortly to appear in that city also, advertising the *Bouillon Supreme*. Mr. Slingsby's products command a large sale in France. The sight would be painful for you, sir.'

'Then where?'

'If I might make a suggestion, sir, why not adhere to your original intention of cruising in Mrs. Travers' yacht in the Mediterranean? On the yacht you would be free from the annoyance of these advertising displays.'

The man seemed to me to be drivelling.

'But the yacht started weeks ago. It may be anywhere by now.'

'No, sir. The cruise was postponed for a month owing to the illness of Mr. Travers' chef, Anatole, who contracted influenza. Mr. Travers refused to sail without him.'

'You mean they haven't started?'

'Not yet, sir. The yacht sails from Southampton on Tuesday next.'

'Why, then, dash it, nothing could be sweeter.'

'No, sir.'

'Ring up Aunt Dahlia and tell her we'll be there.'

'I ventured to take the liberty of doing so a few moments before you arrived, sir.'

'You did?'

'Yes, sir. I thought it probable that the plan would meet with your approval.'

'It does! I've wished all along I was going on that cruise.'

'I, too, sir. It should be extremely pleasant.'

'The tang of the salt breezes, Jeeves!'

'Yes, sir.'

'The moonlight on the water!'

'Precisely, sir.'

'The gentle heaving of the waves!'

'Exactly, sir.'

I felt absolutely in the pink. Gwladys – pah! The posters – bah! That was the way I looked at it.

'Yo-ho-ho, Jeeves!' I said, giving the trousers a bit of a hitch.

'Yes, sir.'

'In fact, I will go further. Yo-ho-ho and a bottle of rum!'

'Very good, sir. I will bring it immediately.'

It has been well said of Bertram Wooster by those who know him best that, whatever other sporting functions he may see fit to oil out of, you will always find him battling to his sixteen handicap at the annual Golf tournament of the Drones Club. Nevertheless, when I heard that this year they were holding it at Bingly-on-Sea, I confess I hesitated. As I stood gazing out of the window of my suite at the Splendide on the morning of the opening day, I was not exactly a-twitter, if you understand me, but I couldn't help feeling I might have been rather rash.

'Jeeves,' I said, 'now that we have actually arrived, I find myself wondering if it was quite prudent to come here.'

'It is a pleasant spot, sir.'

'Where every prospect pleases,' I agreed. 'But though the spicy breezes blow fair o'er Bingly-on-Sea, we must never forget that this is where my Aunt Agatha's old friend, Miss Mapleton, runs a girls' school. If the relative knew I was here, she would expect me to call on Miss Mapleton.'

'Very true, sir.'

I shivered somewhat.

'I met her once, Jeeves. 'Twas on a summer's evening in my tent, the day I overcame the Nervii. Or, rather, at lunch at Aunt Agatha's a year ago come Lammas Eve. It is not an experience I would willingly undergo again.'

'Indeed, sir?'

'Besides, you remember what happened last time I got into a girls' school?'

'Yes, sir.'

'Secrecy and silence, then. My visit here must be strictly incog. If Aunt Agatha happens to ask you where I spent this week, tell her I went to Harrogate for the cure.'

'Very good, sir. Pardon me, sir, are you proposing to appear in those garments in public?'

Up to this point our conversation had been friendly and cordial, but I now perceived that the jarring note had been struck. I had been wondering when my new plus-fours would come under discussion, and I was prepared to battle for them like a tigress for her young.

'Certainly, Jeeves,' I said. 'Why? Don't you like them?'

'No, sir.'

'You think them on the bright side?'

'Yes, sir.

'A little vivid, they strike you as?'

'Yes, sir.'

'Well, I think highly of them, Jeeves,' I said firmly.

There already being a certain amount of chilliness in the air, it seemed to me a suitable moment for springing another item of information which I had been keeping from him for some time. 'Er – Jeeves,' I said.

'Sir?'

'I ran into Miss Wickham the other day. After chatting of this and that, she invited me to join a party she is getting up to go to the Antibes this summer.'

'Indeed, sir?'

He now looked definitely squiggle-eyed. Jeeves, as I think I have mentioned before, does not approve of Bobbie Wickham.

There was what you might call a tense silence. I braced myself for an exhibition of the good old Wooster determination. I mean to say, one has got to take a firm stand from time to time. The trouble with Jeeves is that he tends occasionally to get above himself. Just because he has surged round and – I admit it freely – done the young master a bit of good in one or two crises, he has a nasty way of conveying the impression that he looks on Bertram Wooster as a sort of idiot child who, but for him, would conk in the first chukka. I resent this.

'I have accepted, Jeeves,' I said in a quiet, level voice, lighting a cigarette with a careless flick of the wrist.

'Indeed, sir?'

'You will like Antibes.'

'Yes, sir?'

'So shall I.'

'Yes, sir?'

'That's settled, then.'

'Yes, sir.'

I was pleased. The firm stand, I saw, had done its work. It was plain that the man was crushed beneath the iron heel – cowed, if you know what I mean.

'Right-ho, then, Jeeves.'

'Very good, sir.'

I had not expected to return from the arena until well on in the evening, but circumstances so arranged themselves that it was barely three o'clock when I found myself back again. I was wandering moodily to and fro on the pier, when I observed Jeeves shimmering towards me.

'Good afternoon, sir,' he said. 'I had not supposed that you would be returning quite so soon, or I would have remained at the hotel.'

'I had not supposed that I would be returning quite so soon myself, Jeeves,' I said, sighing somewhat. 'I was outed in the first round, I regret to say.'

'Indeed, sir? I am sorry to hear that.'

'And, to increase the mortification of defeat, Jeeves, by a

blighter who had not spared himself at the luncheon table and was quite noticeably sozzled. I couldn't seem to do anything right.'

'Possibly you omitted to keep your eye on the ball with sufficient assiduity, sir?'

'Something of that nature, no doubt. Anyway, here I am, a game and popular loser and . . .' I paused, and scanned the horizon with some interest. 'Great Scott, Jeeves! Look at that girl just coming on to the pier. I never saw anybody so extraordinarily like Miss Wickham. How do you account for these resemblances?'

'In the present instance, sir, I attribute the similarity to the fact that the young lady *is* Miss Wickham.'

'Eh?'

'Yes, sir. If you notice, she is waving to you now.'

'But what on earth is she doing down here?'

'I am unable to say, sir.'

His voice was chilly and seemed to suggest that, whatever had brought Bobbie Wickham to Bingley-on-Sea, it could not, in his opinion, be anything good. He dropped back into the offing, registering alarm and despondency, and I removed the old Homburg and waggled it genially.

'What-ho!' I said.

Bobbie came to anchor alongside.

'Hullo, Bertie,' she said. 'I didn't know you were here.'

'I am,' I assured her.

'In mourning?' she asked, eyeing the trouserings.

'Rather natty, aren't they?' I said, following her gaze. 'Jeeves doesn't like them, but then he's notoriously hidebound on the matter of leg-wear. What are you doing in Bingley?'

'My cousin Clementina is at school here. It's her birthday and I thought I would come down and see her. I'm just off there now. Are you staying here tonight?'

'Yes. At the Splendide.'

'You can give me dinner there if you like.'

Jeeves was behind me, and I couldn't see him, but at these words I felt his eyes slap warningly against the back of my neck. I knew what it was that he was trying to broadcast – viz. that it would be tempting Providence to mix with Bobbie Wickham even to the extent of giving her a bite to eat. Dashed absurd, was my verdict. Get entangled with young Bobbie in the intricate life of a country-house, where almost anything can happen, and I'm not saying. But how any doom or disaster could lurk behind the simple pronging of a spot of dinner together, I failed to see. I ignored the man.

'Of course. Certainly. Rather. Absolutely,' I said.

'That'll be fine. I've got to get back to London to-night for revelry of sorts at the Berkeley, but it doesn't matter if I'm a bit late. We'll turn up at about seven-thirty, and you can take us to the movies afterwards.'

'We? Us?'

'Clementina and me.'

'You don't mean you intend to bring your ghastly cousin?'

'Of course I do. Don't you want the child to have a little pleasure on her birthday? And she isn't ghastly. She's a dear. She won't be any trouble. All you'll have to do is take her back to the school afterwards. You can manage that without straining a sinew, can't you?'

I eyed her keenly.

'What does it involve?'

'How do you mean, what does it involve?'

'The last time I was lured into a girls' school, a headmistress with an eye like a gimlet insisted on my addressing the chain-gang on Ideals and the Life To Come. This will not happen tonight?'

'Of course not. You just go to the front door, ring the bell, and bung her in.'

I mused.

'That would appear to be well within our scope. Eh, Jeeves?'

'I should be disposed to imagine so, sir.'

The man's tone was cold and soupy: and, scanning his face, I observed on it an 'If-you-would-only-be-guided-by-me' expression which annoyed me intensely. There are moments when Jeeves looks just like an aunt.

'Right,' I said, ignoring him once more – and rather pointedly, at that. 'Then I'll expect you at seven-thirty. Don't be late. And see,' I added, just to show the girl that beneath the smiling exterior I was a man of iron, 'that the kid has her hands washed and does not sniff.'

I had not, I confess, looked forward with any great keenness to hobnobbing with Bobbie Wickham's cousin Clementina, but I'm bound to admit that she might have been considerably worse. Small girls as a rule, I have noticed, are inclined, when confronted with me, to giggle a good deal. They snigger and they stare. I look up and find their eyes glued on me in an incredulous manner, as if they were reluctant to believe that I was really true. I suspect them of being in the process of memorising any little peculiarities of deportment that I may possess, in order to reproduce them later for the entertainment of their fellow-inmates.

With the kid Clementina there was nothing of this description. She was a quiet, saintlike child of about thirteen – in fact, seeing that this was her birthday, exactly thirteen – and her gaze revealed only silent admiration. Her hands were spotless; she had not a cold in the head; and at dinner, during which her behaviour was unexceptionable, she proved a sympathetic listener, hanging on my lips, so to speak, when with the aid of a fork and two peas I explained to her how my opponent that afternoon had stymied me on the tenth.

She was equally above criticism at the movies, and at the conclusion of the proceedings thanked me for the treat with visible emotion. I was pleased with the child, and said as much to Bobbie while assisting her into her two-seater.

'Yes, I told you she was a dear,' said Bobbie, treading on the self-starter in preparation of the dash to London. 'I always insist that they misjudge her at that school. They're always misjudging people. They misjudged me when I was there.'

'Misjudged her? How?'

'Oh, in various ways. But, then, what can you expect of a dump like St. Monica's?'

I started.

'St. Monica's?'

'That's the name of the place.'

'You don't mean the kid is at Miss Mapleton's school?'

'Why shouldn't she be?'

'But Miss Mapleton is my Aunt Agatha's oldest friend.'

'I know. It was your Aunt Agatha who got mother to send me there when I was a kid.'

'I say,' I said earnestly, 'when you were there this afternoon you didn't mention having met me down here?'

'No.'

'That's all right.' I was relieved. 'You see, if Miss Mapleton knew I was in Bingley, she would expect me to call. I shall be leaving tomorrow morning, so all will be well. But, dash it,' I said, spotting the snag, 'how about tonight?'

'What about tonight?'

'Well, shan't I have to see her? I can't just ring the front door bell, sling the kid in, and leg it. I should never hear the last of it from Aunt Agatha.' Bobbie looked at me in an odd, meditative sort of way. 'As a matter of fact, Bertie,' she said, 'I had been meaning to touch on that point. I think, if I were you, I wouldn't ring the front door bell.'

'Eh? Why not?'

'Well, it's like this, you see. Clementina is supposed to be in bed. They sent her there just as I was leaving this afternoon. Think of it! On her birthday – right plumb spang in the middle of her birthday – and all for putting sherbet in the ink to make it fizz!'

I reeled.

'You aren't telling me that this foul kid came out without leave?'

'Yes, I am. That's exactly it. She got up and sneaked out when nobody was looking. She had set her heart on getting a square meal. I suppose I really ought to have told you right at the start, but I didn't want to spoil your evening.'

As a general rule, in my dealings with the delicately nurtured, I am the soul of knightly chivalry – suave, genial and polished. But I can on occasion say the bitter, cutting thing, and I said it now.

'Oh?' I said.

'But it's all right.'

'Yes,' I said, speaking, if I recollect, between my clenched teeth, 'nothing could be sweeter, could it? The situation is one which it would be impossible to view with concern, what? I shall turn up with the kid, get looked at through steel-rimmed spectacles by the Mapleton, and after an agreeable five minutes shall back out, leaving the Mapleton to go to her escritoire and write a full account of the proceedings to my Aunt Agatha. And, contemplating what will happen after that, the imagination totters. I confidently expect my Aunt Agatha to beat all previous records.'

The girl clicked her tongue chidingly.

'Don't make such heavy weather, Bertie. You must learn not to fuss so.'

'I must, must I?'

'Everything's going to be all right. I'm not saying it won't be necessary to exercise a little strategy in getting Clem into the house, but it will be perfectly simple, if you'll only listen carefully to what I'm going to tell you. First, you will need a good long piece of string.'

'String?'

'String. Surely even you know what string is?'

I stiffened rather haughtily.

'Certainly,' I replied. 'You mean string.'

'That's right. String. You take this with you—?'

'And soften the Mapleton's heart by doing tricks with it, I suppose?'

Bitter, I know. But I was deeply stirred.

'You take this string with you,' proceeded Bobbie patiently, 'and when you get into the garden you go through it till you come to a conservatory near the house. Inside it you will find a lot of flower-pots. How are you on recognising a flower-pot when you see one, Bertie?'

'I am thoroughly familiar with flower-pots. If, as I suppose, you mean those sort of pot things they put flowers in.'

'That's exactly what I do mean. All right, then. Grab an armful of these flower-pots and go round the conservatory till you come to a tree. Climb this, tie a string to one of the pots, balance it on a handy branch which you will find overhangs the conservatory, and then, having stationed Clem near the front door, retire into the middle distance and jerk the string. The flower-pot will fall and smash the glass, someone in the house will hear the noise and come out to investigate, and while the door is open and nobody near Clem will sneak in and go up to bed.'

'But suppose no one comes out?'

'Then you repeat the process with another pot.'

It seemed sound enough.

'You're sure it will work?'

'It's never failed yet. That's the way I always used to get in after lock-up when I was in St. Monica's. Now, you're sure you've got it clear, Bertie? Let's have a quick run-through to make certain, and then I really must be off. String.'

'String.'

'Conservatory.'

'Or greenhouse.'

'Flower-pot.'

'Flower-pot.'

'Tree. Climb. Branch. Climb down. Jerk. Smash. And then off to beddy-bye. Got it?'

'I've got it. But,' I said sternly, 'let me tell you just one thing—'

'I haven't time. I must rush. Write to me about it, using one side of the paper only. Good-bye.'

She rolled off, and after following her with burning eyes for a moment I returned to Jeeves, who was in the background showing the kid Clementina how to make a rabbit with a pocket handkerchief. I drew him aside. I was feeling a little better now, for I perceived that an admirable opportunity had presented itself for putting the man in his place and correcting his view that he is the only member of our establishment with brains and resource.

'Jeeves,' I said, 'you will doubtless be surprised to learn that something in the nature of a hitch has occurred.'

'Not at all, sir.'

'No?'

'No, sir. In matters where Miss Wickham is involved, I am, if I may take the liberty of saying so, always on the alert for hitches. If you recollect, sir, I have frequently observed that Miss Wickham, while a charming young lady, is apt—'

'Yes, yes, Jeeves. I know.'

'What would the precise nature of the trouble be this time, sir?'

I explained the circs.

'The kid is A.W.O.L. They sent her to bed for putting sherbet in the ink, and in bed they imagine her to have spent the evening. Instead of which, she was out with me, wolfing the eight-course table-d'hote dinner at seven and six, and then going on to the Marine Plaza to enjoy an entertainment on the silver screen. It is our task to get her back into the house without anyone knowing. I may mention, Jeeves, that the school in which this young excrescence is serving her sentence is the one run by my Aunt Agatha's old friend, Miss Mapleton.'

'Indeed, sir?'

'A problem, Jeeves, what?'

'Yes, sir.'

'In fact, one might say a pretty problem?'

'Undoubtedly, sir. If I might suggest—'

I was expecting this. I raised a hand.

'I do not require any suggestions, Jeeves. I can handle this matter myself.'

'I was merely about to propose—'

I raised the hand again.

'Peace, Jeeves. I have the situation well under control. I have had one of my ideas. It may interest you to hear how my brain worked. It occurred to me, thinking the thing over, that a house like St. Monica's would be likely to have near it a conservatory containing flower-pots. Then, like a flash, the whole thing came to me. I propose to procure some string, to tie it to a flower-pot, to balance the pot on a branch – there will, no doubt, be a tree near the conservatory with a branch overhanging it – and to retire to a distance, holding the string. You will station yourself with the kid near the front door, taking care to keep carefully concealed. I shall then jerk the string, the pot will smash the glass, the noise will bring someone out, and while the front door is open you will shoot the kid in and leave the rest to her personal judgment. Your share in the proceedings, you will notice, is simplicity itself – mere routine-work – and should not tax you unduly. How about it?'

'Well, sir—'

'Jeeves, I have had occasion before to comment on this habit of yours of saying "Well, sir" whenever I suggest anything in the nature of a ruse or piece of strategy. I dislike it more every time you do it. But I shall be glad to hear what possible criticism you can find to make.'

'I was merely about to express the opinion, sir, that the plan seems a trifle elaborate.'

'In a place as tight as this you have got to be elaborate.'

'Not necessarily, sir. The alternative scheme which I was about to propose—'

I shushed the man.

'There will be no need for alternative schemes, Jeeves. We will carry on along the lines I have indicated. I will give you ten minutes' start. That will enable you to take up your position near the front door and self to collect the string. At the conclusion of that period I will come along and do all the difficult part. So no more discussion. Snap into it, Jeeves.'

'Very good, sir.'

I felt pretty bucked as I tooled up the hill to St. Monica's and equally bucked as I pushed open the front gate and stepped into the dark garden. But, just as I started to cross the lawn, there suddenly came upon me a rummy sensation as if all my bones had been removed and spaghetti substituted, and I paused.

I don't know if you have ever had the experience of starting off on a binge filled with a sort of glow of exhilaration, if that's the word I want, and then, without a moment's warning, having it disappear as if somebody had pressed a switch. That is what happened to me at this juncture, and a most unpleasant feeling it was – rather like when you take one of those express elevators in New York at the top of the building and discover, on reaching the twenty-seventh floor, that you have carelessly left all your insides up on the thirty-second, and too late now to stop and fetch them back.

The truth came to me like a bit of ice down the neck. I perceived that I had been a dashed sight too impulsive. Purely in order to score off Jeeves, I had gone and let myself in for what promised to be the mouldiest ordeal of a lifetime. And the nearer I got to the house, the more I wished that I had been a bit less haughty with the man when he had tried to outline that alternative scheme of his. An alternative scheme was just what I felt I could have done with, and the more alternative it was the better I would have liked it.

At this point I found myself at the conservatory door, and a few moments later I was inside, scooping up the pots.

Then ho, for the tree, bearing 'mid snow and ice the banner with the strange device 'Excelsior!'

I will say for that tree that it might have been placed there for the purpose. My views on the broad, general principle of leaping from branch to branch in a garden belonging to Aunt Agatha's closest friend remained unaltered; but I had to admit that, if it was to be done, this was undoubtedly the tree to do it on. It was a cedar of sorts; and almost before I knew where I was, I was sitting on top of the world with the conservatory roof gleaming below me. I balanced the flower-pot on my knee and began to tie the string round it.

And, as I tied, my thoughts turned in a moody sort of way to the subject of Woman.

I was suffering from a considerable strain of the old nerves at the moment, of course, and, looking back, it may be that I was too harsh; but the way I felt in that dark, roosting hour was that you can say what you like, but the more a thoughtful man has to do with women, the more extraordinary it seems to him that such a sex should be allowed to clutter up the earth.

Women, the way I looked at it, simply wouldn't do. Take the females who were mixed up in this present business. Aunt Agatha, to start with, better known as the Pest of Pont Street, the human snapping-turtle. Aunt Agatha's closest friend, Miss Mapleton, of whom I can only say that on the single occasion on which I had met her she had struck me as just the sort of person who would be Aunt Agatha's closest friend. Bobbie Wickham, a girl who went about the place letting the pure in heart in for the sort of thing I was doing now. And Bobbie Wickham's cousin Clementina, who, instead of sticking sedulously to her studies and learning to be a good wife and mother, spent the springtime of her life filling inkpots with sherbet—

What a crew! What a crew!

I mean to say, what a *crew!*

I had just worked myself up into rather an impressive state of moral indignation, and was preparing to go even further, when a sudden bright light shone upon me from below and a voice spoke.

'Ho!' it said.

It was a policeman. Apart from the fact of his having a lantern, I knew it was a policeman because he had said 'Ho!' I don't know if you recollect my telling you of the time I broke into Bingo Little's house to pinch the dictaphone record of the mushy article his wife had written about him and sailed out of the study window right into the arms of the Force? On that occasion the guardian of the Law had said 'Ho!' and kept on saying it, so evidently policemen are taught this as part of their training. And after all, it's not a bad way of opening conversation in the sort of circs, in which they generally have to chat with people.

'You come on down out of that,' he said.

I came on down. I had just got the flower-pot balanced on its branch, and I left it there, feeling rather as if I had touched off the time-fuse of a bomb. Much seemed to me to depend on its stability and poise, as it were. If it continued to balance, an easy nonchalance might still get me out of this delicate position. If it fell, I saw things being a bit hard to explain. In fact, even as it was, I couldn't see my way to any explanation which would be really convincing.

However, I had a stab at it.

'Ah, officer,' I said.

It sounded weak. I said it again, this time with the emphasis on the 'Ah!' It sounded weaker than ever. I saw that Bertram would have to do better than this.

'It's all right, officer,' I said.

'All right, is it?'

'Oh, yes. Oh, yes.'

'What you doing up there?'

'Me, officer?'

'Yes, you.'

'Nothing, sergeant.'

'Ho!'

We eased into the silence, but it wasn't one of those restful silences that occur in talks between old friends. Embarrassing. Awkward.

'You'd better come along with me,' said the gendarme.

The last time I had heard those words from a similar source had been in Leicester Square on Boat-Race Night when, on my advice, my old pal Oliver Randolph Sipperley had endeavoured to steal a policeman's helmet at a moment when the policeman was inside it. On that occasion they had been addressed to young Sippy, and they hadn't sounded any too good, even so. Addressed to me, they more or less froze the marrow.

'No, I say, dash it!' I said.

And it was at this crisis, when Bertram had frankly shot his bolt and could only have been described as nonplussed, that a soft step sounded beside us and a soft voice broke the silence.

'Have you got them, officer? No, I see. It is Mr. Wooster.'

The policeman switched the lantern round.

'Who are you?'

'I am Mr. Wooster's personal gentleman's gentleman.'

'Whose?'

'Mr. Wooster's.'

'Is this man's name Wooster?'

'This gentleman's name is Mr. Wooster. I am in his employment as gentleman's personal gentleman.'

I think the cop was awed by the man's majesty of demeanour, but he came back strongly.

'Ho!' he said. 'Not in Miss Mapleton's employment?'

'Miss Mapleton does not employ a gentleman's personal gentleman.'

'Then what are you doing in her garden?'

'I was in conference with Miss Mapleton inside the house, and she desired me to step out and ascertain whether Mr.

Wooster had been successful in apprehending the intruders.'

'What intruders?'

'The suspicious characters whom Mr. Wooster and I had observed passing through the garden as we entered it.'

'And what were you doing entering it?'

'Mr. Wooster had come to pay a call on Miss Mapleton, who is a close friend of his family. We noticed suspicious characters crossing the lawn. On perceiving these suspicious characters, Mr. Wooster despatched me to warn and reassure Miss Mapleton, he himself remaining to investigate.'

'I found him up a tree.'

'If Mr. Wooster was up a tree, I have no doubt he was actuated by excellent motives and had only Miss Mapleton's best interests at heart.'

The policeman brooded.

'Ho!' he said. 'Well, if you want to know, I don't believe a word of it. We had a telephone call at the station saying there was somebody in Miss Mapleton's garden, and I found this fellow up a tree. It's my belief you're both in this, and I'm going to take you in to the lady for identification.'

Jeeves inclined his head gracefully.

'I shall be delighted to accompany you, officer, if such is your wish. And I feel sure that in this connexion I may speak for Mr. Wooster also. He too, I am confident, will interpose no obstacle in the way of your plans. If you consider that circumstances have placed Mr. Wooster in a position that may be termed equivocal, or even compromising, it will naturally be his wish to exculpate himself at the earliest possible—'

'Here!' said the policeman, slightly rattled.

'Officer?'

'Less of it.'

'Just as you say, officer.'

'Switch it off and come along.'

'Very good, officer.'

I must say that I have enjoyed functions more than that walk to the front door. It seemed to me that the doom had come upon me, so to speak, and I thought it hard that a gallant effort like Jeeves's, well reasoned and nicely planned, should have failed to click. Even to me his story had rung almost true in spots, and it was a great blow that the man behind the lantern had not sucked it in without question. There's no doubt about it, being a policeman warps a man's mind and ruins that sunny faith in his fellow human beings which is the foundation of a lovable character. There seems no way of avoiding this.

I could see no gleam of light in the situation. True, the Mapleton would identify me as the nephew of her old friend, thus putting the stopper on the stroll to the police station and the night in the prison cell, but, when you came right down to it, a fat lot of use that was. The kid Clementina was presumably still out in the night somewhere, and she would be lugged in and the full facts revealed, and then the burning glance, the few cold words and the long letter to Aunt Agatha. I wasn't sure that a good straight term of penal servitude wouldn't have been a happier ending.

So, what with one consideration and another, the heart, as I toddled in through the front door, was more or less bowed down with weight of woe. We went along the passage and into the study, and there, standing behind a desk with the steel-rimmed spectacles glittering as nastily as on the day when I had seen them across Aunt Agatha's luncheon-table, was the boss in person. I gave her one swift look, then shut my eyes.

'Ah!' said Miss Mapleton.

Now, uttered in a certain way – dragged out, if you know what I mean, and starting high up and going down into the lower register, the word 'Ah!' can be as sinister and devastating as the word 'Ho!' In fact, it is a very moot question which is the scalier. But what stunned me was that this wasn't the way she had said it. It had been, or my ears deceived me, a genial 'Ah!' A matey 'Ah!' The 'Ah!' of one old buddy to another. And this startled me so much that, forgetting the dictates of prudence, I actually ventured to look at her again. And a stifled exclamation burst from Bertram's lips.

The breath-taking exhibit before me was in person a bit on the short side. I mean to say, she didn't tower above one, or anything like that. But, to compensate for this lack of inches, she possessed to a remarkable degree that sort of quiet air of being unwilling to stand any rannygazoo which females who run schools always have. I had noticed the same thing when in *statu pupillari*, in my old head master, one glance from whose eye had invariably been sufficient to make me confess all. Sergeant-majors are like that, too. Also traffic-cops and some post office girls. It's something in the way they purse up their lips and look through you.

In short, through years of disciplining the young – ticking off Isabel and speaking with quiet severity to Gertrude and that sort of thing – Miss Mapleton had acquired in the process of time rather the air of a female lion-tamer; and it was this air which had caused me after the first swift look to shut my eyes and utter a short prayer. But now, though she still resembled a lion-tamer her bearing had most surprisingly become that of a chummy lion-tamer – a tamer who, after tucking the lions in for the night, relaxes in the society of the boys.

'So you did not find them, Mr. Wooster?' she said. 'I am sorry. But I am none the less grateful for the trouble you have taken, nor lacking in appreciation of your courage. I consider that you have behaved splendidly.'

I felt the mouth opening feebly and the vocal chords twitching, but I couldn't manage to say anything. I was simply unable to follow her train of thought. I was astonished. Amazed. In fact, dumbfounded about sums it up.

The hell-hound of the Law gave a sort of yelp, rather like a wolf that sees its Russian peasant getting away.

'You identify this man, ma'am?'

'Identify him? In what way identify him?'

Jeeves joined the symposium.

'I fancy the officer is under the impression, madam, that Mr. Wooster was in your garden for some unlawful purpose. I informed him that Mr. Wooster was the nephew of your friend, Mrs. Spenser Gregson, but he refused to credit me.'

There was a pause. Miss Mapleton eyed the constable for an instant as if she had caught him sucking acid-drops during the Scripture lesson.

'Do you mean to tell me, officer,' she said, in a voice that hit him just under the third button of the tunic and went straight through to the spinal column, 'that you have had the imbecility to bungle this whole affair by mistaking Mr. Wooster for a burglar?'

'He was up a tree, ma'am.'

'And why should he not be up a tree? No doubt you had climbed the tree in order to watch the better, Mr. Wooster?'

I could answer that. The first shock over, the old sang-froid was beginning to return.

'Yes. Rather. That's it. Of course. Certainly. Absolutely,' I said. 'Watch the better. That's it in a nutshell.'

'I took the liberty of suggesting that to the officer, madam, but he declined to accept the theory as tenable.'

'The officer is a fool,' said Miss Mapleton. It seemed a close thing for a moment whether or not she would rap him on the knuckles with a ruler. 'By this time, no doubt, owing to his idiocy, the miscreants have made good their escape. And it is for this,' said Miss Mapleton, 'that we pay rates and taxes!'

'Awful!' I said.

'Iniquitous.'

'A bally shame.'

'A crying scandal,' said Miss Mapleton.

'A grim show,' I agreed.

In fact, we were just becoming more like a couple of love-birds than anything, when through the open window there suddenly breezed a noise.

I'm never at my best at describing things. At school, when

we used to do essays and English composition, my report generally read 'Has little or no ability, but does his best', or words to that effect. True, in the course of years I have picked up a vocabulary of sorts from Jeeves, but even so I'm not nearly hot enough to draw a word-picture that would do justice to that extraordinarily hefty crash. Try to imagine the Albert Hall falling on the Crystal Palace, and you will have got the rough idea.

All four of us, even Jeeves, sprang several inches from the floor. The policeman uttered a startled 'Ho!'

Miss Mapleton was her calm masterful self again in a second.

'One of the men appears to have fallen through the conservatory roof,' she said. 'Perhaps you will endeavour at the eleventh hour to justify your existence, officer, by proceeding there and making investigations.'

'Yes, ma'am.'

'And try not to bungle matters this time.'

'No, ma'am.'

'Please hurry, then. Do you intend to stand there gaping all night?'

'Yes, ma'am. No, ma'am. Yes, ma'am.'

It was pretty to hear him.

'It is an odd coincidence, Mr. Wooster,' said Miss Mapleton, becoming instantly matey once more as the outcast removed himself. 'I had just finished writing a letter to your aunt when you arrived. I shall certainly reopen it to tell her how gallantly you have behaved tonight. I have not in the past entertained a very high opinion of the modern young man, but you have caused me to alter it. To track these men unarmed through a dark garden argues courage of a high order. And it was most courteous of you to think of calling upon me. I appreciate it. Are you making a long stay in Bingley?'

This was another one I could answer.

'No,' I said. 'Afraid not. Must be in London tomorrow.'

'Perhaps you could lunch before your departure?'

'Afraid not. Thanks most awfully. Very important engagement that I can't get out of. Eh, Jeeves?'

'Yes, sir.'

'Have to catch the ten-thirty train, what?'

'Without fail, sir.'

'I am sorry,' said Miss Mapleton. 'I had hoped that you would be able to say a few words to my girls. Some other time perhaps?'

'Absolutely.'

'You must let me know when you are coming to Bingley again.'

'When I come to Bingley again,' I said, 'I will certainly let you know.'

'If I remember your plans correctly, sir, you are not likely to be in Bingley for some little time, sir.'

'Not for some considerable time, Jeeves,' I said.

The front door closed. I passed a hand across the brow.

'Tell me all, Jeeves,' I said.

'Sir?'

'I say, tell me all. I am fogged.'

'It is quite simple, sir. I ventured to take the liberty, on my own responsibility, of putting into operation the alternative scheme which, if you remember, I wished to outline to you.'

'What was it?'

'It occurred to me, sir, that it would be most judicious for me to call at the back door and desire an interview with Miss Mapleton. This, I fancied, would enable me, while the maid had gone to convey my request to Miss Mapleton, to introduce the young lady into the house unobserved.'

'And did you?'

'Yes, sir. She proceeded up the back stairs and is now safely in bed.'

I frowned. The thought of the kid Clementina jarred upon me.

'She is, is she?' I said. 'A murrain on her, Jeeves, and may she be stood in the corner next Sunday for not knowing her Collect. And then you saw Miss Mapleton?'

'Yes, sir.'

'And told her that I was out in the garden, chivvying burglars with my bare hands?'

'Yes, sir.'

'And had been on my way to call upon her?'

'Yes, sir.'

'And now she's busy adding a postscript to her letter to Aunt Agatha, speaking of me in terms of unstinted praise.'

'Yes, sir.'

I drew a deep breath. It was too dark for me to see the superhuman intelligence which must have been sloshing about all over the surface of the man's features. I tried to, but couldn't make it.

'Jeeves,' I said, 'I should have been guided by you from the first.'

'It might have spared you some temporary unpleasantness, sir.'

'Unpleasantness is right. When that lantern shone up at me in the silent night, Jeeves, just as I had finished poising the pot, I thought I had unshipped a rib. Jeeves!'

'Sir?'

'That Antibes expedition is off.'

'I am glad to hear it, sir.'

'If young Bobbie Wickham can get me into a mess like this in a quiet spot like Bingley-on-Sea, what might she not be able to accomplish at a really lively resort like Antibes?'

'Precisely, sir. Miss Wickham, as I have sometimes said, though a charming—'

'Yes, yes, Jeeves. There is no necessity to stress the point. The Wooster eyes are definitely opened.'

I hesitated.

'Jeeves.'

'Sir?'

'Those plus-fours.'

'Yes, sir?'

'You may give them to the poor.'

'Thank you very much sir.'

I sighed.

'It is my heart's blood, Jeeves.'

'I appreciate the sacrifice, sir. But, once the first pang of separation is over, you will feel much easier without them.'

'You think so?'

'I am convinced of it, sir.'

'So be it, then, Jeeves,' I said, 'so be it.'

There is a ghastly moment in the year, generally about the beginning of August, when Jeeves insists on taking a holiday, the slacker, and legs it off to some seaside resort for a couple of weeks, leaving me stranded. This moment had now arrived, and we were discussing what was to be done with the young master.

'I had gathered the impression, sir,' said Jeeves, 'that you were proposing to accept Mr. Sipperley's invitation to join him at his Hampshire residence.'

I laughed. One of those bitter, rasping ones.

'Correct, Jeeves. I was. But mercifully I was enabled to discover young Sippy's foul plot in time. Do you know what?'

'No, sir.'

'My spies informed me that Sippy's fiancée, Miss Moon, was to be there. Also his fiancée's mother, Mrs. Moon, and his fiancée's small brother, Master Moon. You see the hideous treachery lurking behind the invitation? You see the man's loathsome design? Obviously my job was to be the task of keeping Mrs. Moon and little Sebastian Moon interested and amused while Sippy and his blighted girl went off for the day, roaming the pleasant woodlands and talking of this and that. I doubt if anyone has ever had a narrower escape. You remember little Sebastian?'

'Yes, sir.'

'His goggle eyes? His golden curls?'

'Yes, sir.'

'I don't know why it is, but I've never been able to bear with fortitude anything in the shape of a kid with golden curls. Confronted with one, I feel the urge to step on him or drop things on him from a height.'

'Many strong natures are affected in the same way, sir.'

'So no *chez* Sippy for me. Was that the front door bell ringing?'

'Yes, sir.'

'Somebody stands without.'

'Yes, sir.'

'Better go and see who it is.'

'Yes, sir.'

He oozed off, to return a moment later bearing a telegram. I opened it, and a soft smile played about the lips.

'Amazing how often things happen as if on a cue, Jeeves. This is from my Aunt Dahlia, inviting me down to her place in Worcestershire.'

'Most satisfactory, sir.'

'Yes. How I came to overlook her when searching for a haven, I can't think. The ideal home from home. Picturesque surroundings. Company's own water, and the best cook in England. You have not forgotten Anatole?'

'No, sir.'

'And above all, Jeeves, at Aunt Dahlia's there should be an almost total shortage of blasted kids. True, there is her son Bonzo, who, I take it, will be home for the holidays, but I don't mind Bonzo. Buzz off and send a wire, accepting.'

'Yes, sir.'

'And then shove a few necessaries together, including golf-clubs and tennis racquet.'

'Very good, sir. I am glad that matters have been so happily adjusted.'

*

I think I have mentioned before that my Aunt Dahlia stands alone in the grim regiment of my aunts as a real good sort and a chirpy sportsman. She is the one, if you remember, who married old Tom Travers and, with the assistance of Jeeves, lured Mrs. Bingo Little's French cook, Anatole, away from Mrs. B. L. and into her own employment. To visit her is always a pleasure. She generally has some cheery birds staying with her, and there is none of that rot about getting up for breakfast which one is so sadly apt to find at country houses.

It was, accordingly, with unalloyed lightness of heart that I edged the two-seater into the garage at Brinkley Court, Worc., and strolled round to the house by way of the shrubbery and the tennis-lawn, to report arrival. I had just got across the lawn when a head poked itself out of the smoking-room window and beamed at me in an amiable sort of way.

'Ah, Mr. Wooster,' it said. 'Ha, ha!'

'Ho, ho!' I replied, not to be outdone in the courtesies.

It had taken me a couple of seconds to place this head. I now perceived that it belonged to a rather moth-eaten septuagenarian of the name of Anstruther, an old friend of Aunt Dahlia's late father. I had met him at her house in London once or twice. An agreeable cove, but somewhat given to nervous breakdowns.

'Just arrived?' he asked, beaming as before.

'This minute,' I said, also beaming.

'I fancy you will find our good hostess in the drawing-room.'

'Right,' I said, and after a bit more beaming to and fro I pushed on.

Aunt Dahlia was in the drawing-room, and welcomed me with gratifying enthusiasm. She beamed, too. It was one of those big days for beamers.

'Hullo, ugly,' she said. 'So here you are. Thank heaven you were able to come.'

It was the right tone, and one I should be glad to hear in others of the family circle, notably my Aunt Agatha.

'Always a pleasure to enjoy your hosp., Aunt Dahlia,' I said cordially. 'I anticipate a delightful and restful visit. I see you've got Mr. Anstruther staying here. Anybody else?'

'Do you know Lord Snettisham?'

'I've met him, racing.'

'He's here, and Lady Snettisham.'

'And Bonzo, of course?'

'Yes. And Thomas.'

'Uncle Thomas?'

'No, he's in Scotland. Your cousin Thomas.'

'You don't mean Aunt Agatha's loathly son?'

'Of course I do. How many cousin Thomases do you think you've got, fathead? Agatha has gone to Homburg and planted the child on me.'

I was visibly agitated.

'But, Aunt Dahlia! Do you realise what you've taken on? Have you an inkling of the sort of scourge you've introduced into your home? In the society of young Thos., strong men quail. He is England's premier fiend in human shape. There is no devilry beyond his scope.'

'That's what I have always gathered from the form book,' agreed the relative. 'But just now, curse him, he's behaving like something out of a Sunday School story. You see, poor old Mr. Anstruther is very frail these days, and when he found he was in a house containing two small boys he acted promptly. He offered a prize of five pounds to whichever behaved best during his stay. The consequence is that, ever since, Thomas has had large white wings sprouting out of his shoulders.' A shadow seemed to pass across her face. She appeared embittered. 'Mercenary little brute!' she said. 'I never saw such a sickeningly well-behaved kid in my life. It's enough to make one despair of human nature.'

I couldn't follow her.

'But isn't that all to the good?'

'No, it's not.'

'I can't see why. Surely a smug, oily Thos. about the house is better than a Thos., raging hither and thither and being a menace to society? Stands to reason.'

'It doesn't stand to anything of the kind. You see, Bertie, this Good Conduct prize has made matters a bit complex. There are wheels within wheels. The thing stirred Jane Snettisham's sporting blood to such an extent that she insisted on having a bet on the result.'

A great light shone upon me. I got what she was driving at.

'Ah!' I said. 'Now I follow. Now I see. Now I comprehend. She's betting on Thos., is she?'

'Yes. And naturally, knowing him, I thought the thing was in the bag.'

'Of course.'

'I couldn't see myself losing. Heaven knows I have no illusions about my darling Bonzo. Bonzo is and has been from the cradle, a pest. But to back him to win a Good Conduct contest with Thomas seemed to me simply money for jam.'

'Absolutely.'

'When it comes to devilry, Bonzo is just a good, ordinary selling-plater. Whereas Thomas is a classic yearling.'

'Exactly. I don't see that you have any cause to worry, Aunt Dahlia. Thos. can't last. He's bound to crack.'

'Yes. But before that the mischief may be done.'

'Mischief?'

'Yes. There is dirty work afoot, Bertie,' said Aunt Dahlia gravely. 'When I booked this bet, I reckoned without the hideous blackness of the Snettishams' souls. Only yesterday it came to my knowledge that Jack Snettisham had been urging Bonzo to climb on the roof and boo down Mr. Anstruther's chimney.'

'No!'

'Yes. Mr. Anstruther is very frail, poor old fellow, and it would have frightened him into a fit. On coming out of which, his first action would have been to disqualify Bonzo and declare Thomas the winner by default.'

'But Bonzo did not boo?'

'No,' said Aunt Dahlia, and a mother's pride rang in her voice. 'He firmly refused to boo. Mercifully, he is in love at the moment, and it has quite altered his nature. He scorned the tempter.'

'In love? Who with?'

'Lilian Gish. We had an old film of hers at the Bijou Dream in the village a week ago, and Bonzo saw her for the first time. He came out with a pale, set face, and ever since has been trying to lead a finer, better life. So the peril was averted.'

'That's good.'

'Yes. But now it's my turn. You don't suppose I am going to take a thing like that lying down, do you? Treat me right, and I am fairness itself: but try any of this nobbling of starters, and I can play that game, too. If this Good Conduct contest is to be run on rough lines, I can do my bit as well as anyone. Far too much hangs on the issue for me to handicap myself by remembering the lessons I learned at my mother's knee.'

'Lot of money involved?'

'Much more than mere money. I've betted Anatole against Jane Snettisham's kitchen-maid.'

'Great Scott! Uncle Thomas will have something to say if he comes back and finds Anatole gone.'

'And won't he say it!'

'Pretty long odds you gave her, didn't you? I mean, Anatole is famed far and wide as a hash-slinger without peer.'

'Well, Jane Snettisham's kitchen-maid is not to be sneezed at. She is very hot stuff, they tell me, and good kitchen-maids nowadays are about as rare as original Holbeins. Besides, I had to give her a shade the best of the odds. She stood out for it. Well, anyway, to get back to what I was saying, if the opposition are going to place temptations in Bonzo's path, they shall jolly well be placed in Thomas' path, too, and plenty of them. So ring for Jeeves and let him get his brain working.'

'But I haven't brought Jeeves.'

'You haven't brought Jeeves?'

'No. He always takes his holiday at this time of year. He's down at Bognor for the shrimping.'

Aunt Dahlia registered deep concern.

'Then send for him at once! What earthly use do you suppose you are without Jeeves, you poor ditherer?'

I drew myself up a trifle – in fact, to my full height. Nobody has a greater respect for Jeeves than I have, but the Wooster pride was stung.

'Jeeves isn't the only one with brains,' I said coldly. 'Leave this thing to me, Aunt Dahlia. By dinner-time tonight I shall hope to have a fully matured scheme to submit for your approval. If I can't thoroughly encompass this Thos., I'll eat my hat.'

'About all you'll get to eat if Anatole leaves,' said Aunt Dahlia in a pessimistic manner which I did not like to see.

I was brooding pretty tensely as I left the presence. I have always had a suspicion that Aunt Dahlia, while invariably matey and bonhomous and seeming to take pleasure in my society, has a lower opinion of my intelligence than I quite like. Too often it is her practice to address me as 'fathead', and if I put forward any little thought or idea or fancy in her hearing it is apt to be greeted with the affectionate but jarring guffaw. In our recent interview she had hinted quite plainly that she considered me negligible in a crisis which, like the present one, called for initiative and resource. It was my intention to show her how greatly she had underestimated me.

To let you see the sort of fellow I really am, I got a ripe, excellent idea before I had gone half-way down the corridor. I examined it for the space of one and a half cigarettes, and could see no flaw in it, provided – I say, provided old Mr. Anstruther's notion of what constituted bad conduct squared with mine.

The great thing on these occasions, as Jeeves will tell you, is to get a toe-hold on the psychology of the individual. Study the individual, and you will bring home the bacon. Now, I had been studying young Thos. for years, and I knew his psychology from caviare to nuts. He is one of those kids who never let the sun go down on their wrath, if you know what I mean. I mean to say, do something to annoy or offend or upset this juvenile thug, and he will proceed at the earliest possible opp. to wreak a hideous vengeance upon you. Only the previous summer, for instance, it having been drawn to his attention that the latter had reported him for smoking, he had marooned a Cabinet Minister on an island in the lake, at Aunt Agatha's place in Hertfordshire – in the rain, mark you, and with no company but that of one of the nastiest-minded swans I have ever encountered. Well, I mean!

So now it seemed to me that a few well-chosen taunts, or jibes, directed at his more sensitive points, must infallibly induce in this Thos. a frame of mind which would lead to his working some sensational violence upon me. And, if you wonder that I was willing to sacrifice myself to this frightful extent in order to do Aunt Dahlia a bit of good, I can only say that we Woosters are like that.

The one point that seemed to me to want a spot of clearing up was this: viz., would old Mr. Anstruther consider an outrage perpetrated on the person of Bertram Wooster a crime sufficiently black to cause him to rule Thos. out of the race? Or would he just give a senile chuckle and mumble something about boys being boys? Because, if the latter, the thing was off. I decided to have a word with the old boy and make sure.

He was still in the smoking-room, looking very frail over the morning *Times*. I got to the point at once.

'Oh, Mr. Anstruther,' I said. 'What ho!'

'I don't like the way the American market is shaping,' he said. 'I don't like this strong Bear movement.'

'No?' I said. 'Well, be that as it may, about this Good Conduct prize of yours?'

'Ah, you have heard of that, eh?'

'I don't quite understand how you are doing the judging.'

'No? It is very simple. I have a system of daily marks. At the beginning of each day I accord the two lads twenty marks apiece.

These are subject to withdrawal either in small or large quantities according to the magnitude of the offence. To take a simple example, shouting outside my bedroom in the early morning would involve a loss of three marks – whistling two. The penalty for a more serious lapse would be correspondingly greater. Before retiring to rest at night I record the day's marks in my little book. Simple, but, I think, ingenious, Mr. Wooster?'

'Absolutely.'

'So far the result has been extremely gratifying. Neither of the little fellows has lost a single mark, and my nervous system is acquiring a tone which, when I learned that two lads of immature years would be staying in the house during my visit, I confess I had not dared to anticipate.'

'I see,' I said. 'Great work. And how do you react to what I might call general moral turpitude?'

'I beg your pardon?'

'Well, I mean when the thing doesn't affect you personally. Suppose one of them did something to me, for instance? Set a booby-trap or something? Or, shall we say, put a toad or so in my bed?'

He seemed shocked at the very idea.

'I would certainly in such circumstances deprive the culprit of a full ten marks.'

'Only ten?'

'Fifteen, then.'

'Twenty is a nice, round number.'

'Well, possibly even twenty. I have a peculiar horror of practical joking.'

'Me, too.'

'You will not fail to advise me, Mr. Wooster, should such an outrage occur?'

'You shall have the news before anyone,' I assured him.

And so out into the garden, ranging to and fro in quest of young Thos. I knew where I was now. Bertram's feet were on solid ground.

I hadn't been hunting long before I found him in the summer-house, reading an improving book.

'Hullo,' he said, smiling a saintlike smile.

This scourge of humanity was a chunky kid whom a too indulgent public had allowed to infest the country for a matter of fourteen years. His nose was snub, his eyes green, his general aspect that of one studying to be a gangster. I had never liked his looks much, and with a saintlike smile added to them they became ghastly to a degree.

I ran over in my mind a few assorted taunts.

'Well, young Thos.,' I said. 'So there you are. You're getting as fat as a pig.'

It seemed as good an opening as any other. Experience had taught me that if there was a subject on which he was unlikely to accept persiflage in a spirit of amused geniality it was this matter of his bulging tum. On the last occasion when I made a remark of this nature, he had replied to me, child though he was, in terms which I would have been proud to have had in my own vocabulary. But now, though a sort of wistful gleam did flit for a moment into his eyes, he merely smiled in a more saintlike manner than ever.

'Yes, I think I have been putting on a little weight,' he said gently. 'I must try and exercise a lot while I'm here. Won't you sit down, Bertie?' he asked, rising. 'You must be tired after your journey. I'll get you a cushion. Have you cigarettes? And matches? I could bring you some from the smoking-room. Would you like me to fetch you something to drink?'

It is not too much to say that I felt baffled. In spite of what Aunt Dahlia had told me, I don't think that until this moment I had really believed there could have been anything in the nature of a genuinely sensational change in this young plugugly's attitude towards his fellows. But now, hearing him talk as if he were a combination of Boy Scout and delivery wagon, I felt definitely baffled. However, I stuck at it in the old bull-dog way.

'Are you still at that rotten kids' school of yours?' I asked.

He might have been proof against jibes at his *embonpoint*, but it seemed to me incredible that he could have sold himself for gold so completely as to lie down under taunts directed at his school. I was wrong. The money-lust evidently held him in its grip. He merely shook his head.

'I left this term. I'm going to Pevenhurst next term.'

'They wear mortar-boards there, don't they?'

'Yes.'

'With pink tassels?'

'Yes.'

'What a priceless ass you'll look!' I said, but without much hope. And I laughed heartily.

'I expect I shall,' he said, and laughed still more heartily.

'Mortar-boards!'

'Ha, ha!'

'Pink tassels!'

'Ha, ha!'

I gave the thing up.

'Well, teuf-teuf,' I said moodily, and withdrew.

A couple of days later I realised that the virus had gone even deeper than I had thought. The kid was irredeemably sordid.

It was old Mr. Anstruther who sprang the bad news.

'Oh, Mr. Wooster,' he said, meeting me on the stairs as I came down after a refreshing breakfast. 'You were good enough to express an interest in this little prize for Good Conduct which I am offering.'

'Oh, ah?'

'I explained to you my system of marking, I believe. Well, this morning I was impelled to vary it somewhat. The circumstances seemed to me to demand it. I happened to encounter our hostess's nephew, the boy Thomas, returning to the house, his aspect somewhat weary, it appeared to me, and travel-stained. I inquired of him where he had been at that early hour – it was not yet breakfast-time – and he replied that he had heard you mention overnight a regret that you had omitted to order the

Sporting Times to be sent to you before leaving London, and he had actually walked all the way to the railway-station, a distance of more than three miles, to procure it for you.'

The old boy swam before my eyes. He looked like two old Mr. Anstruthers, both flickering at the edges.

'What!'

'I can understand your emotion, Mr. Wooster. I can appreciate it. It is indeed rarely that one encounters such unselfish kindliness in a lad of his age. So genuinely touched was I by the goodness of heart which the episode showed that I have deviated from my original system and awarded the little fellow a bonus of fifteen marks.'

'Fifteen!'

'On second thoughts, I shall make it twenty. That, as you yourself suggested, is a nice, round number.'

He doddered away, and I bounded off to find Aunt Dahlia.

'Aunt Dahlia,' I said, 'matters have taken a sinister turn.'

'You bet your Sunday spats they have,' agreed Aunt Dahlia emphatically. 'Do you know what happened just now? That crook Snettisham, who ought to be warned off the turf and hounded out of his clubs, offered Bonzo ten shillings if he would burst a paper bag behind Mr. Anstruther's chair at breakfast. Thank heaven the love of a good woman triumphed again. My sweet Bonzo merely looked at him and walked away in a marked manner. But it just shows you what we are up against.'

'We are up against worse than that, Aunt Dahlia,' I said. And I told her what had happened.

She was stunned. Aghast, you might call it.

'*Thomas* did that?'

'Thos. in person.'

'Walked six miles to get you a paper?'

'Six miles and a bit!'

'The young hound! Good heavens, Bertie, do you realise that he may go on doing these Acts of Kindness daily – perhaps twice a day? Is there no way of stopping him?'

'None that I can think of. No, Aunt Dahlia, I must confess it. I am baffled. There is only one thing to do. We must send for Jeeves.'

'And about time,' said the relative churlishly. 'He ought to have been here from the start. Wire him this morning.'

There is good stuff in Jeeves. His heart is in the right place. The acid test does not find him wanting. Many men in his position, summoned back by telegram in the middle of their annual vacation, might have cut up rough a bit. But not Jeeves. On the following afternoon in he blew, looking bronzed and fit, and I gave him the scenario without delay.

'So there you have it, Jeeves,' I said, having sketched out the facts. 'The problem is one that will exercise your intelligence to the utmost. Rest now, and tonight, after a light repast, withdraw to some solitary place and get down to it. Is there any particularly stimulating food or beverage you would like for dinner? Anything that you feel would give the old brain just that extra fillip? If so, name it.'

'Thank you very much, sir, but I have already hit upon a plan which should, I fancy, prove effective.'

I gazed at the man with some awe.

'Already?'

'Yes, sir.'

'Not *already*?'

'Yes, sir.'

'Something to do with the psychology of the individual?'

'Precisely, sir.'

I shook my head, a bit discouraged. Doubts had begun to creep in.

'Well, spring it, Jeeves,' I said. 'But I have not much hope. Having only just arrived, you cannot possibly be aware of the frightful change that has taken place in young Thos. You are probably building on your knowledge of him, when last seen. Useless, Jeeves. Stirred by the prospect of getting his hooks on five of the best, this blighted boy has become so dashed virtuous that his armour seemed to contain no chink. I mocked at his waistline and sneered at his school and he merely smiled in a pale, dying-duck sort of way. Well, that'll show you. However, let us hear what you have to suggest.'

'It occurred to me, sir, that the most judicious plan in the circumstances would be for you to request Mrs. Travers to invite Master Sebastian Moon here for a short visit.'

I shook the onion again. The scheme sounded to me like apple sauce, and Grade A apple sauce, at that.

'What earthly good would that do?' I asked, not without a touch of asperity. 'Why Sebastian Moon?'

'He has golden curls, sir.'

'What of it?'

'The strongest natures are sometimes not proof against long golden curls.'

Well, it was a thought, of course. But I can't say I was leaping about to any great extent. It might be that the sight of Sebastian Moon would break down Thos.'s iron self-control to the extent of causing him to inflict mayhem on the person, but I wasn't any too hopeful.

'It may be so, Jeeves.'

'I do not think I am too sanguine, sir. You must remember that Master Moon, apart from his curls, has a personality which is not uniformly pleasing. He is apt to express himself with a breezy candour which I fancy Master Thomas might feel inclined to resent in one some years his junior.'

I had had a feeling all along that there was a flaw somewhere, and now it seemed to me that I had spotted it.

'But, Jeeves. Granted that little Sebastian is the pot of poison you indicate, why won't he act just as forcibly on young Bonzo as on Thos.? Pretty silly we should look if our nominee started putting it across him. Never forget that already Bonzo is twenty marks down and falling back in the betting.'

'I do not anticipate any such contingency, sir. Master Travers is in love, and love is a very powerful restraining influence at the age of thirteen.'

'H'm.' I mused. 'Well, we can but try, Jeeves.'

'Yes, sir.'

'I'll get Aunt Dahlia to write to Sippy tonight.'

I'm bound to say that the spectacle of little Sebastian when he arrived two days later did much to remove pessimism from my outlook. If ever there was a kid whose whole appearance seemed to call aloud to any right-minded boy to lure him into a quiet spot and inflict violence upon him, that kid was undeniably Sebastian Moon. He reminded me strongly of Little Lord Fauntleroy. I marked young Thos.'s demeanour closely at the moment of their meeting and, unless I was much mistaken, there came into his eyes the sort of look which would come into those of an Indian chief – Chinchagook, let us say, or Sitting Bull – just before he started reaching for his scalping-knife. He had the air of one who is about ready to begin.

True, his manner as he shook hands was guarded. Only a keen observer could have detected that he was stirred to his depths. But I had seen, and I summoned Jeeves forthwith.

'Jeeves,' I said, 'if I appeared to think poorly of that scheme of yours, I now withdraw my remarks. I believe you have found the way. I was noticing Thos. at the moment of impact. His eyes had a strange gleam.'

'Indeed, sir?'

'He shifted uneasily on his feet and his ears wiggled. He had, in short, the appearance of a boy who was holding himself in with an effort almost too great for his frail body.'

'Yes, sir?'

'Yes, Jeeves. I received a distinct impression of something being on the point of exploding. Tomorrow I shall ask Aunt Dahlia to take the two warts for a country ramble, to lose them in some sequestered spot, and to leave the rest to Nature.'

'It is a good idea, sir.'

'It is more than a good idea, Jeeves,' I said. 'It is a pip.'

You know, the older I get the more firmly do I become convinced that there is no such thing as a pip in existence. Again and again have I seen the apparently sure thing go phut, and now it is rarely indeed that I can be lured from my aloof scepticism. Fellows come sidling up to me at the Drones and elsewhere, urging me to invest on some horse that can't lose even if it gets struck by lightning at the starting-post, but Bertram Wooster shakes his head. He has seen too much of life to be certain of anything.

If anyone had told me that my Cousin Thos., left alone for an extended period of time with a kid of the superlative foulness of Sebastian Moon, would not only refrain from cutting off his curls with a pocket-knife and chasing him across country into a muddy pond but would actually return home carrying the gruesome kid on his back because he had got a blister on his foot, I would have laughed scornfully. I knew Thos. I knew his work. I had seen him in action. And I was convinced that not even the prospect of collecting five pounds would be enough to give him pause.

And yet what happened? In the quiet evenfall, when the little birds were singing their sweetest and all Nature seemed to whisper of hope and happiness, the blow fell. I was chatting with old Mr. Anstruther on the terrace when suddenly round a bend in the drive the two kids hove in view. Sebastian, seated on Thos.'s back, his hat off and his golden curls floating on the breeze, was singing as much as he could remember of a comic song, and Thos., bowed down by the burden but carrying on gamely, was trudging along, smiling that bally saintlike smile of his. He parked the kid on the front steps and came across to us.

'Sebastian got a nail in his shoe,' he said in a low, virtuous voice. 'It hurt him to walk, so I gave him a piggy-back.'

I heard old Mr. Anstruther draw in his breath sharply.

'All the way home?'

'Yes, sir.'

'In this hot sunshine?'

'Yes, sir.'

'But was he not very heavy?'

'He was a little, sir,' said Thos., uncorking the saintlike once more. 'But it would have hurt him awfully to walk.'

I pushed off. I had had enough. If ever a septuagenarian looked on the point of handing out another bonus, that septuagenarian was old Mr. Anstruther. He had the unmistakable bonus glitter in his eye. I withdrew, and found Jeeves in my bedroom messing about with ties and things.

He pursed the lips a bit on hearing the news.

'Serious, sir.'

'Very serious, Jeeves.'

'I had feared this, sir.'

'Had you? I hadn't. I was convinced Thos. would have massacred young Sebastian. I banked on it. It just shows what the greed for money will do. This is a commercial age, Jeeves. When I was a boy, I would cheefully have forfeited five quid in order to deal faithfully with a kid like Sebastian. I would have considered it money well spent.'

'You are mistaken, sir, in your estimate of the motives actuating Master Thomas. It was not a mere desire to win five pounds that caused him to curb his natural impulses.'

'Eh?'

'I have ascertained the true reason for his change of heart, sir.'

I felt fogged.

'Religion, Jeeves?'

'No, sir. Love.'

'Love?'

'Yes, sir. The young gentleman confided in me during a brief conversation in the hall shortly after luncheon. We had been speaking for a while on neutral subjects, when he suddenly turned a deeper shade of pink and after some slight hesitation inquired of me if I did not think Miss Greta Garbo the most beautiful woman at present in existence.'

I clutched the brow.

'Jeeves! Don't tell me Thos. is in love with Greta Garbo?'

'Yes, sir. Unfortunately such is the case. He gave me to understand that it had been coming on for some time, and her last picture settled the issue. His voice shook with an emotion which it was impossible to misread. I gathered from his observations, sir, that he proposes to spend the remainder of his life trying to make himself worthy of her.'

It was a knock-out. This was the end.

'This is the end, Jeeves,' I said. 'Bonzo must be a good forty marks behind by now. Only some sensational and spectacular outrage upon the public weal on the part of young Thos. could have enabled him to wipe out the lead. And of that there is now, apparently, no chance.'

'The eventuality does appear remote, sir.'

I brooded.

'Uncle Thomas will have a fit when he comes back and finds Anatole gone.'

'Yes, sir.'

'Aunt Dahlia will drain the bitter cup to the dregs.'

'Yes, sir.'

'And, speaking from a purely selfish point of view, the finest cooking I have ever bitten will pass out of my life for ever, unless the Snettishams invite me in some night to take pot luck. And that eventuality is also remote.'

'Yes, sir.'

'Then the only thing I can do is square the shoulders and face the inevitable.'

'Yes, sir.'

'Like some aristocrat of the French Revolution popping into the tumbril, what? The brave smile. The stiff upper lip.'

'Yes, sir.'

'Right ho, then. Is the shirt studded?'

'Yes, sir.'

'The tie chosen?'

'Yes, sir.'

'The collar and evening underwear all in order?'

'Yes, sir.'

'Then I'll have a bath and be with you in two ticks.'

It is all very well to talk about the brave smile and the stiff upper lip, but my experience – and I daresay others have found the same – is that they are a dashed sight easier to talk about than actually to fix on the face. For the next few days, I'm bound to admit, I found myself, in spite of every effort, registering gloom pretty consistently. For, as if to make things tougher than they might have been, Anatole at this juncture suddenly developed a cooking streak which put all his previous efforts in the shade.

Night after night we sat at the dinner-table, the food melting in our mouths, and Aunt Dahlia would look at me and I would look at Aunt Dahlia, and the male Snettisham would ask the female Snettisham in a ghastly, gloating sort of way if she had ever tasted such cooking and the female Snettisham would smirk at the male Snettisham and say she never had in all her puff, and I would look at Aunt Dahlia and Aunt Dahlia would look at me and our eyes would be full of unshed tears, if you know what I mean.

And all the time old Mr. Anstruther's visit drawing to a close.

The sands running out, so to speak.

And then, on the very last afternoon of his stay, the thing happened.

It was one of those warm, drowsy, peaceful afternoons. I was up in my bedroom, getting off a spot of correspondence which I had neglected of late, and from where I sat I looked down on the shady lawn, fringed with its gay flowerbeds. There was a bird or two hopping about, a butterfly or so fluttering to and fro, and an assortment of bees buzzing hither and thither. In a garden-chair sat old Mr. Anstruther, getting his eight hours. It was a sight which, had I had less on my mind, would no doubt have soothed the old soul a bit. The only blot on the landscape was Lady Snettisham, walking among the flower-beds and probably sketching out future menus, curse her.

And so for a time everything carried on. The birds hopped, the butterflies fluttered, the bees buzzed, and old Mr. Anstruther snored – all in accordance with the programme. And I worked through a letter to my tailor to the point where I proposed to say something pretty strong about the way the right sleeve of my last coat bagged.

There was a tap on the door, and Jeeves entered, bringing the second post. I laid the letters listlessly on the table beside me.

'Well, Jeeves,' I said sombrely.

'Sir?'

'Mr. Anstruther leaves tomorrow.'

'Yes, sir.'

I gazed down at the sleeping septuagenarian.

'In my young days, Jeeves,' I said, 'however much I might have been in love, I could never have resisted the spectacle of an old gentleman asleep like that in a deck-chair. I would have done *something* to him, no matter what the cost.'

'Indeed, sir?'

'Yes. Probably with a pea-shooter. But the modern boy is degenerate. He has lost his vim. I suppose Thos. is indoors on this lovely afternoon, showing Sebastian his stamp-album or something. Ha!' I said, and I said it rather nastily.

'I fancy Master Thomas and Master Sebastian are playing in the stable-yard, sir. I encountered Master Sebastian not long back, and he informed me he was on his way thither.'

'The motion-pictures, Jeeves,' I said, 'are the curse of the age. But for them, if Thos. had found himself alone in a stable-yard with a kid like Sebastian—'

I broke off. From some point to the south-west, out of my line of vision, there had proceeded a piercing squeal.

It cut through the air like a knife, and old Mr. Anstruther leaped up as if it had run into the fleshy part of his leg. And the next moment little Sebastian appeared, going well and followed at a short interval by Thos., who was going even better. In spite of the fact that he was hampered in his movements by a large stable-bucket which he bore in his right hand, Thos. was running a great race. He had almost come up with Sebastian, when the latter, with great presence of mind, dodged behind Mr. Anstruther, and there for a moment the matter rested.

But only for a moment. Thos., for some reason plainly stirred to the depths of his being, moved adroidy to one side, and, poising the bucket for an instant, discharged its contents. And Mr. Anstruther, who had just moved to the same side, received, as far as I could gather from a distance, the entire consignment. In one second, without any previous training or upbringing, he had become the wettest man in Worcestershire.

'Jeeves!' I cried.

'Yes, indeed, sir,' said Jeeves, and seemed to me to put the whole thing in a nutshell.

Down below, things were hotting up nicely. Old Mr. Anstruther may have been frail, but he undoubtedly had his moments. I have rarely seen a man of his years conduct himself with such a lissom abandon. There was a stick lying beside the chair, and with this in hand he went into action like a two-year-old. A moment later, he and Thos. had passed out of the picture round the side of the house. Thos. cutting out a rare pace but, judging from the sounds of anguish, not quite good enough to distance the field.

The tumult and the shouting died; and, after gazing for a while with considerable satisfaction at the Snettisham, who was standing there with a sandbagged look watching her nominee pass right out of the betting, I turned to Jeeves. I felt quietly triumphant. It is not often that I score off him, but now I had scored in no uncertain manner.

'You see, Jeeves,' I said, 'I was right, and you were wrong.

Blood will tell. Once a Thos., always a Thos. Can the leopard change his spots or the Ethiopian his what-not? What was that thing they used to teach us at school about expelling Nature?'

'You may expel Nature with a pitchfork, sir, but she will always return? In the original Latin—'

'Never mind about the original Latin. The point is that I told you Thos. could not resist those curls, and he couldn't. You would have it that he could.'

'I do not fancy it was the curls that caused the upheaval, sir.'

'Must have been.'

'No, sir. I think Master Sebastian had been speaking disparagingly of Miss Garbo.'

'Eh? Why would he do that?'

'I suggested that he should do so, sir, not long ago when I encountered him on his way to the stable-yard. It was a move which he was very willing to take, as he informed me that in his opinion Miss Garbo was definitely inferior both in beauty and talent to Miss Marlene Dietrich, for whom he has long nourished a deep regard. From what we have just witnessed, sir, I imagine that Master Sebastian must have introduced the topic into the conversation at an early point.'

I sank into a chair. The Wooster system can stand just so much.

'Jeeves!'

'Sir?'

'You tell me that Sebastian Moon, a stripling of such tender years that he can go about the place with long curls without causing mob violence, is in love with Marlene Dietrich?'

'And has been for some little time, he gave me to understand, sir.'

'Jeeves, this Younger Generation is hot stuff.'

'Yes, sir.'

'Were you like that in your day?'

'No, sir.'

'Nor I, Jeeves. At the age of fourteen I once wrote to Marie

Lloyd for her autograph, but apart from that my private life could bear the strictest investigation. However, that is not the point. The point is, Jeeves, that once more I must pay you a marked tribute.'

'Thank you very much, sir.'

'Once more you have stepped forward like the great man you are and spread sweetness and light in no uncertain measure.'

'I am glad to have given satisfaction, sir. Would you be requiring my services any further?'

'You mean you wish to return to Bognor and its shrimps? Do so, Jeeves, and stay there another fortnight, if you wish. And may success attend your net.'

'Thank you very much, sir.'

I eyed the man fixedly. His head stuck out at the back, and his eyes sparkled with the light of pure intelligence.

'I am sorry for the shrimp that tries to pit its feeble cunning against you, Jeeves,' I said.

And I meant it.

In the autumn of the year in which Yorkshire Pudding won the Manchester November Handicap, the fortunes of my old pal Richard ('Bingo') Little seemed to have reached their – what's the word I want? He was, to all appearances, absolutely on plush. He ate well, slept well, was happily married; and, his Uncle Wilberforce having at last handed in his dinner-pail, respected by all, had come into possession of a large income and a fine old place in the country about thirty miles from Norwich. Buzzing down there for a brief visit, I came away convinced that, if ever a bird was sitting on top of the world, that bird was Bingo.

I had to come away because the family were shooting me off to Harrogate to chaperone my Uncle George, whose liver had been giving him the elbow again. But, as we sat pushing down the morning meal on the day of my departure, I readily agreed to pay a return date as soon as ever I could fight my way back to civilisation.

'Come in time for the Lakenham races,' urged young Bingo. He took aboard a second cargo of sausages and bacon, for he had always been a good trencherman and the country air seemed to improve his appetite. 'We're going to motor over with a luncheon basket, and more or less revel.'

I was just about to say that I would make a point of it, when Mrs. Bingo, who was opening letters behind the coffee-apparatus, suddenly uttered a pleased yowl.

'Oh, sweetie-lambkin!' she cried.

Mrs. B., if you remember, before her marriage, was the celebrated female novelist, Rosie M. Banks, and it is in some such ghastly fashion that she habitually addresses the other half of the sketch. She has got that way, I take it, from a lifetime of writing heart-throb fiction for the masses. Bingo doesn't seem to mind. I suppose, seeing that the little woman is the author of such outstanding bilge as *Mervyn Keene, Clubman,* and *Only A Factory Girl,* he is thankful it isn't anything worse.

'Oh, sweetie-lambkin, isn't that lovely?'

'What?'

'Laura Pyke wants to come here.'

'Who?'

'You must have heard me speak of Laura Pyke. She was my dearest friend at school. I simply worshipped her. She always had such a wonderful mind. She wants us to put her up for a week or two.'

'Right ho. Bung her in.'

'You're sure you don't mind?'

'Of course not. Any pal of yours—'

'Darling!' said Mrs. Bingo, blowing him a kiss.

'Angel!' said Bingo, going on with the sausages.

All very charming, in fact. Pleasant domestic scene, I mean. Cheery give-and-take in the home and all that. I said as much to Jeeves as we drove off.

'In these days of unrest, Jeeves,' I said, 'with wives yearning to fulfil themselves and husbands slipping round the corner to do what they shouldn't, and the home, generally speaking, in the melting-pot, as it were, it is nice to find a thoroughly united couple.'

'Decidedly agreeable, sir.'

'I allude to the Bingos – Mr. and Mrs.'

'Exactly, sir.'

'What was it the poet said of couples like the Bingeese?'

' "Two minds with but a single thought, two hearts that beat as one," sir.'

'A dashed good description, Jeeves.'

'It has, I believe, given uniform satisfaction, sir.'

And yet, if I had only known, what I had been listening to that a.m. was the first faint rumble of the coming storm. Unseen, in the background, Fate was quietly slipping the lead into the boxing-glove.

I managed to give Uncle George a miss at a fairly early date and, leaving him wallowing in the waters, sent a wire to the Bingos, announcing my return. It was a longish drive and I fetched up at my destination only just in time to dress for dinner. I had done a quick dash into the soup and fish and was feeling pretty good at the prospect of a cocktail and the well-cooked, when the door opened and Bingo appeared.

'Hullo, Bertie,' he said. 'Ah, Jeeves.'

He spoke in one of those toneless voices: and, catching Jeeves's eye as I adjusted the old cravat, I exchanged a questioning glance with it. From its expression I gathered that the same thing had struck him that had struck me – viz., that our host, the young Squire, was none too chirpy. The brow was furrowed, the eye lacked that hearty sparkle, and the general bearing and demeanour were those of a body discovered after being several days in the water.

'Anything up, Bingo?' I asked, with the natural anxiety of a boyhood friend. 'You have a mouldy look. Are you sickening for some sort of plague?'

'I've got it.'

'Got what?'

'The plague.'

'How do you mean?'

'She's on the premises now,' said Bingo, and laughed in an unpleasant, hacking manner, as if he were missing on one tonsil.

I couldn't follow him. The old egg seemed to me to speak in riddles.

'You seem to me, old egg,' I said, 'to speak in riddles. Don't you think he speaks in riddles, Jeeves?'

'Yes, sir.'

'I'm talking about the Pyke,' said Bingo.

'What pike?'

'Laura Pyke. Don't you remember—?'

'Oh, ah. Of course. The school chum. The seminary crony. Is she still here?'

'Yes, and looks like staying for ever. Rosie's absolutely potty about her. Hangs on her lips.'

'The glamour of the old days still persists, eh?'

'I should say it does,' said young Bingo. 'This business of schoolgirl friendship beats me. Hypnotic is the only word. I can't understand it. Men aren't like that. You and I were at school together, Bertie, but, my gosh, I don't look on you as a sort of mastermind.'

'You don't?'

'I don't treat your lightest utterance as a pearl of wisdom.'

'Why not?'

'Yet Rosie does with this Pyke. In the hands of the Pyke she is mere putty. If you want to see what was once a first-class Garden of Eden becoming utterly ruined as a desirable residence by the machinations of a Serpent, take a look round this place.'

'Why, what's the trouble?'

'Laura Pyke,' said young Bingo with intense bitterness, 'is a food crank, curse her. She says we all eat too much and eat it too quickly and, anyway, ought not to be eating it at all but living on parsnips and similar muck. And Rosie, instead of telling the woman not to be a fathead, gazes at her in wide-eyed admiration, taking it in through the pores. The result is that the cuisine of this house has been shot to pieces, and I am starving on my feet. Well, when I tell you that it's weeks since a beefsteak pudding raised its head in the home, you'll understand what I mean.'

At this point the gong went. Bingo listened with a moody frown.

'I don't know why they still bang that damned thing,' he said. 'There's nothing to bang it for. By the way, Bertie, would you like a cocktail?'

'I would.'

'Well, you won't get one. We don't have cocktails any more. The girl friend says they corrode the stomachic tissues.'

I was appalled. I had had no idea that the evil had spread as far as this.

'No cocktails!'

'No. And you'll be dashed lucky if it isn't a vegetarian dinner.'

'Bingo,' I cried deeply moved, 'you must act. You must assert yourself. You must put your foot down. You must take a strong stand. You must be master in the home.'

He looked at me. A long, strange look.

'You aren't married, are you, Bertie?'

'You know I'm not.'

'I should have guessed it, anyway. Come on.'

Well, the dinner wasn't absolutely vegetarian, but when you had said that you had said everything. It was sparse, meagre, not at all the jolly, chunky repast for which the old tum was standing up and clamouring after its long motor ride. And what there was of it was turned to ashes in the mouth by the conversation of Miss Laura Pyke.

In happier circs., and if I had not been informed in advance of the warped nature of her soul, I might have been favourably impressed by this female at the moment of our meeting. She was really rather a good-looking girl, a bit strong in the face but nevertheless quite reasonably attractive. But had she been a thing of radiant beauty, she could never have clicked with Bertram Wooster. Her conversation was of a kind which would have queered Helen of Troy with any right-thinking man.

During dinner she talked all the time, and it did not take me long to see why the iron had entered into Bingo's soul. Practically all she said was about food and Bingo's tendency to shovel it down in excessive quantities, thereby handing the lemon to his stomachic tissues. She didn't seem particularly interested in my stomachic tissues, rather giving the impression that if Bertram burst it would be all right with her. It was on young Bingo that she concentrated as the brand to be saved from the burning. Gazing at him like a high priestess at the favourite, though erring, disciple, she told him all the things that were happening to his inside because he would insist on eating stuff lacking in fat-soluble vitamins. She spoke freely of proteins, carbohydrates, and the physiological requirements of the average individual. She was not a girl who believed in mincing her words, and a racy little anecdote she told about a man who refused to eat prunes had the effect of causing me to be a non-starter for the last two courses.

'Jeeves,' I said, on reaching the sleeping chamber that night, 'I don't like the look of things.'

'No, sir?'

'No, Jeeves, I do not. I view the situation with concern. Things are worse than I thought they were. Mr. Little's remarks before dinner may have given you the impression that the Pyke merely lectured on food-reform, in a general sort of way. Such, I now find, is not the case. By way of illustrating her theme, she points to Mr. Little as the awful example. She criticises him, Jeeves.'

'Indeed, sir?'

'Yes. Openly. Keeps telling him he eats too much, drinks too much, and gobbles his food. I wish you could have heard a comparison she drew between him and the late Mr. Gladstone, considering them in the capacity of food chewers. It left young Bingo very much with the short end of the stick. And the sinister thing is that Mrs. Bingo approves. Are wives often like that? Welcoming criticism of the lord and master, I mean?'

'They are generally open to suggestions from the outside public with regard to the improvement of their husbands, sir.'

'That is why married men are wan, what?'

'Yes, sir.'

I had had the foresight to send the man downstairs for a plate of biscuits. I bit a representative specimen thoughtfully.

'Do you know what I think, Jeeves?'

'No, sir.'

'I think Mr. Little doesn't realise the full extent of the peril which threatens his domestic happiness. I'm beginning to understand this business of matrimony. I'm beginning to see how the thing works. Would you care to hear how I figure it out, Jeeves?'

'Extremely, sir.'

'Well, it's like this. Take a couple of birds. These birds get married, and for a while all is gas and gaiters. The female regards her mate as about the best thing that ever came a girl's way. He is her king, if you know what I mean. She looks up to him and respects him. Joy, as you might say, reigns supreme. Eh?'

'Very true, sir.'

'Then gradually, by degrees – little by little, if I may use the expression – disillusionment sets in. She sees him eating a poached egg, and the glamour starts to fade. She watches him mangling a chop, and it continues to fade. And so on and so on, if you follow me, and so forth.'

'I follow you perfectly, sir.'

'But mark this, Jeeves. This is the point. Here we approach the nub. Usually it is all right, because, as I say, the disillusionment comes gradually and the female has time to adjust herself. But in the case of young Bingo, owing to the indecent outspokenness of the Pyke, it's coming in a rush. Absolutely in a flash, without any previous preparation, Mrs. Bingo is having Bingo presented to her as a sort of human boa-constrictor full of unpleasantly jumbled interior organs. The picture which the Pyke is building up for her in her mind is that of one of those men you see in restaurants with three chins, bulging eyes, and the veins starting out on the forehead. A little more of this, and love must wither.'

'You think so, sir?'

'I'm sure of it. No affection can stand the strain. Twice during dinner tonight the Pyke said things about young Bingo's intestinal canal which I shouldn't have thought would have been possible in mixed company even in this lax post-War era. Well, you see what I mean. You can't go on knocking a man's intestinal canal indefinitely without causing his wife to stop and ponder. The danger, as I see it, is that after a bit more of this Mrs. Little will decide that tinkering is no use and that the only thing to do is to scrap Bingo and get a newer model.'

'Most disturbing, sir.'

'Something must be done, Jeeves. You must act. Unless you can find some way of getting this Pyke out of the woodwork, and that right speedily, the home's number is up. You see, what makes matters worse is that Mrs. Bingo is romantic. Women like her, who consider the day ill-spent if they have not churned out five thousand words of superfatted fiction, are apt even at the best of times to yearn a trifle. The ink gets into their heads. I mean to say, I shouldn't wonder if right from the start Mrs. Bingo hasn't had a sort of sneaking regret that Bingo isn't one of those strong, curt, Empire-building kind of Englishmen she puts into her books, with sad, unfathomable eyes, lean, sensitive hands, and riding-boots. You see what I mean?'

'Precisely, sir. You imply that Miss Pyke's criticisms will have been instrumental in moving the hitherto unformulated dissatisfaction from the subconscious to the conscious mind.'

'Once again, Jeeves?' I said, trying to grab it as it came off the bat, but missing it by several yards.

He repeated the dose.

'Well, I daresay you're right,' I said. 'Anyway, the point is, P.M.G. Pyke must go. How do you propose to set about it?'

'I fear I have nothing to suggest at the moment, sir.'

'Come, come, Jeeves.'

'I fear not, sir. Possibly after I have seen the lady—'

'You mean, you want to study the psychology of the individual and what not?"

'Precisely, sir.'

'Well, I don't know how you're going to do it. After all, I mean, you can hardly cluster round the dinner-table and drink the Pyke's small talk.'

'There is that difficulty, sir.'

'Your best chance, it seems to me, will be when we go to the Lakenham races on Thursday. We shall feed out of a luncheon-basket in God's air, and there's nothing to stop you hanging about and passing the sandwiches. Prick the ears and be at your most observant then, is my advice.'

'Very good, sir.'

'Very good, Jeeves. Be there, then, with the eyes popping. And, meanwhile, dash downstairs and see if you can dig up another instalment of these biscuits. I need them sorely.'

The morning of the Lakenham races dawned bright and juicy. A casual observer would have said that God was in His Heaven and all right with the world. It was one of those days you sometimes get latish in the autumn when the sun beams, the birds toot, and there is a bracing tang in the air that sends the blood beetling briskly through the veins.

Personally, however, I wasn't any too keen on the bracing tang. It made me feel so exceptionally fit that almost immediately after breakfast I found myself beginning to wonder what there would be for lunch. And the thought of what there probably would be for lunch, if the Pyke's influence made itself felt, lowered my spirits considerably.

'I fear the worst, Jeeves,' I said. 'Last night at dinner Miss Pyke threw out the remark that the carrot was the best of all vegetables, having an astonishing effect on the blood and beautifying the complexion. Now, I am all for anything that bucks up the Wooster blood. Also, I would like to give the natives a treat by letting them take a look at my rosy, glowing cheeks. But not at the expense of lunching on raw carrots. To avoid any rannygazoo, therefore, I think it will be best if you add a bit for the young master to your personal packet of sandwiches. I don't want to be caught short.'

'Very good, sir.'

At this point, young Bingo came up. I hadn't seen him look so jaunty for days.

'I've just been superintending the packing of the lunch-basket, Bertie,' he said. 'I stood over the butler and saw that there was no nonsense.'

'All pretty sound?' I asked, relieved.

'All indubitably sound.'

'No carrots?'

'No carrots,' said young Bingo. 'There's ham sandwiches,' he proceeded, a strange, soft light in his eyes, 'and tongue sandwiches and potted meat sandwiches and game sandwiches and hard-boiled eggs and lobster and a cold chicken and sardines and a cake and a couple of bottles of Bollinger and some old brandy—'

'It has the right ring,' I said. 'And if we want a bite to eat after that, of course we can go to the pub.'

'What pub?'

'Isn't there a pub on the course?'

'There's not a pub for miles. That's why I was so particularly careful that there should be no funny work about the basket. The common where these races are held is a desert without an oasis. Practically a death-trap. I met a fellow the other day who told me he got there last year and unpacked his basket and found that the champagne had burst and, together with the salad dressing, had soaked into the ham, which in its turn had got mixed up with the gorgonzola cheese, forming a sort of paste. He had had rather a bumpy bit of road to travel over.'

'What did he do?'

'Oh, he ate the mixture. It was the only course. But he said he could still taste it sometimes, even now.'

In ordinary circs. I can't say I should have been any too braced at the news that we were going to split up for the journey in the following order – Bingo and Mrs. Bingo in their car and the Pyke in mine, with Jeeves sitting behind in the dickey. But, things being as they were, the arrangement had its points. It meant that Jeeves would be able to study the back of her head and draw his deductions, while I could engage her in conversation and let him see for himself what manner of female she was.

I started, accordingly, directly we had rolled off and all through the journey until we fetched up at the course she gave of her best. It was with considerable satisfaction that I parked the car beside a tree and hopped out.

'You were listening, Jeeves?' I said gravely.

'Yes, sir.'

'A tough baby?'

'Undeniably, sir.'

Bingo and Mrs. Bingo came up.

'The first race won't be for half an hour,' said Bingo. 'We'd better lunch now. Fish the basket out, Jeeves, would you mind?'

'Sir?'

'The luncheon-basket,' said Bingo in a devout sort of voice, licking his lips slightly.

'The basket is not in Mr. Wooster's car, sir.'

'What!'

'I assumed that you were bringing it in your own, sir.'

I have never seen the sunshine fade out of anybody's face as quickly as it did out of Bingo's. He uttered a sharp, wailing cry.

'Rosie!'

'Yes, sweetie-pie?'

'The bunch! The lasket!'

'What, darling?'

'The luncheon-basket!'

'What about it, precious?'

'It's been left behind!'

'Oh, has it?' said Mrs. Bingo.

I confess she had never fallen lower in my estimation. I had always known her as a woman with as healthy an appreciation of her meals as any of my acquaintance. A few years previously, when my Aunt Dahlia had stolen her French cook, Anatole, she had called Aunt Dahlia some names in my presence which had impressed me profoundly. Yet now, when informed that she was marooned on a bally prairie without bite or sup, all she could find to say was: 'Oh, has it?' I had never fully realised before the extent to which she had allowed herself to be dominated by the deleterious influence of the Pyke.

The Pyke, for her part, touched an even lower level.

'It is just as well,' she said, and her voice seemed to cut Bingo like a knife. 'Luncheon is a meal better omitted. If taken, it should consist merely of a few muscatels, bananas and grated carrots. It is a well-known fact—'

And she went on to speak at some length of the gastric juices in a vein far from suited to any gathering at which gentlemen were present.

'So, you see, darling,' said Mrs. Bingo, 'you will really feel ever so much better and brighter for not having eaten a lot of indigestible food. It is much the best thing that could have happened.'

Bingo gave her a long, lingering look.

'I see,' he said. 'Well, if you will excuse me, I'll just go off somewhere where I can cheer a bit without exciting comment.'

I perceived Jeeves withdrawing in a meaning manner, and I followed him, hoping for the best. My trust was not misplaced. He had brought enough sandwiches for two. In fact, enough for three. I whistled to Bingo, and he came slinking up, and we restored the tissues in a makeshift sort of way behind a hedge. Then Bingo went off to interview bookies about the first race, and Jeeves gave a cough.

'Swallowed a crumb the wrong way?' I said.

'No, sir, I thank you. It is merely that I desired to express a hope that I had not been guilty of taking a liberty, sir.'

'How?'

'In removing the luncheon-basket from the car before we started, sir.'

I quivered like an aspen. I stared at the man. Aghast. Shocked to the core.

'You, Jeeves?' I said, and I should rather think Caesar spoke in the same sort of voice on finding Brutus puncturing him with the sharp instrument. 'You mean to tell me it was you who deliberately, if that's the word I want—?'

'Yes, sir. It seemed to me the most judicious course to pursue. It would not have been prudent, in my opinion, to have allowed Mrs. Little, in her present frame of mind, to witness Mr. Little eating a meal on the scale which he outlined in his remarks this morning.'

I saw his point.

'True, Jeeves,' I said thoughtfully. 'I see what you mean. If young Bingo has a fault, it is that, when in the society of a sandwich, he is apt to get a bit rough. I've picnicked with him before, many a time and oft, and his method of approach to the ordinary tongue or ham sandwich rather resembles that of the lion, the king of beasts, tucking into an antelope. Add lobster and cold chicken, and I admit the spectacle might have been something of a jar for the consort. . . . Still. . . all the same . . . nevertheless—'

'And there is another aspect of the matter, sir.'

'What's that?'

'A day spent without nourishment in the keen autumnal air may induce in Mrs. Little a frame of mind not altogether in sympathy with Miss Pyke's views on diet.'

'You mean, hunger will gnaw and she'll be apt to bite at the Pyke when she talks about how jolly it is for the gastric juices to get a day off?'

'Exactly, sir.'

I shook the head. I hated to damp the man's pretty enthusiasm, but it had to be done.

'Abandon the idea, Jeeves,' I said. 'I fear you have not studied the sex as I have. Missing her lunch means little or nothing to the female of the species. The feminine attitude towards lunch is notoriously airy and casual. Where you have made your bloomer is in confusing lunch with tea. Hell, it is well known, has no fury like a woman who wants her tea and can't get it. At such times the most amiable of the sex become mere bombs which a spark may ignite. But lunch, Jeeves, no. I should have thought you would have known that – a bird of your established intelligence.'

'No doubt you are right, sir.'

'If you could somehow arrange for Mrs. Little to miss her tea . . . but these are idle dreams, Jeeves. By tea-time she will be back at the old home, in the midst of plenty. It only takes an hour to do the trip. The last race is over shortly after four. By five o'clock Mrs. Little will have her feet tucked under the table and will be revelling in buttered toast. I am sorry, Jeeves, but your scheme was a wash-out from the start. No earthly. A dud.'

'I appreciate the point you have raised, sir. What you say is extremely true.'

'Unfortunately. Well, there it is. The only thing to do seems to be to get back to the course and try to skin a bookie or two and forget.'

Well, the long day wore on, so to speak. I can't say I enjoyed myself much. I was distrait, if you know what I mean. Preoccupied. From time to time assorted clusters of spavined local horses clumped down the course with farmers on top of them, but I watched them with a languid eye. To get into the spirit of one of these rural meetings, it is essential that the subject have a good, fat lunch inside him. Subtract the lunch, and what ensues? Ennui. Not once but many times during the afternoon I found myself thinking hard thoughts about Jeeves. The man seemed to me to be losing his grip. A child could have told him that that footling scheme of his would not have got him anywhere.

I mean to say, when you reflect that the average woman considers she has lunched luxuriously if she swallows a couple of macaroons, half a chocolate eclair and a raspberry vinegar, is she going to be peevish because you do her out of a midday sandwich? Of course not. Perfectly ridiculous. Too silly for words. All that Jeeves had accomplished by his bally trying to be clever was to give me a feeling as if foxes were gnawing my vitals and a strong desire for home.

It was a relief, therefore, when, as the shades of evening were beginning to fall, Mrs. Bingo announced her intention of calling it a day and shifting.

'Would you mind very much missing the last race, Mr. Wooster?' she asked.

'I am all for it,' I replied cordially. 'The last race means little or nothing in my life. Besides, I am a shilling and sixpence ahead of the game, and the time to leave off is when you're winning.'

'Laura and I thought we would go home. I feel I should like an early cup of tea. Bingo says he will stay on. So I thought you could drive our car, and he would follow later in yours, with Jeeves.'

'Right ho.'

'You know the way?'

'Oh yes. Main road as far as that turning by the pond, and then across country.'

'I can direct you from there.'

I sent Jeeves to fetch the car, and presently we were bowling off in good shape. The short afternoon had turned into a rather chilly, misty sort of evening, the kind of evening that sends a fellow's thoughts straying off in the direction of hot Scotch-and-water with a spot of lemon in it. I put the foot firmly on the accelerator, and we did the five or six miles of main road in quick time.

Turning eastward at the pond, I had to go a bit slower, for we had struck a wildish stretch of country where the going wasn't so good. I don't know any part of England where you feel so off the map as on the by-roads of Norfolk. Occasionally we would meet a cow or two, but otherwise we had the world pretty much to ourselves.

I began to think about that drink again, and the more I thought the better it looked. It's rummy how people differ in this matter of selecting the beverage that is to touch the spot. It's what Jeeves would call the psychology of the individual. Some fellows in my position might have voted for a tankard of ale, and the Pyke's idea of a refreshing snort was, as I knew from what she had told me on the journey out, a cupful of tepid pip-and-peel water or, failing that, what she called the fruit-liquor. You make this, apparently, by soaking raisins in cold water and adding the juice of a lemon. After which, I suppose, you invite a couple of old friends in and have an orgy, burying the bodies in the morning.

Personally, I had no doubts. I never wavered. Hot Scotch-and-water was the stuff for me – stressing the Scotch, if you know what I mean, and going fairly easy on the H_2O. I seemed to see the beaker smiling at me across the misty fields, beckoning me on, as it were, and saying 'Courage, Bertram! It will not be long now!' And with renewed energy I bunged the old foot down on the accelerator and tried to send the needle up to sixty.

Instead of which, if you follow my drift, the bally thing flickered for a moment to thirty-five and then gave the business up as a bad job. Quite suddenly and unexpectedly, no one more surprised than myself, the car let out a faint gurgle like a sick moose and stopped in its tracks. And there we were, somewhere in Norfolk, with darkness coming on and a cold wind that smelled of guano and dead mangel-wurzels playing searchingly about the spinal column.

The back-seat drivers gave tongue.

'What's the matter? What has happened? Why don't you go on? What are you stopping for?'

I explained.

'I'm not stopping. It's the car.'

'Why has the car stopped?'

'Ah!' I said with a manly frankness that became me well. 'There you have me.'

You see, I'm one of those birds who drive a lot but don't know the first thing about the works. The policy I pursue is to get aboard, prod the self-starter, and leave the rest to Nature. If anything goes wrong, I scream for an A.A. scout. It's a system that answers admirably as a rule, but on the present occasion it blew a fuse owing to the fact that there wasn't an A.A. scout within miles. I explained as much to the fair cargo and received in return a 'Tchah!' from the Pyke that nearly lifted the top of my head off. What with having a covey of female relations who have regarded me from childhood as about ten degrees short of a half-wit, I have become rather a connoisseur of 'Tchahs', and the Pyke's seemed to me well up in Class A, possessing much of the *timbre* and *brio* of my Aunt Agatha's.

'Perhaps I can find out what the trouble is,' she said, becoming calmer. 'I understand cars.'

She got out and began peering into the thing's vitals. I thought for a moment of suggesting that its gastric juices might have taken a turn for the worse owing to lack of fat-soluble vitamins, but decided on the whole not to. I'm a pretty close observer, and it didn't seem to me that she was in the mood.

And yet, as a matter of fact, I should have been about right, at that. For after fiddling with the engine for a while in a discontented sort of way the female was suddenly struck with an idea. She tested it, and it was proved correct. There was not a drop of petrol in the tank. No gas. In other words, a complete lack of fat-soluble vitamins. What it amounted to was that the job now before us was to get the old bus home purely by will-power.

Feeling that, from whatever angle they regarded the regrettable occurrence, they could hardly blame me, I braced up a trifle – in fact, to the extent of a hearty 'Well, well, well!'

'No petrol,' I said. 'Fancy that.'

'But Bingo told me he was going to fill the tank this morning,' said Mrs. Bingo.

'I suppose he forgot,' said the Pyke. 'He would!'

'What do you mean by that?' said Mrs. Bingo, and I noted in her voice a touch of what-is-it.

'I mean he is just the sort of man who would forget to fill the tank,' replied the Pyke, who also appeared somewhat moved.

'I should be very much obliged, Laura,' said Mrs. Bingo, doing the heavy loyal-little-woman stuff, 'if you would refrain from criticising my husband.'

'Tchah!' said the Pyke.

'And don't say "Tchah!"' said Mrs. Bingo.

'I shall say whatever I please,' said the Pyke.

'Ladies, ladies!' I said. 'Ladies, ladies, ladies!'

It was rash. Looking back, I can see that. One of the first lessons life teaches us is that on these occasions of back-chat between the delicately-nurtured, a man should retire into the offing, curl up in a ball, and imitate the prudent tactics of the opossum, which, when danger is in the air, pretends to be dead, frequently going to the length of hanging out crêpe and instructing its friends to stand round and say what a pity it all is. The only result of my dash at the soothing intervention was that the Pyke turned on me like a wounded leopardess.

'Well!' she said. 'Aren't you proposing to do anything, Mr. Wooster?'

'What can I do?'

'There's a house over there. I should have thought it would be well within even your powers to go and borrow a tin of petrol.'

I looked. There was a house. And one of the lower windows was lighted, indicating to the trained mind the presence of a ratepayer.

'A very sound and brainy scheme,' I said ingratiatingly. 'I will first honk a little on the horn to show we're here, and then rapid action.'

I honked, with the most gratifying results. Almost immediately a human form appeared in the window. It seemed to be waving its arms in a matey and welcoming sort of way. Stimulated and encouraged, I hastened to the front door and gave it a breezy bang with the knocker. Things, I felt, were moving.

The first bang produced no result. I had just lifted the knocker for the encore, when it was wrenched out of my hand. The door flew open, and there was a bloke with spectacles on his face and all round the spectacles an expression of strained anguish. A bloke with a secret sorrow.

I was sorry he had troubles, of course, but, having some of my own, I came right down to the agenda without delay.

'I say . . .' I began.

The bloke's hair was standing up in a kind of tousled mass, and at this juncture, as if afraid it would not stay like that without assistance, he ran a hand through it. And for the first time I noted that the spectacles had a hostile gleam.

'Was that you making that infernal noise?' he asked.

'Er – yes,' I said, 'I did toot.'

'Toot once more – just once,' said the bloke, speaking in a low, strangled voice, 'and I'll shred you up into little bits with my bare hands. My wife's gone out for the evening and after hours of ceaseless toil I've at last managed to get the baby to sleep, and you come along making that hideous din with your damned horn. What do you mean by it, blast you?'

'Er—'

'Well, that's how matters stand,' said the bloke, summing up. 'One more toot – just one single, solitary suggestion of the faintest shadow or suspicion of anything remotely approaching a toot – and may the Lord have mercy on your soul.'

'What I want,' I said, 'is petrol.'

'What you'll get,' said the bloke, 'is a thick ear.'

And, closing the door with the delicate caution of one brushing flies off a sleeping Venus, he passed out of my life.

Women as a sex are always apt to be a trifle down on the defeated warrior. Returning to the car, I was not well recived. The impression seemed to be that Bertram had not acquitted himself in a fashion worthy of his Crusading ancestors. I did my best to smooth matters over, but you know how it is. When you've broken down on a chilly autumn evening miles from anywhere and have missed lunch and look like missing tea as well, mere charm of manner can never be a really satisfactory substitute for a tinful of the juice.

Things got so noticeably unpleasant, in fact, that after a while, mumbling something about getting help, I sidled off down the road. And, by Jove, I hadn't gone half a mile before I saw lights in the distance and there, in the middle of this forsaken desert, was a car.

I stood in the road and whooped as I had never whooped before.

'Hi!' I shouted. 'I say! Hi! Half a minute! Hi! Ho! I say! Ho! Hi! Just a second if you don't mind.'

The car reached me and slowed up. A voice spoke.

'Is that you, Bertie?'

'Hullo, Bingo! Is that you? I say, Bingo, we've broken down.'

Bingo hopped out.

'Give us five minutes, Jeeves,' he said, 'and then drive slowly on.'

'Very good, sir.'

Bingo joined me.

'We aren't going to walk, are we?' I asked. 'Where the sense?'

'Yes, walk, laddie,' said Bingo, 'and warily withal. I want to make sure of something. Bertie, how were things when you left? Hotting up?'

'A trifle.'

'You observed symptoms of a row, a quarrel, a parting of brass rags between Rosie and the Pyke?'

'There did seem a certain liveliness.'

'Tell me.'

I related what had occurred. He listened intently.

'Bertie,' he said as we walked along, 'you are present at a crisis in your old friend's life. It may be that this vigil in a broken-down car will cause Rosie to see what you'd have thought she ought to have seen years ago – viz: that the Pyke is entirely unfit for human consumption and must be cast into outer darkness where there is wailing and gnashing of teeth. I am not betting on it, but stranger things have happened. Rosie is the sweetest girl in the world, but, like all women, she gets edgy towards tea-time. And today, having missed lunch . . . Hark!'

He grabbed my arm, and we paused. Tense. Agog. From down the road came the sound of voices, and a mere instant was enough to tell us that it was Mrs. Bingo and the Pyke talking things over.

I had never listened in on a real, genuine female row before, and I'm bound to say it was pretty impressive. During my absence, matters appeared to have developed on rather a specious scale. They had reached the stage now where the combatants had begun to dig into the past and rake up old scores. Mrs. Bingo was saying that the Pyke would never have got into the hockey team at St. Adela's if she hadn't flattered and fawned upon the captain in a way that it made Mrs. Bingo, even after all these years, sick to think of. The Pyke replied that she had refrained from mentioning it until now, having always felt it better to let bygones be bygones, but that if Mrs. Bingo supposed her to be unaware that Mrs. Bingo had won the Scripture prize by taking a list of the Kings of Judah into the examination room, tucked into her middy-blouse, Mrs. Bingo was vastly mistaken.

Furthermore, the Pyke proceeded, Mrs. Bingo was also labouring under an error if she imagined that the Pyke proposed to remain a night longer under her roof. It had been in a moment of weakness, a moment of mistaken kindliness, supposing her to be lonely and in need of intellectual society, that the Pyke had decided to pay her a visit at all. Her intention now was, if ever Providence sent them aid and enabled her to get out of this beastly car and back to her trunks to pack those trunks and leave by the next train, even if that train was a milk-train, stopping at every station. Indeed, rather than endure another night at Mrs. Bingo's, the Pyke was quite willing to walk to London.

To this, Mrs. Bingo's reply was long and eloquent and touched on the fact that in her last term at St. Adela's a girl named Simpson had told her (Mrs. Bingo) that a girl named Waddesley had told her (the Simpson) that the Pyke, while pretending to be a friend of hers (the Bingo's), had told her (the Waddesley) that she (the Bingo) couldn't eat strawberries and cream without coming out in spots, and, in addition, had spoken in the most catty manner about the shape of her nose. It could all have been condensed, however, into the words 'Right ho'.

It was when the Pyke had begun to say that she had never had such a hearty laugh in her life as when she read the scene in Mrs. Bingo's last novel when the heroine's little boy dies of croup that we felt it best to call the meeting to order before bloodshed set in. Jeeves had come up in the car, and Bingo, removing a tin of petrol from the dickey, placed it in the shadows at the side of the road. Then we hopped on and made the spectacular entry.

'Hullo, hullo, hullo,' said Bingo brightly. 'Bertie tells me you've had a breakdown.'

'Oh, Bingo!' cried Mrs. Bingo, wifely love thrilling in every syllable. 'Thank goodness you've come.'

'Now, perhaps,' said the Pyke, 'I can get home and do my packing. If Mr. Wooster will allow me to use his car, his man can drive me back to the house in time to catch the six-fifteen.'

'You aren't leaving us?' said Bingo.

'I am,' said the Pyke.

'Too bad,' said Bingo.

She climbed in beside Jeeves and they popped off. There was a short silence after they had gone. It was too dark to see her, but I could feel Mrs. Bingo struggling between love of her mate and the natural urge to say something crisp about his forgetting to fill the petrol tank that morning. Eventually nature took its course.

'I must say, sweetie-pie,' she said, 'it was a little careless of you to leave the tank almost empty when we started today. You promised me you would fill it, darling.'

'But I did fill it, darling.'

'But, darling, it's empty.'

'It can't be, darling.'

'Laura said it was.'

'The woman's an ass,' said Bingo. 'There's plenty of petrol. What's wrong is probably that the sprockets aren't running true with the differential gear. It happens that way sometimes. I'll fix it in a second. But I don't want you to sit freezing out here while I'm doing it. Why not go to that house over there and ask them if you can't come in and sit down for ten minutes? They might give you a cup of tea, too.'

A soft moan escaped Mrs. Bingo.

'Tea!' I heard her whisper.

I had to bust Bingo's daydream.

'I'm sorry, old man,' I said, 'but I fear the old English hospitality which you outline is off. That house is inhabited by a sort of bandit. As unfriendly a bird as I ever met. His wife's out and he's just got the baby to sleep, and this has darkened his outlook. Tap even lightly on his front door and you take your life into your hands.'

'Nonsense,' said Bingo. 'Come along.' He banged the knocker, and produced an immediate reaction.

'Hell!' said the Bandit, appearing as if out of a trap.

'I say,' said young Bingo, 'I'm just fixing our car outside. Would you object to my wife coming in out of the cold for a few minutes?'

'Yes,' said the Bandit, 'I would.'

'And you might give her a cup of tea.'

'I might,' said the Bandit, 'but I won't.'

'You won't?'

'No. And for heaven's sake don't talk so loud. I know that baby. A whisper sometimes does it.'

'Let us get this straight,' said Bingo. 'You refuse to give my wife tea?'

'Yes.'

'You would see a woman starve?'

'Yes.'

'Well, you jolly well aren't going to,' said young Bingo. 'Unless you go straight to your kitchen, put the kettle on, and start slicing bread for the buttered toast, I'll yell and wake the baby.'

The Bandit turned ashen.

'You wouldn't do that?'

'I would.'

'Have you no heart?'

'No.'

'No human feeling?'

'No.'

The Bandit turned to Mrs. Bingo. You could see his spirit was broken.

'Do your shoes squeak?' he asked humbly.

'No.'

'Then come on in.'

'Thank you,' said Mrs. Bingo.

She turned for an instant to Bingo, and there was a look in her eyes that one of those damsels in distress might have given the knight as he shot his cuffs and turned away from the dead dragon. It was a look of adoration, of almost reverent respect. Just the sort of look, in fact, that a husband likes to see.

'Darling!' she said.

'Darling!' said Bingo.

'Angel!' said Mrs. Bingo.

'Precious!' said Bingo. 'Come along, Bertie, let's get at that car.'

He was silent till he had fetched the tin of petrol and filled the tank and screwed the cap on again. Then he drew a deep breath.

'Bertie,' he said, 'I am ashamed to admit it, but occasionally in the course of a lengthy acquaintance there have been moments when I have temporarily lost faith in Jeeves.'

'My dear chap!' I said, shocked.

'Yes, Bertie, there have. Sometimes my belief in him has wobbled. I have said to myself: "Has he the old speed, the ancient vim?" I shall never say it again. From now on, childlike trust. It was his idea, Bertie, that if a couple of women headed for tea suddenly found the cup snatched from their lips, so to speak, they would turn and rend one another. Observe the result.'

'But, dash it, Jeeves couldn't have known that the car would break down.'

'On the contrary. He let all the petrol out of the tank when you sent him to fetch the machine – all except just enough to carry it well into the wilds beyond the reach of human aid. He foresaw what would happen. I tell you, Bertie, Jeeves stands alone.'

'Absolutely.'

'He's a marvel.'

'A wonder.'

'A wizard.'

'A stout fellow,' I agreed. 'Full of fat-soluble vitamins.'

'The exact expression,' said young Bingo. 'And now let's go and tell Rosie the car is fixed, and then home to the tankard of ale.'

'Not the tankard of ale, old man,' I said firmly. 'The hot Scotch-and-water with a spot of lemon in it.'

'You're absolutely right,' said Bingo. 'What a flair you have in these matters, Bertie. Hot Scotch-and-water it is.'

Ask anyone at the Drones, and they will tell you that Bertram Wooster is a fellow whom it is dashed difficult to deceive. Old Lynx-Eye is about what it amounts to. I observe and deduce. I weigh the evidence and draw my conclusions. And that is why Uncle George had not been in my midst more than about two minutes before I, so to speak, saw all. To my trained eye the thing stuck out a mile.

And yet it seemed so dashed absurd. Consider the facts, if you know what I mean.

I mean to say, for years, right back to the time when I first went to school, this bulging relative has been one of the recognised eyesores of London. He was fat then, and day by day in every way has been getting fatter ever since, till now tailors measure him just for the sake of the exercise. He is what they call a prominent London clubman – one of those birds in tight morning-coats and grey toppers whom you see toddling along St. James's Street on fine afternoons, puffing a bit as they make the grade. Slip a ferret into any good club between Piccadilly and Pall Mall, and you would start half a dozen Uncle Georges.

He spends his time lunching and dining at the Buffers and, between meals, sucking down spots in the smoking-room and talking to anyone who will listen about the lining of his stomach. About twice a year his liver lodges a formal protest and he goes off to Harrogate or Carlsbad to get planed down. Then back again and on with the programme. The last bloke in the world, in short, who you would think would even fall a victim to the divine pash. And yet, if you will believe me, that was absolutely the strength of it.

This old pestilence blew in on me one morning at about the hour of the after-breakfast cigarette.

'Oh, Bertie,' he said.

'Hullo?'

'You know those ties you've been wearing. Where did you get them?'

'Blucher's, in the Burlington Arcade.'

'Thanks.'

He walked across to the mirror and stood in front of it, gazing at himself in an earnest manner.

'Smut on your nose?' I asked courteously.

Then I suddenly perceived that he was wearing a sort of horrible simper, and I confess it chilled the blood to no little extent. Uncle George, with face in repose, is hard enough on the eye. Simpering, he goes right above the odds.

'Ha!' he said.

He heaved a long sigh, and turned away. Not too soon, for the mirror was on the point of cracking.

'I'm not so old,' he said, in a musing sort of voice.

'So old as what?'

'Properly considered, I'm in my prime. Besides, what a young and inexperienced girl needs is a man of weight and years to lean on. The sturdy oak, not the sapling.'

It was at this point that, as I said above, I saw all.

'Great Scott, Uncle George!' I said. 'You aren't thinking of getting married?'

'Who isn't?' he said.

'You aren't,' I said.

'Yes, I am. Why not?'

'Oh, well—'

'Marriage is an honourable state.'

'Oh, absolutely.'

'It might make you a better man, Bertie.'

'Who says so?'

'I say so. Marriage might turn you from a frivolous young scallywag into – er – a non-scallywag. Yes, confound you, I *am* thinking of getting married, and if Agatha comes sticking her oar in I'll – I'll – well, I shall know what to do about it.'

He exited on the big line, and I rang the bell for Jeeves. The situation seemed to me one that called for a cosy talk.

'Jeeves,' I said.

'Sir?'

'You know my Uncle George?'

'Yes, sir. His lordship has been familiar to me for some years.'

'I don't mean do you know my Uncle George. I mean do you know what my Uncle George is thinking of doing?'

'Contracting a matrimonial alliance, sir.'

'Good Lord! Did he tell you?'

'No, sir. Oddly enough, I chance to be acquainted with the other party in the matter.'

'The girl?'

'The young person, yes, sir. It was from her aunt, with whom she resides, that I received the information that his lordship was contemplating matrimony.'

'Who is she?'

'A Miss Platt, sir. Miss Rhoda Platt. Of Wistaria Lodge, Kitchener Road, East Dulwich.'

'Young?'

'Yes, sir.'

'The old fathead!'

'Yes, sir. The expression is one which I would, of course, not have ventured to employ myself, but I confess to thinking his lordship somewhat ill-advised. One must remember, however, that it is not unusual to find gentlemen of a certain age yielding to what might be described as a sentimental urge. They appear to experience what I may term a sort of Indian summer, a kind of temporarily renewed youth. The phenomenon is particularly noticeable, I am given to understand, in the United States of America among the wealthier inhabitants of the city of Pittsburg. It is notorious, I am told, that sooner or later, unless restrained, they always endeavour to marry chorus-girls. Why this should be so, I am at a loss to say, but—'

I saw that this was going to take some time. I tuned out.

'From something in Uncle George's manner, Jeeves, as he referred to my Aunt Agatha's probable reception of the news, I gather that this Miss Platt is not of the *noblesse*.'

'No, sir. She is a waitress at his lordship's club.'

'My God! The proletariat!'

'The lower middle classes, sir.'

'Well, yes, by stretching it a bit, perhaps. Still, you know what I mean.'

'Yes, sir.'

'Rummy thing, Jeeves,' I said thoughtfully, 'this modern tendency to marry waitresses. If you remember, before he settled down, young Bingo Little was repeatedly trying to do it.'

'Yes, sir.'

'Odd!'

'Yes, sir.'

'Still, there it is, of course. The point to be considered now is: What will Aunt Agatha do about this? You know her, Jeeves. She is not like me. I'm broad-minded. If Uncle George wants to marry waitresses, let him, say I. I hold that the rank is but the penny stamp—'

'Guinea stamp, sir.'

'All right, guinea stamp. Though I don't believe there is such a thing. I shouldn't have thought they came higher than five bob. Well, as I was saying, I maintain that the rank is but the guinea stamp and a girl's a girl for all that.'

' "For *a*' that," sir. The poet Burns wrote in the North British dialect.'

'Well, "a" that,' then, if you prefer it.'

'I have no preference in the matter, sir. It is simply that the poet Burns—'

'Never mind about the poet Burns.'

'No, sir.'

'Forget the poet Burns.'

'Very good, sir.'

'Expunge the poet Burns from your mind.'

'I will do so immediately, sir.'

'What we have to consider is not the poet Burns but the Aunt Agatha. She will kick, Jeeves.'

'Very probably, sir.'

'And, what's worse, she will lug me into the mess. There is only one thing to be done. Pack the toothbrush and let us escape while we may, leaving no address.'

'Very good, sir.'

At this moment the bell rang.

'Ha!' I said. 'Someone at the door.'

'Yes, sir.'

'Probably Uncle George back again. I'll answer it. You go and get ahead with the packing.'

'Very good, sir.'

I sauntered along the passage, whistling carelessly, and there on the mat was Aunt Agatha. Herself. Not a picture.

A nasty jar.

'Oh, hullo!' I said, it seeming but little good to tell her I was out of town and not expected back for some weeks.

'I wish to speak to you, Bertie,' said the Family Curse. 'I am greatly upset.'

She legged it into the sitting-room and volplaned into a chair. I followed, thinking wistfully of Jeeves packing in the bedroom. That suit-case would not be needed now. I knew what she must have come about.

'I've just seen Uncle George,' I said, giving her a lead.

'So have I,' said Aunt Agatha, shivering in a marked manner. 'He called on me while I was still in bed to inform me of his intention of marrying some impossible girl from South Norwood.'

'East Dulwich, the *cognoscenti* inform me.'

'Well, East Dulwich, then. It is the same thing. But who told you?'

'Jeeves.'

'And how, pray, does Jeeves come to know all about it?'

'There are very few things in this world, Aunt Agatha,' I said gravely, 'that Jeeves doesn't know all about. He's met the girl.'

'Who is she?'

'One of the waitresses at the Buffers.'

I had expected this to register, and it did. The relative let out a screech rather like the Cornish Express going through a junction.

'I take it from your manner, Aunt Agatha,' I said, 'that you want this thing stopped.'

'Of course it must be stopped.'

'Then there is but one policy to pursue. Let me ring for Jeeves and ask his advice.'

Aunt Agatha stiffened visibly. Very much the *grande dame* of the old *régime.*

'Are you seriously suggesting that we should discuss this intimate family matter with your manservant?'

'Absolutely. Jeeves will find the way.'

'I have always known that you were an imbecile, Bertie,' said the flesh-and-blood, now down at about three degrees Fahrenheit, 'but I did suppose that you had some proper feeling, some pride, some respect for your position.'

'Well, you know what the poet Burns says.'

She squelched me with a glance.

'Obviously the only thing to do,' she said, 'is to offer this girl money.'

'Money?'

'Certainly. It will not be the first time your uncle has made such a course necessary.'

We sat for a bit, brooding. The family always sits brooding when the subject of Uncle George's early romance comes up. I was too young to be actually in on it at the time, but I've had the details frequently from many sources, including Uncle George. Let him get even the slightest bit pickled, and he will tell you the whole story, sometimes twice in an evening. It was a barmaid at the Criterion, just before he came into the title. Her name was Maudie and he loved her dearly, but the family would have none of it. They dug down into the sock and paid her off. Just one of those human-interest stories, if you know what I mean.

I wasn't so sold on this money-offering scheme.

'Well, just as you like, of course,' I said, 'but you're taking an awful chance. I mean, whenever people do it in novels and plays, they always get the dickens of a welt. The girl gets the sympathy of the audience every time. She just draws herself up and looks at them with clear, steady eyes, causing them to feel not a little cheesey. If I were you, I would sit tight and let Nature take its course.'

'I don't understand you.'

'Well, consider for a moment what Uncle George looks like. No Greta Garbo, believe me. I should simply let the girl go on looking at him. Take it from me, Aunt Agatha, I've studied human nature and I don't believe there's a female in the world who could see Uncle George fairly often in those waistcoats he wears without feeling that it was due to her better self to give him the gate. Besides, this girl sees him at meal-times, and Uncle George with his head down among the food-stuffs is a spectacle which—'

'If it is not troubling you too much, Bertie, I should be greatly obliged if you would stop drivelling.'

'Just as you say. All the same, I think you're going to find it dashed embarrassing, offering this girl money.'

'I am not proposing to do so. *You* will undertake the negotiations.'

'Me?'

'Certainly. I should think a hundred pounds would be ample. But I will give you a blank cheque, and you are at liberty to fill it in for a higher sum if it becomes necessary. The essential point is that, cost what it may, your uncle must be released from this entanglement.'

'So you're going to shove this off on me?'

'It is quite time you did something for the family.'

'And when she draws herself up and looks at me with clear, steady eyes, what do I do for an encore?'

'There is no need to discuss the matter any further. You can get down to East Dulwich in half an hour. There is a frequent service of trains. I will remain here to await your report.'

'But, listen!'

'Bertie, you will go and see this woman immediately.'

'Yes, but dash it!'

'Bertie!'

I threw in the towel.

'Oh, right ho, if you say so.'

'I do say so.'

'Oh, well, in that case, right ho.'

I don't know if you have ever tooled off to East Dulwich to offer a strange female a hundred smackers to release your Uncle George. In case you haven't, I may tell you that there are plenty of things that are lots better fun. I didn't feel any too good driving to the station. I didn't feel any too good in the train. And I didn't feel any too good as I walked to Kitchener Road. But the moment when I felt least good was when I had actually pressed the front door bell and a rather grubby-looking maid had let me in and shown me down a passage and into a room with pink paper on the walls, a piano in the corner and a lot of photographs on the mantelpiece.

Barring a dentist's waiting-room, which it rather resembles, there isn't anything that quells the spirit much more than one of these suburban parlours. They are extremely apt to have stuffed birds in glass cases standing about on small tables, and if there is one thing which gives the man of sensibility that sinking feeling it is the cold, accusing eye of a ptarmigan or whatever it may be that has had its interior organs removed and sawdust substituted.

There were three of these cases in the parlour of Wistaria Lodge, so that, wherever you looked, you were sure to connect. Two were singletons, the third a family group, consisting of a father bullfinch, a mother bullfinch, and little Master Bullfinch, the last-named of whom wore an expression that was definitely that of a thug, and did more to damp my *joie de vivre* than all the rest of them put together.

I had moved to the window and was examining the aspidistra in order to avoid this creature's gaze, when I heard the door open and, turning, found myself confronted by something which, since it could hardly be the girl, I took to be the aunt.

'Oh, what ho,' I said. 'Good morning.'

The words came out rather roopily, for I was feeling a bit on the stunned side. I mean to say, the room being so small and this exhibit so large, I had got that sensation of wanting air. There are some people who don't seem to be intended to be seen close to, and this aunt was one of them. Billowy curves, if you know what I mean. I should think that in her day she must have been a very handsome girl, though even then on the substantial side. By the time she came into my life, she had taken on a good deal of excess weight. She looked like a photograph of an opera singer of the 'eighties. Also the orange hair and the magenta dress.

However, she was a friendly soul. She seemed glad to see Bertram. She smiled broadly.

'So here you are at last!' she said.

I couldn't make anything of this.

'Eh?'

'But I don't think you had better see my niece just yet. She's just having a nap.'

'Oh, in that case—'

'Seems a pity to wake her, doesn't it?'

'Oh, absolutely,' I said, relieved.

'When you get the influenza, you don't sleep at night, and then if you doze off in the morning – well, it seems a pity to wake someone, doesn't it?'

'Miss Platt has influenza?'

'That's what we think it is. But, of course, you'll be able to say. But we needn't waste time. Since you're here, you can be taking a look at my knee.'

'Your knee?'

I am all for knees at their proper time and, as you might say, in their proper place, but somehow this didn't seem the moment. However, she carried on according to plan.

'What do you think of that knee?' she asked, lifting the seven veils.

Well, of course, one has to be polite.

'Terrific!' I said.

'You wouldn't believe how it hurts me sometimes.'

'Really?'

'A sort of shooting pain. It just comes and goes. And I'll tell you a funny thing.'

'What's that?' I said, feeling I could do with a good laugh.

'Lately I've been having the same pain just here at the end of the spine.'

'You don't mean it!'

'I do. Like red-hot needles. I wish you'd have a look at it.'

'At your spine?'

'Yes.'

I shook my head. Nobody is fonder of a bit of fun than myself, and I am all for Bohemian camaraderie and making a party go, and all that. But there is a line, and we Woosters know when to draw it.

'It can't be done,' I said austerely. 'Not spines. Knees, yes. Spines, no,' I said.

She seemed surprised.

'Well,' she said, 'you're a funny sort of doctor, I must say.'

I'm pretty quick, as I said before, and I began to see that something in the nature of a misunderstanding must have arisen.

'Doctor?'

'Well, you call yourself a doctor, don't you?'

'Did you think I was a doctor?'

'Aren't you a doctor?'

'No. Not a doctor.'

We had got it straightened out. The scales had fallen from our eyes. We knew where we were.

I had suspected that she was a genial soul. She now endorsed this view. I don't think I have ever heard a woman laugh so heartily.

'Well, that's the best thing?' she said, borrowing my handkerchief to wipe her eyes. 'Did you ever! But, if you aren't the doctor, who are you?'

'Wooster's the name. I came to see Miss Platt.'

'What about?'

This was the moment, of course, when I should have come out with the cheque and sprung the big effort. But somehow I couldn't make it. You know how it is. Offering people money to release your uncle is a scaly enough job at best, and when the atmosphere's not right the shot simply isn't on the board.

'Oh, just came to see her, you know.' I had rather a bright idea. 'My uncle heard she was seedy, don't you know, and asked me to look in and make inquiries,' I said.

'Your uncle?'

'Lord Yaxley.'

'Oh! So you are Lord Yaxley's nephew?'

'That's right. I suppose he's always popping in and out here, what?'

'No. I've never met him.'

'You haven't?'

'No. Rhoda talks a lot about him, of course, but for some reason she's never so much as asked him to look in for a cup of tea.'

I began to see that this Rhoda knew her business. If I'd been a girl with someone wanting to marry me and knew that there was an exhibit like this aunt hanging around the home, I, too, should have thought twice about inviting him to call until the ceremony was over and he had actually signed on the dotted line. I mean to say, a thoroughly good soul – heart of gold beyond a doubt – but not the sort of thing you wanted to spring on Romeo before the time was ripe.

'I suppose you were all very surprised when you heard about it?' she said.

'Surprised is right.'

'Of course, nothing is definitely settled yet.'

'You don't mean that? I thought—'

'Oh, no. She's thinking it over.'

'I see.'

'Of course, she feels it's a great compliment. But then sometimes she wonders if he isn't too old.'

'My Aunt Agatha has rather the same idea.'

'Of course, a title *is* a title.'

'Yes, there's that. What do you think about it yourself?'

'Oh, it doesn't matter what I think. There's no doing anything with girls these days, is there?'

'Not much.'

'What I often say is, I wonder what girls are coming to. Still, there it is.'

'Absolutely.'

There didn't seem much reason why the conversation shouldn't go on for ever. She had the air of a woman who had settled down for the day. But at this point the maid came in and said the doctor had arrived.

I got up.

'I'll be tooling off, then.'

'If you must.'

'I think I'd better.'

'Well, pip, pip.'

'Toodle-oo,' I said, and out into the fresh air.

Knowing what was waiting for me at home, I would have preferred to have gone to the club and spent the rest of the day there. But the thing had to be faced.

'Well?' said Aunt Agatha, as I trickled into the sitting-room.

'Well, yes and no,' I replied.

'What do you mean? Did she refuse the money?'

'Not exactly.'

'She accepted it?'

'Well, there, again, not precisely.'

I explained what had happened. I wasn't expecting her to be any too frightfully pleased, and it's as well that I wasn't, because she wasn't. In fact, as the story unfolded, her comments became fruitier and fruitier, and when I had finished she uttered an exclamation that nearly broke a window. It sounded something like 'Gor!' as if she had started to say 'Gorblimey!' and had remembered her ancient lineage just in time.

'I'm sorry,' I said. 'And can a man say more? I lost my nerve. The old *morale* suddenly turned blue on me. It's the sort of thing that might have happened to anyone.'

'I never heard of anything so spineless in my life.'

I shivered, like a warrior whose old wound hurts him.

'I'd be most awfully obliged, Aunt Agatha,' I said, 'if you would not use that word spine. It awakens memories.'

The door opened. Jeeves appeared.

'Sir?'

'Yes, Jeeves?'

' I thought you called, sir.'

'No, Jeeves.'

'Very good, sir.'

There are moments when, even under the eye of Aunt

Agatha, I can take the firm line. And now, seeing Jeeves standing there with the light of intelligence simply fizzing in every feature, I suddenly felt how perfectly footling it was to give this pre-eminent source of balm and comfort the go-by simply because Aunt Agatha had prejudices against discussing family affairs with the staff. It might make her say 'Gor!' again, but I decided to do as we ought to have done right from the start – put the case in his hands.

'Jeeves,' I said, 'this matter of Uncle George.'

'Yes, sir.'

'You know the circs.?'

'Yes, sir.'

'You know what we want.'

'Yes, sir.'

'Then advise us. And make it snappy. Think on your feet.'

I heard Aunt Agatha rumble like a volcano just before it starts to set about the neighbours, but I did not wilt. I had seen the sparkle in Jeeves's eye which indicated that an idea was on the way.

'I understand that you have been visiting the young person's home, sir?'

'Just got back.'

'Then you no doubt encountered the young person's aunt?'

'Jeeves, I encountered nothing else but.'

'Then the suggestion which I am about to make will, I feel sure, appeal to you, sir. I would recommend that you confronted his lordship with this woman. It has always been her intention to continue residing with her niece after the latter's marriage. Should he meet her, this reflection might give his lordship pause. As you are aware, sir, she is a kind-hearted woman, but definitely of the people.'

'Jeeves, you are right! Apart from anything else, that orange hair!'

'Exactly, sir.'

'Not to mention the magenta dress.'

'Precisely, sir.'

'I'll ask her to lunch tomorrow, to meet him. You see,' I said to Aunt Agatha, who was still fermenting in the background, 'a ripe suggestion first crack out of the box. Did I or did I not tell you—'

'That will do, Jeeves,' said Aunt Agatha.

'Very good, madam.'

For some minutes after he had gone, Aunt Agatha strayed from the point a bit, confining her remarks to what she thought of a Wooster who could lower the prestige of the clan by allowing menials to get above themselves. Then she returned to what you might call the main issue.

'Bertie,' she said, 'you will go and see this girl again tomorrow and this time you will do as I told you.'

'But, dash it! With this excellent alternative scheme, based firmly on the psychology of the individual—'

'That is quite enough, Bertie. You heard what I said. I am going. Good-bye.'

She buzzed off, little knowing of what stuff Bertram Wooster was made. The door had hardly closed before I was shouting for Jeeves.

'Jeeves,' I said, 'the recent aunt will have none of your excellent alternative scheme, but none the less I propose to go through with it unswervingly. I consider it a ball of fire. Can you get hold of this female and bring her here for lunch tomorrow?'

'Yes, sir.'

'Good. Meanwhile, I will be 'phoning Uncle George. We will do Aunt Agatha good despite herself. What is it the poet says, Jeeves?'

'The poet Burns, sir?'

'Not the poet Burns. Some other poet. About doing good by stealth.'

' "These little acts of unremembered kindness," sir?'

'That's it in a nutshell, Jeeves.'

*

I suppose doing good by stealth ought to give one a glow, but I can't say I found myself exactly looking forward to the binge in prospect. Uncle George by himself is a mouldy enough luncheon companion, being extremely apt to collar the conversation and confine it to a description of his symptoms, he being one of those birds who can never be brought to believe that the general public isn't agog to hear all about the lining of his stomach. Add the aunt, and you have a little gathering which might well dismay the stoutest. The moment I woke, I felt conscious of some impending doom, and the cloud, if you know what I mean, grew darker all the morning. By the time Jeeves came in with the cocktails, I was feeling pretty low.

'For two pins, Jeeves,' I said, 'I would turn the whole thing up and leg it to the Drones.'

'I can readily imagine that this will prove something of an ordeal, sir.'

'How did you get to know these people, Jeeves?'

'It was through a young fellow of my acquaintance, sir, Colonel Mainwaring-Smith's personal gentleman's gentleman. He and the young person had an understanding at the time, and he desired me to accompany him to Wistaria Lodge and meet her.'

'They were engaged?'

'Not precisely engaged, sir. An understanding.'

'What did they quarrel about?'

'They did not quarrel, sir. When his lordship began to pay his addresses, the young person, naturally flattered, began to waver between love and ambition. But even now she has not formally rescinded the understanding.'

'Then, if your scheme works and Uncle George edges out, it will do your pal a bit of good?'

'Yes, sir. Smethurst – his name is Smethurst – would consider it a consummation devoutly to be wished.'

'Rather well put, that, Jeeves. Your own?'

'No, sir. The Swan of Avon, sir.'

An unseen hand without tootled on the bell, and I braced myself to play the host. The binge was on.

'Mrs. Wilberforce, sir,' announced Jeeves.

'And how I'm to keep a straight face with you standing behind and saying "Madam, can I tempt you with a potato?" is more than I know,' said the aunt, sailing in, looking larger and pinker and matier than ever. 'I know him, you know,' she said, jerking a thumb after Jeeves. 'He's been round and taken tea with us.'

'So he told me.'

She gave the sitting-room the once-over.

'You've got a nice place here,' she said. 'Though I like more pink about. It's so cheerful. What's that you've got there? Cocktails?'

'Martini with a spot of absinthe,' I said, beginning to pour.

She gave a girlish squeal.

'Don't you try to make me drink that stuff! Do you know what would happen if I touched one of those things? I'd be racked with pain. What they do to the lining of your stomach!'

'Oh, I don't know.'

'I do. If you had been a barmaid as long as I was, you'd know, too.'

'Oh – er – were you a barmaid?'

'For years, when I was younger than I am. At the Criterion.'

I dropped the shaker.

'There!' she said, pointing the moral. 'That's through drinking that stuff. Makes your hand wobble. What I always used to say to the boys was: "Port, if you like. Port's wholesome. I appreciate a drop of port myself. But these newfangled messes from America, no." But they would never listen to me.'

I was eyeing her warily. Of course, there must have been thousands of barmaids at the Criterion in its time, but still it gave one a bit of a start. It was years ago that Uncle George's dash at a mesalliance had occurred – long before he came into the title – but the Wooster clan still quivered at the name of the Criterion.

'Er – when you were at the Cri.,' I said, 'did you ever happen to run into a fellow of my name?'

'I've forgotten what it is. I'm always silly about names.'

'Wooster.'

'Wooster! When you were there yesterday I thought you said Foster. Wooster! Did I run into a fellow named Wooster? Well! Why, George Wooster and me – Piggy, I used to call him – were going off to the registrar's, only his family heard of it and interfered. They offered me a lot of money to give him up, and, like a silly girl, I let them persuade me. If I've wondered once what became of him, I've wondered a thousand times. Is he a relation of yours?'

'Excuse me,' I said. 'I just want a word with Jeeves.'

I legged it for the pantry.

'Jeeves!'

'Sir?'

'Do you know what's happened?'

'No, sir.'

'This female—'

'Sir?'

'She's Uncle George's barmaid!'

'Sir?'

'Oh, dash it, you must have heard of Uncle George's barmaid. You know all the family history. The barmaid he wanted to marry years ago.'

'Ah, yes, sir.'

'She's the only woman he ever loved. He's told me so a million times. Every time he gets to the fourth whisky-and-potash, he always becomes maudlin about this female. What a dashed bit of bad luck! The first thing we know, the call of the past will be echoing in his heart. I can feel it, Jeeves. She's just his sort. The first thing she did when she came in was to start talking about the lining of her stomach. You see the hideous significance of that, Jeeves? The lining of his stomach is Uncle George's favourite topic of conversation. It means that he and she are kindred souls. This woman and he will be like—'

'Deep calling to deep, sir?'

'Exactly.'

'Most disturbing, sir.'

'What's to be done?'

'I could not say, sir.'

'I'll tell you what I'm going to do – 'phone him and say the lunch is off.'

'Scarcely feasible, sir. I fancy that is his lordship at the door now.'

And so it was. Jeeves let him in, and I followed him as he navigated down the passage to the sitting-room. There was a stunned silence as he went in, and then a couple of the startled yelps you hear when old buddies get together after long separation.

'Piggy!'

'Maudie!'

'Well, I never!'

'Well, I'm dashed!'

'Did you ever!'

'Well, bless my soul!'

'Fancy you being Lord Yaxley!'

'Came into the title soon after we parted.'

'Just to think!'

'You could have knocked me down with a feather!'

I hung about in the offing, now on this leg, now on that. For all the notice they took of me, I might just have well been the late Bertram Wooster, disembodied.

'Maudie, you don't look a day older, dash it!'

'Nor do you, Piggy.'

'How have you been all these years?'

'Pretty well. The lining of my stomach isn't all it should be.'

'Good Gad! You don't say so? I have trouble with the lining of *my* stomach.'

'It's a sort of heavy feeling after meals.'

'*I* get a sort of heavy feeling after meals. What are you trying for it?'

'I've been taking Perkins' Digestine.'

'My dear girl, no use! No use at all. Tried it myself for years and got no relief. Now, if you really want something that is some good—'

I slid away. The last I saw of them, Uncle George was down beside her on the Chesterfield, buzzing hard.

'Jeeves,' I said, tottering into the pantry.

'Sir?'

'There will only be two for lunch. Count me out. If they notice I'm not there, tell them I was called away by an urgent 'phone message. The situation has got beyond Bertram, Jeeves. You will find me at the Drones.'

'Very good, sir.'

It was latish in the evening when one of the waiters came to me as I played a distrait game of snooker pool and informed me that Aunt Agatha was on the 'phone.

'Bertie!'

'Hullo?'

I was amazed to note that her voice was that of an aunt who feels that things are breaking right. It had the birdlike trill.

'Bertie, have you that cheque I gave you?'

'Yes.'

'Then tear it up. It will not be needed.'

'Eh?'

'I say it will not be needed. Your uncle has been speaking to me on the telephone. He is not going to marry that girl.'

'Not?'

'No. Apparently he has been thinking it over and sees how unsuitable it would have been. But what is astonishing is that he *is* going to be married!'

'He is?'

'Yes, to an old friend of his, a Mrs. Wilberforce. A woman of a sensible age, he gave me to understand. I wonder which

Wilberforces that would be. There are two main branches of the family – the Essex Wilberforces and the Cumberland Wilberforces. I believe there is also a cadet branch somewhere in Shropshire.'

'And one in East Dulwich.'

'What did you say?'

'Nothing,' I said. 'Nothing.'

I hung up. Then back to the old flat, feeling a trifle sand-bagged.

'Well, Jeeves,' I said, and there was censure in the eyes. 'So I gather everything is nicely settled?'

'Yes, sir. His lordship formally announced the engagement between the sweet and cheese courses, sir.'

'He did, did he?'

'Yes, sir.'

I eyed the man sternly.

'You do not appear to be aware of it, Jeeves,' I said, in a cold, level voice, 'but this binge has depreciated your stock very considerably. I have always been accustomed to look upon you as a counsellor without equal. I have, so to speak, hung upon your lips. And now see what you have done. All this is the direct consequence of your scheme, based on the psychology of the individual. I should have thought, Jeeves, that, knowing the woman – meeting her socially, as you might say, over the afternoon cup of tea – you might have ascertained that she was Uncle George's barmaid.'

'I did, sir.'

'What!'

'I was aware of the fact, sir.'

'Then you must have known what would happen if she came to lunch and met him.'

'Yes, sir.'

'Well, I'm dashed!'

'If I might explain, sir. The young man Smethurst, who is greatly attached to the young person, is an intimate friend of mine. He applied to me some little while back in the hope that I might be able to do something to ensure that the young person followed the dictates of her heart and refrained from permitting herself to be lured by gold and the glamour of his lordship's position. There will now be no obstacle to their union.'

'I see. "Little acts of unremembered kindness," what?'

'Precisely, sir.'

'And how about Uncle George? You've landed him pretty nicely in the cart.'

'No, sir, if I may take the liberty of opposing your view. I fancy that Mrs. Wilberforce should make an ideal mate for his lordship. If there was a defect in his lordship's mode of life, it was that he was a little unduly attached to the pleasures of the table—'

'Ate like a pig, you mean?'

'I would not have ventured to put it in quite that way, sir, but the expression does meet the facts of the case. He was also inclined to drink rather more than his medical adviser would have approved of. Elderly bachelors who are wealthy and without occupation tend somewhat frequently to fall into this error, sir. The future Lady Yaxley will check this. Indeed, I overheard her ladyship saying as much as I brought in the fish. She was commenting on a certain puffiness of the face which had been absent in his lordship's appearance in the earlier days of their acquaintanceship, and she observed that his lordship needed looking after. I fancy, sir, that you will find the union will turn out an extremely satisfactory one.'

It was – what's the word I want? – it was plausible, of course, but still I shook the onion.

'But, Jeeves!'

'Sir?'

'She *is*, as you remarked not long ago, definitely of the people.'

He looked at me in a reproachful sort of way.

'Sturdy lower middle class stock, sir.'

'H'm!'

'Sir?'

'I said "H'm!" Jeeves.'

'Besides, sir, remember what the poet Tennyson said: "Kind hearts are more than coronets."'

'And which of us is going to tell Aunt Agatha that?'

'If I might make the suggestion, sir, I would advise that we omitted to communicate with Mrs. Spenser Gregson in any way. I have your suit-case practically packed. It would be a matter of but a few minutes to bring the car round from the garage—'

'And off over the horizon to where men are men?'

'Precisely, sir.'

'Jeeves,' I said. 'I'm not sure that even now I can altogether see eye to eye with you regarding your recent activities. You think you have scattered light and sweetness on every side. I am not so sure. However, with this latest suggestion you have rung the bell. I examine it narrowly and I find no flaw in it. It is the goods. I'll get the car at once.'

'Very good, sir.'

'Remember what the poet Shakespeare said, Jeeves.'

'What was that, sir?'

'"Exit hurriedly, pursued by a bear." You'll find it in one of his plays. I remember drawing a picture of it on the side of the page, when I was at school.'

'What-ho, Jeeves!' I said, entering the room where he waded knee-deep in suitcases and shirts and winter suitings, like a sea-beast among rocks. 'Packing?'

'Yes, sir,' replied the honest fellow, for there are no secrets between us.

'Pack on!' I said approvingly. 'Pack, Jeeves, pack with care. Pack in the presence of the passenjare.' And I rather fancy I added the words 'Tra-la!' for I was in merry mood.

Every year, starting about the middle of November, there is a good deal of anxiety and apprehension among owners of the better-class of country-house throughout England as to who will get Bertram Wooster's patronage for the Christmas holidays. It may be one or it may be another. As my Aunt Dahlia says, you never know where the blow will fall.

This year, however, I had decided early. It couldn't have been later than Nov. 10 when a sigh of relief went up from a dozen stately homes as it became known that the short straw had been drawn by Sir Reginald Witherspoon, Bart, of Bleaching Court, Upper Bleaching, Hants.

In coming to the decision to give this Witherspoon my custom, I had been actuated by several reasons, not counting the fact that, having married Aunt Dahlia's husband's younger sister Katherine, he is by way of being a sort of uncle of mine. In the first place, the Bart. does one extraordinarily well, both browsing and sluicing being above criticism. Then, again, his stables always contain something worth riding, which is a consideration. And, thirdly, there is no danger of getting lugged into a party of amateur Waits and having to tramp the countryside in the rain, singing, 'When Shepherds Watched Their Flocks By Night.' Or for the matter of that, 'Noel! Noel!'

All these things counted with me, but what really drew me to Bleaching Court like a magnet was the knowledge that young Tuppy Glossop would be among those present.

I feel sure I have told you before about this black-hearted bird, but I will give you the strength of it once again, just to keep the records straight. He was the fellow, if you remember, who, ignoring a lifelong friendship in the course of which he had frequently eaten my bread and salt, betted me one night at the Drones that I wouldn't swing myself across the swimming-bath by the ropes and rings and then, with almost inconceivable treachery, went and looped back the last ring, causing me to drop into the fluid and ruin one of the nattiest suits of dress-clothes in London.

To execute a fitting vengeance on this bloke had been the ruling passion of my life ever since.

'You are bearing in mind, Jeeves,' I said, 'the fact that Mr. Glossop will be at Bleaching?'

'Yes, sir.'

'And, consequently, are not forgetting to put in the Giant Squirt?'

'No, sir.'

'Nor the Luminous Rabbit?'

'No, sir.'

'Good! I am rather pinning my faith on the Luminous Rabbit, Jeeves. I hear excellent reports of it on all sides. You wind it up and put it in somebody's room in the night watches, and it shines in the dark and jumps about, making odd, squeaking noises the while. The whole performance being, I should imagine, well calculated to scare young Tuppy into a decline.'

'Very possibly, sir.'

'Should that fail, there is always the Giant Squirt. We must leave no stone unturned to put it across the man somehow,' I said. 'The Wooster honour is at stake.'

I would have spoken further on this subject, but just then the front door bell buzzed.

'I'll answer it,' I said. 'I expect it's Aunt Dahlia. She 'phoned that she would be calling this morning.'

It was not Aunt Dahlia. It was a telegraph-boy with telegram. I opened it, read it, and carried it back to the bedroom, the brow a bit knitted.

'Jeeves,' I said. 'A rummy communication has arrived. From Mr. Glossop.'

'Indeed, sir?'

'I will read it to you. Handed in at Upper Bleaching. Message runs as follows:

'When you come tomorrow, bring my football boots. Also, if humanly possible, Irish water-spaniel. Urgent. Regards. Tuppy.'

'What do you make of that, Jeeves?'

'As I interpret the document, sir, Mr. Glossop wishes you, when you come tomorrow, to bring his football boots. Also, if humanly possible, an Irish water-spaniel. He hints that the matter is urgent, and sends his regards.'

'Yes, that's how I read it, too. But why football boots?'

'Perhaps Mr. Glossop wishes to pay football, sir.'

I considered this.

'Yes,' I said. 'That may be the solution. But why would a man, staying peacefully at a country-house, suddenly develop a craving to play football?'

'I could not say, sir.'

'And why an Irish water-spaniel?'

'There again I fear I can hazard no conjecture, sir.'

'What *is* an Irish water-spaniel?'

'A water-spaniel of a variety bred in Ireland, sir.'

'You think so?'

'Yes, sir.'

'Well, perhaps you're right. But why should I sweat about the place collecting dogs – of whatever nationality – for young Tuppy? Does he think I'm Santa Claus? Is he under the impression that my feelings towards him, after that Drones Club incident, are those of kindly benevolence? Irish water-spaniels, indeed! Tchah!'

'Sir?'

'Tchah, Jeeves.'

'Very good, sir.'

The front door bell buzzed again.

'Our busy morning, Jeeves.'

'Yes, sir.'

'All right. I'll go.'

This time it was Aunt Dahlia. She charged in with the air of a woman with something on her mind – giving tongue, in fact, while actually on the very doormat.

'Bertie,' she boomed, in that ringing voice of hers which cracks window-panes and upsets vases, 'I've come about that young hound, Glossop.'

'It's quite all right, Aunt Dahlia,' I replied soothingly. 'I have the situation well in hand. The Giant Squirt and the Luminous Rabbit are even now being packed.'

'I don't know what you're talking about, and I don't for a moment suppose you do, either,' said the relative somewhat brusquely, 'but, if you'll kindly stop gibbering, I'll tell you what I mean. I have had a most disturbing letter from Katherine. About this reptile. Of course, I haven't breathed a word to Angela. She'd hit the ceiling.'

This Angela is Aunt Dahlia's daughter. She and young Tuppy are generally supposed to be more or less engaged, though nothing definitely Morning Posted yet.

'Why?' I said.

'Why what?'

'Why would Angela hit the ceiling?'

'Well, wouldn't you, if you were practically engaged to a fiend in human shape and somebody told you he had gone off to the country and was flirting with a dog-girl?'

'With a what was that, once again?'

'A dog-girl. One of these dashed open-air flappers in thick boots and tailor-made tweeds who infest the rural districts and go about the place followed by packs of assorted dogs. I used to be one of them myself in my younger days, so I know how dangerous they are. Her name is Dalgleish. Old Colonel Dalgleish's daughter. They live near Bleaching.'

I saw a gleam of daylight.

'Then that must be what his telegram was about. He's just wired, asking me to bring down an Irish water-spaniel. A Christmas present for this girl, no doubt.'

'Probably. Katherine tells me he seems to be infatuated with her. She says he follows her about like one of her dogs, looking like a tame cat and bleating like a sheep.'

'Quite the private Whipsnade, what?'

'Bertie,' said Aunt Dahlia – and I could see her generous nature was stirred to its depths – 'one more crack like that out of you, and I shall forget that I am an aunt, and hand you one.'

I became soothing. I gave her the old oil.

'I shouldn't worry,' I said. 'There's probably nothing in it. Whole thing no doubt much exaggerated.'

'You think so, eh? Well, you know what he's like. You remember the trouble we had when he ran after that singing-woman.'

I recollected the case. You will find it elsewhere in the archives. Cora Bellinger was the female's name. She was studying for Opera, and young Tuppy thought highly of her. Fortunately, however, she punched him in the eye during Beefy Bingham's clean, bright entertainment in Bermondsey East, and love died.

'Besides,' said Aunt Dahlia. 'There's something I haven't told you. Just before he went to Bleaching, he and Angela quarrelled.'

'They did?'

'Yes. I got it out of Angela this morning. She was crying her eyes out, poor angel. It was something about her last hat. As far as I could gather, he told her it made her look like a Pekingese, and she told him she never wanted to see him again in this world or the next. And he said "Right ho!" and breezed off. I can see what has happened. This dog-girl has caught him on the rebound, and, unless something is done quick, anything may happen. So place the facts before Jeeves, and tell him to take action the moment you get down there.'

I am always a little piqued, if you know what I mean, at this assumption on the relative's part that Jeeves is so dashed essential on these occasions. My manner, therefore, as I replied, was a bit on the crisp side.

'Jeeves's services will not be required,' I said. 'I can handle this business. The programme which I have laid out will be quite sufficient to take young Tuppy's mind off love-making. It is my intention to insert the Luminous Rabbit in his room at the first opportunity that presents itself. The Luminous Rabbit shines in the dark and jumps about, making odd, squeaking noises. It will sound to young Tuppy like the Voice of Conscience, and I anticipate that a single treatment will make him retire into a nursing-home for a couple of weeks or so. At the end of which period he will have forgotten all about the bally girl.'

'Bertie,' said Aunt Dahlia, with a sort of frozen calm. 'You are the Abysmal Chump. Listen to me. It's simply because I am fond of you and have influence with the Lunacy Commissioners that you weren't put in a padded cell years ago. Bungle this business, and I withdraw my protection. Can't you understand that this thing is far too serious for any fooling about? Angela's whole happiness is at stake. Do as I tell you, and put it up to Jeeves.'

'Just as you say, Aunt Dahlia,' I said stiffly.

'All right, then. Do it now.'

I went back to the bedroom.

'Jeeves,' I said, and I did not trouble to conceal my chagrin, 'you need not pack the Luminous Rabbit.'

'Very good, sir.'

'Nor the Giant Squirt.'

'Very good, sir.'

'They have been subjected to destructive criticism and the zest has gone. Oh, and Jeeves.'

'Sir?'

'Mrs. Travers wishes you, on arriving at Bleaching Court, to disentangle Mr. Glossop from a dog-girl.'

'Very good, sir. I will attend to the matter and will do my best to give satisfaction.'

That Aunt Dahlia had not exaggerated the perilous nature of the situation was made clear to me on the following afternoon. Jeeves and I drove down to Bleaching in the two-seater, and we were tooling along about half-way between the village and the Court when suddenly there appeared ahead of us a sea of dogs and in the middle of it young Tuppy frisking round one of those largish, corn-fed girls. He was bending towards her in a devout sort of way, and even at a considerable distance I could see that his ears were pink. His attitude, in short, was unmistakably that of a man endeavouring to push a good thing along; and when I came closer and noted that the girl wore tailor-made tweeds and thick boots, I had no further doubts.

'You observe, Jeeves?' I said in a low, significant voice.

'Yes, sir.'

'The girl, what?'

'Yes, sir.'

I tootled amiably on the horn and yodelled a bit. They turned – Tuppy, I fancied, not any too pleased.

'Oh, hullo, Bertie,' he said.

'Hullo,' I said.

'My friend, Bertie Wooster,' said Tuppy to the girl, in what seemed to me rather an apologetic manner. You know – as if he would have preferred to hush me up.

'Hullo,' said the girl.

'Hullo,' I said.

'Hullo, Jeeves,' said Tuppy.

'Good afternoon, sir,' said Jeeves.

There was a somewhat constrained silence.

'Well, good-bye, Bertie,' said young Tuppy. 'You'll be wanting to push along, I expect.'

We Woosters can take a hint as well as the next man.

'See you later,' I said.

'Oh, rather,' said Tuppy.

I set the machinery in motion again, and we rolled off.

'Sinister, Jeeves,' I said. 'You noticed that the subject was looking like a stuffed frog?'

'Yes, sir.'

'And gave no indication of wanting us to stop and join the party?'

'No, sir.'

'I think Aunt Dahlia's fears are justified. The thing seems serious.'

'Yes, sir.'

'Well, strain the brain, Jeeves.'

'Very good, sir.'

It wasn't till I was dressing for dinner that night that I saw young Tuppy again. He trickled in just as I was arranging the tie.

'Hullo!' I said.

'Hullo!' said Tuppy.

'Who was the girl?' I asked, in that casual, snaky way of mine – off-hand, I mean.

'A Miss Dalgleish,' said Tuppy, and I noticed that he blushed a spot.

'Staying here?'

'No. She lives in that house just before you come to the gates of this place. Did you bring my football boots?'

Yes. Jeeves has got them somewhere.'

'And the water-spaniel?'

'Sorry. No water-spaniel.'

'Dashed nuisance. She's set her heart on an Irish water-spaniel.'

'Well, what do you care?'

'I wanted to give her one.'

'Why?'

Tuppy became a trifle haughty. Frigid. The rebuking eye.

'Colonel and Mrs. Dalgleish,' he said, 'have been extremely kind to me since I got here. They have entertained me. I naturally wish to make some return for their hospitality. I don't want them to look upon me as one of those ill-mannered modern young men you read about in the papers who grab everything they can lay their hooks on and never buy back. If people ask you to lunch and tea and what not, they appreciate it if you make them some little present in return.'

'Well, give them your football boots. In passing, why did you want the bally things?'

'I'm playing in a match next Thursday.'

'Down here?'

'Yes. Upper Bleaching versus Hockley-cum-Meston. Apparently it's the big game of the year.'

'How did you get roped in?'

'I happened to mention in the course of conversation the other day that, when in London, I generally turn out on Saturdays for the Old Austinians, and Miss Dalgleish seemed rather keen that I should help the village.'

'Which village?'

'Upper Bleaching, of course.'

'Ah, then you're going to play for Hockley?'

'You needn't be funny, Bertie. You may not know it, but I'm pretty hot stuff on the football field. Oh, Jeeves.'

674

'Sir?' said Jeeves, entering right centre.

'Mr. Wooster tells me you have my football boots.'

'Yes, sir. I have placed them in your room.'

'Thanks. Jeeves, do you want to make a bit of money?'

'Yes, sir.'

'Then put a trifle on Upper Bleaching for the annual encounter with Hockley-cum-Meston next Thursday,' said Tuppy, exiting with swelling bosom.

'Mr. Glossop is going to play on Thursday,' I explained as the door closed.

'So I was informed in the Servants' Hall, sir.'

'Oh? And what's the general feeling there about it?'

'The impression I gathered, sir, was that the Servants' Hall considers Mr. Glossop ill-advised.'

'Why's that?'

'I am informed by Mr. Mulready, Sir Reginald's butler, sir, that this contest differs in some respects from the ordinary football game. Owing to the fact that there has existed for many years considerable animus between the two villages, the struggle is conducted, it appears, on somewhat looser and more primitive lines than is usually the case when two teams meet in friendly rivalry. The primary object of the players, I am given to understand, is not so much to score points as to inflict violence.'

'Good Lord, Jeeves!'

'Such appears to be the case, sir. The game is one that would have a great interest for the antiquarian. It was played first in the reign of King Henry the Eighth, when it lasted from noon till sundown over an area covering several square miles. Seven deaths resulted on that occasion.'

'Seven!'

'Not inclusive of two of the spectators, sir. In recent years, however, the casualties appear to have been confined to broken limbs and other minor injuries. The opinion of the Servants' Hall is that it would be more judicious on Mr. Glossop's part were he to refrain from mixing himself up in the affair.'

I was more or less aghast. I mean to say, while I had made it my mission in life to get back at young Tuppy for that business at the Drones, there still remained certain faint vestiges, if vestiges is the word I want, of the old friendship and esteem. Besides, there are limits to one's thirst for vengeance. Deep as my resentment was for the ghastly outrage he had perpetrated on me, I had no wish to see him toddle unsuspiciously into the arena and get all chewed up by wild villagers. A Tuppy scared stiff by a Luminous Rabbit – yes. Excellent business. The happy ending, in fact. But a Tuppy carried off on a stretcher in half a dozen pieces – no. Quite a different matter. All wrong. Not to be considered for a moment.

Obviously, then, a kindly word of warning while there was yet time, was indicated. I buzzed off to his room forthwith, and found him toying dreamily with the football boots.

I put him in possession of the facts.

'What you had better do – and the Servants' Hall thinks the same,' I said, 'is fake a sprained ankle on the eve of the match.'

He looked at me in an odd sort of way.

'You suggest that, when Miss Dalgleish is trusting me, relying on me, looking forward with eager, girlish enthusiasm to seeing me help her village on to victory I should let her down with a thud?'

I was pleased with his ready intelligence.

'That's the idea,' I said.

'Faugh!' said Tuppy – the only time I've ever heard the word.

'How do you mean, Faugh?' I asked.

'Bertie,' said Tuppy, 'what you tell me merely makes me all the keener for the fray. A warm game is what I want. I welcome this sporting spirit on the part of the opposition. I shall enjoy a spot of roughness. It will enable me to go all out and give of my best. Do you realise,' said young Tuppy, vermilion to the gills, 'that She will be looking on? And do you know how that will make me feel? It will make me feel like some knight of old jousting under the eyes of his lady. Do you suppose that Sir Lancelot or Sir

Galahad, when there was a tourney scheduled for the following Thursday, went and pretended they had sprained their ankles just because the thing was likely to be a bit rough?'

'Don't forget that in the reign of King Henry the Eighth—'

'Never mind about the reign of King Henry the Eighth. All I care about is that it's Upper Bleaching's turn this year to play in colours, so I shall be able to wear my Old Austinian shirt. Light blue, Bertie, with broad orange stripes. I shall look like something, I tell you.'

'But what?'

'Bertie,' said Tuppy, now becoming purely ga-ga, 'I may as well tell you that I'm in love at last. This is the real thing. I have found my mate. All my life I have dreamed of meeting some sweet, open-air girl with all the glory of the English countryside in her eyes, and I have found her. How different she is, Bertie, from these hot-house, artificial London girls! Would they stand in the mud on a winter afternoon, watching a football match? Would they know what to give an Alsatian for fits? Would they tramp ten miles a day across the fields and come back as fresh as paint? No!'

'Well, why should they?'

'Bertie, I'm staking everything on this game on Thursday. At the moment, I have an idea that she looks on me as something of a weakling, simply because I got a blister on my foot the other afternoon and had to take the bus back from Hockley. But when she sees me going through the rustic opposition like a devouring flame, will that make her think a bit? Will that make her open her eyes? What?'

'What?'

'I said "What?"'

'So did I.'

'I meant, Won't it?'

'Oh, rather.'

Here the dinner-gong sounded, not before I was ready for it.

*

Judicious inquiries during the next couple of days convinced me that the Servants' Hall at Bleaching Court, in advancing the suggestion that young Tuppy, born and bred in the gentler atmosphere of the Metropolis, would do well to keep out of local disputes and avoid the football-field on which these were to be settled, had not spoken idly. It had weighed its words and said the sensible thing. Feeling between the two villages undoubtedly ran high, as they say.

You know how it is in these remote rural districts. Life tends at times to get a bit slow. There's nothing much to do in the long winter evenings but listen to the radio and brood on what a tick your neighbour is. You find yourself remembering how Farmer Giles did you down over the sale of your pig, and Famer Giles finds himself remembering that it was your son, Ernest, who bunged the half-brick at his horse on the second Sunday before Septuagesima. And so on and so forth. How this particular feud had started, I don't know, but the season of peace and good will found it in full blast. The only topic of conversation in Upper Bleaching was Thursday's game, and the citizenry seemed to be looking forward to it in a spirit that can only be described as ghoulish. And it was the same in Hockley-cum-Meston.

I paid a visit to Hockley-cum-Meston on the Wednesday, being rather anxious to take a look at the inhabitants and see how formidable they were. I was shocked to observe that practically every second male might have been the Village Blacksmith's big brother. The muscles of their brawny arms were obviously strong as iron bands, and the way the company at the Green Pig, where I looked in incognito for a spot of beer, talked about the forthcoming sporting contest was enough to chill the blood of anyone who had a pal who proposed to fling himself into the fray. It sounded rather like Attila and a few of his Huns sketching out their next campaign.

I went back to Jeeves with my mind made up.

'Jeeves,' I said, 'you, who had the job of drying and pressing those dress-clothes of mine, are aware that I have suffered much at young Tuppy Glossop's hands. By rights, I suppose, I ought to be welcoming the fact that the Wrath of Heaven is now hovering over him in this fearful manner. But the view I take of it is that Heaven looks like overdoing it. Heaven's idea of a fitting retribution is not mine. In my most unrestrained moments I never wanted the poor blighter assassinated. And the idea in Hockley-cum-Meston seems to be that a good opportunity has arisen of making it a bumper Christmas for the local undertaker. There was a fellow with red hair at the Green Pig this afternoon who might have been the undertaker's partner, the way he talked. We must act, and speedily, Jeeves. We must put a bit of a jerk in it and save young Tuppy in spite of himself.'

'What course would you advocate, sir?'

'I'll tell you. He refuses to do the sensible thing and slide out, because the girl will be watching the game and he imagines, poor lizard, that he is going to shine and impress her. So we must employ guile. You must go up to London today, Jeeves, and tomorrow morning you will send a telegram, signed "Angela", which will run as follows. Jot it down Ready?'

'Yes, sir.'

' "So sorry—" . . .' I pondered. 'What would a girl say, Jeeves, who, having had a row with the bird she was practically engaged to because he told her she looked like a Pekingese in her new hat, wanted to extend the olive-branch?'

' "So sorry I was cross," sir, would, I fancy, be the expression.'

'Strong enough, do you think?'

'Possibly the addition of the word "darling" would give the necessary verisimilitude, sir.'

'Right. Resume the jotting. "So sorry I was cross, darling . . ." No, wait, Jeeves. Scratch that out. I see where we have gone off the rails. I see where we are missing a chance to make this the real tabasco. Sign the telegram not "Angela" but "Travers".'

'Very good, sir.'

'Or, rather, "Dahlia Travers". And this is the body of the communication. "Please return at once." '

' "Immediately" would be more economical, sir. Only one word. And it has a stronger ring.'

'True. Jot on, then. "Please return immediately. Angela in a hell of a state." '

'I would suggest "Seriously ill", sir.'

'All right. "Seriously ill." "Angela seriously ill. Keeps calling for you and says you were quite right about hat." '

'If I might suggest, sir—?'

'Well, go ahead.'

'I fancy the following would meet the case. "Please return immediately. Angela seriously ill. High fever and delirium. Keeps calling your name piteously and saying something about a hat and that you were quite right. Please catch earliest possible train. Dahlia Travers." '

'That sounds all right.'

'Yes, sir.'

'You like that "piteously"? You don't think "incessantly"?'

'No, sir. "Piteously" is the *mot juste*.'

'All right. You know. Well, send it off in time to get here at two-thirty.'

'Yes, sir.'

'Two-thirty, Jeeves. You see the devilish cunning?'

'No, sir.'

'I will tell you. If the telegram arrived earlier, he would get it before the game. By two-thirty, however, he will have started for the ground. I shall hand it to him the moment there is a lull in the battle. By that time he will have begun to get some idea of what a football match between Upper Bleaching and Hockley-cum-Meston is like, and the thing ought to work like magic. I can't imagine anyone who has been sporting a while with those thugs I saw yesterday not welcoming any excuse to call it a day. You follow me?'

'Yes, sir.'

'Very good, Jeeves.'

'Very good, sir.'

*

You can always rely on Jeeves. Two-thirty I had said, and two-thirty it was. The telegram arrived almost on the minute. I was going to my room to change into something warmer at the moment, and I took it up with me. Then into the heavy tweeds and off in the car to the field of play. I got there just as the two teams were lining up, and half a minute later the whistle blew and the war was on.

What with one thing and another – having been at a school where they didn't play it and so forth – Rugby football is a game I can't claim absolutely to understand in all its niceties, if you know what I mean. I can follow the broad, general principles, of course. I mean to say, I know that the main scheme is to work the ball down the field somehow and deposit it over the line at the other end, and that, in order to squelch this programme, each side is allowed to put in a certain amount of assault and battery and do things to its fellow-man which, if done elsewhere, would result in fourteen days without the option, coupled with some strong remarks from the Bench. But there I stop. What you might call the science of the thing is to Bertram Wooster a sealed book. However, I am informed by experts that on this occasion there was not enough science for anyone to notice.

There had been a great deal of rain in the last few days, and the going appeared to be a bit sticky. In fact, I have seen swamps that were drier than this particular bit of ground. The red-haired bloke whom I had encountered in the pub paddled up and kicked off amidst cheers from the populace, and the ball went straight to where Tuppy was standing, a pretty colour-scheme in light blue and orange. Tuppy caught it neatly, and hoofed it back, and it was at this point that I understood that an Upper Bleaching versus Hockley-cum-Meston game had certain features not usually seen on the football-field.

For Tuppy, having done his bit, was just standing there, looking modest, when there was a thunder of large feet and the red-haired bird, galloping up, seized him by the neck, hurled him to earth, and fell on him. I had a glimpse of Tuppy's face, as it registered horror, dismay, and a general suggestion of stunned dissatisfaction with the scheme of things, and then he disappeared. By the time he had come to the surface, a sort of mob-warfare was going on at the other side of the field. Two assortments of sons of the soil had got their heads down and were shoving earnestly against each other, with the ball somewhere in the middle.

Tuppy wiped a fair portion of Hampshire out of his eye, peered round him in a dazed kind of way, saw the mass-meeting and ran towards it, arriving just in time for a couple of heavyweights to gather him in and give him the mud-treatment again. This placed him in an admirable position for a third heavyweight to kick him in the ribs with a boot like a violin-case. The red-haired man then fell on him. It was all good, brisk play, and looked fine from my side of the ropes.

I saw now where Tuppy had made his mistake. He was too dressy. On occasions such as this it is safest not to be conspicuous, and that blue and orange shirt rather caught the eye. A sober beige, blending with the colour of the ground, was what his best friends would have recommended. And, in addition to the fact that his costume attracted attention, I rather think that the men of Hockley-cum-Meston resented his being on the field at all. They felt that, as a non-local, he had butted in on a private fight and had no business there.

At any rate, it certainly appeared to me that they were giving him preferential treatment. After each of those shoving-bees to which I have alluded, when the edifice caved in and tons of humanity wallowed in a tangled mass in the juice, the last soul to be excavated always seemed to be Tuppy. And on the rare occasions when he actually managed to stand upright for a moment, somebody – generally the red-haired man – invariably sprang to the congenial task of spilling him again.

In fact, it was beginning to look as though that telegram

would come too late to save a human life, when an interruption occurred. Play had worked round close to where I was standing, and there had been the customary collapse of all concerned, with Tuppy at the bottom of the basket, as usual; but this time, when they got up and started to count the survivors, a sizable cove in what had once been a white shirt remained on the ground. And a hearty cheer went up from a hundred patriotic throats as the news spread that Upper Bleaching had drawn first blood.

The victim was carried off by a couple of his old chums, and the rest of the players sat down and pulled their stockings up and thought of life for a bit. The moment had come, it seemed to me, to remove Tuppy from the *abattoir*, and I hopped over the ropes and toddled to where he sat scraping mud from his wishbone. His air was that of a man who has been passed through a wringer, and his eyes, what you could see of them, had a strange, smouldering gleam. He was so crusted with alluvial deposits that one realised how little a mere bath would ever be able to effect. To fit him to take his place once more in polite society, he would certainly have to be sent to the cleaner's. Indeed, it was a moot point whether it wouldn't be simpler just to throw him away.

'Tuppy, old man,' I said.

'Eh?' said Tuppy.

'A telegram for you.'

'Eh?'

'I've got a wire here that came after you left the house.'

'Eh?' said Tuppy.

I stirred him up a trifle with the ferrule of my stick, and he seemed to come to life.

'Be careful what you're doing, you silly ass,' he said, in part. 'I'm one solid bruise. What are you gibbering about?'

'A telegram has come for you. I think it may be important.'

He snorted in a bitter sort of way.

'Do you suppose I've time to read telegrams now?'

'But this one may be frightfully urgent,' I said. 'Here it is.'

But, if you understand me, it wasn't. How I had happened to do it, I don't know, but apparently, in changing the upholstery, I had left it in my other coat.

'Oh, my gosh,' I said. 'I've left it behind.'

'It doesn't matter.'

'But it does. It's probably something you ought to read at once. Immediately, if you know what I mean. If I were you, I'd just say a few words of farewell to the murder-squad and come back to the house right away.'

He raised his eyebrows. At least, I think he must have done, because the mud on his forehead stirred a little, as if something was going on underneath it.

'Do you imagine,' he said, 'that I would slink away under her very eyes? Good God! Besides,' he went on, in a quiet, meditative voice, 'there is no power on earth that could get me off this field until I've thoroughly disembowelled that red-haired bounder. Have you noticed how he keeps tackling me when I haven't got the ball?'

'Isn't that right?'

'Of course it's not right. Never mind! A bitter retribution awaits that bird. I've had enough of it. From now on I assert my personality.'

'I'm a bit foggy as to the rules of this pastime,' I said. 'Are you allowed to bite him?'

'I'll try, and see what happens,' said Tuppy, struck with the idea and brightening a little.

At this point, the pall-bearers returned, and fighting became general again all along the Front.

There's nothing like a bit of rest and what you might call folding of the hands for freshening up the shop-soiled athlete. The dirty work, resumed after this brief breather, started off with an added vim which it did one good to see. And the life and soul of the party was young Tuppy.

You know, only meeting a fellow at lunch or at the races or loafing round country-houses and so forth, you don't get on to his hidden depths, if you know what I mean. Until this moment, if asked, I would have said that Tuppy Glossop was, on the whole, essentially a pacific sort of bloke, with little or nothing of the tiger of the jungle in him. Yet here he was, running to and fro with fire streaming from his nostrils, a positive danger to traffic.

Yes, absolutely. Encouraged by the fact that the referee was either filled with the spirit of Live and Let Live or else had got his whistle choked up with mud, the result being that he appeared to regard the game with a sort of calm detachment, Tuppy was putting in some very impressive work. Even to me, knowing nothing of the finesse of the thing, it was plain that if Hockley-cum-Meston wanted the happy ending they must eliminate young Tuppy at the earliest possible moment. And I will say for them that they did their best, the red-haired man being particularly assiduous. But Tuppy was made of durable material. Every time the opposition talent ground him into the mire and sat on his head, he rose on stepping-stones of his dead self, if you follow me, to higher things. And in the end it was the red-haired bloke who did the dust-biting.

I couldn't tell you exactly how it happened, for by this time the shades of night were drawing in a bit and there was a dollop of mist rising, but one moment the fellow was hareing along, apparently without a care in the world, and then suddenly Tuppy had appeared from nowhere and was sailing through the air at his neck. They connected with a crash and a slither, and a little later the red-haired bird was hopping off, supported by a brace of friends, something having gone wrong with his left ankle.

After that, there was nothing to it. Upper Bleaching, thoroughly bucked, became busier than ever. There was a lot of earnest work in a sort of inland sea down at the Hockley end of the field, and then a kind of tidal wave poured over the line, and when the bodies had been removed and the tumult and the shouting had died, there was young Tuppy lying on the ball. And that, with exception of a few spots of mayhem in the last five minutes, concluded the proceedings.

I drove back to the Court in rather what you might term a pensive frame of mind. Things having happened as they had happened, there seemed to me a goodish bit of hard thinking to be done. There was a servitor of sorts in the hall, when I arrived, and I asked him to send up a whisky-and-soda, strongish, to my room. The old brain, I felt, needed stimulating. And about ten minutes later there was a knock at the door, and in came Jeeves, bearing tray and materials.

'Hullo, Jeeves,' I said, surprised. 'Are you back?'

'Yes, sir.'

'When did you get here?'

'Some little while ago, sir. Was it an enjoyable game, sir?'

'In a sense, Jeeves,' I said, 'yes. Replete with human interest and all that, if you know what I mean. But I fear that, owing to a touch of carelessness on my part, the worst has happened. I left the telegram in my other coat, so young Tuppy remained in action throughout.'

'Was he injured, sir?'

'Worse than that, Jeeves. He was the star of the game. Toasts, I should imagine, are now being drunk to him at every pub in the village. So spectacularly did he play – in fact, so heartily did he joust – that I can't see the girl not being all over him. Unless I am greatly mistaken, the moment they meet, she will exclaim "My hero!" and fall into his bally arms.'

'Indeed, sir?'

I didn't like the man's manner. Too calm. Unimpressed. A little leaping about with fallen jaw was what I had expected my words to produce, and I was on the point of saying as much when the door opened again and Tuppy limped in.

He was wearing an ulster over his football things, and I wondered why he had come to pay a social call on me instead of proceeding straight to the bathroom. He eyed my glass in a wolfish sort of way.

'Whisky?' he said, in a hushed voice.

'And soda.'

'Bring me one, Jeeves,' said young Tuppy. 'A large one.'

'Very good, sir.'

Tuppy wandered to the window and looked out into the gathering darkness, and for the first time I perceived that he had got a grouch of some description. You can generally tell by a fellow's back. Humped. Bent. Bowed down with weight of woe, if you follow me.

'What's the matter?' I asked.

Tuppy emitted a mirthless.

'Oh, nothing much,' he said. 'My faith in woman is dead, that's all.'

'It is?'

'You jolly well bet it is. Women are a wash-out. I see no future for the sex, Bertie. Blisters, all of them.'

'Er – even the Dogsbody girl?'

'Her name,' said Tuppy, a little stiffly, 'is Dalgleish, if it happens to interest you. And, if you want to know something else, she's the worst of the lot.'

'My dear chap!'

Tuppy turned. Beneath the mud, I could see that his face was drawn and, to put it in a nutshell, wan.

'Do you know what happened, Bertie?'

'What?'

'She wasn't there.'

'Where?'

'At the match, you silly ass.'

'Not at the match?'

'No.'

'You mean, not among the throng of eager spectators?'

'Of course I mean not among the spectators. Did you think I expected her to be playing?'

'But I thought the whole scheme of the thing—'

'So did I. My gosh!' said Tuppy, laughing another of those hollow ones. 'I sweat myself to the bone for her sake. I allow a mob of homicidal maniacs to kick me in the ribs and stroll about on my face. And then, when I have braved a fate worse than death, so to speak, all to please her, I find that she didn't bother to come and watch the game. She got a 'phone-call from London from somebody who said he had located an Irish water-spaniel, and up she popped in her car, leaving me flat. I met her just now outside her house, and she told me. And all she could think of was that she was as sore as a sunburnt neck because she had had her trip for nothing. Apparently it wasn't an Irish water-spaniel at all. Just an ordinary English water-spaniel. And to think I fancied I loved a girl like that. A nice life-partner she would make! "When pain and anguish wring the brow, a ministering angel thou'— I don't think! Why, if a man married a girl like that and happened to get stricken by some dangerous illness, would she smooth his pillow and press cooling drinks on him? Not a chance! She'd be off somewhere trying to buy Siberian eel-hounds. I'm through with women.'

I saw that the moment had come to put in a word for the old firm.

'My cousin Angela's not a bad sort, Tuppy,' I said, in a grave elder-brotherly kind of way. 'Not altogether a bad egg, Angela, if you look at her squarely. I had always been hoping that she and you . . . and I know my Aunt Dahlia felt the same.'

Tuppy's bitter sneer cracked the top-soil.

'Angela!' he woofed. 'Don't talk to me about Angela. Angela's a rag and a bone and a hank of hair and an A1 scourge, if you want to know. She gave me the push. Yes, she did. Simply because I had the manly courage to speak out candidly on the subject of that ghastly lid she was chump enough to buy. It made her look like a Peke, and I told her it made her look like a Peke. And instead of admiring me for my fearless honesty she bunged me out on my ear. Faugh!'

'She did?' I said.

'She jolly well did,' said young Tuppy. 'At four-sixteen p.m. on Tuesday the seventeenth.'

'By the way, old man,' I said, 'I've found that telegram.'

'What telegram?'

'The one I told you about.'

'Oh, that one?'

'Yes, that's the one.'

'Well, let's have a look at the beastly thing.'

I handed it over, watching him narrowly. And suddenly, as he read, I saw him wobble. Stirred to the core. Obviously.

'Anything important?' I said.

'Bertie,' said young Tuppy in a voice that quivered with strong emotion, 'my recent remarks *re* your cousin Angela. Wash them out. Cancel them. Look on them as not spoken. I tell you, Bertie, Angela's all right. An angel in human shape, and that's official. Bertie, I've got to get up to London. She's ill.'

'Ill?'

'High fever and delirium. This wire's from your aunt. She wants me to come up to London at once. Can I borrow your car?'

'Of course.'

'Thanks,' said Tuppy, and dashed out.

He had only been gone about a second when Jeeves came in with the restorative. 'Mr. Glossop's gone, Jeeves.'

'Indeed, sir?'

'To London.'

'Yes, sir?'

'In my car. To see my cousin Angela. The sun is once more shining, Jeeves.'

'Extremely gratifying, sir.' I gave him the eye.

'Was it you, Jeeves, who 'phoned to Miss What's-her-bally-name about the alleged water-spaniel?'

'Yes, sir.'

'I thought as much.'

'Yes, sir?'

'Yes, Jeeves, the moment Mr. Glossop told me that a Mysterious Voice had 'phoned on the subject of Irish water-spaniels, I thought as much. I recognised your touch. I read your motives like an open book. You knew she would come buzzing up.'

'Yes, sir.'

'And you knew how Tuppy would react. If there's one thing that gives a jousting knight the pip, it is to have his audience walk out on him.'

'Yes, sir.'

'But, Jeeves.'

'Sir?'

'There's just one point. What will Mr. Glossop say when he finds my cousin Angela full of beans and not delirious?'

'The point had not escaped me, sir. I took the liberty of ringing Mrs. Travers up on the telephone and explaining the circumstances. All will be in readiness for Mr. Glossop's arrival.'

'Jeeves,' I said, 'you think of everything.'

'Thank you, sir. In Mr. Glossop's absence, would you care to drink this whisky-and-soda ?'

I shook the head.

'No, Jeeves, there is only one man who must do that. It is you. If ever anyone earned a refreshing snort, you are he. Pour it out, Jeeves, and shove it down.'

'Thank you very much, sir.'

'Cheerio, Jeeves!'

'Pip-pip, sir, if I may use the expression.'

It has happened so frequently in the past few years that young fellows starting in my profession have come to me for a word of advice, that I have found it convenient now to condense my system into a brief formula. 'Resource and Tact' – that is my motto. Tact, of course, has always been with me a *sine qua non;* while as for resource, I think I may say that I have usually contrived to show a certain modicum of what I might call *finesse* in handling those little *contretemps* which inevitably arise from time to time in the daily life of a gentleman's personal gentleman. I am reminded, by way of an instance, of the Episode of the School for Young Ladies near Brighton – an affair which, I think, may be said to have commenced one evening at the moment when I brought Mr. Wooster his whisky and siphon and he addressed me with such remarkable petulance.

Not a little moody Mr. Wooster had been for some days – far from his usual bright self. This I had attributed to the natural reaction from a slight attack of influenza from which he had been suffering; and, of course, took no notice, merely performing my duties as usual, until on the evening of which I speak he exhibited this remarkable petulance when I brought him his whisky and siphon.

'Oh, dash it, Jeeves!' he said, manifestly overwrought. 'I wish at least you'd put it on another table for a change.'

'Sir?' I said.

'Every night, dash it all,' proceeded Mr. Wooster morosely, 'you come in at exactly the same old time with the same old tray and put it on the same old table. I'm fed up, I tell you. It's the bally monotony of it that makes it all seem so frightfully bally.'

I confess that his words filled me with a certain apprehension. I had heard gentlemen in whose employment I have been speak in very much the same way before, and it had almost invariably meant that they were contemplating matrimony. It disturbed me, therefore, I am free to admit, when Mr. Wooster addressed me in this fashion. I had no desire to sever a connection so pleasant in every respect as his and mine had been, and my experience is that when the wife comes in at the front door the valet of bachelor days goes out at the back.

'It's not your fault, of course,' went on Mr. Wooster, regaining a certain degree of composure. 'I'm not blaming you. But, by Jove, I mean, you must acknowledge – I mean to say, I've been thinking pretty deeply these last few days, Jeeves, and I've come to the conclusion mine is an empty life. I'm lonely, Jeeves.'

'You have a great many friends, sir.'

'What's the good of friends?'

'Emerson,' I reminded him, 'says a friend may well be reckoned the masterpiece of Nature, sir.'

'Well, you can tell Emerson from me the next time you see him that he's an ass.'

'Very good, sir.'

'What I want— Jeeves, have you seen that play called I-forget-its-dashed-name?'

'No, sir.'

'It's on at the What-d'you-call-it. I went last night. The hero's a chap who's buzzing along, you know, quite merry and bright, and suddenly a kid turns up and says she's his daughter. Left over from act one, you know – absolutely the first he'd heard of it. Well, of course, there's a bit of a fuss and they say to him, "What-ho?" and he says, "Well, what about it?" and they say, "Well, *what* about it?" and he says, "Oh, all right, then, if that's the way you feel!" and he takes the kid and goes off with her out into the world together, you know. Well, what I'm driving at, Jeeves, is that I envied that chappie. Most awfully jolly little girl, you know, clinging to him trustingly and what-not. Something to look after, if you know what I mean. Jeeves, I wish I had a daughter. I wonder what the procedure is?'

'Marriage is, I believe, considered the preliminary step, sir.'

'No, I mean about adopting a kid. You can adopt kids, you know, Jeeves. But what I want to know is how you start about it.'

'The process, I should imagine, would be highly complicated and laborious, sir. It would cut into your spare time.'

'Well, I'll tell you what I could do, then. My sister will be back from India next week with her three little girls. I'll give up this flat and take a house and have them all to live with me. By Jove, Jeeves, I think that's rather a scheme, what? Prattle of childish voices, eh? Little feet pattering hither and thither, yes?'

I concealed my perturbation, but the effort to preserve my *sang froid* tested my powers to the utmost. The course of action outlined by Mr. Wooster meant the finish of our cosy bachelor establishment if it came into being as a practical proposition; and no doubt some men in my place would at this juncture have voiced their disapproval. I avoided this blunder.

'If you will pardon my saying so, sir,' I suggested, 'I think you are not quite yourself after your influenza. If I might express the opinion, what you require is a few days by the sea. Brighton is very handy, sir.'

'Are you suggesting that I'm talking through my hat?'

'By no means, sir. I merely advocate a short stay at Brighton as a physical recuperative.'

Mr. Wooster considered.

'Well, I'm not sure you're not right,' he said at length. 'I *am* feeling more or less of an onion. You might shove a few things in a suit-case and drive me down in the car tomorrow.'

'Very good, sir.'

'And when we get back I'll be in the pink and ready to tackle this pattering-feet wheeze.'

'Exactly, sir.'

Well, it was a respite, and I welcomed it. But I began to see that a crisis had arisen which would require adroit handling. Rarely had I observed Mr. Wooster more set on a thing. Indeed, I could recall no such exhibition of determination on his part since the time when he had insisted, against my frank disapproval, on wearing purple socks. However, I had coped successfully with that outbreak, and I was by no means unsanguine that I should eventually be able to bring the present affair to a happy issue. Employers are like horses. They require managing. Some gentlemen's personal gentlemen have the knack of managing them, some have not. I, I am happy to say, have no cause for complaint.

For myself, I found our stay at Brighton highly enjoyable, and should have been willing to extend it, but Mr. Wooster, still restless, wearied of the place by the end of two days, and on the third afternoon he instructed me to pack up and bring the car round to the hotel. We started back along the London road at about five of a fine summer's day, and had travelled perhaps two miles when I perceived in the road before us a young lady, gesticulating with no little animation. I applied the brake and brought the vehicle to a standstill.

'What,' inquired Mr. Wooster, waking from a reverie, 'is the big thought at the back of this, Jeeves?'

'I observed a young lady endeavouring to attract our attention with signals a little way down the road, sir,' I explained. 'She is now making her way towards us.'

Mr. Wooster peered.

'I see her. I expect she wants a lift, Jeeves.'

'That was the interpretation which I placed upon her actions, sir.'

'A jolly-looking kid,' said Mr. Wooster. 'I wonder what she's doing, biffing about the high road.'

'She has the air to me, sir, of one who has been absenting herself without leave from her school, sir.'

'Hallo-allo-allo!' said Mr. Wooster, as the child reached us. 'Do you want a lift?'

'Oh, I say, can you?' said the child, with marked pleasure.

'Where do you want to go?'

'There's a turning to the left about a mile farther on. If you'll put me down there, I'll walk the rest of the way, I say, thanks awfully. I've got a nail in my shoe.'

She climbed in at the back. A red-haired young person with a snub nose and an extremely large grin. Her age, I should imagine, would be about twelve. She let down one of the spare seats, and knelt on it to facilitate conversation.

'I'm going to get into a frightful row,' she began. 'Miss Tomlinson will be perfectly furious.'

'No, really?' said Mr. Wooster.

'It's a half-holiday, you know, and I sneaked away to Brighton, because I wanted to go on the pier and put pennies in the slot-machines. I thought I could get back in time so that nobody would notice I'd gone, but I got this nail in my shoe, and now there'll be a fearful row. Oh, well,' she said, with a philosophy which, I confess, I admired, 'it can't be helped. What's your car? A Sunbeam, isn't it? We've got a Wolseley at home.'

Mr. Wooster was visibly perturbed. As I have indicated, he was at this time in a highly malleable frame of mind, tender-hearted to a degree where the young of the female sex was concerned. Her sad case touched him deeply.

'Oh, I say, this is rather rotten,' he observed. 'Isn't there anything to be done? I say, Jeeves, don't you think something could be done?'

'It was not my place to make the suggestion, sir,' I replied, 'but, as you yourself have brought the matter up, I fancy the trouble is susceptible of adjustment. I think it would be a legitimate subterfuge were you to inform the young lady's school-mistress that you are an old friend of the young lady's father. In this case you could inform Miss Tomlinson that you had been passing the school and had seen the young lady at the gate and taken her for a drive. Miss Tomlinson's chagrin would no doubt in these circumstances be sensibly diminished if not altogether dispersed.'

'Well, you *are* a sportsman!' observed the young person, with considerable enthusiasm. And she proceeded to kiss me – in connection with which I have only to say that I was sorry she had just been devouring some sticky pieces of sweetmeat.

'Jeeves, you've hit it!' said Mr. Wooster. 'A sound, even fruity, scheme. I say, I suppose I'd better know your name and all that, if I'm a friend of your father's.'

'My name's Peggy Mainwaring, thanks awfully,' said the young person. 'And my father's Professor Mainwaring. He's written a lot of books. You'll be expected to know that.'

'Author of the well-known series of philosophical treatises, sir,' I ventured to interject. 'They have a great vogue, though, if the young lady will pardon my saying so, many of the Professor's opinions strike me personally as somewhat empirical. Shall I drive on to the school, sir?'

'Yes, carry on. I say, Jeeves, it's a rummy thing. Do you know, I've never been inside a girl's school in my life.'

'Indeed, sir?'

'Ought to be a dashed interesting experience, Jeeves, what?'

'I fancy that you may find it so, sir,' I said.

We drove on a matter of half a mile down a lane, and, directed by the young person, I turned in at the gates of a house of imposing dimensions, bringing the car to a halt at the front door. Mr. Wooster and the child entered, and presently a parlourmaid came out.

'You're to take the car round to the stables, please,' she said.

'Ah!' I said. 'Then everything is satisfactory, eh? Where has Mr. Wooster gone?'

'Miss Peggy has taken him off to meet her friends. And cook says she hopes you'll step round to the kitchen later and have a cup of tea.'

'Inform her that I shall be delighted. Before I take the car to the stables, would it be possible for me to have a word with Miss Tomlinson?'

A moment later I was following her into the drawing-room.

Handsome but strong-minded – that was how I summed up Miss Tomlinson at first glance. In some ways she recalled to my mind Mr. Wooster's Aunt Agatha. She had the same penetrating gaze and that indefinable air of being reluctant to stand any nonsense.

'I fear I am possibly taking a liberty, madam,' I began, 'but I am hoping that you allow me to say a word with respect to my employer. I fancy I am correct in supposing that Mr. Wooster did not tell you a great deal about himself?'

'He told me nothing about himself, except that he was a friend of Professor Mainwaring.'

'He did not inform you, then, that he was *the* Mr. Wooster?'

'*The* Mr. Wooster?'

'Bertram Wooster, madam.'

I will say for Mr. Wooster that, mentally negligible though he no doubt is, he has a name that suggests almost infinite possibilities. He sounds, if I may elucidate my meaning, like Someone – especially if you have just been informed that he is an intimate friend of so eminent a man as Professor Mainwaring. You might not, no doubt, be able to say off-hand whether he was Bertram Wooster the novelist, or Bertram Wooster the founder of a new school of thought; but you would have an uneasy feeling that you were exposing your ignorance if you did not give the impression of familiarity with the name. Miss Tomlinson, as I had rather foreseen, nodded brightly.

'Oh, *Bertram* Wooster!' she said.

'He is an extremely retiring gentleman, madam, and would be the last to suggest it himself, but, knowing him as I do, I am sure that he would take it as a graceful compliment if you were to ask him to address the young ladies. He is an excellent extempore speaker.'

'A very good idea,' said Miss Tomlinson decidedly. 'I am very much obliged to you for suggesting it. I will certainly ask him to talk to the girls.'

'And should he make a pretence – through modesty – of not wishing—'

'I shall insist.'

'Thank you, madam. I am obliged. You will not mention my share in the matter? Mr. Wooster might think that I had exceeded my duties.'

I drove round to the stables and halted the car in the yard. As I got out, I looked at it somewhat intently. It was a good car, and appeared to be in excellent condition, but somehow I seemed to feel that something was going to go wrong with it – something serious – something that would not be able to be put right again for at least a couple of hours.

One gets these presentiments.

It may have been some half-hour later that Mr. Wooster came into the stable-yard as I was leaning against the car enjoying a quiet cigarette.

'No, don't chuck it away, Jeeves,' he said, as I withdrew the cigarette from my mouth. 'As a matter of fact, I've come to touch you for a smoke. Got one to spare?'

'Only gaspers, I fear, sir.'

'They'll do,' responded Mr. Wooster, with no little eagerness. I observed that his manner was a trifle fatigued and his eye somewhat wild. 'It's a rummy thing, Jeeves, I seem to have lost my cigarette-case. Can't find it anywhere.'

'I am sorry to hear that, sir. It is not in the car.'

'No? Must have dropped it somewhere, then.' He drew at his

gasper with relish. 'Jolly creatures, small girls, Jeeves,' he remarked, after a pause.

'Extremely so, sir.'

'Of course, I can imagine some fellows finding them a bit exhausting in – er—'

'*En masse*, sir?'

'That's the word. A bit exhausting *en masse*.'

'I must confess, sir, that that is how they used to strike me. In my younger days, at the outset of my career, sir, I was at one time page-boy in a school for young ladies.'

'No, really? I never knew that before. I say, Jeeves – er – did the – er – dear little souls *giggle* much in your day?'

'Practically without cessation, sir.'

'Makes a fellow feel a bit of an ass, what? I shouldn't wonder if they usedn't to stare at you from time to time, too, eh?'

'At the school where I was employed, sir, the young ladies had a regular game which they were accustomed to play when a male visitor arrived. They would stare fixedly at him and giggle, and there was a small prize for the one who made him blush first.'

'Oh, no, I say, Jeeves, not really?'

'Yes, sir. They derived great enjoyment from the pastime.'

'I'd no idea small girls were such demons.'

'More deadly than the male, sir.'

Mr. Wooster passed a handkerchief over his brow.

'Well, we're going to have tea in a few minutes, Jeeves. I expect I shall feel better after tea.'

'We will hope so, sir.'

But I was by no means sanguine.

I had an agreeable tea in the kitchen. The buttered toast was good and the maids nice girls, though with little conversation. The parlourmaid, who joined us towards the end of the meal, after performing her duties in the school dining-room reported that Mr. Wooster was sticking it pluckily, but seemed feverish.

I went back to the stable-yard, and I was just giving the car another look over when the young Mainwaring child appeared.

'Oh, I say,' she said, 'will you give this to Mr. Wooster when you see him?' She held out Mr. Wooster's cigarette-case. 'He must have dropped it somewhere. I say,' she proceeded, 'it's an awful lark. He's going to give a lecture to the school.'

'Indeed, miss?'

'We love it when there are lectures. We sit and stare at the poor dears, and try to make them dry up. There was a man last term who got hiccups. Do you think Mr. Wooster will get hiccups?'

'We can but hope for the best, miss.'

'It would be such a lark, wouldn't it?'

'Highly enjoyable, miss.'

'Well, I must be getting back. I want to get a front seat.'

And she scampered off. An engaging child. Full of spirits.

She had hardly gone when there was an agitated noise, and around the corner came Mr. Wooster. Perturbed. Deeply so.

'Jeeves!'

'Sir?'

'Start the car!'

'Sir?'

'I'm off!'

'Sir?'

Mr. Wooster danced a few steps.

'Don't stand there saying "sir?" I tell you I'm off. Bally off! There's not a moment to waste. The situation's desperate. Dash it, Jeeves, do you know what's happened? The Tomlinson female has just sprung it on me that I'm expected to make a speech to the girls! Got to stand up there in front of the whole dashed collection and talk! I can just see myself! Get that car going, Jeeves, dash it all. A little speed, a little speed!'

'Impossible, I fear, sir. The car is out of order.'

Mr. Wooster gaped at me. Very glassily he gaped.

'Out of order!'

'Yes, sir. Something is wrong. Trivial, perhaps, but possibly a matter of some little time to repair.' Mr. Wooster, being one of those easygoing young gentlemen who will drive a car but never take the trouble to study its mechanism, I felt justified in becoming technical. 'I think it is the differential gear, sir. Either that or the exhaust.'

I am fond of Mr. Wooster, and I admit I came very near to melting as I looked at his face. He was staring at me in a sort of dumb despair that would have touched anybody.

'Then I'm sunk! Or' – a slight gleam of hope flickered across his drawn features – 'do you think I could sneak out and leg it across country, Jeeves?'

'Too late, I fear, sir.' I indicated with a slight gesture the approaching figure of Miss Tomlinson, who was advancing with a serene determination in his immediate rear.

'Ah, there you are, Mr. Wooster.'

He smiled a sickly smile.

'Yes – er – here I am!'

'We are all waiting for you in the large school-room.'

'But, I say, look here,' said Mr. Wooster, 'I – I don't know a bit what to talk about.'

'Why, anything, Mr. Wooster. Anything that comes into your head. Be bright,' said Miss Tomlinson. 'Bright and amusing.'

'Oh, bright and amusing?'

'Possibly tell them a few entertaining stories. But, at the same time, do not neglect the graver note. Remember that my girls are on the threshold of life, and will be eager to hear something brave and helpful and stimulating – something which they can remember in after years. But, of course, you know the sort of thing, Mr. Wooster. Come. The young people are waiting.'

I have spoken earlier of resource and the part it plays in the life of a gentleman's personal gentleman. It is a quality peculiarly necessary if one is to share in scenes not primarily designed for one's co-operation. So much that is interesting in life goes on apart behind closed doors that your gentleman's gentleman, if he is not to remain hopelessly behind the march of events, should exercise his wits in order to enable himself to be – if not a spectator – at least an auditor when there is anything of interest toward. I deprecate as vulgar and undignified the practice of listening at keyholes, but without lowering myself to that, I have generally contrived to find a way.

In the present case it was simple. The large school-room was situated on the ground floor, with commodious French windows, which, as the weather was clement, remained open throughout the proceedings. By stationing myself behind a pillar on the porch or veranda which adjoined the room, I was enabled to see and hear all. It was an experience which I should be sorry to have missed. Mr. Wooster, I may say at once, indubitably excelled himself.

Mr. Wooster is a young gentleman with practically every desirable quality except one. I do not mean brains, for in an employer brains are not desirable. The quality to which I allude is hard to define, but perhaps I might call it the gift of dealing with the Unusual Situation. In the presence of the Unusual, Mr. Wooster is too prone to smile weakly and allow his eyes to protrude. He lacks Presence. I have often wished that I had the power to bestow upon him some of the *savoir-faire* of a former employer of mine, Mr. Montague-Todd, the well-known financier, now in the second year of his sentence. I have known men call upon Mr. Todd with the express intention of horsewhipping him and go away half an hour later laughing heartily and smoking one of his cigars. To Mr. Todd it would have been child's play to speak a few impromptu words to a schoolroom full of young ladies; in fact, before he had finished, he would probably have induced them to invest all their pocket-money in one of his numerous companies; but to Mr. Wooster it was plainly an ordeal of the worst description. He gave one look at the young ladies, who were all staring at him in an extremely unwinking manner, then blinked and started to pick feebly at his coat-sleeves. His aspect reminded me of that of a bashful young man who, persuaded against his better judgment to go on the platform and assist a conjurer in his entertainment, suddenly discovers that rabbits and hard-boiled eggs are being taken out of the top of his head.

The proceedings opened with a short but graceful speech of introduction from Miss Tomlinson.

'Girls,' said Miss Tomlinson, 'some of you have already met Mr. Wooster – Mr. *Bertram* Wooster, and you all, I hope, know him by reputation.' Here, I regret to say, Mr. Wooster gave a hideous, gurgling laugh and, catching Miss Tomlinson's eye, turned a bright scarlet. Miss Tomlinson resumed: 'He has very kindly consented to say a few words to you before he leaves, and I am sure that you will all give him your very earnest attention. Now, please.'

She gave a spacious gesture with her right hand as she said the last two words, and Mr. Wooster, apparently under the impression that they were addressed to him, cleared his throat and began to speak. But it appeared that her remark was directed to the young ladies, and was in the nature of a cue or signal, for she had no sooner spoken them than the whole school rose to its feet in a body and burst into a species of chant, of which I am glad to say I can remember the words, though the tune eludes me. The words ran as follows:

> 'Many greetings to you!
> Many greetings to you!
> Many greetings, dear stranger,
> Many greetings,
> Many greetings,
> Many greetings to you!
> Many greetings to you!
> To you!'

Considerable latitude of choice was given to the singers in the matter of key, and there was little of what I might call co-operative effort. Each child went on till she had reached the end, then stopped and waited for the stragglers to come up. It was an unusual performance, and I, personally, found it extremely exhilarating. It seemed to smite Mr. Wooster, however, like a blow. He recoiled a couple of steps and flung up an arm defensively. Then the uproar died away, and an air of expectancy fell upon the room. Miss Tomlinson directed a brightly authoritative gaze upon Mr. Wooster, and he blinked, gulped once or twice, and tottered forward.

'Well, you know—' he said.

Then it seemed to strike him that this opening lacked the proper formal dignity.

'Ladies—'

A silvery peal of laughter from the front row stopped him again.

'Girls!' said Miss Tomlinson. She spoke in a low, soft voice, but the effect was immediate. Perfect stillness instantly descended upon all present. I am bound to say that, brief as my acquaintance with Miss Tomlinson had been, I could recall few women I had admired more. She had grip.

I fancy that Miss Tomlinson had gauged Mr. Wooster's oratorical capabilities pretty correctly by this time, and had come to the conclusion that little in the way of a stirring address was to be expected from him.

'Perhaps,' she said, 'as it is getting late, and he has not very much time to spare, Mr. Wooster will just give you some little word of advice which may be helpful to you in after-life, and then we will sing the school song and disperse to our evening lessons.'

She looked at Mr. Wooster. He passed a finger round the inside of his collar.

'Advice? After-life? What? Well, I don't know—'

'Just some brief word of counsel, Mr. Wooster,' said Miss Tomlinson firmly.

'Oh, well— Well, yes— Well—' It was painful to see Mr. Wooster's brain endeavouring to work. 'Well, I'll tell you something that's often done *me* a bit of good, and it's a thing not many people know. My old Uncle Henry gave me the tip when I first came to London. "Never forget, my boy," he said, "that, if you stand outside Romano's in the Strand, you can see the clock on the wall of the Law Courts down in Fleet Street. Most people who don't know don't believe it's possible, because there are a couple of churches in the middle of the road, and you would think they would be in the way. But you can, and it's worth knowing. You can win a lot of money betting on it with fellows who haven't found it out." And, by Jove, he was perfectly right, and it's a thing to remember. Many a quid have I—'

Miss Tomlinson gave a hard, dry cough, and he stopped in the middle of a sentence.

'Perhaps it will be better, Mr. Wooster,' she said, in a cold, even voice, 'if you were to tell my girls some little story. What you say is, no doubt, extremely interesting, but perhaps a little—'

'Oh, ah, yes,' said Mr. Wooster. 'Story? Story?' He appeared completely distraught, poor young gentleman. 'I wonder if you've heard the one about the stockbroker and the chorus-girl?'

'We will now sing the school song,' said Miss Tomlinson, rising like an iceberg.

I decided not to remain for the singing of the school song. It seemed probable to me that Mr. Wooster would shortly be requiring the car, so I made my way back to the stable-yard, to be in readiness.

I had not long to wait. In a very few moments he appeared, tottering. Mr. Wooster's is not one of those inscrutable faces which it is impossible to read. On the contrary, it is a limpid pool in which is mirrored each passing emotion. I could read it now like a book, and his first words were very much on the lines I had anticipated.

'Jeeves,' he said hoarsely, 'is that damned car mended yet?'

'Just this moment, sir. I have been working on it assiduously.'

'Then, for heaven's sake, let's go!'

'But I understood that you were to address the young ladies, sir.'

'Oh, I've done that!' responded Mr. Wooster, blinking twice with extraordinary rapidity. 'Yes, I've done that.'

'It was a success, I hope, sir?'

'Oh, yes. Oh, yes. Most extraordinarily successful. Went like a breeze. But – er – I think I may as well be going. No use outstaying one's welcome, what?'

'Assuredly not, sir.'

I had climbed into my seat and was about to start the engine, when voices made themselves heard; and at the first sound of them Mr. Wooster sprang with almost incredible nimbleness into the tonneau, and when I glanced round he was on the floor covering himself with a rug. The last I saw of him was a pleading eye.

'Have you seen Mr. Wooster, my man?'

Miss Tomlinson had entered the stable-yard, accompanied by a lady of, I should say, judging from her accent, French origin.

'No, madam.'

The French lady uttered some exclamation in her native tongue.

'Is anything wrong, madam?' I inquired.

Miss Tomlinson in normal mood was, I should be disposed to imagine, a lady who would not readily confide her troubles to the ear of a gentleman's gentleman, however sympathetic his aspect. That she did so now was sufficient indication of the depth to which she was stirred.

'Yes, there is! Mademoiselle has just found several of the girls smoking cigarettes in the shrubbery. When questioned, they stated that Mr. Wooster had given them the horrid things.' She turned. 'He must be in the garden somewhere, or in the house. I think the man is out of his senses. Come, mademoiselle!'

It must have been about a minute later that Mr. Wooster poked his head out of the rug like a tortoise.

'Jeeves!'

'Sir?'

'Get a move on! Start her up! Get going and *keep* going!'

I applied my foot to the self-starter.

'It would perhaps be safest to drive carefully until we are out of the school grounds, sir,' I said. 'I might run over one of the young ladies, sir.'

'Well, what's the objection to that?' demanded Mr. Wooster with extraordinary bitterness.

'Or even Miss Tomlinson, sir.'

'Don't!' said Mr. Wooster wistfully. 'You make my mouth water!'

'Jeeves,' said Mr. Wooster, when I brought him his whisky and siphon one night about a week later, 'this is dashed jolly.'

'Sir?'

'Jolly. Cosy and pleasant, you know. I mean looking at the clock and wondering if you're going to be late with the good old drinks, and then you coming in with the tray always exactly on time, never a minute late, and shoving it down on the table and biffing off, and the next night coming in and shoving it down and biffing off, and the next night – I mean, gives you a sort of safe, restful feeling. Soothing! That's the word. Soothing!'

'Yes, sir. Oh, by the way, sir—'

'Well?'

'Have you succeeded in finding a suitable house yet, sir?'

'House? What do you mean, house?'

'I understood, sir, that it was your intention to give up the flat and take a house of sufficient size to enable you to have your sister, Mrs. Scholfield, and her three young ladies to live with you.'

Mr. Wooster shuddered strongly.

'That's off, Jeeves,' he said.

'Very good, sir,' I replied.

In these disturbed days in which we live, it has probably occurred to all thinking men that something drastic ought to be done about aunts. Speaking for myself, I have long felt that stones should be turned and avenues explored with a view to putting a stopper on the relatives in question. If someone were to come to me and say, 'Wooster, would you be interested in joining a society I am starting whose aim will be the suppression of aunts or at least will see to it that they are kept on a short chain and not permitted to roam hither and thither at will, scattering desolation on all sides?', I would reply, 'Wilbraham,' if his name was Wilbraham, 'I am with you heart and soul. Put me down as a foundation member.' And my mind would flit to the sinister episode of my Aunt Dahlia and the Fothergill Venus, from which I am making only a slow recovery. Whisper the words 'Marsham Manor' in my ear, and I still quiver like a humming-bird.

At the time of its inception, if inception is the word I want, I was, I recall, feeling at the top of my form and without a care in the world. Pleasantly relaxed after thirty-six holes of golf and dinner at the Drones, I was lying on the *chez Wooster* sofa doing the *Telegraph* crossword puzzle, when the telephone rang. I could hear Jeeves out in the hall dealing with it, and presently he trickled in.

'Mrs. Travers, sir.'

'Aunt Dahlia? What does she want?'

'She did not confide in me, sir. But she appears anxious to establish communication with you.'

'To talk to me, do you mean?'

'Precisely, sir.'

A bit oddish it seems to me, looking back on it, that as I went to the instrument I should have had no premonition of an impending doom. Not psychic, that's my trouble. Having no inkling of the soup into which I was so shortly to be plunged, I welcome the opportunity of exchanging ideas with this sister of my late father who, as is widely known, is my good and deserving aunt, not to be confused with Aunt Agatha, the werewolf. What with one thing and another, it was some little time since we had chewed the fat together.

'What ho, old blood relation,' I said.

'Hullo, Bertie, you revolting young blot,' she responded in her hearty way. 'Are you sober?'

'As a judge.'

'Then listen attentively. I'm speaking from an undersized hamlet in Hampshire called Marsham-in-the-Vale. I'm staying at Marsham Manor with Cornelia Fothergill, the novelist. Ever heard of her?'

'Vaguely, as it were. She is not on my library list.'

'She would be, if you were a woman. She specializes in rich goo for the female trade.'

'Ah, yes, like Mrs. Bingo Little. Rosie M. Banks to you.'

'That sort of thing, yes, but even goo-ier. Where Rosie M. Banks merely touches the heart strings, Cornelia Fothergill grabs them in both hands and ties them into knots. I'm trying to talk her into letting me have her new novel as a serial for the *Boudoir*.'

I got the gist. She has since sold it, but at the time of which I speak this aunt was the proprietor or proprietress of a weekly paper for the half-witted woman called *Milady's Boudoir*, to which I once contributed an article – a 'piece' we old hands call it – on What The Well-Dressed Man Is Wearing. Like all weekly papers, it was in the process of turning the corner, as the expression is, and I could well understand that a serial by a specialist in rich goo would give it a much-needed shot in the arm.

'How's it coming?' I asked. 'Any luck?'

'Not so far. She demurs.'

'Dewhat's?'

'Murs, you silly ass.'

'You mean she meets your pleas with what Jeeves would call a *nolle prosequi*?'

'Not quite that. She has not closed the door to a peaceful settlement, but, as I say, she de—'

'Murs?'

'Murs is right. She doesn't say No, but she won't say Yes. The trouble is that Tom is doing his Gaspard-the-Miser stuff again.'

Her allusion was to my uncle, Thomas Portarlington Travers, who foots the bills for what he always calls *Madame's Nightshirt*. He is as rich as creosote, as I believe the phrase is, but like so many of our wealthier citizens he hates to give up. Until you have heard Uncle Tom on the subject of income tax and supertax, you haven't heard anything.

'He won't let me go above five hundred pounds, and she wants eight.'

'Looks like an impasse.'

'It did till this morning.'

'What happened this morning?'

'Oh, just a sort of break in the clouds. She said something which gave me the impression that she was weakening and that one more shove would do the trick. Are you still sober?'

'I am.'

'Then keep so over this next week-end, because you're coming down here.'

'Who, me?'

'You, in person.'

'But why?'

'To help me sway her. You will exercise all your charm—'

'I haven't much.'

'Well, exercise what you've got. Give her the old oil. Play on her as on a stringed instrument.'

I chewed the lip somewhat. I'm not keen on these blind dates. And if life has taught me one thing, it is that the prudent man keeps away from female novelists. But it might be, of course, that a gay house-party was contemplated. I probed her on his point.

'Will anyone else be there? Is there any bright young society, I mean?'

'I wouldn't call the society young, but it's very bright. There's Cornelia's husband, Everard Fothergill the artist, and his father Edward Fothergill. He's an artist, too, of a sort. You won't have a dull moment. So tell Jeeves to pack your effects, and we shall expect you on Friday. You will continue to haunt the house till Monday.'

'Cooped up with a couple of artists and a writer of rich goo? I don't like it.'

'You don't have to like it,' the aged relative assured me. 'You just do it. Oh, and by the way, when you get here, I've a little something I want you to do for me.'

'What sort of a little something?'

'I'll tell you about it when I see you. Just a simple little thing to help Auntie. You'll enjoy it,' she said, and with a cordial 'Toodle-oo' rang off.

It surprises many people, I believe, that Bertram Wooster, as a general rule a man of iron, is as wax in the hands of his Aunt Dahlia, jumping to obey her lightest behest like a performing seal going after a slice of fish. They do not know that this woman possesses a secret weapon by means of which she can always bend me to her will – viz. the threat that if I give her any of my lip, she will bar me from her dinner table and deprive me of the roasts and boileds of her French chef Anatole, God's gift to the gastric juices. When she says Go, accordingly, I do not demur, I goeth, as the Bible puts it, and so it came about that toward the quiet evenfall of Friday the 22nd inst. I was at the wheel of the old sports model, tooling through Hants with Jeeves at my side and weighed down with a nameless foreboding.

'Jeeves,' I said, 'I am weighed down with a nameless foreboding.'

'Indeed, sir?'

'Yes. What, I ask myself, is cooking?'

'I do not think I quite follow you, sir.'

'Then you jolly well ought to. I reported my conversation with Aunt Dahlia to you verbatim, and you should have every word of it tucked away beneath your bowler hat. To refresh your memory, after a certain amount of kidding back and forth she said "I've a little something I want you to do for me", and when I enquired what, she fobbed me off. . . is it fobbed?'

'Yes, sir.'

'She fobbed me off with a careless "Oh, just a simple little thing to help Auntie." What construction do you place on those words?'

'One gathers that there is something Mrs. Travers wishes you to do for her, sir.'

'One does, but the point is – what? You recall what has happened in the past when the gentler sex have asked me to do things for them. Especially Aunt Dahlia. You have not forgotten the affair of Sir Watkyn Basset and the silver cow-creamer?'

'No, sir.'

'On that occasion, but for you, Bertram Wooster would have done a stretch in the local hoosegow. Who knows that this little something to which she referred will not land me in a similar peril? I wish I could slide out of this binge, Jeeves.'

'I can readily imagine it, sir.'

'But I can't, I'm like those Light Brigade fellows. You remember how matters stood with them?'

'Very vividly, sir. Theirs not to reason why, theirs but to do and die.'

'Exactly. Cannons to right of them, cannons to left of them volleyed and thundered, but they had to keep snapping into it regardless. I know just how they felt,' I said, moodily stepping on the accelerator. The brow was furrowed and the spirits low.

Arrival at Marsham Manor did little to smooth the former and raise the latter. Shown into the hall, I found myself in as cosy an interior as one could wish – large log fire, comfortable chairs and a tea-table that gave out an invigorating aroma of buttered toast and muffins, all very pleasant to encounter after a long drive on a chilly winter afternoon – but a single glance at the personnel was enough to tell me that I had struck one of those joints where every prospect pleases and only man is vile.

Three human souls were present when I made my entry, each plainly as outstanding a piece of cheese as Hampshire could provide. One was a small, thin citizen with a beard of the type that causes so much distress – my host, I presumed – and seated near him was another bloke of much the same construction but an earlier model, whom I took to be the father. He, too, was bearded to the gills. The third was a large spreading woman wearing the horn-rimmed spectacles which are always an occupational risk for penpushers of the other sex. They gave her a rather remarkable resemblance to my Aunt Agatha, and I would be deceiving my public were I to say that the heart did not sink to some extent. To play on such a woman as on a stringed instrument wasn't going to be the simple task Aunt Dahlia appeared to think it.

After a brief pause for station identification, she introduced me to the gang, and I was on the point of doing the civil thing by asking Everard Fothergill if he had been painting anything lately, when he stiffened.

'Hark!' he said. 'Can you hear a mewing cat?'

'Eh?' I said.

'A mewing cat. I feel sure I hear a mewing cat. Listen!'

While we were listening the door opened and Aunt Dahlia came in. Everard put the 64,000-dollar question squarely up to her.

'Mrs. Travers, did you meet a mewing cat outside?'

'No,' said the aged relative. 'No mewing cat. Why, did you order one?'

'I can't bear mewing cats,' said Everard. 'A mewing cat gets on my nerves.'

That was all about mewing cats for the moment. Tea was dished out, and I had a couple of bits of buttered toast, and so the long day wore on till it was time to dress for dinner. The Fothergill contingent pushed off, and I was heading in the same direction, when Aunt Dahlia arrested my progress.

'Just a second, Bertie, before you put on your clean dickey,' she said. 'I would like to show you something.'

'And I,' I riposted, 'would like to know what this job is you say you want me to do for you.'

'I'll be coming to that later. This thing I'm going to show you is tied in with it. But first a word from our sponsor. Did you notice anything about Everard Fothergill just now?'

I reviewed the recent past.

'Would you describe him as perhaps a bit jumpy? He seemed to me to be stressing the mewing cat motif rather more strongly than might have been expected.'

'Exactly. He's a nervous wreck. Cornelia tells me he used to be very fond of cats.'

'He still appears interested in them.'

'It's this blasted picture that has sapped his morale.'

'Which blasted picture would that be?'

'I'll show you. Step this way.'

She led me into the dining-room and switched on the light.

'Look,' she said.

What she was drawing to my attention was a large oil painting. A classical picture, I suppose you would have called it.

Stout female in the minimum of clothing in conference with a dove.

'Venus?' I said. It's usually a safe bet.

'Yes. Old Fothergill painted it. He's just the sort of man who would paint a picture of Ladies Night In A Turkish Bath and call it Venus. He gave it to Everard as a wedding present.'

'Thus saving money on the customary fish-slice. Shrewd, very shrewd. And I gather from what you were saying that the latter does not like it.'

'Of course he doesn't. It's a mess. The old boy's just an incompetent amateur. But being devoted to his father and not wanting to hurt his feelings Everard can't have it taken down and put in the cellar. He's stuck with it, and has to sit looking at it every time he puts on the nose-bag. With what result?'

'The food turns to ashes in his mouth?'

'Exactly. It's driving him potty. Everard's a real artist. His stuff's good. Some of it's in the Tate. Look at this,' she said, indicating another canvas. 'That's one of his things.'

I gave it a quick once-over. It, too, was a classical picture, and seemed to my untutored mind very like the other one, but presuming that some sort of art criticism was expected of me I said:

'I like the patina.'

That, too, is generally a safe bet, but it appeared that I had said the wrong thing, for the relative snorted audibly.

'No, you don't, you miserable blighter. You don't even know what a patina is.'

She had me there, of course. I didn't.

'You and your ruddy patinas! Well, anyway, you see why Everard has got the jitters. If a man can paint as well as he can, it naturally cuts him to the quick to have to glue his eyes on a daub like the Venus every time he sits down to break bread. Suppose you were a great musician. Would you like to have to listen to a cheap, vulgar tune – the same tune – day after day? Or suppose that every time you went to lunch at the Drones you had to sit opposite someone who looked like the Hunchback of Notre Dame? Would you enjoy that? Of course you wouldn't. You'd be as sick as mud.'

I saw her point. Many a time at the Drones I have had to sit opposite Oofy Prosser, and it had always taken the edge off a usually keen appetite.

'So now do you grasp the position of affairs, dumb-bell?'

'Oh, I grasp it all right, and the heart bleeds, of course. But I don't see there's anything to be done about it.'

'I do. Ask me what.'

'What?'

'You're going to pinch that Venus.'

I looked at her with a wild surmise, silent upon a peak in Darien. Not my own. One of Jeeves's things.

'Pinch it?'

'This very night.'

'When you say "pinch it", do you mean "*pinch it*"?'

'That's right. That's the little something I was speaking of, the simple little thing you're going to do to help Auntie. Good heavens,' she said, her manner betraying impatience, 'I can't see why you're looking like a stuck pig about it. It's right up your street. You're always pinching policemen's helmets, aren't you?'

I had to correct this.

'Not always. Only as an occasional treat, as it might be on a Boat Race night. And, anyway, pinching pictures is a very different thing from lifting the headgear of the Force. Much more complex.'

'There's nothing complex about it. It's as easy as falling off a log. You just cut it out of the frame with a good sharp knife.'

'I haven't got a good sharp knife.'

'You will have. You know, Bertie,' she said, all enthusiasm, 'it's extraordinary how things fit in. These last weeks there's been a gang of picture-thieves operating in this neighbourhood. They got away with a Romney at a house near here and a Gainsborough from another house. It was that that gave me the idea. When his Venus disappears, there won't be a chance of old Fothergill suspecting anything and having his feelings hurt. These marauders are connoisseurs, he'll say to himself, only the best is good enough for them. Cornelia agreed with me.'

'You told her?'

'Well, naturally. I was naming the Price of the Papers. I said that if she gave me her solemn word that she would let the *Boudoir* have this slush she's writing, shaving her price to suit my purse, you would liquidate the Edward Fothergill Venus.'

'You did, did you? And what did she say?'

'She thanked me brokenly, saying it was the only way of keeping Everard from going off his rocker, and I told her I would have you here, ready to the last button, this week-end.'

'God bless your old pea-pickin' heart!'

'So go to it, boy, and heaven speed your efforts. All you have to do is open one of the windows, to make it look like an outside job, collect the picture, take it back to your room and burn it. I'll see that you have a good fire.'

'Oh, thanks.'

'And now you had better be dressing. You haven't much time, and it makes Everard nervous if people are late for dinner.'

It was with bowed head and the feeling that the curse had come upon me that I proceeded to my room. Jeeves was there, studding the shirt, and I lost no time in giving him the low-down. My attitude towards Jeeves on these occasions is always that of a lost sheep getting together with its shepherd.

'Jeeves,' I said, 'you remember me telling you in the car that I was weighed down with a nameless foreboding?'

'Yes, sir.'

'Well, I had every right to be. Let me tell you in a few simple words what Aunt Dahlia has just been springing on me.'

I told him in a few simple words, and his left eyebrow rose perhaps an eighth of an inch, showing how deeply he was stirred.

'Very disturbing, sir.'

'Most. And the ghastly thing is that I suppose I shall have to do it.'

'I fear so, sir. Taking into consideration the probability that, should you decline to co-operate, Mrs. Travers will place sanctions on you in the matter of Anatole's cooking, you would appear to have no option but to fall in with her wishes. Are you in pain, sir?' he asked, observing me writhe.

'No, just chafing. This has shocked me, Jeeves. I wouldn't have thought such an idea would ever have occurred to her. One could understand Professor Moriarty, and possibly Doctor Fu Manchu, thinking along these lines, but not a wife and mother highly respected in Market Snodsbury, Worcestershire.'

'The female of the species is more deadly than the male, sir. May I ask if you have formulated a plan of action?'

'She sketched one out. I open a window, to make it look like an outside job—'

'Pardon me for interrupting, sir, but there I think Mrs. Travers is in error. A broken window would lend greater verisimilitude.'

'Wouldn't it rouse the house?'

'No, sir, it can be done quite noiselessly by smearing treacle on a sheet of brown paper, attaching the paper to the pane and striking it a sharp blow with the fist. This is the recognised method in vogue in the burgling industry.'

'But where's the brown paper? Where the treacle?'

'I can procure them, sir, and I shall be happy to perform the operation for you, if you wish.'

'You will? That's very white of you, Jeeves.'

'Not at all, sir. It is my aim to give satisfaction. Excuse me, I think I hear someone knocking.'

He went to the door, opened it, said 'Certainly, madam, I will give it to Mr. Wooster immediately,' and came back with a sort of young sabre.

'Your knife, sir.'

'Thank you, Jeeves, curse it,' I said, regarding the object with a shudder, and slipped sombrely into the mesh-knit underwear.

After deliberation, we had pencilled in the kick-off for one in the morning, when the household might be expected to be getting its eight hours, and at one on the dot Jeeves shimmered in.

'Everything is in readiness, sir.'

'The treacle?'

'Yes, sir.'

'The brown p.?'

'Yes, sir.'

'Then just bust the window, would you mind.'

'I have already done so, sir.'

'You have? Well, you were right about it being noiseless. I didn't hear a sound. Then Ho for the dining-room, I suppose. No sense in dillying, or, for the matter of that, dallying.'

'No, sir. If it were done when 'tis done, then 'twere well it were done quickly,' he said, and I remember thinking how neatly he puts these things.

It would be idle to pretend that, as I made my way down the stairs, I was my usual debonair self. The feet were cold, and if there had been any sudden noises, I would have started at them. My meditations on Aunt Dahlia, who had let me in for this horror in the night, were rather markedly lacking in a nephew's love. Indeed, it is not too much to say that every step I took deepened my conviction that what the aged relative needed was a swift kick in the pants.

However, in one respect you had to hand it to her. She had said the removal of the picture from the parent frame would be as easy as falling off a log – a thing I have never done myself, but one which, I should imagine, is reasonably simple of accomplishment – and so it proved. She had in no way overestimated the goodness and sharpness of the knife with which she had provided me. Four quick cuts, and the canvas came out like a winkle at the end of a pin. I rolled it up and streaked back to my room with it.

Jeeves in my absence had been stoking the fire, and it was now in a cheerful blaze. I was about to feed Edward Fothergill's regrettable product to the flames and push it home with the poker, but he stayed my hand.

'It would be injudicious to burn so large an object in one piece, sir. There is risk of setting the chimney on fire.'

'Ah, yes, I see what you mean. Snip it up, you think?'

'I fear it is unavoidable, sir. Might I suggest that it would relieve the monotony of the task if I were to provide whisky and a syphon?'

'You know where they keep it?'

'Yes, sir.'

'Then lead it to me.'

'Very good, sir.'

'And meanwhile I'll be getting on with the job.'

I did so, and was making good progress, when the door opened without my hearing it and Aunt Dahlia beetled in. She spoke before I was aware of her presence in my midst, causing me to shoot up to the ceiling with a stifled cry.

'Everything pretty smooth, Bertie?'

'I wish you'd toot your horn,' I said, coming back to earth and speaking with not a little bitterness. 'You shook me to the core. Yes, matters have gone according to plan. But Jeeves insists on burning the *corpus delicti* bit by bit.'

'Well, of course. You don't want to set the chimney on fire.'

'That was what he said.'

'And he was right, as always. I've brought my scissors. Where is Jeeves, by the way? Why not at your side, giving selfless service?'

'Because he's giving selfless service elsewhere. He went off to get whisky.'

'What a man! There is none like him, none. Bless my soul,' said the relative some moments later, as we sat before the fire and snipped, 'how this brings back memories of the dear old school and our girlish cocoa parties. Happy days, happy days! Ah, Jeeves, come right in and put the supplies well within my reach. We're getting on, you see. What is that you have hanging on your arm?'

'The garden shears, madam. I am anxious to lend all the assistance that is within my power.'

'Then start lending. Edward Fothergill's masterpiece awaits you.'

With the three of us sparing no effort, we soon completed the work in hand. I had scarcely got through my first whisky and s. and was beginning on another, when all that was left of the Venus, not counting the ashes, was the little bit at the south-east end which Jeeves was holding. He was regarding it with what seemed to me a rather thoughtful eye.

'Excuse me, madam,' he said. 'Did I understand you to say that Mr. Fothergill senior's name was Edward?'

'That's right. Think of him as Eddie, if you wish. Why?'

'It is merely that the picture we have with us appears to be signed "Everard Fothergill", madam. I thought I should mention it.'

To say that aunt and nephew did not take this big would be paltering with the truth. We skipped like the high hills.

'Give me that fragment, Jeeves. It looks like Edward to me,' I pronounced, having scrutinised it.

'You're crazy,' said Aunt Dahlia, feverishly wrenching it from my grasp. 'It's Everard. Isn't it, Jeeves?'

'That was certainly the impression I formed, madam.'

'Bertie,' said Aunt Dahlia, speaking in a voice of the kind which I believe is usually called strangled and directing at me the sort of look which in the days when she used to hunt with the Quorn and occasionally the Pytchley she would have given a hound engaged in chasing a rabbit, 'Bertie, you curse of the civilised world if you've burned the wrong picture . . .'

'Of course I haven't,' I replied stoutly. 'You're both cockeyed.

But if it will ease your mind, I'll pop down to the dining-room and take a dekko. Amuse yourselves somehow till my return.'

I had spoken, as I say, stoutly, and hearing me you would no doubt have said to yourself 'All is well with Bertram. He is unperturbed.' But I wasn't. I feared the worst, and already I was wincing at the thought of the impassioned speech, touching on my mental and moral defects, which Aunt Dahlia would be delivering when we forgathered once more. Far less provocation in the past had frequently led her to model her attitude toward me on that of a sergeant dissatisfied with the porting and shouldering arms of a recruit who had not quite got the hang of the thing.

I was consequently in no vein for the receipt of another shock, but I got this when I reached journey's end, for as I entered the dining-room somebody inside it came bounding out and rammed me between wind and water. We staggered into the hall, locked in a close embrace, and as I had switched on the lights there in order to avoid bumping into pieces of furniture I was enabled to see my dance partner steadily and see him whole, as Jeeves says. It was Fothergill senior in bedroom slippers and a dressing-gown. In his right hand he had a knife, and at his feet there was a bundle of some sort which he had dropped at the moment of impact, and when I picked it up in my courteous way and it came unrolled, what I saw brought a startled 'Golly!' to my lips. It deadheated with a yip of anguish from his. He had paled beneath his whiskers.

'Mr. Wooster!' he . . . quavered is, I think, the word. 'Thank God you are not Everard!'

Well, I was pretty pleased about that, too, of course. The last thing I would have wanted to be was a small, thin artist with a beard.

'No doubt,' he proceeded, still quavering, 'you are surprised to find me removing my Venus by stealth in this way, but I can explain everything.'

'Well, that's fine, isn't it?'

'You are not an artist—'

'No, more a literary man. I once wrote an article on What The Well-Dressed Man Is Wearing for *Milady's Boudoir*.'

'Nevertheless, I think I can make you understand what this picture means to me. It was my child. I watched it grow. I loved it. It was part of my life.'

Here he paused, seeming touched in the wind, and I threw in a 'Very creditable' to keep the conversation going.

'And then Everard married, and in a mad moment I gave it to him as a wedding present. How bitterly I regretted it! But the thing was done. It was irrevocable. I saw how he valued the picture. His eyes at meal times were always riveted on it. I could not bring myself to ask him for it back. And yet I was lost without it.'

'Bit of a mix-up,' I agreed. 'Difficult to find a formula.'

'For a while it seemed impossible. And then there was this outbreak of picture robberies in the neighbourhood. You heard about those?'

'Yes, Aunt Dahlia mentioned them.'

'Several valuable paintings have been stolen from houses near here, and it suddenly occurred to me that if I were to – er – remove my Venus, Everard would assume that it was the work of the same gang and never suspect. I wrestled with the temptation . . . I beg your pardon?'

'I only said "At-a-boy!".'

'Oh? Well, as I say, I did my utmost to resist the temptation, but tonight I yielded. Mr. Wooster, you have a kind face.'

For an instant I thought he had said 'kind of face' and drew myself up, a little piqued. Then I got him.

'Nice of you to say so.'

'Yes, I am sure you are kind and would not betray me. You will not tell Everard?'

'Of course not, if you don't want me to. Sealed lips, you suggest?'

'Precisely.'

'Right ho.'

'Thank you, thank you. I am infinitely grateful. Well, it is a little late and one might as well be turning in, I suppose, so I will say good-night,' he said, and having done so, buzzed up the stairs like a homing rabbit. And scarcely had he buzzed, when I found Aunt Dahlia and Jeeves at my side.

'Oh, there you are,' I said.

'Yes, here we are,' replied the relative with a touch of asperity. 'What's kept you all this time?'

'I would have made it snappier, but I was somewhat impeded in my movements by pards.'

'By what?'

'Bearded pards. Shakespeare. Right, Jeeves?'

'Perfectly correct, sir. Shakespeare speaks of the soldier as bearded like the pard.'

'And,' said Aunt Dahlia, 'full of strange oaths. Some of which you will shortly hear, if you don't tell us what you're babbling about.'

'Oh, didn't I mention that? I've been chatting with Edward Fothergill.'

'Bertie, you're blotto.'

'Not blotto, old flesh and blood, but much shaken. Aunt Dahlia, I have an amazing story to relate.'

I related my amazing story.

'And so,' I concluded, 'we learn once again the lesson never, however dark the outlook, to despair. The storm clouds lowered, the skies were black, but now what do we see? The sun shining and the blue bird back once more at the old stand. La Fothergill wanted the Venus expunged, and it has been expunged. Voila!' I said, becoming a bit Parisian.

'And when she finds that owing to your fatheadedness Everard's very valuable picture has also been expunged?'

I h'med. I saw what she had in mind.

'Yes, there's that,' I agreed.

'She'll be madder than a wet hen. There isn't a chance now that she'll let me have that serial.'

'I'm afraid not. I had overlooked that. I withdraw what I said about the sun and the blue bird.'

She inflated her lungs, and it could have been perceived by the dullest eye that she was about to begin.

'Bertie—'

Jeeves coughed that soft cough of his, the one that sounds like a sheep clearing its throat on a distant mountain side.

'I wonder if I might make a suggestion, madam?'

'Yes, Jeeves? Remind me,' said the relative, giving me a burning glance, 'to go on with what I was saying later. You have the floor, Jeeves.'

'Thank you, madam. It was merely that it occurs to me as a passing thought that there *is* a solution of the difficulty that confronts us. If Mr. Wooster were to be found here lying stunned, the window broken and both pictures removed, Mrs. Fothergill could, I think, readily be persuaded that he found miscreants making a burglarious entry and while endeavouring to protect her property was assaulted and overcome by them. She would, one feels, be grateful.'

Aunt Dahlia came up like a rocket from the depths of gloom in which she had been wallowing. Her face, always red owing to hunting in all weathers in her youth, took on a deeper vermilion.

'Jeeves, you've hit it! I see what you mean. She would be so all over him for his plucky conduct that she couldn't decently fail to come through about the serial.'

'Precisely, madam.'

'Thank you, Jeeves.'

'Not at all, madam.'

'When, many years hence, you hand in your dinner pail, you must have your brain pickled and presented to the nation. It's a colossal scheme, don't you think, Bertie?'

I had been listening to the above exchange of remarks without a trace of Aunt Dahlia's enthusiasm, for I had spotted the flaw in the thing right away – to wit, the fact that I was not lying stunned. I now mentioned this.

'Oh, that?' said Aunt Dahlia. 'We can arrange that. I could give you a tap on the head with . . . with what, Jeeves?'

'The gong stick suggests itself, madam.'

'That's right, with the gong stick. And there we'll be.'

'Well, good-night, all,' I said. 'I'm turning in.'

She stared at me like an aunt unable to believe her ears.

'You mean you won't play ball?'

'I do.'

'Think well, Bertram Wooster. Reflect what the harvest will be. Not a smell of Anatole's cooking will you get for months and months and months. He will dish up his Sylphides à la creme d'écrevisses and his Timbales de Ris de Veau Toulousaines and what not, but you will not be there to dig in and get yours. This is official.'

I drew myself to my full height.

'There is no terror, Aunt Dahlia, in your threats, for . . . how does it go, Jeeves?'

'For you are armed so strong in honesty, sir, that they pass by you like the idle wind, which you respect not.'

'Exactly. I have been giving considerable thought to this matter of Anatole's cooking, and I have reached the conclusion that the thing is one that cuts both ways. Heaven, of course, to chew his smoked offerings, but what of the waistline? The last time I enjoyed your hospitality for the summer months, I put on a full inch round the middle. I am better without Anatole's cooking. I don't want to look like Uncle George.'

I was alluding to the present Lord Yaxley, a prominent London clubman who gets more prominent yearly, especially seen sideways.

'So,' I continued, 'agony though it may be, I am prepared to kiss those Timbales of which you speak goodbye, and I, therefore, meet your suggestion of giving me taps on the head with the gong stick with a resolute *nolle prosequi*.'

'That is your last word, is it?'

'It is,' I said, and it was, for as I turned on my heel something struck me a violent blow on the back hair, and I fell like some monarch of the forest beneath the axe of the woodman.

What's that word I'm trying to think of? Begins with a 'c'. Chaotic, that's the one. For some time after that conditions were chaotic. The next thing I remember with any clarity is finding myself in bed with a sort of booming noise going on close by. This, the mists having lifted, I was able to diagnose as Aunt Dahlia talking. Hers is a carrying voice. She used, as I have mentioned, to go in a lot for hunting, and though I have never hunted myself, I understand that the whole essence of the thing is to be able to make yourself heard across three ploughed fields and a spinney.

'Bertie,' she was saying, 'I wish you would listen and not let your attention wander. I've got news that will send you dancing about the house.'

'It will be some little time,' I responded coldly, 'before I go dancing about any ruddy houses. My head—'

'Yes, of course. A little the worse for wear, no doubt. But don't let's go off into side issues, I want to tell you the final score. The dirty work is attributed on all sides to the gang, probably international, which has been lifting pictures in these parts of late. Cornelia Fothergill is lost in admiration of your intrepid behaviour, as Jeeves foresaw she would be, and she's giving me the serial on easy terms. You were right about the blue bird. It's singing.'

'So is my head.'

'I'll bet it is, and as you would say, the heart bleeds. But we all have to make sacrifices at these times. You can't make an omelette without breaking eggs.'

'Your own?'

'No, Jeeves's. He said it in a hushed voice as he stood viewing the remains.'

'He did, did he? Well, I trust in future . . . Oh, Jeeves,' I said, as he entered carrying what looked like a cooling drink.

'Sir?'

'This matter of eggs and omelettes. From now on, if you could see your way to cutting out the former and laying off the latter, I should be greatly obliged.'

'Very good, sir,' said the honest fellow. 'I will bear it in mind.'

The shades of night were falling fairly fast as I latchkeyed self and suit-case into the Wooster G.H.Q. Jeeves was in the sitting-room messing about with holly, for we would soon be having Christmas at our throats and he is always a stickler for doing the right thing. I gave him a cheery greeting.

'Well, Jeeves, here I am, back again.'

'Good evening, sir. Did you have a pleasant visit?'

'Not too bad. But I'm glad to be home. What was it the fellow said about home?'

'If your allusion is to the American poet John Howard Payne, sir, he compared it to its advantage with pleasures and palaces. He called it sweet and said there was no place like it.'

'And he wasn't so far out. Shrewd chap, John Howard Payne.'

'I believe he gave uniform satisfaction, sir.'

I had just returned from a week end at the Chuffnel Regis clinic of Sir Roderick Glossop, the eminent loony doctor or nerve specialist as he prefers to call himself – not, I may add, as a patient but as a guest. My Aunt Dahlia's cousin Percy had recently put in there for repairs, and she had asked me to pop down and see how he was making out. He had got the idea, I don't know why, that he was being followed about by little men with black beards, a state of affairs which he naturally wished to have adjusted with all possible speed.

'You know, Jeeves,' I said some moments later, as I sat

quaffing the whisky-and-s. with which he had supplied me, 'life's odd, you can't say it isn't. You never know where you are with it.'

'There was some particular aspect of it that you had in mind, sir?'

'I was thinking of me and Sir R. Glossop. Who would ever have thought the day would come when he and I would be hobnobbing like a couple of sailors on shore leave? There was a time, you probably remember, when he filled me with a nameless fear and I leaped like a startled grasshopper at the sound of his name. You have not forgotten?'

'No, sir, I recall that you viewed Sir Roderick with concern.'

'And he me with ditto.'

'Yes, sir, a stiffness certainly existed. There was no fusion between your souls.'

'Yet now our relations are as cordial as they can stick. The barriers that separated us have come down with a bump. I beam at him. He beams at me. He calls me Bertie. I call him Roddy. To put the thing in a nutshell, the dove of peace is in a rising market and may quite possibly go to par. Of course, like Shadrach, Meshach and Abednego, if I've got the names right, we passed through the furnace together, and that always forms a bond.'

I was alluding to the time when – from motives I need not go into beyond saying that they were fundamentally sound – we had both blacked our faces, he with burned cork, I with boot polish, and had spent a night of terror wandering through Chuffnel Regis with no place to lay our heads, as the expression is. You don't remain on distant terms with somebody you've shared an experience like that with.

'But I'll tell you something about Roddy Glossop, Jeeves,' I said, having swallowed a rather grave swallow of the strengthening fluid. 'He has something on his mind. Physically I found him in excellent shape – few fiddles could have been fitter – but he was gloomy ... distrait ... brooding. Conversing with him, one felt that his thoughts were far away and that those thoughts were stinkers. I could hardly get a word out of him. It made me feel like that fellow in the Bible who tried to charm the deaf adder and didn't get to first base. There was a blighter named Blair Eggleston there, and it may have been this that depressed him, for this Eggleston . . . Ever hear of him? He writes books.'

'Yes, sir. Mr. Eggleston is one of our angry young novelists. The critics describe his work as frank, forthright and fearless.'

'Oh, do they? Well, whatever his literary merits he struck me as a fairly noxious specimen. What's he angry about?'

'Life, sir.'

'He disapproves of it?'

'So one would gather from his output, sir.'

'Well, I disapproved of him, which makes us all square. But I don't think it was having him around that caused the Glossop gloom. I am convinced that the thing goes deeper than that. I believe it's something to do with his love life.'

I must mention that while at Chuffnel Regis Pop Glossop, who was a widower with one daughter, had become betrothed to Myrtle, Lady Chuffnel, the aunt of my old crony Marmaduke ('Chuffy') Chuffnell, and that I should have found him still single more than a year later seemed strange to me. One would certainly have expected him by this time to have raised the price of a marriage licence and had the Bishop and assistant clergy getting their noses down to it. A redblooded loony doctor under the influence of the divine passion ought surely to have put the thing through months ago.

'Do you think they've had a row, Jeeves?'

'Sir?'

'Sir Roderick and Lady Chuffnel.'

'Oh no, sir. I am sure there is no diminution of affection on either side.'

'Then why the snag?'

'Her ladyship refuses to take part in the wedding ceremony

while Sir Roderick's daughter remains unmarried, sir. She has stated in set terms that nothing will induce her to share a home with Miss Glossop. This would naturally render Sir Roderick moody and despondent.'

A bright light flashed upon me. I saw all. As usual, Jeeves had got to the very heart of the matter.

A thing that always bothers me when compiling these memoirs of mine is the problem of what steps to take when I bring on the stage a dramatis persona, as I believe the expression is, who has already appeared in some earlier instalment. Will the customers, I ask myself, remember him or her, or will they have completely forgotten her or him, in which case they will naturally want a few footnotes to put them abreast. This difficulty arises in regard to Honoria Glossop, who got into the act in what I suppose would be about Chapter Two of the Wooster Story. Some will recall her, but there may be those who will protest that they have never heard of the beazel in their lives, so perhaps better be on the safe side and risk the displeasure of the blokes with good memories.

Here, then, is what I recorded with ref. to this H. Glossop at the time when owing to circumstances over which I had no control we had become engaged.

'Honoria Glossop,' I wrote, 'was one of those large, strenuous, dynamic girls with the physique of a middleweight catch-as-catch-can wrestler and a laugh resembling the sound made by the Scotch Express going under a bridge. The effect she had on me was to make me slide into a cellar and lie low there till they blew the All Clear.'

One could readily, therefore, understand the reluctance of Myrtle, Lady Chuffnell to team up with Sir Roderick while the above was still a member of the home circle. The stand she had taken reflected great credit on her sturdy commonsense, I considered.

A thought struck me, the thought I so often have when Jeeves starts dishing the dirt.

'How do you know all this, Jeeves? Did he confer with you?' I said, for I knew how wide his consulting practice was. 'Put it up to Jeeves' is so much the slogan in my circle of acquaintance that it might be that even Sir Roderick Glossop, finding himself on a sticky wicket, had decided to place his affairs in his hands. Jeeves is like Sherlock Holmes. The highest in the land come to him with their problems. For all I know, they may give him jewelled snuff boxes.

It appeared that I had guessed wrong.

'No, sir, I have not been honoured with Sir Roderick's confidence.'

'Then how did you find out about his spot of trouble? By extra-whatever-it's-called?'

'Extra-sensory perception? No, sir. I happened to be glancing yesterday at the G section of the club book.'

I got the gist. Jeeves belongs to a butlers and valets club in Curzon Street called the Junior Ganymede, and they have a book there in which members are required to enter information about their employers. I remember how stunned I was when he told me one day that there are eleven pages about me in it.

'The data concerning Sir Roderick and the unfortunate situation in which he finds himself were supplied by Mr. Dobson.'

'Who?'

'Sir Roderick's butler, sir.'

'Of course, yes,' I said, recalling the dignified figure into whose palm I had pressed a couple of quid on leaving that morning. 'But surely Sir Roderick didn't confide in him?'

'No, sir, but Dobson's hearing is very acute and it enabled him to learn the substance of conversations between Sir Roderick and her ladyship.'

'He listened at the keyhole?'

'So one would be disposed to imagine, sir.'

I mused a while. So that was how the cookie crumbled. A pang of p. for the toad beneath the harrow whose affairs we were discussing passed through me. It would have been plain to a far duller auditor than Bertram Wooster that poor old Roddy was in a spot. I knew how deep was his affection and esteem for Chuffy's Aunt Myrtle. Even when he was liberally coated with burned cork that night at Chuffnell Regis I had been able to detect the lovelight in his eyes as he spoke of her. And when I reflected how improbable it was that anyone would ever be ass enough to marry his daughter Honoria, thus making his path straight and ironing out the bugs in the scenario, my heart bled for him.

I mentioned this to Jeeves.

'Jeeves,' I said, 'my heart bleeds for Sir R. Glossop.'

'Yes, sir.'

'Does your heart bleed for him?'

'Profusely, sir.'

'And nothing to be done about it. We are helpless to assist.'

'One fears so, sir.'

'Life can be very sad, Jeeves.'

'Extremely, sir.'

'I'm not surprised that Blair Eggleston has taken a dislike to it.'

'No, sir.'

'Perhaps you had better bring me another whisky-and-s., to cheer me up. And after that I'll pop off to the Drones for a bite to eat.'

He gave me an apologetic look. He does this by allowing one eyebrow to flicker for a moment.

'I am sorry to say I have been remiss, sir. I inadvertently forgot to mention that Mrs. Travers is expecting you to entertain her to dinner here tonight.'

'But isn't she at Brinkley?'

'No, sir, she has temporarily left Brinkley Court and taken up residence at her town house in order to complete her Christmas shopping.'

'And she wants me to give her dinner?'

'That was the substance of her words to me on the telephone this morning, sir.

My gloom lightened perceptibly. This Mrs. Travers is my good and deserving Aunt Dahlia, with whom it is always a privilege and pleasure to chew the fat. I would be seeing her, of course, when I went to Brinkley for Christmas, but getting this preview was an added attraction. If anyone could take my mind off the sad case of Roddy Glossop, it was she. I looked forward to the reunion with bright anticipation. I little knew that she had a bombshell up her sleeve and would be touching it off under my trouser seat while the night was yet young.

On these occasions when she comes to town and I give her dinner at the flat there is always a good deal of gossip from Brinkley Court and neighbourhood to be got through before other subjects are broached, and she tends not to allow a nephew to get a word in edgeways. It wasn't till Jeeves had brought the coffee that any mention of Sir Roderick Glossop was made. Having lit a cigarette and sipped her first sip, she asked me how he was, and I gave her the same reply I had given Jeeves.

'In robust health,' I said, 'but gloomy. Sombre. Moody. Despondent.'

'Just because you were there, or was there some other reason?'

'He didn't tell me,' I said guardedly. I always have to be very careful not to reveal my sources when Jeeves gives me information he has gleaned from the club book. The rules about preserving secrecy concerning its contents are frightfully strict at the Junior Ganymede. I don't know what happens to you if you're caught giving away inside stuff, but I should imagine that you get hauled up in a hollow square of valets and butlers and have your buttons snipped off before being formally bunged out of the institution. And it's a very comforting thought that such precautions are taken, for I should hate to think that there was any chance of those eleven pages about me receiving wide publicity. It's bad enough to know that a book like that – pure dynamite, as you might say – is in existence.

'He didn't let me in on what was eating him. He just sat there being gloomy and despondent.'

The old relative laughed one of those booming laughs of hers which in the days when she hunted with the Quorn and Pytchley probably lifted many a sportsman from the saddle. Her vocal delivery when amused always resembles one of those explosions in London streets you read about in the papers.

'Well, Percy had been with him for several weeks. And then you on top of Percy. Enough to blot the sunshine from any man's life. How is Percy, by the way?'

'Quite himself again. A thing I wouldn't care to be, but no doubt it pleases him.'

'Little men no longer following him around?'

'If they are, they've shaved. He hasn't seen a black beard for quite a while, he tells me.'

'That's good. Percy'll be all right if he rid himself of the idea that alcohol is a food. Well, we'll soon buck Glossop up when he comes to Brinkley for Christmas.'

'Will he be there?'

'He certainly will, and joy will be unconfined. We're going to have a real old-fashioned Christmas with all the trimmings.'

'Holly? Mistletoe?'

'Yards of both. And a children's party complete with Santa Claus.'

'With the vicar in the stellar role?'

'No, he's down with flu.'

'The curate?'

'Sprained his ankle.'

'Then who are you going to get?'

'Oh, I'll find someone. Was anyone else at Glossop's?'

'Only a fellow of the name of Eggleston.'

'Blair Eggleston, the writer?'

'Yes, Jeeves tells me he writes books.'

'And articles. He's doing a series for me on the Modern Girl.'

For some years, helped out by doles from old Tom Travers, her husband, Aunt Dahlia had been running a weekly paper for women called *Milady's Boudoir*, to which I once contributed a 'piece', as we journalists call it, on What The Well-Dressed Man Is Wearing. The little sheet has since been sold, but at that time it was still limping along and losing its bit of money each week, a source of considerable spiritual agony to Uncle Tom, who had to foot the bills. He has the stuff in sackfuls, but he hates to part.

'I'm sorry for that boy,' said Aunt Dahlia.

'For Blair Eggleston? Why?'

'He's in love with Honoria Glossop.'

'What!' I cried. She amazed me. I wouldn't have thought it could be done.

'And is too timid to tell her so. It's often that way with these frank, fearless young novelists. They're devils on paper, but put them up against a girl who doesn't come out of their fountain pen and their feet get as cold as a dachshund's nose. You'd think, when you read his novels, that Blair Eggleston was a menace to the sex and ought to be kept on a chain in the interest of pure womanhood, but is he? No, sir. He's just a rabbit. I don't know if he has ever actually found himself in an incense-scented boudoir alone with a girl with sensual lips and dark smouldering eyes, but if he did, I'll bet he would take a chair as far away from her as possible and ask her if she had read any good books lately. Why are you looking like a half-witted fish?'

'I was thinking of something.'

'What?'

'Oh, just something,' I said warily. Her character sketch of Blair Eggleston had given me one of those ideas I do so often get quick as a flash, but I didn't want to spill it till I'd had time to think it over and ponder on it. It never does to expose these brain waves to the public eye before you've examined them from every angle. 'How do you know all this?' I said.

'He told me in a burst of confidence the other day when we

were discussing his Modern Girl Series. I suppose I must have one of those sympathetic personalities which invite confidences. You will recall that you have always told me about your various love affairs.'

'That's different.'

'In what way?'

'Use the loaf, old flesh and blood. You're my aunt. A nephew naturally bares his soul to a loved aunt.'

'I see what you mean. Yes, that makes sense. You do love me dearly, don't you?'

'Like billy-o. Always have.'

'Well, I'm certainly glad to hear you say that—'

'Well deserved tribute.'

'– because there's something I want you to do for me.'

'Consider it done.'

'I want you to play Santa Claus at my children's Christmas party.'

Should I have seen it coming? Possibly. But I hadn't, and I tottered where I sat. I was trembling like an aspen. I don't know if you've ever seen an aspen – I haven't myself as far as I can remember – but I knew they were noted for trembling like the dickens. I uttered a sharp cry, and she said if I was going to sing, would I kindly do it elsewhere, as her ear drum was sensitive.

'Don't say such things even in fun,' I begged her.

'I'm not joking.'

I gazed at her incredulously.

'You seriously expect me to put on white whiskers and a padded stomach and go about saying "Ho, ho, ho" to a bunch of kids as tough as those residing near your rural seat?'

'They aren't tough.'

'Pardon me. I've seen them in action. You will recollect that I was present at the recent school treat.'

'You can't go by that. Naturally they wouldn't have the Christmas spirit at a school treat in the middle of summer. You'll find them as mild as newborn lambs on Christmas Eve.'

I laughed a sharp, barking laugh.

'*I* shan't.'

'Are you trying to tell me you won't do it?'

'I am.'

She snorted emotionally and expressed the opinion that I was a worm.

'But a prudent, level-headed worm,' I assured her. 'A worm who knows enough not to stick its neck out.'

'You really won't do it?'

'Not for all the rice in China.'

'Not to oblige a loved aunt?'

'Not to oblige a posse of loved aunts.'

'Now listen, young Bertie, you abysmal young blot . . .'

As I closed the front door behind her some twenty minutes later, I had rather the feeling you get when parting company with a tigress of the jungle or one of those fiends with hatchet who are always going about slaying six. Normally the old relative is as genial a soul as ever downed a veal cutlet, but she's apt to get hot under the collar when thwarted, and in the course of the recent meal, as we have seen, I had been compelled to thwart her like a ton of bricks. It was with quite a few beads of persp. bedewing the brow that I went back to the dining-room, where Jeeves was cleaning up the debris.

'Jeeves,' I said, brushing away the b. of p. with my cambric handkerchief, 'you were off stage towards the end of dinner, but did you happen to drink in any of the conversation that was taking place?'

'Oh yes, sir.'

'Your hearing, like Dobson's, is acute?'

'Extremely, sir. And Mrs. Travers has a robust voice. I received the impression that she was incensed.'

'She was as sore as a gumboil. And why? Because I stoutly refused to portray Santa Claus at the Christmas orgy she is giving down at Brinkley for the children of the local yokels.'

'So I gathered from her obiter dicta, sir.'

'I suppose most of the things she called me were picked up on the hunting field in her hunting days.'

'No doubt, sir.'

'Members of the Quorn and Pytchley are not guarded in their speech.'

'Very seldom, sir, I understand.'

'Well, her efforts were . . . what's that word I've heard you use?'

'Bootless, sir?'

'Or fruitless?'

'Whichever you prefer, sir.'

'I was not to be moved. I remained firm. I am not a disobliging man, Jeeves. If somebody wanted me to play Hamlet, I would do my best to give satisfaction. But at dressing up in white whiskers and a synthetic stomach I draw the line and draw it sharply. She huffed and puffed, as you heard, but she might have known that argument would be bootless. As the wise old saying has it, you can take a horse to the water, but you can't make it play Santa Claus.'

'Very true, sir.'

'You think I was justified in being adamant?'

'Fully justified sir.'

'Thank you, Jeeves.'

I must say I thought it pretty decent of him to give the young master the weight of his support like this, for though I haven't mentioned it before it was only a day or two since I had been compelled to thwart him as inflexibly as I had thwarted the recent aunt. He had been trying to get me to go to Florida after Christmas, handing out a lot of talk about how pleasant it would be for my many American friends, most of whom make a bee line for Hobe Sounds in the winter months, to have me with them again, but I recognised this, though specious, as merely the old oil. I knew what was the thought behind his words. He likes the fishing in Florida and yearns some day to catch a tarpon.

Well, I sympathised with his sporting aspirations and would have pushed them along if I could have managed it, but I particularly wanted to be in London for the Drones Club Darts Tournament, which takes place in February and which I confidently expected to win this year, so I said Florida was out and he said 'Very good, sir', and that was that. The point I'm making is that there was no dudgeon or umbrage or anything of that sort on his part, as there would have been if he had been a lesser man, which of course he isn't.

'And yet, Jeeves,' I said, continuing to touch on the affair of the stricken aunt, 'though my firmness and resolution enabled me to emerge victorious from the battle of wills, I can't help feeling a pang.'

'Sir?'

'Of remorse. It's always apt to gnaw you when you've crushed someone beneath the iron heel. You can't help thinking that you ought to do something to bind up the wounds and bring the sunshine back into the poor slob's life. I don't like the thought of Aunt Dahlia biting her pillow tonight and trying to choke back the rising sobs because I couldn't see my way to fulfilling her hopes and dreams. I think I should extend something in the way of an olive branch or *amende honorable*.'

'It would be a graceful act, sir.'

'So I'll blow a few bob on flowers for her. Would you mind nipping out tomorrow morning and purchasing say two dozen long-stemmed roses?"

'Certainly, sir.'

'I think they'll make her face light up, don't you?'

'Unquestionably, sir. I will attend to the matter immediately after breakfast.'

'Thank you, Jeeves.'

I was smiling one of my subtle smiles as he left the room, for in the recent exchanges I had not been altogether frank, and it tickled me to think that he thought that I was merely trying to apply a soothing poultice to my conscience.

Mark you, what I had said about wanting to do the square thing by the aged relative and heal the breach and all that sort of thing was perfectly true, but there was a lot more than that behind the gesture. It was imperative that I get her off the boil, because her co-operation was essential to the success of a scheme or plan or plot which had been fizzing in the Wooster brain ever since the moment after dinner when she had asked me why I was looking like a half-witted fish. It was a plan designed to bring about the happy ending for Sir R. Glossop, and now that I had had time to give it the once over it seemed to me that it couldn't miss.

Jeeves brought the blooms while I was in my bath, and having dried the frame and donned the upholstery and breakfasted and smoked a cigarette to put heart into me I started out with them.

I wasn't expecting a warm welcome from the old flesh and blood, which was lucky, because I didn't get one. She was at her haughtiest, and the look she gave me was the sort of look which in her Quorn and Pytchley days she would have given some fellow-sportsman whom she had observed riding over hounds.

'Oh, it's you?' she said.

Well, it was, of course, no argument about that, so I endorsed her view with a civil good morning and a smile – rather a weak smile, probably, for her aspect was formidable. She was plainly sizzling.

'I hope you thoroughly understand,' she said, 'that after your craven exhibition last night I'm not speaking to you.'

'Oh, aren't you?'

'Certainly not. I'm treating you with silent contempt. What's that you've got there?'

'Some long-stemmed roses. For you.'

She sneered visibly.

'You and your long-stemmed roses! It would take more than long-stemmed roses to change my view that you're a despicable cowardy custard and a disgrace to a proud family. Your ancestors fought in the Crusades and were often mentioned in despatches, and you cringe like a salted snail at the thought of appearing as Santa Claus before an audience of charming children who wouldn't hurt a fly. It's enough to make an aunt turn her face to the wall and give up the struggle. But perhaps,' she said, her manner softening for a moment, 'you've come to tell me you've changed your mind?'

'I fear not, aged relative.'

'Then buzz off, and on your way home try if possible to get run over by a motor bus. And may I be there to hear you go pop.'

I saw that I had better come to the *res* without delay.

'Aunt Dahlia,' I said, 'it is within your power to bring happiness and joy into a human life.'

'If it's yours, I don't want to.'

'Not mine. Roddy Glossop's. Sit in with me in a plan or scheme which I have in mind, and he'll go pirouetting about his clinic like a lamb in Springtime.'

She drew a sharp breath and eyed me keenly.

'What's the time?' she asked.

I consulted the wrist-w.

'A quarter to eleven. Why?'

'I was only thinking that it's very early for anyone, even you, to get pie-eyed.'

'I'm not pie-eyed.'

'Well, you're talking as if you were. Have you got a piece of chalk?'

I tut-tutted impatiently.

'Of course I haven't. Do you think I go about with pieces of chalk on my person? What do you want it for?'

'I would like to draw a line on the carpet and see if you can walk along it, because it's being borne in upon me more emphatically every moment that you're stewed to the gills. Say "Truly rural".'

I did so.

'And "She stood at the door of Burgess's fish sauce shop, welcoming him in".'

Again I passed the test.

'Well,' she said grudgingly, 'you seem as sober as you ever are. What do you mean about bringing happiness and joy into old Glossop's life?'

'The matter is susceptible of a ready explanation. I must begin by saying that Jeeves told me a story yesterday that shocked me to the core. No,' I said in answer to her query, 'it was not the one about the young man of Calcutta. It had to do with Roddy's love life. It's a long story, but I'll condense it into a short-short, and I would like to stress before embarking on my narrative that you can rely on it being accurate, for when Jeeves tells you anything, it's like getting it straight from the mouth of the stable cat. Furthermore, it's substantiated by Mr. Dobson, Roddy's butler. You know Myrtle, Lady Chuffnell?'

'I've met her.'

'She and Roddy are betrothed.'

'So I've heard.'

'They love each other fondly.'

'So what's wrong with that?'

'I'll tell you what's wrong. She stoutly declines to go centre-aisleing with him until his daughter Honoria gets married.'

I had expected this to make her sit up, and it did. For the first time her demeanour conveyed the impression that she wasn't labelling my utterances as just delirious babble from the sick bed. She has always been fond of R. Glossop and it came as a shock to her to learn that he was so firmly established in the soup. I wouldn't say she turned pale, for after years of following the hounds in all weathers she can't, but she snorted and I could see that she was deeply moved.

'For heaven's sake! Is this true?'

'Jeeves has all the facts.'

'Does Jeeves know everything?'

'I believe so. Well, you can understand Ma Chuffnell's

attitude. If you were a bride, would you want to have Honoria a permanent resident of your little nest?'

'I wouldn't.'

'Exactly. So obviously steps must be taken by Roddy's friends and well-wishers to get her married. And that brings me to the nub. I have a scheme.'

'I'll bet it's rotten.'

'On the contrary, it's a ball of fire. It flashed on me last night, when you were telling me that Blair Eggleston loves Honoria. That is where hope lies.'

'You mean you're thinking that he will marry her and take her off the strength?'

'Precisely.'

'Not a chance. I told you he was too much of a rabbit to suggest a merger. He'll never have the nerve to propose.'

'Unless helped by a push from behind.'

'And who's going to give him that?'

'I am. With your co-operation.'

She gave me another of those long keen looks, and I could see that she was again asking herself if her favourite nephew wasn't steeped to the tonsils in the juice of the grape. Fearing more tests and further references to pieces of chalk, I hastened to explain.

'Here's the idea. I start giving Honoria the rush of a lifetime. I lush her up at lunch and dinner. I take her to theatres and night clubs. I haunt her like a family spectre and cling to her closer than a porous plaster.'

I thought I heard her mutter 'Poor girl', but I ignored the slur and continued.

'You meanwhile . . . Will you be seeing something of Eggleston?'

'I see him daily. He brings me his latest views on the Modern Girl.'

'Then the thing's in the bag. You say he has already confided in you about his warmer-and-deeper-than-ordinary-friendship feelings concerning Honoria, so it won't be difficult for you to bring the subject up in the course of conversation. You warn him in a motherly way that he's a sap if he goes on not telling his love and letting concealment like a worm in the bud feed on his damask cheek – one of Jeeves's gags. I thought he put it rather well – and stress the fact that he had better heat up his feet and grab the girl while the grabbing's good, because you happen to know that your nephew Bertram is making a heavy play in her direction and may sew up the deal at any moment. Use sufficient eloquence, and I can't see how he can fail to respond. He'll be pouring out his love before you know where you are.'

'And suppose she doesn't feel like getting engaged to him?'

'Absurd. Why, she was once engaged to *me*.'

She was silent for a space, plunged in thought, as the expression is.

'I'm not sure,' she said at length, 'that you haven't got something.'

'It's a snip.'

'Yes, I think you're right. Jeeves has a great brain.'

'What's Jeeves got to do with it?'

'Wasn't it his idea?'

I drew myself up rather haughtily – not an easy thing to do when you're sitting in an arm-chair. I resent this universal tendency to take it for granted that whenever I suggest some particularly ripe scheme, it must be Jeeves's.

'The sequence was entirely mine.'

'Well, it's not at all a bad one. I've often said that you sometimes have lucid intervals.'

'And you'll sit in and do your bit?'

'It will be a pleasure.'

'Fine. Can I use your phone? I want to ask Honoria Glossop to lunch.'

I should imagine that it has often been said of Bertram Wooster that when he sets his hand to the plough he does not readily sheathe the sword. I had told Aunt Dahlia that I was going to give Honoria the rush of a lifetime, and the rush of a lifetime was precisely what I gave her. I lunched, dined and on two occasions nightclubbed her . . . It ran into money, but you can put up with a few punches in the pocketbook when you're working in a good cause. Even when wincing at the figures at the foot of the bill I was able to console myself with the thought of what all this was in aid of. Nor did I grudge the hours spent in the society of a girl whom in normal circs. I would willingly have run a mile in tight shoes to avoid. Pop Glossop's happiness was at stake, and when a pal's happiness is at stake, the undersigned does not count the cost.

Nor were my efforts bootless. Aunt Dahlia was always ringing me up to tell me that Blair Eggleston's temperature was rising steadily day by day and it seemed to her only a question of time before the desired object would be achieved. And came a day when I was able to go to her with the gratifying news that the d.o. had indeed been a.

I found her engrossed in an Erle Stanley Gardner, but she lowered the volume courteously as I entered.

'Well, ugly,' she said, 'what brings you here? Why aren't you off somewhere with Honoria Glossop, doing your South American Joe act? What's the idea of playing hooky like this?'

I smiled one of my quiet smiles.

'Aged relative,' I said, 'I have come to inform you that I think we have reached the end of the long long trail,' and without further preamble I gave her the low-down. 'Have you been out today?'

'I went for a stroll, yes.'

'The weather probably struck you as extraordinarily mild for the latter part of December. More like spring than winter.'

'You haven't come here to talk about the weather?'

'You will find it is germane to the issue. Because the afternoon was so balmy—'

'Like others I could name.'

'I beg your pardon?'

'I didn't speak. Go on.'

'Well, as it was such a nice day I thought I would take a walk in the Park. I did so, and blowed if the first thing I saw wasn't Honoria. She was sitting on a chair by the Serpentine. I was about to duck, but it was too late. She had seen me, so I had to heave alongside and chat. And suddenly who should come along but Blair Eggleston.'

I had enchained her interest. She uttered a yip.

'He saw you?'

'With the naked eye.'

'Then that was your moment. If you'd had an ounce of sense, you'd have kissed her.'

I smiled another of my quiet ones.

'I did.'

'You *did*?'

'Yes, sir, I folded her in a close embrace and let her have it.'

'And what did Eggleston say?'

'I didn't wait to hear. I pushed off.'

'But you're sure he saw you?'

'He couldn't have missed. He was only a yard or two away, and the visibility was good.'

It isn't often that I get unstinted praise from my late father's sister, she as a rule being my best friend and severest critic, but on this occasion she gave me a rave notice. It was a pleasure to listen to her.

'That should have done it,' she said after handing me some stately compliments on my ingenuity and resource. 'I saw Eggleston yesterday, and when I mentioned what fun you and Honoria were having going about together, he looked like a blond Othello. His hands were clenched, his eyes burning, and if he wasn't grinding his teeth, I don't know a ground tooth when I hear one. That kiss was just what he needed to push him over the edge. He probably proposed to her the moment you were out of the way.'

'That's how I had it figured out.'

'Oh, hell,' said the ancestor, for at this moment the telephone rang, interrupting us just when we wanted to go on discussing the thing undisturbed. She reached for it, and a long onesided conversation ensued. I say onesided because her contribution to it consisted merely of Ohs and Whats. Eventually whoever was at the other end appeared to have said his or her say, for she replaced the receiver and turned a grave face in my direction.

'That was Honoria,' she said.

'Oh, really?'

'And what she had to tell me was fraught with interest.'

'Did matters work out according to plan?'

'Not altogether.'

'How do you mean, not altogether?'

'Well, to begin with, it seems that Blair Eggleston, no doubt inflamed by what I told you I had said to him yesterday, proposed to her last night.'

'He did?'

'And was accepted.'

'That's good.'

'Not so good.'

'Why not?'

'Because when he saw you kiss her, he blew his top and broke the engagement.'

'Oh, my God!'

'Nor is that all. The worst is yet to come. She now says she's going to marry you. She said she quite realised your many defects but is sure she can correct them and mould you, and even though you aren't the mate of her dreams, she feels that your patient love should be rewarded. Obviously what happened was that you made yourself too fascinating. There was always that risk, I suppose.'

Long before she had concluded these remarks I had gone into my aspen act again. I goggled at her, stunned.

'But this is frightful!'

'I told you it wasn't so good.'

'You aren't pulling my leg?'

'No, it's official.'

'Then what shall I do for the best?'

She shrugged a moody shoulder.

'Don't ask me,' she said. 'Consult Jeeves. He may be able to suggest something.'

Well, it was all very well to say consult Jeeves, but it wasn't as simple as she seemed to think. The way I looked at it was that to place him in possession of the facts in what you might call pitiless detail would come under the head of bandying a woman's name, which, as everybody knows, is the sort of thing that gets you kicked out of clubs and cut by the County. On the other hand, to be in a jam like this and not seek his counsel would be a loony proceeding. It was only after profound thought that I saw how the thing could be worked. I gave him a hail, and he presented himself with a courteous 'Sir?'.

'Oh, Jeeves,' I said, 'I hope I'm not interrupting you when you were curled up with your Spinoza's Ethics or whatever it is, but I wonder if you could spare me a moment of your valuable time?'

'Certainly, sir.'

'A problem has arisen in the life of a friend of mine who shall be nameless, and I want your advice. I must begin by saying that it's one of those delicate problems where not only my friend must be nameless but all the other members of the personnel. In other words, I can't mention names. You see what I mean?'

'I understand you perfectly sir. You would prefer to term the protagonists A and B.'

'Or North and South?'

'A and B is more customary, sir.'

'Just as you say. Well, A is male, B female. You follow me so far?'

'You have been lucidity itself, sir.'

'And owing to . . . what's that something of circumstances you hear people talking about? Cats enter into it, if I remember rightly.'

'Would concatenation be the word for which you are groping?'

'That's it. Owing to a concatenation of circumstances B has got it into her nut that A's in love with her. But he isn't. Still following?'

'Yes, sir.'

I had to pause here for a moment to marshal my thoughts. Having done so, I proceeded.

'Now until quite recently B was engaged to—'

'Shall we call him C, sir?'

'Caesar's as good a name as any, I suppose. Well, as I was saying, until quite recently B was engaged to Caesar and A hadn't a worry in the world. But now there has been a rift within the lute, the fixture has been scratched, and B is talking freely of teaming up with A, and what I want you to bend your brain to is the problem of how A can oil out of it. Don't get the idea that it's simple, because A is what is known as a preux chevalier, and this hampers him. I mean when B comes to him and says "A, I will be yours," he can't just reply "You will, will you? That's what *you* think." He has his code, and the code rules that he must kid her along and accept the situation. And frankly, Jeeves, he would rather be dead in a ditch. So there you are. The facts are before you. Anything stirring?'

'Yes, sir.'

I was astounded. Experience has taught me that he generally knows all the answers, but this was certainly quick service.

'Say on, Jeeves. I'm all agog.'

'Obviously, sir, B's matrimonial plans would be rendered null and void if A were to inform her that his affections were engaged elsewhere.'

'But they aren't.'

'It would be necessary merely to convey the impression that such was the case.'

I began to see what he was driving at.

'You mean if I – or, rather, A – were to produce some female and have her assert that she was betrothed to me – or I should say him – the peril would be averted?'

'Precisely, sir.'

I mused.

'It's a thought,' I agreed, 'but there's the dickens of a snag – viz. how to get hold of the party of the second part. You can't rush about London asking girls to pretend they're engaged to you. At least, I suppose you can, but it would be quite a nervous strain.'

'That, sir, is the difficulty.'

'You haven't an alternative plan to suggest?'

'I fear not, sir.'

I confess I was baffled, but it's pretty generally recognised at the Drones and elsewhere that while you can sometimes baffle Bertram Wooster for the nonce, he rarely stays baffled long. I happened to run into Catsmeat Potter-Pirbright at the Drones that night, and I suddenly saw how the snag to which I had alluded could be got around.

Catsmeat is on the stage and now in considerable demand for what are called juvenile roles, but in his early days he had been obliged, like all young hams, to go from agent to agent seeking employment – or trying to get a shop, as I believe the technical term is, and he was telling me anecdotes about them after dinner. And it struck me like a blow in the midriff that if you wanted a girl to exhibit as your fiancée, a theatrical agent was the very man to help you out. Such a bloke would be in an admirable position to supply some resting artiste who would be glad to sit in on an innocent deception in return for a moderate fee.

Catsmeat had told me where these fauna were to be found. The Charing Cross Road is apparently where most of them hang out, and on the following morning I might have been observed entering the premises of Jas Waterbury on the top floor of a building about halfway up that thoroughfare.

The reason my choice had fallen on Jas was not that I had heard glowing reports of him from every side, it was simply because all the other places I had tried had been full of guys and dolls standing bumper to bumper and it hadn't seemed worth while waiting. Entering *chez* Waterbury I found his outer office completely empty. It was as if he had parted company with the human herd.

It was possible, of course, that he had stepped across the road for a quick one, but it was also possible that he was lurking behind the door labelled Private, so I rapped on it. I hadn't expected anything to start into life, but I was wrong. A head popped out.

I've seen heads that were more of a feast for the eye. It was what I would describe as a greasy head. Its summit was moist with hair oil and the face, too, suggested that its proprietor after the morning shave had thought fit to rub bis cheeks with butter. But I'm a broad-minded man and I had no objection to him being greasy, if he liked being greasy. Possibly, I felt, if I had had the privilege of meeting Kenneth Molyneux, Malcolm McCullen, Edmund Ogilvy and Horace Furnival, the other theatrical agents I had visited, I would have found them greasy, too. It may be that all theatrical agents are. I made a mental note to ask Catsmeat Potter-Pirbright about this.

'Oh, hullo, cocky,' said this oleaginous character, speaking thickly, for he was making an early lunch on what looked like a ham sandwich. 'Something I can do for you?'

'Jas Waterbury?'

'That's me. You want a shop?'

'I want a girl.'

'Don't we all? What's your line? Are you running a touring company?'

'No, it's more like amateur theatricals.'

'Oh, those? Well, let's have the inside story.'

I had told myself that it would be embarrassing confiding one's intimate private affairs to a theatrical agent, and it was embarrassing, but I stiffened the upper lip and had at it, and as my narrative proceeded it was borne in upon me that I had sized up Jas Waterbury all wrong. Misled by his appearance, I had assumed him to be one of those greasy birds who would be slow on the uptake and unable to get hep to the finer points. He proved to be both quick and intelligent. He punctuated my remarks with understanding nods, and when I had finished said I had come to the right man, for he had a niece called Trixie who would fill the bill to my complete satisfaction. The whole project, he said, was right up Trixie's street. If I placed myself in her hands, he added, the act must infallibly be a smash hit.

It sounded good, but I pursed my lips a bit dubiously. I was asking myself if an uncle's love might not have made him give the above Trixie too enthusiastic a build-up.

'You're sure,' I said, 'that this niece of yours would be equal to this rather testing job? It calls for considerable histrionic skill. Can she make her role convincing?'

'She'll smother you with burning kisses, if that's what you're worrying about.'

'What I had in mind was more the dialogue. We don't want her blowing up in her lines. Don't you think we ought to get a seasoned professional?'

'That's just what Trixie is. Been playing Fairy Queens in panto for years. Never got a shop in London owing to jealousy in high places, but ask them in Leeds and Wigan what they think of her. Ask them in Hull. Ask them in Huddersfield.'

I said I would, always provided I happened to come across them, and he carried on in a sort of ecstasy.

'"This buxom belle" – *Leeds Evening Chronicle*. "A talented bit of all right" – *Hull Daily News*. "Beauty and dignity combined" – *Wigan Intelligencer*. Don't you fret yourself, cocky,

Trix'll give you your money's worth. And talking of that, how much does the part pay?'

'I was thinking of a fiver.'

'Make it ten.'

'Right ho.'

'Or, rather, fifteen. That way you'll get every ounce of zest and co-operation.'

I was in no mood to haggle. Aunt Dahlia had rung up while I was breakfasting to tell me that Honoria Glossop had told her that she would be looking in on me at four o'clock, and it was imperative that the reception committee be on hand to greet her. I dished out the fifteen quid and asked how soon he could get hold of his niece, as time was of the essence. He said her services would be at my disposal well ahead of zero hour, and I said Fine.

'Give me a ring when it's all set,' I said. 'I'll be lunching at the Drones Club.'

This seemed to interest him quite a bit.

'Drones Club, eh? You a member there? I've got some good friends at the Drones Club. You know Mr. Widgeon?'

'Freddie Widgeon? Yes, very well.'

'And Mr. Prosser?'

'Yes, I know Oofy Prosser.'

'Give them my best, if you see them. Nice lads, both. And now you can trot along and feed your face without a care in the world. I'll have contacted Trixie before you're halfway through your fish and chips.'

And I was called to the 'phone while having the after-luncheon coffee in the smoking-room. It was, as I had anticipated, Jas Waterbury.

'That you, cocky?'

I said it was, and he said everything was under control. Trixie had been contacted and would be up and doing with a heart for any fate in good time for the rise of the curtain. What, he asked, was the address they were to come to, and I told him and he said they would be there at a quarter to four without fail. So that was all fixed, and I was full of kindly feelings towards Jas Waterbury as I made my way back to the smoking-room. He was a man whom I would have hesitated to invite to come with me on a long walking tour and I still felt that he would have been well advised to go easier on the grease as regarded both his hair and his person, but there was no getting away from it that if circumstances rendered it necessary for you to plot plots, he was the ideal fellow to plot them with.

During my absence from the smoking-room Catsmeat Potter-Pirbright had taken the chair next to mine, and I lost no time in sounding him out on the subject of Jas Waterbury.

'You remember you were telling me about theatrical agents, Catsmeat. Did you ever happen to come across one called Waterbury?'

He pondered a while.

'The name seems vaguely familiar. What does he look like?'

'Nothing on earth.'

'That doesn't place him. All theatrical agents look like nothing on earth. But it's odd that I seem to know the name. Waterbury? Waterbury? Ha! Is he a greasy bird?'

'Very greasy.'

'And is his first name Jas?'

'That's right.'

'Then I know the chap you mean. I never met him myself – I doubt if he was going at the time when I was hoofing it from agent to agent – but I've heard of him from Freddie Widgeon and Oofy Prosser.'

'Yes, he said they were friends of his.'

'He'd revise that view if he could listen to them talking about him. Oofy in particular. Jas Waterbury once chiselled him out of two thousand pounds.'

I was amazed.

'He chiselled *Oofy* out of two thousand pounds?' I gasped, wondering if I could believe my e. Oofy is the Drones Club millionaire, but it is well known that it's practically impossible to extract as much as five bob from him without using chloroform and a forceps. Dozens have tried it and failed.

'That's what Freddie Widegon told me. Freddie says that once Jas Waterbury enters your life, you can kiss at least a portion of your holdings goodbye. Has he taken anything off you?'

'Fifteen quid.'

'You're lucky it wasn't fifteen hundred.'

If you're saying to yourself that these words of Catsmeat's must have left me uneasy and apprehensive, you are correct to the last drop. A quarter to four found me pacing the Wooster carpet with furrowed brow. If it had been merely a matter of this grease-coated theatrical agent tapping Freddie Widgeon for a couple of bob, it would have been different. A child can tap Freddie. But when it came to him parting Oofy Prosser, a man in whose wallet moths nest and raise large families, from a colossal sum like two thousand pounds, the brain reeled and one sought in vain for an explanation. Yet so it was. Catsmeat said it was impossible to get the full story, because every time Jas's name was mentioned Oofy just turned purple and spluttered, but the stark fact remained that Jas's bank balance was that amount up and Oofy's that amount down, and it made me feel like a fellow in a novel of suspense who suddenly realises that he's up against an Octopus of Crime and hasn't the foggiest how he's going to avoid the menacing tentacles.

But it wasn't long before Reason returned to its throne and I saw that I'd been alarming myself unnecessarily. Nothing like that was going to happen to me. It might be that Jas Waterbury would have a shot at luring me into some business venture with the ultimate aim of leaving me holding the baby, but if he did he would find himself stymied by a firm *nolle prosequi*, so, to cut a long story s., by the time the front door bell rang Bertram was himself again.

I answered the bell, for it was Jeeves's afternoon off. Once a week he downs tools and goes off to play Bridge at the Junior Ganymede. I opened the door and Jas and his niece came in, and I stood gaping dumbly. For an instant, you might say I was spellbound.

Not having attended the performance of a pantomime since fairly early childhood, I had forgotten how substantial Fairy Queens were, and the sight of Trixie Waterbury was like a blow from a blunt instrument. A glance was enough to tell me why the dramatic critic of the *Leeds Evening Chronicle* had called her buxom. She stood about five feet nine in her short French vamps and bulged in every direction. Also the flashing eyes and the gleaming teeth. It was some moments before I was able to say Good Afternoon.

'Afternoon,' said Jas Waterbury. He looked about him approvingly. 'Nice little place you've got here. Costs a packet to keep up, I'll bet. This is Mr. Wooster, Trixie. You call him Bertie.'

The Fairy Queen said wouldn't 'sweetie-pie' be better, and Jas Waterbury told her with a good deal of enthusiasm that she was quite right.

'Much more box office,' he agreed. 'Didn't I say she would be right for the part, cocky? You can rely on her to give a smooth West End performance. When do you expect your lady friend?'

'Any moment now.'

'Then we'd better be dressing the stage. Discovered, you sitting in that chair with Trixie on your lap.'

'What!'

He seemed to sense the consternation in my voice, for he frowned a little under the grease.

'We're all working for the good of the show,' he reminded me austerely. 'You want the scene to carry conviction, and there's nothing like a sight gag.'

I could see there was much in what he said. This was not a time for half measures. I sat down. I don't say I sat blithely, but

I sat, and Wigan's favourite Fairy Queen descended on my lap with a bump that made the stout chair tremble like an aspen. And scarcely had she started to nestle when the door bell rang.

'Curtain going up,' said Jas Waterbury. 'Let's have that passionate embrace, Trixie, and make it good.'

She made it good, and I felt like a Swiss mountaineer engulfed by an avalanche smelling of patchouli. Jas Waterbury flung wide the gates, and who should come in but Blair Eggleston, the last caller I was expecting.

He stood goggling. I sat goggling. Jas Waterbury goggled, too. One could understand how he was feeling, Anticipating the entrance of the female star and observing coming on left centre a character who wasn't a member of the cast at all, he was pardonably disconcerted. No impresario likes that sort of thing.

I was the first to speak. After all, I was the host and it was for me to get the conversation going.

'Oh, hullo, Eggleston,' I said. 'Come along in. I don't think you've met Mr. Waterbury, have you. Mr. Eggleston, Mr. Jas Waterbury. And his niece Miss Trixie Waterbury, my fiancée.'

'Your *what*?'

'Fiancée. Betrothed. Affianced.'

'Good Lord!'

Jas Waterbury appeared to be feeling that as the act had been shot to pieces like this, there was no sense in hanging around.

'Well, Trix,' he said, 'your Bertie'll be wanting to talk to his gentleman friend, so give him a kiss and we'll be getting along. Pleased to have met you, Mr. What-is-it,' and with a greasy smile he led the Fairy Queen from the room.

Blair Eggleston seemed still at a loss. He looked at the door through which they had passed as if asking himself if he had really seen what he thought he had seen, then turned to me with the air of one who intends to demand an explanation.

'What's all this, Wooster?'

'What's all what, Eggleston? Be more explicit.'

'Who on earth is that female?'

'Weren't you listening? My fiancée.'

'You're really engaged to her?'

'That's right.'

'Who is she?'

'She plays Fairy Queens in pantomime. Not in London owing to jealousy in high places, but they think a lot of her in Leeds, Wigan, Hull and Huddersfield. The critic of the Hull *Daily News* describes her as a talented bit of all right.'

He was silent for a space, appearing to be turning this over in his mind. Then he spoke in the frank, forthright and fearless way these modern novelists have.

'She looks like a hippopotamus.'

I conceded this.

'There is a resemblance, perhaps. I suppose Fairy Queens have to be stoutish if they are to keep faith with their public in towns like Leeds and Huddersfield. Those audiences up North want lots for their money.'

'And she exudes a horrible scent which I am unable at the moment to identify.'

'Patchouli. Yes, I noticed that.'

He mused again.

'I can't get over you being engaged to her.'

'Well, I am.'

'It's official?'

'Absolutely.'

'Well, this will be great news for Honoria.'

I didn't get his drift.

'For Honoria?'

'Yes. It will relieve her mind. She was very worried about you, poor child. That's why I'm here. I came to break it to you that she can never be yours. She's going to marry me.'

I stared at him. My first impression was that even though the hour was only about four-thirty he was under the influence of alcoholic stimulants.

'But I learned from a usually reliable source that that was all off.'

'It was, but now it's on again. We have had a complete reconciliation.'

'Well, fancy that!'

'And she shrank from coming and telling you herself. She said she couldn't bear to see the awful dumb agony in your eyes. When I tell her you're engaged, she'll go singing about the West End of London, not only because of the relief of knowing that she hasn't wrecked your life but because she'll be feeling what a merciful escape she's had. Just imagine being married to you! It doesn't bear thinking of. Well, I'll be going along and telling her the good news,' he said, and took his departure.

A moment later the bell rang. I opened the door and found him on the mat.

'What,' he asked, 'was that name again?'

'Name?'

'Your fiancée's.'

'Trixie Waterbury.'

'Good God!' he said, and pushed off. And I returned to the reverie he had interrupted.

There was a time when if somebody had come to me and said 'Mr. Wooster, I have been commissioned by a prominent firm of publishers to write your biography and I need some intimate stuff which only you can supply. Looking back, what would you consider the high spot in your career?', I would have had no difficulty in slipping him the info. It occurred, I would have replied, in my fourteenth year when I was a resident pupil at Malvern House, Bramley-on-Sea, the private school conducted by that prince of stinkers, Aubrey Upjohn, M.A. He had told me to present myself in his study on the following morning, which always meant six of the juiciest with a cane that bit like a serpent and stung like an adder, and blowed if when morning came I wasn't all over pink spots. I had contracted measles and the painful interview was of course postponed *sine die*, as the expression is.

That had always been my supreme moment. Only now was I experiencing to an even greater extent the feeling of quiet happiness which comes to you when you've outsmarted the powers of darkness. I felt as if a great weight had been lifted off me. Well, it had of course in one sense, for the Fairy Queen must have clocked in at fully a hundred and sixty pounds ringside, but what I mean is that a colossal burden had been removed from the Wooster soul. It was as though the storm clouds had called it a day and the sun come smiling through.

The only thing that kept the moment from being absolutely perfect was that Jeeves was not there to share my hour of triumph. I toyed with the idea of ringing him up at the Junior Ganymede, but I didn't want to interrupt him when he was probably in the act of doubling six no trumps.

The thought of Aunt Dahlia presented itself. She of all people should be the one to hear the good news, for she was very fond of Roddy Glossop and had shown herself deeply concerned when informed of his in-the-soup-ness. Furthermore, she could scarcely not be relieved to learn that a loved nephew had escaped the fate that is worse than death – viz. marrying Honoria. It was true that my firm refusal to play Santa Claus at her children's party must still be rankling, if that's the word, but at our last meeting I had found her far less incandescent than she had been, so there was reason to suppose that if I looked in on her now I should get a cordial reception. Well, not absolutely cordial, perhaps, but something near enough to it. So I left a note for Jeeves saying where I'd gone and hared off to her address in a swift taxi.

It was as I had anticipated. I don't say her face lit up when she saw me, but she didn't throw her Perry Mason at me and she called me no new names, and after I had told my story she was all joviality and enthusiasm. We were saying what a wonderful Christmas present the latest development would be for Pop

Glossop and speculating as to what it would feel like being married to his daughter Honoria and, for the matter of that, being married to Blair Eggleston, and we had just agreed that both Honoria and Blair had it coming to them, when the telephone rang. The instrument was on a table near her chair, and she reached for it.

'Hullo?' she boomed. 'Who?' Or, rather, WHO, for when at the telephone her vocal delivery is always of much the same calibre as it used to be on the hunting field. She handed me the receiver. 'One of your foul friends wants you. Says his name's Waterbury.'

Jas Waterbury, placed in communication with self, seemed perplexed. In rather an awed voice he asked:

'Where are you, cocky? At the Zoo?'

'I don't follow you, Jas Waterbury.'

'A lion just roared at me.'

'Oh, that was my aunt.'

'Sooner yours than mine. I thought the top of my head had come off.'

'She has a robust voice.'

'I'll say she has. Well, cully, I'm sorry I had to disturb her at feeding time, but I thought you'd like to know that Trix and I have been talking it over and we both think a simple wedding at the registrar's would be best. No need for a lot of fuss and expense. And she says she'd like Brighton for the honeymoon. She's always been fond of Brighton.'

I was at something of a loss to know what on earth he was talking about, but reading between the lines I gathered that the Fairy Queen was thinking of getting married. I asked if this was so, and he chuckled greasily.

'Always kidding, Bertie. You will have your joke. If you don't know she's going to get married, who does?'

'I haven't a notion. Who to?'

'Why, you, of course. Didn't you introduce her to your gentleman friend as your fiancée?'

I lost no time in putting him straight.

'But that was just a ruse. Surely you explained it to her?'

'Explained what?'

'That I just wanted her to pretend that we were engaged.'

'What an extraordinary idea. What would I have done that for?'

'Fifteen quid.'

'I don't remember any fifteen quid. As I recall it, you came to me and told me you'd seen Trixie as the Fairy Queen in Cinderella at the Wigan Hippodrome and fallen in love with her at first sight, as so many young fellows have done. You had found out somehow that she was my niece and you asked me to bring her to your address. And the moment we came in I could see the love light in your eyes, and the love light was in her eyes, too, and it wasn't five minutes after that that you'd got her on your lap and there you were, as snug as two bugs in a rug. Just a case of love at first sight, and I don't mind telling you it touched me. I like to see the young folks getting together in springtime. Not that it's springtime now, but the principle's the same.'

At this point Aunt Dahlia, who had been simmering gently, intervened to call me a derogatory name and ask what the hell was going on. I waved her down with an imperious hand. I needed every ounce of concentration to cope with this misunderstanding which seemed to have arisen.

'You're talking through your hat, Jas Waterbury.'

'Who, me?'

'Yes, you. You've got your facts all wrong.'

'You think so, do you?'

'I do, and I will trouble you to break it to Miss Waterbury that those wedding bells will not ring out.'

'That's what I was telling you. Trixie wants it to be at the registrar's.'

'Well, that registrar won't ring out, either.'

He said I amazed him.

'You don't want to marry Trixie?'

'I wouldn't marry her with a ten foot pole.'

An astonished 'Lord love a duck' came over the wire.

'If that isn't the most remarkable coincidence,' he said. 'Those were the very words Mr. Prosser used when refusing to marry another niece of mine after announcing his betrothal before witnesses, same as you did. Shows what a small world it is. I asked him if he hadn't ever heard of breach of promise cases, and he shook visibly and swallowed once or twice. Then he looked me in the eye and said "How much?" I didn't get his meaning at first, and then it suddenly flashed on me. "Oh, you mean you want to break the engagement," I said, "and feel it's your duty as a gentleman to see that the poor girl gets her bit of heart balm," I said. "Well, it'll have to be something substantial," I said, "because there's her despair and desolation to be taken into account." So we talked it over and eventually settled on two thousand quid, and that's what I'd advise in your case. I think I can talk Trixie into accepting that. Nothing, mind you, can ever make life anything but a dreary desert for her after losing you, but two thousand quid would help.'

'BERTIE!' said Aunt Dahlia.

'Ah,' said Jas Waterbury, 'there's that lion again. Well, I'll leave you to think it over. I'll come and see you tomorrow and get your decision, and if you feel that you don't like writing that cheque, I'll ask a friend of mine to try what he can do to persuade you. He's an all-in wrestler of the name of Porky Jupp. I used to manage him at one time. He's retired now because he broke a fellow's spine and for some reason that gave him a distaste for the game. But he's still in wonderful condition. You ought to see him crack Brazil nuts with his fingers. He thinks the world of me and there's nothing he wouldn't do for me. Suppose, for instance, somebody had done me down in a business transaction, Porky would spring to the task of plucking him limb from limb like some innocent little child doing She-loves-me she-loves-me-not with a daisy. Good night, good night,' said Jas Waterbury, and rang off.

*

I would have preferred, of course, after this exceedingly unpleasant conversation to have gone off into a quiet corner somewhere and sat there with my head between my hands, reviewing the situation from every angle, but Aunt Dahlia was now making her desire for explanatory notes so manifest that I had to give her my attention. In a broken voice I supplied her with the facts and was surprised and touched to find her sympathetic and understanding. It's often this way with the female sex. They put you through it in no uncertain manner if you won't see eye to eye with them in the matter – to take an instance at random – of disguising yourself in white whiskers and stomach padding, but if they see you are really up against it, their hearts melt, rancour is forgotten and they do all they can to give you a shot in the arm. It was so with the aged relative. Having expressed the opinion that I was the king of the fatheads and ought never to be allowed out without a nurse, she continued in gentler strain.

'But after all you are my brother's son whom I frequently dandled on my knee as a baby, and a subhuman baby you were if ever I saw one, though I suppose you were to be pitied rather than censured if you looked like a cross between a poached egg and a ventriloquist's dummy, so I can't let you sink in the soup without a trace. I must rally round and lend a hand.'

'Well, thanks, old flesh and blood. Awfully decent of you to want to assist. But what can you do?'

'Nothing by myself, perhaps, but I can confer with Jeeves and between us we ought to think of something. Ring him up and tell him to come here at once.'

'He won't be home yet. He's playing Bridge at his club.'

'Give him a buzz, anyway.'

I did so, and was surprised when I heard a measured voice say 'Mr. Wooster's residence'.

'Why, hullo, Jeeves,' I said. 'I didn't expect you to be home so early.'

'I left in advance of my usual hour, sir. I did not find my Bridge game enjoyable.'

'Bad cards?'

'No, sir, the hands dealt to me were uniformly satisfactory, but I was twice taken out of business doubles, and I had not the heart to continue.'

'Too bad. So you're at a loose end at the moment?'

'Yes, sir.'

'Then will you hasten to Aunt Dahlia's place? You are sorely needed.'

'Very good, sir.'

'Is he coming?' said Aunt Dahlia.

'Like the wind. Just looking for his bowler hat.'

'Then you pop off.'

'You don't want me for the conference?'

'No.'

'Three heads are better than two,' I argued.

'Not if one of them is solid ivory from the neck up,' said the aged relative, reverting to something more like her customary form.

I slept fitfully that night, my slumbers much disturbed by dreams of being chased across country by a pack of Fairy Queens with Jas Waterbury galloping after them shouting Yoicks and Tally ho. It was past eleven when I presented myself at the breakfast table.

'I take it, Jeeves,' I said as I started to pick at a moody fried egg, 'that Aunt Dahlia has told you all?'

'Yes, sir, Mrs. Travers was most informative.'

Well, that was a relief in a way, because all that secrecy and A-and-B stuff is always a strain.

'Disaster looms, wouldn't you say?'

'Certainly your predicament is one of some gravity, sir.'

'I can't face a breach of promise action with a crowded court giving me the horse's laugh and the jury mulcting. . . . Is it mulcting?'

'Yes, sir, you are quite correct.'

'And the jury mulcting me in heavy damages. I wouldn't be able to show my face in the Drones again.'

'The publicity would certainly not be agreeable, sir.'

'On the other hand, I thoroughly dislike the idea of paying Jas Waterbury two thousand pounds.'

'I can appreciate your dilemma, sir.'

'But perhaps you have already thought of some terrific scheme for foiling Jas and bringing his greasy hairs in sorrow to the grave. What do you plan to do when he calls?'

'I shall attempt to reason with him, sir.'

The heart turned to lead in the bosom. I suppose I've become so used to having Jeeves wave his magic wand and knock the stuffing out of the stickiest crises that I expect him to produce something brilliant from the hat every time. Though never at my brightest at breakfast I could see that what he was proposing to do was far from being what Jas Waterbury would have called box office. Reason with him, forsooth! To reason successfully with that king of the twisters one would need brass knucks and a stocking full of sand. There was reproach in my voice as I asked him if that was the best he could do.

'You do not think highly of the idea, sir?'

'Well, I don't want to hurt your feelings—'

'Not at all, sir.'

'– but I wouldn't call it one of your top thoughts.'

'I am sorry, sir. Nevertheless—'

I leaped from the table, the fried egg frozen on my lips. The front door bell had given tongue. I don't know if my eyes actually rolled as I gazed at Jeeves, but I should think it extremely likely, for the sound had got in amongst me like the touching off an ounce or so of trinitrotoluol.

'There he is!'

'Presumably, sir.'

'I can't face him as early in the morning as this.'

'One appreciates your emotion, sir. It might be advisable if you were to conceal yourself while I conduct the negotiations. Behind the piano suggests itself a suitable locale.'

'How right you are, Jeeves!'

To say that I found it comfortable behind the piano would be to give my public a totally erroneous impression, but I secured privacy, and privacy was just what I was after. The facilities, too, for keeping in touch with what was going on in the great world outside were excellent. I heard the door opening and then Jas Waterbury's voice.

'Morning, cocky.'

'Good morning, sir.'

'Wooster in?'

'No, sir, he has just stepped out.'

'That's odd. He was expecting me.'

'You are Mr. Waterbury?'

'That's me. Where's he gone?'

'I think it was Mr. Wooster's intention to visit his pawnbroker, sir.'

'What!'

'He mentioned something to me about doing so. He said he hoped to raise, as he expressed it, a few pounds on his watch.'

'You're kidding! What's he want to pop his watch for?'

'His means are extremely straitened.'

There was what I've heard called a pregnant silence. I took it that Jas Waterbury was taking time off to allow this to sink in. I wished I could have joined in the conversation, for I would have liked to say 'Jeeves, you are on the right lines' and offer him an apology for ever having doubted him. I might have known that when he said he was going to reason with Jas he had the ace up his sleeve which makes all the difference.

It was some little time before Jas Waterbury spoke, and when he did his voice had a sort of tremolo in it, as if he'd begun to realize that life wasn't the thing of roses and sunshine he'd been thinking it. I knew how he must be feeling. There is no anguish like that of the man who, supposing that he has found the pot of gold behind the rainbow, suddenly learns from an authoritative source that he hasn't, if you know what I mean. To him until now Bertram Wooster had been a careless scatterer of fifteen quids, a thing you can't do if you haven't a solid bank balance behind you, and to have him presented to him as a popper of watches must have made the iron enter into his soul, if he had one. He spoke as if stunned.

'But what about this place of his?'

'Sir?

'You don't get a Park Lane flat for nothing.'

'No, indeed, sir.'

'Let alone a vally.'

'Sir?'

'You're a vally, aren't you?'

'No, sir. I was at one time a gentleman's personal gentleman, but at the moment I am not employed in that capacity. I represent Messrs. Alsopp and Wilson, wine merchants, goods supplied to the value of three hundred and four pounds, fifteen shillings and eightpence, a bill which Mr. Wooster finds it far beyond his fiscal means to settle. I am what is technically known as the man in possession.'

A hoarse 'Gorblimey' burst from Jas's lips. I thought it rather creditable of him that he did not say anything stronger.

'You mean you're a broker's man?'

'Precisely, sir. I am sorry to say I have come down in the world and my present situation was the only one I could secure. But while not what I have been accustomed to, it has its compensations. Mr. Wooster is a very agreeable young gentleman and takes my intrusion in an amiable spirit. We have long and interesting conversations, and in the course of these he has confided his financial position to me. It appears that he is entirely dependent on the bounty of his aunt, a Mrs. Travers, a lady of uncertain temper who has several times threatened unless he curbs his extravagance to cancel his allowance and send him to Canada to subsist on a small monthly remittance. She is of course under the impression that I am Mr. Wooster's personal attendant. Should she learn of my official status, I do not like to envisage the outcome, though if I may venture on a pleasantry, it would be a case of outgo rather than outcome for Mr. Wooster.'

There was another pregnant s., occupied, I should imagine, by Jas Waterbury in wiping his brow, which one presumes had by this time become wet with honest sweat.

Finally he once more said 'Gorblimey'.

Whether or not he would have amplified the remark I cannot say, for his words, if he had intended uttering any, were dashed from his lips. There was a sound like a mighty rushing wind and a loud snort informed me that Aunt Dahlia was with us. In letting Jas Waterbury in, Jeeves must have omitted to close the front door.

'Jeeves,' she boomed, 'can you look me in the face?'

'Certainly, madam, if you wish.'

'Well, I'm surprised you can. You must have the gall of an Army mule. I've just found out that you're a broker's man in valet's clothing. Can you deny it?'

'No, madam. I represent Messrs. Alsopp and Wilson, wines, spirits and liqueurs supplied to the value of three hundred and four pounds fifteen shillings and eightpence.'

The piano behind which I cowered hummed like a dynamo as the aged relative unshipped a second snort.

'Good God! What does young Bertie do – bathe in the stuff? Three hundred and four pounds fifteen shillings and eight-pence! Probably owes as much, too, in a dozen other places. And in the red to that extent he's planning, I hear, to marry the fat woman in a circus.'

'A portrayer of Fairy Queens in pantomime, madam.'

'Just as bad. Blair Eggleston says she looks like a hippopotamus.'

I couldn't see him, of course, but I imagine Jas Waterbury

drew himself to his full height at this description of a loved niece, for his voice when he spoke was stiff and offended.

'That's my Trixie you're talking about, and he's going to marry her or else get sued for breach of promise.'

It's just a guess, but I think Aunt Dahlia must have drawn herself to her full height, too.

'Well, she'll have to go to Canada to bring her action,' she thundered, 'because that's where Bertie Wooster'll be off to on the next boat, and when he's there he won't have money to fritter away on breach of promise cases. It'll be as much as he can manage to keep body and soul together on what I'm going to allow him. If he gets a meat meal every third day, he'll be lucky. You tell that Trixie of yours to forget Bertie and go and marry the Demon King.'

Experience has taught me that except in vital matters like playing Santa Claus at children's parties it's impossible to defy Aunt Dahlia, and apparently Jas Waterbury realised this, for a moment later I heard the front door slam. He had gone without a cry.

'So that's that,' said Aunt Dahlia. 'These emotional scenes take it out of one, Jeeves. Can you get me a drop of something sustaining?'

'Certainly, madam.'

'How was I? All right?'

'Superb, madam.'

'I think I was in good voice.'

'Very sonorous, madam.'

'Well, it's nice to think our efforts were crowned with success. This will relieve young Bertie's mind. I use the word mind loosely. When do you expect him back?'

'Mr. Wooster is in residence, madam. Shrinking from confronting Mr. Waterbury, he prudently concealed himself. You will find him behind the piano.'

I was already emerging, and my first act was to pay them both a marked tribute. Jeeves accepted it gracefully, Aunt Dahlia with another of those snorts. Having snorted, she spoke as follows.

'Easy enough for you to hand out the soft soap, but what I'd like to see is less guff and more action. If you were really grateful, you would play Santa Claus at my Christmas party.'

I could see her point. It was well taken. I clenched the hands. I set the jaw. I made the great decision.

'Very well, aged relative.'

'You will?'

'I will.'

'That's my boy. What's there to be afraid of? The worst those kids will do is rub chocolate eclairs on your whiskers.'

'Chocolate eclairs?' I said in a low voice.

'Or strawberry jam. It's a tribal custom. Pay no attention, by the way, to stories you may have heard of them setting fire to the curate's beard last year. It was purely accidental.'

I had begun to go into my aspen act, when Jeeves spoke.

'Pardon me, madam.'

'Yes, Jeeves?'

'If I might offer the suggestion, I think that perhaps a maturer artist than Mr. Wooster would give a more convincing performance.'

'Don't tell me you're thinking of volunteering?'

'No, madam. The artist I had in mind was Sir Roderick Glossop. Sir Roderick has a fine presence and a somewhat deeper voice than Mr. Wooster. His Ho-ho-ho would be more dramatically effective, and I am sure that if you approached him, you could persuade him to undertake the role.'

'Considering,' I said, putting in my oar, 'that he is always blacking up his face with burned cork.'

'Precisely, sir. This will make a nice change.'

Aunt Dahlia pondered.

'I believe you're right, Jeeves,' she said at length. 'It's tough on those children, for it means robbing them of the biggest laugh they've ever had, but they can't expect life to be one round of pleasure. Well, I don't think I'll have that drink after all. It's a bit early.'

She buzzed off, and I turned to Jeeves, deeply moved. He had saved me from an ordeal at the thought of which the flesh crept, for I hadn't believed for a moment the aged r.'s story of the blaze in the curate's beard having been an accident. The younger element had probably sat up nights planning it out.

'Jeeves,' I said, 'you were saying something not long ago about going to Florida after Christmas.'

'It was merely a suggestion, sir.'

'You want to catch a tarpon, do you not?'

'I confess that it is my ambition, sir.'

I sighed. It wasn't so much that it pained me to think of some tarpon, perhaps a wife and mother, being jerked from the society of its loved ones on the end of a hook. What gashed me like a knife was the thought of missing the Drones Club Darts Tournament, for which I would have been a snip this year. But what would you? I fought down my regret.

'Then will you be booking the tickets.'

'Very good, sir.'

I struck a graver note.

'Heaven help the tarpon that tries to pit its feeble cunning against you, Jeeves,' I said. 'Its efforts will be bootless.'

'Had P. G. Wodehouse's only contribution to literature been Lord Emsworth and Blandings Castle, his place in history would have been assured. Had he written of none but Mike and Psmith, he would be cherished today as the best and brightest of our comic authors. If Jeeves and Wooster had been his solitary theme, still he would be hailed as The Master. If he had given us only Ukridge, or nothing but the recollections of the Mulliner family, or a pure diet of golfing stories, Wodehouse would nonetheless be considered immortal. That he gave us all those and more – so much more – is our good fortune and a testament to the most industrious, prolific and beneficent author ever to have sat down, scratched his head and banged out a sentence.'   Stephen Fry

We hope you have enjoyed this book. With over ninety novels and around 300 short stories to choose from, you may be wondering which Wodehouse to choose next. It is our pleasure to introduce...

UNCLE FRED

Uncle Dynamite

Meet Frederick Altamount Cornwallis Twistleton, Fifth Earl of Ickenham. Better known as Uncle Fred, an old boy of such a sunny and youthful nature that explosions of sweetness and light detonate all around him.

Cocktail Time

Frederick, Earl of Ickenham, remains young at heart. So his jape of using a catapult to ping the silk top hat off his grumpy half-brother-in-law, is nothing out of the ordinary – but the consequences abound with possibilities.

UKRIDGE

Ukridge

Money makes the world go round for Stanley Featherstonehaugh Ukridge – looking like an animated blob of mustard in his bright yellow raincoat – and when there isn't enough of it, the world just has to spin a bit faster.

MR MULLINER

Meet Mr Mulliner

Sitting in the Angler's Rest, drinking hot scotch and lemon, Mr Mulliner has fabulous stories to tell of the extraordinary behaviour of his far-flung family. This includes Wilfred, whose formula for Buck-U-Uppo enables elephants to face tigers with the necessary nonchalance.

Mr Mulliner Speaking

Holding court in the bar-parlour of the Angler's Rest, Mr Mulliner reveals what happened to The Man Who Gave Up Smoking, what the Something Squishy was that the butler delivered on a silver salver, and what caused the dreadful Unpleasantness at Bludleigh Court.

MONTY BODKIN

The Luck of the Bodkins

Monty Bodkin, besotted with 'precious dream-rabbit' Gertrude Butterwick, Reggie and Ambrose Tennyson (the latter mistaken for the late Poet Laureate), and Hollywood starlet Lotus Blossom, complete with pet alligator, all embark on a voyage of personal discovery aboard the luxurious liner, *S. S. Atlantic*.

JEEVES
The Novels

Thank You, Jeeves

Bertie disappears to the country as a guest of his chum Chuffy – only to find his peace shattered by the arrival of his ex-fiancée Pauline Stoker, her formidable father and the eminent loony-doctor Sir Roderick Glossop. When Chuffy falls in love with Pauline and Bertie seems to be caught in flagrante, a situation boils up which only Jeeves (whether employed or not) can simmer down . . .

Jeeves and the Feudal Spirit

A moustachioed Bertie must live up to 'Stilton' Cheesewright's expectations in the Drones Club darts tournament, or risk being beaten to a pulp by 'Stilton', jealous of his fiancée Florence's affections . . .

Much Obliged, Jeeves

What happens when the Book of Revelations, the Junior Ganymede Club's recording of their masters' less than perfect habits, falls into potentially hostile hands?

Aunts Aren't Gentlemen

Under doctor's orders, Bertie moves with Jeeves to a countryside cottage. But Jeeves can cope with anything – even Aunt Dahlia.

Jeeves in the Offing

When Jeeves goes on holiday to Herne Bay, Bertie's life collapses; finding his mysterious engagement announced in *The Times* and encountering his nemesis Sir Roderick Glossop in disguise, Bertie hightails it to Herne Bay. Then the fun really starts . . .

The Code of the Woosters

Purloining an antique cow creamer under the instruction of the indomitable Aunt Dahlia is the least of Bertie's tasks, for he has to play Cupid while feuding with Spode.

The Mating Season

In an idyllic Tudor manor in a picture-perfect English village, Bertie is in disguise as Gussie Fink-Nottle, Gussie is in disguise as Bertram Wooster and Jeeves, also in disguise, is the only one who can set things right . . .

Ring for Jeeves

Patch Perkins and his clerk are not the 'honest bookies' they seem, but Bill, the rather impoverished Ninth Earl of Rowcester, and his temporary butler Jeeves. When they abscond with the freak winnings of Captain Biggar, Jeeves's resourcefulness is put to the test . . .

Stiff Upper Lip, Jeeves

Bertie Wooster visits Major Plank in an attempt to return a work of art which Stiffy had told Bertie had been effectively stolen from Plank by Sir Watkyn Bassett. Thank goodness for Chief Inspector Witherspoon – but is he all he seems?

Right Ho, Jeeves

Bertie assumes his alter ego of Cupid and arranges the engagement of Gussie Fink-Nottle to Tuppy Glossop. Thankfully, Jeeves is ever present to correct the blundering plans hatched by his master.

Joy in the Morning

Trapped in rural Steeple Bumpleigh with old flame Florence Craye, her new and suspicious fiancé Stilton Cheesewright, and two-faced Edwin the Boy Scout, Bertie desperately needs Jeeves to save him . . .

JEEVES

The Collections

Carry on, Jeeves

In his new role as valet to Bertie Wooster, Jeeves's first duty is to create a miracle hangover cure. From that moment, the partnership that is Jeeves and Wooster never looks back . . .

Very Good, Jeeves

Endeavouring to give satisfaction, Jeeves embarks on a number of rescue missions, including rescuing Bingo Little and Tuppy Glossop from the soup . . . Twice each.

The Inimitable Jeeves

In pages stalked by the carnivorous Aunt Agatha, Bingo Little embarks on a relationship roller coaster and Bertie needs Jeeves's help to narrowly evade the clutches of terrifying Honoria Glossop . . .

The World of Jeeves

A complete collection of the Jeeves and Wooster short stories, described by Wodehouse as 'the ideal paperweight'.

BLANDINGS

Something Fresh

The first Blandings novel, featuring the delightfully dotty Lord Emsworth and introducing the first of many impostors who are to visit the Castle.

Pigs Have Wings

Can the Empress of Blandings avoid a pignapping to win the Fat Pigs class at the Shropshire Show for the third year running?

Leave it to Psmith

Lady Constance Keeble, sister of Lord Emsworth of Blandings Castle, has both an imperious manner and a valuable diamond necklace. The precarious peace of Blandings is shattered when her necklace becomes the object of dark plottings, for within the castle lurk some well-connected jewel thieves. Among them, a pair of American crooks: Lord Emsworth's younger son Freddie, desperate for money to establish a bookie's business, and Psmith, hoping to use a promised commission to finance his old school friend Mike's purchase of a farm to secure his future happiness.

Service with a Smile

When Clarence, Ninth Earl of Emsworth, must travel to London for the opening of Parliament, he grudgingly leaves his beloved pig, the Empress of Blandings, at home. When he returns, he must call upon Uncle Fred to restore normality to the chaos instilled during his absence . . .

Summer Lightning

The first appearance in a novel of the Empress of Blandings, the prize-winning pig and all-consuming passion of Clarence, Ninth Earl of Emsworth, which has disappeared. Suspects within the Castle abound . . . Did the butler do it?

Full Moon

When the moon is full at Blandings, strange things happen. Including a renowned painter being miraculously revivified decades after his death to paint a portrait of the beloved pig, the Empress of Blandings . . .

Uncle Fred in the Springtime

Uncle Fred believes he can achieve anything in the springtime. However, disguised as a loony doctor and trying to prevent prize pig, the Empress of Blandings, from falling into the hands of the unscrupulous Duke of Dunstable, he is stretched to his limit . . .

A Pelican at Blandings

Skulduggery is afoot, involving the sale of a modern nude painting, which, in Lord Emsworth's eyes, resembles a pig. Inundated with unwelcome guests, Clarence embarks on the short journey to the end of his wits. Fortunately Galahad Threepwood is on hand to solve all the mysteries . . .

The World of Blandings (Omnibus)

This wonderfully fat omnibus (containing three short stories and two full novels) spans the dimensions of the Empress of Blandings herself, surely the fattest pig in England . . .

Blandings Castle

The Empress of Blandings, potential silver medal winner in the Fat Pigs Class at the Shropshire Agricultural show, is off her food. Clarence, absent-minded Ninth Earl of Emsworth, is engaged in a feud with Head Gardener McAllister. But first of all, the vexed matter of the custody of the pumpkin must be resolved. This collection also includes Mr Mulliner's stories about Hollywood.

And Some Other Treats...

What Ho!

Introduced by Stephen Fry, this is a bumper anthology, providing the cream of the crop of Wodehouse's hilarious stories, together with verse, articles and all manner of treasures.

The Heart of a Goof

From his favourite chair on the terrace above the ninth hole, the Oldest Member reveals the stories behind his club's players, from notorious 'golfing giggler' Evangeline to poor, inept Rollo Podmarsh.

The Clicking of Cuthbert

A collection of stories, including that of Cuthbert, golfing ace, hopelessly in love with Adeline, who only cares for rising young writers. But enter a Great Russian Novelist with a strange passion, and Cuthbert's prospects might be looking up . . .

Big Money

Berry Conway, employee of dyspeptic American millionaire Torquil Patterson Frisby, has inherited a large number of shares in the Dream Come True copper mine. Of course they're worthless . . . aren't they?

Hot Water

In the heady atmosphere of a 1930s French chateau, J. Wellington Gedge only wants to return to his life in California, where everything is as it seems . . .

Laughing Gas

Joey Cooley, golden-curled Hollywood child film star, and six-foot-tall boxer Reginald, Earl of Havershot, are both under anaesthetic at the dentist's when their identities are swapped in the fourth dimension.

The Small Bachelor

It's Prohibition America and shy young George Finch is setting out as an artist – without the encumbrance of a shred of talent. Will George triumph over the social snob Mrs Waddington and successfully woo her stepdaughter?

Money for Nothing

Two households, both alike in dignity, in fair Rudge-in-the-Vale, where we lay our scene . . . Will the love of John Carmody and Pat Wyvern survive the bitter feud between their fathers, miserly Lester Carmody and peppery Colonel Wyvern?

Summer Moonshine

Poor Sir Buckstone Abbott owns in Walsingford Hall one of the least attractive stately homes in the country, so when a rich continental princess seems willing to buy it, he's overjoyed. But will the deal be completed?

The Adventures of Sally

When Sally Nicholas inherits some money, her life becomes increasingly complicated; with a needy brother, a handsome fiancé, who is not all he seems, and a naive generosity of spirit, Sally must turn to doting, clueless Ginger Kemp to set things right . . .

Young Men in Spats

Meet the Young Men in Spats – all innocent members of the Drones Club, all hopeless suitors, and all busy betting their sometimes non-existent fortunes on highly improbable outcomes. That is when they're not recovering from driving their sports cars *through* Marble Arch . . .

Piccadilly Jim

It takes a lot of effort for Jimmy Crocker to become Piccadilly Jim – nights on the town roistering, and a string of broken hearts. When he eventually succeeds, Jimmy ends up having to pretend he's himself, possibly the hardest pretence of all . . .

A Damsel in Distress

The Earl of Marshmoreton just wants a quiet life pottering around his garden, supported by his portly butler Keggs. However, when his spirited daughter, Lady Maud, is placed under house-arrest due to an unfortunate infatuation, and the American, George Bevan, determines to claim her heart, the Earl is allowed no such reprieve . . .

The Girl in Blue

Young Jerry West has a few problems, including uncles with butlers who aren't all they seem, and a love for the woman he is not due to marry. When his uncle's miniature Gainsborough, *The Girl in Blue*, is stolen, Jerry sets out on a mission to find her . . . Will everything come right in the process?